THE MOST OF
LEWIS GRIZZARD

THE MOST OF LEWIS GRIZZARD

FIVE TITLES COMPLETE IN ONE VOLUME

Kathy Sue Loudermilk, I Love You

Won't You Come Home, Billy Bob Bailey?

Don't Sit Under the Grits Tree
With Anyone Else But Me

Elvis Is Dead, And I Don't Feel
So Good Myself

Shoot Low, Boys—
They're Riding Shetland Ponies

Galahad Books ▪ New York

CONTENTS

Kathy Sue Loudermilk, I Love You

To
Christine and H. B.

FOREWORD

Lewis Grizzard asked me to write the foreword to this book. I'm flattered, because Lewis is one of my favorite people.

Also, he saved my marriage, perhaps even the roof over my head. I will explain. I will begin at the beginning, when I personally discovered Lewis Grizzard.

It was 1968, when I was executive sport editor of the *Atlanta Journal*. We needed to hire a beginning sports writer, and I went about finding one in my usual scientific way.

I went to a certain coach, whom I knew to be paranoid, ill-tempered and, on occasion, inclined to lie. "Coach," I said, "who is the worst young sports writer you know?"

"Lewis Grizzard," he replied, "that jerk who works for the *Athens Daily News*."

I hired Lewis that very afternoon.

He was an instant hit in the sports department. Being from Moreland, Georgia, he talked like people are supposed to and he understood the importance of getting the Friday night wrestling results into the Saturday paper.

He was twenty-one years old, had a pretty blonde wife, a wornout Volkswagen, and he did everything I told him to do.

Lewis was on his way to becoming the best wrestling writer in Atlanta when our sports slot man quit.

In every sports department there is an individual called the "man who does the slot." It's just a sexy term for the one who does all the work while the rest of us cover the World Series and the Sugar Bowl.

The slot man comes to work at four in the morning and sometimes works until two the next morning. But he doesn't have to worry about filling out an overtime slip because he qualifies as a supervisor.

1

That's the job I had fallen into shortly after Grizzard came aboard. My wife had not seen me fully awake in three months and my children actually thought I was deceased.

My wife called the office one midnight and made it fairly clear: "Get somebody to do the slot or get a lawyer," she said.

"Lewis," I said. "How would you like to do the slot?"

"Remember," I said, "you get a $5 raise and Saturday off."

I didn't explain that I meant every third Saturday in July. Grizzard took the job. Three months later his wife divorced him.

One day I took Lewis out for a beer. "Kid," I said, "you've got a great future in this business. What do you really want to do with your life?"

"Someday, I want to have my own barbecue place," he answered. "With sliced pork pig sandwiches and cold beer in longneck bottles. With a jar of pickled pigs feet next to the cash register and an ol' hound dog next to me. Most afternoons I would close up and go fishing, and some afternoons I would even put bait on the hook."

I knew Lewis was a comer. When I somehow became managing editor of the *Atlanta Constitution*, Lewis got my old job as executive sports editor at the *Journal*, the youngest ever. He moved on to become associate city editor at the *Journal*, and special assignments editor at the *Constitution*.

Later (I forget the details) he wound up sports editor of the *Chicago Sun-Times*.

I went up there to visit him once. He took me out to lunch, and the wind was so strong they had a *rope* you had to hold onto walking from the newspaper to the restaurant. We had to write out our order because the waitress couldn't understand us. Stray dogs in Moreland might not have eaten what they served us.

After about two years in Chicago, Lewis started calling me every night. Collect.

"I'm looking out my window," he'd say, "watching a guy mug a little old lady."

Or, "Thirty-third day in a row below zero."

Or, "Just had another bowl of boiled Polish cabbage."

He was down to 124 pounds and having fainting spells.

One night I casually mentioned I was trying to hire a columnist for the *Constitution*.

"Hire me!" Grizzard screamed.

Nevermind that he'd never written a newspaper column.

Nevermind that he's already quit the Atlanta papers about six times.

If they can't take a joke, to hell with 'em, I decided.

Besides, the long-distance charges were getting impossible to explain.

So Grizzard came back to Atlanta to write a column for the *Constitution*.

He's up to 189 pounds, and if you think you'll ever catch him in the office you're kidding yourself.

He's the hottest thing on Southern newsprint.

Everywhere I go people ask me if I know Lewis Grizzard.

"Do you ever get to talk to him?" they ask.

"No," I reply. "But one day on the elevator he nodded to me."

And one day he did.

Jim Minter
Managing Editor
The *Atlanta Journal*

CONTENTS

1

COMING HOME IS A ONE-WAY TRIP

I lived in Chicago for two years before returning to Atlanta to begin writing a daily column for the Atlanta Constitution. *Chicago's not a bad town. But the weather didn't suit me, and the food didn't suit me, and people talked funny.*

When I lived in Chicago, I used to think of the line from the country song that went, "If I ever get back to Georgia, I'm gonna nail my feet to the ground." What the following columns about home and where my heart is should say is, I finally got back to Georgia and I'll be dipped in hot buttered grits before I'll leave again.

CHICAGO—What this neighborhood must have been fifty years ago! Eight blocks north on Lincoln Avenue is the Biograph Theatre where they shot John Dillinger down. The Biograph lives on with nostalgia flicks. Bogart and Davis in *Petrified Forest* for $1.50. Four blocks north on Clark Street is the site of the Saint Valentine's day Massacre, now the site of a home for old people who don't have homes. Capone, I am told, operated south. This was Bugs Moran's territory.

Today, it is ethnic and Democratic, congested and overpriced. It is alternately charming and frustrating. An automobile is an albatross. There is no place to park it. But this has been home for two years, and these are the very last moments.

The dwarfish old man who delivers for the liquor store on the corner has already made two runs on my street, and it's barely ten o'clock. Bloody Mary mix mostly. Bloody Marys are big anywhere on Sunday mornings. On the near north side of Chicago, they are a way of life.

The line is already forming for brunch at R. J. Grunts. For $3.50—fork in one hand, plate in the other—you can shovel through a cornucopia somebody grossly underestimated and called a salad bar. Hash browns are extra with the eggs. Hash browns are a bad joke Chicago restaurants play on breakfast.

7

The Loop is only ten minutes away. The most poignant memory will be the bleak, snowy afternoon a fire department ambulance, followed by four black limousines and a cadre of policemen on motorcycles, drove solemnly up Michigan Avenue, past the Wrigley Building and across the river, while all the power and force that is Chicago commerce came to a reverent halt. Inside the ambulance rode the corpse of Richard J. Daley.

Lake Michigan and the endless high rises on Lakeshore Drive's gold coast are just across Lincoln Park where, on days that weather permits, thousands flock to walk on something that is not asphalt or concrete. It is warm this morning, and thank God for that. Chicago has two seasons, they like to say: Winter and the Fourth of July.

Songs and poems are written about saying goodbye because it is one of those things in life that is usually impossible to do gracefully if it is worth doing at all. I got mine out of the way a day early. "If you're ever in Atlanta. . . ."

Slowly, a final order does come to the mess that is necessary for the moving of all one's earthly belongings. My plane is at noon. There is one last run through the back bedrooms, and the movers left a box. Anybody need a dart board, a rickety lawn chair, and forty-five slightly-used tennis balls?

The cab pulls out on North Cleveland, left to Fullerton, and on to the Kennedy Expressway where it's every man for himself to O'Hare. Some of it I have liked a great deal. Some of it I may have even loved. There were parts I hated. Regardless. It's over.

****

Living in a city other than Atlanta was something I had never considered. I am not native, but close. And Atlanta—even when the Dinkler Plaza was the big stop and Terminal Station was busy at midnight—was a mecca for those of us in the Coweta County hinterlands. "Atlaner" they called it where I lived, and a lot of people went there on Friday nights. Those who didn't stop at the Farmer's Market drove on to the city auditorium for the wrestling matches. No, the *rasslin'* matches.

Predictably, my first job out of school was in Atlanta. The changes were already at hand. Up jumped the Stadium and in came the Braves, the Falcons, the Hawks, and the Flames. Underground flourished and the *New York Times* did front page stories. Boddy Dodd retired, Lester Maddox faded, and Hartsfield went international. And everybody from Keokuk and Three Rivers showed up in his leisure suit for the hardware convention at the Marriot or the Regency. The Nitery? One block up and two over.

I left Atlanta two years ago for Chicago, figuring what the hell, horizons are for stretching. I was homesick at the first stop light in Cartersville. Horizons without a red clay motif are somebody else's horizons.

I did keep up while I was gone. Jimmy Carter, a Georgian, became president, and that helped. Suddenly, it was fashionable at Hotspurs and Arnie's in Chicago to be able to explain the difference between poke salet and pot likker. A man stood on the corner of Rush and State and called another a "sumbitch." I swear.

Time Magazine even devoted a special issue to explaining the South. I noted with no small measure of pride that it no longer considered H. L. Mencken's dismissal of the cultural South as the "intellectual Gobi or Lapland" to be operative.

Ted Turner was front page in Chicago. "Is he a little goofy?" I was asked more than once. Midwesterners can't really distinguish between Georgia Tech and just plain Georgia, but when Pepper upset Notre Dame last fall the question did come up. *Playboy* said the women were great in Atlanta. *Sports Illustrated* said the sports teams were lousy. Could be worse, I said. What if it were the other way around?

I am sure a lot has changed. The new hotels are supposed to be incredible. One allegedly has a lake in the lobby. It is rumored liquor may be purchased on Sunday. Parts of the city, I understand, have disappeared altogether in the wake of MARTA bulldozers. And Mr. Young has gone to New York and Mr. Fowler has gone to Washington in his place.

But folks still talk nice to you, don't they? And Harold's Barbecue hasn't closed? Northside Drive from the expressway to West Paces has not gone commercial? And late on summer afternoons what of that stillness, that cooling, that sundown in the Deep South that makes whatever happened during the day worth it and whatever may transpire that night even better? Has the Fox been saved?

I hope so. The commitment is made.

The Delta lady on the other end of the phone was talking. "There is space available on the noon flight to Atlanta," she said a few days ago. "Will this be round trip?"

I just let it hang there, savoring the moment.

"No, m'am," I answered. "One way."

No Spot Is So Dear . . .

On a cold day last week, I stood outside the church in my hometown of Moreland, Georgia, that is so dear to my childhood and tried

to remember how long it had been since I was inside. Ten years? At
least that long. But if there weren't still roots here, would I come
back so often in my mind?

Church was about all we had. Sunday school was at ten, but
preaching was only twice a month. We shared sermons and the
preacher with another flock down the road.

What did they call it on Sunday night? MYF? We had a couple of
rowdy brothers in town who broke into a store. They were juvenile
first offenders. Their punishment was to attend Methodist Youth
Fellowship for six months. First night they were there, they beat up
two fifth-graders and threw a Cokesbury hymnal at the lady who
met with us and always brought cookies.

She ducked in time and then looked them squarely in their devilish
eyes. Soft as the angel she was, she said, "I don't approve of what
you boys did here tonight, and neither does Jesus. But if He can
forgive you, I guess I'll have to."

She handed them a plate of cookies, and last I heard, both are
daddies with steady jobs and rarely miss a Sunday. That was the
first miracle I ever saw.

Revivals at the church were the highlight of the summer. I remember a young visiting preacher talking about the night he was
converted.

"I was drunk in an Atlanta bar," he said, "and I was lost. But Jesus
walked in and sat down beside me. Praise His name, because that's
the reason I'm with you here tonight."

That frightened me. If Jesus could find that fellow in an Atlanta
bar, he certainly wouldn't have any trouble walking up on me smoking behind the pump house in Moreland. I always took an extra look
around before lighting up after that.

Workers were smoking one day in the attic of our church. They left
a cigarette. It took less than an hour for flames to destroy that old
building. I didn't cry, but grown men did.

We built it back—of brick this time. Country folks will dig deep in
the name of the Lord.

The best fried chicken I ever ate, the best iced tea I ever drank
were the fried chicken and the iced tea on Homecoming Day at the
church. Dinner on the grounds, we called it. The chickens had been
walking in someone's backyard earlier in the morning. The tea went
into a galvanized washtub. A piece of block ice kept it cold.

The day Red Murphy died, they announced it in the church. The
congregation wept as one. Everyone loved Red Murphy. He ran the
little post office and took children on pony rides.

Maxine Estes taught my Sunday school class. In rural Georgia in the fifties, she was big on being kind to your neighbor no matter the color of his skin. I learned to sing Hymn No. 153, "Love, Mercy and Grace," in that church. And "What a Friend We Have in Jesus." And the one I still break into occasionally today, "Precious Memories." They do linger.

My mother married my stepfather inside that church. And one hot Saturday afternoon a long time ago, a pretty nineteen-year-old girl married me at the same altar. I told her I would never forget her, and I haven't.

It's easy to fall away from the church, no matter the closeness to it in times past. I have done it. So have you. Grown people can do as they please. The 10:30 Sunday morning movie is even an excuse I use. So are Saturday nights that should have ended a lot earlier.

I never could bring myself to walk inside my old church last week. But some Sunday morning soon, maybe I will. And maybe I'll put a ten in the collection plate, and maybe they'll have chicken and iced tea, and maybe afterward I'll make a habit of it.

There is a new country song out. An old man is singing to a group of fellow derelicts. "Lean on Jesus," goes the chorus, "before He leans on you."

I'm not one to panic, but it's something to think about.

Country Store

There is no sign, but the lady inside at Bailey's General Store assured me this was, in fact, Jones Crossroads.

"The Joneses don't own the land anymore," she said, "but they still call it 'Jones Crossroads.'" Who's being picky?

Jones Crossroads is one country store and a house or two and some nice trees at the intersection of Georgia highways 18 and 219 half the distance between West Point and Pine Mountain. The population depends on how many people needed to go to the store that day.

I have a thing about country stores, a love affair that goes back to my youth and a wonderful place called Cureton and Cole's. I could never quite understand why Cureton and Cole's was owned by Lee Evans and J. W. Thompson, but again, who's being picky?

You name it, they sold it at Cureton and Cole's in downtown Moreland, as long as it was coal, sacks of guano, corn meal, Sugar Daddy all day suckers, Hollywood candy bars, Zero candy bars, Zagnut candy bars, snuff, work shirts, work pants, work shoes, kerosene, soda crackers, Vienna sausage, Home Run cigarettes, po-tatoes—sweet and Irish—Blue Horse notebook paper, ice cream in cups with lids that if you licked the ice cream off the underside you would uncover the picture of a movie star like Yvonne DeCarlo, Prince Albert in a can, chicken feed, thread, seed, moon pies, and cold drinks such as R.C. Colas, Nehi oranges, Double Colas, and NuGrapes from a box filled with chunks of block ice, and other of life's necessities.

Sadly, Cureton and Cole's has been boarded shut, never to open again. At least they haven't torn it down and put up a disco. I can see it now: J. W.'s Juke Joint.

Bailey's General Store in Jones Crossroads is a lot like Cureton and Cole's. It has a front porch and two chairs for just sittin'. It has a screened front door and a thermometer so old men can look at it and greet one another with, "Hot enough for you?"

Inside, there are hardwood floors and an air-conditioning system—a floor fan. I saw some flies. A fly is never at home until it is buzzing about a country store on a hot afternoon.

The lady inside said her daddy, Mr. Bailey, ran the store before he died. Worked hard all his life, she said, until the day he found out he had cancer. He lived five more weeks.

"Daddy did a lot of business here," she said. "Mama took it over after he died. Things have sort of gone down hill since then."

I checked out the merchandise. In the back were sacks of hog pellets and scratch feed for chickens. There was a meat box with bologna, the kind you cut directly from the loaf. A yard rake was for sale.

There was a classic candy display case. Zagnut must be out of business. Behind the counter was more snuff than your grandmother could dip in a lifetime of evenings in the front porch rocking chair. There was Bruton's snuff, and Dental snuff, and Tops snuff, and I think I spotted a can of Rooster.

I couldn't resist any longer. From inside Bailey's drink box I pulled out a Nehi orange bellywasher. From the cookie and cracker rack I plucked a "Big Town" chocolate moon pie.

I walked outside and sat me down on the front porch. The marsh-mallow filling inside the moon pie had become runny from the heat, but the cold rush of the orange bellywasher released its hold from the roof of my mouth.

For a moment I had been ten again, with a dime burning a hole in my jeans, and with all the pleasures a child could imagine encircling me and dazzling me. For a moment, I thought I could hear Lee Evans talking to J. W. Thompson. For a moment, that moon pie was cha-teaubriand and my big orange was a gentle and soothing nectar of the gods.

It's Okay to Cry

Things my mother told me would come true when I was grown that I really didn't believe at the time:

The older you get, the harder it is to quit smoking.

You might turn up your nose at turnip greens now, but there will come a time you can't get them and you will want them more than T-bone steak.

Love is the greatest gift one person can give to another.

Money can't buy love.

The kind it might buy isn't worth having.

People will tell you they love you when they don't mean it.

There are no answers in the bottom of a cocktail glass.

Its easy to go into debt. Getting out is next to impossible.

Marriage is a two-way street.

You will never meet a good woman in a night club.

One lie begets another.

If you don't take care of yourself when you are young, you might not live to regret it.

Even if you don't agree with everything the preacher says, it won't hurt you to sit still for thirty minutes and listen to him.

It's okay to cry.

Never let a friend down. You will need him someday.

You don't need to talk dirty to prove you are a man.

The Lord listens to your prayers.

He doesn't answer all of them.

The best way to tell somebody you care is to show them first.

It's not written anywhere that life is supposed to be fair.

Money doesn't grow on trees.

Always wear clean underwear. You might be in a wreck.

Children and old people appreciate kindness.

So do dogs.

Be careful when you buy a used car or an insurance policy.

Pay attention when somebody older tells you something. You can learn a lot from people who have already been down the road.

Being stubborn won't get you anywhere.

Women don't like men who drink too much.

There will be times when you are very lonely. Just remember your mother loves you and always will.

People who shout to make themselves heard usually don't know what they are talking about.

When you get older, your back will hurt and it won't be that easy to get to sleep.

Someday, a man will walk on the moon. And Pepsi Colas will cost a quarter.

Pretty faces can be deceiving.

Always say "Thank you" when somebody does you a favor. You will get more favors that way.

Ball games aren't the most important thing in the world.

Income tax will eat you alive.

You will regret not keeping up your piano lessons.

A Mother Will Worry

I have always disliked hospitals. They even smell like people are sick. And everybody who works there dresses all in white. That makes me uncomfortable, too.

Every moment I am visiting in a hospital, I expect one of those people in white to attempt to puncture my body with a needle. In medical science, when in doubt, grab a needle and look for a victim.

She was lying there in her hospital bed, asleep and attached to a strange looking machine. There was a needle in her arm. It was attached to a tube which led to a bottle of solution.

The solution, a drop at a time, rolled down to the tube, into the needle, and into her body. Each time a drop fell from the bottle, the machine made a clicking sound. The Chinese, I am certain, are behind such a torture-rendering machine.

I don't know what awakened her. Perhaps it was simply my presence in the room. I hadn't made a sound.

She looked tired. I have seen her like this so many times before. Once, when I was a child, she was sick and in the hospital for a long time. That was for something else, something she eventually whipped.

I am praying for an encore this time.

My mother first fell ill to her disease fifteen years ago. She went through a long, treacherous operation the day John Kennedy was buried.

She was better for a time after that, and then worse, and then better and then worse again. One day last week she said, "I haven't felt this good in years."

But it was no time before she was back in the hospital again and I was standing over her again, trying to say something that would help and instead talking mostly about myself.

One thing I never bring up to my mother is any involvement I might be having with the opposite sex, but she always asks about it because one thing she would like to be—like most mothers, I suppose—is a grandmother, and so far, she hasn't been close.

"There's plenty of time for that," I always tell her.

"Maybe for me," she laughs, "but how about you?"

The preacher came by. He was a soft man, who literally crept into the room and introduced himself to me by saying, "Hello, I'm a Baptist preacher."

He told my mother he was praying for her, and she thanked him. He didn't stay long.

"He goes by to see just about everybody," my mother explained. Visit the sick and calm the grieving. Nobody does it better than a small-town preacher.

I was there maybe a couple of hours. I finally pulled a chair near the bed toward the end of my visit. I think my mother sensed I would be leaving soon.

I am thirty-two years old. I have a good job. A car. A nice place to live. Friends. And more health than I deserve.

My mother is sick, lying in a hospital bed with a Chinese Solution Torture Machine attached to her arm. But here is how our visit ended:

"Are you eating well, son?"

"Sure."

"Remember to eat well. Sweets are bad for your teeth."

"I'll remember that."

"Don't ever pick up a stranger when you're driving at night."

"I would never do that."

"Do you have enough cover for your bed?"

"Plenty."

"I wish you would stop smoking."

"I've tried."

"Try harder."

"I'll try harder."

"Don't bother to get me anything for Christmas. I don't need a thing."

"I want to get you *something*."

"And don't worry about me."

"I can't help that."

"Do you have enough cover for your bed?"

"Plenty, mother. Plenty."

Mother's Day

She married late in life, compared to other women of her day. When she finally found her man, he would soon leave her and go off to war.

He was a brave soldier and performed many heroic deeds, and he lived through it all. When he returned, she loved him dearly and he loved her. A boy child was born one October morning.

But came another war that took her man away again.

She got the news from a yellow telegram. The child was playing in the yard, chasing butterflies and wrestling a playful bird dog. He can still remember her scream from within the house. He can still remember her tears. He was too young to understand why she was crying, but he tried to comfort her the best he could.

Her brave soldier, said the telegram, was missing in action. An enemy force had overrun his company's position on some barren hill a million miles away in Korea.

The child wondered about this "Korea," what it was, where it was, and why his daddy was there.

On Christmas Eve, there was a telephone call, followed by more tears. The soldier was alive. He was calling from a hospital in Pearl Harbor. He would be home soon.

"Do you still love me?" he asked his son.

The child did not yet understand the telephone. He nodded a "yes."

"Of course, he does," the mother assured the father. "And so do I."

He returned in triumph. He had been captured and imprisoned by the enemy. He had been tortured. But he had escaped. For weeks, he was hidden in an underground cave and cared for by a South Korean boy who brought him rice and kept him alive until he could make his way back to his lines.

He was weak from the diet and the fear. His feet were so severely frostbitten, they would crack open and bleed each day of the rest of his life.

He was a patriot, still. He made speeches throughout the land, his wife and son at his side. He told of his experiences and he assailed those who would keep American forces out of distant lands threatened by the spread of Communism.

He would say many times, "There is no soldier like the American soldier. The rest of the world needs us to keep it free."

But those many years of combat had taken their toll. He had changed. When he returned, the woman thought their long periods of separation were over. She would be disappointed again.

He brooded. He awakened nights in a cold sweat, screaming. He drank only a little at first. But then he would sit up those nights, alone with a bottle.

The Army, despite his many decorations for valor and his years of service, decided him unfit for further military duty. He wandered aimlessly, at a loss for a purpose.

The mother and the child would see him whenever they could. They would visit him in other cities and she would pretend someday they would be together again.

But she knew they wouldn't. A thousand nights, thinking the child next to her was asleep, she prayed aloud for help.

Finally, she gave up on her husband. She had no other choice. He was a hopeless alcoholic, a man lost in an imagined shame that was nearly demonic in its possession of his life.

She educated herself. She struggled to work each day and to evening classes at night. Somehow, she still managed to bring her son toward manhood and she told him, "Always respect your father, no matter what."

She would eventually remarry. She would take a man steady and kind to her and to her son. She would find at least a share of the contentment and security that had avoided her for so long.

The father, the brave soldier, would die alone. The son would grow and leave her. But he would think of his mother and her plight often. On occasion, he would remember to thank her for the sacrifices she made in his behalf.

Sadly, her burdens have never ceased totally. Today, it is an illness she battles. The doctors say it is incurable. She *deserves* a miracle.

She wanted to be with her son today, and he wanted to be with her on Mother's Day. He wonders if he made the right decision to put off a visit because of business demands.

He did send roses, however. And because she means so much to him, and because she was strong on his mind, and because he wanted to remind himself of the long road she's been down, he spent an afternoon and half a night writing what you just read.

2

OFF THE WALL

People ask me, "Where do you get your ideas for columns?" I never know how to answer that question. Sometimes I look under rocks. I think that is where I got the ideas for the following pieces. At any rate, I do hate liver and I remain convinced the world would be better off without airplanes.

They Gave the Ball Without Me

For the thirty-second consecutive year, I did not receive an invitation to the annual Harvest Ball at the Piedmont Driving Club. Obviously, there has been some kind of mistake.

Every year, I anxiously await the arrival of the white envelope beckoning me to what is certainly one of Atlanta's most prestigious and gala social events.

And every year, I am disappointed. Could the problem be I have moved around too much and they don't know where to find me?

I could just drop by the club and pick it up, you know, and I promise to leave the truck on the street.

What happens at the Harvest Ball is some of the city's loveliest and tenderest and most charming young girlpersons, whose daddies also have a big stash, make their "debuts" to society.

That makes them "debutantes." I have never quite understood exactly what a debutante is, but I'm sure there are lots of good things to eat and drink at their parties.

"When a girl makes her debut," somebody who should know told me, "it means her parents are presenting her to their friends and that she is now a part of the social scene."

I think the male comparison to that—on a lower social strata—is your old man taking you for a beer at the VFW and letting you shoot pool with Scooter Haines who was once eight ball champion of all Heard County.

They held this year's Harvest Ball last week and, again, I had to be satisfied with reading about it in the paper.

19

It was a grand affair. Proud fathers, said the report, beamed as their daughters curtsied to the audience in their expensive and chic gowns.

One of the debs did express concern her escort might get too drunk to cut in on her father when it came time for the evening's waltz. That shocked me.

I can understand getting too drunk to shoot eight ball with Scooter Haines, but the Piedmont Driving Club ain't the Moose Lodge, sport.

Dinner was divine, the story went on. Everybody had tomato aspic with shrimp, breast of chicken, spinach souffle with artichokes and almond mousse and even Scooter Haines, who once went all the way to Houston for a pool tournament, never wrapped his gums around anything like that.

Sadly, the closest I have ever come to a debutante ball was the annual Fourth of July Street Dance in front of the knitting mill on the square in downtown Moreland with a live band that played "Down Yonder" over and over again because that's all the band knew except for "Alabama Jubilee" which it didn't play so well.

What always happened at the dance was farmers from as far away as Luthersville and Arno-Sargent showed up with truckloads of daughters they wanted to marry off. If any of them had teeth, they got to ride up front in the cab.

Some grand old girls got out of trucks at those street dances. The only curtseying they did, however, was over behind the depot where nobody could see them. We were a polite society, too.

There was Cordie Mae Poovey. Cordie Mae always came in her "bermudalls." That's a pair of overalls cut off just above the knee. Cordie Mae couldn't dance a lick, but don't tell her that because she weighed a good 220 and was stronger than she smelled.

And who could forget Lucille Garfield? Lucille carried her pet pig everywhere she went. The way you could tell the pig from Lucille was the pig wore a hat and was the better conversationalist of the two.

Betty Jean Turnipseed didn't miss a dance for fifteen years. Betty Jean wasn't very smart. One time somebody brought an armadillo to school for show-and-tell and she thought it was a possum on the half-shell

But Kathy Sue Loudermilk came to the street dances, too, and when she danced, even the preacher broke a sweat. Nature blessed that child beyond the limits of this timid vocabulary.

It's like my boyhood friend and idol, Weyman C. Wannamaker Jr., a great American, said of her: "That dog can hunt."

So I'll probably never make the Harvest Ball. But I would have paid to have seen Kathy Sue Loudermilk debuting at the Piedmont Driving Club.

One curtsey from ol' Kathy Sue in something tight and low cut and the whole crowd would have been knocked squarely on their tomato aspics.

Interviewing Myself

I get letters from journalism students and other assorted weirdos wanting to know how I go about putting together a column five days a week.

"I have to write a term paper for my JRL 101 class," began one recent letter, "and I have chosen you as my topic. I want to know, in at least 2,000 words, how you go about putting together a column five days a week.

"I need your response no later than two weeks from Friday. Please double-space and try to avoid typographical errors as the instructor counts off for that."

The student who wrote that letter will probably grow to be a good columnist. Getting other people to do your work is a cornerstone of this profession.

Since it is impossible for me to answer all such inquiries, I have decided today to interview myself on the subject of writing a column for the benefit of interested students and my boss.

I know my boss is interested because just the other day he asked me, "Grizzard, how can you do this to me five days a week?"

Here, then, is the interview, conducted in my office, which is located near the men's rest room and which recently got new carpet the color of river water near a chemical dump. I am using an IBM Selectric II typewriter which makes strange sounds like a semi hauling hogs through Holly Springs, Mississippi, on a hot July afternoon:

What does a semi hauling hogs through Holly Springs, Mississippi, on a hot, July afternoon sound like?"

"Grrrrrrrrrrrooooooooink!"

When your IBM Selectric II typewriter makes that sound, what do you think of?

The odor of overcrowded hogs in a steam bath and possible death by electrocution.

Has anybody ever suffered serious injury or even death in an accident involving an electric typewriter?

Yes. One day a skinny religion reporter got his tie hung in the paper roller of his electric typewriter. In a vain attempt to remove it, he rolled his head into his machine and was typed to death by a lower case 'j' and an out-of-control ampersand.

Do readers sometimes call and suggest column ideas to you?

Every day. Recently, an anonymous caller suggested I do a column on the most handsome, best-dressed sportcaster on Atlanta television.

Did you follow up on the suggestion?

Of course not. I knew it was Harmon the minute he mispronounced "Robert Hall."

As a columnist, do you have opportunities for exciting travel and adventure?

You betcha. Just in the last two months, I have been to Memphis and Birmingham. Memphis was closed after dark and under martial law, but the hotel in Birmingham had one of those neat, revolving restaurants like the Regency Hyatt in Atlanta. Unfortunately, the one in Birmingham was in the basement.

Last year, I got to go to the Indianapolis 500 automobile race. What an interesting event that was. It was the most mental illness I have seen at one time.

Approximately, what are your working hours?

I am on call twenty-four hours a day. No story is ever too big or too small for a good columnist. If the bartender forgot to tell you the office called, however, it's not your fault.

Who are the most difficult people to interview?

Those whose names recently appeared in the obituary column, anybody in Harrison's on Friday night with a wedding ring in his pocket, and Korean soccer players.

Is it a strain on your health to write five columns a week?

Absolutely not. I have migraine headaches, stomach pains, dizzy spells, nightmares, hallucinations, ingrown toenails, smoker's cough, and my back is stiff. Other than that, I am in perfect health for a sixty-five-year-old malaria victim.

Is it necessary to drink to be a good columnist?

That is a common myth, but a young person setting out on a career as a columnist should avoid drinking at all costs. It is certainly not necessary to drink to be a good columnist. It is a great help on the days you are a bad one, however.

In summary, then, what is the most difficult part of writing a daily column: (a) the research; (b) the actual writing; (c) the need for a constant flow of the creative juices; or (d) crazies threatening to break your hands?

(E) Admitting to myself I can't hold down a regular job.

Liver Is a Fraud

Eating used to be so simple. A couple of eggs with grits, bacon, toast and coffee in the morning, a quick hamburger and fries at noon, and evening was your basic meat and potatoes.

Give me something with character in the evenings. A steak. Pork chops. Fried chicken. My mother would occasionally try to slip liver into my diet.

"Eat liver, live longer," she would say.

I'm still taking my chance. Who wants a long life that includes eating liver? I don't even like to be in the same room with it.

After I left my mother's table, eating became a bit more complicated. Restaurant food can make eating more of a chore than a joy.

When I lived in Chicago, I nearly starved. Chicago is filled with ethnic restaurants that are fun once. But man can not live on a steady diet of veal marsala and things that still have their heads and eyes.

He must also have cornbread and collards and an occasional barbecue pork-pig sandwich. Otherwise, scurvy and rickets are distinct possibilities.

Today, eating has become a major problem. That is because all the things we used to think were good for us are actually bad for us. Like light bread and biscuits. Light bread and biscuits, somebody told me, are fattening, have no food value and can lead to heart attack and cancer. Say it ain't so.

The same goes for too much milk and eggs. They cause cholesterol and cholesterol causes your arteries to clog and clogged arteries are one-way tickets to the coronary wing.

You have probably heard bacon and hamburgers cause cancer. My doctor told me not to eat pork. That's a problem. A week without barbecue, and I hallucinate and get shortness of breath.

I was hoping they would find something wrong with liver. I always figured it probably caused the spread of communism if nothing else.

"Eat liver, live longer," said my doctor, the dirty pinko.

What we are supposed to be eating today are natural foods. Foods that have not been processed. Foods that have no chemical additives and preservatives. Foods that give us bulk and fibre.

All that sounds like good advice on how to keep your lawnmower engine in tune, but I decided to at least seek more information on the matter.

I have a friend who eats nothing but natural foods. Actually, he doesn't eat. He grazes. I went to him for advice.

"Breakfast," he said, "is the most important meal of the day. I eat natural cereals with low-fat milk and no sugar.

"Or, I mix natural yogurt, a banana, a teaspoon of raw honey and miller's bran together. It gives me enough food value to last me until lunch time when I eat raw vegetables and nuts.

"The dinner meal is usually a large salad, a bowl of celery or asparagus soup, a glass of natural fruit juice and maybe a piece of cheese. The cheese is optional."

Never introduce a man with a diet like that to your house plants. I know horses and goats who eat better.

My friend explained further about people in other parts of the world whose diets include nothing but natural foods. I remembered the yogurt commercials on television. Eat a lot of yogurt and grow up to be a 112-year-old Russian. Who needs it?

"Don't laugh," he said. "Cultures whose diets are totally natural have no traces of heart disease or cancer or other such diet-related diseases. If Americans would turn to natural foods, it would do wonders for the health of our nation."

That, and eat plenty of liver, I added.

"No liver," he said. "Liver stores all the residues and chemicals the animal takes in from eating his own processed foods. I wouldn't touch liver."

I knew it! Anything that tastes as bad as liver has to be the devil's own doing. Finally, I am absolved. Liver is a lying, indigestible fraud.

Praise the Lord, and pass the roots and berries.

My House and a Word or Two About Cats

I have lived in apartments most of my adult life. I have lived in apartments all over Atlanta. I have lived in two different apartments in Chicago.

My first apartment in Chicago was on the fifth floor of a five-floor building. I had space on the roof and an excellent view of the alley behind the building.

Space on the roof is important in Chicago because that is where you go for cookouts and parties with other residents the two months you wouldn't freeze to death or be blown half way to Gary, Indiana by the wind.

Cookouts and parties on a roof in Chicago are equivalent to cookouts and parties in the backyard in Atlanta. Such occasions are more of an adventure on a roof, however, because you can't get wall-eyed and fall off a backyard.

A good view of the alley is also something nice to have in a Chicago apartment because otherwise you might go days without seeing a single mugging.

My second apartment in Chicago was on the second floor. The people downstairs had cats. Cats are snooty and wouldn't fetch a stick on a bet. They also scratch. I dislike cats.

One night a cat belonging to the people downstairs came into my apartment while I was having dinner. It jumped onto the table and walked in the mashed potatoes. I attempted to drown the cat in the gravy. Never attempt to drown a cat in gravy.

The people downstairs refused to pay for the stitches.

Several years ago, I lived in an apartment on the south side of Atlanta near the airport. It had one of those fancy, English names like Hampshire on the Lake. Or Oyster on the Half-Shell. I forget which.

Regardless, the noise from airplanes landing and taking off from Hartsfield gave me migraine headaches, and the first time it rained, the apartment flooded.

Pleas to the resident manager's office for help and a pump went unheeded. Finally, I wrote her a letter. "I can no longer live in this carpeted rice paddy," is what I wrote. She finally came over to inspect my apartment and brought her cat. It drowned.

My last apartment was on the northwest side of the city, and the most interesting thing about it was the pool and the girl who sat by it wearing nothing but two strategically placed R.C. caps and a polka-dot loin cloth.

My apartment pool was also where off-duty airline stewardesses came to sunbathe. The girl with the two R.C. caps and the polka-dot loin cloth was *not* an airline stewardess, however.

She was an ex-biology teacher who got fired for adding new dimensions to show-and-tell time.

The purpose for all this background on my apartment living adventures is to tell you I have finally given up apartment living, not to mention another deposit.

I bought a house. One with windows and doors and a leaking faucet in the bathtub. One with trees in the yard and squirrels and birds in the trees. One with gutters to clean and grass to cut. One with taxes and insurance and a high interest rate and dogs who roam in the yard and who had a dinner party in the first batch of garbage I dumped in my very own curbside garbage container.

One my old furniture insults. I have bought automobiles for what a couch and a coffee table costs these days. One with windows to wash and carpets to clean and leaves to rake.

One with bathroom tile that needs *grouting*. Until I bought a house, I thought grouting was something only consenting adults should do and only with the lights off.

But one the sun shines into in the mornings. And one I hoped for and saved for and looked high and low for.

One I wouldn't mind sharing someday.

Maybe I'll buy a cat.

Don't Get Gypped When You Need a Crypt

I started not to write this column. It's about cemetery plots. This is only my third sentence, but I've already got the creeps.

When I was a kid, the old folks used to gather and talk about their cemetery plots. I would leave the room.

When I returned, they had usually progressed to the Fire on Judgment Day. I would leave the room again.

"Where is your plot, Myrtle?" one of the old folks would ask another.

"On the hill."

"Not much shade up there," the dialogue would continue.

"It's peaceful, though. And I overlook the front of the church."

"I'm under the oak tree, next to Maude Bates."

"Won't it be cold in the wintertime?"

"I'm wearing my wool suit."

"The gray one?"

"Gray with black checks."

"You'll be pretty as a picture. If you don't break out."

"Why should I break out?"

"Wool. Maude Bates wore wool, you know. She broke out something awful."

"How do you know that?"

"Her sister Ruby told me. Ruby's on the hill next to me. We're wearing cotton prints."

I can take almost anything else. Dandruff, roaches in the sink, your last proctoscope examination. But not cemetery plots. Cemetery plots are personal, like your underwear size.

And deliver me from advertisements about cemetery plots and their accompanying paraphernalia. Classified ads in the newspaper sell plots like used cars:

"WESTVIEW—4-grave. Terrace B. Shaded, Curbside. Reasonable. Leaving state. Quick sale."

What's so important about being "curbside"? You're going to catch a bus?

Another ad caught my eye the other day:

"DAWN MEMORIAL, (2) plots with vaults, markers and perpetual maintenance. Must sell. Need money!"

That's obvious. Anybody needing money bad enough to hock his own burial vault and marker is one broke hombre.

Television commercials for cemetery plots are even worse. There was the one I borrowed from to begin this column: "We started not to make this commercial," the announcer would open.

And for good reason. It stunk.

". . . But the Deep Six Burial Company wants you to plot now for what the future holds for all of us. Don't be left out in the cold *when that time comes.* You and your loved ones will be eternally grateful you acted now."

I would be eternally grateful if I never saw that commercial again.

Some things simply shouldn't be hard-sold. Cemetery plots head the list. The announcer is somber-slick. The music is sleepy-soft. The plan is "Pay now, die later."

Any day, I expect a commercial for cemetery plots with a singing jingle:

"Pay just two-ninety-five
While you're still alive
So you won't get gypped
When you need a crypt."

I admit I'm easily spooked when it comes to this matter. And I admit I'm in the same mortal boat with everybody else. I will, in fact, need a place to lay me down for the ages.

But I don't want to be reminded of that unsettling fact as I sit in my own living room.

Among other things, it is depressing and causes me to break out like Maude Bates, rest her woolly soul.

I Don't Have Any Children

We were all close once. I thought it had been six, maybe seven years. Somebody else said it had been more like twelve or thirteen.

It was a chance reunion. There was some beer, and we told a few of the old stories again. One was about the time we had Ben E. King at the spring formal at a big, downtown hotel.

A fight broke out. We couldn't remember who started it or who won, but we did recall a lot of glass breaking and being asked never to come back to that particular big, downtown hotel.

They all introduced me to their wives, none of whom seemed particularly interested in hearing a few of the old stories again. Then they pulled out their wallets and showed me pictures of their children.

That's exactly what I needed to see, pictures of their children, but I always make polite remarks at a time like that.

"She's a sweetheart."

"This is when she was an angel in the church play."

"Looks just like you."

"His teacher says he's the brightest kid in her class."

"Fine-looking young man."

"He plays fullback."

They asked if I had any children. Somebody will always ask that, and I will normally answer while staring at the floor.

"No, I don't," I will say. What am I doing? Apologizing? Why do I always feel like I need to offer an explanation?

I don't have any children because I just don't have any. We talked about it. We even tried a couple of times, but nothing ever happened.

And by that time, it was obvious that trying to have a child, under the circumstances, would be . . . stupid. I think that's exactly the word I used. "Stupid."

I have been congratulated often for my farsighted approach to the situation.

"You're better off," people have said to me.

I've also been told I was "lucky."

"You're lucky you never had any children. When you have children, it just makes things a lot worse."

I think it was one of my aunts who said, "At least there weren't any little children to get hurt."

But I like children. Maybe that's a little strong. I don't have anything against children, and from what limited knowledge I have of them, there is apparently at least some appeal to their company.

They seem to forgive easily, like dogs, and I am impressed by that.

When they first awaken, they look around for somebody to hold them. I know the feeling.

Thunder frightens children. I'm still not at peaceful terms with thunder, either.

Children give you a fair shot before they decide they don't like you.

They look fresh and cute dressed up, especially when they are dressed up and walking into a church holding their mother's hand.

Children think it's a big deal when you give them a quarter.

I've always wanted to teach a little boy which end of a baseball bat to hold. You would think little boys would be born with that knowledge, but they aren't.

One of the men who was showing me pictures of his children said when you have children you hear the word, "daddy," about a thousand times a day.

That can't be all bad.

Once I took a friend's child on a carnival ride, the Octopus. In the middle of the ride, she said she had to go to the bathroom. I explained the Octopus does not stop when you have to go to the bathroom.

I am positive she did everything in her power to wait until the Octopus ride was over.

The beer gave out about midnight. We promised each other we would get together again soon. Likely, we won't.

You know how it is when you have children.

Airplanes Are Unsafe

I was having a conversation with an airline stewardess. We were not in an airplane, however. I avoid traveling by airplane. Don't get me wrong. I'm not afraid to fly. It is crashing and burning that bothers me. If God had intended man to fly, He would have never given him the rental car and unlimited mileage.

"That's silly," said the stewardess when I told her of my aversion to air travel. "Don't you know that you are safer in an airplane than in an automobile?"

I've heard that bunk before. Anything that goes five miles into the air at 500 miles per hour and they make you strap yourself inside can't be safe.

Automobiles are much safer than airplanes because they don't go as high nor as fast, and they can be pulled over and parked and abandoned, if necessary, at a moment's notice. Try pulling an airplane into the emergency lane when the engine overheats.

I only fly in airplanes in extreme emergencies. Like when the train doesn't go there, the bus company is on strike, or I go temporarily insane.

I even hate airports. First thing you see at an airport is a sign that says "terminal." Airports are noisy, crowded and usually a $15 cab ride from the hotel, plus tip.

The stewardess said she has been flying for twelve years. "I've only been in one real emergency," she said. "I was in a two-engine prop and we lost power in both engines. We were directly over Palm Beach, so we just glided in for a safe landing."

Nothing to it. But engines don't always go out over Palm Beach. Try gliding in to Brasstown Bald, for instance.

I have tried to overcome my difficulties with flying. I decided drinking before boarding would be the answer. I scheduled a flight and then went to the airport bar. A day before the flight.

There isn't enough booze on earth, I discovered, to make me relax on an airplane.

A number of bad things have happened to me on airplanes. Once, I stepped on a woman's violin case while trying to get past her to a window seat. She called me awful names for two hours and tried to hit me with what used to be a violin.

Another time, I had to sit next to a religious nut on an airplane. I had rather be hit on the head with a broken violin than to sit next to a religious nut.

"Brother," he said to me, "do you know the Lord?" I said I knew *of* Him.

"Are you ready to meet Him?" he continued.

I looked out the window. We were 20,000 feet and climbing.

"I thought this was the Milwaukee flight," I said.

I do have some faith in airplane pilots, however. Especially Robert Stack and John Wayne. I know pilots go through rigorous training, and I know they are checked regularly to make sure their hands are still steady on the stick.

When I fly, I like for the pilot to have gray hair and a gorgeous woman awaiting his arrival at our destination. Something to live for, in other words.

"I dated a pilot five years," said the stewardess. "I'll never forget the day we broke up. He called me from the airport, just before takeoff. We had an awful fight and I hung up on him."

"Was he mad?" I asked her.

"Was he mad? He pulled the plane away from the gate and rammed one of the wings into another plane. He always was one to pout."

A pouting pilot. I think I am going to be sick.

My Kind of Town

Chicago isn't really a city. It's a train wreck. Five or six or seven million people live there against their will. Chicago has a river that runs through the middle of town. You can walk across it in the wintertime because it's frozen. You can walk across it in the summertime because it is thick with various forms of waste. Like floating bodies.

Chicago's political system is "vote for the Democrat, or I'll break your arms." It is not safe to ride the city's transit system. Dial "el" for murder.

It is not safe to drive on the city's streets. Every year, hundreds of motorists are lost after driving into potholes which the city repairs once a decade whether they need to or not.

Say something nice about Chicago for a change. OK. There hasn't been a mass murder there in nearly three weeks.

The worst thing about Chicago, of course, is the weather. There is no autumn in Chicago, and there is no spring. Summer lasts an hour and a half. The rest of the time it is winter.

I lived in Chicago two years. It was so cold, my precinct captain was Frosty the Snowman. A precinct captain is the one who gives you the bottle of whiskey on election day.

The current winter in Chicago has been the worst since 1912, the year Mayor Daley was elected. Already this month, there have been two blizzards. I saw it snow in May once. Welcome to Ice Station Zero.

There is some humor in all this, however. Something new called Chicago jokes. A few were offered in a Chicago newspaper the other day:

How many Chicagoans does it take to drive a car in winter?
Seven. One to steer, six to push.
Why do Chicago-style pizzas have such thick crusts?
What isn't eaten can be used for insulation.
How do you drive a Chicagoan crazy?
Send him or her a $5 gift certificate toward a Florida vacation.
I thought of some Chicago jokes of my own.
How do they start the baseball season in Chicago?
The mayor thaws out the first ball.
How does a robber disguise himself while holding up a Chicago liquor store in the wintertime?
He takes off his ski mask.
Where had your wife rather live than in Chicago?
Wait a minute. Alaska.

I feel sorry for people who still live in Chicago. They should have their heads examined for brain warts. I especially felt sorry for them Thursday. Thursday was a spring day in January in Atlanta.

I even called one of my old Lincoln Avenue haunts—the Twenty-Three Fifty Pub—to inquire about the health and well-being of some of my old drinking buddies, the ones who used to insist Chicago is a nice place to live.

"Your mother's a polar bear," I would say to them just before the beer-throwing started.

Chuck Dee came to the phone. He runs the joint. I asked about the weather.

"Colder'n (something I can't print)," he said. "Thirty inches of snow on the ground and more falling."

"Nearly sixty degrees here," I told him.

"That's cold," he said.

"Sixty ABOVE, dummy," I said.

"Go to (somewhere it's at least warm)," he said back.

Chuck lives near the pub.

"The people on my street got together and hired two snowplows to come dig us out," he explained. "The drivers took one look and refused. I'm the only one who can get out. But I had to buy a four-wheel drive jeep to do it."

Some people never learn, which reminds me of another Chicago joke I made up Thursday.

What do you say to a smart Chicagoan?

Welcome South, brother.

3

COLD BEER AND COUNTRY MUSIC

I fell in love with country music when I was nine years old and somebody slipped a nickel into the juke box at Steve Smith's truck stop in my hometown of Moreland, Georgia, and played a hurtin' song by Hank Williams. Everybody likes beer, of course.

The Best Beer Joint in Georgia

Jim Stone led me inside the "No-Name" beer joint. "This place just ain't been the same," he said, a certain sadness and longing in his voice, "since the monkey died."

The monkey and its passing are another story I will get around to later. Before that, meet the winner of the Lucille's Memorial Best Beer Joint Search Contest, Jim Stone.

Several months ago, I asked for nominations for the best beer joint in the state of Georgia and named it for Lucille, who sold me my first beer. There were contest rules. The juke box had to be all-country, there couldn't be any mixed drinks or cheeseburgers on sale, wives or girlfriends of regulars weren't allowed, neither were smart-aleck college students, and a bottle of imported beer within thirty miles of the place would be grounds for automatic disqualification.

Jim Stone entered the "No-Name" beer joint in Willacoochee. It is called the "No-Name" because it doesn't have a name. A broken Pabst sign outside is the only evidence the one-room building is where a man can break a dry spell. Otherwise:

—— The jukebox is all-country.

—— Beer costs 55 cents. *All* beer, including gloriously cold long-necks.

—— Cans of Vienna sausage adorn the back counter.

—— There is a sign that says, "No Bumming and No Begging." ("They ain't kiddin'," said a regular.)

——— There is another sign that says, "No Gambling: Anybody caught gambling will be 'prosuted.'"

——— There are two pool tables in the back, which is the reason for the gambling sign.

——— There is no air-conditioning. The windows and doors are kept open in the summer, closed in the winter.

——— There is a new paint job on the outside toilet, despite the fact an indoor facility was installed a month ago.

——— You can still use the outdoor toilet if you want to.

——— The regulars inside do a lot of pulpwooding in the swamp, but they are friendly.

——— The bartender's name is "Hoss," and he chews tobacco.

First prize in the Lucille's Memorial Best Beer Joint Search Contest was that I come to the winner's favorite spot and we drink beer and I pick up the tab.

We started as the evening sun was going down on Willacoochee, which straddles the Seaboard Coast Line tracks and Highway 82 between Pearson and Alapaha, on the west end of Atkinson County, a hard day's ride from Atlanta in the flats and piney woods of deep south Georgia.

Jim Stone had driven in from Douglas, where he works for South Georgia College. "A lot of folks come here from Douglas," he explained. "Willacoochee is to Douglas sort of what Hyannis Port is to Boston."

"Hoss" was behind the bar, his jaw bulging. Luther, one of the regulars in overalls, had dropped by. So did Lace Futch, the mayor of Willacoochee, a man of constant good humor. Amos, the jailer, was there and so was Henry, who owns the No-Name.

Henry was proud to know his place had won the contest.

"I can use the business," he said.

"You ain't doing so bad, are you, Henry?" asked Jim Stone.

"I ain't saying for sure," replied Henry, "but I got three head of young'uns at the house, and ain't none of 'em mssing no meals."

We sat ourselves down at one of the two tables, the one nearest the jukebox, which Henry turned up because we asked him to. We proceeded with the longnecks.

The hot south Georgia sun poured in through the windows. Tired and thirsty men who sweat for a living poured in through the doors in search of relief for dusty and parched throats. The jukebox blared.

She stood outside the door, not daring to come in. She wore bermudas. She was barefoot in the sand. She held an infant at her hip.

"Your old lady's out there," Henry said to a young man as he pulled on a tall bottle. The young man finished his beer. But slowly.

Only then did he walk outside and disappear with his family west on Highway 82.

A slow Seaboard freight passed on the tracks outside. Somebody said Mayor Futch ws ready to take on the entire Seaboard Coast Line.

"They got boxcars parked right in the middle of town, and they won't move 'em," the mayor said.

"How long have they been there?" I asked.

"Eight years," he answered.

Jim Stone finally got around to the monkey story. It is fairly complicated.

A few years back, there was a girl in town who was an excellent basketball player. Her family gave her a pet monkey for high school graduation. But the monkey was messy. Her parents told the girl to give the monkey away.

"She brought it here," said Jim Stone. "It was some kind of smart monkey. They trained it to take the change off the table anytime anybody passed out. Everybody's got to earn his keep."

I had to ask how the monkey died.

"Bad diet," Jim Stone explained. "You can't live that long on just beer and peanuts."

"That ain't nothing," interrupted Mayor Futch. "They used to have a coon in here, too. People would come in and the coon would crawl up on their table. They'd fill the ashtrays full of beer and the coon would drink it all."

We were pondering that when the mayor spoke up again.

"I'll tell you something else," he said, "about half drunk, that was one mean coon."

The tab for the entire afternoon was less than $30, and that even included a round of Vienna sausages and Conway Twitty's "We're Not Exactly Strangers" five times on the juke box.

Somebody said it was the only thing the monkey and the coon ever agreed on. It was their favorite song.

Zell and Fuzz

NASHVILLE—The distinguished lieutenant governor of Georgia, Zell Miller, is a big man in Nashville. He knows practically all the country music stars, and they know him.

Zell Miller was instrumental, a lovely choice of words, in helping Don Williams acquire a new drummer for his band from England recently.

For the uninformed, Don Williams was named male vocalist of the year Monday night at the spiffy Country Music Association awards program here.

Zell is also big buddies with Bill Anderson. Ronnie Milsap, who has reached superstar status, was a student of his at Young Harris College. Zell Miller is a country music expert, a country music superfan, and if he is ever elected governor, I would not be surprised if he didn't start work on moving the Grand Ole Opry to Marietta. Make that "May-retta."

Monday afternoon in Nashville, the lieutenant governor went down to old Music Row to The Alamo, Nashville's top shop for rhinestone suits, boots and cowboy hats.

He tried on hats. He priced a $350 pair of boots. But all he bought was a jar of boot polish and a pair of gray socks.

"This is the same way I feel state government should be run," he said, counting out the $3.50 total to the cashier. "You look around at everything you would like to have, but in the end, you buy only the necessities and make do."

A wonderful thing happened to Zell Miller in Nashville this week at the CMA awards show.

Zell met country comedian Jerry Clower, who is from Yazoo City, Mississippi, and who tells funny stories in person and on records for a living. He used to be a fertilizer salesman.

"I've been wanting to meet you, Lieutenant Governor Miller," Jerry Clower said, "'cause I have done used one of your stories on my latest album, and I give you credit for it. I say, 'This story comes from the lieutenant governor of the great state of Georgia.'"

News that George Busbee had just abdicted the governorship couldn't have made Zell Miller happier.

Later, I asked him to tell me the story. There was a reason for that. He's our lieutenant governor, the story happens in Georgia, and we deserve to hear it before the rest of the world.

Ladies and gentleman, Jerry Clower's budding ghostwriter, Zell Miller:

"This is a true story. It happened up in my hometown of Young Harris. Young Harris is a very small town. We didn't even have a fire department. Not even a volunteer fire department.

"One day, a house caught fire. The whole town gathered around to watch it. We were helpless to put it out. About that time, we saw a pickup truck come over the ridge. It was a local character named Fuzz Chastain. He had his wife with him, all their kids, a cousin or two, and some aunts and uncles.

"Fuzz drove right down to where we were all standing, but he didn't stop. He drove that pickup right into the middle of the fire. He jumped out and so did everybody else. They started beating the fire with anything they could find—even their clothes.

"It took 'em thirty minutes, but danged if they didn't put out the fire. The mayor of Young Harris was there. He said, 'This is the most courageous thing I have ever seen in Young Harris. Let's pass the hat for Fuzz Chastain.'

"They raised $17. The mayor presented the mony to Fuzz. 'Fuzz,' he said, 'the people of Young Harris appreciate this heroic act of yours.' Fuzz's hair was singed. His clothes were burned and torn.

"'But Fuzz, there is one thing I'd like to know,' the mayor went on, 'What are you going to do with this money?'

"Fuzz thought a minute and then said, 'Well, Mr. Mayor, I guess the first thing I ought to do is get the brakes fixed on that pickup.'"

If Zell Miller's new "career" takes off, don't worry if he can mix show business with politics. Lest we forget, in many respects, they're the same.

Dreaming at the Twilite

It was Ladies Night at the Twilite Club down on Stewart Avenue, but it was too cold for a crowd. Nights like this are for covering up early, even if the bedroom is a lonely place. There is always the cat.

The band was allegedly country. Mostly, it was loud and did too many Elvis numbers. The singer's shirt was unbuttoned nearly all the way down. That's not country.

"Y'all got any requests?" he asked the sparse audience.

"Yeah," said an old girl sitting at the table next to mine. She was drinking salty dogs. "Turn that thang down."

Big Jim Cook had an easy night. He's the bouncer. The Twilite Club isn't a rough place, by any means, but like the lady who runs it said, "We're getting a little more riff-raff since the Nugget Club burned down."

Jim Cook is twenty-seven and big as a Haggard hit single. He's 6-4 and 240 and he still goes home to Milner, which is near Griffin, on the weekends to see his mother. "I ain't nothing," he says, "but an old country boy from the woods."

He probably could have been more than that, and may yet be. That is his story. Jim Cook was a good enough high school basketball player that Georgia Tech offered a scholarship. He turned it down. "I just didn't know what I wanted to do," is his explanation. That's not the best reason in the world to pass up a free college education, but like the man said, ten years later it will have to do.

The band *was* loud, but we talked between ear-splitting choruses, and I found out what Jim Cook wants to be more than anything else is a famous professional wrestler. Granny says *rassler*.

He used to be skinny, he said, but he wandered into one of those health spas one day and now he could walk around with a Datsun on his back.

"Some of the wrestlers come in here," he said. "They got me interested. You can make a lot of money."

You can. You can also get thrown on the floor and crab-locked and full-Nelsoned until you are a walking bruise. And you can spend a great deal of your time jumping around in your underwear in front of screaming crowds packed into tank town high school gymnasiums. Wrestling has its bush leagues, too. Verne Gagne and Lou Thetz stayed at the Ritz and drank call brands. Jim Cook is doing Carrollton and Porterdale.

He was married, but that ended in divorce and one child. He was a yardman at an auto transport company in Atlanta. That ended when he was laid off. A wrestler now retired, one Rocket Monroe, helped him learn the basics, and Jim Cook took off for California and Canada to seek his wrestling fortune.

He didn't find it. Vancouver can be rotten lonely and rainy. He worked his way back South, back through Kansas City and Oklahoma. A man in Oklahoma told him to go home and find somebody to teach him to wrestle.

"That's the problem," the big man said. "Most of the guys I know have to wrestle every night. They don't have the time to train me."

He insists wrestling isn't fake. "You can get hurt if you don't know what you're doing," he said. No matter where he wrestles, the place is packed. Watching wrestling is like eating collards. If you're hooked, you're hooked.

He's gone against some of the biggies in the area: The Anderson Brothers, Stan Hansen, Dick Slater, a Korean guy whose name he can't spell, Bill White, and a masked fellow who calls himself The Executioner. Mostly, he loses. "But I'm a good guy," he explained. "The people always cheer me on."

Jim Cook stayed around until the Twilite Club went dark for a few restful hours. "The only time we really have trouble," he had said, "is when somebody comes in from another part of town and doesn't know what kind of place this is. Usually, by the time anybody is ready to do more than talk, he's too drunk to fight."

When he finally went home, it was to a room at the Alamo Plaza Motel, a southside relic. There would hopefully be the chance to work out the following day. And maybe there will also be the chance someday to get off the bottom of the cards, to get out of the preliminaries and into the main events. To make a name. To make a buck. To be there in the City Auditorium on Friday nights when the masses come and the lights are shining brightly.

A country boy from Milner has a dream.

The Den Mother of Country Music

NASHVILLE—They put Tootsie Bess to rest on a snowy hillside in Nashville Tuesday afternoon. When she died of cancer at sixty-four the other day, they should have lowered every flag in the city to half-mast. She was somebody. She was the den mother of country music.

Without her, there might not have been the stardom and the music of people like Tom T. Hall. Or Kris Kristofferson. Or Roger Miller. Or Johnny Rodrigues. Or Hank Williams, or any number of pickers and singers who have made what otherwise would have been nothing more than Chattanooga North into a multi-million dollar recording Mecca called Music City U.S.A.

Without her, many who stayed and finally caught their dreams might have long since caught the next bus back home. Like a man said at Tootsie's funeral Tuesday, "You can find rhinestones and applause in Nashville, but before you do, it can be the loneliest place in the world."

Hattie Louise "Tootsie" Bess ran a beer joint in Nashville at Fifth and Broadway called Tootsie's Orchid Lounge. There was a back door. It led to an alley that led to the stage entrance of the old Ryman Auditorium, for years the home of the Grand Ole Opry.

Grant Turner, the Opry announcer, said, "You could leave Tootsie's at 7:58 and still be on stage at the Opry at 8 o'clock." So many did just that.

When Tom T. Hall first came to Nashville, he nearly starved. Tootsie fed him. Tootsie encouraged him. Tootsie gave him pocket money. Today, Tom T. Hall sells millions of records and trucks on television.

Kris Kristofferson worked construction and swept floors in Nashville while trying to peddle his music. He was one of Tootsie's pets. She kept him going until another star was born.

Roger Miller was a Nashville bellhop. He would write one of his biggest hits, "Dang Me," in a booth at Tootsie's.

"She ran a beer joint," said Tom T. Hall, "but to young songwriters and musicians, she was a small finance company, a booking agent, and a counsellor."

Maybe Ernest Tubb put it even better. "Tootsie," he said, "was the softest touch in town."

I was in her place only once. But I remember the beer being cold and the atmosphere being warm and Tootsie saying as my party left, "Y'all come back when you can stay longer."

Her juke box had million sellers. It also had non-sellers. When nobody else would play a youngster's record, Tootsie would put it next to "Hello Walls," and give the kid the best chance she could.

She kept order with a hatpin. Get rowdy and out you went at the point of her hatpin. Come back tomorrow and apologize, and all was forgiven.

There were five inches of fresh snow on the ground in Nashville Tuesday. Still, the funeral home was packed with people and flowers.

The registry was a country music who's who. Mel Tillis sent flowers. There was a wreath from Ben Smathers and his mountain cloggers. Ernest Tubb and his son Justin sent a heart-shaped arrangement. There was a break in the middle of the heart. It was pierced with a hatpin.

Roy Acuff sat down front for the services. One of the Wilburn Brothers was close to him. Included in the grieving family was Tootsie's son-in-law, who is an Opry drummer. Tom T. Hall was one of the pallbearers. Grant Turner got up and said a few words. And Connie Smith stood behind Tootsie's lavender casket and sang "In the Sweet By and By," "Amazing Grace," and "How Great Thou Art." She has never sounded better.

Tootsie had friends who weren't stars. "She was just as happy to see a ditch digger walk in as the biggest name in town," said a friend. Sitting next to a millionaire singer at the funeral was a man in a service station outfit. He hadn't had time to wash the grease off his hands.

The preacher read a telegram from Tennessee Sen. Howard Baker. He talked about the necessity of loving one another and said Mrs. Bess, as he called her, performed that task exactly as the Good Book intended.

It could be the Good Lord likes the company of a bighearted saloonkeeper, too.

Willie at the White House

WASHINGTON—People wearing bags over their heads and carrying signs that screamed about "massacres" in their native Iran paraded in front of the White House Wednesday evening.

To the north of the city at Camp David, three powerful leaders of three powerful nations struggled to find a way to bring peace to another troubled land.

The papers were filled with stories of death and destruction in Nicaragua, and half the world is on strike.

But the night was clear, and cool and the moon was full and bright in Washington Wednesday. And out on the south lawn of the White House, a million miles from everything else, a bearded man wearing a red bandana took a long pull from a wine bottle and commenced to sing.

He sang "Whiskey River" first; then he sang "Crazy" and "Amazing Grace" and "Georgia" and something called "Blue Eyes Crying in the Rain." As he sang "Blue Eyes Crying in the Rain" I had a thought, probably an outrageous one, but at least worth a moment of consideration:

Jimmy Carter didn't make his own party Wednesday night, the one he threw to honor stockcar drivers. His wife announced to the crowd that "only something the magnitude of the summit talks would have kept him away."

He made a mistake by not coming. And he made a mistake by not bringing Egypt's Sadat and Israel's Begin with him.

Sit the two of them down together in front of Willie Nelson, I thought. Bring the people with the bags over their heads inside, too. Give them all a cold beer and let them listen to Willie Nelson. After "Blue Eyes Crying in the Rain," who would still want to fight?

Wednesday night was Jimmy Carter fulfilling a promise. When he was governor of Georgia, he made it an annual practice to host stockcar drivers and even sportwriters at the mansion on West Paces Ferry.

You know about the stockcar racing. Stockcar racing isn't Watkins Glen or spiffy gentlemen in sleek Porsches and Ferraris. It is Talledega and Daytona and Atlanta International Raceway and beer and fried chicken and a punch in the nose because you said a Chevrolet can whip a Dodge or, worse, you insulted the glorious memory of Fireball Roberts.

"Jimmy told us if he ever got to be president," explained driver David Pearson, "we would share in some of the glory. Here we are."

And there they were. Pearson, Petty, Waldrip, Yarborough, and Bill France, the head kabolla of stockcar racing. And even some sportswriters and even Billy Carter, and especially Willie Nelson, who sang with Amy and Rosalynn and Billy's wife, Sybil.

The night was heavy with doubleknit and denim.

The Washington papers the next day didn't quite know what to make of the affair. They said it did prove we are under the reign of a populist president. They went into great detail concerning the Carters' love for stockcar racing and explained stockcar racing grew in the South from an earlier preoccupation with running moonshine.

"I ain't never run moonshine," Richard Petty told a reporter, "but I don't know about the rest of my family."

I go back to those parties at the governor's mansion. The first one was a flop because Rosalynn had charge of the food and entertainment. She offered an exotic menu that included fish-like things that still had their eyes. The entertainment was an operatic trio.

I can still see A. J. Foyt shifting uncomfortably from one cowboy boot to another and Jabe Thomas driving to the front of the mansion in his mechanic's truck. I can still hear somebody saying, "This would make Curtis Turner roll over in his grave." Rosalynn Carter stepped onto the bandshell behind the White House Wednesday night and apologized for all that. She had learned her lesson. The fare this evening was beer and wine and roast beef and ham and corn bread. The program announced, "Selections by Willie Nelson."

I could probably dabble around in all this for some hidden political meaning. But the heck with that.

What happened Wednesday night at the home of the president of the United States was a large group of mostly Southern people got together in the backyard for a picnic and to listen to one of their own sing his red bandana off. Andy Jackson used to give the same kind of parties here, and he wound up on the $20 bill.

In the middle of that singing, when people had squared off to clog on the lawn, a fellow I know from Georgia came to my table and whispered in my ear:

"My great-grandfather was wounded at the Battle of Sharpsburg. He was captured at Gettysburg. He had to limp all the way home to Georgia. If he could see this tonight, he'd think we won after all."

Sweet Innocence

That was her daddy, the girl said, playing with the country band that performed, sort of, in one corner of the room. They played the old songs—hungry songs and cheatin' songs—and they made them sound even older.

Her mama was in and out, too. She was a stout, tightfaced woman and she gave the appearance of running things. A would-be rowdy was rendered nearly peepless after mama suggested his conduct was reaching the bouncing stage.

It doesn't matter the name of the town or the name of the joint, because there are maybe a million towns and million joints just like them.

Picture a two-lane highway running through what seems like nowhere on a warm Georgia spring night. Suddenly, up ahead, the glare of neon is blinking and beckoning. Park some trucks around. Behold, the local fast crowd in its natural habitat.

The girl worked feverishly behind the bar while daddy played and mama patrolled. She was pretty. Dark hair and dark eyes. Plump, a little, but pleasingly so. She wore pink chiffon. Tight pants and a blouse that exposed little, but enough to gather the eyes of the gentleman customers seated around on the bar stools.

I judged her innocent somehow, and trained to perform. At her obviously tender age, could she know what her audience was thinking as she moved gracefully back and forth behind the bar? Likely not.

They ordered beer, of course, and from some unseen cache she produced it in cold, longneck bottles. They were emptied nearly as fast as she could bring more.

There was booze, too. That was surprising, this far into the hinterlands. I wondered to a man next to me how long the county had had liquor.

"Long as there's been anybody around to drink it, I guess," he said. Then, he corrected himself. "You mean how long's it been legal? Four or five years, I guess."

And the Baptists and the bootleggers are still fighting it, somebody added.

I watched the girl. She had been trained well. Her performance was splendid. I waited for a slip, something that would unveil that innocence that seemed unfit for midnight in a smoky, backroads saloon. It never came.

A youngster sat alone at the end of the bar, nursing a beer.

"One more?" the girl asked.

The youngster nearly blushed from her attention. He held the bottle against a light. It was nearly empty.

"Believe I've had enough," he said.

"Just one more?" the girl persisted. "For me?"

"One more," the youngster said. He seemed pleased he had pleased her.

She even sang. Daddy played while she sang. The place was hers all over again.

"Sounds just like Linda Ronstadt, don't she?" the man with the liquor information said to me.

I agreed. It's smart, I figured, for a stranger to agree.

The band took a break, and the girl asked nobody in particular for money to play the jukebox. To a man, her subjects reached into their pockets for change.

The chosen one marched to the jukebox and obediently pushed the buttons as the girl called out the numbers of her favorite songs.

The crowd began to thin later. There were no more calls for drinks. The girl walked to where I was sitting and propped herself on the bar. She asked where I was from. I told her.

"I was in Atlanta once," she said. She named the hotel. "I didn't like it. That place is too big for me."

There it was. Simple girl, simple tastes. Maybe one day she can leave this, I thought. Find some nice fellow with a good job and raise a family.

"Daddy gone?" the girl asked a waitress, who nodded yes.

"Mama, too?" she asked next. Mama was gone, too.

"Damn, it's about time," said the girl, reaching for a bottle of vodka on the shelf. She filled a glass and heaved down its contents in one hard gulp.

4

THOSE WERE THE DAYS

The first column in this section is about my fifteenth year high school reunion that turned out to be a tremendous success. One of my ex-wives came. She looked terrific. Dudley Stamps, who was a good friend in school, also came to the reunion.

He said to me, "I see your damn picture in the newspaper sometimes, but I don't read any of that garbage." When we had some beer later, I hugged his neck anyway.

The last column in this section is about Bill Johnson, who was a classmate in college. He died. I wish I could hug his neck one more time.

The Class of '64

The fellow who was president of my high school senior class called the other day to ask a favor. He wants me to write something witty and clever to be used as an invitation to our fifteenth year class reunion next summer.

We never had a tenth year reunion, which was just as well with me. The principal's office statute of limitations probably doesn't run out in ten years. They might still have had something on me.

Like there was the book I never got around to returning to the school library. The posse didn't come back until the early seventies. Our librarian was also the principal's wife, and she ran the library with an iron hand. Nuclear power plants are maintained with less regimentation.

I was remembering some of the library rules at my high school:

—— Thou shalt not touch a book unless your hands have been scrubbed clean and thoroughly inspected by the head librarian. ("A smudge on a book is an insult to literature.")

45

—— Thou shalt not wear wristwatches or bracelets into the library because a wristwatch or a bracelet could make a scratch on one of the library tables, God forbid.

(I am convinced anybody caught scratching a library table at my high school would have been draggd out behind the auditorium and shot, not to mention having his or her library privileges taken away.)

—— Thou shalt not talk while in the library, nor giggle nor grunt nor pull a chair from under a table so as to make the noise a chair being pulled from under a table will inevitably make.

(Once a fat girl, who was stronger than I, punched me in the belly in the library because I wouldn't give her the sports section of the newspaper. I grunted from the punch and attempted to flee for fear of further blows.

(In my haste, I pulled my chair from under the table and it made a noise. I had to stay after school every day for a week and my stomach hurt for a month. The fat girl's nickname was "Mean Mama," incidentally.)

Irregardless—which isn't a word but was used a hundred times a day by one of the coaches—I still look back on my high school years with favor.

I was on the baseball team and the basketball team, and I was in the Key Club and I had a steady girlfriend, which is another reason I wasn't particularly disturbed when we had no tenth year reunion.

The last time I saw my steady girlfriend, who later became much more than that, she was loading our living room furniture, my stereo, the bed, and the washer and dryer into the back of a truck.

Who knows what she might still have been in the market for?

Frankly, I am puzzled as to what to write witty and clever for the invitation.

I can say we'll all drink a few beers, likely, and we won't have to hide behind Robert's and Alf's drive-in to do it.

We'll take a look at one another and say things like, "You haven't changed a bit" when what we really mean is, "I wouldn't have known you in a million years because the last time I saw you, you had hair."

We'll see who is fat now who didn't used to be, and who lost weight and who is still obnoxious and who got rich and who wouldn't kiss you goodnight for love nor money in school but has been pregnant practically every day since graduation. And who has retained all his hair and his slim, boyish figure. Like me.

We'll listen to the old songs and tell a lie or two.

And maybe for old times' sake, I'll even have a dance with my steady girlfriend who later became much more than that while somebody sings, "In the Still of the Night."

Come to think of it, fifteen years later is a perfect time to have a high school reunion. It's a short enough period for the good memories to be fresh and for the ravages of age to have taken only a soft toll.

And long enough to have forgiven an overdue library book, a punch in the belly, and even the night I walked into an empty house and found out for the first time adulthood isn't all it was cracked up to be.

They Were Playing Our Songs

The three of us were children of the forties, but we had left the campus when the trouble began. We were born of men back from the war and the women who waited for them to come home.

We barely remember Korea. My daddy was gone two years, and I really never knew why. The name Harry Truman rings a vague bell. The thing I remember most about Ike was how the people down home cursed him for spending too much time playing golf at Augusta.

Kennedy was ours, but we lost him in high school. Vietnam was festering during our college days, but on a sleepy Deep South campus, it would take longer for the explosion of dissent to finally come.

After school, one of us—ordered to do so—went to the fight. The other two, lucky as hell, stayed home and learned about making a living.

We made the same fraternal pledge fifteen years ago. That tie still binds us somehow. One of us is losing his hair. Another has put on a few pounds. I get down in my back occasionally and I don't sleep as well as I used to.

Monday night was a reunion of sorts. It is rare we can be together as a threesome for an evening out anymore.

But this was special. They were playing our songs at a club called the Harlequin. We wouldn't have missed it.

First, you must get this picture: The year is 1964. The band is black and loud. Beer cans are illegal on campus. There was such a thing in those days, however, as "Humdinger" milkshake cups. They would hold two full cans until they became soggy and fell apart. A date must be selected carefully. She must not mind beer on her skirt. There were a lot of good women like that in 1964.

And the band would play until midnight, time to beat the curfew back to the girls' dorms. The frolic before was always grand and glorious because, as that campus anthem went, we came to college not for knowledge, but to raise hell while we're here.

Our music was a soulful strut. Maurice Williams and the Zodiacs, "Stay;" The Isley Brothers, "Twist and Shout;" The Temptations, "My Girl;" The Drifters, "Save the Last Dance for Me;" Marvin Gaye and the classic, "Stubborn Kind of Fellow."

And two more groups, hallowed be their names: The Atlanta Tams. The Showmen.

We were on the edge of our seats Monday night. And then, there they were. Four black men from Norfolk, Virginia. Four black men who can dance and sing and take you back where, the Lord knows, you never wanted to leave in the first place.

Four black men called The Showmen who put "39-21-46" on a record years ago.

"We're gonna take the roof off this place," they said, and they did.

The Tams were next. "Atlanta's own Atlanta Tams," announced the announcer. They have aged, the Tams. But their voices still blend in perfect, deep harmony, and when they sang "What Kind of Fool?" everybody in the house was nineteen years old again.

As is the custom, we went down front to the stage before the night was over. We sang and we danced along. Our parents did the same to Big Band swing. A group of teenyboppers went crazy over a child named Shaun Cassidy at the Omni the other night. Who knows what sound will attract our children?

But does it really matter? Music, any kind of music, is memories and sometimes hope for the future. Music can soothe, music can hurt. Music can be lost loves and old friends. Music can give advice worth heeding.

"Listen to that," said one of us to the other two Monday night. "They're right, you know."

The Tams were singing. It was one of their old songs. You have missed something if you have never heard it. Three fellows bound for middle-age gathered in every word:

"Be Young.

"Be Foolish.

"Be Happy."

When the Smoke Had Cleared

Dorsey Hill still laughs about the night I came through fraternity rush at the Sigma Pi house in Athens.

"Damn'dest sight I ever saw," he says. "You were wearing white socks and black, pointed-toe shoes, and your head was skinned. I mean *skinned*. I said, 'Where on earth did THAT come from?'"

But they took in the skinhead anyway at the house on Milledge Avenue, the one with the white columns, and there were some high times the next four years.

I forget exactly who went to put the Chi Omega owl to the torch. The Chi Omega sorority house was across the street from ours, and they were an uppity bunch. One year they built a paper owl, a huge thing, for rush.

We were sitting on our front porch in those marvelous rocking chairs, and somebody thought it would be a good idea to burn the owl.

Every firetruck in Athens showed up to put it out. So did Dean Tate, dean of University of Georgia men. When the smoke had cleared, we were on something called "social probation."

That meant we couldn't have another party until every member had graduated from school, had fulfilled his military obligation, and had fathered at least two legitimate children.

In retrospect, it was worth it. Fifty silly sorority girls, outraged and bewildered, watching their precious paper owl go up in a glorious blaze. Strike another one for dear old Sigma Pi.

I could do this all day. There was the basement we called the "Boom-Boom Room." Beware, young coed, to enter there. It was in the "Boom-Boom Room" where we administered a water-drinking torture called "Cardinal Puff" during initiation. A pledge almost died after "Cardinal Puff" one night.

Maybe that is what started it. Sigma Pi once thrived. We had the captain of the football team, the captain of the basektball team. But hard times came along.

I heard they had to sell that beautiful old house to pay their way out of debt. I heard the membership had fallen off to almost nothing. I heard the university had even taken away the charter and that Sigma Pi had died a quiet, slow death on the campus.

I shed a quick tear, but nothing more. It's been a long time.

But there was a telephone call last week. It was from a Georgia coed. She had a sense of urgency in her voice.

"You've got to help," she said.

"Help who?" I answered.

"Sigma Pi at Georgia," she went on. "I'm dating this guy who's a member. They're trying to make a comeback, but they're about to go bankrupt. They lost a couple of pledges who were supposed to move into the house. They needed their money for rent. One of them joined the Navy."

I called the Sigma Pi house in Athens. The president answered the telephone. We used to have eighty members. "We've got eleven," he said. We sent more than that to burn the Chi Omega owl.

The new house is being rented from a university faculty member, the young man said. The current members are trying to hold on to the house until more members can be pledged. More members, more money.

"We even keep the heat turned off," he said, "to save money." There are no parties, the president told me, because there is no money for parties. There are no meals at the house because who can afford cooks? What Sigma Pi in Athens needs and wants is some help from the alumni. A donation, maybe, at least a visit to help with rush.

"Just some encouragement," said the president.

That's not much to ask. I'll try to get up a group and come over, I said. We'll have a few cold ones and talk about it. And afterwards maybe we'll all go over to Chi Omega and apologize.

In a pig's eye, we will.

Sweetheart of Sigma Chi

How I got invited to a University of Georgia fraternity party at my age isn't the story here. The story is what I saw when I went there.

It was the Sigma Chi's annual gathering to select a chapter sweetheart. Sigma Chis the nation over take selecting a chapter sweetheart seriously because somebody once immortalized young ladies so chosen with a popular song entitled, appropriately enough, "Sweetheart of Sigma Chi."

A banquet preceded the party. I don't know what I expected. I had seen *Animal House*. I knew that it was only a short time ago the college campus was a social battleground. Sometimes, it was just a battleground.

But what, I asked myself, are the prevailing moods and customs of the campus on this, the eve of the 1980s?

I knew about the early sixties. It was button-down, slick-it-back, eat, drink and chase Mary in the tight skirt and monogrammed sweater. The late sixties and early seventies were angry and hip and taking things that made you crazy and wearing clothes to look the part.

The Sigma Chis on this night came dressed as a *GQ* ad. They were three-pieced and button-downed and blown-dried almost to a man. Their dates were clones from the Phi Mu house fifteen years ago.

The chapter president, whose hair was shorter than mine, opened with a moving invocation. Gentlemen rose from their seats when ladies excused themselves from the tables. The dinner lasted well over an hour. Nobody threw a single morsel of food.

When the new sweetheart was introduced, the chapter stood as one and sang her their delicate, obviously inspired rendition of the sweetheart song while she cried. Donna Reed would have played her part. John Belushi would have been asked to leave.

There was some loosening up when the party began, but the frolic that followed wouldn't have qualified as even a mild public disturbance.

The band played Marvin Gaye's "Stubborn Kind of Fellow," "Sixty Minute Man," and the Temptations' "My Girl." I know all the words to all three songs. A young man asked for something by Jackie Wilson, and the band gave him "Lonely Teardrops." Who turned back the time machine?

The booze was mostly beer. Somebody had a half-gallon of Jim Beam bourbon and was pouring it into Coca-Cola. The smokers I saw were pulling on Marlboros.

Later in the evening, a small ice fight broke out—it always did— and everybody danced the "Gator." I know grown people who still dance the "Gator," which involves lying on the floor and acting like a half-crazed reptile with a bad case of the shakes.

The University of Georgia was never a leader in the radical league and the war is over now and things are quieter everywhere, but it did occur to me after the Sigma Chi party that perhaps life on the campus has returned to normal, sis-boom-bah.

—— Fraternities and sororities, spurned by many students just a few years ago, are making a big comeback at Georgia. "We are nearly overrun during rush," a Sigma Chi told me.

—— Pot smoking is still prevalent among some students, I was told, but "drinking is back stronger than ever." Sigma Chi fines members caught smoking pot in the fraternity house.

—— Political activism is down on the Georgia campus. SDS is dead and gone. The student body president ran with a bag over his head, the "Unknown Candidate" with no platform. He won in a walk.

The strongest and most active group on campus, believe it or not, is the Young Americans for Freedom, a conservative, pro-Reagan outfit.

"They don't want to stop a war," said an editor at the student newspaper, "they want to start one."

Wonders never cease, and spring quarter approaches. Let's go get a six-pack and have a panty raid.

One for Bill Johnson

ATHENS—Winter quarter was a sinus headache that seemed to linger on and on. The glory of the fall and football had passed. Springtime on the University of Georgia campus was always brightness and color and cold beer in tall cups and young things from Fitzgerald and Dalton whose mommas would have fainted had they known their babies were parading around in public dressed like that. And would it all ever return again and save us from January's gloom?

There was only a trickle of people about the campus Monday. Joggers ran up Lumpkin Street. Will this generation's legacy be a pair of worn running shoes and a green sweatshirt? The Campus Crusade for Christ is presenting *Master of Illusion* this week. One of the sorority houses has a banner hanging outside congratulating a sister for being accepted to the Harvard Law School. Girls used to go to college to find a husband.

But things change. There is even a sign now at the entrance to the athletic department training room in the Georgia Coliseum that reads, "Women are in the training room. Remember to wear your shorts." I was thinking of some names like Rissmiller and Swinford and Ridlehuber as I read that sign. Would they have stood for such encroachment? Women in the training room, indeed.

Who can come back here—even in the depths of the winter doldrums—and not launch himself into a sentimental journey? Boys become men here. Gangly, chirping girls become sophisticated women. How many of us had that first, heady taste of sin on these grounds? I recall being anxious to leave. I was out of my mind.

Bill Johnson loved Georgia. He loved everything about it. We were in the same, overloaded boat. We both had school, and we both—by choice—had work as well. Bill Johnson was employed by an Athens radio station. I worked for an Athens newspaper.

How do friendships begin? He was "the voice" of Athens High School sports. I was second on a two-man sports department totem pole. The boss covered the Bulldogs. I had Athens High. My friend Bill Johnson and I were together in a thousand rickety, crowded press boxes in places like Gainesville and Augusta and Hartwell and Elberton.

He was good at what he did. Bill Johnson was barely past twenty, but there could be no question as to his promise as a sportscaster. His voice was smooth, yet strong. There were those nights after games we would drive back to Athens together and fantasize about our futures.

"Do you think," he would ask, "we'll ever get to the big time?"

I reckoned that we would. We promised if one of us made it and the other did not, the friendship would last. I have never made a more sincere promise.

There is something about those days of dreaming. There are no limits in an ambitious mind. Bill Johnson would be as good and as important as Ed Thilenius someday. And I would be paid to write a story about a ball game for an Atlanta newspaper.

The last time I saw Bill Johnson was the day he graduated from Georgia. We had a few last beers together and said how much we would miss each other. He also had to leave a young wife in Athens for a short military obligation. But then he would be back and look out, Lindsey Nelson.

That was March 1966. Spring quarter was beautiful that year. We wrote back and forth. He was stationed somewhere in Texas.

Came the autumn and a wonderful Georgia football team. You remember. Kirby Moore. Kent Lawrence. George Patton. Bill Stanfill.

There was the second half comeback at Auburn that gave Vince Dooley his first Southeastern Conference title. Undefeated Georgia Tech fell the next week in Stanford Stadium. And Georgia would go on to the Cotton Bowl and belittle Southern Methodist.

Somewhere tucked away I have Bill Johnson's last letter. He was ill, he said. It was the first I knew about it. Some crazy blood infection. But he said don't worry. He said the doctors were thinking of letting him go to Dallas to see Georgia in the Cotton Bowl.

A week later, on December 7, Bill Johnson died. He was twenty-three.

The church up in Summerville, his hometown, was packed. When we carried him through town to the cemetery, the old men stopped on the streets and covered their hearts with their hats. The young widow cried hard.

Monday, as I walked across the campus, I remembered another promise. I told Bill Johnson I would mention him one day in a column if I ever got a job with a big city newspaper.

This is that mention. It's for a friend, a long time gone.

5

THE VIEW FROM LEFT FIELD

I knew it was time for me to get out of sportswriting when I covered the 1978 Super Bowl game between Dallas and Denver and enjoyed the halftime show that featured dogs catching frisbees more than I did the football game.

I will still fall into a sports column now and then, however. It's comfortable there, like an old pair of sneakers.

At the Ball Game With My Dad

I would have taken my father out to the ball game Tuesday night. I would have taken him to the Atlanta Stadium to see Pete Rose try to break Wee Willie Keeler's hitting streak record.

His birthday is Saturday. He would have been sixty-six. A trip to the ball game would have been a nice present from a son to his father.

He was an athlete himself, my dad. And he was a strapping man with alleged blinding speed in his youth. He was taller than Pete Rose, but similar in stocky frame. One time he picked up the back of a 1949 Hudson. I saw him do it.

My father would have loved Tuesday night at the ball park. Nice summer evening. Big, noisy crowd. My father always enjoyed singing the national anthem at baseball games.

He had a big voice, a booming voice that could cut you down at one hundred yards when it broke into "He Leadeth Me" or our national anthem, his two favorite songs. He always sang along when they played the national anthem, no matter where or what event. One time I said to him, "I wish you wouldn't sing so loud. It's embarrassing."

He said to me, "Son, it's embarrassing when you don't sing along with me."

55

Tuesday night, just before Pete Rose stepped up to bat, going for forty-five straight, my father and I would have stood shoulder-to-shoulder and sung the national anthem together.

Pete Rose is my father's kind of man, I was thinking when Rose approached the plate in the first inning. Just before the game began, he had his picture made with a crippled boy and put his hat on the crippled boy's head.

"Look at the way that man moves," my father would have said of Rose. "He doesn't waste a motion. He has speed. He has strength. He has determination. That's the kind of man you want in a foxhole with you."

My father was a soldier. A damn good one.

His only objection to Pete Rose might have been Rose's hair. I noticed it precariously near his shoulders. His ears disappeared weeks ago. My father wore a crew cut. He thought everybody else should.

"I'll never get used to long hair on a ballplayer or a soldier," he might have said as Larry McWilliams of the Braves threw the first pitch of the ball game—a curve—"It's not what the Lord intended."

The curve to Rose is low for ball one. And then a foul deep to right that misses being a double by five feet. A fast ball outside, a curve catches the inside corner, the count goes full, two more fouls, then ball four. The streak holds at forty-four.

I never saw a major league baseball game with my father. We saw plenty of service ball together. He once coached the Fort Benning team. Coached in a Hawaiian shirt and a straw hat.

Later, we bummed around South Georgia one summer. My father had fallen on hard times, but he kept a ten-year-old fed and cared for during three of the best months of my life.

That summer, we spent night after hot South Georgia night fighting gnats and eating peanuts in broken-down Class D parks in Waycross and Moultrie and Tifton where something called the Georgia-Florida League still had life.

There is something special about a man with his son at a baseball game. A man and his son sat next to me Monday night when Pete Rose extended his batting streak to forty-four. As Pete strode to the plate for the first time, the boy asked his dad if he would take him to the rest room.

"Not now, son," said the father. "Not now. Pete Rose is batting."

The boy held on, uncomfortably, but appearing to understand the necessity of the effort.

When a man takes his son to a baseball game, I think, it establishes a link, one that won't easily be broken even in the face of a subsequent premature parting that might leave other scars.

I know that to be a fact.

Rose came up for a second time. "Let's go, Pete," my father would have screamed, loud enough to be heard in LaGrange. What the heck. Let him have his fun.

First pitch, Rose swings. A shot up the middle. Young McWilliams' gloved hand appears from nowhere and spears the drive. Rose drops his bat and gives the youngster a hand. Mostly, my father would have enjoyed the game Tuesday night because it was a vivid American scene. It was an act of patriotism, somehow, to have been there.

He would have looked at his fellow Americans eating hot dogs and drinking beer, he would have heard their cheers for the home runs by Horner and Murphy, and he would have said something like, "This is why your daddy went to war, son. This is what we fought to keep."

Rose is up again. The inning is the fifth. The game is tied, 3-3. A fake bunt, ball one. Another ball. Then a ground out to short. The tension builds.

Now, it is the seventh. The brutal Gene Garber is pitching for the Braves. A runner is on. One out. A fast ball strike on the outside corner. Two straight balls. A foul tip, the count is even. Then, another shot by Rose, toward left, the opposite field. But Horner is there for the out and a double play.

A final chance, and only that, remains. The ninth. The game has turned to slaughter. The Reds, for once, are the victims, 16-4. Atlanta has twenty-one hits. Even Garber has one. Pete Rose, whose name even sounds like a line drive, has none.

Two outs. Rose at the bat. "Pete! Pete! Pete!" the stadium is begging.

The first pitch from Garber. An attempted drag bunt to third goes foul. Two straight balls. A foul tip.

The ball leaves Garber's hand. A split second later, we will know.

Strike three. Swinging. It is over.

What Pete Rose did—hit safely in forty-four straight games— wasn't a man on the moon, I reminded myself as the stadium lights dimmed. It wasn't a lonely flight across the Atlantic or the first heart transplant.

But it was a good and honorable thing, a fierce man with a bat in his hand, playing a boy's game as it was meant to be played.

And I am thankful I had the chance to witness part of it, even the bitter end.

Tuesday night at the ball game, me and my dad had a helluva good time.

A Case of the Bleeps

I missed Pete Rose's post-game television interview Tuesday night after he had failed to extend his batting streak.

I was busy typing in the press box. I never promised the news editor a Rose column, but it seemed the thing to do what with the excitement the hitting streak had generated.

I understand it was an interesting interview. Ted Turner's nation-wide network carried it, and little old ladies coast-to-coast were swallowing their snuff.

Pete Rose, American Hero, said some dirty words. There were cameras all around him. He didn't know one was live. Ah, the magic of television.

I know some of the words Pete Rose said. Randy Donaldson of the Braves staff told me. Obviously, I can't print any of them here, but one has four letters and the other two have seven.

One of the other two may be hyphhenated, come to think of it. Spelling dirty words can be a tricky business, because most of them aren't in the dictionary. It's anybody's guess.

What we use in the newspaper for dirty words people say is "bleep." Using "bleep" shows how the influence of the electronic media is even slipping into real journalism.

When Johnny Carson says a dirty word on television, you don't hear the dirty word, you hear an electronic sound that goes "Bleep." Ah, the magic of television.

Wednesday, I was reading one of the local sportswriters' stories from the Rose interview. He quoted Pete as saying to Atlanta pitcher, Larry McWilliams, who robbed him of a base hit with a grand catch. "Why the hell did you catch that bleep-bleep ball?"

"Hell" is now OK in the newspaper. It is finally off the bleep list, in other words. Calling it a "bleep-bleep" ball also seems to indicate my earlier suspicions were correct. "Bleep-bleep" must be a hyphenated dirty word.

The sportswriter also quoted Rose as saying to all the sportswriters Tuesday night, "I'm going to miss you bleeps."

That bleep is no mystery to me at all. I know what ballplayers call sportswriters. Once, a ballplayer said to me, "You bleeping bleep, get your bleeping bleep away from my locker, or I'm going to knock the bleep out of you, and you can print that in your bleeping news-paper, and I don't give a bleep if you bleeping do."

I ran for the door. To save my bleep.

I am sure there were viewers Tuesday night offended by Rose's language. I just hope nobody was surprised that a big league baseball player curses. Cursing is a part of the game. Like spitting tobacco juice, scratching and adjusting, and becoming a free agent.

The first curse word I ever heard was at a baseball game. We chose up sides in the second grade and my team's first baseman, a fat boy named Roy who should have been in the fifth-grade game, chased a foul ball. He stumbled into a gully where there were many briars.

"Bleep!" he said as he picked the briars from his bleep, which was sore for a week.

The only thing Pete Rose said Tuesday night that surprised me was his expression of displeasure that the Braves' Gene Garber would pitch to him in the ninth inning "like it was the seventh game of the World Series."

What did Rose expect from a professional like Garber? Gene Garber pitches like Pete Rose bats. With the intensity of a runaway locomotive. Would Rose have eased up had it been Garber going for some sort of pitching record?

I know a word worse than any Pete Rose used on television Tuesday night. As much as I admire the man, I insist it must be applied to his remarks concerning Garber.

I has four letters, too.

B-U-S-H.

Scooter T. Washington: Blue Chipper

It was all over the Sunday paper about the recruiting of young athletes to play football at large universities in the region. It's that season. Children are snatched away from their mothers' arms back home in Twobit County and the next thing you know, the Head Coach is saying, "Ol' Dram Bowie from down in Twobit County is the finest prospect since Jiggy Smaha." Which brings up that musical question, has anybody seen Jiggy Smaha lately?

Recruiting is important. "You gotta have the horses," a coach once told me, "before you can pull the wagon." Coaches talk like that. Translated, it means if he doesn't get off his tail and sign some talent, he'll be selling tires at K-Mart the next time toe meets leather.

What I hear is that Tennessee is making a big move into Georgia this year in search of recruits to rebuild the once-mighty Volunteer program. You don't sign to go to Knoxville. You are sentenced there. Clemson is also usually heavy into seeking Georgia material. A Clemson raid especially makes Georgia Tech people mad.

"You know that tractorcade this weekend?" one asked me.

"They weren't farmers," he said. "They were Clemson fans on their way to Sears to buy clothes for the Gator Bowl."

From the various sources around the Southeast, I have come into possession of the list of the most-wanted high school athletes in the state. None have been signed yet. They are known as "blue-chippers" to the alumni. Coaches call them "job-savers." Here's the list.

ARDELL GROVER—Linebacker from Atlanta. Missed half his senior season with terminal acne. "He'll hit you," say the recruiters. Especially if you call him "Zit head," which a tenth-grader did shortly before Ardell rendered him unconscious during fifth-period study hall.

MARVIN PALAFOX—Marvin is a tight end. He's from Macon. Wears No. 82. Scored same number on his college boards. "Great hands," say the coaches. So do the cheerleaders.

SCOOTER T. WASHINGTON—Half-back from Savannah. Olympic speed. Expensive tastes. Wants two Cadillacs and a mink coat like Reggie Jackson's to sign. Answers the telephone, "You need the loot to get the Scoot." Contact through his agent Sam the Fly at the Wise Owl Pool and Recreation Hall, Savannah.

BILLY BOB WALTON—Offensive tackle from Moultrie. Extremely offensive. Friends call him "Dump Truck" because that's how big he is and he could eat all the pork chops and mashed potatoes out of the back of one. Made *Tifton Gazette* All-Area team. Makes Junior Samples look like David Niven. Loves buttermilk, but can't spell it.

LAVONNE (The Rolling Stone) LARUE—Led Columbus school in interceptions. Also led burglary ring to back entrance of Harry's One-Stop Stereo Shop. Got one-to-five, but sentence suspended when entire student body turned out as character witnesses after suggestion they do so by several of The Stone's "acquaintances."

"Can start for any college team in the country," says his coach, who didn't start him once and still carries the scars.

IRVING BOATRIGHT III—Quarterback for a fashionable northside Atlanta private school. Father prominent Atlanta attorney with homes on Hilton Head and Sea Island. Can't play a lick, but the head coach gets free legal advice and either house three weeks each summer. Started every game during high school career. Bed-wetter.

BARTHANATOMAY RIMJOB—Place-kicker. Son of Pakistani professor of Eastern philosophy at Clayton Junior College. Kicks soccer style. Made 110 straight extra points during prep career. Does not speak English and goes through fifteen-minute ancient ritual before every kick. Weighs ninety pounds soaking wet. Once scored winning touchdown on fake field goal by hiding ball in his turban.

ALBERT WARTZ JR.—From South Georgia. 6-4, 250. Plays quarterback. Questionable student. Thinks Henry Cabot Lodge is a motel in Bainbridge. Filled out recruiting questionnaire. By "sex," wrote: "Not since Mavis Wilson moved out of Hahira."

"This kid," says his high school coach, "doesn't know the meaning of 'quit.'" Doesn't know the meaning of third-grade arithmetic either. Leaning toward Alabama.

Super Girls

NEW ORLEANS—Actually, the Dallas Cowboys cheerleaders wear a lot of clothes, comparatively speaking. Seen *Sports Illustrated*'s annual porno issue this week? The cover is a lovely Brazilian child named Maria Joao, who is on the beach in Bahia. She is not naked, but you have to look closely to see that she isn't.

Inside the magazine, which is usually reserved for pictures of huge men perspiring in the name of sport, are more pictures of Maria and other Brazilian girls, all of whom would make a good man leave home for south of the border. I was especially impressed by a photograph of the same Maria Joao posing in much less than what underpants used to be in a fruit stand in Itapoa. Yes, she has some bananas.

Sports gets sexy occasionally. *High Society*, which makes Larry Flynt's *Hustler* look like *National Geographic*, is out with a picture spread (a bad choice of words) of girls cavorting in hockey uniforms. We recently went through the annual girl-in-the-dorm story with Arkansas. Jim Bouton's *Ball Four* was a study in major league voyeurism and the latest rumor is San Francisco leads all leagues in homosexual athletes. What more do you expect from the gay bay?

It is the Cowboys cheerleaders in their white hot pants and short halters, however, who currently rank first in sporting sensuality. Who cares if Roger Staubach will occasionally run out of the pocket? He doesn't even shave his legs. If he played in San Francisco he might, but that is beside the point.

There are thirty-two of them. The *Dallas Cowboys Weekly*, a publication sponsored by the team that will play the Denver Broncos here Sunday in Super Bowl XII, calls them "luscious lovelies." I'll hit some highlights:

There is Cheri Jo Adams. Have mercy. There is Monica Muehlhause. There ought to be a law. There is Debbie and Charyl and Connie and Lisa and Janice Garner, I think I love you.

Some of the other National Football League teams have tried to start their own cheerleading corps. Chicago has the Honey Bears. It's too cold in Chicago to show your navel after Labor Day. Curt Mosher, who was instrumental in founding the Cowboy cheerers, started the Atlanta Falconettes this past season. Get the hook. Denver has the Bronco Belles. They will compete sideline-to-sideline with the Cowboy cheerleaders here Sunday. I'm giving the Cowboy cheerleaders and three wiggles.

Steve Perkins is editor of *Dallas Cowboys Weekly* which has over 40,000 circulation. Each week of the season, the paper features a centerfold of one of the Cowboy cheerleaders. That is the main reason circulation is over 40,000.

"There were times," a Dallas man was saying, "when the pictures really got risque. Perkins didn't want to run them, but Tex Schramm (Cowboys president) said go ahead."

Perkins is here for the Super Bowl. The cheerleaders will be in Sunday. Perkins gives Schramm the credit for the cheerleaders' success and popularity. Watch a Dallas game and see the cheerleaders in action between almost every play. Television cameramen are no dummies.

"What Tex wants," says Perkins, "Tex gets. He demands the best in everything. He gets the right girls. He doesn't take any chances on them if he thinks they might cause a scandal."

So far, so good. Many of the cheerleaders are students. There are also legal secretaries, even a check-out girl at a supermarket. Some are married. There has been only one near-miss in the problem department.

A well-endowed young lady walked into a Corpus Christi topless bar recently and told the owner she was a Cowboy cheerleader and she was available for duty. The owner broke his neck getting an advertisement into the local newspaper. Schramm got wind of the hoax and informed the owner his new talent was no cheerleader. The show was cancelled.

Nearly 700 girls showed up for tryouts in Dallas last year. Those chosen are paid $15 per game. They are choreographed by a lady named, appropriately enough, Texi Waterman. The big bucks come later for personal appearances.

"It's a very lucrative situation for them," Perkins explained. "They might get $200 to go to San Antonio for the opening of an auto dealership. Five went to Little Rock the other day to open a store. They come from all over to try out. If a girl from Houston, say, makes the squad, she'll just move to Dallas.

The hottest-selling poster in the country pictures the Cowboy girls. The same photograph adorns T-shirts. They are on sale throughout the New Orleans French Quarter. Farrah in her wet suit is now a distant second. The first twenty days the posters were on the market, sales reached 20,000.

A number of questions remain concerning the Dallas darlings:

Do any of the players date cheerleaders?

Randy White rolled out of bounds late in a Dallas rout and asked one of the girls to dinner. She accepted.

Do any of the cheerleaders also have brains? Vanessa Baker, a six-year veteran, was recently awarded her master's degree in education from Texas Woman's University. She made all A's.

How can I get a Dallas Cowboy cheerleader of my very own?

A man from Hollywood called one of the cheerleaders last year and told her he had seen her on television and she was beautiful and he wanted to give her a screen test.

She went to see him. Not once, but twice, and then a third time. The last time, the man was no longer with the studio. He was fired for flying a Dallas Cowboy cheerleader to California three times when there were no jobs available at the studio.

Lest We Forget

For the past two weekends, the Falcons, Flames, Hawks, Techs, and Georgias have all been winners, and Losersville is surely dead they say. What miracles next? Wyman C. Lowe winning an election? MARTA making a friend?

In New York, they celebrate winning the World Series. Dallas holds the Super Bowl trophy. Even tiny Green Bay rejoices. It leads the league again. Here, we celebrate winning weekends. Atlanta is a sports cancer patient that just got the word its head cold is clearing up.

But forgive us our headiness over what others might consider routine. Little things mean a lot when the suffering has been long and constant.

Georgia Tech people are talking about a bowl game. Georgia's football team—and we can claim it as being at least "local"—was supposed to embarrass the basketball squad. Now, it has a chance to win the Southeastern Conference title.

A Falcon placekicker actually attempted a field goal in the waning moments of a game and made it for victory. The basketball Hawks defeated powerful Denver. And the Flames defeated Montreal in hockey. That's impossible. Montreal invented ice.

Sound the trumpets for the lame and downtrodden. A Polish boy has grown up to be pope, and Atlanta may be slowly rising from the ashes of athletic ruin.

(The only words of caution I might offer are not to forget that the Braves open spring training in just five months, and you remember what happened to the last pope.)

But before the seedy and checkered past of Atlanta sports is dumped into history's garbage pile, I would like to recall briefly a few of the dumpees. We simply cannot say goodbye to Losersville that quickly.

Now without at least a mention of some of our classic losers and the moments they gave us:

—— In the final game of the 1972 season, Falcon running-back Dave Hampton became the first player in the team's history to gain over 2,000 yards in a season. Play was stopped, and he was awarded the game ball. On the next snap, Hampton was thrown for a big loss and time ran out before he could regain the lost 1,000th.

—— In his first major league game, Braves' rookie shortstop Leo Foster booted the first ground ball hit to him. In his first major league at-bat, he hit into a triple play.

—— How did Losersville maintain itself year after year? Here are some of the names of Number One draft choices of Atlanta professional teams:

Skip Harlika, Gerald Tinker, Ron Broaddus, Tom Workman, John Small, Greg Marx, John Valleley, Joe Profit, Gene Hobart, George Trapp and Leo Carroll.

Of that group, Leo Carroll is the most notable. Drafted by the Falcons to improve their offensive line, he disappeared one night from training camp.

All he left was his Tiny Tim "Tiptoe Through the Tulips" record.

—— Early in their history, the Flames launched an ad campaign warning fans all season tickets would soon be gone, the demand being so great. A few years later, management was begging city leaders for donations to help meet the team payroll.

—— The closest the Falcons ever came to making the playoffs was in 1973. They won seven straight, but then collapsed and lost back-to-back to Buffalo and St. Louis to be eliminated from post-season play.

The head coach, Norman Van Brocklin, blamed it all on "Peachtree Street whores and bartenders."

—— In the middle of a thirteen-game losing streak, the Braves' team bus got lost in the middle of a swamp between the airport and downtown in Philadelphia.

—— Great Trades Number One: The Falcons gave Minnesota their top quarterback, Bob Berry, and their top draft choice for the coming year in return for the Vikings' number two linebacker, Lonnie Warwick, and number two quarterback, Bob Lee. The Vikings later used the draft choice to obtain a player named Chuck Foreman.

—— Great Trades Number Two: The Hawks gave Pete Maravich to the New Orleans Jazz.

—— For opening game 1977 the Braves asked Bert Lance to throw out the first ball. He was stuck in a stadium elevator for thirty minutes and finished the season lower than the pitiable team he had launched.

—— Falcons' quarterback Randy Johnson, sacked several times this given Sunday, led his team out of the huddle and lined up behind a guard.

—— That's nothing. Falcon fullback Art Malone and tight end Jim Mitchell went into an Atlanta huddle and got into a fistfight before the next play could be called.

—— Georgia Tech's 1971 football team was invited to the Peach Bowl, but voted not to go, much to the relief of head coach Bud Carson. Athletic officials demanded that another vote be taken, however, and the pressured players this time voted "yes."

Tech lost the game 41-18 in the mud and Carson got fired.

—— The first Falcons game ever was an exhibition at the Stadium against Philadelphia in 1966. The Falcons were to kick off to launch themselves into the National Football League.

The whistle blew and kicker Wade Traynam approached the ball. He whiffed it.

Third Down and Praise the Lord

A few years ago, I talked to a wonderful preacher named William Holmes Borders, pastor of the Wheat Street Baptist Church, about the political problems Atlanta was having at the time.

The conversation was background work for a series the *Atlanta Constitution* produced called "City in Crisis." A lot of people didn't like what "City in Crisis" said. It said Atlanta had polarized politically, our leaders were more interested in bickering than progressing, and the City Too Busy To Hate was growing ornery.

What I remember most about that conversation was William Holmes Borders saying, "What we need in this city more than anything else is for our sports teams to get off their behinds and give us something to cheer. The Lord willing, maybe someday they will."

"The Lord willing . . ." is the key phrase here. I will be the first to admit the recent rise to prominence of our local sporting heroes is nothing short of miraculous, but never have I heard so much credit given to Providence for athletic success.

Take the Falcons. The Falcons have seven victories and only four losses, and Sunday in New Orleans, the tipped-pass-for-a-touchdown that defeated the Saints in the final seconds was hailed by one reporter as the "Immaculate Reception."

The phraseology is superb. The man who threw the ball, oft-injured and maligned Steve Bartkowski, makes Lazarus look like an amateur. He has risen time and again from the quarterbacking graveyard, and he has also announced he has been "born again."

Another writer wondered, "Now that he has found the Lord, will he be able to find his secondary receivers?"

Here is what Steve Bartkowski said Sunday after his prayerful pass was answered:

"I just said, 'Praise the Lord.' He was with us. I was praying real hard."

You would think if anybody was going to get help from Above, it would have been the Saints, who are named for those with, I would imagine, heavy influence when it comes to heavenly decisions.

I don't know how much the Flames figure God has had to do with their resurrection. It wasn't that long ago there was talk of the franchise going broke, but now the Great Goalie in the Sky is certainly smiling down on Omni center ice.

Last time I looked, the Hawks were only a game behind in their division. Holy turnover! Sadly, the only team yet to be saved from the fiery depths of the league cellar is the Braves. Let's all stand and sing the first and last verses of "Just As I Am."

Even our collegiate athletes are in the spirit. Just about the time I had decided Vince Dooley had sold out to the devil for his Georgia team's incredible 8-1 season, I find out the Bulldog quarterback, Jeff Pyburn, has linked up with the Almighty.

And recall what happened a few weeks back when Georgia played Kentucky. Kentucky led 16-0 in the third quarter. But with seconds to play, there stood kicker Rex Robinson with a field-goal attempt to win the game.

"I just put my faith in the Lord," Robinson said after the kick was good, "and He blessed me."

Eddie Lee Ivery, the Georgia Tech running back who set an NCAA single-game rushing record against Air Force Saturday? He's deeply religious and occasionally offers a locker-room sermon.

And to think Atlanta used to have athletes like Alex Hawkins, the former Falcons receiver, who, admittedly, once made the Fellowship of Christian Athletes' all-opponent team.

I certainly don't want to cast aspersions on other people's faith—athletes included—but I do sort of wonder what with the Middle East (which is sort of God's home town), starvation, crime, and discos, does He really have time to bless a field goal or a touchdown pass?

Since I couldn't get a direct interview, I can only speculate the answer would probably be: Only when it is absolutely necessary. Like when Notre Dame is playing for the national championship.

The best religion-in-sports story I know is an old one, but one I would suggest every athlete and fan who thinks God gives an angel's feather about third-and-long should hear again.

A spectator at a boxing match was sitting next to a priest. When the bell rang, one of the fighters crossed himself before heading to the middle of the ring.

"Will that help him, Father?" asked the spectator.

"Not if he can't fight," said the priest.

Dwayne Sanders

DURHAM, N.C.—On September 19, 1978—a sweltering, late summer Saturday—Duke and Georgia Tech played a game of college football in a tattered, half-empty stadium named after an old coach.

Georgia Tech will remember the occasion as a nightmare, its second, thanks to Duke, in less than a year.

The Tech sidelines, as the end drew near, was an outdoor death row. Men and boys, condemned to bitter and solid defeat, cursed themselves, cursed the officials, and cursed the heat. Mostly, they cursed the heat.

A giant Tech lineman, his body bloody and drenched in sweat, looked toward the sky and spat at the sun.

Football, when you are losing, is a game of reassurance. We are surrounded by a million Indians, but any minute now the Cavalry will appear and the day will be saved. Sure, it will.

"We'll win it," said a Tech assistant at halftime, the score 10-3 in favor of Duke. "I can feel it."

"The second half," added a player, "belongs to us."

There was agreement all about. But help never came. The bugles never blew. And the heat—damn the heat—grew worse, completing the agony.

September 9, 1978: Duke 28, Georgia Tech 10.

Remember the day, if you favor the White and Gold, as an ungodly day of frustration.

Then, forget it. And put your mind to the misfortune of a young man who had a stinking Saturday, too.

His loss was worse than any silly football game ever played. As Duke was kicking Georgia Tech Saturday afternoon, he was in the Duke University Hospital fighting for the use of the bottom two-thirds of his body.

It happened shortly before the game began. Dwayne Sanders, who is eighteen, was warming up with his fellow Georgia Tech cheerleaders.

It was to be his first game as a cheerleader. He's a sophomore at Tech. "About the hardest worker we got," said one of his partners.

Dwayne Sanders, from Atlanta's Henderson High School, did a few flips on the trampoline in front of the Tech supporters.

Then, he did one more. The kickoff was near. The bands were playing, balloons filled the air. Duke was worrying about the running of Eddie Lee Ivery. Tech was worrying about the passing of Stanley Driskell.

"He made the flip okay," a Tech cheerleader explained it, "but when he did his roll coming out, that's when he got hurt."

It took the ambulance a half hour to arrive. Dwayne Sanders lay on the grass, unable to move the bottom portion of his body.

His neck was broken. His removal from the field was barely noticed. The remaining Tech cheerleaders gave him a good-luck cheer.

At this writing, Dwayne Sanders was in intensive care at the Duke Hospital. He was to undergo diagnostic surgery. A doctor explained:

"It's too early to know what the outcome will be. Depending on the swelling and the pressure, he could regain his movement. It was a freak thing. The only thing you can do is hope."

The doctor crossed both his fingers.

Another doctor said, "Had the injury been higher, it could have been fatal."

So scream if you will about Georgia Tech's football ineptness Saturday. Granted, the defense leaked. And the offense proved why Pepper Rodgers doesn't like the forward pass. And there were questionable calls by the officials at times. "Welcome to the Atlantic Coast Conference," somebody said.

And, of course, focus the blame for it all squarely upon the shoulders of the head coach, for that is the American way of losing.

But do it quickly and then get along to concern for Dwayne Sanders. There will be other Saturdays and other chances for Tech's football team. Believe it or not at this point, there will even be times to praise it.

On such occasions, may Dwayne Sanders, the Lord willing, be there to lead the cheers.

(*Dwayne Sanders did not recover. He remains confined to a wheelchair.*)

Baseball's Spittin' Image

Watching baseball on television offers a rare opportunity to see the players up close. The Big Eye can put you nose-to-nose with your favorite stars, most of whom apparently do not shave on a regular basis.

Thurman Munson of the Yankees, for instance, looks like Pancho Villa after a two-week binge. Davy Lopes of the Dodgers looks like the guy who waters his horse.

The reason television has so much time to show closeup shots of the players during a game is there is a lot of standing around in baseball. Baseball is the only sport where three-fourths of the game is a time out.

Here comes the batter towards the plate. Watch him take a few practice swings, knock the dirt out of his spikes, fondle the tar rag, and scratch and adjust. (When a game is on national television, players should be reminded to cut down on the scratching and adjusting.)

There stands the pitcher on the mound. Watch him tug at his cap, pound the ball in the glove, pick up the resin bag, throw it down again, lean over for the sign, shake it off, nod agreement to the next one, and then throw over to first.

The batter steps out and here we go again, more practice swinging, dirt-knocking, and, if you must know, more scratching and adjusting.

Television even goes into the dugouts now. Dugouts used to be off-limits to civilians. A player could scratch and adjust and yawn and figure tax shelters until the last man was out, and who would know?

"Now," a ballplayer told me, "you have to act interested in the game for nine full innings."

Seeing the players close up on television during this year's Yan-kees-Dodgers World Series has also brought to my attention another interesting thing about men who play baseball for a living.

They spit more than anybody else. I don't suppose they spit on each other that much, but they spit on everything else. Home plate. The bases. The on-deck circle. Their hands. They used to spit on the ball, but that was outlawed. Leo Durocher once spit on an umpire.

Many baseball players chew tobacco. They all look like they have cheek tumors, but at least you expect them to spit. God help them if they didn't.

But watching the World Series games, I've noticed even baseball players who chew nothing at all also spit a lot.

Take Reggie Jackson of the Yankees. He spits constantly, even when he is figuring tax shelters in the dugout. He spits walking to the plate. He spits while he is there. He spits on balls. He spits on strikes.

Reggie Jackson spits with style. He has two distinct spits. There is the straight "ptui!" spit where he simply applies cheek and lip pressure.

His deluxe, superstar spit—typically flamboyant—is his through-the-teeth-line-drive-spit, however. He can fire away five to ten quick streams through the gap in his two front teeth faster than a Ron Guidry fastball.

One of the advantages to playing major-league baseball, I suppose, is it is one of the few professions that allows you to spit on national television and not be considered uncouth.

Other professional athletes don't have that luxury. Imagine Jack Nicklaus walking away from a putt on the scenic sixteenth green at Augusta and spitting. Basketball players wouldn't spit on a shiny hardwood floor. Hockey players might spit on the ice if they had more teeth. Jockeys don't spit during horse races out of concern for their fellow riders to the rear.

A private citizen certainly can't spit in public. It is considered nasty, and it could spread disease. It's like a New Yorker mentioned to me recently.

"Strange thing about the subways in New York," he said. "You spit and they fine you $25, but you can throw up for nothing."

I really don't have anything against baseball players spitting. Maybe what bothers me is television insists upon showing them doing it close up.

Then, again, perhaps I should count my blessings. Television has gone face-to-face with the players and into their dugouts today. Tomorrow, the showers?

Georgia 28, Georgia Tech 28

ATHENS—I was totally biased about the Georgia-Georgia Tech football game they played here Saturday. I admit it. Openly, and without shame. None of that I'm-just-here-to-report-the-facts nonsense for me.

I wanted a tie, dammit. When Georgia scored a touchdown in the waning moments to make the score 28-27 in favor of Georgia Tech, I hoped Bulldog Coach Vince Dooley would momentarily lose hold of his faculties and go on for a one-point conversion.

It's happened to him before. Just two weeks ago in Auburn.

Why should anybody have to lose a game like this? A tie at Auburn cost Georgia the Southeastern Conference title and the Sugar Bowl trip.

A tie Saturday, and neither Tech nor Georgia would have suffered the slightest pain. The Yellow Jackets would still have had their Peach Bowl bid, and the Bulldogs would have kept their date in Houston's Bluebonnet, and ABC would still have had the hit of their collegiate telecast season.

Tech-Georgia 1978 was more than a game. It was a spectacle. A classic. One team, Georgia Tech, builds an early lead. Twenty-to-nothing. But the other team, Georgia, fights back and with the stadium falling in, scores to lead 21-20.

But Georgia Tech won't hold, either. Drew Hill runs the kickoff back 102 yards for a touchdown, and the score is 28-21. ABC should double its payment to both schools for the right to show the rest of the nation such a show.

It isn't over. Here come the Bulldogs behind a boy-child quarterback named Buck Belue. And Georgia scores. Twenty-eight-to-twenty seven. Two minutes, twenty-four seconds remaining.

Of course, Vince Dooley went for the two points and the victory. And his people in red were successful in the attempt, and despite what I thought, somebody did have to lose Saturday—Georgia Tech.

Twenty-nine to twenty-eight.

"It was the best Tech-Georgia game I have ever seen," said Georgia publicist and historian, Dan Magill.

Georgia celebrated into the dusk. There is something Bulldog fans say at a time like this. They say, "How bout them Dawgs?", a grammatical insult, but it gets the point across.

There is something Georgia Tech people say at a time like this too, and player after player was saying it in the Tech dressing quarters after the game. That's as far as I will go. Use your imagination.

I had rather be a brain surgeon than a big-time college football coach. There's less pressure. Lose in brain surgery, and you can say you did your best, and you still get paid.

"What are they doing over on the winner's side?" asked Pepper Rodgers, a big-time college football coach who wished he had chosen another line of work after the heartbreak of Saturday.

The Tech players were stunned. They sat there, staring at nothing, slowly pulling off equipment and tossing it into a heap of tape and bloodied jerseys on the floor.

I've been to funerals more lively. And speaking of funerals, Rodgers did: "This is like a death in the family," he said.

"I want it to hurt! I want it to hurt!" a Georgia fan, flowing in the spirit, said to the Tech team as it filed off the field. He got his wish.

Georgia was brilliant in its comeback. And credit the Bulldog faithful. At 20-0, Tech, they were still on their feet, beseeching their team to recover from enough early mistakes to lose five games. The crowd was worth at least a touchdown.

And Georgia Tech was so close. Had Eddie Lee Ivery, the best player on the field, not been injured in the second half, the Jackets would have likely been able to hold their lead that vanished at the eleventh hour.

"It was like losing a tennis match when the last shot hits the tape," said Rodgers.

There is something both sides should remember after the events of Saturday. It's something a Georgia man said to me once.

It was a dozen years ago, and I was talking to Bulldog lineman John Kasay, now a Dooley assistant. Georgia had won a big game. The Bulldog dressing room was New Year's Eve.

But John Kasay looked around him and put the moment in its proper perspective.

"Why is it," he asked, "the highs are never as high as the lows are low?"

There is another way to put it. Losing hurts worse than winning feels good.

A tie, dammit. Georgia 28. Georgia Tech 28. Everybody shake hands and go home happy.

Larry Munson: Better Than Being There

Sometime in the wee hours of Sunday morning, my telephone rang. Even the ring sounded drunk. Among a number of other bad things, alcohol in large quantities dulls the ability of the user to tell time.

I muttered a groggy, hesitant, "Hello?"

"Gooooooo Daaaawgs!" was the reply from the other end. Deliver me from Billy Bulldog when it's the middle of the night, Georgia won, and the whiskey hasn't run out.

"That you, Dorsey?" I asked. It had to be. It had to be Dorsey Hill, the world's biggest Bulldog fan. Dorsey Hill thinks when you die you go to Vince Dooley's house. He can't wait.

Last year, when Georgia lost to Kentucky, 33-0, Dorsey claimed it didn't count because Kentucky was on probation for recruiting violations and had too many players from New Jersey.

"Best team money could buy," is how he described the victorious Wildcats, who went on to tie for the Southeastern Conference title. Dorsey dies hard.

I was awake enough by now to realize why the telephone call. Only hours before, Georgia had avenged last season's loss to Kentucky with a thrilling 17-16 victory in Lexington. The Bulldogs had trailed 16-0 in the third quarter.

"I never gave up," Dorsey said. "After the miracle at Grant Field Saturday, I knew the Lord would give us one, too."

He was referring to Georgia Tech's equally thrilling 17-13 defeat of Florida Saturday afternoon. Dorsey doesn't like Georgia Tech or anybody who does.

"I like it when we sweep a double-header," he explains. "That's when Georgia wins and Tech loses."

I have never quite understood that thinking, but there are those among the Georgia Tech followers who feel the same about the Bulldogs.

"I wouldn't pull for Georgia," a Tech man once told me, "with one engine out on the team plane."

I thought Saturday was one of the grandest days in Georgia collegiate football history. Tech wins its sixth straight and Grant Field hasn't been that full of life in years. That old house on North Avenue literally trembled with delight when Eddie Lee Ivery scored the Yellow Jackets' winning touchdown.

And Georgia's drive to the Rex Robinson field goal in the final moments was a classic profile in sporting courage. Georgia is only two victories—Florida and Auburn—away from another SEC championship and a trip to the Sugar Bowl. That is astounding when you consider that in the pre-season, the Bulldogs bore a strong resemblance to Vanderbilt.

I am almost frightened to consider the ramifications of a Falcons' victory over the Rams Monday night at the Stadium. If the clinkers win, close the schools and banks and I demand a parade.

There was one other hero Saturday besides the Eddie Lee Iverys, the Willie McClendons and the Rex Robinsons. He is a fiftyish fellow from Minnesota.

He worked in Wyoming for a time, and then spent years and years in Nashville. He moved to Atlanta only a few months ago, but he is one of us now.

"The traffic here," he says, "is murder."

Larry Munson has been broadcasting Georgia football games for thirteen years. Saturday night was his finest hour. His description of the closing moments of the Georgia-Kentucky game, said a man listening with me, "is Bobby Thomson's home run against the Dodgers all over again."

It was so good, the Sunday paper reprinted Munson's call of the winning Georgia field goal word-for-word.

"It's set down, it looks good—watch it! YEAH! YEAH! YEAH! YEAH! Three seconds left! Rex Robinson put 'em ahead, 17-16"

It was so good, Dorsey Hill said, "listening to Larry Munson was better than being there."

Frame that one, Larry. There is no higher praise.

Two Little Girls

Two little girls went out to play in the sun one day. One wore a pretty yellow dress. She was tall, and she wore her hair in a pigtail.

The other little girl wore blue shorts. She was shorter, and her hair was red. She had many freckles.

It was very hot this day.

"What should we play?" asked the little girl with the pigtail.

"How about tennis?" said the little girl with red hair.

"That sounds like fun," said her friend. "I'll serve."

The two little girls played tennis for a long, long time.

The little girl with the pigtail won the first five games. Her friend won the sixth game, but soon the first set was over. The score was 6-1.

The little girl with red hair played much better the second set and won by the same score. Six games to one.

"Let's play one more," she said.

"I'll serve," said her friend.

The two little girls played on and on. The redheaded girl led 2-0. Then, she lost three straight games. The score became 5-5. Golly, what a neato match. Back and forth and back and forth went the tennis balls. There were crosscourt backhands and down-the-line forehands. There were deep lobs and excellent gets and much top-spin.

One time, the little girl with red hair had a match point against her. She hit a drop-shot winner. Jimmy Conners wouldn't try a drop-shot winner facing a match point.

The little girl with the red hair was not old enough to know better.

It was very exciting, but suddenly the two little girls weren't having as much fun as they thought they would. So tense was the little girl with the pigtail, she began to cry after missing an easy shot.

She cried and cried, and she stomped her foot and she contorted her face into an awful shape.

The little girl with red hair did not cry, but when she missed a shot, it hurt her very badly. Once, she hit herself on the head with her racquet because she missed a shot.

"Dummy," she muttered to herself.

By this time, the little girls were covered in perspiration and their cute play outfits were soaking wet.

The sun beat down on them ferociously during the final game. The little girl with red hair was leading 6-5, serving for the match.

She had three match points, but each time the little girl with the pigtail sent the game back to duece. The little girl with the pigtail cried between almost every point.

"I wish we had decided to play something else," she thought to herself.

Suddenly, it was over. The little girl with the pigtail hit a back-hand over the baseline. She said, "Nice match" to her friend and then she cried some more.

Many people had gathered to watch the two little girls play tennis because they played so well. "There is probably a quarter of a million dollars worth of lessons between them," said a man.

Other men made wagers on the outcome of the tennis match be-tween the two little girls who will probably grow up to be million-airesses.

The two little girls each received a silver dish for playing so well. The little girl with the red hair got a bigger dish because she won the match.

Her name was Margaret Hopkins, and she lives in Illinois. Her friend was Cari Hagey. She lives in California. They played at the Bitsy Grant Tennis Center in Atlanta.

Margaret Hopkins, because she beat Cari Hagey, is now the top-ranked twelve-year-old girl tennis player in all of the nation. When the match was over, she smiled and showed her braces.

It was the first time either of the two little girls had smiled in over two hours.

Wow. Tennis is such fun.

Eighty-Pound Lawsuit

I have always been a bit skeptical about organized athletics for children not old enough to have all their permanent teeth.

What is it about a society that will put a bat in the hand of a six-year-old, dress him in a baseball uniform, and ask him to perform on a diamond with real bases and everything, including umpires, coaches, and shouting spectators?

There is something called the "T-League." That's for kids who have just graduated from potty training. How can a child who hasn't learned his ABCs yet be expected to know to hit the cutoff man?

In the T-League, there is no pitcher. The ball is placed on a tee at the plate and the batter takes his cuts. Once I saw a T-League game where there was a close play at the plate. The runner was called out.

The runner's coach disputed the call. A grown man who would argue with an umpire at a baseball game involving toddlers is a sick person.

As the rhubarb continued, the opposing team's centerfielder became bored with the proceedings. He took off his glove, sat down in the outfield and began playing in the sand next to the fence.

Now, the other coach came storming out of his dugout. "Johnny!" he screamed to the youngster. "Do you want to play baseball, son?"

The child, still engrossed in the sand, studied his coach's inquiry for a moment, and then answered him by shaking his head, "No." Sand is marvelous when you are six, but it's lonely in centerfield.

I read an incredible story in the newspaper the other day about children playing organized athletics. It happened in Cobb County. Two midget football teams, nine-to-eleven year olds, play a game Saturday that ended in an 8-8 tie.

The winner would have gone on to the league playoffs that lead to an eventual "Super Bowl" championship. I am convinced adults organize children's athletic teams for their own enjoyment and glorification. Otherwise, who would care which team of nine-to-eleven year olds would emerge as champions over other teams of nine-to-eleven year olds?

Since the game ended in a tie, neither team qualified for more play. Wait until next year, and let's all go home and play with the dog.

But, first, let's file a lawsuit.

Adults involved with the Mableton team claimed the other team, South Cobb, had hired its own officials for the game and had not gone by rules stating officials should be named by something called the Cobb County Midget Football Conference.

They wanted the game played over. They filed a protest to the conference. Protest denied. They hired an attorney. He asked a Superior Court judge to stop the playoffs until the matter could be settled.

"When you set up an organization, you say you are going to go by the rules," attorney for the plaintiff, Laurie Davis, told me. "But when there is a clear violation and nobody will listen to you, where do you go?

"Do you have a fistfight to settle it? No, you try to find somebody who will listen and make a fair decision."

That is Laurie Davis' explanation of why an issue involving eighty-pound football players was taken to court.

Good for Judge Luther Hames. Why he even agreed to hear the case is a puzzle, but at least he denied the request to stop the league playoffs and found there was no reason whatsoever for the court to get involved further.

Why not let children be children while they have the chance? Whatever happened to games where you chose sides and played in the yard and made up your own rules and never invited the over-grown kid across the street because he could hit the ball too far?

Whatever happened to damming creeks and climbing trees and playing in mud and marbles?

And what do you tell your ten-year-old son, the quarterback, when he asks, "Hey, dad, what's a lawsuit?"

Gatewood Dooper at the Masters

AUGUSTA—The press corps that covers the Masters at Augusta National ranks just above the guys with the pointed sticks who go around the course picking up paper "the best gallery in golf" strews from Flowering Paranoia to Blooming Threeputtomia.

I was lucky enough this year not to qualify for a Genuine, Official, Keep-It-Pinned-on-Your-Person-at-All-Times press badge.

So I have set up shop in a tree overlooking the beautiful par-three twelfth. I have disguised myself as Tom Weiskopf having a nervous breakdown.

Tom Weiskopf is one of my favorite golfers. Last year, he shot a bad round in the Masters and stormed out of the locker room with a number of reporters in hot pursuit. He slammed the screen door that leads to the clubhouse grill with such force it knocked the frown off a Pinkerton man.

"Tommy takes a bad round hard," somebody said. They should take away his shoelaces and hide all sharp objects while Weiskopf is on the grounds.

The toughest thing about being a member of the press corps for the Masters tournament is the players' interviews. Contending players sit on a platform in the press barn while grown men from Tokyo to Tuscaloosa write down everything the golfers say concerning their day's rounds.

The fun part is when a golfer "goes over his round." Going over one's round is describing in full detail every blow struck for eighteen holes. . . .

"On number 1, I hit a driver 267 yards just to the right, hit an eight-iron twenty-three feet, six inches from the pin, etc., etc."

It is not as boring as watching wheelchair needlepoint, but it is close. I have this recurring fantasy about listening to a golfer go over his round. I know what Nicklaus did. He hit a drive down the middle 4,000 yards, hit a wedge to the stick and tapped it in with his middle finger. On 16, he walked across the water to the green after holing his tee shot. That's everyday stuff.

I want them to bring in Gatewood Dooper from the Clubfoot Links in Oshkosh who got into the tournament by some strange quirk of Masters eligibility fate and then played like a goat with muscular distrophy.

Let me hear *him* go over his round with the world's press assembled. Here is Gatewood Dooper describing his 107, worst round in Masters history.

"On the first tee, I wet my pants. That's a two-stroke penalty and very embarrassing. I was hitting three on my opening drive. It landed in a trap. I wound up with a nine. My wife went back to the car.

"On 2, I went into the trap again. The one behind number 3 green. I managed to save double bogey. My sponsor made an obscene gesture and went looking for my wife.

"On 3, 4 and 5, I had bogeys. My caddy agreed to stay for one more hole. I triple-bogeyed 6 and he went back to my car, too. To slice my tires.

"At 7, I hit a spectator. I had to. He came at me with a rock.

"I made the turn at seventeen-over. Before I teed off on 10, the tournament committee asked me to withdraw, my wife came back to the course and asked me for a divorce, and my sponsor stripped his company's name off my bag and hat.

"I fell into the lake on 12. One of the marshals pushed me. My drive went into the crowd lining the fairway at 13. I had to take another penalty. They hid my ball.

"Number 14 and number 15 were both disasters. At 16, they threw beer at me. At 17, I twisted my ankle. My playing partner tripped me. At 18, they sang 'Turkey in the Straw' while I tried to hit out of the rough.

"After I finally putted out, they put my card in the paper shredder and I had to hightail it to the locker room. The tournament committee had ordered sniper fire from the roof of Ike and Mamie's cottage."

Tough luck, Gatewood, but hang in there. From the nearest magnolia. Incidentally, Tommy Weiskopf usually brings extra rope.

I Am the Wind

I have received a lot of nasty mail from joggers lately. All I said was joggers make lousy conversationalists and their feet smell bad.

Even Gayle Barron, the famous runner, agreed with me in part. "The last thing I want to talk about at a party," she told me, "is how far everybody ran that week."

Gayle Barron is the prettiest jogger I know. It's OK if her feet smell bad.

I am not against physical fitness. I am against talking about it night and day. There are too many other topics that interest me more. Like famous left-handed Chinese yacht racers.

A man from Sandy Springs finally got to me. "The reason you don't like joggers," he wrote, "is you are jealous. I'd like to see you run the Peachtree Road Race. You wouldn't make the first one hundred yards."

I can't believe he said that. I took it as a dare. Never let it be said I am the kind of man who would back down from a challenge. My boyhood friend and idol Weyman C. Wannamaker Jr., a great American, once dared me to put a dead frog down the front of Kathy Sue Loudermilk's dress in biology class.

I would have done it, too, but there was a problem. There wasn't room for anything else down the front of Kathy Sue's dress, that lovely child.

I won't run in the Peachtree race Tuesday with the 12,000 official entrants. It is a matter of principle.

Let Hal Gulliver, our editor, carry the *Constitution*'s banners. Hal

Gulliver, incidentally, is the perfect example of what can happen to a person who jogs. Before he started jogging, he looked like Tarzan. There was a picture of him in his running clothes in the paper. Now he looks like Jane.

I didn't want to mention it, but the smart-aleck letters have forced me to reveal I have already run the Peachtree Road Race 6.2-mile course.

I did it over the weekend. Alone. Just me, my swim suit, and a pair of slightly used jogging shoes I borrowed from my neighbor who recently gave up running.

"I had to," he explained. "My wife wouldn't run, and I didn't think we could survive a mixed marriage."

I made my run under the cloak of darkness. I wanted no publicity, no spectators, no big-name hoofers to run behind.

I departed Lenox Square from what will be Tuesday's starting line at 3 A.M. I crushed out a final cigarette, took a deep breath of the humid air and jogged away into the night.

Lonely is the nocturnal runner. The only sound was the rhythmic beat of the soles of my neighbor's jogging shoes. *Clop! Clop! Clop!* The first mile fell to its knees behind me.

Like an eagle swept through the air by some unseen current, I reached the International House of Pancakes, which was closed, still in a smooth, graceful glide.

Only an occasional passing motorist and an empty MARTA bus broke my solitude. That and a wino asleep in the entrance to an adult movie house in Buckhead and two fellows strolling on the sidewalk near West Wesley. I think they were more than pals.

I imagined myself upon a gallant steed, loping toward the dawn and the liquor store, which was also closed, at the top of the next hill.

On past Brookwood station and past Spring street. I reach Colony Square, slowing down, but still in forceful stride.

I am the wind.

I turned left on Twelfth Street, crossed Piedmont, and swept into the park. I rounded the lake and headed toward what will be Tuesday's finish line. My strength was fading, but my courage was not. Frank Shorter was on my heels. I left him in my wake.

Finally, it was over. The eagle had landed. My time is not important, for I ran not for glory. I ran simply to prove to a clod in Sandy Springs with jock itch on the brain I could conquer his silly 6.2 miles of asphalt.

Mission accomplished.

The Grief Passes Slowly

Billy Henderson has one of the last crew cuts in captivity. When he talks, he talks about how much he enjoys doing a job that involves young people, and there is no doubting his sincerity. Saturday is an important day in his life. In the evening, the football team he coaches, Clarke Central High School, will play Valdosta High for the state AAA championship. The game will be played in Athens.

Billy has been the full twenty yards during his career. Once he played before 73,000 people in the Sugar Bowl. Wally Butts was his coach. Georgia was his school. And he has seen the view from the other side, too. Before he moved to Clarke Central, he coached at tiny Mt. de Sales, a private school near Macon. When he went to Athens to interview, the nuns at Mt. de Sales held a mass and beseeched Providence to keep him in their fold. It was Clarke Central's prayers that were answered.

Billy took his team to Jekyll Island for its preseason training camp back in August.

Four months and thirteen games later, it is still undefeated. And it still remembers what happened on Jekyll the day it broke camp. These things are always so sudden. But the shock lingers. And the grief passes so slowly.

It was August 19, at 1:20 P.M. to be precise. Barry Malcom was sixteen. Billy Henderson, who cared for him deeply, recalls every detail.

"We were having our final lunch before heading back to Athens. Some of the players' families always come down for a few days at the beach together.

"We were about to eat when Mr. Malcom, Barry's dad, came up to me and asked if Barry could join the family. I invited him to stay for lunch. He said he'd come back later.

"After we ate, Barry left with his dad for their motel. We left for Athens. I was listening to the radio later that afternoon. The news came on. A youngster had been struck by lightning and killed on Jekyll. I froze. I was speechless. It was Barry."

Barry Malcom was a guard on the Clarke Central team. He weighed only 150 pounds. "But he would tackle a giant," said Billy Henderson. "He was a shining example."

Barry was standing outside, fifty yards from the front door of the Jekyll motel, when the bolt struck. Every effort was made to revive him. His father put him in his car and drove him into the hospital in Brunswick. At four o'clock that afternoon, he was pronounced dead.

"We drove on into Athens," the coach said. "There was the tendency to turn around and go back, but we knew there was nothing we could do. When we pulled into the parking lot at the high school, cars were lined up for blocks. They didn't know if we had heard the news."

What still hurts Billy Henderson is to talk about the Malcom family's drive back to Athens that night. "I don't know how they did it," he said. "They came all that way, with that burden, in the rain."

Life goes on. The season would open soon, against rival Cedar Shoals. "The team wanted to do something," Billy said. "They wanted to do something that was a tribute to Barry."

Barry Malcom would have worn number '65'. That number is on the top of every Clarke Central player's jersey. The mothers did the sewing.

Barry Malcom's parents have seen every game this season. They will be at the field behind Clarke Central High School Saturday night for the game of the year.

"They are wonderful people," said Billy Henderson. "It's not a wealthy family, but they have stuck by us. They are a part of us."

As we talked, Billy had to choke some of the words out. Death took a favorite player. It is obvious, his coach is still taking it hard.

Thirteen years ago, he had gone through the same thing. Billy Henderson was coaching football at Willingham High in Macon. His team opened with a 21-0 victory over Warner Robins.

Monday was Labor Day. One of his players was parked at a stop sign in Macon with his girl. Somebody ran the stop sign and crashed into them. Both the player and the girl were killed.

The player was Billy Henderson's quarterback. He was also sixteen. His name was Brad. Brad Henderson, Billy's eldest son.

Boston

BOSTON—As I sit on my rump smoking cigarettes and typing this, I can still see runners coming in from the suburb of Hopkinton, 26 miles and 385 yards from the Boston Marathon finish line at the downtown Prudential Center.

It will be hours before the last of the 7,800 official entrants, and maybe a couple of thousand more who ran anyway, finally come to the end of their exhausting journey.

The big names arrived to the cheering throngs what is now nearly two hours ago. Bill Rodgers was first. Actually, a cop on a motorcycle was first, but Bill Rodgers was right behind him with a record

time of two hours, nine minutes, and twenty-seven seconds. It was
his second straight Boston Marathon victory.

Appropriately, Bill Rodgers is from Boston and he sells sneakers.
For accomplishing his feat, Bill Rodgers had a laurel wreath placed
upon his head, and a medallion was hung around his neck by the
governor of Massachusetts, Edward King. The crowd booed Edward
King on Patriots Day in Boston.

What else the winner of the Boston Marathon gets is a bowl of beef
stew. I hope they never change that. What occurred here Monday in
cold and drizzling rain was a sporting event—a human event—that
is still relatively pure and unspoiled by promoters and agents and
television, not to mention candybar and beer companies that want to
get their names in the newspapers.

Bill Rodgers crossing the finish line at the Boston Marathon Monday was as thrilling a moment as I have seen in sport. My goosepim-
ples from the cold doubled in size.

But what is even more thrilling is watching now, watching the
stragglers, the "nobodies"—the teachers, the housewives, the doctors, maybe even a cop or two, or Joe Futz the insurance salesman
from Pottsdown—push their tired and worn bodies to limits they
probably never believed possible when they ended a two-pack-a-
day habit and decided to become athletes.

Grown men are hugging each other at the finish line. Many are
finishing in tears. A medical center is located in a nearby garage.
Freezing, cramping runners are wrapped in cellophane sheets and
placed on cots. Doctors move from cot to cot treating frightful blisters. It's the rescue center after an earthquake.

I asked a man who looked like he was dying was it worth it.

"I ran the sonuvabitch," he said, "and I beat it." On his soaked T-
shirt were the words, "Human Power."

As I looked at him, I thought about Bob Horner of the Braves
and Pete Rose and what's-his-name Parker with the Pirates and
Reggie Jackson of the Yankees, as well as Jim Rice of the Red
Sox, who at that moment was only a few blocks away at Fenway
Park, lolling around in left field for something like $50,000 a
game.

Columnist Leigh Montville of the Boston Globe was apparently
thinking of the same sports millionaires' club when he so aptly
advanced the Boston Marathon Monday morning.

"There are no agents involved today," he wrote. "There are no
options being played out, no deals being made, no fleets of Mercedes
being pulled into any special parking lot.

"The athlete of the day is an athlete, period, not some modern

Clark Gable figure, some *Photoplay* sports god, cast in bubblegum and set atop some big rock-candy mountain.

"He is one of us again. As he runs the grand promenade from Hopkinton to the Prudential Center, he beckons us to come along, to sweat and enjoy. . . .

"The runner in the eighty-third Boston Marathon returns fun and games to fun and games. Somehow, he makes the rest of the sports page seem silly on this day."

You sense the trend vividly here, the fitness trend that has 20 million Americans running, the trend that has the rest of us at least thinking every time we light up a cigarette or spend another wasted, stinking afternoon watching overpaid balloonheads perform on that wretched talking box in our living rooms.

Grandmothers and grandfathers ran in the Boston Marathon Monday. A woman was telling her dinner companions in Boston Sunday night about announcing to her husband two years ago she was going to run in this race. His reply can't be printed here. But Monday, she showed him. There was a wheelchair brigade in the race. There were no fat people. A husband and wife, wearing matching outfits, finished together in an embrace.

Human Power. May the first promoter with the idea to turn this event into $100,000 Colgate Foot Race of Champions and move it to Las Vegas be shot at the next available sunrise, and may Howard Cosell never get close to it.

For the record, the Boston Marathon champion, Bill Rodgers, made a salary of $7,000 last year selling shoes. He drives a dented, 1963 Volkswagen. He lives with his wife, and they pay $165 a month in apartment rent.

Somebody once asked him what he thought of golf as a sport.

"You get about the same exercise in a hand of canasta," he said.

In the same interview, he was asked if he thought Joe Namath was a great athlete because he could throw a football straight.

"I'll be running over his grave," was Bill Rodgers' answer.

Farewell to Sports

I saw my first major league baseball game in Clark Griffith Stadium in Washington, D.C., in July of 1959. You don't forget your first major league baseball game.

The White Sox were visiting the Senators. Billy Pierce pitched for Chicago. Camilo Pascual pitched for Washington. It was a warm night.

There was no score until the top of the seventh. Nellie Fox, who is dead now, singled home two runs for the Sox. Jim Landis brought Fox home with a sacrifice fly. Chicago led, 3-0.

Pierce had a no-hitter into the eighth. Ron Samford broke it up with a double to left field that scored a runner who had walked. The final score was 3-1.

Harmon Killebrew struck out three times. Luis Aparicio made two great plays at shortstop. I drank three Cokes and ate two boxes of popcorn and one bag of peanuts. At one point during the game, I looked around at the stadium and spotted an enclosed seating area behind home plate. There were men inside.

"Who are those people?" I asked my adult companion.

"Sportswriters," he said.

"Do they see all the games?" I went on.

"It's their job," he said. "They don't even have to pay to get in."

That settled it. I was twelve. Anybody, I figured, could become a doctor or a lawyer or a car dealer. Nineteen years later, I don't own a boat, but I've seen a lot of ball games free. And once I went to Callaway Gardens for four days to cover a water-ski tournament and the newspaper paid for it. I made the right choice of professions.

A week from Sunday, I am moving my typewriter to another part of the building. My boss and I went through lengthy negotiations concerning the switch.

"Grizzard," he said, "your column is moving out of sports."

"Okay," I said.

Both the *Constitution* and the *Journal* are taking on new graphic faces, and I am to be relocated in a new section that will concern itself with news of city and state. I am told I can still write about sports but that when I choose not to, I won't have to feel guilty about it anymore.

I'm not very good at goodbyes, but before I go, there's a few more things I wanted to say:

—— I will never get used to Al Ciraldo not broadcasting Georgia Tech basketball games and Whack Hyder not coaching the team.

—— The best place to watch a baseball game is Wrigley Field in Chicago. The worst place is Yankee Stadium because crazy people go there.

—— My favorite sportswriter is Dan Jenkins. My favorite sports book is *Semi-Tough*, which he wrote. My favorite sports movie is not *Semi-Tough*. It is *Bless the Beasts and Children*, a movie about shooting buffalo.

—— Soccer and hockey are boring. Horse racing is exciting only if you have money on the race. The Indianapolis 500 should be against the law. Wrestling is fake. Organized sports are harmful to children under twelve. Tennessee has the most obnoxious fans in college football. Alabama is second. I'll be glad when Woody Hayes retires.

—— Jesse Outlar wrote the best line I ever read about the National Basketball Association's long-winded playoff system: "If the NBA had been in charge of World War II, Japan and Germany would still be in the running."

—— I still miss Harry Mehre.

—— The sixteenth hole at Augusta National on a Sunday in April is the prettiest place in the world.

—— There will never be another pitcher like Sandy Koufax, another college quarterback like Joe Namath, another stockcar driver like Fireball Roberts, another stockcar writer like Bill Robinson, another golfer like Arnold Palmer, and I wish Rod Laver were twenty years old.

—— I loved it when Dan Jenkins wrote, "The only thing worse than track is field."

—— Al McGuire is beautiful. Once he said, "The only time winning is important is in surgery and war."

—— The second best line I ever read about the NBA's long-winded playoff system came from a guy in Philadelphia who said, "The only uncomfortable thing that lasts longer than an NBA season is pregnancy."

—— Of all the people I have met in sports, Dan Magill, the Georgia tennis coach, is the most unforgettable. "Can I help you?" asks the waitress. "A Heineken's, honeykins," replies Magill, "and a sliced, barbecue, pork-pig sandwich."

—— If Alex Hawkins says that pot was planted in his car, I believe him.

6

FERGIT, HELL!

I make no apologies for anything that appears in this chapter. I was born in the South and I love the South and once my grandmother told me we had a relative who fought with Stonewall Jackson. That would be Uncle Beauregard Grizzard who died in 1882, singing "Dixie" and hating Yankees.

Homer Southwell, Author

Occasionally, Ludlow Porch of WRNG radio calls me on the telephone. That is because I knew him before he was a star. I knew him when he was a mild-mannered insurance claims adjuster with a secretary and a messy desk in Decatur. Ludlow wasn't as much fun in those days, but he caused less trouble.

What Ludlow Porch does for a living now is host two hours of madness on Atlanta's all-talk WRNG. Five days a week, he is set loose on the air to say anything he wants to. Listeners call in and the result is the city's most popular radio show.

You may recall Ludlow's revealing the "Montana Myth." There is no Montana, he said. Or the Great Parsley Debate. Ludlow claimed parsley causes several rare blood diseases and shortness of breath.

Recently, he set about to prove smoking is the cause of homosexuality. He also interviewed an official from HEW who announced all marriage licenses issued in the seven Southern states—"and parts of Florida"—since 1958 were void because they were issued outside HEW guidelines.

"The only exceptions," Ludlow explained, "are marriages conducted on navigable waterways or in a Winnebago."

Ludlow called last week to tell me about Homer Southwell.

Homer Southwell, it turns out, has been a frequent guest on the Porch program. He is the alleged author of books assailing the constant flow of Northerners southward.

"First he wrote, *Yankee Go Home*," Ludlow said, "and then followed it with a sequel, *And Stay There*. He is terribly disturbed about Yankees who come South because of our warm weather and good food."

Homer Southwell has stirred the masses. Calls come by the thousands when he is a Porch guest. Irate transplanted Northernpersons want him lynched. Southerners who share his feelings concerning Yankee emigration want his statue erected on the grounds of the state capitol. A Porch sponsor canceled.

I caught up with Homer Southwell Thursday as he worked away in his East Cobb County home.

"I'm starting my first novel," he said. "It's called *Return to Marietta* or *East of the Big Chicken*."

The hero of his latest literary endeavor, Homer said, will be a fellow named Jimmy James Cheetwood.

"Jimmy James is a real person I knew growing up in Cobb County," Homer explained. "He was the meanest man I have ever seen. He was so mean, he was *born* with a tattoo. They think he inherited it from his mama."

I probed deeply into Homer Southwell's disdain for Northern infiltration into the South. After all, I pointed out, the war has been over 113 years.

"So what?" Homer asked. "They're flocking down here by the millions. What will happen to our wonderful Southern way of life if we let every fast-talking Yankee who wants to live on our precious soil?"

Homer immediately launched into a tirade. I hurriedly copied down all the remarks I could follow:

—"I wouldn't go North for a three-week orgy with 'Charlie's Angels.'"

—"I encourage ripping-off of Yankee tourists on the interstates. You don't even need a mechanic to do it. You just tell 'em you're going to change their shocks and then don't."

—"The greatest form of birth control known to man is a Bronx accent."

—"God lives somewhere in the Alpharetta area."

—"I once made the mistake of dating a woman from Des Moines. She had hairy legs. All Yankee women have hairy legs."

Frankly, I had suspicions Homer Southwell might be a fraud, a figment of Ludlow Porch's weirdo imagination.

Then I asked him what he did for fun and relaxation when there is a break from the rigors of writing and Yankee-hating.

"I have a hobby I have enjoyed for years," Homer said. "Reading the *New York Times* obituary page."

Fergit, hell.

The Cyclorama: A Disgrace

The strains of "Dixie" come up softly at first and then grow louder and louder. Recorded musket fire bristles in the background. There is a vague human cry from somewhere in the background. There is a vague human cry from somewhere in the distance. Perhaps it is a Rebel yell, or perhaps it is some mother's child catching a bullet 114 years ago.

"Ladies and gentlemen," booms a familiar voice, "this is Victor Jory."

I remember Victor Jory. Last time I saw him, he had a whip in his hand.

There are a couple of things that have always bothered me about the Battle of Atlanta production in Atlanta's Cyclorama:

The painting is from Milwaukee, and the man who does the narration, Victor Jory, played the part of a most hateful carpetbagger in *Gone with the Wind*. I don't forgive easily.

Today is Confederate Memorial Day. All state offices will be closed. The United Daughters will celebrate. I prepared by spending a morning revisiting the Cyclorama. It had been a few years.

The guns are still blazing out of Hurt House. Sherman still watches the "inferno" from his mounted perch. The Wisconsin farmer's eagle still soars above the battle. And there remains the classic portrait of brother meeting brother in the midst of hell.

One is dying. The other, his enemy, gives him water to ease the pain. "This," roars Victor Jory, "is not a memorial to the decay of brotherhood, but a memorial to the birth of freedom. . . ."

For a time Tuesday morning, I was alone with the *Battle of Atlanta*. Tourists weren't exactly tearing through the turnstiles.

I paid my two dollars. A young black woman took my ticket. She was polite and urged me to hurry. "The next presentation," she said, "is about to begin."

I noticed posters on the walls, posters asking donations for the Cyclorama. I walked up the winding staircase that leads to history in the round.

It took 8,000 pounds of paint to put the *Battle of Atlanta* on canvas. It has faded now. There are visible cracks.

Red is the dominant color around me. Victor Jory announces the earthen floor of the painting's three-dimensional foreground is "actual Georgia red clay." What did he expect?

Red covers the faces and chests of the dying and wounded figures that seem as real now as they did the first time a child looked upon them in amazement. ". . . Die they do by the thousands," says Victor

Jory of a Confederate charge that was, perhaps, the South's last charge, on that day, July 22, 1864.

Once there was talk of moving the Cyclorama to another site. The building is old. It leaks. There was a fight for restoration funds, and somebody said, "If we don't do something soon, it will be too late."

It appears the Cyclorama will be restored now. Improvement can't come too soon.

Four ladies from someplace like Akron finally joined me and broke my solitude Tuesday morning. When the presentation was over, we walked outside. I heard one of the ladies say to the others, "From the looks of this place, the South has finally forgotten the war."

This shrine is, frankly, a disgrace. The years of neglect are taking their toll. And we really don't have "Dixie" to play anymore. "Dixie" is considered offensive.

One of the papers had to remind Atlanta readers that today is Confederate Memorial Day. Most of them wouldn't have known, otherwise. I heard a woman on a radio show the other day say, "We celebrate Confederate Memorial Day up North. We call it a tribute to Yankee marksmanship." That got a big laugh from a group of southerners.

I don't want to rally around the Rebel flag again. I don't have a picture of Stonewall Jackson over my fireplace.

I do know, however, Robert E. Lee once said of the men we are supposed to be honoring today, "They were asked to give more than should have been expected of them," and I know that they gave it.

That's good enough for me.

The Truth About General Lee

Dr. Emory Thomas came on the line from Athens where he is a professor of history at the University of Georgia.

My question was quick and to the point:

"Is it true," I asked, "what they are saying about Gen. Robert E. Lee?"

No true sons or daughters of the Confederacy have had a decent night's sleep since President Carter, of all people, visited Gettysburg the other day and said His Majesty General Lee made a "big mistake" in the key battle of the Civil War.

Heresy. Pure and simple.

To make matters worse, there is a new book concerning Lee, *The Marble Man*, in which a Nashville military historian named Thomas Connelley fires further salvos at Our Hero and Leader.

Lee, says Connelley, was a man obsessed with failure, who suffered from "repressed vibrance." ("He would have been a hell-raiser if he had had the opportunity" is Dr. Thomas' translation of that phrase.)

Connelley also says Lee was depressive because of an unhappy marriage to a woman prematurely arthritic and that he used religion as a crutch.

Dr. Thomas recently reviewed *The Marble Man* for *Virginia Magazine*.

"The reference to religion," he explained, "is basically that if Lee met anything he couldn't deal with or didn't want to deal with, he would simply put it off on Almighty Providence."

But that didn't answer my original question. Did, I asked Dr. Thomas—a Civil War authority and a native of Richmond, by-God Virginia—Robert E. Lee blow Gettysburg?

"Lee, himself, said it was all his fault," Dr. Thomas began, "and it was."

Allow the shock to wear off, and then we will continue. Recall that Lee had invaded the North in hopes of a major confrontation with the enemy. Although there was no clear-cut victor at Gettysburg, the loss of manpower and supplies Lee's Army of Northern Virginia suffered was the knockout blow of the war to the South.

I pressed for more details from Dr. Thomas as a tear rolled down my cheek.

"My interpretation," he went on, "is that Lee got up there, figured he had come all that way, and had gone to all that trouble and that it was maybe his last chance to do it big and do it right.

"He wanted a showdown battle. He had tried to turn the left and he had tried to turn the right. Finally, he said to hell with it, and went right up the middle.

"It was suicide."

Dr. Thomas does take some of the blame away from Lee. Ewell, he explained, didn't occupy Cemetery Ridge the first day he arrived, allowing the Yankees to take that strategic position.

Lee wanted Longstreet to take Little Roundtop. Longstreet could have, had he moved earlier.

"One of the problems," said Dr. Thomas, "was that the Army of Northern Virginia was basically a command of gentlemen. Lee didn't give his commanders specific orders. He just suggested what they *might* do."

Lee ordered a charge, said the professor, "at the geographic center of the entire Yankee army."

Get the picture: Flags are flying, bugles blowing, bands playing. And men dying. Fifteen thousand Confederate soldiers tried to take

Cemetery Ridge from the Yankees. Maybe 300 made it to the top. They were easily repulsed.

"They were doomed," said Dr. Thomas, "before they started."

We talked more. About Pickett's tears after the battle. About his dislike for Lee after the war. About Lee making the same mistake in the Seven Days Battle. About Lee's words, "It is good that war is so terrible, else men would grow too fond of it."

My heart breaking, an idol from my first history class crushed to mortal dust, I had to ask one more question:

Would the South have been better off with somebody else in charge of its military besides Lee?

"The best answer for that," Dr. Thomas said, "is certainly it would. Then, it would have lost the war about two years earlier."

7

ON THE ROAD

My favorite place to be is home. I know all the bartenders and where to get great barbecue. But a man can have an occasional high time in Memphis, the music is good in Dallas, Washington isn't such a bad place if you don't have to work there, and they like to hear me talk in New York.

And once an angel cooked my breakfast in Tellico Plains, Tennessee. . . .

"Honk If You Love Elvis"

MEMPHIS—I don't know what I expected Wednesday at Graceland on the first anniversary of the death of Elvis Presley. Graceland is the walled mansion in Memphis where Elvis, the late King, lived and died and is buried behind the swimming pool, next to his mother.

I didn't expect dignity because neither Elvis' life nor his death was dignified. He lived in a world of glitter and rhinestones and $50,000 automobiles, and he died in his pajamas on his bathroom floor.

One doctor said death was from "acute blood pressure changes," caused by straining for a bowel movement.

But I expected at least a certain reverence. A certain respect for Elvis' memory. A man born to near-poverty rose to fame and the millions that went with it. And I have read so much about the love of his fans.

A sign on a car in downtown Memphis this week read, "Elvis—We Will Love You Forever." Another said, "Honk If You Love Elvis."

I expected respect and reverence at least. I found a circus. Worse, I found a carnival of money-changers.

It was hell-hot Wednesday morning, and the line in front of the wall at Graceland was long and barely moving. Thousands waited hours for a chance to file past the gravesite.

Across the street from the mansion were rows of Elvis souvenir shops. Hawkers were at every corner, and they worked the ready-to-buy crowd with the intensity of a worrisome fly. They had to be shooed away.

93

For sale: Elvis T-shirts, Elvis posters, Elvis plates, Elvis clocks, Elvis portraits, pictures of Elvis riding horses, pictures of Elvis riding motorcycles.

For sale: Elvis belt buckles, Elvis hats, Elvis bumper stickers, Elvis black armbands, and a game called "King of Rock 'n Roll," a sort of Elvis Presley monopoly board with play money, lots of it.

For sale: copies of Elvis' driver's license, copies of Elvis' birth certificate, copies of Elvis' high school report card (F's in English), copies of Elvis' marriage license, and for $5, get your picture taken sitting in Elvis' first Cadillac, a 1956 purple El Dorado.

For sale: Elvis Frisbees.

Flowers and a picture of a hound dog covered the Graceland lawn. Flowers covered the gravesite. A pink teddybear had been placed nearby. "I love you, Elvis," read a card around its neck. It was signed "Your teddybear, Columbus, Ohio."

Back at the gate, national guardsmen, in the city because of the police and firemen's strike, had stopped allowing people inside the gates.

"The family wants a little time to itself," said a burly sergeant.

In came Vester Presley, Elvis' uncle, blowing the horn of his Cadillac. His books are on sale at the gate. In came Ginger Alden, Presley's girlfriend who was with him at the time of his death. She rode in the back of a car with two men in the front.

Later she would be driven out again. She would be in the back seat, crying. Twenty people would rush to the window of the car to snap pictures of her. Look for those pictures on sale here next year.

A Memphis garbage truck pulled out of the Graceland driveway Wednesday after its daily pickup.

A man standing in the line said to his wife, "Grab a sack of that garbage, honey. No telling what it would sell for."

Texas Chic

DALLAS—There are a lot of things I like about Texas, but let me start at the top: in Texas, they sell barbecue downtown.

Take the lovely city of Dallas, for instance. A person can step right out of his hotel onto bustling Commerce Street, walk into Neiman-Marcus for a little shopping, and then lunch at Gus's or the Copper Cow or the Golden Steer and feast upon sliced barbecue sandwiches in a modern, urban setting of glass and steel and taxi and bus exhaust fumes.

You can't do that in most other cities.

There are good barbecue places accessible *from* Atlanta—like Harold's at the federal pen—but in mid-city, the closest thing to barbecue is a truckload of hogs in a traffic jam on the downtown connector.

Regardless of where barbecue is eaten, its flavor and enjoyment are always enhanced by something cold to drink—preferably beer.

In Texas, you can have Coors beer with your downtown barbecue. Coors, the Colorado light nectar, is the favorite beer of Americans who can't get it. Coors isn't sold in Atlanta. It is smuggled into the city by airline stewardesses who fly out West.

I was in Dallas over the weekend for the Texas-Oklahoma football game, a good excuse for three-fourths of the population of both states to get drunk for three days.

Before the game, I stepped out of my motel room onto bustling Commerce Street, walked into Nieman-Marcus for a little shopping, and then had lunch at the Golden Steer in a modern urban setting of glass and steel and taxi and bus exhaust fumes.

I ordered two sliced barbecue sandwiches and a Coors and settled into thinking about why Texas has suddenly become so popular and chic. Do you realize New York City has even discovered Texas?

One of the hottest spots in town is a country music bar where they serve the Texas state beer, Lone Star, in longneck bottles, and the clientele wears cowboy hats and boots and is attempting to learn the correct pronunciation of "sumbitch."

I asked a Texas native about the phenomenon.

"Texas just *feels* good," he said, and "it encompasses about everything. We're out West, but we're also down South. And look what we've done for the culture of this country."

The list of Texas' cultural donations is staggering. Texas gave us chicken-fried steak and Walter Cronkite. It gave us Dan Jenkins and his marvelous book, *Semi-Tough.*

Don Meredith is from Texas. So is Phyllis George, and I would imagine most of the Dallas Cowboys cheerleaders. Which brings up the musical question: Whatever happened to the Kilgore Junior College dancing rangerettes?

And you know who else is from Texas. Willie Nelson. His buddy, Waylon Jennings, says everybody in Austin thinks when they die, they go to Willie's house.

Dallas is my favorite big city in Texas.

"It's nothing more than a big Mineola," said another native. "Dallas is made up of all the people who left the farm and learned to count."

But the people are friendly in Dallas. A hotel clerk didn't ask me for a major credit card and actually said when I checked in, "Nice to have you with us."

And Dallas is the home of the annual State Fair of Texas, perhaps the last of the great expositions of its kind in America. It opened Saturday and it will run two weeks and attract over 3 million visitors.

There will be horse shows and a rodeo, and livestock exhibits and gospel and country singing. The carnival midway is massive. See the world's smallest woman for a quarter. She's only four inches tall. See Emmett, the Alligator Boy. Billy Earl and his wife, Clovis, come every year all the way from Lubbock.

"This is where we spent our honeymoon," Clovis smiled proudly. Billy Earl looked embarrassed and disappeared to look at the tons of prime meat on the hoof down at the cattle barn.

Texans are a proud and courageous lot. Remember the Alamo. The University of Texas football team, incidentally, had about the same chance against Oklahoma Saturday at Dallas' Cotton Bowl. But they are a little crazy when it comes to football in Oklahoma, where the school president once said, "We want a university the football team can be proud of."

Texans simply know themselves, what they like, and what they expect of each other. I heard it put this way from across the bar after a few more Coors at the Golden Steer Saturday: "If you don't like Willie Nelson, longneck beers, long-legged women, rodeos, football, barbecue, the state fair, and an occasional fist fight, then you ain't no Texan. You just live here."

Cash Only

WASHINGTON—Here I sit in a big hotel room.

What fun.

When I was a kid, I liked hotel rooms because I could jump on the beds. Now, I like them because I can throw towels on the floor and somebody else will pick them up.

Washington is full of big hotels, because this is an important city and a lot of people from other places come here to work and to visit and to be politicians.

I suppose that the reason they always give you a booklet on security when you check into a Washington hotel is that there are lots of politicians here.

My booklet says, "Do not leave money, jewelry or other valuables in your room."

It also says, "Please bolt your door. This will shut out all keys. Also, insure that the security chain is engaged and that the connecting room door is locked."

Some rooms in Washington come with their own German shepherds. They are the ones nearest the Capitol.

This is a classy hotel I'm in. I knew it was classy when I saw the room service menu. The only thing cheaper than the $4.95 cheeseburger is a cup of coffee, which is $1.50.

One morning, I saw a fight between two taxicab drivers in the parking lot of my hotel. They were arguing about whose turn it was to pick up a fare. One driver bopped the other driver in the face, thus settling the argument. The other driver threw a rock at his colleague's cab as it sped away with the fare. Like I said, this is a classy hotel.

Hotel front desks are usually manned and womanned by young people who are very clean, wear expensive clothes and have a habit of acting snooty. Whatever happened to the friendly night clerk in his undershirt reading tomorrow's race entries?

Even the bellmen have come up in the world in today's hotels. The bellmen here wear red uniforms like the one Omar Sharif wore when he danced with Julie Christie at the Leningrad ball.

There is one staggering problem in hotels today, however. Hotels do not like to deal in cash. They abhor cash, as a matter of fact, along with anybody who would deface their front desk with it.

I deal in cash. Credit cards are financial heroin.

"May I see a credit card?" the snooty young woman at the front desk asked me when I arrived at my Washington hotel.

"Don't carry them," I said.

She called over the assistant manager.

"He doesn't carry credit cards," she said to him.

A lady behind me gasped in horror.

The assistant manager called over the manager.

"He doesn't carry credit cards," the manager was told.

I rattled my change as loudly as possible.

"If you don't have a credit card, sir" the manager asked me, his hands squarely on the hips of his designer trousers, "then how do you propose to pay your bill?"

Now, he had me.

"Cash," I said. "American," I quickly added, hoping to regain at least some face.

They wanted to see it.

A half hour passed before a decision was made. Finally, after I paid in advance, I was allowed to proceed to my room. They gave me a little card to read on the way up, however.

It said, "Because you have made a cash payment and did not present a major credit card at the time of your arrival, our operational procedure is to request that you make all futher payments in restaurants, bars, and the gift shop at the time the bills are presented."

How can you trust a man who carries cash?

The only time cash is accepted cheerfully in a hotel is when you give it to a bellman in the form of a tip.

After the experience of checking in, I followed a squatty version of Omar Sharif at the Leningrad ball up to my room.

He put up my bags, switched on the lights and the air-conditioner, and then waited impatiently by the door for his tip.

"Got change for a hundred?" I asked.

"No," he answered, "but I can get it from the front desk. I heard some yahoo just checked in using cash."

We both got a big laugh over that.

Disco Zoo

NEW YORK—The hottest spot in town is Studio 54, a disco on West 54th Street, appropriately enough. Not just anybody can get into Studio 54.

Here is how it works: every evening at midnight, a throng gathers outside and waits to be chosen for entrance. The lucky ones are then allowed to pay $20 per couple for admission. Once inside, there is a huge dance floor, flashing lights, and music to give birth to a buffalo by.

The dancing and the music and the lights go nonstop until dawn, when many of the customers must scurry back to the sewers. These are the beautiful people? A regular had mentioned to me earlier, "Go stand by the men's room. You might see Andy Warhol."

I'm not certain by what criteria entrants are selected. Judging from some of the clientele I saw, it would appear to be in your favor to come from another planet. Besides the men's and ladies' rooms, there is one marked "it."

I was given some advice on getting inside: "Make sure you dress in something unusual, or grease the doorman with a fifty."

I needed the fifty for breakfast the next morning. I wore my college rush outfit—a navy blazer, gray slacks, yellow Polo tie and Weejuns.

I was inside in a New York second.

"Funky outfit," said the doorman. To him, a wetsuit tux and snow shoes are normal.

"Disco" is our nation's latest nervous breakdown. Studio 54 is the home office. Truman Capote might drop by with Norman Mailer. For that matter, Godzilla might shake his booty with Yasser Arafat while Leon Spinks plays the flute. This is a strange place.

There was a movie made about disco, *Saturday Night Fever*. In the movie, they danced the hustle, and the moves were graceful and with style.

In Studio 54, they dance something that resembles a monkey halfway there on an LSD trip. Say it ain't so, John Revolta.

I paid my admission and went directly to the men's room to interview Andy Warhol. He wasn't there. Fan Man was. Fan Man wore a ribbon in his hair, lipstick, a long skirt and peered out from behind a fan.

"Funky outfit," he said as I walked past him.

There was more. Golden Boy strolled through. He was a stunning blond. For the evening, he had chosen a sleeveless blouse, open to the navel. He carried a gold purse and wore a gold lamé skirt and gold bedroom slippers from the Aladdin collection.

Later, he danced with Peter Punk. Peter Punk came in his father's old bowling shirt, which he wore outside his mother's jodphurs. He had a black ring painted around his left eye.

There was a girl in fatigues carrying a hula hoop. There was another girl in a wraparound evening dress she had fashioned from a bedsheet. She had washed her hair in Thousand Island dressing and blown it dry with an acetylene torch. Fan Man was looking better all the time.

My companion and I eventually braved the dance floor. We immediately provoked stares. My companion was a girl person in a chiffon, ankle-length dress, appropriate for dinner at "21."

"Funky outfit," said the girl in the bedsheet dancing with Hoola-Hoop Hattie next to us.

Studio 54 is loud and kinky and, on this night at least, predominantly gay. Teenage boys wait tables in silver underpants, tennis shoes and nothing else. After they clean your table, they dance on it.

Two models show up in running shorts, pull off their blouses and dance barebreasted. Shirtless men dance with other shirtless men. I puffed a Marlboro. Most of the crowd rolled their own.

In the wee hours, it was time to leave. There was still the mob scene outside. As I walked through the crowd, a breathless girl grabbed my arm.

"How did you get in?" she asked, in full swoon.

With an air of self-assurance, I replied, "My funky outfit," and disappeared down the street into a fog of reality.

"Chicken" and the "Worm"

PLAINS—A regular walked into Billy Carter's Service Station one hot afternoon last week and greeted Leon, the man who takes up money for gas and beer.

"Last time I saw you," he said, "we were both drunk."

"Believe we were," agreed Leon.

"We go in them bad places, don't we?" the man continued.

"Them dives," said Leon.

"Them places we go in," the man went on, "are so bad they got blood on the ceiling. Place with blood on the floor don't worry me. Place with blood on the ceiling, that's a tough place."

He noticed a jar on the side of the bar. The jar had money inside it.

"What's that for?" he asked Leon.

"For 'Chicken'," Leon replied. "We're gonna get him in the state senate. You gonna help us?"

"Damn right," said the man. "I'd do anything to get rid of that damn Hugh Carter."

Some introductions are probably necessary. The Hugh Carter here is Cousin Hugh Carter Sr., antique dealer, state senator, worm grower and author of the book *Cousin Beedie and Cousin Hot*, in which he wrote all sorts of things about First Cousin Jimmy and First Cousin Billy and anybody else who came to mind.

Hugh Carter Sr. lives in Plains, and he is running for re-election as state senator from the Fourteenth District. The primary approaches on August 8th.

"Chicken" is another story. He is Malcolm "Chicken" Wishard, a local farmer with no political experience to speak of. He's the man the regulars at Billy Carter's Service Station want to see whip the pants off Hugh Carter in the election.

That includes Billy himself.

"Miss Lillian's with us, too," said Leon. "She said she would spend every dime she had to see Chicken whip that damn Hugh Carter. Billy's done give his dime."

It took some talking and a six-pack, but I finally got to the bottom of this split in the Carter political camp. For one thing, Hugh's book didn't set well with the family. And for another, said a woman at

Billy's, "there never has been no love lost between Billy and Hugh, and Miss Lillian and Billy are just alike."

Chicken Wishard's campaign was cranking up full blast at Billy's this afternoon. Leon passed out cards that read, "Help Chicken Take the Worm."

The "Worm" reference is to Hugh Carter, of course, the self-styled "Nation's Worm King." Even Mrs. Chicken dropped by for a visit.

"Why do they call Chicken 'Chicken'?" she was asked.

"When he was a little boy," she answered, "He was the first one in the family to get chickenpox."

Leon calls him "One-Eyed Chicken."

"That's because he ain't got but one good eye," said Leon. Leon also had a stack of campaign posters with Chicken's smiling face. Somebody put an empty beer can on the stack of posters.

"Get that off of there," Leon screamed. "You might get beer in Chicken's good eye."

I pressed for more details on campaign issues.

"Only issue I know," said Leon, "is we can't stand Hugh Carter and we finally got somebody to run against him. You can talk to Chicken. He's loud and if he walked in here right now, you'd think he was half a fool. But he ain't. He's a good man."

Billy Carter would eventually drop by the station. He was sipping something clear over ice. The tourists flocked around him. He signed autographs, posed for pictures, and sold six-packs of Billy Beer for $2.60. The local line is, "Jimmy's making $200,000 a year running the country, and Billy's already made $500,000 running his mouth."

And Billy would do his best for Chicken too.

"We need two things from you to help Chicken," he said to a farmer who came in for refreshment.

"What's that?" asked the farmer.

"Your vote and your money," said Billy.

I had to ask Billy Carter how he could go against his own flesh and blood. "Isn't this man your cousin?" I said.

"He ain't my cousin" Billy answers. "I gave him away."

Riding the High Lonesome

ON A GEORGIA BACKROAD—There are only two sounds out here. Four tires are humming as they hug the taxpayers' asphalt on Georgia 15. And the radio—God bless an automobile radio—has me in touch with you wouldn't believe the faraway places.

I am constantly turning the dial. Voices with no faces fade in and voices with no faces fade out. But at least there are voices, and without them the loneliness would creep even closer.

I have just departed from Sandersville, northbound through the deep-hole blackness the night brings to middle-eastern Georgia. There was a shooting in Louisville, clear-channel WHAS reports, but invading static keeps me from the details.

Dallas comes in loud and clear. It will be nice in Dallas tomorrow, with highs in the mid-seventies. I even pick up Cleveland.

You know they tried to recall the mayor in Cleveland. Now, the city council has been charged with accepting kickbacks. Things are tough all over.

Chicago's country WMAQ, an old friend, is beaming to thirty-eight states and Canada. A man sings a song that includes the line, "Plant them 'taters, and pull up another tomorrow."

It is difficult to avoid a hockey game, turning the dial on latenight radio. Hockey is enough of a problem for me in person. On the radio, it might as well be the noon news from Mars.

"Ro-jay brings the puck to center ice! Marcham-bo checks him there. Jablare intercepts, and there is a whistle for icing the puck!"

I am on the fringes of Hancock County, Georgia, listening to a man from Fort Wayne, Indiana, describe the actions of twelve foreigners on ice skates, chasing a rubber disc.

I turn back to Cleveland.

My headlights tunnel through the darkness. The tall pines frame the road, and two beady pearls of light suddenly appear in the distance.

This is the Halloween season, but a stray dog crossing the road has simply turned its head toward the lights of the car, and its eyes have reflected back.

Give me a dime for every stray dog on every Georgia back road, and my creditors can relax. I'll take a quarter for every dead possum.

I am trying to make Atlanta and home before sleep takes me over. Interstate 20 is somewhere ahead, just out of a place called Siloam in Greene County. The interstate is an auto jet-stream after crawling over two-lane. There is no other traffic because of the late hour and because country people have been in bed for hours. They get up early out here, you know. Don't let the sun catch you a-restin'.

There are tiny frame houses here and there, but not a sign of life to go with them. I grew up in a frame house that went dark at an early hour. The peace and comfort it held until morning has been difficult to relocate.

Downtown Sparta approaches. There are street lights, but no people. The old tavern in the middle of town, a historic landmark, looks haunted. It probably is.

Sparta lasts thirty seconds. The village of White Plains will be next. I cross Copeland Creek and Whitter Creek. There is a newscast coming in from WCAU, Philadelphia. Damn, I'm a long ways from Philadelphia.

What I am thinking is maybe everybody ought to do this occasionally. I am at least free with my thoughts here. Out like this, a man can talk to himself and it seems perfectly natural. You can ask yourself a question on a Georgia back road and get an honest answer.

Finally, Siloam. Siloam won't awaken for hours yet. The interstate approaches, laden with eighteen-wheeled monsters with big eyes and loaded backs bound for the city.

Parting with Georgia 15 is more difficult than I figured it would be. I will be home in just over an hour, but I realize that out on that primitive stretch I had maybe stumbled upon one of the modern urbanite's last escapes. I had ridden about all that remains of the High Lonesome on a pony with automatic transmission.

Cleveland has faded off the radio. I turn the dial again and a preacher is chasing the devil out of Tulsa. "Be saved or be damned!" is his warning.

Rolling along the interstate, I search for another hockey game.

Covering the Arrival of Spring

HILTON HEAD ISLAND, S.C.—Soft rain is falling, the wind is blowing, and the skies are cloudy. But the temperature is pleasantly mild, and for three days previous to this one, late winter's coastal sun has shown brilliantly. I will be leaving here soon, and that thought saddens me.

I will miss my duck. There has never been such a duck. I don't know much about ducks, but this one lives in a lagoon outside my bedroom window and makes a sould like, "Braaaack! Braaaack!"

He works the night shift. His job is keeping the alligators awake. Ditto for any other creature within the sound of his quack.

He begins precisely at sundown. He doesn't hush until the dawn. I have nicknamed him "Hosea."

News from the outside world filters in slowly to a place like this. A big story here is that a cosmetic surgeon is moving to the island from Florida to take the wrinkles out for the summer parties at the Sea Pines Club.

That announcement brought an interesting remark in a local paper from a man identified as an "island punster."

"Instead of having your face lifted," he asked, "why not have your body lowered?"

So the Reggie Eaves controversy rages on back in Atlanta, does it? Here, they are more concerned about the bleak outlook for shrimp. No white shrimp have been seen in coastal waters for five weeks. The cost of appetizers goes up and up.

Coal strike? What coal strike? Bless my Lincoln Continental, the cost of a membership to the Sea Pines Club will go up from $3,000 to $5,000 come April 1.

There has been some interest, however, in the story out of Arkansas where the preacher put his deceased eighty-year-old mother in a freezer locker and then tried to raise her from the dead. The older retirees here are keeping a close eye on his progress.

I came here to cover the arrival of spring. It comes two weeks earlier to coastal paradise.

I lived without any spring at all for a couple of years. There are only two seasons in Chicago. Winter and the Fourth of July. A year ago today, I was in snow navel-high to a tall Yankee.

Missing springtime is like missing a woman. You never really noticed her and then she was gone, and all that she was returns and makes the separation even more painful.

I think I read this somewhere. "Springtime is the land awakening. The March winds are the morning yawn."

People are already on bicycle jaunts around the island here. Sunbathers were on the beach at Turtle Cove over the weekend. Two couldn't wait and hit the surf in mid-seventies temperatures.

Squirrels cavort everywhere, I saw a bluebird and a starling. Four deer crossed a road in the Sea Pines Plantation and loped casually through front yards of island residents.

Soon will come another sign of the season. I usually gauge the appearance of spring by the arrival south of the professional golf tournaments. Hilton Head's annual Heritage Classic, a prelude to Augusta National's Masters, is only a week away.

"The boats are already coming in," said a man in Harbor Town Tuesday. "The Heritage and spring brings them south."

Let It Be is docked from Ithaca. Taranak is here from Plymouth, Maine. Ravissant came down from Wilmington, Delaware. I see them and think of the old line about nobody ever retiring north.

The rain has stopped. There is a mist hanging over the marsh behind the Harbor Town Links' sixteenth green. The wind has ceased, and the stillness that has followed offers an added comfort.

Let them fight it out at City Hall, and where on earth is South Molucca, anyway? Spring is rushing in, and me and my duck wish you were here.

New York Subways

NEW YORK—I had planned to ride a lot of commuter trains around New York to practice for when Atlanta's new rapid rail system opens. That will be just as soon as the excavation is completed and the city is put back together again.

Presently, Atlanta looks like what Sherman would have left if he had been carrying bulldozers and jackhammers.

Also, I figured the subway would be the best means of transportation around New York, following the big snowstorm last week. After the snow came warmer temperatures and rain. The snow melted and the streets flooded.

The crud that normally just sits on the streets of New York started floating. Egg shells, potato peelings, and salami sandwich parts I stepped over on 52nd Street passed by me again as I tried to cross 63rd.

I decided, however, to brave the flooded streets and to look for nonexistent empty taxicabs rather than attempt to take subway trains. That is because the snow and flooding were causing problems underneath New York, too.

One train on its way to New Jersey quit running in what they call a PATH tube somewhere underneath the Hudson River, speaking of floating crud. The people inside the train were three hours getting out.

"Everybody stayed calm," said one of the passengers. "We sang songs to pass the time."

If I were on a stranded commuter train on the way to New Jersey in a tube somewhere underneath the Hudson River, I would not stay calm, nor would I sing songs. That is because I can't panic and sing at the same time.

I heard some other horror stories about subway trains from native New Yorkers who ride them all the time.

"We were going along one morning," a young woman told me, "and it became quite obvious the train was going faster than it should have been. Everybody got a little nervous.

"Suddenly, the motorman walked out of his little compartment and threw up. He was drunk. At the next stop, they came and took him away."

Another commuter topped that.

"You never know what you'll see," he said. "I was on my way to Queens. A guy and his wife or girlfriend got on the train having a big argument.

"They argue for four or five stops. They get louder and louder. Finally, the guy takes all he can stand and starts choking the woman. He chokes her until she's blue.

"Another man nearby grabs him and pulls him away from the woman and belts him one to settle him down. Soon as that happens, the woman cranks up and bops the poor guy who saved her life on the head with her pocketbook. He's out cold.

"At the next stop, the couple gets off and walks away arm-in-arm."

You simply have to know certain rules about riding commuter trains. Here are some I picked up in New York for Atlantans to remember in the future:

—— If somebody decides to choke his lover on a commuter train, don't interfere unless you want your head bashed in.

—— No matter how crowded a car looks, it will always hold one more.

—— Let sleeping drunks lie. Unless one happens to be driving your train. In that case, launch an immediate search of the cars for a priest.

—— In case of an emergency, like having to walk out of a tunnel, avoid the third rail. Ignore this rule and that sizzling sound is you, Bacon Face.

—— Discourage pickpockets and thieves. Swallow your wallet before entering the train.

—— If several young men in black leather jackets appear and ask for your wallet, do not tell them you swallowed it. Notice the fellow passenger who did is now minus one wallet and bleeding to death.

—— Never shove a friend off a platform in front of a speeding commuter train as a practical joke. Unless he gave you a hot foot when you were packed in like sardines during rush hour the day before. Then it's OK. You owe him one.

—— If you are now frightened about riding Atlanta's new commuter trains after reading all of the above, don't be. Remember none of that could ever happen in our city.

Saltines and Solzhenitsyn

TELLICO PLAINS, TENN.—I had been days without newspaper, locked away in a careless world of mountains, rivers, dirt roads, and a supply of Vienna sausage and sardines and a gift for which we can never offer enough gratitude: the saltine cracker.

God bless the saltine cracker, for it is constantly loyal in its service to enhance the flavor of even the barest edible. You could eat dirt with a packet of saltine crackers on the side.

I can't go many days without a newspaper because I can't go many days without certain information necessary to my peace of mind.

I need to make sure the world hasn't been blown away, and I need to keep up with the Dodgers. In this rustic village, which is located at the foot of some mountains near the Tennessee-North Carolina border, I purchased a newspaper and found the world still in one piece, which is more than I could say for the Dodgers.

Interest in the Dodgers is a carryover from my youth, but must a man have to explain every quirk of his character? The Dodgers, I read, have sunk to a lowly third. And the Giants, whom I hate, are still holding to first place. So help me Junior Gilliam, my favorite all-time Dodger, that can't last.

My companion and I needed a hot breakfast, if for no other reason than to take a brief leave from the joys of saltines. We walked into a place in Tellico Plains that was a combination beer joint and restaurant, mostly beer joint. The regulars were already at their stations. A card game of some variety was in progress, and an old man in a hat played the game with a boy-child on his knee.

"You have grits?" I asked the lady.

"Not grits," she said. She was missing some teeth. "I could fix you potatoes."

Where does it say an angel must have teeth?

Over eggs and country ham and fried potatoes—the kind that are round and thin—I read the rest of the newspaper. Carter this. Carter that. All hail Proposition 13. And a bearded man had made a speech in the Harvard Yard and had said some nasty things about our country. He made the speech in his native tongue, Russian.

The man, who has never been to Tellico Plains, Tennessee, said we ought to eat dirt for awhile because we have become fat and too interested in material goods, like nice places to live and motorboats. He said we are suffering from a "moral poverty."

He said if he could change his country, which would put him in jail if he went back to it, he wouldn't use our country as a model.

I finished my breakfast and the newspaper, left a nice tip for the lady and walked out on the streets of Tellico Plains.

It was a gorgeous late spring day. Just beyond the fruited plain that surrounds the village was a mountain majesty more green than purple, but stunning nevertheless.

Passing by me were simple folk, dedicated to the day's work and the simple pleasures. Most of them, I am sure, had never heard of the Harvard Yard, much less of the bearded, exiled Russian author who spoke there.

A pickup truck passed through town, its rear bumper bearing a message I don't entirely agree with, but one I needed at the moment. The Dodgers were going badly and what the Russian had said upset me.

"America," read the sticker, "love it or leave it."

But where would you go, Mr. Solzhenitsyn? Where would you go?

8

RAILROAD BLUES

One day there won't be anymore trains to ride, and a part of me will die. The part that enjoys good conversation in the club car, morning coffee crossing the Potomac into Washington in the dining car, and little boys and old men who, as long as there are passenger trains, will stand beside the tracks and wave at them.

She Goes Bump in the Night

ABOARD THE FLORIDIAN—She used to have a more romantic name. She was The South Wind, and Johnny Cash mentioned her in a song: "She left me on The South Wind. . . ." When she was younger, she dazzled them with her speed and grace for over 2,000 miles of railed opulence.

Now, she is a tattered, financial mess that is unloved and unwanted. By way of introduction she is Amtrak's Chicago-to-Miami Floridian. She is old, she is slow, and she goes bump in the night.

The Floridian, nine cars and a brightly painted engine with a red snub-nose, left Miami just after dawn the morning before. The feminine personification is hardly applicable anymore. "It" passed through Fort Lauderdale and Orlando and rolled into Jacksonville nearly eight hours later.

Then, there was a westward swing through the flatlands of south Georgia, through Waycross, Valdosta and Thomasville, before a turn north into Alabama and Dothan, Montgomery and Birmingham.

The Floridian is notorious for running behind schedule. It is supposed to make the 2,576-mile journey between Chicago and Miami in just over thirty-seven hours, two full days and one night.

It is due in Birmingham's old Louisville and Nashville railroad station—located in the middle of downtown—at 1:48 A.M. The rest of Birmingham sleeps unaware in a soft rain.

A station agent, a baggage clerk and four passengers await the train on a platform outside the station. Precisely at its expected time of arrival, the Floridian's headlight peers around a corner south of

109

the station. "Train comin'," says the station agent. Train comin' right on time, for a change.

I have made this trip before—Birmingham to Chicago, Chicago to Birmingham—aboard The Floridian. Nashville and Louisville are two of the stops in between. Rail travel remains a personal adventure, despite the hardships it often entails. Although Amtrak, the government-subsidized authority that runs most of the nation's remaining passenger trains, has managed to upgrade some of its service, much of it remains a frayed relic of the past. The Floridian falls into that category.

This train is one of Amtrak's biggest losers. This train, to borrow from songwriter Steve Goodman, "got them disappearin' railroad blues." This train is bound for a permanent siding if a providential solution isn't found that would increase its ridership and cut down its annual losses. The yearly deficit runs into millions.

One problem is its patronage is seasonal. "We are packed in the summer," the dining car steward will tell me during the trip. "We'll get two or three hundred people—most of them on vacation to Florida—every day. After school starts back, that changes."

When the Floridian arrives in Louisville the next day at noon, there will be twenty-one passengers on board.

A route change was one of the possible solutions Amtrak was looking into before its management recommended complete scrapping of the train. One proposal would have sent the Floridian south out of Nashville into Atlanta, then to Macon and Savannah—or to Macon, Albany, and Jacksonville. Public hearings were held in Atlanta and in cities on the Floridian's route.

If Amtrak's board of directors goes along with management, Atlanta will remain the nation's largest city not receiving Amtrak service. Southern Railway, which is not an Amtrak member, operates its own passenger train, the Southern Crescent, daily between Atlanta and Washington, D.C., and three times a week between Atlanta, Birmingham, and New Orleans.

It is 713 rail miles between Birmingham and Chicago. Arrival in Chicago is scheduled at 9:02 P.M., nineteen hours after the Birmingham departure.

I am asleep thirty minutes out of Birmingham, despite a ride reminiscent of the tilt-a-whirl from county fairs past. For $71.50, I have purchased a first-class, one-way ticket that entitles me to a roomette accommodation—a private room with a bed that folds out of the wall. There is also a tiny toilet, a tiny lavatory, and a tiny closet inside.

A regular ticket—you sleep in a reclining seat in one of the day coaches—costs $35.00. Amtrak offers a number of special fares on the Floridian, including a Florida package that provides free use of a rental car for a week.

I can sleep on a train. Most people can't. I talked with a companion from the sleeper the next morning at breakfast.

"Sleep well?" I asked.

"No," he replied. "There are only three ways to go to sleep on this train. Be dead tired, dead drunk, or just plain dead."

The equipment was old when Harry and Bess were in the White House. It is vintage thirties and forties. It includes a baggage car, one Pullman, four day coaches, a diner, a rounded-end observation lounge car and a mail car tagging along at the end.

One of the coaches has a domed top with huge windows for sightseeing. It is located behind the diner. The greasy smoke from the diner's kitchen exhaust has opaqued the windows in the sightseeing dome car. The view from the back of the rounded-end observation lounge car is the front of the mail car. Nobody has ever accused Amtrak of planning ahead.

Two middle-aged women boarded the train in Louisville. They will go to Chicago, spend the night, and board another train the following evening for California. They will arrive almost three days later.

"The train is the only way to fly," one tells me.

"It's the ONLY way I'll fly," laughs her companion.

They are sitting in the lounge car, drinking beer. They have at least six beers each between Louisville and Chicago. When we reach Chicago, they are flying higher than anybody else on the train.

Out of Birmingham, the Floridian crosses Sand Mountain. There are two tunnels. It gradually rolls down into the Tennessee Valley and into Decatur, Alabama, where it crosses huge Wheeler Lake, a TVA reservoir. Dawn catches up just outside Nashville.

The terrain is hilly, the scenery is autumn-in-the-country. We are in Nashville's crumbling Union Station at 7 A.M. We cross the Cumberland River and travel on into the Kentucky morning. There is a quick stop in Bowling Green and then another river, the Barren. A brochure describing the Floridian's route says that near the Barren River is Lost River Cave, once the reputed hideout of the James Gang. The James Gang used to rob a lot of trains.

Out of Louisville, we cross the Ohio river after a forty-five minute wait for our turn on the bridge. "This is what kills us," says the dining car steward. "If it's between a freight and us, we always have to wait for the freight to pass first."

Across the river is Indiana. Indiana, I notice, is mostly small towns, with miles of pig farms, cow farms and horse farms and acres of dying corn stalks in between.

I also notice it is difficult for most people not to wave at a train when it passes by them. As long as there are passenger trains, there will be old men and little boys to wave at them.

At Bedford, Indiana, we stop for the southbound Floridian to pass. It is nearly empty, too.

My sleeping car porter is classic in the railroad sense. He is black, with a full crop of gray hair. He is smart in his black trousers and starched white frock. He is polite, patient and helpful. We talked about this train.

"I told 'em they ought to put this train through Atlanta five years ago," he says. "They ought to run it like the old Dixie Flyer that went to Atlanta and Albany and Jacksonville out of Chicago.

"That was some kind of a train. It left Jacksonville at night and got to Atlanta the next morning. The businessmen used to ride it. A lot of people down there might ride it up to Atlanta now if Atlanta had any ball teams that were any good. But I don't believe Atlanta will ever have any ball teams that are any good. Do you?"

I said we would probably see pigs fly first.

The young man introduced himself as a songwriter from Nashville. He said the work was indoors and there was no heavy lifting, but he was having a hard time feeding himself.

"All day," he began, "I've been sitting here trying to write a good song about trains. 'City of New Orleans' really ran trains down. I just can't think of anything good to say."

The Floridian has been called the "dirtiest and smelliest" train on the Amtrak fleet. It isn't dirty. The smell is from another coat of fresh paint. The train is simply worn out and tired from overuse.

The cars were taken from the pool of equipment donated by the nation's freight-minded railroads when Amtrak was established in 1971. Some of the shorter runs are now using modern equipment built for Amtrak. The Floridian gets mostly scraps.

The Amtrak color scheme inside is a horrid scarlet and purple. The lounge car decoration is something from topless-a-go-go. It is kept spotless, however, by a pleasant bartender. Drinks are $1.50. Beer is 80 cents. The sterling of years past is gone from the dining car, but on each table sits a pair of fresh carnations.

The rest rooms are usable. In each are two signs. One is the familiar, "Kindly flush after each use EXCEPT when train is standing in the station." The other is, "It is impossible to clean rest rooms after every use. Please consider the next passenger."

It has been my experience that people who do not consider the next passenger—or people who can't read—are usually responsible for dirty rest rooms on trains.

The Floridian has had a number of accidents, although none has resulted in a passenger fatality. Once I was on this train and the bartender, a woman, passed around color photographs of a recent wreck. It was an unsettling experience.

A couple of months ago near Plant City, Florida, the Floridian hit a camper as the camper attempted to cross the tracks. Ten people in the camper died.

Some of the waiters were talking about train wrecks at lunch.

"My wife told me to get off this train," says one. "She say it's always trying to jump off into the woods."

"It's better than being on one of those big planes when it goes down," interrupts another. Everybody agrees to that.

One of the waiters was on the train when it hit the camper. He gives all the details. It is a gruesome description.

"Everybody is always wantin' to beat the train across the tracks," he says. "All they got to do is be patient for a couple of minutes and then go on about their business. Those people in the camper got plenty of time now," he goes on. "All the time they need."

Food is not included in the price of a ticket. A breakfast example is juice, two eggs, bacon or sausage, and coffee for $2.75. Lunch is a cheesburger and potato chips for $2.35. Or an Amtrak Chef's Salad Bowl for $3.

Dinner might be a ten-ounce sirloin for $7.50. Or red snapper filet for $4.25. Or broiled chicken for $4.25. Wine is $2 per half-bottle.

The food is only fair. But the service is excellent. A conductor told me about the food on the old South Wind.

"The railroad raised its own pork," he said. "And everybody knew it had the best country ham anywhere. Everything was cooked right on the train. First thing the cooks would do is start baking. They baked all their own pies.

"Breakfast was something. Country ham, red-eye gravy on the grits, and hot biscuits. People would ride that train just to have the breakfast."

Grits aren't listed on the Floridian's menu. You have to ask for them. They are instant grits.

Smoking is not permitted in any of the coaches or in the dining car. You can smoke in the rest rooms, in private rooms, or in the lounge car. If you do not smoke, you will appreciate all that on a long train ride. If you do, it will drive you slightly crazy.

We arrive in Bloomington, Indiana, 200 miles out of Chicago, on time. Same for Lafayette, where the train station is the Lahr Hotel in the middle of town. There are two hours to go. The route has straightened. It is smoother than before, which is saying very little. At times, we have crept along. After Lafayette, the train picks up speeds that reach eighty miles per hour. Just before sundown, I looked out the window near Cloverdale, Indiana, and saw three deer huddled together in a clearing in the woods.

Chicago comes at us suddenly. The lights of the Hancock Building and the Sears Tower are visible for miles over what is now flat terrain. At seven minutes until nine—nine minutes early—we are standing in Chicago's massive Union Station. A miracle has occurred.

I can't recommend the ride, but I can't curse it, either. There were no telephone calls. There was time to read, and time to think. A man who made the entire trip from Miami said he felt "defloovicated." I suppose that meant drained from the experience.

There was another conductor on the trip. His name was McWhirter. He had been on this run for twenty-five years. Promotion, he felt, would have been the Floridian's saviour.

"There is nothing wrong with this train some advertising couldn't change," he began. "I pick up the paper everyday and see these big advertisements on airplanes. I never see anything on Amtrak.

"Why don't they spend a million dollars advertising this train? It would get 'em 5 million back. Nobody knows about us."

As he talked, I remembered a conversation with a Birmingham bartender long before Amtrak's management decided the Floridian should be scuttled. I asked him if people in Birmingham were concerned they might lose their train to Atlanta.

"What train?" he asked back.

Jimmy Harmon

It wasn't that long ago all little boys loved trains. Most of them grew out of it. Some of us didn't.

Jimmy Harmon, who was thirty-one, didn't. He knew the joy of dinner in the diner and watching America go by at eye level.

He knew about the lights of Washington passing behind the Southern Crescent as it pulls away from Union Station on its daily run to Atlanta. He knew about crossing the Potomac and catching pitch darkness in the woodlands of northern Virginia, rolling gently on Southern rails.

And morning on the Southern Crescent, he knew about that. Breakfast at sunrise in the mountains near Toccoa. Then, Gainesville, and finally Atlanta.

Atlanta is bustling and traffic-snarled as the train arrives here shortly before 9 o'clock. And Atlanta in her morning greenery from the window of a train can be a magnificent way to welcome another day.

Just a few days ago, Jimmy Harmon experienced all that again. He rode the train from Atlanta to Washington and from Washington back through Atlanta and on to New Orleans—the Southern Crescent from start to finish.

It was his idea—he was a news film photographer for Channel 11—to put together a thirty-minute documentary on the Southern Crescent for his television station. The train's future is in doubt. Southern Railway wants to orphan it to Amtrak.

Jimmy Harmon went to work with John Pruitt, the new man at Channel 11 who was lured away from Channel 2. They took the long ride up and down the Southern line together.

John Pruitt was telling me Wednesday, "I didn't know anything about trains, but Jimmy did. He was a train freak. He could tell me what kind of diesels were pulling the train. I didn't even know that train Arlo Guthrie sings about, the 'City of New Orleans,' was a real train. Jimmy told me it was, an Illinois Central train."

The documentary will be aired as planned on Channel 11 sometime in September. It will be dedicated to Jimmy Harmon—news photographer, husband, father—who died Wednesday trying to make the product just a little better.

From a number of sources, here is what likely happened to him:

The filming of the documentary was actually completed. But he had been out each morning this week, trying for even more footage of the train's arrival in Atlanta.

Wednesday morning, there was fog in Atlanta. Jimmy Harmon may have envisioned a shot of the Southern Crescent rolling out of that fog.

He set up two cameras on a relatively new trestle that crosses North Druid Hills Road near Peachtree Road in DeKalb County.

One camera, a sound camera, was rolling at one side of the tracks where the train would soon pass. A silent camera, small enough to be embedded in the gravel between the tracks, would perhaps pick up a dramatic shot of the train roaring directly over it.

There are two buttons to be pushed to activate the silent camera. One button starts the camera. The other locks it into the "on" position.

Jimmy Harmon apparently tried to wait until the last moment before the train's arrival from around a curve to activate his camera.

He moved too slowly. The engineer of the train said he was directly in front of the huge diesel when he was swept underneath the train and dragged 600 feet.

"I've just come to work here," John Pruitt was saying, "and I hadn't really known Jimmy that long. But we worked closely together on the documentary. I feel like I've lost my best friend."

They called Jimmy Harmon a "damn good photographer" at 11. They talked about the grief of his wife, Donna, his son, Cary, twelve, and his daughter, Shana, six. They were working at the station to produce for the evening news broadcasts a sensitive goodby to one of their own.

A little boy never lost his love for trains. Wednesday, in the line of duty, it killed him.

The Smiling Chef

Yeah, I knew Lewis Price. I have eaten his cooking, and I have shaken his hand. And what comes back now is the recollection of the morning I poked my sleepy head into his office—the kitchen of the Southern Crescent passenger train dining car—and inquired as to the state of his general health and well-being.

We were northbound, a few hours out of Washington. He had been up for hours and busy every minute. He made his own bran muffins for breakfast, a South Crescent speciality.

He replied to my inquiry, smiling. "Everything is beautiful, Cap'n. Everything is beautiful." The man used all his face when he smiled.

He went to work as a chef on the Southern in 1941, and for thirty-seven years to come, he would practice his arts midst the grease and smoke and crowded dining-car kitchen facilities.

Company executives, the story goes, often tried to lure him away from the passengers to their private cars. And once he left the rails altogether to become chef at the Alabama governor's mansion. He could cook, understand.

But he was back on the trains shortly. "Too many female bosses" is why Lewis Price said he departed Montgomery.

He died Sunday morning. Lewis Price, sixty-four and a native of Athens and a resident of Atlanta, was one of six people killed when the Southern Crescent left the tracks in Virginia shortly before dawn on its daily Atlanta-to-Washington run.

The smiling chef—wearing his starched white frock—was preparing breakfast when the crash occurred.

The photographs of the wreck were horrible. Twisted cars strewn about the tracks. I make a habit of riding the Southern Crescent. I might have been in the dining car talking to Lewis Price.

He leaves a widow. He leaves five children—the youngest a daughter enrolled at Georgia State—and five grandchildren.

Larry Price is one of his sons. He is twenty-nine and a real estate developer. He was at his father's Burbank Drive home Monday, awaiting news of when his father's body would be returned from Virginia.

"We waited all day Sunday to hear the inevitable," he said. "Finally, at about six o'clock in the evening, we heard the news."

I asked him to talk about his father. He complied without further persuasion.

"He had an eighth-grade education," Larry Price began. "And what he wanted most was for his children to have the education, the independence, the chances he never had.

"When he went to work for the railroad, black people didn't have that many choices. But he liked the railroad, and he worked hard at his job because he wanted to provide for his family.

"And he did provide. We never lived in Sandy Springs or anything like that, but we never wanted for much, either. We were never hungry. We were never cold. And we never went barefooted.

"I never heard him talk about it, but I suppose he thought something like this could happen. There is always that chance.

"All his children were close to him. He taught us to have pride in ourselves. He instilled that in us. And he made us happy."

The Southern Crescent's future is in doubt, of course. Southern Railway wants to discontinue the train because of heavy operating losses.

"That bothered my father," Larry Price said. "He was thinking about retiring early because of it. I think he would have retired next year if the train had been stopped."

I will remember Lewis Price mostly for his smile and his food and the fact he was a vanishing breed. Passenger trains and the people who made them the Grand Conveyance of another time are running thirty years behind schedule and losing ground.

"All my father would want," the son said, "is to be remembered as loyal to the Southern Crescent. It was his life."

Engine Ride

ABOARD THE SOUTHERN CRESCENT—This weirdo little kid I know who loves passenger trains and wouldn't give you a dime for what the Wright Brothers thought was such a big deal got to ride in the head engine of the Southern Crescent twice this week.

North to Greenville, South Carolina, in the evening, and south back to Atlanta early the next morning.

I went along as a sort of chaperon.

It was the kid's last opportunity to experience such an adventure. Wednesday night, Southern Railway got out of the passenger train business, 149 years after it began, when the last Southern Crescent pulled out of Atlanta's Peachtree Station bound for Washington, D.C.

As of Thursday, Amtrak controls Atlanta's only passenger train. It is now called, simply, "The Crescent," and even its future may be limited.

This kid should have his head examined. Once he paid $50 for a conductor's hat. He wears it when he listens to his record of train sounds. He has pictures of trains on his walls, and once he even spent a honeymoon night on a train.

He's a mature kid.

He climbed up the side of the green and gold Southern engine Number 6914 shortly before 7:30 P.M. at Peachtree Station, and he heard the conductor from the back of the train, "Train Number Two, the blue flag is down! Let's leave here!"

He remembered to go to the bathroom before his trip began. That is important for a little kid because riding in the engine of a passenger train is very exciting.

He got to sit next to the engineer and watch him pull back the throttle and turn on the air brakes and blow the whistle of the ancient, snorting diesel when school buses approached crossings.

There are fifty-two crossings between Atlanta and the train's first stop, Gainesville. The whistle must be blown before reaching each one. Two long blows. One short. Another long.

That is 208 pulls on the train whistle the first hour of the trip.

"I love my job," said the engineer, "But people at crossings will drive you crazy. I fear school buses and tank trucks. In that order."

Occasionally, people attempt to beat trains across road crossings. Occasionally, they don't make it and get themselves wiped out.

The engineer's name was M.D. Hester, a man steady-handed, clear-eyed, and steel-jawed. He wore a green baseball cap and said he has been at his job for thirty-nine years, the last six of which have been spent driving the Southern Crescent between Atlanta and Greenville.

He will continue to drive the train for Amtrak "until I get disgusted." You know how working for the government can be.

A passenger train engineer stays busy. He reads signals that tell him which track to take because there is a freight train on the other one. He reads orders to tell him now how fast to run the train.

His maximum speed on curves is sixty miles per hour. His maximum speed on straight track is seventy-nine. In December, the Southern Crescent ran off the track in Virginia because the train was going too fast for a curve. Six people died.

A foreman in the engine explained how that happened. The engineer had sent the fireman, his co-pilot, back into the engine because of a power malfunction.

Alone in the cab, the engineer was busy with controls at his back and did not notice he had reached the curve at a speed of eighty miles an hour. Once he realized his mistake, he attempted to brake the train. When he applied the emergency braking system, the second engine came off the tracks and all hell broke loose.

Human error, they call it.

M.D. Hester was driving the Southern Crescent into Atlanta one morning and hit a local television cameraman filming his train. The cameraman was killed.

It wasn't Mr. Hester's fault, but he doesn't want to talk about it, other than to say he still has trouble sleeping at night.

He did say, however, the person driving the train is often in danger, too.

"We're sitting ducks up here," he explained. "People throw things off overpasses and hang things off overpasses for us to hit. Once I hit a concrete block hanging from a rope off an overpass."

Why aren't people who would do things like that in institutions?

"You never know what you will see," the engineer went on. "One morning I was coming in and a man appeared at the side of the train. He wore a hat he had made out of honeysuckles, a pair of clodhoppers and nothing else.

"He ran along the side of the train, flapping his arms trying to fly." Probably somebody late for work at the state capitol.

We were thirty-four minutes behind schedule leaving Atlanta for Greenville. You cross Piedmont Road, then Interstate 285, on and on out through Duluth and Buford and Flowery Branch.

We whisked past Bill Miner's Crossing, named for the last person to hold up a Southern Railway passenger train. That was 1907. He got $18,000 in gold but was captured a few days later, passed out drunk in a Dahlonega hotel room.

There is a downhill glide into Toccoa, taken at a smooth sixty, and there is a tall trestle to cross over the river into South Carolina.

Clemson is a flagstop. More than the normal number of passengers boarded the train at the old station in Greenville, northbound for such places as Charlotte, Greensboro, Danville, Lynchburg, and finally, Washington, at shortly past eight the next morning.

The sun rises on the southbound Southern Crescent in the still-icy hills of Banks, Habersham and Hall. Greeting morning in the engine of a passenger train, with three other engines behind you making the noise of the devils of 10,000 hells, is something Freud should have experienced and interpreted.

The little kid loved every minute of it. When we had left the engine back at Peachtree Station, I asked him what he thought of Brock Adams, Jimmy Carter's secretary of transportation, who is trying to do away with 10,000 miles of the Amtrak system, including the route of the Crescent.

"Why doesn't he go to lunch with a highway construction lobbyist and leave the rest of us alone?" the little kid asked back.

I didn't have an answer for him.

Besides, his eyes were still wide and his heart was still pounding from what the engineer had allowed him to do as the train had approached the station moments before.

He let the little kid blow the whistle, on the Southern Crescent.

And his life was complete.

Saying Goodby

ABOARD THE SOUTHERN CRESCENT—I don't know exactly where we were. Between Spartanburg and Charlotte perhaps. Midnight approached. Four hours earlier, the Southern Crescent had pulled out of Atlanta's Peachtree Station bound for Washington with three green-and-gold engines, thirteen cars and a pack of riders come to attend the funeral-on-wheels of America's last privately owned overnight luxury passenger train.

"I just wanted to say goodby in person," said a man who had boarded in Gainesville for a half hour ride to Toccoa.

There were three of them. The big one had a full beard, and he wore a cowboy hat. Somebody said his daddy was a big wheel with Southern Railway. You could have fooled me.

From somewhere in the back of the train they had each pulled out a guitar, and the music they were making had hushed what moments before had been a noisy, close-to-rowdy crowd that had gathered in the lounge car to drink its final respects to the Southern Crescent.

A black man and a black woman, wearing white starched coats in the South tradition, poured.

Train songs. Naturally we wanted train songs. The guitar trio obliged. The big one with the hat and beard had a voice on him.

They began with "The Glendale Train." Somebody robbed it. They played "City of New Orleans," of course, and everybody sang along.

People took pictures. Channel 5 rolled its film. A girl got drunk and suggested we all greet the waiting passengers in Charlotte with a group "moon." The vote was close against her. A passenger ordered more beer for the singers, and I was in the middle of thanking the Lord for letting me be there when in walked Graham Claytor.

Graham Claytor is secretary of the Navy. Before Jimmy Carter gave him that job, he was president of Southern Railway and a fine friend to people who like to ride in passenger trains.

It was Graham Claytor who had insisted that the Southern Crescent continue running—and continue its excellence of service—when all others around him wanted it stopped. He was a paying passenger this night, however. He had his own goodbys to say.

The big one cut down on "Wreck of Old '97," a damn fine train song, and Mr. Secretary of the Navy Claytor soloed to the top of his voice.

It was a poignant moment in the storied history of railroading.

He lingered with the passengers after his song. He even signed autographs, and he assured those who asked that Amtrak, which assumed control of the Southern Crescent Thursday, would continue the train's branch of service.

"This isn't the end of anything," Graham Claytor said.

But the Department of Transportation Secretary Brock Adams has proposed doing away with even the Amtrak version of the train.

"I don't think that will happen," said Claytor. "The political reality is this train will continue."

Another round for the singers, please.

Southern's plush office car number 11, fit for the company brass it carried, brought up the rear of the train Wednesday night. Atlantan Jack Martin, a power in the National Association of Railroad Passengers—the group that would like to hang Brock Adams—was on board. And somebody said they spotted Marvin Hamlisch. Marvin Hamlisch, among other things, wrote the music for A Chorus Line.

There were reporters and photographers and television people. And a group from the Atlanta that would ride northbound to Salisbury, North Carolina, and then return on the final southbound Southern Crescent at 2:30 in the morning.

One Atlanta man had ridden the train from Atlanta to New Orleans Tuesday then boarded again Wednesday morning for the full trip back to Washington.

"It's my birthday present to myself," he said.

Southern also had extra security on the train. That was to keep souvenir-seeking passengers from stripping it. Extra security didn't help that much. Menus disappeared by the dozens from tables in the dining car.

So did napkins and coasters, and a sleeping-car porter was missing his platform stool.

"My God," said a conductor, "I'm glad the toilets are bolted down."

There was one ugly incident. A young woman who had driven from Jacksonville to Atlanta to ride the train had her purse stolen. Security men finally located the culprit in a dark coach. They retrieved the purse and put the thief off the train in the cold and dark of Greensboro, North Carolina, at 3 in the morning, which is exactly what he deserved.

The Southern Crescent had been ten minutes late in arriving in Atlanta from New Orleans. With maybe a couple of hundred standing in the cold night to watch. The train finally poked its nose around the corner, gave a blast of its horn, and there was scattered applause.

"It's a sad day," said a man taking pictures.

Over the Peachtree Station loudspeaker came the Southern Crescent's final call. The caller sang it out: "Here comes the Southern Crescent, all the way from New Orleeeens!"

He added, "Thank you for riding Southern all these years." A touch of class.

All these years were 149 of them. Southern Railway opened regularly scheduled passenger service in the United States in 1830. The Southern Crescent was born the Washington and Southwestern Vestibuled Limited in January of 1893. Timetables advertised trips to Atlanta, the "Queen City of the New South."

Gainesville was the first stop Wednesday night. Then Toccoa, Clemson, Greenville, Spartanburg, Gastonia, Charlotte, Salisbury, High Point, Greensboro, Danville, Lynchburg, Charlottesville, Culpeper, Alexandria and finally across the Potomac River into cold and windy Washington and Union Station. Twenty minutes later than the advertised 8:50 A.M.

There were no bands, no speeches. The train pulled in. The train stopped. The people got out. An era passed.

I own a book called *A Portrait of the Rails*. A man named David Morgan wrote the introduction. As I left the Southern Crescent for the last time Thursday morning, I thought about a line from that introduction.

The unmatched adventure of rail and steel is nearly over. I admit that. So does David Morgan. But at least he sounded hopeful when he wrote, "Oh, Lord, but it will take some doing for America to get that adventure out of her soul."

9

AIN'T LOVE GRAND?

Somewhere in this chapter is a column that expresses my feelings about homemade biscuits and their relationship to love and marriage. You would think a column like that would not make anybody mad.

You would think wrong. They came at me with hatpins. One militant women's rights group wanted to chase me down Peachtree Street with large sticks.

I have always considered myself an expert on women's liberation. In the last fifteen years, I have given two their freedom myself.

Valentine's Day Massacre

This may be an inappropriate time to break such news. Then, again, today is Valentine's, and this is a love story, or what's left of it.

It began when I was in the third grade. So was my boyhood friend and idol, Weyman C. Wannamaker Jr., a great American.

The summer break had passed, and it was the first day of the new school year. We were standing, Weyman and I, by the playground swing set where Weyman ran a thriving porno business.

Weyman's older brother was in the Navy. He came home on leave and brought Weyman a deck of playing cards with pictures you didn't see that often in those timid times.

For a dime, you got a blind draw out of Weyman's deck, and you didn't have to give the card back until lunch period. Weyman sold out almost every morning, and by the time the cards and pictures were too worn for further rentals, he had a downpayment on a movie projector, which is another story.

"There's a new girl in our class," Arnold Bates walked up and told us. Arnold, who was one of Weyman's best customers, got all the inside information at school because his mother taught sixth grade.

Arnold also wore thick glasses and got extra dessert in the lunch-room. "Arnold ain't worth killing" is what Weyman thought of him.

This time, however, Weyman was keenly interested in what Arnold had to say. I knew that because when Arnold wouldn't tell him the new girl's name unless Weyman rented him his favorite card for free, Weyman belted him one.

"Kathy Sue Loudermilk," said Arnold, picking himself up off the playground dirt. You didn't make deals with the third grade god-father.

It was love at first sight. Weyman already had a stable of grade-school lovelies that even included a fifth-grader, Margie Roundtree, who wore lipstick and was talked about in faculty meetings.

"She's headed for nothing but trouble," is what Arnold Bates said his mother heard the principal say about her. Weyman simply wanted to be there when she arrived.

But there was something special about Kathy Sue Loudermilk. Even at eight, she made a tight sweater seem much more than a woolen garment.

I had never seen Weyman act as he did over the new girl in class. He brought her candy. He walked her home from school every day. He tried to break Arnold Bates' arm for talking to her during morn-ing recess. He even offered her one of his playing cards for half price. Weyman was *delirious* with love.

As the years passed, nothing changed. When Weyman was six-teen, he bought his first car, a 1953 Ford. He covered the backseat with a chenille bedspread, put shag carpets on the floorboard, and hung a pair of foam rubber dice from the rearview mirror.

It was in this romantic setting that they spent evening after eve-ning parked in the pecan grove behind the Line Creek Fundamental Back-to-the-Bible Church.

One night the preacher dropped by the church to prepare his Sunday sermon. He caught Weyman and Kathy Sue as they were about to drive away. The lint on her skirt was a dead giveaway.

"My children," asked the preacher, "have you sinned?"

"I don't know about her," said Weyman, "but I did all I could."

Nobody knows the real reason they never married. Weyman bought a truck and went into the produce business. Kathy Sue had already filled out her ambitions by the time she was out of high school. They retired her sweater when she graduated.

Weyman called the other day. I could tell something was wrong.

"Hear about Kathy Sue?" he asked.

I hadn't.

"Ran off and got married," Weyman said.

"I'm sorry," is all I could think to say. "Anybody I know?"

"Arnold Bates," Weyman answered, choking back the tears. He was sacking a load of onions at the time.

He will eventually get over the hurt, of course. Not Weyman. Arnold. Weyman went on to mention he had given the happy groom a wedding present. They'll take the cast off in six weeks.

Charlie and Julia

I called the Atlanta federal pen to inquire about Charlie Hines, Number 31579-120. Charlie, who is sixty-four, robbed a bank down in Florida a couple of years ago. After his conviction, he was shipped off to the "Big A."

"Yep," said a most unpleasant voice on the other end of the phone, "we still got 'im."

And probably will have for some time to come.

Charlie sent me something in the mail once. It was a copy of an article by a *Florida Times-Union* reporter named Ken Cruickshank. The article explained how Charlie became a bank robber.

I'll take the story from Cruickshank's article. He said he didn't mind.

Charlie got married in 1968 to a lady named Julia. Cruickshank told me, "They were a very devoted couple."

But hard times soon followed the marriage. Charlie had trouble with his feet. He was a diabetic. He had managed an amusement park in Tampa, but his health forced him to quit.

He bought some property in Tampa and opened a tavern and restaurant.

But Charlie Hines was in and out of the hospital and was eventually declared disabled by the Social Security Administration. He and his wife were trying to live on $156 a month.

In 1973 their problems worsened. Julia had to have an operation for cancer.

Charlie tried to go back to work to pay for her medicine. He tried a paper route of 125 miles for eleven months. Because of his health, he lost money on the route and was forced to quit again.

The bank took the tavern and restaurant away. Charlie turned sixty-two. His disability payments stopped. Social Security payments started. Now, Charlie and Julia Hines were trying to live on $137.10 a month.

Julia was in terrible pain, the story continues. Her medicine was expensive. Liquor was cheap. She began drinking heavily.

"I would mix her a drink to ease her," Charlie told Ken Cruickshank. "That's how it started."

Charlie's condition hadn't improved, either. He was having dizzy spells and periodic blackouts. A doctor ordered a brain scan.

"I couldn't do it, though," Charlie explained. "I didn't have that kind of money."

It was May 1977 and Charlie Hines was desperate. He borrowed a .22 pistol and took five times his normal amount of painkillers—"so I could walk"—and went out to look for a bank to rob.

He found one in Inverness, Florida. Charlie doesn't know exactly how much money he took. He never got a chance to count it. He was captured an hour later, fifteen miles away. He tried to plead insanity, but the jury wouldn't listen.

"I thought I was dying anyway," he said. "We had no food, no money and no prospect of getting any. So I went in and robbed that bank."

Last I heard, Charlie hadn't seen his wife since his interview with Ken Cruickshank. She can't come for visits.

Julia Hines, who accompanied her husband everywhere, was outside in the car that day while Charlie was inside robbing the bank.

Her number, incidentally, is 01129-179, Women's Unit, Lexington, Kentucky. She got fifteen months.

What made me think of Charlie and Julia was the exciting news that heiress Patty Hearst, who was also convicted of robbing a bank, had been freed from prison in time for her upcoming wedding to her former bodyguard.

It may be "the biggest wedding California has ever seen," said one news story, or just a "simple, private ceremony."

Whatever, they can afford it.

Let's all wish the happy couple well.

Lovin' in the Oven

Jerry Clower, the funniest man alive, does a routine on one of his records about biscuits. Jerry says the absence of homemade biscuits at the American breakfast table is one reason the divorce rate is going up.

"Saddest sound in this world," Jerry once told me, "is the sound of them little canned biscuits being popped open early evah mawnin' in evah house in the neighborhood."

Jerry goes, "Whop! Whop! Whop!" as an illustration. It's enough to make a grown man cry.

I agree with Jerry Clower. Give a man homemade biscuits in the morning, and he'll come home to you at night. The Pillsbury Doughboy, with his dratted canned biscuits, is a lousy home-wrecker.

There was a time, especially in the South, when the woman arose early enough in the morning to prepare homemade biscuits for her husband and family. It was a simpler time. Before mixed doubles replaced sex.

Women in those days served plates of piping hot biscuits. Big, fluffy biscuits. Cut one open. Slap a portion of butter between the halves and then cover that with your choice of jam or jelly.

"A breakfast without biscuits," went a famous saying, "is like a day without sunshine."

But what, if anything, endures? The last homemade biscuit I saw was in a museum behind a glass case.

It is time, women of America, to come to your senses. Halt the alarming increase in the divorce rate! Bring the homemade biscuit back to your breakfast table! We can all work together! You make 'em, we'll eat 'em. What could be more fair?

I must insist on taking a hard line on this matter. Any woman within the range of this column who subsequently serves her family canned biscuits for breakfast in anything but an extreme emergency is a brazen hussy who smokes filterless cigarettes, drinks beer from a can and doesn't shave her legs.

I called the editor of a famous cookbook, *A Taste of Georgia*, for help. She lives in Newnan and later this month, she is taking her book to the White House to present a copy to Rosalynn Carter.

A Taste of Georgia is in homes all over the country, including Alaska, where the Eskimos are now eating grits with their whale blubber. The book contains thousands of Deep South recipes, including some for biscuits.

The editor of *A Taste of Georgia* is Mrs. White. Mrs. John N. White. *Martha* White. I swear.

"It's not that hard to make biscuits in the morning," said Martha White. "It's just that it takes a lot of time. Most women these days simply don't want to spend that much time in the kitchen in the morning when there are so many other options open to them."

Like watching "Donahue"? Like playing in the Wednesday Morning Serve and Chat Doubles? Like running for political office? Like marching on a nuclear plant?

I accept no excuses, and there is nothing uglier than a hairy-legged girl. I asked Martha White if she cooked biscuits in the mornings for her family.

"Not on weekdays," she said. "Besides, my husband doesn't like a big breakfast."

Mr. White could not be reached for comment.

I looked in *A Taste of Georgia* for a biscuit recipe. One is for "Angel Biscuits."

You need flour, baking soda, salt, baking powder, sugar, shortening, yeast and buttermilk. Cook for twelve minutes. Sounds divine.

And one more thing, an ingredient most important. The last woman to cook biscuits for me in the mornings was a lady I lived with for seventeen years. I can remember asking her, "What makes these biscuits so good?"

"Love, son," she would say. "I put in lots of love."

Homemade biscuits for breakfast, ladies? At least once? And soon?

He'll taste the love. I promise.

Making Up

I remain convinced love conquers all, even in this day and time of rampant divorces and the breakdown of the family.

Take the recent example of the lovely Oregon couple, John and Greta Rideout. Greta called the cops on her husband one day and claimed he had raped her.

John said everybody knows you can't rape your own wife. That would be like stealing your own car.

A messy and much-publicized trial resulted. Besides raping her, Greta said, another thing she didn't like about her husband was he didn't keep his fingernails trimmed and clean. John countered and said Greta had these weirdo sexual fantasies thet didn't include him.

Luckily for husbands everywhere, the jury said, "Not guilty."

But that was not the end of the story. Almost before the jury could get out of its box, Greta and John announced they had resolved their differences and were returning home to live as husband and wife.

If John and Greta Rideout can patch things up again, anybody can. Including the Marietta couple that was divorced last week.

I couldn't believe my eyes as I read news reports of what finally put their marriage asunder. It happened last October. On Halloween night.

There stood the wife, who was separated from her husband at the time, minding her own business in her kitchen. Into the room walked the muscular figure of the man she married.

He's an avid weightlifter, so the story goes. Apparently, that's not all of his problem.

He was dressed in the costume of the television character, the "Incredible Hulk," all green and scary looking. On television, the "Incredible Hulk" is a quiet, unassuming, puny physicist who has this chemical imbalance in his body.

When riled, the physicist swells to several times his normal size, and his face changes into something that would scare a dog off a meat wagon.

Frightening his wife right out of her apron wasn't enough for the Cobb Clonker, by day a pharmacist.

According to the news story, he also pounded his wife one to the head, rendering her unconscious as they say at police headquarters.

He denied belting her and said he had simply dropped by her kitchen on his way to a Halloween party where he later won "best costume" after eating the glass punch bowl.

The divorce was granted last week. I called authorities in Cobb County for further details. I was told the man is presently free on a $3,000 peace bond following another assault on his wife.

I also found out policemen hate dealing with this sort of situation because it can be extremely dangerous duty.

"What drives us crazy," a Cobb officer said, "is when you go into one of these things where the man has beaten up his old lady and she wants him thrown in jail, sometimes she'll turn on you if you have to take him out by force.

"These officers went into a house one night. The woman was all bloody and bruised. Two or three young'uns were crying, and the man was drunk. They tried to take him to jail, and he put up a fight.

"Before you knew it, the woman and the young'uns were breaking things over the officers' heads. They knocked the brim clean off one officer's Stetson."

That's what I was saying. When the going gets tough, love can still overcome the greatest obstacles. I think there is definite hope for the ex-couple from Marietta.

He wants to be the "Incredible Hulk." Fine. She could dress up like "Wonder Woman." Give and take. That's the answer.

Just like the Rideouts. John is going to get a manicure, and Greta, sweet thing, has promised to try to work him into at least two fantasies a week.

My Little Cupcake

Dear "Sweetie-Poo,"

Bet you thought you'd never hear me call you that again. Cupcake, we may be living apart now, but there are some things I will never forget about the six weeks we had together.

Just the other day, I was remembering how I started calling you that name, "Sweetie Poo." Do you remember, Dovey? I used to leave little notes on my pillow before I left for work so you would find them when you awakened later.

I would write, "Roses are red, violets are blue, and I love my Sweetie-Poo." I know you enjoyed them because you would always call me the minute you turned over and found them.

I'm sorry I was hardly ever in the office when you called, but the boss insisted we knock off for lunch at one o'clock on the dot.

Darling, I've been doing a lot of thinking about what happened to our Little Blue Heaven. I have never had a shock like the one you gave me when you said you believed we should separate and I should move out because marriage was stifling your career.

Honey, I still believe you could be married and teach bridge at the club, too, but I suppose it's too late to turn back now. I guess you know your lawyer has talked to mine and we'll be going to court soon to get the divorce.

Maybe you didn't know. I ran into your best friend Gladys, and she said you've been traveling a lot. Aspen, huh? I'll bet you turned a few heads on the slopes with those new ski outfits you bought for the trip.

Didn't think I knew about that, did you, Pumpkin? The bill you had the department store send me came this morning. We've worked something out so I can pay a little at the time. It probably helped that your old man owns the joint.

Incidentally, if Gladys mentions anything about my saying I hoped you broke your leg in five places, I was only kidding, ma chérie.

Drove by the house the other night to pick up the broom and dustpan set you gave me as a wedding present, but I was afraid to come in. It looked like you might be having a party.

The band sounded tremendous. I know you are going to think I'm crazy, but for a moment, I thought I could see you and your lawyer dancing without any clothes on by the pool. Silly me. Just my imagination, I'm sure, or the lighting from the Japanese lanterns.

By the way, was that a new car I saw parked in the driveway? Gladys also said something about your Dad giving you a new Jag to help you get over the grief of our sudden breakup.

Love that color! You always did look good in red. Besides, the burnt orange Porsche he gave you for your birthday last month simply wasn't you, Cutes.

Sorry I got so upset last month when you said you had run out of money again and I'd have to make the house payment. I had some fool notion you could put what I send you together with the allowance from your old man and have plenty for the mortgage and some left over.

But you're right. I had no idea the price of tennis outfits had gone up so much, and I didn't know your father had cut you to a grand a week because of the way his stocks have fallen off.

I managed to scrape by. The watch my grandfather gave me on his deathbed was worth a pretty penny at the pawn shop, and I sold a few pints of blood to get the rest.

I'm doing just fine in my new place, Gumdrop. The landlord said he couldn't do anything about the rats for a while, but I'm getting used to them. It's nice to have some pleasant company for a change. (Ha! Ha! Still kidding, my little Sweet Potato.)

Better close for now, Puddin'. Know you're busy. Me, too. Working two jobs can sure keep a fellow hopping. One more thing, I really laughed when Gladys made that crack that you and your lawyer planning to "take me to the cleaners" in divorce court. You're a regular riot, Loveykins.

All for now. Write soon.

Always,
Your "Precious Lamb"

P.S.: My lawyer just called and told me the Supreme Court has ruled that women with a lot of money may now have to pay alimony to their husbands.

P.P.S. See you in court, Snorkel-Face.

Hope

ELLIJAY—The day has grown old gracefully in Ellijay, where the mountains are about to begin, and as is the custom in such settings, men with nothing better to do have gathered around the courthouse. In this case, it is the Gilmer County courthouse. There is a tree in front. And benches.

I still love a courthouse because it was on the steps of one I learned to play checkers and dominoes, and I learned about the Book of Revelation, which is what the old men would talk about after they tired of checkers and dominoes.

"Gon' be an awful day That Day," one old man would say at the courthouse.

"Gon' be a lot of folks caught short That Day," another would reply.

I even tried to read Revelation once. I stopped. It spooked me.

Standing with the men under the tree in front of the Gilmer County courthouse, I noticed the heat again—it remained stifling despite the approaching dusk—and perhaps that is what brought back Revelation's fiery warnings so vividly.

I am in Ellijay to watch the campaign tactics of Mary Beth Busbee, wife of the governor who is the first man in our state's modern history to seek a second consecutive term to that post.

I watch her closely and decide she loves her husband deeply or she wouldn't be working with such fervor. That feels good to me. He is campaigning south. She is campaigning north. Mary Beth Busbee says to people, "I'm Mary Beth Busbee, and I hope you will vote for my husband."

As I watch her, I think about marriage and how it has failed me— or how I have failed it—and I wonder if there is hope for those of us who have seen only marriage's bad side.

Earlier, Mary Beth Busbee had walked into a book and magazine store on the Ellijay courthouse square. "I'm Mary Beth Busbee," she said to the woman working there, "and I hope you will vote for my husband."

The woman spoke up quickly, "I lost my husband, you know. A year ago. He had a massive heart attack."

Mrs. Busbee listened. The woman's voice cracked with emotion. A year later, her voice still cracked with emotion.

The governor's wife introduced herself to the group standing at the courthouse.

A man in a T-shirt said, "If I was runnin' for office, the last person I'd want out tryin' to get me votes is my wife."

Mrs. Busbee wanted to know why.

"'Cause," the man went on, "she ain't never said nothin' good about me at home, and I know she ain't gonna say nothin' good about me out in public."

That brought a laugh all around. A good marriage needs a little levity, I was thinking.

Grady was there, and he met Mrs. Busbee, too. Grady is wearing overalls. His hat is twice my age. Remnants of the day's snuff encircle his mouth. For every courthouse, there is a Grady.

"Grady's ninety-three," somebody said.

"He still gets up and preaches over at the Holiness Church," somebody else said.

"That's my wife over there," Grady said to me. I looked and saw a little lady in a print dress, sitting on one of the benches alone. She drank water from a tall soft-drink bottle. There was evidence she dips now and then, too.

"How long you been married?" I asked Grady.

"Twelve years," he answered. "She's a good woman."

As I drove from Ellijay, I looked back once at the courthouse. Grady and his bride were walking away. It may have been my imagination, but I think I saw him take her hand.

Only one thing spooks me more than Revelation. Marriage. But Mary Beth loves George, a woman in a store grieves a year later, a husband makes a loving joke, and a ninety-three-year-old newlywed still feels the spark.

There is hope. There is hope.

10

A STINKING
PLACE TO DIE

A good father. A good cop. A good friend. And a porno hustler who saw the light. Death and near-death from Guyana to Lawrenceville, Georgia.

Don Harris

Ray Tapley is a man I have known for a long time. He has a good job with an insurance company in Atlanta, but he continues to insist upon working for the newspaper on Saturday nights.

Ray Tapley writes headlines and edits stories that appear in the Sunday sports section.

Saturday night, he said he only glanced at the front page when the final Sunday edition came up to the newsroom for a final read-down.

"I saw the headlines about Congressman Ryan possibly being killed in Guyana," Ray said, "but I didn't look at the story any closer. Only after I got home and read the entire report did I know about Don Harris.

"And it took me a minute to recall 'Don Harris' was Darwin Humphrey's television name."

Don Harris—or Darwin Humphrey—was the NBC reporter from Los Angeles who was murdered along with Rep. Leo J. Ryan, two other newsmen and a member of the suicidal People's Temple settlement in the Saturday ambush at Port Kaituma, Guyana.

I am still not certain where Guyana is, or even *what* it is, but I do know it is a million miles from Vidalia, Georgia, and one stinking place to die.

Darwin Humphrey was from Vidalia, down Route 297 off Interstate 16, in the heart of tobacco country. Vidalia is 11–12,000 people. Ray Tapley says it is the largest town between Dublin and Savannah. He also says it is the largest town in Georgia—outside a metro area—that is not a county seat. Lyons keeps the courthouse in Toombs County.

137

Ray is also from Vidalia. He and Darwin Humphrey used to ride the school bus together thirty years ago.

"Both our families lived in the country," Ray Tapley was saying Tuesday. He would be leaving his office soon to return home to Vidalia for Thanksgiving. And for Darwin Humphrey's funeral Wednesday morning.

"His mother always came out on the front porch to see Darwin when he got on the bus in the morning and when he got off in the afternoon."

Later, Ray Tapley's family and Darwin Humphrey's family—there were two younger brothers—both moved into Vidalia, country folks come to town. They settled around the corner from each other. "I saw Darwin grow up," Ray said. "He was only fifteen when he started announcing for our radio station. They were a middle-class family, good people. His father worked behind the vegetable counter at the supermarket."

Darwin Humphrey left Vidalia for Statesboro and Georgia Southern. He had a radio job while in school. Then, it was Charleston and a stop here and a stop there and a name change to a more flattering-for-television "Don Harris," and on to Los Angeles and NBC.

And finally to that airstrip in Guyana where a shotgun blast ended his life. He was forty-two, the father of three.

There is more about Darwin Humphrey. His speech teacher at the high school in Vidalia says that in twenty-five years, he was her most gifted student. Another is a New York actress.

Both his younger brothers followed him into radio careers. A daughter—Claire, sixteen—has lived in Los Angeles for five years. She says, "Vidalia is my home."

I talked to Claire Humphrey Tuesday afternoon at her grandmother's house in Vidalia. She says she is proud of her daddy.

"He was always leaving, we were used to that," she explained. Her voice was strong. "We knew what he was going to do was dangerous, but he did other dangerous things. We expected him back in a week.

"He was a very brave man. We are proud of him."

I don't know if Darwin Humphrey was aware of it before he died, but his daughter told me something Tuesday that would have made him proud.

"My brother is seventeen," she said. Her brother's name is Jeff. And he has already decided upon his future.

"He wants to be a television reporter," said Claire. "Like his father was."

Jesse Frank Frosch

Jesse Frank Frosch of Speedway, Indiana, was twenty-seven when he died. We had both struggled together on a struggling daily newspaper in Athens, and I looked up to him because he was a genius.

Frank Frosch was a brilliant writer. Once he wrote a story about what it's like in his hometown the night before the Indianapolis 500 automobile race.

That story remains the best sports story I have ever read.

Besides teaching English at the University of Georgia, Frank also led the band at a rural high school near Athens. He was well qualified to do that because he played something like thirty musical instruments.

Frank raised dogs, too. Basset hounds. When they sent Frank off to Vietnam in 1968, he asked me to keep one of his dogs while he was away. The dog's name was "Plato" and his pedigree reached for miles. Frank had paid $500 for the dog.

When he came back from Vietnam, the dog and I had become very close. I was prepared to pay Frank any amount of money to keep "Plato."

That wasn't necessary. Frank gave me to the dog. That's a friend.

Frank Frosch was an Army intelligence officer in Vietnam. He knew all about what had happened at My Lai, and after leaving the Army, he detailed his knowledge in a masterful piece in *Playboy*.

He later went to work for United Press International in the Atlanta bureau. That job bored him. He wanted to go back to Southeast Asia, this time as a reporter.

He got his chance. They would eventually make young Frank Frosch the UPI bureau manager in Phnom Penh, Cambodia. Like I said, he was a genius.

I took "Plato" over to Frank's house in Atlanta a couple of days before he left on his new mission. We sat on his front porch and took turns patting the dog, and I recall asking Frank if it ever occurred to him he could get killed.

"If I do," he laughed, "at least it won't be because a beer truck ran over me on my way to cover a stupid county commission meeting."

There were all sorts of stories about what actually happened to Frank Frosch. There were even rumors maybe Frank knew too much about My Lai and political motives were at the dark bottom of his death.

Nine years later, the details are still sketchy.

Frank was working in his office in Phnom Penh. A report came in of fighting on the outskirts of the city.

Frank grabbed a photographer. They jumped into a Volkswagen and drove out in search of the reported action.

When they didn't return for several hours, other reporters went searching for them.

They found both Frank Frosch and the photographer dead in an open field near their car. They had been shot several times by automatic rifle fire.

There was blood in the car. They had apparently been ambushed.

UPI now gives an annual Frank Frosch award for meritorious service to journalism. And his dog lived a long, full live. One hot day when he was fourteen, "Plato" curled up in a cool creek and died in his sleep.

Why I'm discussing Frank Frosch should be obvious. Another American newsman trying to get a story in a foreign country was murdered Wednesday.

The television film of the cold-blooded execution of ABC's Bill Stewart in Managua was sickening. He was unarmed. He was helpless. And some animal kicked him and then blew his head off at point-blank range.

The list of American correspondents killed in stinking places like Cambodia, Guyana and Nicaragua grows while the rest of us in this business wrap up our days with tax relief, gasoline shortages and a four-column headline on the Astros' winning streak.

Frank Frosch of UPI. Ron Harris of NBC. Bill Stewart of ABC. And all the others, rest their brave souls.

At least they didn't die because a beer truck ran over them on the way to cover a stupid county commission meeting.

Mournful Silence for Steve Vann

On a cloudy day, spring's first rain approaching, they came by the hundreds to mourn the death of Steve Vann. One of the preachers got up and said, "This is the Christian act of mourning. That is why we are here."

The chapel was packed with people who had known him, who had loved him. Who still did. Perhaps now more than ever. The hallways outside the chapel were also crowded. Those who couldn't find standing room inside waited in silence outside. Grief is rarely loud.

He was seventeen. He was a senior at Lakeside High School in DeKalb County. He was a quarterback on the football team. He lived in an upper middle-class neighborhood. He had a lot of friends. He had parents who gave him their time and their attention and, of course, their love.

Saturday morning, somebody found him dead in a creek.

"There were all sorts of rumors going around," said a classmate at the funeral. "Somebody at first said he had been stabbed. I knew that wasn't true. If Steve had an enemy, I never heard about it."

The county coroner was on television trying to explain it. Steve Vann died of exposure to cold. He was found in creek water that had been below freezing the night before. The temperatures the night before were also below freezing.

Evidence of drugs were found in Steve Vann's body. There was no overdose, but there were drugs.

I talked to more classmates at the funeral.

"I don't guess anybody will really ever know what happened," said one. "He went to a party Friday night, but Steve just wasn't the type to take anything. He might have smoked some grass, most everybody else does; but I can't see him drinking and taking pills."

"Somebody could have slipped him something," added another. "I knew him as well as anybody in school, and he knew better."

The death has been ruled an accident. The most popular conjecture is Steve Vann, because of drugs, became disoriented, wandered into the creek and remained there—unconscious—until the cold killed him.

Something like this shouldn't happen here, I was telling myself at the funeral. Look around you, I said. This isn't the ghetto. This is suburbia, good life America.

Steve Vann was no mindless punk.

He was an athlete. He was the second-string quarterback, but Lakeside is a state power with a huge student body from which to draw its talent.

"He had the best arm on the team," somebody said. "It hurt him that he wasn't a starter, but he threw a touchdown pass in one of the last games. He must have thrown the ball sixty yards."

But it happened. Steve Vann's death was drug-related. There is no way to hide it.

A young man standing outside the chapel said, between puffs on a cigarette, "If this don't make you think nothing will."

I could make this a sermon. Parents tell your children. Teachers shout it. Drugs kill. What I had rather do is take you back to the funeral. There can be no more drastic lesson.

There were flowers, always there are flowers, and their scent inside a funeral home is a sickening sweet.

The casket was a metallic blue. There were flowers on top of it. The mother cried hard. The father appeared stunned. Old people hung their heads. Young people stared in disbelief.

An organ played softly. A man sang, "Will the Circle Be Unbroken?" and "I Come to the Garden Alone" and "The Lord's Prayer."

One preacher said, "We are all in shock."

Another said, "This is a great tragedy."

A third said, "He esteemed his elders, he respected his leaders, he was growing into a man of worth."

And at the end, the father walked to the podium and spoke from his breaking heart.

"If any of you are ever in trouble," he told his son's friends, "if any of you need any help, or need to talk, then come to me. This," he went on, looking at the casket before him, "is enough."

God bless him for saying that.

One Year Later: A Father's Pain

The longer I sat and talked with Ed Vann last week, the more I realized what had happened to him since the last time I saw him.

That was at a DeKalb County funeral chapel. He was standing behind a flower-draped casket telling the young people who had gathered there not to take drugs.

Inside the casket was the body of his seventeen-year-old son who had been found dead in a shallow creek one year ago today.

Steve Vann's death shocked the community in which he had lived. He had been an athlete, quarterback at Lakeside High, an upper middle-class suburban school that is an annual football power.

He had scores of friends. The teary young eyes at the funeral home said that. And he was certainly no foggy-brained junkie. He had no prior record of ever having taken drugs.

But evidence of drugs was found in his body. What on earth could have happened?

Conjecture at the time—still undisputed—was Steve Vann had possibly taken some pills at a party he attended the night before his body was found.

Later, because of the effect of the pills, he had become disoriented and he had wandered into the tiny creek. Unconscious, he died there from exposure to the wet and cold of the March night.

Ed Vann still isn't satisfied with the investigation of his son's death by police. "Somebody gave my son bad pills," he said last week.

And he will never be satisfied with his performance as a father.

"Maybe Steve needed something to pick him up, maybe he was tired and was being pushed too hard to excel," Ed Vann said. "I did a lot of talking to him, but that was the problem. What I didn't do was listen. Everybody wants to talk to kids. But nobody ever listens to them."

What has happened to Ed Vann is he is haunted by guilt. Unnecessarily so, probably, but the agony that has lingered this long runs deep within him. "Living hell" is what they call this.

He and Steve's mother are no longer living together. He said she has had her own problems, coping with their son's death.

Ed Vann has taken a small apartment, one he had already leased to give to his son after his high school graduation.

He writes poems about his son. He carries them with him at all times.

He grasps at every straw. He asked a family friend along when we met last week. The friend claimed to have seen a vision at Steve's funeral.

"I was standing in the back of the chapel," the man said, "and suddenly everything in the chapel disappeared and in its place came another picture.

"I saw a spring day and a green hill. I saw Steve walking up the hill with Christ. When they reached the top of the hill, Steve turned and waved goodbye. Then, they both disappeared over the hill."

Others have seen similar visions, Ed Vann told me. Another friend, he said, claims to have seen his son twice in the past year.

He even attaches significance to the fact his hair, solid gray a year ago, is now getting darker.

"Who ever heard of that?" he asked. "I don't know what is happening here, but all these experiences must mean something."

Ed Vann's emotional plea to his son's friends at the funeral received a great deal of publicity. That bothers him, too. "Ed Vann Joins Fight Against Drugs" is one of the headlines he can recall.

"I don't want that," he said. "My son was a wonderful human being. You wouldn't believe the things his friends have told me he did for them. I'm not the one who should be praised for anything. The good one, my son, is gone."

I didn't have any answers for Ed Vann last week. I don't know what it is to lose a son. But I do know if a person doesn't eventually accept death, no matter how difficult that might be, he will eventually go straight up a wall.

All I can offer is a couple of suggestions. First, let go, Ed. Forget the visions. Forget your guilt and bitterness. They will destroy you.

And what you might do to help purge those feelings is whenever you see a man with his children still by his side, simply remind him to enjoy and cherish every minute of it.

You would probably be surprised how many fathers need that reminder.

Frank Schlatt: Don't Forget

The story didn't make the front page the other day, and I doubt the television stations even bothered with it. It was filled with a lot of legal-beagle mumbo-jumbo, and it didn't have anything to do with the price of oil, cracks in big airliners, or who's running—or not running—for the U.S. Senate.

"Slaton Appeals Ruling," whispered the uninspired headline.

So what? So this:

The story told about Fulton County District Attorney Lewis Slaton's efforts to convince the Georgia Supreme Court to reconsider a ruling it made May 31.

On May 31, the Georgia Supreme Court cited a technicality and overturned the murder conviction and life sentence of somebody named David Burney, Jr.

The court said that when David Burney, Jr. was tried, the trial judge had erroneously disallowed his request to act as his own co-counsel.

The legalese in the story was taxing, but from what I could gather, the trial judge had decided that since David Burney, Jr. already had two defense lawyers, granting him the right to act as his own co-counsel would have led to "undue disruption" of the trial.

District Attorney Slaton said a trial judge has the inherent authority to make decisions like that.

I don't know one end of a gavel from the other, and I would certainly hate to see David Burney, Jr.'s right to a fair trial violated, so I'm not about to take a stand for or against the Georgia Supreme Court's ruling.

After reading the story, however, I did want to bring up three other persons who have a fair stake in all this. They are the ones usually lost in the shuffle in such high-level maneuverings by men carrying law books. They come under the heading of "victims."

They shouldn't be forgotten.

There was Frank R. Schlatt, who was thirty-one. He was an Atlanta policeman. One day he answered a robbery call in a local furniture store.

David Burney, Jr. and three other goons were at the store. One of them blew off Officer Schlatt's head.

I went to his funeral. It was a pretty day and lots of people came. The chapel was packed. Fellow officers wearing white gloves stood at each side of Officer Schlatt's casket.

Somebody blew "Taps." Lester Maddox sat down front. High commissioners and police department czars arrived in limousines.

The preacher talked about what a good life Officer Schlatt had lived. I remember him trying to explain, then, how the Lord could allow such a good man to die. I forget his explanation.

At the graveside later, a policeman said to me, "We'll find the animals who did this, no matter how long it takes."

Then there was Officer Schlatt's widow. She was young and pretty. For a time, she held together well, but then the reality of the moment hit her again, and she cried hard and long.

God, there is nothing that tears at the heart like the sight of a young widow crying.

By her side under the funeral tent that day was Officer Schlatt's little girl.

What a brave little girl, everybody said. She was nine, I think. She fought off her own grief and tried to console her sobbing mother.

There was an American flag on Officer Schlatt's casket. Atop the flag lay a single flower. The little girl had placed it there for her daddy.

For as long as I live, I will never forget the moment an honor guard solemnly folded the flower into the flag and handed it to the grieving widow and daughter.

I don't really have an ending for this. I just wanted to make sure Officer Frank Schlatt and his family were at least mentioned while our judicial system contemplates how it can best serve David Burney, Jr.

Death of a Stripper

People are killing other people in droves in this city. So far in 1979, there have been 109 murders in Atlanta. In 1978, there had been "only" seventy-three murders by this date.

One hundred-and-nine citizens shot, stabbed, and strangled by other citizens.

Sometimes it happens in the nice neighborhoods, and it's page one. But mostly it happens where the sun doesn't shine. The victims wind up no more than statistics in the roundup of brutal crimes in the next morning's newspaper.

Young Hui Griffin, for instance. They called her "Young." She was thirty-two and petite and pretty. She was a native of South Korea. She married an American serviceman, and he brought her to this country.

The couple had a child, a daughter. Later, they divorced. Young Hui Griffin had to go to work to support herself and her child.

She took a daytime job, but that didn't bring in enough money. So she took a nighttime job, too.

She was a dancer at a place called the Purple Onion on Stewart Avenue. I don't need to tell you what kind of dancer.

She danced without her clothes.

Young Hui Griffin needed money. Young sent her daughter to live with the child's grandmother during the school year. Grandmother lives in the country.

"She didn't want the kid growing up in the city," a friend of Young's explained. "She had to live in a bad neighborhood. She was afraid to leave the kid in her apartment while she worked. She was saving to buy a house so the two of them could be together all the time."

There were also Young's relatives back in South Korea. She was sending as much as $500 a month home so that two brothers and a sister could receive the education she never had.

Young Hui Griffin made the papers this week, inside section, in a roundup story headed, "Four Slayings Boost City's Total to 109."

Police had received a report of her screams. Evidence, said the story, indicated she had staggered into her living room after being stabbed in a bedroom.

So far, there are no suspects.

The man at the Purple Onion this week said he would be glad to talk about Young Hui Griffin.

"She was a damn good person," said Mike Acker, the manager. "You know about how she was trying to help her kid and her relatives, don't you?"

I said I did.

"She was like that. She worked here off and on for three years. She was a good worker. She had a reputation as always being respectful to management.

"She was never late, and if she was going to miss work or something, she would always let you know about it in advance."

I asked Mike Acker about his place, the Purple Onion.

"It used to be a little rough," he said, "but we moved, and we get just about all kinds in here now. We get the men who fly the airplanes, and we get the ones who load 'em. We get construction foremen, and we get construction workers.

"Young danced topless. She would do Oriental dances, like with fans, to basic rock 'n' roll music. A lot of customers really got off on that. She would dance two numbers, and then wait tables.

"Know what else she would do? She was some kind of cook. She was always bringing in things like egg rolls for the other employees to eat. We'll miss that."

There had been some talk around, Mike Acker said, some talk that maybe Young had taken some crazy home with her and that's how she got killed.

"I don't pay any attention to that, though," he said. "What she did after she left this place was none of my business. And we'd probably all be surprised how many working girls leave their regular jobs and turn tricks for money or kicks or whatever."

I'll tell you what else would probably surprise us. To find out those 109 Atlanta murder victims were real people, not faceless, nameless statistics. Real people with hopes and dreams and crosses to bear like the rest of us.

Real people like Young Hui Griffin, a topless dancer who got her throat cut. But she was also mother to a daughter, and a sister who cared to a family who loved her and needed her and, no doubt, hates like hell that she's gone.

A Right to Private Grief

This is when it is hell working for a newspaper.

A young woman is driving home from a party in Cobb County nearly a year ago. She is twenty-five and single, her best years still ahead of her.

She has friends and loving parents. She has a boyfriend.

She never makes it home that night. She disappears with no traces whatsoever. Police can turn up no clues.

And the months and months of grief begin for those close to Nancy Carol Campbell.

The rain was pelting down all over the metro area Wednesday. Most of the talk in the newsroom of the *Constitution* concerned Tuesday's election.

Then, the call came. A car had been found submerged in water alongside the route Nancy Campbell was believed to have taken the night of her disappearance.

Slowly, the details came in. It was Nancy Campbell's car, and she was inside it. Early reports said her death appeared to have been accidental. It's a lousy job, but it has to be done. The softies say, "Leave her family and friends alone. They have enough to bear."

But this is a big city, and this is big city journalism and somebody has to make those calls.

I tried the parents' home first. What would their reaction be? Relief? What were those months and months of no answers like? Another reporter, who had worked on the Nancy Campbell story from the beginning, was with me.

"I don't believe I could do it," she said. "I don't believe I could talk to the parents after what they've been through."

The phone rang at the Campbell home. A woman answered. I identified myself. My hands were shaking.

"I'm sorry," said the woman, "but the Campbells aren't taking any calls. You must understand."

I understood. Frankly, I was relieved.

There were other calls by other reporters. To Colorado, the last known address of John Kurtz, Nancy Campbell's boyfriend. There were calls to an Atlanta friend who has since moved to California. No luck.

I tried a former sorority sister of Nancy Campbell's. She answered. I told her what had happened.

"Oh, my God," said Peggy Reese. "I'm in shock."

We talked maybe fifteen minutes. Peggy Reese, who teaches school, said she had been "very close" to Nancy Campbell, that she had always felt something "bizarre" had happened to her friend.

I asked how they became so close.

"We were at Georgia together," she said, "and I had been in a car accident. My leg was all bandaged up, and I was telling Nancy how bored I was because I wasn't getting to go out.

"Nancy got me a date. We wound up dating these two guys who were friends, and we saw a lot of each other after that."

After Georgia, Peggy Reese and Nancy Campbell stayed in touch. They talked on the telephone, about their lives, about their futures. "I really believe Nancy was a happy person," Peggy Reese said. "She like her job. She was doing some photography which she enjoyed.

"She and John had been dating a long time, but I don't think she was ready to get married. We are in that age group where we are looking for a lot of things in life."

We talked about Nancy's parents.

"I just went to see them several times," Peggy said. "It was awful. They were so down, so depressed. I was convinced they would never breathe another happy breath.

"What happened today will be rough on them right now, but maybe in the long run, it will be better they know."

Later, I thought about trying to call Nancy Campbell's parents again.

I decided not to. To hell with big city journalism on a dreary Wednesday afternoon. People have a right to grieve in private.

Religion and Larry Flynt

It was the prettiest day of late winter. Larry Flynt was somewhere between life and death on an operating table in Button Gwinnett Hospital. Lawrenceville radio station WLAW was on the air with its daily gospel hour.

The first record, the announcer said, was the number one gospel tune in the country, "I'm A Believer Since Jesus Showed Me The Way."

Some nut gunned down Larry Flynt and one of his lawyers on a Lawrenceville street Monday. "Nothing like this has ever happened here before," said an old man at the hospital. Larry Flynt was on trial here for peddling dirty books. Larry Flynt said recently he is a believer since Jesus showed him the way.

Many people don't believe that.

One woman was talking to another woman outside the hospital emergency room.

"I bet the Mafia done it," she said. "He made too much money for the Mafia not to be in on this."

The other woman agreed.

Somebody else said it was probably "some religious fanatic." Larry Flynt gave his views on religion at the trial last week. Some didn't hold to the strictest of Christian doctrine. I remember one of the things he said: "The Bible is a tool to live by, but it shouldn't be an obstacle course."

Flowers were already pouring in for Flynt. There were roses from somebody named Stan Coakley in Killbruck, Ohio. The card read, "Hang in there."

Another arrangement came in from a Bob Flamm. There was no address. The card read, "You showed me how fear can shake a mountain and how faith could move it. Keep the faith. I'm pulling for you all the way."

One of the flower-bearers at the hospital said, "You haven't seen anything. We're making one up from the PTL Club that's gonna be six-foot tall."

PTL stands for "Praise The Lord." The PTL Club is a Christian television program that is shown all over America, Canada and Latin America. Atlantans see it on Channel 36. Its headquarters are in Charlotte. A man named Jim Bakker founded it, runs it and is the television program host.

He sent the flowers.

I couldn't reach Jim Bakker Monday. I talked to his assistant, Robert Manzano, by telephone. Here is what he told me about Larry Flynt and religion:

"Some of our members met Larry Flynt in New York and invited him to Charlotte to talk with Jim Bakker on the PTL Club.

"He came but he was not put on the show. He and Jim Bakker went into another room and talked about religion off the record. Jim was concerned about Mr. Flynt's sincerity concerning his recent conversion.

"The interview was taped, and when it ended, Jim Bakker said he really believed Mr. Flynt was a born-again Christian and that he was honest and sincere.

"He said he was a brandnew Christian and confused and not clear in his philosophy. We caught a lot of flak from religious groups for having anything to do with Larry Flynt at all.

"But Jim Bakker said because he was a new Christian and confused, we needed to love him and help him rather than reject him. He said, 'It is the job of a Christian to love and not to judge.'"

I asked the man to repeat that for me. I wanted to make sure I had it straight.

"It is the job of a Christian," he said, "to love and not to judge."

The woman with the Mafia idea was talking to her friend again.

"You reckon he REALLY got religion?" she asked.

"If he didn't before," her friend said, looking into the emergency room, "I bet he's got it now."

11

SOME OLD PEOPLE

Come to think of it, the one burning ambition in my life is to live long enough to become an old man. . . .

Smokey Bailey

The past few months had been good ones for Ottis "Smokey" Bailey, a friend of mine. Smokey Bailey is the man who collects Bibles and then gives them away to people he thinks "need a good talkin' from the Lord."

I first met him in the cool of a springtime evening as he sat in his favorite chair under some trees behind the big apartment buildings at 2450 Peachtree. Smokey worked there as the building custodian. He lived in the basement.

"I come out here in the evenings," he told me, "to study the Book. Every answer to every question ever been is in the Book."

I wrote a couple of columns about Smokey, and you responded with hundreds of Bibles for him. He beamed each time I brought over a new load.

Later, I would see him on street corners from Buckhead to Brookwood, preaching to anybody who would listen—preaching to anybody.

There was the sweltering day in Buckhead. Smokey, long sleeves and a hat, stood in the park across from the old Capri Theater, Bible held high in one hand, the other hand waving toward the heavens.

He was glad to see me.

"Done give every one of them Bibles away," he said. "Lot of folks out there got the Word wouldn't have had it if you hadn't brought me them Bibles."

I passed along the credit to those who had taken the time, who had gone to the expense to load Smokey's Biblical arsenal.

151

Smokey Bailey is nearly sixty. He's a color-blind black man without family, without a purpose other than to do what he thinks the Lord has insisted he do.

For his custodial work at the apartment buildings, he was paid $200 a month. Most of that went for new Bibles. He had layaway accounts at Buckhead book stores. Smokey was always busted, and Wednesday his world caved in.

There are several versions to the story. Aycock, the management company that runs Smokey's building, said Smokey was evicted Wednesday because the building owner, Mrs. Dorothy Johnson, instructed that it be done.

"He wasn't doing his job," said Garvin Aycock. "All I could do was what the law directs me to do."

Mrs. Johnson has refused comment.

A resident who asked that her name not be used ("or I'd be evicted, too") said, "A lot of it was racial. One of the men residents here complained that Smokey put his hand on some of the women's shoulders. He put his hand on my shoulder. And then he'd say, 'God bless you.'

"There wasn't that much work for Smokey to do in the first place. Mrs. Johnson didn't like him preaching either. Whatever else Smokey was, he was harmless. What happened today broke my heart."

Smokey was fired from his job and kicked out on the street. A half-dozen sheriff's deputies came and moved his meager belongings from his basement apartment out to the sidewalk on Peachtree.

Smokey *had* been warned. His checks had been stopped. "I didn't know where else to go," Smokey told me later. "I didn't know they would do me that way. That ain't no way to do anybody."

People from Atlanta's Housing Support Service came to help Smokey. They hired a truck to move away his belongings. Bibles were scattered up and down the sidewalk. A chair wouldn't fit in the truck. A passerby stopped and purchased it for seven dollars. The movers gave the money to Smokey.

He was eventually taken to the Salvation Army, which has agreed to house him for ten days. Somebody paid to have his few possessions stored.

I can't place any blame here. Maybe Smokey should have spent more time on his custodial duties before heading for his streetside pulpit. And he did have notice that the eviction was coming.

But an old man with a big heart and a message of love is homeless today, and that makes me sick to my stomach.

I do remember something Smokey said to me once, however. It had to do with not being overly concerned with personal gains and security while running in the human race.

"Money ain't never worried me," he said, "'cause my wages are comin' later. The Lord's been holdin' 'em for me."

Pauline Jones

Pauline Jones had enough troubles as it was. She is crippled and in a wheelchair. Arthritis. She was married once, but that was a long time ago. There were no children.

She has two sisters in Atlanta, but they have health problems of their own. They can't help. Pauline is sixty-eight. And she is alone in the city.

What keeps her going is her stubbornness. You need that, and a good measure of it, when you fight The Big Red Tape Machine.

Two months ago, she entered a hospital for surgery on her legs. Doctors say there is a possibility she may even walk again. Pauline is still in the hospital going through a period of rehabilitation.

But it has been slow. Slower than normal because she doesn't know if she will have a place to live when the hospital releases her.

It all began months ago when the Atlanta Housing Authority ordered her to leave her apartment at the AHA high-rise at 2240 Peachtree.

The other tenants were complaining. Mrs. Jones drinks too much, they said. She gets frightened in the middle of the night and calls the fire department, they said. And she keeps cats in her apartment. There is a rule against pets in AHA apartments.

Pauline wouldn't budge. "Somebody's poisoned one of my cats," she says. "I had two kittens left in my apartment. They are all I have."

The AHA took her to court. Tenants from her apartment came by bus to testify. The jury ruled she must leave. Her attorney managed to hold off any further action by appealing to a higher court. Recently, the higher court ruled against Pauline Jones again.

She got that bad news in the hospital the other day from her own law firm, which decided to inform her in a rather matter-of-fact letter that also mentioned she might be evicted within ten days. Pauline didn't need that. "Physically, she is coming along fine," said a doctor at her bedside. "But psychologically, all this hasn't helped a bit."

I talked with two lawyers and one housing authority spokesperson about Pauline Jones this week. "We had no choice," they said. "We had the other tenants to think about. We even offered her another apartment, but she wouldn't take it." Graciously, the AHA says it will not evict Pauline from her apartment until the higher court sends down its final order to the lower court. "Then," said the spokeperson, "we will proceed."

The AHA's suggestion for Pauline Jones is a private nursing home.

I looked to finger a heavy here, but I don't know exactly who it is.

The housing authority is legally within its rights to evict resident Pauline Jones. The other tenants, just as needy, were howling. Fire trucks in the middle of the night aren't exactly what elderly people living in a high-rise apartment building need to see.

And the AHA had offered Pauline another place to live. It had warned her of the consequences if she didn't vacate.

And she *is* stubborn, and she *is* eccentric, but at sixty-eight, she has every right to be.

She doesn't understand how bureaucracies work, and she doesn't understand legalese. And the thought of moving frightened her.

And when it gets lonely in the night, who can begrudge her a drink and a couple of cats to keep her company?

And when she asked me last week, "Where will I go when I leave the hospital? How can I afford a nursing home on $188.40 a month?" I didn't have an answer for her.

It's a big-city dilemma. An urban-living standoff. Nobody to blame. Nobody to go to for help. And a little old lady nobody seems to want is caught squarely in the middle of it all.

The Man With No Socks

He was an old man out of a picture book, and I am a sucker for old men. We would get along famously, I was certain. I would ask questions about the mysteries of life and living and he would provide answers based on the truths experience had taught him.

I watched him totter across the street toward the bus stop in downtown. He wore a tattered baseball cap. If I live long enough to be an old man, I will wear a tattered baseball cap.

His shirt was wrinkled. His pants were baggy. There were no strings in his shoes and he wore no socks. Why, on such a fine spring morning, should a man have to lace his shoes and wear socks if he chooses not to?

He carried a newspaper under his arm. He shaved sometime last week. If I live long enough to be an old man, I will browse over the newspaper at my leisure in the morning and shave only when I damn well please.

He peered at the first bus that came by and chose not to board it. He asked the obnoxious dude standing next to him had such-and-such bus been by. He got no reply. The young tough ignored the old man. The young tough also wore an ear ornament. Never trust or strike up conversations with men who decorate their ears.

It was my chance to talk to the old man.

"Need any help?" I asked.

"Help?" He asked back. "I don't need any help. I need a bus. I ain't stayin' down here all day."

I apologized. Old men can be stubborn and independent. If I live long enough to be an old man, I will be stubborn and independent and defy anybody to treat me like an old man.

"I came down here to get my check," he went on. "The government gives me enough to live on. I don't need much. I don't smoke. I don't drink. I used to drink, but I don't drink anymore. And I don't fool with no women. That's what costs money, foolin' with women."

I was pressing my luck, I knew, but I wanted to keep the conversation going.

I asked if he had any family.

"I had a wife," he said. "She's been dead thirty-five years."

And children?

"A houseful. That's why I never did marry again. You get that many young'uns to raise, you ain't got no time to be out chasin' around for another wife."

A bus came by. He squinted through the morning sun and tried to see the sign above the front window. It wasn't his bus. I was glad. I wanted to hear more.

"You believe I'm eighty-one years old?" he asked me.

He looked every day of it, but I lied. I told him I couldn't believe he was eighty-one.

"Well, I'm not," he laughed. "I'm just eighty. But if the Lord lets me live another month, I'll be eighty-one."

He was rolling now, the old man. He talked about his children. Some were successful. One son had a house with eight rooms in it. Some were not so successful. He had a daughter who had been in a wreck.

"Drinkin' caused it," he said. "She had $35,000 worth of doctor bills. I told her to quit the bottle. She wouldn't listen to me. I knew something bad was going to happen to her, and it did."

He had another daughter bad, too, he said. The old man said he went to her house last week and gave her $37 and some food stamps and then went back later and found her and her husband at the kitchen table drinking beer.

"I'm through with 'em now," he said. "I tried one time to get 'em to come live with me, but they won't. You know why?"

I didn't have the slightest.

"'Cause every morning I get me some good preachin' and some good gospel singin' on the radio, and they don't want to listen to that," he said. "I guess they're afraid it might do 'em some good."

His bus finally arrived. We shook hands and he was gone in a cloud of MARTA fumes. If I live long enough to be an old man, I'll play my preachin' and singin' as long and as loud as I please and the devil with any of my ungrateful children who don't have the good sense to listen to it.

Invitation

The speeding Metroliner from Washington to New York last week had already passed through Baltimore and its railside ghetto that seems to stretch into an endless prairie of shacks from the window of the train.

Wilmington would be next. Then Philadelphia, and on to Trenton, through the ruins of Newark, and into the tunnel that leads to Pennsylvania Station.

I had seen all this before. I know every junkyard by heart. This is one train ride where the scenery is a liability to those who would espouse the benefits of downtown-to-downtown rail travel.

I do not want to be accused of provincial prejudice. I sat next to a man from New Jersey on this same trip once. I'll let him describe the view traveling by train up the eastern seaboard:

"One big dump," is how he put it.

You look for diversions on a trip like this. A newspaper will last you barely past Capital Beltway, the first stop out of Washington. I like to pass the time talking to people who will talk back.

Like the old man who sat down bside me out of Baltimore and ordered up a cup of coffee, cream and sugar. One gulp into his refreshment and he was gushing with conversation.

A lot of people won't listen to old men. A lot of people are stupid.

His clothes were wrinkled and tired, but he had at least bothered to wear what was left of his tie. There was a dignity about him.

When he talked, his blue eyes danced about. His hair was solid in post-gray white. He was a little man, but not stooped.

"Goin' to New York, sir?" he asked me. I said I was. He said he was, too. The traveler's ice was broken. Imagine, I thought to myself, this old man addressing me as "sir."

"I'm seeing the ball game today at Yankee Stadium," he continued. "I live in Baltimore, but I go to see the Yankees. The Orioles have no team, no team at all. Now, the Yankees, there is a team."

I used to talk a lot of baseball with my grandfather. He barely got out of Heard County, Georgia, in his seventy-three years, but he knew some baseball.

"Do you know, sir," the old man went on, "I saw Mr. George Herman Ruth hit his first home run in Yankee Stadium? That was fifty-six years ago. Nineteen-and-twenty-three.

"They talk about ball players today. There are no ball players today like we used to have ball players. Ever hear of Mr. Ty Cobb, sir?"

I said I had heard of him.

"Hit three-sixty-something lifetime. LIFETIME! Can you imagine somebody hittin' three-sixty-something lifetime today?"

He took another gulp of coffee.

"Did you know, sir, Mr. George Herman Ruth was also a pitcher? He was also one fine pitcher. Held some records for shutout innings in the World Series. He was the greatest ball player of all time. I saw him hit his first home run in Yankee Stadium in Nineteen-and-twenty-three."

If I had seen something like that, I would repeat myself, too.

"I know all about the Yankees," the old man said. We were coming into Wilmington. "I could name you the starting lineup of the 1923 Yankees, sir, do you believe I could do that?"

I didn't have time to answer. He was already off and naming. Few of the names meant anything to me, but his feat was impressive, nevertheless. I can name the starting lineup of the 1959 Dodgers and White Sox. It didn't seem worth bringing up, however.

Philadelphia was next. When they finally close Thirtieth Street Station in Philadelphia, they can use it for a dungeon. Trenton. Then, Newark. I would hate to live in Newark.

Five minutes into the tunnel that leads to New York, the conductor announced Pennsylvania Station. The old man was still talking. Among other things, he predicted the Yankees would win the World Series again because Tommy John keeps his pitches low.

"You're a busy man?" he asked me. Very, I said.

Later, after he had tottered away, and I had departed the station for a task that wasn't all that important in retrospect, I concluded the old man had probably considered asking me if I wanted to go to the ball game at Yankee Stadium with him. But I was too busy, I had said. A lot of people are stupid.

Barney

Barney Wisdom is dead. It happened Monday. Everybody has a right to an obituary, I was thinking. Even old winos. This is Barney's. It's the least I can do.

It won't be that complete, however, because nobody knew much about Barney—and he could barely talk—except he was a pitiful sight hobbling around the Howell Mill-Collier Road area in Northwest Atlanta looking for his next drink.

"I'm not that sad Barney died," a lady from the neighborhood told me. "It's probably a blessing. It just breaks my heart he had to live the way he did."

Barney was sixty-nine. A policeman found that out. Somebody said he was a native of Alabama and used to work in a sawmill. Somebody else said he had a son in Florence. There was talk he might have a sister in Summerville in north Georgia, and I even heard once he had a brother over in Lawrenceville.

A man at the coroner's office told me Wednesday he had tried to contact a relative to claim Barney's body from the Grady morgue.

"So far," he said, "nothing."

Barney was the *quintessential* wino. He worked at it all his waking hours. His favorite drinking perch was atop a bench on the side of Springlake Pharmacy at the corner of Howell Mill and Collier.

Barney never bothered anybody that I knew of. Give him a buck and he would return a toothless smile that was certainly not without charm. Barney was the subject of another column of mine a few months back.

Two rascal children were throwing rocks at him as he sat beside the drugstore one Saturday afternoon. I wrote about the incident in the newspaper. I heard the two children moved out of town. Good riddance.

Barney slept in the woods off Howell Mill. Or in the basement of a neighborhood laundromat. Or, when the weather became unbearable, down at Atlanta's Union Mission, thanks to rides by caring Atlanta policemen.

That's where he died. A passing motorist found him nearly comatose on the sidewalk Monday afternoon. Barney had been fading fast lately. A few months back, there was even a rumor he had died, but Barney showed up again, thirsty as ever.

The motorist took him to the Union Mission. One of the spokesmen there told me what happened:

"Barney was in bad shape," he said. "The first thing we do is give them a shower and then find some clean clothes. We gave him the shower, and then he just fell over dead."

He was taken to the Grady morgue. Police investigated and did find Barney had a small bank account.

"I believe he has enough to bury him," explained a teller at the bank. "I hope so. He didn't have a very good life. I would at least like to see him put away nicely."

The alternative, of course, is a pauper's funeral at county expense.

I live in the Howell-Collier area, and I always marveled at the special—and surprising—interest the neighborhood had in Barney, the old boozer who was as much a local landmark as Springlake Pharmacy, home of the world's finest limeade coolers.

I made a speech to the local Garden Club last week. After the speech, I asked for questions:

"How's Barney?" was the first response from a little, gray lady.

Capital City Liquor store is across the street from Springlake Pharmacy. Needless to say, Barney spent a great deal of time there.

"We cashed his social security checks," said one of the men there. "Barney didn't beg when he was out of money. He'd just stand there and look at you.

"He could wear you down psychologically. I wish I had a nickel for every fifty cents he got from me."

I hope some of Barney's relatives—if there are any—read this, and I hope they show enough interest to make sure one of his own is standing by when shovels of dirt cover his last remains.

Everybody has a right to blood kin at his funeral, I was thinking.

Even old winos.

Won't
You
Come Home,
Billy Bob
Bailey?

To Kathy,
Who loves me anyway

CONTENTS

1

TAKE MY ADVICE . . . PLEASE!

Grits Billy Bob

There are probably some things more important than learning how to cook good grits—or, learning how to cook grits good—but I can't think of any off the top of my head, so that is why this book begins with the following piece, written by my good friend, Billy Bob Bailey of Fort Deposit, Alabama.

Billy Bob writes my newspaper column for me occasionally, like when I have to get a haircut, and he has become quite popular with my readers, except those who are from the North. They are quite offended by Billy Bob.

Of course, they don't like grits, either, which is how all the following got started in the first place.

My name is Billy Bob Bailey, and I live down in Fort Deposit, Alabama, which ain't close to nothing but the ground. Plumbing maintenance is my game—you name it and I can unstop it—but on the side I write a newspaper column for the local weekly.

It's called "The Straight Flush with Billy Bob." My dog Rooster's the one who thought up that name.

Me and Lewis Grizzard go way back. We knew each other before Studebaker went broke. He's a good ol' boy, Lewis, but he's bad to get into what I call one of his sorry spells. Too sorry to work, and too sorry to care if he don't.

If his hind end ever gets any weight on it, they ought to hang the lazy scoundrel.

So here I am bailin' him out again while he takes another day off. I bet his time card's got more empty spaces on it than the doctors saw when they examined the Penn State football team for brain damage after it was run slap over by the University of Aladamnbama in the Sugar Bowl.

We're still celebrating knocking Four-Eyed Joe Paterno out of the national championship. It's true we got us an Auburn man sittin' in the governor's chair in Montgomery now, but it's Mr. Paul Bryant who's still the king, roll Tide.

Football ain't what's on my mind today, though, but I've got something to talk about that's just about as important.

Grits.

You heard me right. G—for "good"—r-i-t-s, grits. This all started a week ago when me and Rooster went down to the diner to have breakfast.

Sittin' in the diner were these two Yankee tourists who got lost trying to find Florida, which ain't exactly hard to locate like Rhode Island or Kansas. You just drive that big black Buick until everybody you see is two years older than Lydia E. Pinkham's hat.

Clovis, the waitress, asked the two Yankees if they wanted grits with their eggs, and they turned up their noses and said they'd rather eat mud first.

Clovis blanched, and it was all I could do to keep Rooster still. I don't know why it is people from up North who come South want to make fun of the way we eat and talk.

Before I got down in my back, I used to have a special way of dealing with riff-raff like that. After they got out of the hospital, they couldn't wait to get back to New Jersey where it smells like what it took me half a day to unclog at the bus station last week.

But Billy Bob ain't as young as he used to be, and I'm learning to be a little more tolerant about ignorance. This is a free country, and if somebody ain't got the good sense God gave a sweet potato, it ain't up to me to move his nose over to the side a little.

The reason Yankees don't like grits is nobody ever told 'em how to eat 'em. If you don't doctor up grits a little, I'll be the first to admit they taste like something I wouldn't even say.

Grits need a little help, and what I'm going to do today is give out my famous recipe for Grits Billy Bob, and if you have anything to do with any Yankees, you might pass it along.

Grits Billy Bob:

First, don't fool with no instant grits. The idiot who invented instant grits also thought of frozen fried chicken, and they ought to lock him up before he tries to freeze-dry collards.

Get yourself some Aunt Jeminas or some Jim Dandys. Cook 'em slow and stir every chance you get. Otherwise, you'll have lumps, and you don't want lumps.

Salt and pepper and stir in enough butter to choke a goat. Fry some bacon and sausage on the side and crumble that in, and then come right on top of that with all the cheese the law will allow.

Grits Billy Bob ought not to run out of the pot. They ought to crawl. Serve hot. Cold Grits Billy Bob are harder than a steel-belted radial.

Speaking of tires, it was a shame the bad luck those two Yankees had before they could get out of town. All four of their tires blew out right in front of Clovis's brother's service station. His name is Harvey.

Harvey made 'em a good deal on a new set, though. Said he never had seen tires punctured that way. Said they looked like something with real sharp teeth had gnawed right through 'em.

Rooster said he figured they ran over a possum.

On Living Alone

This was written before I got married—again—which will all be explained at the end of the book. But for those of you who are still living alone, or who are planning to give it a try, there should be some excellent advice for you here. Like the part about underwear. Clean underwear doesn't grow on trees, you know.

I'm not certain who digs up such information, or who pays for the digging, but there was an item on the evening news about more and more Americans living alone these days.

I can think of at least three reasons for that:

1. People are waiting around longer before they get married.

2. Those who didn't wait around to get married are getting divorced in droves.

3. Maybe there are more nurdy-type people who can't find anybody who will live with them.

I am sort of an expert on all this becaue I live alone. I could go into details as to why, but that isn't really necessary. Just check somewhere between aforementioned reasons-for-living-alone "2" and "3."

A lot of people actually enjoy living alone. There are certain advantages:

1. People who live alone can leave their underwear lying around all over the floor.

2. There are never any arguments over what to watch on television. If you live alone, you can even watch "The Dating Game," and who will know?

3. The phone is always for you.

4. You never have to hear, "Honey, there's something I've been meaning to talk to you about," when Dallas is fourth-and-one on the Washington two-yard line.

5. If you find a hair in your soup, you know for certain whose it is.

I could go on, but those are the highlights. Perhaps what I am trying to say is, if you are sharing a dwelling and think you would like to kick the bum or old bag out, think twice.

The item on the evening news went on to say people who live alone tend to die younger than others.

I think I know why. I can only speak for the male of the species, but there are certain shocks that will come the minute she's gone, fellows.

Let's go back to the underwear for a second. You probably think your underwear walks to the washing machine, dives in, and after washing itself, marches back to your dresser, gets inside, and folds itself.

Soon after I was cast adrift, I wore all my underwear once, and then looked in the dresser for another fresh pair. My underwear was where I had left it—lying around all over the floor.

A man of my standing and upbringing certainly wasn't going to wash his own underwear, so I did a second-time-around on the dirties. After that I had no choice. I went to K-Mart where they were having a special and bought a six-month supply of undershorts.

When they were dirty, I did what any other just-divorced American male would do. I threw them away and bought another six-month supply.

There are other similar problems. Toilet paper and fresh towels don't grow in the bathroom. Strange green things do if you don't clean it, however.

Light bulbs. Light bulbs will drive you crazy. They are always burning out. You have to take the time from your busy schedule to go out and BUY more light bulbs and then bring them home and screw them in. That alone can take years off your life.

Food. You live alone, you try cooking for yourself. You cook for yourself, you can get poisoned, and then there are the dishes. You don't cook, you eat a lot of heat-and-serve Mexican dinners, which annually kill thousands of men who live alone.

Beer cans. Who is going to throw his own beer cans in the garbage? Let me tell you something about beer cans. You leave a couple of empty beer cans around, and the next time you look there will be four beer cans, and then eight, and pretty soon, you are up to your eyeballs in empty beer cans.

If you are about to strike out alone, big boy, I don't mean to frighten you with this, so to soften the blow, maybe I should offer one more advantage to living by yourself:

If you do happen to die young, maybe the end will come before you finally have to break down and change your sheets.

The Truth About Dentists

Nearly every society has had its element of cruel and sadistic monsters, preying on the helpless and innocent. We call ours "dentists."

Get ready for this, because I don't want you to be caught off guard. The American Dental Association has launched a new propaganda scheme aimed at people who will do anything to stay out of the dentist's office—people like me.

We are not small group. According to its own figures, the ADA says only half the population goes to the dentist each year.

The purpose of its scheme is to get the other 50 percent strapped into that chair so the dentist can scrape and pull and drill and make the poor suckers hurt and bleed and then charge them for his trouble.

The scheme includes sending out ADA "ambassadors" all over the country to tell you incredible lies, such as, it doesn't hurt to go to the dentist anymore.

One of those "ambassadors" is a lady dentist named Dr. Sheva Rapoport, of Allentown, Pennsylvania. I read a newspaper account of some of the baloney she is peddling.

Get a load of this song and dance. According to Dr. Rapoport:

• Dentists' offices now offer a more pleasant environment than before.

• Dentists are now more aware of their patients' feelings.

• Dental equipment has been improved.

• If you ask for one, a dentist will provide a cost estimate before he starts excavating in your mouth.

Big deal. So dentists have put in Muzak and hung a few pictures, and now you can find out about their outrageous prices ahead of time.

What the ADA wants to do is double root-canal sales, and I, for one, will not be fooled by its would-be clever trick.

Do not listen to the ADA, America. Listen to your Uncle Lewis, who knows all there is to know about dentists, because he was held prisoner by one until he was old enough to escape without parental consent.

The *truth* about dentists—clip and save:

• Of course, it still hurts to go to the dentist, because dentists WANT it to hurt. They like to watch you squirm, they like to hear your muffled cries of agony, they like to fill your mouth with cotton and then ask you, So who do you like Monday night? The Cowboys or the Steelers?

• Dental equipment will be improved only when the heinous drill is totally silent, has a rubber tip, and tickles, rather than feels like someone has taken to your mouth with the first cousin to a jackhammer.

• When a dentist says, "This may sting a little," he really means, "How high can you jump?"

• Oral Roberts University is not a school of dentistry.

• Beware any dentist whose nickname is "Mad Dog" or "Nick the Grinder."

• Beware any dentist with a nervous twitch.

• Beware any dentist who is missing one or more fingers.

• Beware any dentist who is wearing an inordinate amount of leather and whose chair has straps.

• Beware dating dental assistants. They kiss with their teeth, and floss in public.

• Despite what the American Dental Association says, there are worse things than having all your teeth rot out.

• I would gladly list a couple, but it's late and I have to go gum dinner.

Learning to Mix With the Idle Rich

I am the only person in my family ever to have spent a weekend at The Cloister on Sea Island, or anywhere like it. However, my Uncle Gaylord once spent a weekend in Tulsa, where he finished second in a pool tournament and met his fourth wife, who was performing on

the tables in the motel lounge. Uncle Gaylord always knew how to
live.

Sea Island, Ga.

Soon, I wll be checking out of The Cloister, a famous resort hotel for rich people. Soon, I will be penniless again.

A weekend here costs four houses and a mortgage on Marvin Gardens. Harley Devonshire Billups III, the big butter and egg man from Shreveport, might have that kind of stash, but I was hoping somebody would put me on scholarship before settle-up time came at the cashier's window in the lobby.

This place is so spiffy, you have to wear a tuxedo for tennis. The Cloister, people always say, is full of "old world charm." That means that if you don't own at least one small European country, you'll choke when you see your bill.

The bigs come here. Corporation presidents, heads of state, politicians who haven't been caught yet, and wealthy baseball players like Pete Rose, would come, if they had any class.

All weekend, I have felt like a leisure suit at the club's spring formal.What if the other guests, I kept asking myself, discover a charlatan has slipped into their midst?

I took extra precautions, like wearing dark socks and parking the truck off the island, but rich people can usually sniff out a taxpayer. We fold our wallets inside out.

One fellow almost caught me over drinks in one of the club rooms. He was from New York and several other places. I think he owned Canada or something.

"What's your game, old chap?" he asked me.

"Newspapers," I said.

"Buying or selling?" he persisted.

I took a long sip from my drink, a Rednecker. That's an amaretto straight-up with a long-neck Bud chaser.

"Buying," I said, which isn't a total lie. When I can't rip off my daily copy from the boss's office, I have to pop for a quarter and go to the rack like everyone else.

There is a lot to do at The Cloister, located on the opulent Golden Isles of Georgia and a million miles from the back room of Harold's Barbecue in Atlanta, one of my other favorite vaction spots.

You can go for a walk on the beach, or play tennis, golf, croquet, lawn bowls, shuffleboard, and bridge. You can shoot skeet at the gun club, go horseback riding, take dancing lessons, or drink afternoon tea with the older folk.

It is true that a lot of older people do visit here. In fact, the line on The Cloister goes, it's the spot for "newlyweds and nearly-deads." Often, young couples honeymoon here who fit both categories after a week of bundling in their ocean-front bungalows.

One of the older people I met here was a delightful man they call "The Colonel." The Colonel is a West Pointer, class of '15. Eisenhower was one of his classmates. He is looking forward to his next reunion.

"Only nineteen of us left now," said the Colonel as he gunned down a final prune juice and left for his dancing lesson.

The reason I did this—took a room at The Cloister for the week-end—is I deserved it. The rigors of work have been piling up, the heap I drive blew a gasket, the moths ate another hole in my sports-coat, and I left my favorite Willie Nelson album on a window ledge the other morning and the sun warped it, which is why Willie sounds like Kate Smith with a bucket over her head.

So I came here to get away from it all. I had patio breakfasts overlooking the gray Atlantic. One morning I even ordered Kadota figs fresh from South Kadota. I dined in graceful elegance, played tennis, rubbed and bent elbows with the landed gentry, and dozed in the sunshine with the Colonel.

It's like they say in those beer commercials, "You only go around once . . ." so grab all the cucumber aspic you can.

Besides, next week I can eat the soap I stole off the maid's cleaning cart.

How to Survive an Airplane Crash

A lot of people aren't really serious about their fear of flying. I am. I once rode a bus from Atlanta to El Paso and back to avoid flying. Don't knock it. The bus station in Shreveport, where you stop for dinner, has terrific meat loaf, which is impossible to find on any airline in the country.

A reader who obviously knows of my problems with air travel has passed along a clipping of an article about how to survive if you happen to be in one of those winged monsters and worst comes to absolute worst.

The article is entitled, appropriately enough, "How to Survive a Plane Crash," by former flight attendant Sarah Uzzel-Rindlaub, who has miraculously survived two.

I read the article with great interest. There ARE things that frighten me more than flying—nuclear war, losing my travelers' checks in Tehran—but not very many.

One, I don't understand flying. I don't understand how anything that big goes that high and stays up there that long and is able to come down softly.

Two, I have this thing about being burned to a crisp or getting separated from myself, both of which can happen in an airplane crash.

Sarah Uzzel-Rindlaub survived a crash at Kennedy airport and, six weeks later, another during a landing in Istanbul.

A normal person would take a bus next time. Not Sarah. She is now emergency procedures instructor for United Airlines.

In a couple of words, she says you will have a better shot at living through a plane crash if you "don't panic."

Somehow, I knew she was going to say that. Every time I tell somebody how much it frightens me to ride in an airplane and how afraid I am it will fall out of the sky and I will die, they say, "Don't panic."

I panic dialing the airlines for reservations.

I panic getting a shoeshine before my flight.

In flight, it is Terror City at 30,000 feet.

I dare not eat anything. In order to eat, I would have to loosen my grip on the seat.

I dare not have a conversation with a fellow passenger. I must remain completely quiet in order to listen for changes in engine tone.

I dare not go to the restroom when I fly, either, because once I did. The plan hit turbulence and a light came on in the restroom that said, "Return to your seat immediately."

When you are in the restroom on an airplane, it is not always possible to return to your seat immediately. What did I do? I panicked, of course, but I will spare you the details.

I gave up flying once for six years. I rode a bus through Alabama, took a cross-country train trip or two, and one night I was driving through a lonely stretch of Arkansas and had a blowout, and my jack was bent.

Along came a semi hauling hogs. I hitched a ride to the next town, seventy-five miles away. The stench was awful. Hogs have poor personal hygiene.

"Sorry about that smell," said the driver.

"No problem, good buddy," I replied, "at least I'm not flying."

But it is next to impossible to live in today's fast-paced world without occasionally having to board an airplane.

My first flight after my absence from the skies was leaving at two o'clock in the afternoon. By ten in the morning, I had already broken out in some hideous rash and had checked and rechecked my will.

I decided to call a friend, an ex-Air Force pilot, for encouragement. Perhaps he could calm me.

"I've flown thousands of hours," he began. "If anything happens to the plane, or there is any sign of trouble, just do the following:

"Bend down as far as you can behind the seat in front of you. Grab each ankle securely. Bend your head between your legs, and. . . . "

"I know," I interrupted him, "'don't panic.'"

"No," he said, "kiss your bohunkus goodby."

I know the reader who sent me Sarah what's-her-name's article was just trying to help. Next time, don't bother; I'm beyond it.

Fun and Games at Home

It could happen, you know. No gasoline, and there you are, stuck at home. Make the best of it with my Treasure Chest of Homespun fun.

According to an article in the *Wall Street Journal*, Americans are staying home these days in droves because of the gasoline shortage.

(For the record, I have never purchased a copy of the *Wall Street Journal*, but a junior executive friend of mine buys one every day to wear to work. He passes his copies to me, along with an occasional pair of dark over-the-calf-socks.)

The *Journal* article said resort areas can expect to start taking financial beatings because people are beginning to find all sorts of ways to entertain themselves in their very own homes.

The article mentioned sitting by your pool, watching cable television and videotape machines, and riding bicycles.

Since the average price of a house is closing in on six figures, it does make a great deal of sense to spend a little more time where you get your mail.

Our is the only country in the world where we pay $150,000 for a house and then leave it for two weeks every summer to go sleep in a tent.

The obvious problem here, however, is not all of us can afford swimming pools, cable television and videotape machines, and riding bicycles is hard work.

I have no swimming pool, no cable television, no videotape machine; and the last time I rode a bicycle I was twelve and obviously mentally retarded, or I would have known to take a taxi.

But as an experiment in lifestyle-changing, I stayed home a couple of days and entertained myself. I discovered a person doesn't have to go bowling to have a good time.

Right in the comfort of your own home, no matter how modest it might be, you can have loads of fun and tell the Arab oil peddlers to go eat some sand.

What follows is Grizzard's Treasure Chest of Homespun Fun. Planning a trip to Disney World? Who needs it?

Stay home, America, and:

• PLAY WITH THE KIDS: You remember your kids. Skeeter is eleven. Barney is eight. After you have played with your kids for a while, lock the little boogers in a closet and have a couple of belts.

But remember to let them out in time for tomorrow's roof climb and picnic.

• EAT: Fun for the entire family. Instead of three meals a day, eat twelve. If you take an hour for each meal, and an hour in between, that's an entire day and it's time to eat again.

Soon, the opportunity will arise for other fun home games. Like trying to find Mom's original chin. Hide-and-go-seek in Dad's trousers. And pin the tail on the "Whale," baby sister's new nickname.

• TAKE BATHS: Rub-a-dub-dub, just relaxing in the tub. Invite your neighbors. If things go well, you may never want to leave home again.

• CLEAN OUT YOUR ATTIC OR BASEMENT: Who knows what you might find there? Remember your Uncle Fred, who's been missing since 1958? Dust him off and you've got another entry for the houseplant-swallowing tournament.

• STOMPING ANTS: There are always a lot of ants around the house. How many ants can you stomp?

• COUNTING STOMPED ANTS: Tedious as heck, but a great way to relax after stomping a few hundred thousand ants.

• SETTING THE GARAGE ON FIRE: Wow! See the bright red fire engines! Hear the shrill of their sirens! See the brave firemen battle the blaze! See the friendly insurance man deliver the check!

• MEMORIZE THE PHONE BOOK: "Aaron" to "Zzbowski," hours of good, clean fun. Unless, of course, you live in Yellville, Arkansas, where it will take you approximately nine minutes.

• MONOPOLY: Four can play, but Monopoly may have changed a bit since you played it last. "Free Parking" is now a condominium complex, and when you pass "GO" you have to PAY $200.

Also, you can't take a ride on the Reading anymore. With the gasoline shortage, trains are booked solid.

The Pass-the-Maalox Diet

More advice for singles: If you don't cook, follow this simple diet and you'll be dead in a year, which is better than having to face breakfast at McDonald's indefinitely.

There are all sorts of diets to choose from today. Diets for people who are overweight, diets for people who want to live a long time. Scarsdale diets. Pritikin diets.

There is no diet, however, for the segment of our population that is always being left out—the American Single Person Who Lives Alone and Would Probably Starve to Death Were It Not for Chinese Take-Out Restaurants.

I am one of those persons. I am not married, I live alone, and if I eat one more cardboard box full of fried rice and chicken almondine, I may start quacking like a Peking duck.

I do not cook. I cannot cook. I refuse to cook. Cooking takes a lot of time and causes greasy pots. Weird things that are green grow on greasy pots when they are not washed in several weeks.

But I survive, and I still have my slim, boyish figure. Unfortunately, I also still have sunken eyes, protruding ribs, and a daily bout with acid indigestion that would gag Mother Tums.

A lot of people are making a lot of money writing books about their diets. I do not have time to write a book, because I have to finish this in a hurry so I can meet somebody at Long John Silver's for lunch.

Therefore, I will make it quick and simple: The Grizzard Diet for Single Non-Cookers Who Are in a Hurry.

Eat, drink, and be merry, for tomorrow you may get lockjaw and your troubles will be over:

MONDAY

BREAKFAST—Who can eat breakfast on a Monday? Swallow some toothpaste while you are brushing your teeth.

LUNCH—Send your secretary out for six "gutbombers," those little hamburgers that used to cost a dime and now cost thirty-five cents. Also, order French fries, a bowl of chili, a soft drink, and have your secretary stop on the way back for a bottle of Maalox, family size.

AFTERNOON SNACK—Finish off the bottle of Maalox.

DINNER—Six-pack of beer and Kentucky Fried Chicken three-piece dinner. Don't eat the cole slaw.

TUESDAY

BREAKFAST—Eat the cole slaw.

LUNCH—Go to the office vending area and put ninety-five cents into the machine and close your eyes and push a button. Whatever comes out, swallow it whole. Chewing that garbage increases the inevitable nausea.

DINNER—Four tacos and a pitcher of sangria at El Flasho's.

WEDNESDAY

BREAKFAST—"Jaws" couldn't eat breakfast after a night at El Flasho's.

LUNCH—Rolaids and a Pepsi.

DINNER—Drop in at a married friend's house and beg for table scraps.

THURSDAY

BREAKFAST—Order out for pizza.

LUNCH—Your secretary is out sick. Check Monday's "gut-bomber" sack for leftovers.

DINNER—Go to a bar and drink yourself silly. When you get hungry, ask the bartender for olives.

FRIDAY

BREAKFAST—Eggs, sausage, and an English muffin at McDonald's. Eat the Styrofoam plate and leave the food. It tastes better and it's better for you.

LUNCH—Skip lunch, Fridays are murder.

DINNER—Steak, well-done, baked potato, and order the asparagus, but don't eat it. Nobody really likes asparagus.

SATURDAY

BREAKFAST—Sleep through it.

LUNCH—Ditto.

DINNER—Steak, well-done, baked potato, and order the Brussels sprouts, but don't eat them. Take them home and plant them in a hanging basket.

SUNDAY

BREAKFAST—Three Bloody Marys and half a Twinkie cake.

LUNCH—Eat lunch, waste a good buzz. Don't eat lunch.

DINNER—Chicken noodle soup. Call your mom, and ask her about renting your old room.

2

FAMOUS PEOPLE YOU HAVE NEVER HEARD OF

Mama Willie

Soon after dying, "Mama Willie" went to the heaven it talked about in her Bible, and she is presently very happy there. For some reason, I am absolutely certain of that.

Moreland, Ga.

Willie Smith Word died last week, and they took her down to the little cemetery on the south end of town and put her next to the only man in her life, Charles Bunyon Word, who will have been gone twenty years come April.

Willie Word lived to be almost eighty-nine. She was the mother of five children. I can't begin to count the grandchildren, great-grand-children, and even great-great-grandchildren.

The funeral was what Willie Word—we called her "Mama Wil-lie"—would have wanted, two hard-shell Baptist preachers shaking the rafters in the tiny church and duet renditions of her favorite hymns, "Amazing Grace" and "Precious Memories."

"I've known this good woman all of my life," one of the preachers said. "She was solid as a rock."

She was. I knew Willie Word all of my life, too. I think you would have liked her.

She laughed a lot. I will always remember that. And she enjoyed a little dip of snuff before bed, and she knew a number of important things she passed along to those fortunate enough to find a place under her wing.

Important things. Like thunder won't hurt you, but running with a pointed object can. Like if you don't take a nap after lunch, you could get polio; and Jesus said the red words in the Bible.

She could cook. The woman never failed at a pie or a cake, and she must have fried 10,000 chickens in her lifetime. I hope I remembered to thank her for the portion that wound up on my plate.

She was born dirt poor in another century. Think of the changes she saw in her eighty-eight-plus years:

Two world wars, the Great Depression, running water, the automobile, the airplane, radio, television, William McKinley to Jimmy Carter, horses and buggies to moon shots.

This was the same woman who never missed a rasslin' match on television and dared anyone to suggest the punches might be pulled.

She saw some troubles. A son died young. Her man went suddenly. And her last years were filled with pain.

She was taken from her little frame house a couple of years ago and hospitalized, never to come home again. There was no hope. But she lingered on and on, barely conscious of her surroundings.

"How she must have suffered," a daughter was saying at the funeral.

The modern technology that can send a man to the moon and can even stall death may be thanked.

Willie Word lingered with only the support of drugs and devices, and perhaps she did suffer; and she died in somebody else's bed, and I think she deserved better.

Who's to blame? We all are, because those prolonging drugs and devices say we still haven't accepted the fact that when a life ceases to be precious, it is an affront to that life not to allow its natural—and dignified—leave.

My family—and other families in similar situations—might not have wanted to be reminded of that, but I think Willie Smith Word, my grandmother, would have wanted me to say it anyway.

The Lady at the Diner

I've heard a lot of highly-educated women say that what's wrong with most men is we go around looking for somebody to mother us all the time. They're right, you know. We do.

She sits there behind the cash register every day with her bad leg, and she takes the money from the people who have been through the line and filled their plates with the wonders of Southern cooking.

They ruin us early in the South. Our mothers do it. Heaping plates of country-fried steak, smothered in gravy, and the like. And when they cook vegetables, they cook them in conjunction with something known as "fatback," which is something left over from a pig, and the resulting taste defies description.

And we are taught not to leave a morsel. There was a fellow I knew from Alabama who tried to explain his 400-pound frame.

"I grew up during the war," he said. "Every night, my mother would fill my plate and say, 'Don't leave anything, son. Every time you leave something on your plate, you're wasting food and feeding Hitler.'

"Hell, I tried to starve the entire German army."

We never quite get over that. We leave our mothers' tables and then we roam endlessly in search of a reasonable facsimile of her servings, and more often than not, the search is fruitless.

That is why the lady behind the cash register and her little diner down in a shaky part of town are so important to me.

The food is genuine. Monday is spare ribs. Tuesday is the country-fried steak, praise the Lord. Wednesday might be fried chicken, Thursday is ham and maybe some homemade chicken pot pie, and on Friday there's fried fish, and every day the strong beans and the squash with onions and the baby limas will take your breath.

The lady behind the register was gone for a time with the leg, and her husband, as gentle and kind as she, handled both their duties. Now she is back, but he is gone with an illness of his own.

And the neighborhood is going down as the crime rate in the city soars.

Derelicts line the sidewalks and pass around their paper sacks with the drunken dreams inside. Gangs of toughs are all about.

I stopped in the diner last week and took a corner booth.

Three urchins from the street, eight or nine or ten, had entered through a side door. Near the line of food is a counter of candies and tobaccos. The smallest of the three snatched something and then bolted for the door.

It was a nickel crime in progress. The lady behind the cash register never left her stool, but bellowed out:

"Come back here! All three of you, come here to me right now!"

There was something in her voice. Another lady I know used the same tone to me maybe a thousand times.

The trio of urchins walked to her, eyes down to the floor. The little one, the guilty one, was pushed to the front.

"I saw what you did," the lady said. "Do you know what I do to little boys who take things from me and then run away?"

The little one shook his head.

"I cut their ears off," the lady said. "You wouldn't look so good without ears, would you?"

The little one shook his head again.

And then he looked up at her—he was filled with terror—but she was smiling down at him now, and she said, "You're not going to do anything like that again, are you?"

And he shook his head another time and replied softly, meekly, "No, ma'am." He left the diner with his ears intact, and maybe he will never forget his rookie attempt at theft.

Most of us long gone from home forget too soon the magic of a mother's touch, be it at her table or when the need for a lesson to be learned is great.

God bless the lady behind the cash register for an occasional reminder.

Warren Newman

If Warren Newman had lived long enough to have had a book published, he would have mentioned me in it, I am sure. It's been months since he died. Sometimes, late at night, I still miss him hard.

Warren Newman, for a country boy from Sandersville, Georgia, was quite sophisticated. He didn't like clichés, nor anything that was "hokey." I have put quotations around that word, "hokey," because it was a word Warren used a great deal.

The man was an idealist, was what he was. That, and a perfectionist.

He disliked such things as plastic flowers and neon cowboys. What he liked were old people who sat in front of country stores, dozing and telling good stories, dogs, and Vienna sausages eaten directly from a can on a riverbank.

I suppose knowing all that about Warren Newman is what is making writing this so difficult. The last thing he would have wanted would have been—as he would have put it—"one of those God-awful sad stories about what a great guy I was."

But here I sit on a bright Sunday morning in May writing one of those God-awful sad stories about what a great guy he was.

Maybe the only thing I can do to temper this is to leave out a lot of gush about how much I loved him and how much I will miss him and just stick to the parts about how he cracked me up and how a number of us who knew him best often wondered if he were really from this planet.

Warren had a bizarre sense of humor, and his ideas and thoughts must have come from some celestial left field where the rest of us could never reach for inspiration.

There was his Lyndon Johnson impression. He did Lyndon Johnson announcing he would not seek re-election better than Lyndon Johnson. I can still hear him—Warren, not Lyndon Johnson—pronouncing, "Mah feller Amuricahns. . . ."

There was his small-town disc-jockey voice. I think somewhere in Warren's past he had been a small-town disc jockey.

The act was a riot, and I stole it from him and I use it when I make a speech.

And there was the thing he did about a fellow getting arrested for murder down in Sandersville and what he told the authorities when they came to get him, but I couldn't come close to capturing it in print, and another thing that makes me sad is now that Warren is gone, so is that story. Forever.

What else. He was an artist. He did sketches, and they were quite good. He played guitar. He was an expert on the Civil War.

He owned a famous dog, "Springfield," the last of the long-nosed Egyptian coon hounds, which is another story.

He snored with the best of them. I shared a tent with him for seven nights on a wilderness river somewhere out in Arkansas last summer, so I ought to know.

The funny thing that happened on that trip was one morning as we started to launch our canoes, we discovered a rattlesnake in Warren's. The three adults on the trip were all afraid to remove the snake, but, luckily, there was a fifteen-year-old along who wasn't old enough to be frightened of rattlesnakes. We let him handle the situation while the three of us hid behind a tree.

One other thing. Warren Newman was a talented writer. Three years ago, he was a bartender. Then, he got a job at the newspaper helping count football contest ballots. Soon after that, he moved to some boring job on the desk. Soon after that, he became the *Atlanta Constitution*'s brightest sports star. The man was moving up fast.

He would have left sports eventually, I am certain, and written of the world as he saw it. Damn, we missed something there.

Warren Newman, thirty-one, ran into a tree in his automobile Saturday morning, and he is dead. I went over to his house Saturday afternoon and petted his dog and talked to his pretty, heartbroken wife.

She told me about a short poem she had written about her husband a couple of months ago. She read it to me and said she was thinking about having it put on his gravestone. She asked me if I though it was "hokey."

Here's the poem:

> Son of the Southland,
>   A dreamer, kind and wise.
> More than most men dare imagine
>   Shone clearly in his eyes.

That's not "hokey." That says it. That says it all.

Dudley Stamps

Of all the people I have met in my life, Dudley is one of them, which is the one of the nicest things anybody ever said about him.

It was great to see Dudley Stamps at my fifteenth high school reunion. It was great to see everybody, but seeing Dudley was special.

Dudley and I used to hang out together and do weird things. Actually, Dudley did weird things and I would go along to see what he was going to do next.

Dudley enjoyed driving motorized vehicles as fast as they could possibly go. The fastest I have ever traveled on land was inside the 1960 Thunderbird Dudley's parents bought him for his sixteenth birthday.

Often I questioned Dudley's parents' judgment in buying him that car, because he spent his entire junior and senior years in high school attempting suicide in this 1960 Thunderbird.

One night, the highway patrol stopped Dudley and gave him a ticket for speeding. The patrol man said he had clocked Dudley at 110 miles per hour.

Dudley was incensed. He swore he had been going at least 120.

Dudley also owned a truck. We were driving around in Dudley's truck and he said to me, "I wonder if trucks will float."

An idle thought, I figured. I figured wrong. Dudley was a man of action. He immediately drove his truck into the middle of White Oak Creek.

I learned a lot of important things hanging out with Dudley Stamps. One thing I learned is trucks won't float.

Dudley also enjoyed climbing. He would climb anything that wouldn't climb him first, like forest ranger towers, water towers, statues on the town square in the middle of the night, etc.

I was in the front seat, and Dudley was driving. We passed a tall water tower. Dudley stopped his car and attacked the water tower. I remained in the car where it was safe. It was never safe around Dudley.

Soon, I began to hear large objects crashing onto the top of Dudley's car.

Dudley had filled his pockets with large rocks before he climbed the water tower. He thought it great sport to frighten me by dropping large rocks onto the top of his car.

When Dudley eventually traded his car, for a case of beer and several back issues of Guns magazine, it looked like it had been through the Third Punic War.

The best fist fight I ever saw involved Dudley Stamps. It was the heavyweight championship of the ninth grade, between Dudley and the school bully.

The school bully was a dummy. He verbally assaulted Dudley one afternoon in study hall when the teacher went out of the room.

It was a close fight; but the judges, one of the tenth grade girls and myself, gave Dudley the decision. Soon afterwards, the school bully joined the drama club.

About half the class turned out for the reunion. We had a picnic in the afternoon and a dance at the Elks Club that night. They played the old songs.

We also gave out awards. I won most divorces. One of the people who helped me win that award was there. I don't mind admitting it. She looked terrific.

A couple of my classmates are now lawyers. One is president of a company. The girls who were pretty in high school still are.

I was proud of myself because several of my classmates walked up to me and said they read what I write in the newspaper. Some even mentioned they enjoy it.

I imagined Dudley as a hired gun. Or at least a steeplejack. He's married and has a child. He farms a little and repairs Volkswagens, he said.

We had a brief conversation.

"I see your ugly picture in the newspaper sometimes," Dudley said to me.

"Oh, yeah?"

"Yeah. But I don't read the garbage," he continued.

"Oh, no?"

"No. And the only time I see your picture is when I need some paper to put under a car so it won't leak oil on my garage floor. I look down and say, 'There's that damn fool with oil all over his stupid face.'"

Thanks, Dudley. I needed that.

"Flash" Noles

Since LeRoy "Flash" Noles died, incidentally, the Atlanta Constitution *has been struggling to right itself. The jury is still out as to whether we will make it without him.*

The funeral is over now, and LeRoy "Flash" Noles, celebrated copyboy of the *Atlanta Constitution*, has been put to rest on a day hung with mist and pall, an appropriate day for a funeral, as if there can be such a thing.

Flash died Saturday. Somebody said he had a heart attack. He was sixty-three. He had worked here for forty-two years. His "office"—a supply room marked, simply, "Flash"—was next to my own.

Flash never married, but he had a good dog once. His aunt cried on the front pew of the funeral home chapel.

What the man did for an honest living was carry newspapers and good cheer throughout the building at 72 Marietta Street.

We talked a lot. Flash enjoyed fishing. Once, he showed me a picture of himself holding a mess of catfish.

"Them things are the devil to clean," he said, "but they make good eatin'."

I will remember him. Floppy hat, boots, a limp. Over lunch after the funeral, they were saying how he thought Conway Twitty hung the musical moon.

The newspaper sent Flash away in style. His obit made page one of a section front in Sunday's paper. They even ran his picture.

Columns and editorials followed.

"I think I'm going to do something on Flash for tomorrow," I was saying.

"Not much left to say," a co-worker replied.

"I'm going to do something anyway," I said.

Flash never wrote a line of copy for the *Constitution*. He never made an editorial decision, never took a picture, never wrote a headline.

But to anyone looking around at the funeral, his importance could not be doubted. The biggies were there, publisher, editor, managing editors, and their assistants. A columnist also came and wondered if he would have drawn the same heavy crowd.

And if Flash Noles' death accomplished anything, it at least brought those of us who cover a rather hectic and complicated world, and grow cynical from the effort, into contact with an element of simplicity some of us had forgotten, and many of us had likely never known. Flash had a country funeral. There is no other description, that is the only description. The last country funeral I saw was the one they gave for my grandfather in a hot Head County church twenty years ago.

The organ was playing softly, tenderly. It was playing selections from a brown Cokesbury hymnal of my youth.

"In the Sweet By and By" was one selection. "I Love to Tell the Story" was another. And then a girl wearing glasses sang "Precious Memories." How they linger. A woman across the aisle from me dabbed at her eyes with a crumpled tissue. The women always bring crumpled tissues to a country funeral.

The preacher wore his best suit, three pieces of blue that were snug. He read the twenty-third Psalm.

He preached a "warning" service. A "warning" service is where the preacher looks down at the casket and says we're all going to be in the same shape one of these days, and we'd better get ready. Or else.

It's the "or else" part that spooks me, but truth is normally frightening. At a country funeral, they figure nothing more can be done for the dead, so let the living take heed.

That's about it. If there is a deeper message, I frankly don't feel like searching for it. Just a couple of more things.

One, the only bad thing I ever knew Flash to do was occasionally cuss a slow elevator, but that is certainly a forgivable sin, so I'm not concerned about his address in the hereafter.

Two, I just figured out why I went ahead and wrote this anyway. I wanted the late, great LeRoy "Flash" Noles, forty-two years at his post, to have something to do with one more edition of the *Atlanta Constitution*.

Courage in the Pulpit

Good news. Some months after I wrote this, the preacher and his wife decided to give it another try.

It is one of those big downtown churches—a "rich folks' church," they would have called it back home.

There are a couple of assistant preachers who handle the preliminaries at the Sunday morning service, and then the head preacher delivers his message through a microphone. A radio station carries it out to the "shut-ins," a good church word you may or may not remember.

All the preachers wear long robes and have important-sounding degrees, and the choir sings difficult arrangements you can't tap a toe to, and people around you would probably look at you funny if you did.

There is carpet and there are expensive windows, and you feel like the Lord *expects* something more than a few loose coins when they come around with the collection plate.

I have been there in the congregation a few Sundays, and despite all the "luxury," for the lack of a better term, the fellow worshipers are friendly and the head preacher, when he finally takes command, is a bright and forceful man who sprinkles his sermons with humor.

I have always liked a preacher with a sense of humor. So many of them seem never to take off their funeral faces.

I don't see the need to be specific here, as far as the name of the church or the name of the head preacher, the man who can smile and fan a hell-fire at the same time.

It could happen to anybody. But when it happens to a preacher in a big church with fancy windows, tongues wag and eyebrows are lifted and you hear people saying, "What is the world coming to?"

The preacher's wife left him a few weeks ago. That happens to lawyers and doctors and insurance salesmen and ditch-diggers and newspaper columnists, but it doesn't happen to preachers because they know all the answers, and the good they do, you figure, protects them from such.

A shock wave went through the church.

"I always thought they looked so happy together," somebody said.

"You can never tell about things like that," said somebody else.

The preacher offered to resign. Could he continue to be effective with this wart on his face?

Good for the church. Sure, there was gossip, but the resignation wasn't accepted. Had it been, I would never have gone back. Not that I'm a regular or serve on committees, but I hate snootiness in any form.

It would have been *snooty* to let the man walk away. It would also have been cruel.

The preacher took some time off to put his life back in order, if that is possible, which it is not. He wrote a letter to every member of the church. Attached to his letter was a letter from his wife.

"Being a minister's wife," the gist of her explanations for the breakup went, "is very difficult. I can't handle it."

That's her business. His letter asked for understanding and prayers. Yes, there were children involved.

He came back to the pulpit last week. I caught him on the radio. Those who were there said he looked a little drained, but that he handled himself well.

That's an understatement. "Today," he said, "I have to go public with a private disaster in my own life." Few things are more difficult.

I felt for him throughout the sermon. He quoted scripture—Psalms, I think—and he asked for more understanding, and he said, "I know you have been praying for me already . . . I can feel them working."

I could sense his embarrassment, his "gnawing pain" as he put it. At the end of the sermon, he even called for others with similar problems to meet him at the altar afterwards for some safety-in-numbers reassurance.

Give him credit. Looking out on that sea of curious faces Sunday morning, he must have recalled a familiar lament that never has an answer—"Why me, Lord?"

Or maybe it does have an answer. Why you, preacher? Because you are only human.

Your flock will forget that occasionally. For your own peace of mind, don't you.

Preacher Jackson

Wayne Jackson did everything he could to keep my father from the devil in the bottle.

What made me think to look up Preacher Jackson after all these years was the news about Billy Carter that came on the heels of the news about Herman Talmadge.

Billy Carter, the president's brother, and Herman Talmadge, the millionaire United States senator from Georgia, are both now admitted alcoholics.

Talmadge was recently released from the Long Beach Naval Hospital in California, where they treat people with drinking problems. Billy Carter checked in this week.

Not just anybody can get help at Long Beach, but neither Talmadge nor Carter had any problems. The Secretary of the Navy intervened in Billy's behalf. Both men are obviously capable of paying the $266-a-day rate.

Long Beach is sort of the Hilton of rehabilitation centers. Betty Ford got help there once for a pill problem. Talmadge emerged after five weeks, went the news reports, looking "tan and fit."

Billy Carter, said the Nashville agent, will come out "a new man." Good luck. Alcoholism is a bear to whip.

Preacher Jackson knows that better than anybody. He's been at the business of trying to help people give up booze for sixteen years out in the sticks at a place called Hope Haven near Jefferson, Georgia.

"When you do what I do," he told me Wednesday, "frustration becomes a way of life."

Preacher Jackson is fifty-three. His first name is Wayne. He's a God-fearing Baptist, and he started Hope Haven in 1963. He had two bucks in his pocket.

He renovated an old school building and opened the doors to any man who would voluntarily submit to what he calls "Christian rehabilitation."

He uses no fancy drugs. He doesn't have any. There is no place to get a suntan. There are no jogging tracks.

"We don't have any carpet on the floor," he said, "because we can't afford it. We operate on faith." That means donations.

I asked him how many men come to him and leave with their drinking problem licked.

"The percentage is very, very low," he said. "I've had maybe 1,400-1,500 men come through here. If you keep a man sober for a day, you've helped him.

"But completely rehabilitated? Maybe 2 percent. The odds are just too high."

I first met Pracher Jackson—that's what everybody calls him—maybe ten or twelve years ago when I went to visit a patient of his, a man the preacher remembered well.

"How could we ever forget him?" he laughed.

"I retrieved him out of a lot of hotel rooms," he said, "and I spent a lot of time with him over the years. He'd come in with bleary eyes and needing a shave. Then, he'd hit the showers.

"He'd find a clean shirt somewhere, and get somebody to press his pants. He always wanted a crease in them. Then, he'd look for a bow tie. He always wore bow ties.

"Next thing you knew, he'd walk out looking like a million. He used to really liven this place up, too.

"We had a singing group here one time, and he joined them on the piano. I'll never forget it. He started playing 'When the Saints Go Marching In,' and about the third time around, he had everybody jumping up and down.

"We don't know exactly what made him drink. He lived in a fantasy world, I think, and he had some strong guilt about something.

"We used to get a lot of calls from him when things were going bad. He'd call and tell us how much he loved us. I used to say, 'Why don't you tell us that when you're sober?'"

I said the same thing to him a thousand times.

The man Preacher Jackson and I were remembering was one of the 98 per cent who couldn't overcome alcoholism. It finally killed him. He died a pauper. "What a waste of talent," said the preacher.

Yeah, and I wonder sometimes if it could have been salvaged in a swanky place like Long Beach.

Probably not. And what's the use of such speculation? Rich people and famous people who have drinking problems are called "alcoholics." The others are called "drunks."

I should count my blessings. A drunk I loved a great deal got the best help money couldn't buy from Wayne Jackson and Hope Haven, and I should never have waited this long to thank them for their efforts.

A Dying Man

August 12, 1979, Claxton, Georgia. The devil in the bottle, and perhaps a thousand more that inevitably hound a fallen hero, finally won the battle.

Claxton, Ga.

There are scenes that will never leave you. One such, for me, took place here ten years ago in little Claxton, where they make fruit-cakes. Ten years. I can't believe it has been that long.

It was an August morning, hot and damp outside. I stood inside a tiny hospital room where a fifty-eight-year-old man was near death.

Around me stood a few others who also cared about him, too. One was a preacher. As the end neared, the preacher asked that we all bow our heads, and he prayed.

He asked the Lord to take the soul about to depart the ravaged body on the bed. I said a prayer of my own. I asked the Lord to ignore the preacher and leave the soul where it was.

That was the only miracle I have ever prayed for. I wasn't ready to give the man up just yet, and, frankly, I thought the preacher was rushing things a bit.

I had never seen anybody die before. I envisioned death rattles and twitching and gasping and one final heave of breath, and then the last hold of air rushing out.

It was nothing like that. The man, who was unconscious, breathed, and then he wasn't breathing anymore.

So much for my miracle.

The preacher asked that we bow our heads again, and we did, and he prayed again, but I forget about what this time.

I wanted to say something dramatic when he had finished, some-thing befitting the life we had just seen pass. I said something stupid, instead. I said, "He hated hot weather, you know."

The only comfort I could find in the moment was that the man wouldn't have to live through the oppressive Georgia heat the after-noon was certain to offer. He was a big man, a fat man, and the heat was always his dreaded enemy, I recalled. You think of the strangest things at times like those.

I had held his hand during the final minutes, and I will always be thankful for that. I have often wondered since if, somewhere in his fleeting subconscious, he had known I was there.

Probably not, but it is a fantasy worth keeping. He was alone a great deal during his life, which was the real cause of his death, and I will always hope he had some faint knowledge of the fact that there was an audience for the last act he performed.

How he happened to die here, in this outpost, is still somewhat of a mystery to me. Better, I thought then and I think now, years before on a battlefield of some historic worth.

Seven of his fifty-eight years had been devoted to combat, and he had distinguished himself and had inspired others, I have heard.

Better he had gone in the midst of some heroic adventure, even at a much younger age, than here between white hospital sheets.

He had found nothing but unhappiness since his last war, Korea, and he had wandered alone and lost. He was just passing through this, his last stop, when some vital organ stopped its function.

The nurse came in. Then the doctor, who noted the time before he pulled the sheet over the man's blue face.

Later, someone handed me his earthly belongings in a plastic bag. It was a small bag. Inside were shoes, socks, underwear, trousers, a shirt, an empty wallet, an old watch, and a cheap ring. Fifty-eight years, and they can put what is left of you in a small plastic bag.

I was just passing through here the other day myself, but there was time, as I drove away, to put the scene back together again. I owe the man that much—to ponder occasionally how his end had come.

I owe him a lot more than that. He's the one who gave me this name, for one thing. For another, he left me with a stockpile of stories, some of which are even true, that keep a roof over my head.

3

GREAT ISSUES

Sports Cars: Pro and Mostly Con

If you are currently thinking of buying a sports car, read this. Afterwards, if you still want to buy a sports car, you deserve one.

Sooner or later, everybody goes through the stage of wanting to own a sports car. I think it has something to do with being deprived as a child.

I had plenty to eat as a child, and I was warm at night. But I never had the real necessities, like a trip to Europe after high school graduation or a sports car.

I have owned all sorts of cars. My first car was a red-and-white 1956 Chevrolet. Tennis racquets cost more today than I paid for my first car.

I have also owned a Volkswagen, several Pontiacs and a Vega. Of all the cars I have owned, the Vega is the one I have never forgiven.

It was brown and hard to crank. I used to park it in bad neighborhoods and leave the keys on the hood, hoping somebody would steal it.

Somebody tried once. I was hiding in a nearby alley watching with a pair of jumper cables just in case. When the Vega wouldn't crank, I appeared with the jumper cables and offered my services to the thief.

"Forget it," he said. I gave him taxi fare home for his efforts and called a tow truck.

I finally got rid of my Vega by giving it to my ex-wife. I am a bad person.

A year-and-a-half ago, I decided it was time I had my first sports car. The eagle inside me cried for the opportunity to soar.

Get the picture:

The open road lies ahead, begging to be conquered. I wind my way along it, two steady, gloved hands sure upon the wheel of my classic new sports car. The sleek lines are unmistakable. The perfectly balanced hum of the engine is a purr.

197

I pass through Barletta as a streaking blur. And on through Trani, Bisceglie, Molfetta, toward Monopoli, along the Italian shore, the blue waters of the Adriatic shimmering in the sun.

My road hat sits deftly upon my head, tilted at precisely the correct, cocksure angle. My scarf treads the breeze behind me. As the road straightens, I press the toe of my right Gucci against the accelerator, and the naked eye cannot still the motion I command.

The woman beside me? A long and most unbelievable story, my friend. It began only a fortnight ago as I stood on the balcony of my hotel room in Roma. . . .

Picture that in a brown Vega that won't crank and has a lot of empty beer cans in the hatchback.

The sports car I finally bought is a British import, one of those sexy little numbers with the racing stripes and plaid seat covers. The man who sold it to me is from Tupelo, Mississippi, and chews gum. His leisure suit matched the seat covers of the car.

"Sassy chassis, ain't it?" he remarked as we looked at the car. Somehow, I thought buying a sports car would be like shopping for rare art treasures. It ain't.

I am now an expert on sports cars because I have owned one for a year-and-a-half.

Here are the advantages of owning sports cars:

1. They're cute.

Here are the disadvantages of owning sports cars:

1. Sitting in a shoebox is more comfortable.

2. Try finding somebody to work on one on a hot Sunday afternoon in Cooper, Texas.

3. While riding with the top down it is impossible to talk, smoke, listen to the radio, or keep the part in your hair. Also, bugs occasionally fly into your mouth at sixty miles per hour.

4. A lot of silly teenage girls have one, too.

5. If you hit a trailer truck head-on in a sports car, they'd be lucky to find all your movable parts in a week, despite a three-county search.

What I am trying to say here is I have passed through my sports car stage, and it was a miserable experience. The latest bad thing to happen was Tuesday morning. I was backing out of my driveway, and the steering wheel broke off the column.

Luckily, the car came to a halt against a large tree. I don't know where the steering wheel finally landed.

And in order to leave this with a clear conscience, I must also admit I never drove along the Italian coast or the shimmering Adriatic.

I made all that up on the way to work today. My neighbor's cleaning woman gave me a ride in her Vega.

The High Price of Ice Cream

Some of you may not think seventy-five cents for one scoop of ice cream is outrageous. So if you're that spiffy, what are you doing reading a book like this?

I read about inflation and recession and depression and the portents of economic doom that are hanging over our heads like vultures. I read about the plight of the American consumer and his never-ending battle to make ends meet.

I imagine a nation on its collective way to the poorhouse. Hitchhiking. Who can afford gasoline?

And then I pick up a copy of *Newsweek* magazine and read about people gladly paying seventy-five cents for one scoop of ice cream.

Seventy-five cents for ONE scoop of ice cream.

Hard times is when people start adding water to the soup. NOT when they can still pay seventy-five cents for one scoop of ice cream.

Newsweek reports a boom in the sales of premium-quality, top-priced ice cream in the country. Ice cream like New York's Haagen-Dazs, which sounds Dutch, carries a Scandinavian label, and is made in New Jersey.

Haagen-Dazs costs seventy-five cents a scoop, and get this, $3.50 for a quart.

"If it's good," the magazine quotes a Haagen-Dazs freak as saying, "I'll buy it."

So buy it. Haagen-Dazs is described as rich-and-creamy and naturally flavored. But should you EAT it? It seems a wiser investment to WEAR it instead, like on your tie or on the front of your shirt to upgrade your wardrobe.

You are dealing with an ice cream expert here, a man who has consumed gobs and gobs of it, who lusts for it and dreams about it, but a man who thinks seventy-five cents for a single scoop of ice cream is outrageous.

We didn't need a top-of-the-line, state-of-the-art, better ice cream. Ice cream was fine the way it was.

The trouble actually began with all the new flavors introduced by people like Baskin-Robbins. What was wrong with your basic vanilla, chocolate, and strawberry?

I am, and always have been, a vanilla person, myself. One of those sex guides for the sensuous woman mentioned that men who eat vanilla ice cream usually make love the same way. Plain, Jane. I won't go into what the book said about a man who prefers tutti-frutti.

Now, we have ice cream flavors like butterscotch brandy, creamy caramel, rum raisin, and even ice cream that tastes like coffee, and bubble gum.

But don't get me wrong. I'm not a total straight arrow when it comes to ice cream. I have, shall we say, "experimented" with ice cream in its more exotic forms.

Ice cream sandwiches, for instance. An occasional ice cream sandwich is harmless, but the cake-like outer covering will stick to the roof of your mouth, and it takes two Big Orange bellywashers to loosen its grip.

Fudgesicles. I've done fudgesicles. Once at a party somebody had some groovy "dreamsicles," fruit-flavored ice cream on a stick. The danger there, of course, is where might it lead? Dreamsicles today. Eskimo Pies tomorrow?

The best, and safest, way to eat ice cream is out of a cup, with a spoon. Cones are messy, and they taste like wet plywood.

I would like to see the return of individual cups of ice cream like they sold for a nickel when I was a kid, the ones with pictures of movie stars on the underside of the lids.

Lick the ice cream off the underside of the lid, and there was a picture of Victor Mature, or maybe even Dorothy Malone.

My boyhood friend and idol, Weyman C. Wannamaker, Jr., a great American, had this thing about Dorothy Malone. Once, he bought fifteen individual cups of ice cream. He got one Debra Paget, two Joseph Cottens, three Debbie Reynolds, four Victor Matures, and FIVE Dorothy Malones.

All that for what one lousy scoop of Haagen-Dazs costs today. Haagen-Dazs, Haagen-Smazs.

It's like Weyman said after he ate all that ice cream and licked all those lids for five pictures of Dorothy Malone.

"It ain't worth it."

People Who Talk to God

I received a great many nasty letters after writing the following. Anytime you mention God, I have discovered, you get a lot of nasty letters.

I have just completed reading a newspaper interview with a woman named Margaret Schroeder of Murphy, North Carolina, who has written a book about the fact she talks to God.

Everybody who believes in prayer can make that claim, of course, but Mrs. Schroeder says God talks back to her. As a matter of fact, she says that in the past ten years, God has sent her 13,000 personal messages.

Her book is entitled *Love, Acts of the Apostles*, and it costs $3.95, a rare bargain. If I were getting personal messages from God, I would write a book, too, but I would charge a sight more than $3.95 to let the rest of the world in on our conversations.

Mrs. Schroeder says her messages from God have to do with such things as the importance of loving one another, sacrifice, and eternal life.

I am not going to say I think Mrs. Schroeder is trying to pull a fast one, because I don't doubt much of anything these days. Billy Carter stopped drinking, the mayor of Chicago is a womanperson, and a baseball team from a foreign country has challenged for a spot in the World Series.

But I must admit I have always been a bit skeptical of people who say they get messages from God.

There was a man in my hometown who claimed to have gotten a message from God—Uncle Jake Gaines, the laziest man in town. One Sunday morning, Uncle Jake stood up in church and described his experience.

"His words were written across the sky," be began. "They said, 'Uncle Jake—go preach the gospel.'"

You never know, so they let Uncle Jake preach the morning sermon. Billy Graham he wasn't.

After the service, my grandfather took Uncle Jake aside. "I think you may have misread the message, Jake," he whispered. "You sure God didn't say, 'Go plow your corn'?"

What else bothers me about people who say they talk to God, like Mrs. Schroeder, is they never get any specific information.

One of the messages Mrs. Schroeder says God sent was, "Body is a great sounding board; it is the mystic chord struck by the mind."

If God decided to give out information to twentieth century mortals, I frankly don't think He would beat around the bush.

I honestly do not want this to come off as overt irreverence, but after reading about Mrs. Schroeder, I couldn't help making myself a list of specific questions I would like to ask, given the opportunity for two-way conversation with the Almighty:

What REALLY happened at Chappaquiddick? It's urgent.

How long before you do something about Howard Cosell?

Is disco a sin?

Is there life after gasoline?

Has Anita Bryant become a total embarrassment?

Did Elvis go to heaven?

Can rabbits swim?

Is Oral Roberts on the level?

Does the name "Margaret Schroeder" ring a bell?

Are Cheerleaderrs Really Necessary?

Of course, cheerleaders aren't necessary, but we keep them around anyway. They're the parsley of athletic competition.

Last football season, I wrote a column in which I implied cheerleaders are a waste of everybody's time. I received a great deal of mail about the column:

"You are a jerk!" —Pipsie McQueen, Farrah Fawcett High, Kilgore, Texas.

"Go blow your nose!" —Precious Sweeney, University of Arkansas at Stuttgart.

"May Tony Dorsett run over your face." —Phyllis G. Brown, Kentucky.

I frankly didn't realize people felt that strongly about cheerleaders, so I attempted to enter this season with an open mind.

Say something nice about cheerleaders for a change, I reminded myself. OK. They don't perspire as much as the players.

But that is as far as I can go. This season, I have attended both professional and college games, and I would be untruthful if I said my stance on cheerleaders has changed.

It has not. They are still a waste of time.

One, cheerleaders don't really lead cheers, because most of the people who go to football games are either too involved in beating the point spread or too bombed to pay attention to them.

Two, cheerleaders usually have silly names. Like "Pipsie" and "Precious."

Three, cheerleaders, especially at professional games, do little more than wiggle their navels for a couple of hours.

Four, most cheers are stupid:

> *Wiggle your navel left!*
> *Wiggle your navel right!*
> *Wiggle your navel up and down!*
> *And fight! Fight! Fight!*

Pressed, I suppose I can abide a cheerleader or two at college games because sis-boom-bah is part of the appeal of the collegiate game, and there needs to be somebody around who remembers the words to the alma mater.

But I would like to put all professional cheerleaders on a permanent taxi squad. Autumn Sunday afternoons have become one big pompom shaking in the face of America. There are exceptions to everything, of course; but, basically, when you have seen one shaking pompom, you have seen them all.

I blame the Dallas Cowboys for this. There was a time when professional football teams wouldn't even think of allowing a group of women to stand around in their underpants on the sidelines and bump and grind for four quarters.

But later came National Football League expansion, and a team was placed in Dallas, where the men spend a lot of time out on the range with their cattle.

Spend enough time out on the range with your cattle, and football won't be enough to occupy your mind totally on the weekends either, Tex.

That's how the Dallas Cowboys Cheerleaders came to be. Watch the game, watch the girls, too, and get along, little dogie.

Soon, practically every team in the league had its cheerleaders, with the notable exception of the Pittsburgh Steelers, who said,

"We're here to play football. Get them broads off the sidelines." The Steelers, incidentally, are Super Bowl champions.

Before the letters start to pour in again, let me offer my assurance that this column was not written from a sexist point of view.

I don't like boy cheerleaders, either. Sometimes, you see boy cheerleaders at college games. What bothers me is, what will boy cheerleaders tell their sons when they ask, "What did you do in the Big Game, daddy?"

And they will be forced to answer, "I jumped around like an idiot and screamed my fool head off."

I am even more concerned about boy baton twirlers, but that is another story entirely.

The Old Chinchilla Game

All you've ever wanted to know about why NOT to invest in chinchillas, which have an alarming tendency to go bald.

What I knew about chinchillas, furry little animals that sometimes wind up as expensive coats, you could have put on the tip end of a chinchilla's tail, only I didn't even know if chinchillas have tails. (Later, I was to discover they most certainly do.)

What aroused my interest in chinchillas was an advertisement that ran in the newspaper last week.

"Own Your Own Business," said the advertisement. "Opportunity to Earn $30,000 Raising Chinchillas. Start in a spare room, garage, basement, outbuilding, etc."

The company that placed the advertisement was International Furriers Ltd.

I could use the thirty big ones, and I have a spare room. Also, there was a picture of a chinchilla included in the advertisement. Chinchillas are cute little boogers.

I talked to a Mr. Flowers of International Furriers Ltd. He became angry and defensive when I told him I worked for the newspaper. I don't think he believed I was serious about wanting to learn about chinchillas so I could possibly go into business raising them.

I think he thought I was trying to stir up trouble just because a few thousand people get ripped off in chinchilla-raising schemes every year.

Mr. Flowers assured me his company would never knowingly fleece a customer. He said people who go into chinchilla-raising and lose their shirts are just dummies who do not give their animals the proper care and handling.

After he settled down a bit, I was able to get even more vital information about chinchillas.

He said chinchillas were originally from South America, but now they all live in cages in spare rooms, garages, basements, outbuildings, etc.

He said they are nocturnal animals of the rodent family. They are about the size of rabbits, he went on, and it costs a penny a day to feed one chinchilla on Ralson-Purina Chinchilla Chow.

"Do they have tails?" I asked.

"They most certaily do," Mr. Flowers assured me.

He also said he would sell six chinchillas—one boy and five girls—for $3,400 and he would even throw in the cages.

I also wanted to know how much a ready-for-market chinchilla is worth and how many people are actually making $30,000, but that's where Mr. Flowers became testy again and I decided it would be best to hang up.

What I did next was call the Governor's Office of Consumer Affairs, to ask would it be smart for a person to get involved in raising chinchillas.

Not by the hair of your chinny chinchilla, said a spokesperson. Here's why:

1. Contrary to what a chinchilla salesman might tell you, chinchillas are NOT easy to raise. They are subject to a variety of diseases, traumas, and even emotional breakdowns which affect their breeding habits and the quality of their offspring. There is nothing worse than a chinchilla gone bonkers.

2. Chinchillas make a lot of noise at night. They're nocturnal, remember? Unfortunately, most of the suckers who get involved in raising them aren't.

3. Sometimes, chinchillas lose all their hair. A bald chinchilla is a worthless chinchilla.

4. Sometimes, even worse things happen. Sometimes, they gnaw their feet off.

5. Chinchilla salesmen often claim chinchillas reproduce three times a year. That's a bunch of Chinchilla Chow.

6. Spare rooms, garages, basements, outbuildings, etc., are NOT conducive to raising chinchillas. A New York chinchilla scam recently had people trying to raise chinchillas in their bedrooms. They are the same people who keep Florida swampland salesmen in business.

7. Companies that put people in the chinchilla business have a tendency to move around a lot.

8. Most chinchilla buying and selling is done through large associations. And the chinchilla market right now is lousy.

I wanted this to be a thorough investigation, so I also looked for somebody who has actually had a chinchilla-raising experience. I found somebody.

His name is Bill Paulidis and he is a furrier for S. Baum and Co., an Atlanta firm.

Mr. Paulidis once tried to raise chinchillas on Ponce de Leon Avenue. He had 180 of them. They all got sick and lost their hair. In one night, Mr. Paulidis had to put thiry-nine chinchillas out of their misery.

He lost $25,000.

"Anybody who puts money into chinchillas," said Mr. Paulidis, "is crazy."

End of investigation.

Me and My Guccis

Sometime later, someone stole the very pair of Guccis I am writing about here. I left them in the locker room of where I play tennis, and when I returned, they were gone, which made me feel very good. At least one person I hang around with at the tennis courts has some class. I never would have guessed it.

All my adult life, I have attempted to rise above my humble beginnings. Take shoes, for example. Now that I have steady work and live in the city, I like to wear nice shoes.

In the boondocks, we didn't wear shoes unless it was an absolute necessity. Like your feet would freeze if you didn't, or there was a funeral.

My boyhood friend and idol, Weyman C. Wannamaker, Jr., a great American, didn't wear shoes even on those occasions, but he did wash his feet twice a week whether they needed it or not.

The first time I saw Weyman in a pair of shoes they were forced upon him.

We were in the sixth grade, and the teacher organized a field trip to Atlanta to hear a performance by the symphony orchestra. As the bus pulled away from the school, she noticed Weyman was barefooted.

Horrified, she ordered the bus driver to stop at the nearest shoe store, where she bought Weyman a pair of shoes. He protested, but the teacher hit him in the mouth and Weyman didn't mention the shoes again.

During the performance of the symphony orchestra, however, Weyman's feet began hurting him, so he took off his shoes and hung his bare feet over the railing of the balcony. Unfortunately, he was between washes.

The entire percussion section and two flute players stopped in the middle of Chopin's Movement No. 5 to search for what had obviously passed away days earlier.

I always think of Weyman when I pull on a new pair of shoes. Lately, some of the fellows down at the lodge have been giving me the business because I now own a pair of stylish loafers by Gucci, the famous Italian leatherperson.

I prefer to think their boorish, catty remarks stem from ignorance, sprinkled with at least a tad of jealousy.

"I knew him," said one of the buzzbrains, wearing a pair of hideous lace-ups named for something you eat with fried catfish, "when he wore high-top tennis shoes and ran rabbits"

How utterly crude. And untrue. I wore low-cuts.

My new Guccis were a gift from a lady friend who brought them back from Palm Beach, where they have a Gucci store. They don't have Gucci stores except in spiffy places like Palm Beach. It's easier to move an NFL expansion franchise team into town.

My lady friend is always bringing me nice gifts when she goes on trips. Once she went to the drugstore and brought me a giant bottle of mouthwash and some extra-strength Tegrin shampoo.

I must do something nice for her. Maybe I'll take her bowling.

What makes a pair of stylish Italian loafers by Gucci so appealing is their softness, their master workmanship, and their price.

I've bought cars for less. Walk into a Gucci store, and they ask for your shoe size second. First, they want a quick glance at your Dun and Bradstreet.

Not just anybody can wear a pair of Gucci shoes, of course. Those crass dolts down at the lodge, for instance.

"You get a purse, too?" cracked one of the sorry lot, a hint of white socklet peering outside the top of his brogans.

Disgusting.

My new Guccis are an unpretentious oxblood, accented perfectly with buckles and slightly raised heels.

The cushioned inner soles wear the proud Gucci crest with the subtle, but effective announcement, "Made in Italy," as if there were any doubt.

When I am in the company of individuals with the proper breeding to appreciate such hallmarks of style, I am not hesitant to remove one of my new shoes to prove I am wearing the Real McCoy.

"Have you noticed I am wearing Guccis?" I asked the hostess at a dinner party.

"Frankly, I haven't," she said.

I took off one of my shoes and showed her the proud Gucci crest on the cushioned inner soles. I didn't want to stay at her stupid dinner party anyway.

I also called Weyman C. Wannamaker, Jr., back home and told him I am now wearing Guccis. I knew he would be proud.

"You wearing them shoes," he said, "is like putting perfume on a hog."

My Kind of Beauty Queen

. . . And whatever happened to Barbi Benton?

The wires carried an interesting interview the other day with the newly-crowned Miss Universe, an eighteen-year-old from Venezuela.

I take that back. It was not an interesting interview at all. As a matter of fact, it was a very dull interview, because it was like every other interview with beauty queens.

Beauty queens today have a thing about denying they are sex objects. That's nothing. So do girls who pose with no clothes on in magazines.

Open a magazine and pull out the centerfold, and there is the Lustlady of the Year revealing everything but her shoe size.

"I can't stand a man who wants me only for my body," she is saying in the caption. "I have a brain, too, and I can use it. I know six state capitals and once I went to a museum."

If I've read where one beauty queen was saying there is more to her than what she has managed to stuff inside her tight-fitting swimsuit, I've read where a thousand more were making the same irrelevant remarks.

If brains were all that important in a beauty contest, you could enter wearing a Hefty Bag.

The current Miss Universe is Maritza Sayalero. She is from Caracas. Her father is an engineer, which has nothing to do with anything but is the kind of incidental information they put in interviews with beauty queens to help fill up space.

Maritza was posing for tourists in New York City in her tight-fitting swimsuit in front of the statue of Prometheus at Rockefeller Center, and, sure enough, some reporter asked her if she considered herself a sex symbol.

And, sure enough, Miss Universe wiggled and giggled and said, "Even though I am beautiful, I don't consider myself a sex symbol."

Even though she is beautiful, what does she consider herself? Posing at Rockefeller Center in her tight-fitting swimsuit, one of those eye-poppers with slits down the sides, she was no sack of potatoes, por favor.

The interview also carried information concerning Miss Universe's plans for when her reign is over and she returns to Caracas.

She wants to be an architect.

"I want to design beautiful buildings," she said, "but with a purpose—for the poor."

I am sure the poor people in Caracas will appreciate that. Give them a few beautiful buildings and maybe they will quit complaining about being cold and hungry.

Give me a beauty queen who understands the rules of the game. Give me a beauty queen like Kathy Sue Loudermilk, who won the coveted Miss Collard Festival Queen title seven years running back home, breaking Cordie Mae Poovy's string of four in a row.

That's not the only string Kathy Sue broke. When the one that held up the top of her swimsuit snapped, that's how she ousted Cordie Mae in the first place.

Kathy Sue Loudermilk knew what a beauty contest was all about. Every year, she ordred a new swimsuit from the Sears catalog and every year, she was living proof that you could, in fact, stuff one hundred pounds of collards into a fifty-pound sack if you squeezed and packed and pushed long and hard enough.

Even the Baptist preacher always turned out to watch Kathy Sue in action at the pageant. Once, he even allowed himself a bellowing, "Hallelujah!" when Kathy Sue, sensing she might be in trouble with the judges for missing a question concerning the current price of hog vaccine, gave a couple of quick hip-flips to make up the lost points.

The county seat newspaper always dispatched a photographer and a reporter to cover the festival, and one year they posed Kathy Sue in her swimsuit on a tractor.

The reporter asked, "Miss Loudermilk, do you consider yourself a sex symbol?"

Kathy Sue never blinked.

"Does a duck have lips, Four-Eyes?" she replied as she cranked the John Deere, did a quick wheelie and disappeared down a dirt road.

I said it then, and I will say it now: "There goes my kind of beauty queen."

A Hero Unmasked

Do cowboys ever cry? Sure, even the Lone Ranger . . .

I spent an entire afternoon and part of an evening trying to reach the Lone Ranger on the telephone. You don't just pick up the telephone and ask information for the number of the Lone Ranger, but I finally resorted to that when all other efforts failed.

"I am trying to reach a Mr. Clayton Moore," I said to the operator in California. "He's the Lone Ranger."

"Is that a person or a business, sir?" she asked.

"A person," I said. "You've never heard of the Lone Ranger?"

"The rock singer?" she replied.

I hung up. Probably some mindless nineteen-year-old, high on a Hostess Twinkie.

Perhaps it was best I never reached him. What would I have said to "the masked rider of the plains"?

"Tough luck"?

"Hang in there"?

"How's Tonto"?

They stuck it to Clayton Moore, who portrayed the Lone Ranger from 1949 to 1956 on television, in a Southern California court the other day.

A judge ordered him to take off his mask and go ride off somewhere and drop dead. At least, that's what it sounded like to me.

I didn't understand all the legal mumbo jumbo—and I really didn't try—but the judge said Clayton Moore no longer has any claim to the role he made famous and ordered that he no longer make any public appearances wearing his mask.

They're making a new film about the legendary western hero of my youth, and the film company said Moore, who is sixty-four, is too old to play the character. They wanted him to remove his mask "to avoid confusion."

That's a lot of trail dust. Buddy Ebsen, who is certainly no tenderfoot, can still bring'em to justice as Barnaby Jones, so why put Clayton Moore in mothballs before his time?

According to the news, Clayton Moore cried when the judge handed down his decision. The dirty galoot.

I go all the way back to the early fifties with Clayton as the Lone Ranger and Jay Silverheels as Tonto, and Silver and Scout, who played themselves.

Merita Bread sponsored the show. "Come with us now to those thrilling days of yesteryear . . . etc."

I even remember a Lone Ranger joke. It was funny the first time I heard it, when I was ten or eleven, and it is even funnier now because Indians quit taking any grief a few year back.

The Lone Ranger and his trusty sidekick Tonto—who was always referred to as an "Injun" by badmen and other insensitive creeps on the show—were surrounded by ten million original Americans all dressed up in war paint and carrying bows and arrows and tomahawks and rifles they had borrowed from the local cavalry fort.

"Well, Tonto," says the Lone Ranger in Clayton Moore's deep, resonant voice, "it looks like we've finally come to the end of our trail."

Tonto, meanwhile, had other ideas. He replies:

"What's this 'we' business, white-eyes?"

Things have been tough all over for Old West television stars lately. Roy's got a bum ticker, you may have heard.

Hoppy died. Lash LaRue, the last word I had, was cracking the whip for Jesus in a tent crusade.

And now, this. A judge has taken the mask off the Lone Ranger.

Maybe if I had reached Clayton Moore on the telephone, I could have given him a message from his fans, and I know I could have spoken for all of them.

Maybe I could have said something like, "It's no big thing, Kemo Sabe. You're still the Lone Ranger to us, and we'll always love you."

He would have probably liked to have heard that. Especially the "we" part.

Shafting the Kids: Part I

Most of the time, the biggest trouble with young people is adults.
That is what I was trying to say in the next two pieces, which are
about alcohol and sex.

Sometimes I dislike being in the company of young adults. That is
because sometimes they ask probing, thoughtful questions I cannot
answer. I find what I do most when talking to young people is make
apologies and excuses for their elders.

It will happen to me again. I will be with a group of young adults,
and they will ask me why the would-be grown folks who make the
laws of the state are trying to put the screws to them again.

But damned if I will hide from the truth this time. The Georgia
General Assembly, which often resembles recess at the playschool,
is considering depriving eighteen-year-olds—possibly even nineteen-year-olds and twenty-year-olds, too—of the right to purchase
alcoholic beverages legally.

That is outrageous.

We lowered the legal drinking age from twenty-one to eighteen in
this state during the Vietnam War. That was because we could no
longer face ourselves knowing we could send a young man to die for
no apparent reason in a war that made no apparent sense and still
deprive him of a full citizenship.

But "times have changed," read an editorial last week that favored
raising the drinking age again.

What on earth does that mean? That full citizenship is only valid
when we are in the middle of an idiotic war? What if we get ourselves involved in another one? Times haven't changed enough that
we wouldn't. And if there is a next time, guess who would get the
call to duty and death again? That same eighteen-year-old the state
legislature is trying to tell he must now relinquish his right to buy
booze.

The state legislature giveth. I am all for that. But I personally get
very nervous when any body of lawmakers or law enforcers starts
trying to taketh away. Rights are not to be dangled in front of the
citizenry as candy before a drooling baby.

There is, of course, the argument that because the drinking age has
been lowered to eighteen, it is now easier for high school students to
obtain alcohol. The proponents of raising the drinking age point to
an increase in teenage alcoholism.

Teenagers drink because they are programmed to do so by adults who can't hold any function without a cocktail beforehand. By adults like the state legislators who had a cocktail party scheduled every night of the first week of their current session.

Television, movies, and advertising—all run by adults—picture drinking as chic, as fun, as almost necessary in order to be functional within our society. Until all that is changed, teenage drinking will continue to increase, and a tub full of ridiculous regulations won't even begin to reverse the trend.

Also, I find it terribly unfair to ask an eighteen-year-old, who can vote, pay taxes, and reproduce the species, to give up his or her right because we can't convince a sixteen-year-old to wait a couple of years.

The drinking age for me was twenty-one. I had no trouble whatsoever in a town of 300, getting my hands on enough beer to turn me green when I was fifteen.

When I was eighteen, I registered, by law, for the draft, I entered college, held down a job, paid taxes, successfully proposed marriage to another eighteen-year-old, and was told I could vote.

If there was anything I wasn't ready to do yet, it was vote. One afternoon in 1964, I got blitzed at the fraternity house and went out and cast a ballot for Lyndon Johnson.

We have put the shaft to young adults long enough. We have told them one thing and meant another. We have preached to them one thing and practiced another. We have insisted they pay support to and help defend our society, but at the same time we have tried to tell them they cannot enjoy all the privileges of it.

"Bless the Beasts and the Children." It was a song from a movie of the same name. And there was the lyric: "Bless the beasts and the children/For in this world, they have no voice/They have no choice."

If the Georgia General Assembly wants to take away somebody's right to drink, then so be it.

I would be solidly in favor of a new law making it illegal for any state legislator to get himself soused in an Atlanta bar before going out looking for hookers while he was supposed to be at the business of taking care of the welfare of the citizens he represents.

Let's see a vote on that one, boys.

Shafting the Kids: Part II

There was no such thing as sex education when I was in school. I take that back. There was plenty of sex education in my school, but

214 WON'T YOU COME HOME, BILLY BOB BAILEY?

classes were conducted behind the grandstand of the baseball diamond and the teacher usually had only a couple of years on his students.

We did have "health" classes in school. That is where you learned clean fingernails are important, if you don't brush your teeth regularly your teeth will fall out, and you can get all the Vitamin D you need by spending a lot of time out in the sun.

We also had biology classes where we did hear something about sex, but only if it involved a couple of frogs.

But times changed. Educators finally began to realize that perhaps the reason so many of their female students were getting pregnant—some at ridiculous ages like twelve and thirteen—was because all they knew about sex was the basics of how to perform it.

So, gradually, sex education has been introduced into many of our schools. There has been protest, of course, because some parents and school board members still think it best for children to learn about sex in other places.

Like behind the grandstand of a baseball diamond.

Take Cobb County, for instance. They are always fighting about something in the Atlanta suburb of Cobb County. This time, it is whether to introduce a unified sex education program into the sixth, seventh, and eighth grades.

Those in favor of the program argued at a recent school board meeting that it is important because an estimated 30,000 American girls under the age of fifteen will get pregnant this year.

Those against the program had a good argument, too. Cobb County school board member John McClure said students need less sex education and more teaching of "self-respect, discipline, and patriotism."

He also suggested sex education be handled in the home.

"But not everybody has a home," countered a Cobb County high school senior who came to the meeting.

"Hmmmp!" said board member McClure, who could be suffering from chalk dust on the brain.

We think nothing of teaching our children all about wars. Half of the time I was in school, I was learning about a war, the Third Punic all the way to the Great WWII.

People get maimed and killed in wars. Sex has to do with loving. Teach 'em about war, but ignore the little brats when they ask about sex.

The new sex education plan didn't pass at the Cobb school board meeting. The vote was 3-3, but the superintendent has already said he would not ask his teachers to teach the program if the board were split on such a "controversial issue."

I don't know if this will help, but it is probably worth a try. For those Cobb students who will be deprived of sex education for at least another year, here is my own sex short-course.

Clip and save:

• Having sex, even if you are only twelve, can make babies.

• Having a baby while you are still a kid is a bummer.

• If you are determined to have sex no matter what anybody tells you, there are ways to avoid making a baby. They are called "contraceptives." Ask an older friend who won't go berserk how to obtain them.

• There is nothing dirty about sex. It is a beautiful and necessary part of life.

• Many grown people would be better off if they realized that.

The Rumored Closing of Harold's Barbecue

Harold's lives on to this day. The barbecue and the crackling cornbread are still good, the posters about Jesus are still on the wall, and there's still no beer.

There is a nasty rumor going around the city that I would like to quash immediately.

Harold's Barbecue, that wonderful haven for lovers of pork down past Atlanta Stadium, is not going to close.

I repeat, is NOT going to close.

I first heard the nasty whisperings a couple of weeks ago when a friend, a fellow barbecue junkie, walked into my office, pale as a sheet.

"They can't do this!" he screamed. "I won't stand for it! I'll write Herman Talmadge!"

Better hurry, I said, if you want to write ol' Herman.

"OK," my friend went on, "I'll write Guy Sharpe! But somebody has to put a stop to this!"

Stop to what?

"You haven't heard?" my friend asked. "Harold's Barbecue is selling out to a trucking company, and there are no plans to reopen."

You could have knocked me over with a sliced sandwich, outside meat, toast the bread.

As I have mentioned before, to my taste, there are three great barbecue joints in Georgia. You could not rate Ruth, Gehrig, DiMag-

gio. Neither could you rate Harold's Barbecue in Atlanta, Sprayber-
ry's in Newman, and Sweat's, Soperton branch.

They are all superior places to eat barbecue, the Holy Barbecue
Triumvirate, if you will.

Harold's close? Harold's is one of the reasons I went through all
the trouble to escape Chicago.

I dialed the number with shaking hands. I said a little prayer,
"Lord, don't let it be true."

I talked to Harold himself. Harold is Harold Hembree. His father
opened Harold's Barbecue thirty-two years ago. The son has operated the business for twenty-two years.

"Harold," I began, "are you going to close?"

"Good Lord, no!" he replied.

Marvelous, absolutely marvelous.

"That rumor gets out all the time," Harold went on. "There's a
trucking company close to us, and one time we talked about selling
them this property.

"But they were going to give us a new place nearby and build
whatever we wanted, but that never worked out.

"I have no plans to close, now or ever. I've been at this too long to
try anything else."

I could go on about the quality of the barbecue at Harold's, but
that would only start an argument. People feel strongly about their
barbecue.

What I do want to say about Harold Hembree's establishment is it
looks like a good barbecue joint ought to look. It's small. It's not
fancy. There is no glass, no potted plants, no wicker.

The food is simple. Barbecue sandwiches, barbecue plates,
chopped or sliced. Potato chips. Pickles. Brunswick stew. Cornbread. *Crackling* cornbread.

"That was mama's idea," Harold said.

Harold's is a total family operation.

"Counting nieces, sisters, and wives," Harold said, "there are
about thirteen of us working here."

I also like the way the walls are decorated. Harold's family is
serious about its religion.

"God Is My Co-Pilot." "Lean on Jesus." There are a lot of religious
posters around on the walls at Harold's.

There was one other rumor I wanted to check out as long as I had
Harold on the line, the one that said maybe it wouldn't be long before
you could get a beer along with your barbecue at Harold's.

"No truth to that, either," he said. "Mama wouldn't stand for it."

Some things, some people endure the ravages of progress. I will
sleep better tonight knowing that.

Golf, or a Reasonable Facsimile Thereof

*Golf is the favorite game of insurance salesmen, car thieves, and
Methodist ministers. I don't know exactly what that means, but it is
certainly worth pondering.*

What's always been wrong with golf is, any way you slice it, golf
is a dull game.

The players are dull, robots carrying sticks. They don't even spit
or scratch their privates like other athletes. The spectators are dull.
They applaud even when some guntz hits a good shot.

The television announcers are dull, too. If Dave Marr cracks you
up, you probably think Bernard Kalb is a riot.

Take the United States Open golf tournament, played somewhere
near Toledo last week. Dull. A couple of players tried to put a little
life in the stodgy proceedings, but all those stuffy United States Golf
Association (USGA) officials in their long-sleeved white shirts
nearly had a hissy.

(All my life I have wanted to know the exact definition of the word
"hissy." I think it means turning red in the face and stomping and
raving around like something crazy.)

One of the players, Lon Hinkle, discovered it was closer from tee
to green on a par-five hole to hit his drive into another fairway. To
show you how dull golf is, that was front-page sports news for days.

The USGA would have nothing of it. They ordered a tree planted
near the tee so Lon Hinkle couldn't take the scenic route.

Put the USGA in charge of sex and it would eliminate body
contact.

Then there was young Bobby Clampett. Young Bobby Clampett
missed the cut, but they asked him to play along the next day
anyway because somebody still in the field needed a partner.

Graciously, Bobby Clampett agreed and took a busman's holiday.
He also hit a few of his tee shots from his knees and joked around
with the gallery.

It didn't matter Bobby Clampett's knee-shots were long and
straight. It didn't matter there is nothing in the rules of golf that says

you can't hit the ball from a kneeling position. And what's wrong with joking around with the gallery?

"Watch me hit this ball on my knees," said Bobby Clampett.

"Ha! Ha!" laughed the gallery.

The hilarity is killing me.

Anybody seen Bobby Clampett lately? Of course not. He was dragged away from the thirteenth hole by USGA officials and shot.

I played golf last week. I hadn't played golf in ten years. I quit because I was a lousy golfer and because I didn't like to walk around in the woods. There are spiders and snakes in there.

Also, it was making me a dull person. After a round of golf, I thought a big night out was a couple of hands of canasta with my neighbor, Mr. Forndyce. Mr. Forndyce was a nice enough fellow, but he was also eighty-three and had been declared legally dead from his eyebrows down thirty years earlier.

But I finally found a way to play golf that is fun. I played in the annual Busch Bash, formerly the Old Milwaukee Open, at the Newnan Country Club. Two grown men named Joe Lawson and Jim Mottola are in charge of it. If Joe Lawson and Jim Mottola ran the U.S. Open, Bobby Clampett could hit balls standing on his head and they wouldn't care.

The Busch Bash involves playing twenty-seven holes of golf and drinking a beer on each one. There are some terrific rules:

• If you don't want to hit the ball, you can throw it. I didn't hit the ball so well, but I made some excellent throws.

• If you don't want to hit the ball or throw it, fine. Drink another beer.

• If you hit the ball into the woods, forget it. Hit somebody's ball that didn't go into the woods.

• You can wear tennis shoes.

• Wives and girlfriends of participants are enouraged to stay away from the trailer parked behind the seventeenth green.

• The night before the tournament, there is a party from seven until nine o'clock that lasts until three in the morning.

• The night after the tournament, there is a party that still may be going.

There are always prizes at the annual Busch Bash, but tournament officials never remember to give them out. In fact, at the party after the tournament, I asked Joe Lawson who won, and he said, "Who knows?"

That's my kind of golf tournament. I only wish some officials from the USGA, the pompous old goats, could have been there. They would have had a hissy. A double.

4

FIGHTING CITY HALL

Grizzard for Mayor

My campaign never got off the ground. I was selling bumper stickers for $17.50 each to raise money. Counting the one my mother didn't buy, I didn't sell any. Also, I got some sage political advice from one of my readers who reminded me, "Grizzard, the only thing you ought to run for is the city limits."

I know you are all going to fall down laughing when you read this, but it wasn't my idea. It came from a group of dentists over at Emory University.

They wrote me a letter that began, "Atlanta is ready for, and in need of, responsible leadership in city government."

The understatement of the year. Our City Council is a monkey show, at best, and our mayor—you read it here first—was dropped on his head as a small boy, which explains some of his delirious actions like making plans to run in a statewide election against Senator Herman Talmadge.

Outside Atlanta, they think Maynard Jackson is the name of a new hog vaccine.

You also have to question the mayor's recruiting abilities. He gave the city A. Reginald Eaves, remember. And he is also responsible for Tweedle-Dum and Tweedle-Dee, Brown and Napper, over at police headquarters.

Their crack leadership of the police force has the rest of us looking for places to hide, as the crime rate soars. A friend in Des Moines called the other day and said, "I was planning to come visit you in Atlanta, but now I'm not sure. Shouldn't we plan to meet somewhere safer? Like Juarez or Newark?"

219

The dentists over at Emory have strongly suggested that because I am always writing as if I know it all, maybe I should run for mayor of Atlanta in the upcoming 1981 election.

Pull yourselves together. It's not that damned funny. I was treasurer of my freshman class in high school, and when I was a kid, I used to shovel out what the horses left in the barn. I know a little something about politics.

(What does shoveling out what horses leave in the barn have to do with politics? I don't think I have to answer that question.)

Dr. Thomas W. McDonald has appointed himself campaign chairman of the "Grizzard for Mayor in '81 Committee," and he lists Dr. George Ulrich and Dr. George Pryles as his associates.

Their letter drafting my candidacy further stated, "Campaign strategy and meetings are under way, and an effective bumper sticker blitz has been initiated."

I must say I'm flattered. "Mayor Lewis Grizzard." "Mr. Mayor Lewis Grizzard." "His Honor, Mayor Lewis Grizzard." They all have a certain ring.

But I would have some problems of my own as mayor. For one thing, I don't really need a car; and when someone else drives, it makes me nervous. And all those bodyguards scurrying around and opening my doors would make me feel a bit pompous.

I probably would do something dumb like fire my bodyguards; because I happen to think if anybody needs bodyguards in this town, it's not the mayor, it's the working stiff who has to brave the raging streets alone.

And then I would have all those fat-cat jobs to hand out, the ones you give to your pals, or former pals, like A. Reggie.

All my friends already have good jobs.

And I have no idea what to do about Central City Park, the downtown zoo. Yes, I do, but electric fencing is so expensive. I don't get free drinks at Billy's, and would that much of an outsider really have a fighting chance at getting elected?

I'll just stick here, fighting the daily battle to produce a column for a great, metropolitan newspaper. Besides, you'll have plenty of choices for a new mayor in 1981, without my getting in the way.

Statesmen like A. Reggie and Mike Lomax, who has a cute beard and knows some rock stars, will probably be in the battle. And if Leroy Johnson, the new head of the Stadium Authority, can pass out enough big cigars and free parking at Falcons games to the right people, who knows about him?

I am not now, nor will I ever be, a candidate. But collector's item "Grizzard for Mayor" bumper stickers are available. Send $17.50, or more if you can spare it, and my staff of volunteers will see that your sticker is in the mail promptly.

Sure, I'll make a few quick bucks for doing nothing. But I already told you I know a little something about politics.

Adventures of the Drug Fairy

City Councilman James Bond is one of my favorite Atlanta politicians. His tailor, incidentally, is the same guy who designed the Hefty Bag.

I called a detective in the auto theft division of the Atlanta Police Department Wednesday and promised him if he answered a few of my questions candidly, I wouldn't use his name. Sometimes such tactics are necessary in big-time journalism.

He agreed.

What would happen, I began, if I called the police emergency number, like any ordinary citizen would do, to report a theft of a radio and a tape system from my car?

"We would send over a uniformed officer," said the detective, "and he would make out a report."

What would happen, I went on, if I called the chief of police directly with such a complaint?

"You wouldn't do that," said the detective.

"But what if I did?"

"If you got through, I suppose he would just send over a uniformed officer, and he would make out a report."

There was one more question. What would happen if I were a city councilman and a member of the Public Safety Committee, which overlooks police department matters, and I called the chief with my complaint? Would I get special treatment? Would I, for instance, be sent a detective rather than a uniformed cop?

"I see what you mean," said the detective. "But let's face it, that kind of thing has *always* gone on, and it always will. Who do you think they would send over if Jimmy Carter called and said somebody had broken into his car?"

Good point. We take care of our own on nearly every level of government. It's an American tradition. Like Bunker Hill, remembering the *Maine*, and fixing traffic tickets.

That brings us to the recent case of Atlanta City Councilman James Bond, who just happens to be a member of the Public Safety Committee which overlooks the police department.

Somebody broke into his car and took his radio and tape system. He did not call the police emergency number. He called Chief George Napper. Who came to Bond's house to investigate? Not Charlie the Cop, but Detective R. T. Ford.

Detective Ford did a thorough job in his investigation. This wasn't Joe Doe he was dealing with, remember.

Detective Ford did too good a job. Somebody should talk to Detective Ford. Know what he found in Councilman Bond's car besides a missing radio and tape system? He found something that looked a lot like marijuana cigarettes, fellow citizens.

He found one unsmoked cigarette behind the front seat. He found nine already-smoked cigarettes in Councilman Bond's ashtray. Just to prove himself wrong of his suspicions, Detective Ford sent the substance to the Georgia Crime Lab for identification.

Holy Case Dismissed! The substance was marijuana! Marijuana is against the law! There must be an explanation!

There was. Chief Napper handled the matter himself. After all, this had been his baby from the start.

"There is no reason to believe the owner of the car had any responsibility for placing the marijuana there," said the chief, adding, "Somebody other than the owner could have placed it there."

Of course. The Drug Fairy, for one. The chief even mentioned the thief might have done it. That's logical. A thief decides to rip off Councilman Bond's car. He opens the door with a coat hanger and lies down in the seat to partake of the goodies.

While he is there, he decides to mix a little pleasure with business and smokes nine marijuana cigarettes in the minute-and-a-half it takes to dislodge Councilman Bond's radio and tape system. At least he had the courtesy to crush out all nine in the ashtray and leave one unsmoked joint behind the front seat for the next thief.

Just so nobody gets any wrong ideas, Chief Napper has assured Atlanta citizens that Councilman Bond's high position in the city government had absolutely nothing to do with his decision not to file charges against Bond.

Even the Drug Fairy wouldn't fall for that one.

A Toast to the Poor People

The hero of this story is A. Reginald Eaves, who once bought an expensive love seat for his office when he was Atlanta's public safety commissioner, and who likes big, chauffeur-driven limos and lots of bodyguards and shiny suits. Isn't it sad poor people in other parts of the country besides Atlanta don't have a guy like A. Reginald Eaves on their side?

In the past, when I read articles about the possibility of A. Reginald Eaves' becoming mayor of Atlanta, I would get down on the floor and roll around and laugh.

Stone Mountain will crumble, the Peachtree Plaza will fall before that will happen, I would say.

My attitude changed Tuesday night. I am now convinced A. Reggie, former public safety commissioner, current county commissioner, and a big man in a number of local discos, could become the next mayor of Atlanta.

How does that feel to me? How does it feel to stand around and wait for a homemade H-bomb to go off?

A. Reggie, as you probably know, was against the idea to raise the local sales tax. Maynard Jackson, the current Atlanta mayor, was for it, and so was his hand-picked successor, Michael Lomax.

The sales tax hike was soundly trounced in Tuesday's election. Said the political experts, "The sales tax defeat showed the strong base of support for A. Reginald Eaves."

A. Reggie didn't want anybody to forget that, so as soon as he could find somebody with a microphone, he started campaigning. I watched his performance on the eleven o'clock news.

"This is a great victory for the poor people," said A. Reggie. As soon as a person starts talking about great victories for the poor people, you can bet the farm he is campaigning.

A. Reggie wore a pin-striped gangster suit for the occasion and was celebrating in a hotel room with a lot of others, who may or may not have been drinking champagne out of the glasses they were holding.

I think they probably were drinking champagne, because that's what you usually drink when the poor people win one.

I will be the first to admit A. Reggie is smarter than I originally thought. I used to think he was a complete dummy. Now, I think he is only a half-dummy, which makes him one of our most intelligent local politicians.

Recall, he was fired as public safety commissioner by the mayor, the same fellow who hired him on the basis that they were old friends. It is difficult to get fired from a job where your boss is an old chum, but A. Reggie managed it.

Yet A. Reggie landed on his feet. He could have left town in disgrace. Instead, he chose to become a martyr. Martyrs have a big edge in elections, and that is how A. Reggie got elected to the county commission.

Then he started going around winning great victories for the poor people. The Falcons' playoff win over Philadelphia last season, for instance.

"Great victory for the poor people," said A. Reggie.

He gave away such jobs as personal bodyguard and chauffeur to poor people like county policemen, and when he walks into a local disco, he buys the first ten poor people to recognize him a drink.

There are a number of things that bother me about the possibility of A. Reginald Eaves' becoming mayor of Atlanta.

• He forever loused up the police department when he was chief. Imagine what he could do as mayor.

• I don't think he really cares about poor people. I think he cares more about personal bodyguards and chauffeurs.

After the sales tax vote was in Tuesday night, A. Reggie also said, "The people have more intelligence than we gave them credit for."

Let's hope so. God, let's hope so.

Frontier Mayor

It is very helpful to a newspaper columnist when the local mayor is taken to doing weird things, thus giving the newspaper columnist a topic. I would like to thank Atlanta Mayor Maynard Jackson for all his help through the years . . .

I've been sleeping much more soundly recently since I read about Mayor Maynard Jackson's one-man battle against crime in Atlanta.

We have a great deal of crime in Atlanta: murder, robbery, rape, jacking up cars on the streets.

The other day, the mayor was riding around town in his limousine. People probably said, "Look, there's Mayor Jackson riding around town in his limousine. Why isn't he back at his office trying to do something about the rising crime rate?"

That's the people for you. What the chumps don't realize is, you can't stop crime sitting behind a desk pushing a pencil.

"Frontier Mayor" Maynard Jackson wasn't just riding around town. He was on patrol.

Suddenly, he spotted a crime in progress. Not murder. Not robbery. Not rape. But *jacking cars up on the streets.* The mere sound of the words themselves is enough to make your skin crawl.

"Whoa!" shouted "Frontier Mayor" Maynard to his limo driver. Disregarding his own safety, the mayor leaped from the limo, opening his own door in the process, and marched right into J. K. Ramey's tire store on Walton Street.

Out front of J. K. Ramey's store were several cars jacked up for tire changes. In broad daylight.

"Mr. Ramey," said the mayor, "you've got to cut that out."

At least that's what the mayor said he said to Mr. Ramey. Mr. Ramey says the mayor also said, "I'm going to put your bleep out of business"—not because of the cars jacked up on the street, but because of Mr. Ramey's involvement with plans to erect a police protest sign in the city.

The mayor denies all that. "He was breaking the law," the mayor stated, "and if my own father was violating the law, and I was in charge of enforcing it, I would enforce the law."

I heard Matt Dillon say that very same thing once to Miss Kitty over a few beers at the Long Branch.

I happen to think Mayor Jackson is absolutely correct in putting his foot down to stop the heinous practice of illegal car-jacking.

"It's a negative reflection on the city," he said. "There are oil spots on the street where he (Mr. Ramey) had cars out there changing tires."

Oil spots today, leaking transmission fluid puddles tomorrow, and pretty soon, the entire city is down the drain.

Just to prove he wasn't picking on J. K. Ramey, the mayor also pointed out another "bust" he made recently against another rampant crime spree in the city. Illegally parked cars.

The mayor was patrolling in his trusty limo on Peachtree Street and spotted illegally parked cars in front of Salvatore's Restaurant.

"You better cut that out," he said to the owner of Salvatore's Restaurant. A couple of months later, the mayor made a routine check of Salvatore's again and, sure enough, he found two illegally parked cars in front of the restaurant. He called a wrecker and had them towed away.

Justice is swift at the hand of "Frontier Mayor" Maynard.

The mayor also announced he is personally involved in trying to halt the rise of a couple of other crimes in our city.

Not murder. Not robbery. Not rape. But illegal newspapers on the street, and throwing things out of car windows.

"I see a newspaper on the street," the mayor said, "and I pick it up."

"I see somebody throw something out a car window," he continued, "and I stop them and make them come back and pick it up."

Does this man's bravery know no bounds?

Those same ungrateful people who complain about the mayor riding around town in his limo are probably saying now, if he's so effective at stopping crimes like jacking up cars and throwing garbage out of windows, why doesn't he also tackle such crimes as murder, robbery, and rape?

That's simple. "Frontier Mayor" Maynard is no dummy. Drive around in that big limo on the dark Atlanta streets where people are being murdered and robbed and raped in record numbers and he could get HIS bleep put out of business, too.

Permanently.

Pink Flamingos for MARTA

Atlanta's new rapid rail transit system successfully opened in July 1979—just a few months after this column was written—WITHOUT expensive pieces of sculpture in the stations. You can't win 'em all, however. The inside of the Decatur station looks like the inside of the Holiday Inn Disco and Lounge at the airport in Oklahoma City.

Contrary to what you may have been led to believe, not everybody who has something to do with MARTA, Atlanta's public transportation company, is a dumbhead.

You take K. A. McMillon from suburban Gwinnett County. He is a member of the MARTA Development Committee. At a meeting of his committee this week, he actually stood up and said something that made good sense.

He said it was stupid to spend $145,000 on a sculpture MARTA was going to buy for one of its new rail stations.

"I think it's ridiculous we can't come to a meeting without having to listen to this garbage from the liberals who want to throw away MARTA's money," said Mr. McMillon.

He added, "I don't think we should spend any more on such as that until we've built the railroad first."

Two liberals fainted and another had to go to the bathroom when Mr. McMillon said that.

He is also against paying MARTA secretaries who don't know their ampersands from a hole in the ground at Forsyth Street $20,000 a year, but he's saving that one for later.

The sculpture issue has been around for a while. Atlanta artist Curtis Patterson designed the piece for the new Hightower Station.

I was very interested to find out what a $145,000 piece of sculpture looks like. Thursday, I called around.

"Abstract steel," was one description.

"One of them modernistic-looking things," was another.

A MARTA official who swore he would break my neck if I quoted him said it was "a hunk of iron."

I eventually had to go straight to the artist himself. Strangely, Curtis Patterson wasn't talking.

"I am afraid anything I say will be misinterpreted," he said.

"You won't even describe your work to me?" I pressed on.

"No comment," he persisted.

The best I can determine, then, is that MARTA's $145,000 hunk of iron is abstract, modernistic, and is probably bigger than a bread box.

Mr. McMillon won out in his battle against the sculpture and the garbage-headed liberals. He persuaded four other members of the committee to vote with him against three who voted to purchase the sculpture. Hooray!

Supporters of the sculpture were very angry, because they said some type of art work was needed in MARTA rail stations to make them aesthetically pleasing to transit riders.

I agree. All K. A. McMillon and I are saying is, you can dress up a rail station and not have to fork over $145,000 for one piece of bent iron.

Those pink flamingos with the long legs they sell on the side of the highway are cheap, for instance. Throw a couple of those around the lot, and if there are any trees, you could always paint the trunks white.

And here's an idea: what happens to worn MARTA bus tires? What you can do with worn tires is move them over to the rail station, paint them white, and plant flowers inside them.

Hang a bullfighter picture or two, and you've got yourself one finely appointed rail station.

Also, you can usually count on the transit riders to do some decorating themselves. In New York, for instance, they paint colorful slogans like "Mao Lives!" and "Keel the Gringos" on station walls.

I would be willing to pop for maybe one big statue at the main MARTA station, a statue saluting all the people who paid the taxes that enabled MARTA to be constructed and provided jobs for a lot of fat cats.

Just show some poor sucker standing on a street corner with his pockets turned out and his collar turned up. And make him look hungry.

That modernistic enough for you?

5

HAIL TO THE CHIEF!

The Perfect President

I think it was my boyhood friend and idol, Weyman C. Wanna-maker, Jr., a great American, who said it best. In the fifth grade, the teacher asked him, "Weyman, would you like to be president when you grow up?"

Weyman replied, "Hell, no. Only an idiot would want to be president."

Being president used to be a nice job. Make a few speeches, sign a few bills into law, declare war to rousing cheers, go throw out the first ball at a Senators' game.

Practically everybody liked you, or at least respected the fact you were doing the best you could. They played "Hail to the Chief" and old men saluted and pretty girls smiled when your train pulled into town.

But all that has changed. Being president now is like being sentenced to four years of wearing your jockey shorts too tight.

The president can't please anybody anymore. Our nation is so diverse in its special interests and its needs and desires, that the president automatically becomes the national whipping boy for everybody with a gripe.

Take Jimmy Carter. We elected him president because he wasn't a member of the Washington establishment. He was one of us, a simple peanut farmer from Georgia.

Read his reviews lately? Richard Nixon was in better shape, and he barely escaped a lynching on the White House lawn.

It seems a cinch now Jimmy Carter won't be reelected president in 1980. Why? Because he isn't a member of the Washington establishment, and what does a simple peanut farmer from Georgia know about being president?

Frankly, I don't think the Democrats can elect anybody president in 1980—not even Teddy Kennedy, who has terrific hair. Polls show Americans deserting the Democratic party in droves.

And who are the Republican choices? Howard Baker? Too slick. Robert Dole? Too slimy. John Connally? Too tricky. Ronald Reagan? Too dangerous. He's from California.

Name any potential candidate, and he has warts. Name any potential candidate, and I will name a faction that will eventually want his head on a platter.

Who we need for president is somebody who is perfect.

I've got just the guy.

We need a president who can unite us again, someone who can bring Anita Bryant together with the Gay Liberationists. Bring Joan Baez together with Jane Fonda. Bring Martin and Lewis together again for *Jumping Jacks II*.

We need a president who can get this country moving, who can give us an energy program that will fill the tank of every big, black Buick from Maine to California at thirty cents a gallon.

If anybody could pull off that miracle, you say, why not get him to raise the dead, too? Stay tuned.

Could he help the farmers? Of course he could. He could lower the price of fertilizer and raise the price of peas so fast the farmers would be dancing in their fields rather than clogging up the interstate with tractorcades.

Same for the truckers. Could he help the truckers in their fight against high diesel-fuel prices and idiotic government regulations? Does a semi hauling hogs pollute?

Taxes. Now there is a problem. The people with the least money pay the most taxes. My candidate would jump on that imbalance feet first.

He knows what it means to be poor. If you think Abe Lincoln had it tough as a kid, you should have seen where this guy was born.

Human rights? My man with the plan for 1980 swears by human rights. No, he doesn't. He doesn't swear. Or drink, or smoke, or lust.

SALT II? Who needs it? The Russians would be eating out of his hands.

Feed the starving? He could do it. It's a long story, but nobody knows more about how to make a little food go a long way.

My candidate could bridge all our gaps, solve all our problems. He could make George Meany a sweetie.

And if elected, there would be no need to change the towels in the White House. He has the same initials as the current president.

Unfortunately, he's probably too busy to run. But the poor sucker who winds up with the job in 1980 will still be expected to live up to all his standards.

It's the new fact of life for the American presidency. If you can't walk on water, you need not apply.

First Sister

You must admit, the Carter family has been one of the most colorful in the nation's history of presidential families. "Colorful" is a nice way to say it.

My first thought when I read about the president's sister Gloria being arrested for playing a harmonica in a late-night diner in Americus was, so let her play it.

That is mild compared to other things I have seen people do in late-night diners. I have seen egg-throwings, plate-breakings, cigarette-machine destroyings, domestic-quarrelings, and one night I saw a man dump his grits on the floor because they were lumpy.

And they most certainly were. When he dumped them on the floor, they didn't splatter. They rolled underneath the jukebox, causing an electrical shortage right in the middle of Conway Twitty and Loretta Lynn's duet.

The president's sister, Gloria Spann—heretofore known mostly for riding on motorcycles and in tractorcades—told her version of the incident in Tuesday's papers.

She and her husband and some friends went to the McWaffles restaurant in Americus early Sunday morning for a late snack. Gloria broke into "I'm so Lonesome I Could Cry" on her harmonica. She would have been happy to play something else, but that's the only tune she knows.

Moments later, a waitress came to her table and asked that she cut out the harmonica. The other customers were complaining they couldn't hear the jukebox.

No way. "Back me into a corner," says Gloria, "and I'll come out blowing my harmonica." That's the old Carter family spirit. Too bad Jimmy can't use it. As many corners as he's been in lately, he'd need a symphony orchestra with extra tubas to get out.

The waitress was no pushover, either. She called the law. It's not every night you get a call to a diner where the sister of the president of the United States is playing her harmonica so the other customers can't hear the jukebox.

But Americus was ready. Three police cars showed up to quell the disturbance. Gloria and her husband were arrested for refusing to leave the restaurant when three carloads of policemen asked them to.

"Good thing I didn't bring my guitar," Gloria said. "I might have gotten five years."

There are two sides to every story, of course. I called the restaurant to get the other side. The manager came to the phone. Her name is Chrystal Bailey. She said there was trouble with harmonicat Gloria and her gang the minute they walked in.

"We have a rule on the weekend you have to order from the counter after eleven o'clock," Chrystal said. "That's because we get so many in here who are wild and drinkin'. I couldn't keep help because they didn't want to go to the tables and serve people like that.

"This group wouldn't order from the counter. They wanted table service. I didn't know who she (Gloria) was, but it wouldn't have mattered. If I gave her table service, I'd have to give it to everybody else, too, and then I wouldn't have anybody still working here.

"They got loud, and they got rowdy. I'm not against anybody having a good time, but they were disturbing others, and they were asked twice to be quiet.

"I can't have that. This place used to be really bad when it was a Hasty House because of such carrying-on. We've tried to get rid of that reputation."

I asked Chrystal Baily if she thought the Spann party might possibly have been drinking before their arrival at McWaffles.

"I do," she said. "I think drinkin' is what it was."

I can't blame Gloria and her friends for that. Not everybody who goes into a late-night diner has been out boozing, but it helps. Sober, you would notice the grease hanging in the air and the tattoos on the cook's arms, and that might spoil your appetite.

Now that I have finally reached the bottom of all this, I think the entire matter has been blown out of proportion. Playing harmonica in a late-night diner is no big deal, but Chrystal Baily has her problems, too.

So what's the big fuss about? A day without one of the president's relatives getting into hot water and embarrassing the White House would be like a day without new allegations against Bert Lance.

What we should do is be thankful there was another Carter to take up the slack until Billy gets out of the hospital.

The Plain(s) Truth About Killer Rabbits

I'll bet covering Millard Fillmore was never this much fun . . .

It's not that I didn't believe President Carter when he reported being attacked by a "killer rabbit" during his recent fishing trip in Plains, but my vast knowledge of rabbits has left me with a number of questions I would like to ask him about the "attack."

I know a lot about rabbits, because I spent a great portion of my boyhood trying to trap one in a box. The idea is, prop a box on a stick and put something under the box a rabbit might like to eat.

When the rabbit goes under the box to take the bait, he knocks away the stick and the box falls down over him, and you have yourself a rabbit.

Sounds good on paper, but it doesn't work. The rabbit will take the bait every time, but he is also smart enough to avoid contact with the stick, and I wasted a lot of good lettuce and carrots and okra—rabbits like okra, believe it or not—before I realized that fact.

What else I know about rabbits is (a) they are lousy swimmers, (b) they are afraid of their own shadows, and (c) the president has been under a great deal of stress and strain lately, which had nothing to do with rabbits until one tried to attack his canoe in the middle of a South Georgia pond.

Since the White House would not even release an alleged photograph of the rabbit in question—some clever soul called it a "Banzai Bunny"—I don't suppose I will ever get the opportunity to question the president face-to-face on the matter.

I won't, however, be pushed aside that easily. When the man with his finger on the nuclear button starts seeing killer rabbits in ponds, I think it is time the American people got an explanation.

I submit the following list of questions to the president as a public service. Dare he not respond?

1. Have you, Mr. President, ever had similar experiences?

2. If so, how often?

3. Are these experiences often accompanied by headaches and/or dizzy spells?

4. Was Hamilton Jordan along on the trip?

5. Did he see the rabbit, too?

6. Your report concerning the incident said the rabbit, as it attacked your canoe, was "hissing menacingly." Did at any time the rabbit make a sound that could be called a "snort"?

7. Did Hamilton Jordan at any time make such a sound?

8. How tall was the rabbit?

9. One foot? Two feet?

10. Think deeply, Mr. President, but could the rabbit have been as tall as SIX feet?

11. When you were a little boy in Plains, Mr. President, did you have, uh, "playmates" that were not really there?

12. Were any of them rabbits?

13. Did you talk to them and play fun games with them, and when Miss Lillian prepared your lunch, did you ask her to set an extra place for them?

14. How old were you when Miss Lillian explained to you that people were beginning to talk about your, uh, "playmates"?

15. As a child, were you ever completely shut out at an Easter egg hunt and the other children threw rocks at you and called you names because your basket was empty?

16. If I say, "Here Comes Peter Cottontail, hopping down the bunny trail, hippity-hoppity, Easter's on its way," what is the first thing that comes into your mind?

17. The report of the incident said you "beat back" the rabbit with your canoe paddle. As a childish prank, Mr. President, did you ever put your cat in a dryer at the laundromat?

18. Are you absolutely certain the animal that attacked your canoe was a rabbit?

19. Could it have been a beaver? An otter with long ears?

20. Bob Dole in his bunny pajamas?

Who's Ready for Teddy?

It should become very obvious while reading this that I do not consider Teddy Kennedy to be one of the great leaders of our time. I do think he looks nice in a suit, however.

There was one big headline after another recently concerning Ted Kennedy's entry into the 1980 presidential race. Some of the news was earthshaking.

• First, Teddy's mom said it was OK for him to run.

• Second, Teddy's wife said if he got elected she would go live with him in the White House. I thought that was big of her.

• Third, Teddy allegedly thinks of President Carter as a "political cripple" and told Carter he'd be smart to go beat a rabbit in the head and leave the presidenting to him.

• Fourth, everybody involved said that was a bunch of "horse manure."

• Fifth, President Carter's mom, Miss Lillian, got into the act, too. She said if Teddy runs she hopes "nothing happens to him."

According to news reports, Miss Lillian's statement, made at a chicken barbecue in New Hampshire, sent a shock wave through the Democratic party.

Jerry Brown was there. He was shocked. State Democratic party chairman Romeo Dorval was there. He was shocked, too. So were Kennedy backers in the audience.

They were so shocked, they booed Miss Lillian (who is eighty-one). I wasn't shocked. I happen to think if you are eighty-one, you can say anything you damn well please, especially if your son is the president and you've been on "The Johnny Carson show" a couple of times.

There has always been something about Teddy Kennedy that bothered me, but I could never quite put my finger on it.

Now I know what it is. It is not Teddy who bothers me so much; it is people who think he would make a good president.

They really don't know why Teddy Kennedy would make a good president, and they boo little old eighty-one-year-old ladies.

"Why do you think he would make a good president?" I have asked a number of draft-Kennedyites recently.

"Because," begins the usual reply, "He, uh, well . . .

"He, uh, LOOKS like a president."

I have heard that, uh, brilliant line of political thinking before. That's how Henry Fonda got his part in *Fail Safe*, but, unfortunately, we aren't casting a movie here.

So what do you LOOK like when you look like a president?

I remember a calendar we had in elementary school. It had the pictures of all the presidents, up through Eisenhower, who had just been elected president.

Ike was bald and looked like he had just knocked his tee shot in the lake at the par-three twelfth at Augusta National.

Herbert Hoover looked uncomfortable, Abe Lincoln had a big nose, and although you couldn't tell it by his picture on the calendar, George Washington had bad teeth.

Teddy Kennedy has long hair, a pleasant smile, and he wears dopey glasses to make himself look more sophisticated. They said the same thing about Warren G. Harding.

I did find one Kennedy backer willing to list some other qualifications Teddy has to be president. Relax, this will only take a second:

• He has a good speaking voice.

• His mother is a courageous person.

• He probably learned a lot about running the country from his two brothers.

Brilliant, I was sitting here trying to think of a way to end this, and I just thought of it. What do you say to people when they fumble and stumble and try to tell you why they think Teddy Kennedy, just another pretty face who got a big break the day he was born, would make a good president?

You say, uh, two little words.

Horse manure.

The Official Candidate Quiz

I wrote this one cold afternoon during the 1980 New Hampshire primary. I seriously doubt I was sober at the time.

Manchester, N.H.

Now that we have completed caucuses in Iowa and Maine and primaries here in New Hampshire, with extensive news coverage of all three, it is high time the voters of America were well acquainted with the candidates who want to be their next president.

This is the beauty of a system that no longer allows its presidential nominees to be hand-picked in smoke-filled rooms. The people finally have something to do with the nomination process.

You may be asking yourself, "I think I am up-to-date on the candidates and the issues, but how can I be certain?"

Worry not. To get a reading on your knowledge of the 1980 presidential race, all you need do is take the following test which asks pertinent questions concerning the run for the White House.

The test, concocted by yours truly, who has been trapped in New Hampshire with babbling brooks and babbling political-types for what seems like months, is simple and easy to understand.

Mark your answers with a No. 2 lead pencil only, and make no unnecessary smudges or marks on the test paper. Correct answers will be printed in the classified ad section of the Fargo, North Dakota, *Fleaflicker-Herald* on Inauguration Day, 1981.

If you answer all the questions correctly, you are qualified to read a Joseph Kraft political column and then pretend you understood it. If you miss less than five, you probably remember who Tom Eagleton was. If you miss between five and ten, you probably think Dewey hung on to win, and if you miss more than that, your penalty should be a week locked in a room with a Right-to-Lifer, an opponent of gun control, Paul Harvey, and two anti-nukes who are protesting the Three-Mile Island incident by refusing to bathe.

The test follows. Take as long as necessary to complete. Ready? Begin.

1. Of the following, pick the most boring aspect of President Jimmy Carter's current administration.

A. His hemorrhoid condition. B. Walter Mondale.

2. Which of the previously held positions would Republican candidate George Bush say helped him LEAST in preparing him for the possibility of serving as president?

A. Congressman from Texas. B. Head of the CIA. C. Ambassador to China. D. Houston Roto-Rooter man.

3. Ronald Reagan was born in:

A. 1612. B. 1613. C. 1614. D. 1615. E. Poland.

4. The primary difference between Reagan and fellow Republican candidate John Anderson is:

A. Grecian Formula 9.

5. Which of the following are LEAST likely to win the 1980 Democratic nomination?

A. Hodding Carter. B. Bo Derek. C. The Fog. D. Jerry Brown.

6. True or false: Republican Philip Crane of Illinois is a figment of his imagination.

7. Who is shorter than a fire hydrant and speaks with a Southern Accent?

A. Little Jimmy Dickens. B. Amy Carter. C. A Vidalia onion. D. Howard Baker.

8. In the space provided below, list all the intelligent comments rock singer Linda Ronstadt made while campaigning in New Hampshire for boyfriend Jerry Brown.

9. Robert Dole is:

A. A senator from Kansas. B. A former vice-presidential candidate. C. A pineapple. D. Wasting his time. E. All of the above.

10. Which of the following embarrassing situations DID NOT involve Ted Kennedy?

A. Chappaquiddick. B. CBS interview with Roger Mudd. C. Harvard cheating scandal. D. Idiotic comments concerning the Shah of Iran. E. Seward's Folly.

11. President Carter has called for an American boycott of the 1980 Summer Olympics in Moscow. Challenger Kennedy's alternatives to that are:

A. Boycotting the 1980 NBA playoffs, instead.

12. One of the lesser-known candidates who ran in the New Hampshire Democratic primary is named "LaRouche." His first name is:

A. Anita. B. Boom-Boom. C. Lady Bird. D. Lash.

13. Former President Gerald Ford would like to throw his hat in the 1980 political ring, but he can't remember where he put his hat. Where would you suggest he look?

A. In his closet. B. In his golf bag. C. Under his pillow. D. On his head.

14. True or false? John Connally.

Political Pain in the "Neck"

Another problem with being president is somebody is always sticking his nose in your, uh, business.

Things have been tough for the president lately. Egypt and Israel still can't come to terms for peace, there has been no SALT agreement, angry farmers disrupted his holiday visit to Plains, and then there was the messy business of kicking Taiwan out of bed in favor of Red China.

I have a great deal of faith in the president, however, and I am certain he will eventually find a way to deal with those lingering issues.

But one other problem facing President Carter could lead to his eventual downfall. It might even become the battleground on which the Republicans decide to fight for reentry into the White House in 1980.

The president of the United States, the honorable James Earl Carter, Jr., has a bad case of hemorrhoids.

I am all for the public's right to know, but I was a bit shocked when the news of the president's condition came blasting over the radio one evening during the holidays.

How did such private information leak out? I called one of my White House sources to find out.

"We tried our best to keep it quiet," he said, "but the president sent Jody Powell out for 'Preparation H' and that was the ballgame."

"Preparation H" is the medicine most prescribed by doctors for relief of the painful condition known as hemorrhoids.

When I first heard the news, I laughed. But then I realized the painful condition known as hemorrhoids is no laughing matter, especially when it is the president of a large, powerful nation who has them.

"He's hurting and he's hurting bad," *Newsweek* magazine quoted a White House spokesperson as saying about President Carter's case.

It is probably not in good taste to discuss exactly what hemorrhoids are and how they affect their victims. But they make it hurt where you sit and often cause drastic changes in the sufferer's personality.

I once worked for a man who had hemorrhoids. Most of the time, he was the nicest guy you would ever want to meet. When his condition flared up, he was Attila the Hun with a hangover.

During a particularly painful bout with his ailment, he attempted suicide in the middle of the office as a means of relief. Only the actions of a quick-thinking secretary saved his life.

Two weeks later, when the pain returned, he fired her. A man suffering from hemorrhoids cannot be held responsible for his actions.

Which brings me back to the president. Suppose he had another flareup in the middle of serious negotiations with, say, Soviet President Brezhnev?

The pain having siphoned his good senses, who knows what the president might say in the midst of a testy situation?

"Leonid, you pork-faced imbecile!" is simply not good diplomatic phraseology.

I can hear the Republicans asking the question of the American people already: Can we feel secure knowing the leader of the free world, the man with his finger on the nuclear bomb, is suffering from the horrid fate and agony of you-know-what?

"It's a ticklish situation for sure," admitted my White House source.

"Ticklish?" I asked.

"Poor choice of words," he replied. "But I think the president can handle it. He's had experience with this sort of thing all his life, you know."

I didn't know. The president has had hemorrhoids all his life?

My source explained. "First, he had to grow up with a brother like Billy. Then, when he was governor, he had to deal with Lester Maddox.

"Now, he's got the farmers on him, the Taiwanese are marching, the Iranian dissidents are mad because he has supported the Shah, Ted Kennedy may run against him in '80, and Barry Goldwater has called him a coward."

But what, I asked, do they have to do with hemorrhoids?

"They're all a big pain in the . . ."

"Neck?" I interrupted.

"Have it your way," said my source.

6

IT'S BEEN ONE HASSLE AFTER ANOTHER

Looking for Mr. Goodwrench

How many days does it take me to screw in a light bulb? Four. Three to fool around with it myself, and one to round up an electrician to finish the job.

A man from the city water department came to my house last week and cut off my water. He had some absurd reason for doing that. I think he mentioned I hadn't paid my bill on time.

I attempted to explain. Maybe there were some goats in the neighborhood, and one was nosing around in my mailbox and ate my payment to the city water department.

You can't explain *anything* to a man with a wrench.

So there I was for a couple of days, with no water. It was a learning experience.

I learned it is virtually impossible to brush your teeth using orange juice.

I learned if you wet your face with milk and then try to shave, the pain will be incredible.

I learned if you don't shower for a couple of days, you won't have to put up with worrisome people like your friends and fellow employees.

I learned if you don't wash coffee cups, something green will grow inside of them.

I also learned that I still don't know anything about anything that is mechanical in nature. I couldn't change the oil in my salad.

241

Here's what happened:

I finally reached the city water department—the telephone there had been busy for forty-eight hours—and the woman who answered agreed with me that it was probably all a big mistake that my water had been cut off.

She apologized on behalf of the mayor and the city for the inconvenience and said if I would pay my bill, along with an additional six-dollar service charge, the man with the wrench would return to my house and turn the water back on.

Naturally, I accepted her apology and her kind offer to right the department's wrong.

I returned home that evening, expecting to find running water. Instead, I found a note in my door from Mr. Goodwrench.

"Dear Sir," it began, "I turned the water back on in your meter. However, I left it off in your property valve because of an indication there was a faucet open in your house.

"You can turn the water on in your property valve. It is located approximately twelve inches down in a metal pipe that is located approximately ten feet behind your water meter. Thanks."

Thank you. But I don't know anything about water meters and property valves. I can barely operate my shower curtain.

I called the water department again, and they tried to explain to me where to locate my property valve. They tried to explain it several times.

"You'd better talk to Mr. Something-or-Other," a woman said. Mr. Something-or-Other became impatient and said, "If you don't know where your property valve is, you'll just have to look in your yard until you find it."

It was raining outside. I searched for my property valve for half an hour. It occurred to me that I wouldn't know my property valve if it walked up to me and played the flute.

I called the department again. It was after five o'clock Friday afternoon. I went into Plan "B." I started crying.

Another half-hour search, and I finally located what I determined to be my water meter. It was located in some tall grass I should cut, but when I pull the starter cord on my lawn mower, nothing happens.

I walked approximately ten feet behind my water meter and, sure enough, there was a metal pipe like the note said. I reached twelve inches inside it and, sure enough, there was my property valve, along with a lot of dirt and bugs and worms.

I suffered a mild coronary, ruined a shirt and a pair of pants, but I finally turned my property valve and immediately felt a sensation of great satisfaction.

I went back inside my house, took a shower, and watered the green things growing in the coffee cups.

I Hate the Beach

I forgot to mention one other thing that will drive a person crazy at the beach. Is there a more uncomfortable feeling on this earth than pulling on a cold, wet bathing suit?

Kiawah Island, S.C.

Every six months or so I get a little crazy in the city and I say to myself, "What I need are a few days at the beach."

So here I am at Kiawah Island, near Charleston. Kiawah Island used to be inhabited by bugs, large birds, and alligators, but then some smart money from Kuwait came in and built condominiums, a golf course, tennis courts, and one of those trinket shops where a lamp made out of sea shells costs $175.

I like my room here at the Kiawah Inn. It overlooks the shimmering Atlantic, and at these prices, I will turn the thermostat down to any level I please.

Scenes from the nearby low-country marsh adorn the walls, and the soap in the bathroom is individually boxed.

At Howard Johnsons and Holiday Inns, the soap in the bathroom comes wrapped in paper. How gauche.

What I don't like about Kiawah Island, and what I don't like about all seaside resorts, is the beach itself. I never thought I would admit this, but I have been a closet beach-hater for years.

What I hate most about the beach is the sand. If beaches had outdoor carpet or Astro Turf, maybe I would feel differently. Sand is the pits.

There is no way to go to the beach without getting completely covered with sand. Sand in your topsiders, sand in your hair, sand in your bologna sandwiches, and if you are not careful, sand in your bathing trunks.

Sand in your bathing trunks makes a person crabby and uncomfortable and causes all sorts of unspeakable rashes.

Once you are covered with sand, it is impossible to wash it all off. No matter how long you shower after a day at the beach, there will always be sand in your bed.

Cracker crumbs in your bed are just as bad as sand in your bed, but I would rather sleep with a South Carolina three-eyed marsh hog than with sand or cracker crumbs.

I also hate the sun at the beach. Two minutes in the sun, and I look like I've been roasted on the devil's own spit. People with nothing better to do but lie around getting suntans DESERVE skin cancer and early wrinkling and smelling like *eau de Valvoline*.

Another thing I dislike about the beach is young, musclebound boys with deep tans who cavort in skimpy bathing suits and throw frisbees. Throwing frisbees is a mindless exercise designed for people with the IQs of jellyfish, which is another reason the beach is no place for the sane.

What's under that water? Jellyfish, stingrays, things with no eyes, things with teeth, like sharks. Once I read what to do in case you are in the water and a shark approaches.

"Do not run. Do not splash water. Do not shout. Wait until the shark swims close enough and then strike it on the head with a blunt instrument."

Fine. I'll just stand here without running or splashing water or shouting, and when the shark swims close enough, I'll pull this tire tool I keep in the pocket of my bathing trunks and belt him right between his bloodthirsty eyes.

I could go on. I could even make a tacky remark like, may a giant oil spill cover every beach in the world and see if I care.

But I won't. A lot of people enjoy the beach. Children, musclebrains, and exhibitionists, for instance.

Let them all go bake their brains. I'll just sit here in my room in my overcoat and play with the knobs on my air conditioner.

Return of the Wethead

If every man in America would stop using his electric hair dryer for one week, we could save enough in energy costs to send a dozen kids to barber school. Think about it.

I took a long look at my electric hair dryer the other morning. It was a Christmas gift, and I cherished it once. Its sleek, modern styling hinted macho, but at the same time said its owner would be a man of sensitivity, a man in touch with the necessity for good grooming habits.

I recall how the handle felt in my hand the morning of that first dry. It fit perfectly. It was a part of me, an added appendage for countless mornings to come.

I began in warm, shifted to medium in mid-dry, and then gunned it to high for the finish. My hair fluffed as it had never fluffed before. One spark, however, and meet the human torch.

I realize there are a number of important issues that probably should be discussed in a forum such as this, but occasionally, the real issues of the day are hidden deep behind the headlines. Occasionally, one must stand and be heard on a matter that at first glance might seem trivial.

The time has come, America, to speak out on the electric hair dryer for men.

It came to me as I stood, nurd-like, holding my dryer to my head. Like all mornings, I had showered and shampooed with a shampoo the fragrance of blossoming apricots, the color of the dawning sky.

This, I thought, is ridiculous. This is insane. This is a horrid, useless waste of time I can do without.

I figure I have spent five minutes every morning for the past five years blow-drying my hair. That is six days of my life spent with Flash Gordon's ray gun pointed at my brain, which probably has windburn by now.

It all began with cosmetics commercials screaming at us on television. Our forefathers rallied behind "54-40 or Fight!" and "Remember the Alamo!" and "A Chicken in Every Pot!" For this generation, it has been, "The Wethead Is Dead!" Pour out your Wildroot Creme Oil, Charlie, it's a blow-dry kind of day.

What followed was a mad rush by America's male population to grow hair. Then dry it. Then spray it so it wouldn't budge in a hurricane. No longer did men comb their hair. They raked it. Hair wasn't "cut," it was "styled."

Ears disappeared from Maine to California, and ten million bottles of Vitalis sat lonely and gathering dust, an oily relic of the past.

Young and old alike, we all bought electric hair dryers. Even athletes and probably truck drivers.

I know not what course others may take, but as for me, I have plugged in my electric hair dryer for the last time.

I despise the effort and time wasted on it, and I despise its high-pitched hum. Put an electric hair dryer to your head and you couldn't hear the 7:05 flight to Cleveland take off in the kitchen.

Left completely alone, I have discovered, hair will dry itself in less than an hour. I will save time, conserve energy, and never be mistaken for a skinny sheepdog again.

I threw my electric hair dryer in the garbage. Along with my banana creme rinse somebody said would give my hair body. I don't want body. Along with my shampoo the fragrance of blossoming apricots. The fragrance of blossoming apricots is for girls and boys who drink whiskey sours and eat the cherries.

Join me if you dare, men. Wetheads, arise again and stand tall! If you must, even slick it down and part it on the side and look up your old barber.

You never know. He may still be in business.

The Doctor, Revisited

My doctor read this and called me in for an immediate reexamination. I was sore for a month.

It had been a long time since my last complete physical examination, and I was in no hurry to have another one.

When I was eleven, a doctor examined me from head to toe before my trip to Camp Thunder and pronounced me fit for everything from overnight hiking trips to towel fights in the shower.

I didn't want to go to Camp Thunder and secretly hoped he would find some horrible malady like bumps on my head, which would have kept me away from camp and couldn't have been as bad as the towel fights in the showers there.

A towel fight in a shower involves inflicting physical harm upon a fellow camper. My boyhood friend and idol, Weyman C. Wannamaker, Jr., a great American, was the king of the towel fighters.

He would wet one end of a large beach towel and fling that lethal end toward the uncovered hindparts of his victim, snapping it back on impact with a resounding, "Whap!"

Bend over to retrieve your soap in a shower with Weyman C. Wannamaker, Jr., and his beach towel, and you would be standing for campfire vespers the entire week.

I had no bumps on my head when I was eleven, and I went on to Camp Thunder. I solved the towel fight problem. I didn't take a shower for seven days.

I sat alone at campfire vespers. But I sat.

I don't know what came over me last week to have another physical examination. Doctors spook me. Their offices spook me. Their nurses spook me, and all their receptionists just got off the boat from Transylvania where their last jobs were in a blood bank.

"You vil take a seat, please," they begin. "It vil only be a little while."

It vil never be a little while. It vil be an eternity if you are as frightened of doctors as I am. Doctors' offices even smell like impending doom.

Last week, while I waited for my doctor, I tried to read a magazine. Why are magazines in doctors' offices always out of date?

I picked up a *Newsweek*. Roosevelt was on the cover. Teddy.

My doctor was a nice enough fellow. First, he asked me a lot of questions.

Do you smoke?

Yes.

Do you drink?

Yes.

Do you eat regular, balanced meals?

No.

Do you get plenty of rest and exercise?

No.

Do you ever get dizzy spells?

Only when I run out of cigarettes or have a drink before "The Today Show" goes off the air.

Then, he took me into a small room with only one door, which he closed, and examined me. He examined my head, my nose, my ears, my throat, my neck, my chest, my back, my stomach, my legs, my feet, and my toes.

I still don't have any bumps on my head, but one of my toes has an ingrown nail which he mashed, prompting a scream. That is how he pays his receptionist. She loves screaming.

He did other things to my person as well, but I can't mention any of them here except to say they were indignities that shouldn't happen to a rabid dog.

"It's for your own good," the doctor said.

Jack the Ripper told his patients the same thing.

Later, he turned me over to a nurse who put needles in me and gave me an X-ray. I have also wondered why, if there is nothing dangerous about X-rays, the nurse who administers them always stands behind a lead screen?

The doctor didn't put it in so many words, but I suppose I will live.

Otherwise, the receptionist—Countess Rubellina in the old country—wouldn't have asked, "Vil you be paying now, or shall ve bill you later?"

"Later, sweetheart," I said. "Later."

Deliver Me From Sausage Balls

I even know people who give cocktail parties you go to before you go to another cocktail party. Isn't being grown-up fun?

Standing around at a cocktail party the other evening, in honor of somebody getting married or getting a divorce or running for president—I forget which—the thought suddenly occurred to me, "I'm sick of standing around at cocktail parties."

I don't have an actual count, but I am certain I have been to somewhere near a million cocktail parties since I became old enough to stop cruising around in a car drinking beer, which is what you do until you become old enough to get invited to cocktail parties.

At first, I thought cocktail parties were sort of neat. The booze was free, and normally in great abundance, and before I had eaten several thousand of those little sausage balls they always serve as an *hors d'oeuvre*, I thought they were quite tasty. Now, the very mention of one makes me quite ill.

And, after a time, I found myself actually dreading cocktail parties and concocting all sorts of excuses to get out of them.

My best excuse to get out of a cocktail party is, "Thank you very much for inviting me, but I'm supposed to be involved in a serious automobile accident that evening."

Americans will give a cocktail party for nearly every occasion and for nearly everybody.

I have been to cocktail parties in honor of Canadian consuls, Japanese piano players, a man from Louisiana who makes duck calls, the birth of twins, the buying of a new house, the selling of an old one, the opening of a play, and the closing of a number of newspapers and magazines and even a used-car dealership. (The owner had liquidated with plans to go into the ministry. It's a long story.)

Regardless of the occasion, however, all cocktail parties are generally alike.

• There is never anywhere to sit down, and it is my firm belief that drinking is a sit-down sort of endeavor.

• You get drunker faster when you drink standing up and are therefore more liable to do something you will regret the next day.

• Somebody always does something he regrets the next day, like saying *Kramer vs. Kramer* stunk, or barging in on the hostess in the bathroom.

• You have to talk a lot at a cocktail party, and the conversation is always the same. Dull, unless someone knows some juicy gossip about somebody who wasn't invited.

• You can never find an ashtray.

• While you are listening to some juicy gossip and eating one of those little chicken wings, which are always near the sausage balls, the little plate where you are supposed to put your bones will be taken away, and you will have to stand there like an idiot holding one of those little chicken-wing bones.

• The solution to that problem is to find a person you don't like and drop the bone into his or her coat pocket while he or she isn't looking.

There simply must be more original ways for people to gather and bore one another.

Charades, for instance. Terrific game. You make a complete fool of yourself, just like at a cocktail party, but this way you have all the guests' undivided attention while you do it.

Croquet. Remember croquet? Everybody gathers in the back yard and knocks the little balls through the wire hoops. Nobody really likes to play croquet because it's a stupid game, but at least you don't have to talk.

I can think of all sorts of alternatives to cocktail parties. Doesn't anybody give wienie roasts anymore? What about hayrides?

Hayrides are for bumpkins, you say. Hayrides are kid stuff. That's all you know.

Once I went on a hayride with Kathy Sue Loudermilk, bless her heart. I was gone six days and woke up in Ocala, Florida, with a tattoo.

That, believe me, beats the absolute fool out of standing around half-crocked trying to talk to a Japanese piano player with a mouthful of sausage balls.

Interviewing Miss Fruit Fly

I admit it. This is one of those columns I wrote because I didn't have anything else to write about. I still don't want to interview any little girl ice skaters, however.

A lot of people call and write suggesting ideas for columns. I appreciate that. It should be obvious by now I need all the help I can get.

But not all the ideas I get are good ones. In fact, some of the ideas I get are insane.

There is a man who writes to suggest a column about him because he is Jesus. You would be surprised how many people think they are Jesus.

"I have followed your work closely," he says, "and I want you to be the first to have my story."

It's a dilly, I admit, but I've already heard it.

Out of sheer curiosity, I called the man who thinks he is Jesus. I got a recording. "This is Jesus Christ," it began. "I have stepped away for a few moments. . . ."

Another group of people who want to be written about are people who think they know who really killed John Kennedy. I think there are more of them than people who think they are Jesus.

"Can you talk?" a voice asked on the other end of the telephone.

"About what?" I replied.

"About what happened in Dallas."

A sports nut, I figured.

"I know who really killed JFK," said the voice.

"Who?" I asked, off the top of my head.

"I'll have to call you back," the voice said. "I hear the nurse coming."

Another group of nuts who want publicity are nuts who own talking animals. Talking dogs, talking cats, talking mules, talking rabbits, talking pigs, and the woman who called to say she had taught her parakeet to recite the pledge of allegiance to the flag.

The parakeet's name was Cindy.

"Cindy's so smart," said the woman, "next, I'm going to teach her to sing 'God Bless America.'"

God bless a milk cow before I'm going to interview a flag-waving parakeet that thinks it's Kate Smith.

In order to save us all a lot of trouble, I have compiled a list of other things I refuse to write columns about. I don't want to offend anyone, but if you were planning to call or write to suggest any of the following, go talk to your cat and leave me alone:

• BALLOON RACES: I am not interested in balloon races. I am not interested in balloon racers. I get all the hot air I can handle interviewing politicians.

• LITTLE GIRL ICE SKATERS: I don't have anything against little girl ice skaters, I just don't want to talk to one. After you have asked a little girl ice skater, "Do you really enjoy the skating?" and her mother has answered, "She just loooooves it," that's the ball-game.

Besides, all little girl ice skaters grow up to marry quarterbacks, which is what can happen if you spend too much time spinning your brain around.

• RATTLESNAKE HUNTS: Television stations love rattlesnake hunts because they can get film of some clod walking around with a sackful of live rattlesnakes and peddle it at eleven o'clock as news. I am interested in rattlesnake hunts only if somebody is bitten at one, preferably somebody from a television station.

I agree with philosopher Dupree Jenkins, who once pointed out, "Finding a rattlesnake when you are looking for one is not exciting. When you ain't, and you find one anyway, now there's an attention-grabber."

• BEAUTY QUEENS: Ever try to interview Miss Fruit Fly?

• MISTREATMENT OF BABY SEALS: If I knew any baby seals personally, I might feel differently. I'd rather help the rattlesnakes. People are all the time milking rattlesnakes, poking forked sticks in their faces and taking them to weirdo churches. You'd bite back, too.

• SOCCER: If we ignore soccer long enough, I am convinced it will finally go away.

• RUGBY: See "SOCCER."

• UFO SIGHTINGS: Don't tell me about UFOs, bring me one. Put it on my desk and let me talk to the driver. Otherwise, go sniff some more swamp gas.

• TROUBLES WITH THE IRS: About this time every year, I begin to hear from people complaining about how they've been screwed by the IRS. I don't want to hear your whining and petty gripes. It is the duty of every American citizen to pay his or her taxes cheerfully and respectfully.

Besides, I don't want to be reminded of what the lousy blood-suckers are trying to do to me.

How I Stop Pedxxx Smookxing

To be quite honest, I did write the following piece without a ciga-rette, and I am proud to announce I finally kicked the nasty tobacco habit after fifteen years. Do I still want a cigarette occasionally? Given a chance, I would eat one.

I am going to attempt the impossible. I am going to attempt to write this entire column without smoking a cigarette. I have never written anything without relying heavily on the soul of tobacco.

The doctor was firm in his insistence I give up a fifteen-year, two-pack-a-day habit.

"And what if I don't?" I asked him.

"A number of things could happen," he answered. "All of them end in somebody collecting your life insurance a lot sooner than you expected."

I have tried to stop smoking before. A friend and I agreed to stop smoking together. We made it eight days. I called his home one evening to see how he was doing. His wife answered the phone.

"He smoked a cigarette," she said. "He was sitting in a chair watching television. Suddenly, he got out of the chair, jumped up on the coffee table, lit a cigarette, and looked to the sky and said, 'God wants me to smoke!'"

It made sense that if God wanted my friend to smoke, He would have felt the same about me.

There are a number of things I can do without having a cigarette while I am doing them. I don't need a cigarette while sleeping, swimming, taking a shower, playing with dynamite, or eating collards.

But write without a cigarette?

So far, I have made it this far, but I have begun to hallucinate, which always happens to me when I attempt to quit smoking. A penguin just walked into the office.

It would be just about here I would normally have a cigarette while writing a column. I need both hands to type, so I would stop typing, pull one out of the pack, light it, take two or three puffs and return to the typewriter.

Sometimes when I smoke while writing my column, I forget I am smoking and the cigarette burns down to a point where it falls out of the ashtray.

That is very dangerous with all the paper that is usually strewn about my desk. Last week, the April issue of *Playboy*, my desk calendar, and a press release from the annual Armadillo Confab and Exposition in Victoria, Texas, were burned to a crisp.

What helped me make the decision to attempt to quit smoking is some news I heard the other night at the baseball game.

I was sitting next to Sports Editor Jesse Outlar, who smokes, and he was telling me Henry Aaron had quit smoking.

"He smoked all those years he was playing ball every day," said Jesse, "and then when he's retired, he decides to give up smoking. If he had quit fifteen years ago, he might have hit a thousand home runs."

But it is more difficult for a writer to quit smoking than for anybody else because smoking sort of goes with writing. I would normally have another cigarette about here while pausing to figure out how to end this piece, which is now into the home stretch.

I think what I will do is type just as fast as I can because thisis a boutto driveme crayz, If I couldhave a cigaretteer ight xxx right now, I notonly would smokeit, I would eat thefil ter.

Ithas also occurred tome thatif I xxx reallyhad to have a cigarette, xxxI couldgo a head and smoooooooke itand who would knowthe difference?

Inother words, I could lieabout this whole thing andwrite how I got through thiscolumn without having a cigar xxxxette, and have allthe cigarxx ettes Iwanted to becasueyou can't seeme whil Iam writing this.

Trust me.

A Case of the Cutes

I am always looking for ways to serve the public. Here, I discuss one of the average citizen's greatest problems: How to tell whose rest-room is whose in a restaurant. Please read carefully.

Historians may look back to the current period of American life and call it our "cute" phase and wonder what happened to all the adults.

We are all driving cute little cars with funsie little names, "Rabbit" and "Pinto" and "Sunbird." Blow their cute little horns and hear the cute little sound: "Beep! Beep!"

We read cute little magazines like *People* and *Us*, and we watch cute little television programs starring cute little people with cute little names like "Mork" and "Mindy."

Imagine trying to carry on an intelligent, grownups' conversation with somebody named "Mork" or "Mindy." I'd rather try to talk to the air filter on a Pinto station wagon.

We also dress in cute little clothes nowadays, jeans and T-shirts and orange sneakers, and we wear them to do cute things like go roller skating.

Bleech!

We even have a "cutie" running for president. He is Jerry Brown, the governor of California. He even thinks he has a chance to win.

How cute.

Restaurants are the worst offenders, however. They have gone "cute crazy." Clowns serve hamburgers and waiters are in pirate suits, and the menu is printed on a balloon you can keep.

Restaurants also serve cute dishes. "Happy Meals" in a box. Seafood restaurants serve "Cap'n's Delight," which is crab meat with hollandaise, and the bottom of the plate has real barnacles.

Zowie, what fun!

You can also get all sorts of darling little drinks before you eat in a restaurant. Piña coladas, apricot daiquiris, rum and Dr. Pepper.

Also, there are those precious little green bottles with nothing but water inside that fuzz-brains drink.

Restaurants have even gotten cute with their restrooms. That makes me very angry. Going to the restroom is a serious matter, and it should be kept as simple as possible.

It used to be that when you went to a restroom in a restaurant, all you had to do was ask directions and then find the door marked "men" or "women" or in spiffy places, "ladies" or "gentlemen." You chose the appropriate door and then walked through it to take care of your needs.

That has all changed. Restaurant restrooms are no longer marked plainly "men" or "women" or "ladies" or "gentlemen." Go into a restaurant that serves Mexican food. The restroom doors will be marked "señors" or "señoritas." If the management is really into "cute," they may be marked, "muchachos" and "muchachas."

It's the same for other restaurants that serve ethnic foods. If you don't speak the language, you could be in trouble.

I suppose people with at least a fair amount of intelligence can usually select the correct restroom in those instances, but there are occasions when the choices are not that clear.

Watch yourself in restaurants that specialize in fried chicken. They often use "roosters" and "hens" on their restroom doors.

I happen to know the difference. I am "rooster." But I have an advantage. As a child, one of my chores was to gather the eggs from the henhouse. You pick up who's what in chickens rather quickly that way.

Others might not be so fortunate as to have that background, however, and there is nothing quite so embarrassing as strolling unannounced into the wrong roost.

I could go on, but I don't want to lose any more of my temper. It is simply time grownups started demanding grownup products and grownup services.

If for no other reason, there is too much else for an adult to worry about today to have to go through potty training again.

Don't laugh. Been in one of those western steak houses lately? Some western steak houses don't even bother with names on their restroom doors. They just have pictures of cowboys and cowgirls.

Whom do you favor more, Roy or Dale?

Careful, Tex. They both wore boots, you know.

7

VIOLENCE: FIVE VICTIMS

Officer Frank Schlatt

Frank Schlatt was a good cop who was blown away in the line of duty. His daughter must be nearly grown by now. And the man who shot him probably doesn't have that long before he is eligible for parole.

To the man who shot Frank Robert Schlatt:

You should have been there Tuesday morning. You should have been there at the funeral service they held for your victim.

Was it easy to pull that trigger? Was it easy to point that sawed-off shotgun at Frank Robert Schlatt and shoot him in the face?

What happened? Did you panic? You and your accomplices were robbing a furniture store. In walked Officer Frank Robert Schlatt of the Atlanta Police Department. You shot him. Three hours later, he was dead.

I want to tell you about the funeral, and I pray to God you read this. You should know about the pain, the heartbreak, the grief you caused.

Officer Schlatt was thirty-one. He was only thirty-one. It's like the priest said Tuesday morning. "How can we explain death when it occurs in the midst of a life with so much potential unfulfilled?" Could you have explained that Tuesday morning?

It was a beautiful spring day. The chapel out in Forest Park was packed with people. That many again waited outside.

You have probably been to a funeral before. You probably know how haunting organ music in the background can be. As the people filed into the chapel, the organ was playing "The Battle Hymn of the Republic."

A number of important people came. The mayor was there, along with commissioners and ex-commissioners and even an ex-governor, Lester Maddox. He sat alone to pay his respects to the man you killed.

There were flowers everywhere. There was even a police badge made of white and blue flowers.

Policemen from all over came to mourn Officer Schlatt. They came from as far away as Phenix City, Alabama. One would tell me, "When a fellow officer dies, it's like something inside you dying. It is infuriating."

You know what he said about you? He said: "I don't see how that killer can live with his conscience . . . if he has a conscience."

An honor guard brought in the casket. Three members of the honor guard had worked all-night shifts, but volunteered to be at the funeral Tuesday morning. That is how they felt about the man you killed.

The priest said something I wish you could have heard. He was talking about death not being final. Officer Schlatt, he said, "was a good man. And you cannot bury a good man."

The casket was bronze. It was draped with an American flag. The honor guard marched in. They wore white hats and white gloves. As the services continued, two members of the guard stood at strict attention on either side of the casket. One was white. One was black.

"These men fight among themselves all the time," said a man who is paid to monitor the police department, "but at a time like this, they all come together."

That should worry you. They will find you and bring you to justice. You can count on it.

I wish you could have been standing with me outside when they brought Officer Schlatt's body from the chapel.

Scripture was read. There was a prayer. The family sat under a tent in folding chairs, just a few feet from the one they loved so much.

There was Officer Schlatt's father. He gazed ahead in shock and disbelief. There was his mother, a tiny, graying lady who wept openly. Another relative fainted.

There was also the widow. She wore black, her shoulders covered in a white shawl. I watched her as she tried to say The Lord's Prayer aloud. She choked on every word. She was such a pretty woman, even in her grief. She was blonde and small. Young widows can break the coldest heart. Maybe even yours.

I wish you could have seen the honor guard fold the flag. Their leader broke down. I wish you could have seen the mayor hand the flag to Officer Schlatt's widow. I wish you could have heard the bugler blow taps.

More than anything, I wish you could have seen your victim's daughter. She is twelve. Her name is Jodie. She cried, too. She cried hard and she cried long.

There was a small flower on top of the casket. It was red and white. When the honor guard folded the flag, they folded the flower inside it.

It was Jodie's flower. She had placed it on her daddy's casket.

You should have been there.

Two Good Soldiers

Islamabad, Pakistan. December, 1979. A group of screaming idiots attack and burn the United States Embassy. Brian Ellis and Steven Crowley, two American servicemen, are killed. Lest we forget.

Citizens have been complaining about the American servicemen who were released as hostages from the United States Embassy in Iran.

They are complaining because the soldiers accepted their releases.

"What kind of men do we have in our armed services today?" a reader asked in a letter to the newspaper.

"Those released from the embassy in Iran should have refused to leave and stayed on to protect the others and to show Iran the American military has the guts and fortitude to stick out any situation."

People who write letters like that have mush for brains.

One, it is rather doubtful that the young soldiers had any choice in the matter.

Two, what could they have realistically accomplished by staying, other than making a few mushbrains back home "feel proud to be Americans"?

Three, if there is so much concern about the courage and integrity of American servicemen, why doesn't somebody write something in the newspaper about the two soldiers at our embassy in Islamabad, Pakistan, who also came home recently?

In boxes.

It's been only two weeks since they died. Would one in a thousand Americans even remember their names?

Brian Ellis, an army warrant officer, died in Islamabad. He was thirty. They found his charred remains in the rubble that was the embassy after the attack.

The exact details of his death aren't known, but a Baptist minister in his hometown of Spring Lake, North Carolina, said Brian Ellis "loved his country and the army. He was committed to the defense of his country."

That is at least a hint that he died trying to protect American lives and American property.

Marine Cpl. Steven Crowley also died in Islamabad, one day after the second anniversary of his Marine Corps enlistment.

He was twenty. The posthumous Bronze Star citation he was awarded included what details the Marine Corps knows about his death.

When the attack came, Corporal Crowley took his post on the roof of the embassy. He was immediately exposed to a barrage of rocks and whatever else the attackers could find to throw, as well as small-arms fire.

He never budged. He was able to give valuable information to those on the inside, and he was able to act as a diversion to buy time for them to reach the safety of the embassy security vault.

A man at Marine headquarters in Washington told me over the telephone, "Corporal Crowley got it in the head. We don't know if he was shot or if he was hit by a flying missile. We do know, however, it was pretty bad. There was some debate about whether to open the casket at his funeral."

Steven Crowley was one of nine children. After his father died, said those who knew him, Steven Crowley helped support his mother and younger brothers and sisters, even when he was in high school.

He was a good Catholic. He was a member of his high school track team. He was on the staff of his high school newspaper. He was an expert cabinet maker. He worked to keep classmates away from drugs.

After his death, his hometown church in Port Jefferson, New York, carried an insert in the Sunday morning worship program, giving other details of Steven Crowley's life. The insert included these words: "He was a thoughtful young man who was personally concerned with the well-being of others."

The reader was worried about what kind of men we have in our armed services today.

I can't answer that, except to say that now there are two less damn good ones.

Morris Galanti

The problem with writing about murder in a big city is you could write the same thing every day. Just change the names. God help us.

The Atlanta police officers at the scene Tuesday morning, the beginning of a bright autumn day, were not in a pleasant mood. They were investigating a robbery murder that had taken place the day before.

Two men had robbed King's Food Market at 559 Boulevard N. E., a small grocery store that catered to lower income customers. Morris S. Galanti, who was fifty-seven, had been in business at that location for fifteen years.

"I thought the world of him," said a man standing outside the store. "It tore me up when I heard what happened. I did all my business with him."

What really did happen is still mostly a matter of speculation. Police think Morris Galanti may have been forced to lie face-down on the floor near one of his cash registers while the robbery was taking place. At least that is where and how they found him.

With a bullet in his back. He died later at Grady Hospital.

One officer was talking about what might be the mood of the killer now. That is apparently important in order to determine what might be his subsequent actions following the crime.

"I'll bet he thinks he's big . . . now," said the officer. "He's killed a man."

"If we could break out the rubber hoses," said another, "we might could put a stop to things like this."

"Scumbags," said a third policeman. "That's what we are dealing with here. Dirty, rotten scumbags."

These things happen all the time in a big city, you tell yourself. Neighborhood grocery stores are prime targets for robberies.

The papers report them the next day, but they are rarely page-one news, and soon another victim has been recorded. A couple of blocks down the street, much less across town, who even notices?

Sgt. H. W. McConnell of homicide was in the store Tuesday morning. He has seen his share of such waste of human life. He finally walked out of the store to the street and leaned against his car.

"Look at the wreath on the door," he said. "Isn't that something? A man works fifteen years and all that's here today to symbolize it is a damn green wreath."

He remembered a similar incident two blocks up the street six years before. An old man had been shot in his shoe store.

"I rode to Grady with him," he said. "Before he died, he could talk a little. I asked him who shot him. He said, 'Man did . . . Man did.'" I said, "I know a man shot you, but who was it?"

"We finally found out they called the one who shot him 'Man.' His dying words gave us what we needed."

There have been no such breaks in the case of Morris Galanti.

"There was a lot of animosity toward the ones who did this when we got here Monday," said Sgt. McConnell, "but it's still hard to get people to talk. They either don't want to get involved or they feel bitterness for the police, too."

How, I wanted to know, can storekeepers avoid losing their lives during a robbery attempt? Should they attempt to stop the robbery? What did Morris Galanti do wrong?

"He didn't do anything wrong. That's the hell of it," said Sgt. D. V. Lee. "But don't ever argue with a man with a gun, and don't ever resist him. Just give him everything he wants. He doesn't have that much to lose by killing you.

"And remember one thing: You can get more money, but you can't get another life."

Good advice. But the wreath, the green wreath on the door to Morris Galanti's store, had already said that.

Patti Barry

I was very angry when I wrote this column. After it was completed, I had second thoughts about running it in the newspaper. Maybe I had gone too far, I said to myself.

But then I thought of Patti Barry again. So young. So pretty. So full of life. It was her birthday, and some street goon gunned her down.

The column received more favorable reaction than anything I have ever written. The letters and calls numbered in the thousands. Not because I said anything new, but because I said what the people were thinking.

In fact, the only negative call I received came for a guy over at City Hall, the mayor's press secretary.

It is four-thirty in the afternoon as I write this. My deadline is approaching. I will never make it. Let 'em wait a couple of minutes.

What I have to say, I have to say. Not for the editors. Not even for you, the readers. But for myself.

I love this city. I left it once. I missed it harder than anything I have ever missed in my life.

I have cried like a baby twice as an adult. Once when I left Atlanta because I knew I had made a mistake, and once when I returned because I knew I had finally rectified it.

But this city is going to hell. It may already be there.

I don't care what the mayor says. The mayor is more concerned about his future political ambitions than the welfare of the citizens of this city.

I don't care what the Chamber of Commerce says. The Chamber of Commerce looks and sees dollar signs.

I don't care what the big-dog police commissioners say. They are the mayor's puppets.

This city is going to hell because you can get yourself killed walking its streets in broad daylight.

The details are elsewhere in this newspaper. Quickly, her name was Patricia Barry. She was twenty-six. She worked for a law firm.

It was her birthday. She and a friend were walking the streets of Atlanta at noon. They were walking to lunch to celebrate Patricia Barry's birthday.

At Peachtree and Forsyth—I walk there nearly every day—a goon shot Patricia Barry dead. "Just shot her," said her friend.

Then, the goon shot himself. He died, the coward.

Patricia Barry was the 185th homicide victim in Atlanta in 1979. My God, we've got two-and-one-half months to go.

What is wrong with this city is downtown is a zoo. A zoo. A month ago, I took an hour's walk from 72 Marietta Street down and around Central City Park and back to 72 Marietta Street again.

Drunks and punks were everywhere. Drunks and punks get crazy. They get mean. They rob. They steal. They kill.

Why doesn't somebody get the drunks and punks off the streets of Atlanta?

Why doesn't somebody, like the governor, order the state patrol back? Why doesn't somebody, like the governor, put a trooper on every corner in downtown until we can go an entire week without a citizen getting blown away?

Why doesn't somebody, like the governor, order the national guard in, if that is what it takes, to make this city safe again?

I am sick of Maynard Jackson. Maynard Jackson complains this newspaper overreacts to the city's increasing crime rate.

Call me, Maynard. I am overreacting to the point my hands are shaking.

I am sick of Lee Brown and George Napper. Let them tell Patricia Barry's family and friends, like they tell the rest of us, about the terrific job they are doing.

The *Atlanta Journal* carried the first story about Wednesday's downtown murder. Near the end of the article was a sentence that read, "The shooting was sure to revive controversy over the safety of downtown streets."

"Controversy"? What "controversy"? You mean there are those who would still question the fact there is a war zone down here?

That is exactly what we have on the streets of Atlanta. A war. The drunks and the punks against the rest of us.

And we're losing, goddammit. We're losing.

8

CRITIC-AT-LARGE

"Dallas": Pass the Trash

I heard from a lot of other "Dallas" fans after writing this. One even sent me a bumper sticker. It read, "Free Sue Ellen."

I stumbled into my very first episode of the television hit, "Dallas," the other evening. I really don't know what I expected.

It sounded like a western—gunfights and a lot of horses and somebody is always getting hanged—but westerns rode off into the television sunset years ago.

Maybe it was quiz show. Guess how high a Dallas cowboys cheerleader can count, and win a weekend at the Fish or Cut Bait Dude Ranch near Tyler.

Or perhaps it was another cop series. Sort of a cow-town version of "CHIPS," which, incidentally, is a cowchip version of Broderick Crawford's old "Highway Patrol," ten-four.

"Dallas" turned out to be none of the above. It is a prime-time soap opera—who's pregnant this week?—and what do you that about that, buckaroos?

Previously, only housewives and lazy scoundrels who wouldn't work could watch soap operas because soap operas were never shown after dark.

But with "Dallas" comes the opportunity for the rest of us to get in on the fun, even the kids, who can learn a lot watching the program, like the intelligence of adults is probably vastly overrated.

"Dallas" is a CBS production, the same network that gives us Walter Cronkite. It sits high atop the Nielsen ratings. It appears on Friday nights at ten o'clock, nine o'clock central. Check your local listings if you live somewhere it gets late earlier.

In case you have missed "Dallas" so far, don't worry. A soap opera is like a large plate of cold, boiled rutabagas. Even if you start in the middle, you haven't missed a thing.

I can, however, offer you considerable background after viewing just one episode.

"Dallas" involves the trials and tribulations of the Ewing family of Southfolk Ranch, which is located a short hop in the ol' Mercedes from downtown "Big D."

There is Jock Ewing, the head of the family, who got filthy rich in shady oil dealings. He is played by Jim Davis, who used to play "Railroad Detective" and whose face looks like it finished second in a pick-axe fight.

His wife is Miss Ellie, who seems like a nice person, but we will probably find out she doesn't shave her legs and spends a curious amount of time hanging out at rodeos.

There is J. R., number one son. J. R. runs the family business now. You wouldn't trust J. R. in the same room with your Doberman.

Sue Ellen is J. R.'s wife. Bobby is J. R.'s brother. Pam is his wife. Lucy is his cute, little blonde niece, who is bound to get invovled in something just awful because she's built like a brick hay barn and has that look about her.

J. R. and Sue Ellen have a lousy marriage, so J. R. is sleeping with Kristin, Sue Ellen's sister. Sue Ellen is no fool. Sue Ellen, somebody said, used to ride the range with Pam's brother, Cliff, but now she has roped a cowboy, whose name escapes me, ooh-la-la.

Bobby, meanwhile, has something going with an old childhood sweetheart, but you can't blame him for that because Pam went to Paris with her boss for the weekend.

Confused? You should be. "It would take a motelkeeper to know who was in what bed in the Ewing family, and why," said *Time* magazine of the "Dallas" plots and subplots.

Utter trash is what I say of "Dallas." Sex, sex, and more sex. The fact "Dallas" sits high atop the Nielsen ratings is further proof our television tastebuds are located south of where they were originally intended.

If "Dallas" were a movie, it would be rated "R." For "rotten."

If it were a sport, it would be love wrestling.

And if I miss tonight's episode, I'll die.

The Demise of Drive-Ins

There are still a few drive-in movies around, but they're not packed like they were in the old days. It is a shame an entire generation of Americans will grow up having never had to learn their way around the back seat of a 1957 Chevrolet.

Bang the drum slowly. An institution passes from our midst. The obituary appeared in last week's newspaper. Drive-in movie theaters were for watching movies out-of-doors. Then I went to one with Kathy Sue Loudermilk, bless her heart. She was a lovely child and a legend before her sixteenth birthday. She was twenty-one, however, before she knew an automobile had a front seat.

Dressed in something tight, Kathy Sue could have stopped traffic at the Indianapolis 500. When she graduated from high school, they retired her sweater.

The last time I was at a drive-in theater, come to think of it, it was with Kathy Sue. I forget what was playing. I remember it didn't matter in the least.

You had to be careful at our drive-in because of the theater patrolman, Hascal "The Rascal" Pitts. Hascal's favorite thing was to slip behind a seemingly abandoned car and surprise the couple inside with his flashlight, the biggest and brightest the hardware store had to offer.

"Ah, ha!" he would scream in delight at his discoveries. On a busy night, Hascal could run through an entire set of batteries before the end of the second feature.

Hascal did have a tough job, but he was paid well for his efforts. He got twenty-five dollars a week and all he could see.

Drive-ins have been going downhill steadily. That much was obvious when the motel industry boomed. Now they have motels with adult movies inside the rooms. That seems a waste. Once the door is locked and the curtains are drawn, most couples don't need an instructional film.

There are people, I suppose, who go to drive-ins simply to watch the movies, and they have gone low-budget, low-quality.

Macon County Line was a drive-in biggie. So was *Return to Macon County Line*. All seven *Walking Talls* played at drive-ins, and *Saturday Night Fever* should have if it didn't.

I checked the current drive-in features in the Atlanta area this week. Wonder why nobody goes to drive-ins anymore? Check this line-up:

• *Tintorera—Tiger Shark*. Another *Jaws* spin-off, filmed in one afternoon in the producer's bathtub. Stars Susan George, Fiona Lewis, Jennifer Ashley, Hugo Tiglitz, and Andres Garcia as a rubber duck gone berserk.

• *Eaten Alive.* Spin-off of *Tintorera—Tiger Shark.* Stars Susan George, Fiona Lewis, Jennifer Ashley, Hugo Tiglitz, and Andres Garcia, who should turn in overtime.

• *Chain Gang Women.* Wrenching story of lust in rural prison camp. Rated "S" for "stinks."

• *Buckstone County Prison.* Wrenching story of lust in rural prison camp. Rated "R" for "ripoff."

• *The Tool Box Murder.* Stars Cameron Mitchell, Pamelyn Ferdin, Wesley Eure, and Andres Garcia as the tool box. Intriguing drama on how to wipe out an entire neighborhood using only a Phillips-head screwdriver and four tacks.

• *Starship Invasion.* Cousin of *Close Encounters.* Greyhound bus stops in Moultrie, Georgia, and strange creature emerges. Turns out it's only Hickey Bates, local druggist, in his new beige leisure suit he picked up on sale in Macon.

A Zillion Light Years From Virginia City

"Battlestar Galactica" didn't turn out to be a smash hit, and the last time I saw Lorne Greene, he was back down to earth in his cowboy boots selling dog food.

This is the week for television's fall premieres. This is also the week the television industry should be made to take the first moon shuttle out of town.

The new shows don't concern me that much. I am too disappointed some of the old ones are back. "Starsky and Hutch," for instance. I can never remember which one is Starsky and which one is Hutch, but I do think they make a cute couple.

I would like to see a combination episode of some of the old programs. Say, "Starsky and Hutch" with "Laverne and Shirley." What happens is, Starsky and Hutch pistol-whip Laverne and Shirley during a Milwaukee drug bust and then are devoured themselves by a Channel 17 rerun of *The Blob.*

The new fall rage is supposed to be a space adventure called "Battlestar Galactica" that premiered for three hours on ABC Sunday night. Three hours is a long time for anything to premiere. In fact, the only uncomfortable television program I have seen last longer is a Braves game.

Space adventure is hot because of the smashing box office of the move *Star Wars*. I never saw *Star Wars*, but a friend of mine did.

"Saw it twice," he said. "Once straight and once stoned."

I think he meant the second time he saw *Star Wars*, he was somewhere out in space himself.

I tried the same tactic Sunday night while watching the premiere of "Battlestar Galactica." I was high on a plate of butterbeans.

Space adventure is nothing new on television. In my youth, we had "The Adventures of Flash Gordon," starring Buster Crabbe, the famous swimmer.

Flash Gordon wore a Peter Pan outfit and battled the evil Ming, who was uglier than both Laverne and Shirley and meaner than Starsky and Hutch beating up a drunk in the park.

What Flash did mostly was save Dr. Zarkov's semi-beautiful daughter—I forget her name—from Ming's soldiers, all of whom looked like tree stumps with beards.

After viewing the opening segment of "Battlestar Galactica," I contend nothing much has changed about television space adventure.

You've seen one television spaceship, you've seen them all. Flash Gordon toured the heavens in something that looked like empty pork-and-bean cans covered in aluminum foil, and so did the cast of "Battlestar Galactica."

And the highlight of any space adventure is still a ray-gun battle. Ray guns make people disappear instead of blowing holes in them. If Starsky and Hutch had ray guns, their programs wouldn't be nearly as bloody, and kids wouldn't have to stay up so late to watch them.

I am conceding "Battlestar Galactica" had a plot, but it was difficult to follow. A group of people-people were involved in a deadly conflict with reptile-people and grasshopper-people and machine-people. The machine-people looked like what you might do with the rest of the empty pork-and-bean cans and a couple of leftover rolls of aluminum foil.

What upset me most about "Battlestar Galactica" was who played the head human. Lorne Greene. The last time I saw Lorne Greene, he was petting a puppy on a dog food commercial.

Sunday night, he stood behind the controls of the "Battlestar Galactica," a zillion light years from Virginia City.

Lorne Greene, who ran the grandest ranch in all of Nevada, who was "Pa" to Little Joe and Hoss, who fought outlaws and Indians and anything else the western wilds could throw at him, wore a black dress and a jeweled necklace.

I suppose a good actor can make any sort of transition, but it is a blessing, I was thinking, Hoss didn't live to see his daddy dressed up like a dance hall girl.

Tom Snyder, by Golly

"Prime Time Sunday" later became "Prime Time Saturday," which improved that show greatly because I'm never home to watch television on Saturday nights.

The big news in television is now there is somebody else to hate and say nasty things about besides Howard Cosell of ABC. He is NBC's Tom Snyder, who has bushy eyebrows and goes around saying, "By golly."

Frankly, Tom Snyder may have pushed Howard Cosell all the way to second place as the television personality who makes the most viewers sick to their stomachs.

Nobody does Howard Cosell impressions at parties anymore. Now, everybody is doing Tom Snyder impressions. He's much easier to do than Cosell.

You sit in a chair at one o'clock in the morning, light a cigarette, and say something stupid.

Cosell could not be reached for comment on the dramatic developments, but a representative at ABC in New York did quash the rumor that Cosell, missing since late December, was recently eaten alive by the defensive unit of the Pittsburgh Steelers at a banquet in McKeesport.

Tom Snyder has been on television hosting talk shows and giving the news for a long time in cities like Milwaukee, Savannah, Atlanta, Philadelphia, Los Angeles, and New York.

Mostly, he has been on television so late at night that small children and normal people had better sense than to stay up and watch him.

So much for small blessings. Besides his nightly "Tomorrow" appearances where he interviews himself, Tom Snyder is now available for viewing on Sunday evenings during prime time. NBC is calling the new show "Prime Time Sunday." They have some real thinkers at NBC.

"Prime Time Sunday" is NBC's answer to the ever-popular CBS program, "60 Minutes." That's like answering a Russian Backfire bomber with a Messerschmidt armed with water balloons.

NBC even had the shameless audacity to hire Mike Wallace's kid for its "PTS" show. Mike Wallace, the star of "60 Minutes," is a Doberman pinscher. Unfortunately, his son Chris has all the forceful technique of a cocker spaniel puppy.

In many ways, Tom Snyder and Howard Cosell are alike. They are both arrogant and oft putrescent, and they use too many big words.

But Tom Snyder is more dangerous than Cosell. He involves himself in serious topics like our gasoline shortage and religious nuts begging money at airports.

All Cosell ever does is ramble on about the Dallas punter's hang time.

I watched Tom Snyder perform during his first two "Prime Time Sunday" programs. I wanted to hit him in the mouth.

He also had dumb shows. He sits in front of a large screen and talks to people from somewhere in Canada and Decatur, Illinois, who are nervous and don't know exactly what to say or when to say it.

They also perspire a great deal. An NBC biography of Tom Snyder says he has "shown a remarkable ability to illuminate issues and personalities." It doesn't say anything about his remarkable ability to make some poor stiff standing in a Canadian oil field sweat like a racehorse.

There was also a "Prime Time Sunday" segment where the program unveiled the earthshaking information that Americans were planning to do a lot of camping on the Fourth of July. It was a thirty-second bit. Unfortunately, it lasted eleven minutes.

But there are usually two sides to every story. There must be something nice that can be said for Tom Snyder.

There is. I decided long ago what this country needs desperately to do is let Elvis Presley rest in peace and quit complaining about Howard Cosell.

Nobody has released a tribute-to-the-King record in months, and Tom Snyder has taken our minds off Howard Cosell.

By golly, that's the best news since Phyllis George disappeared.

"... And Now for the Weather ..."

If local television news were an animal, it would be a duck.
                                           —Old Journalism School Saying.

I was watching the local television news program the other evening, and a man walked onto the screen and talked for nearly five minutes about the weather. *For nearly five minutes.*

Television news has done it again, I said to myself. Gone slap overboard.

I can recall when the entire local television news program lasted only fifteen minutes. "President Eisenhower said today . . . ," and what followed was quick and concise.

No would-be clever repartee between the anchor person and his underlings. No "live-action" reports from the site of an afternoon fender-bender.

You got the news, a few ball scores, and then out came a man in a baggy suit with the weather report. He drew a few raindrops and snowflakes and happy suns on a big map and said, "Today, it will rain. Tomorrow, it won't."

That was the weather report. That was enough.

But local television news is always looking for a better way to do something that was fine in the first place. So Baggy Suit was eventually canned, and what followed him was the smiling "weathergirl-person."

"And what can I do for you, young lady?" asked the station manager.

"I want to be a smiling weathergirlperson," said the sensuous blonde, crossing her legs.

"Can you draw raindrops and snowflakes and happy suns?" the station manager probed.

"No, but I'm a fast learner," replied the blonde.

"You're hired," said the station manager.

So for years, we got our television weather reports from smiling weathergirlpersons.

"What's the weather for tomorrow, Bonnie Sue?" asked the eleven o'clock anchor man.

"A tornado will touch down at noon and wipe out half the city," answered Bonnie Sue, smiling.

But even that approach to television weather is dying. What stations, especially those in major markets, are doing today is hiring full-fledged, card-carrying meteorologists to give the weather, and their forecasts all have the stamp of approval of the American Meteorological Society, which sounds important even if it probably doesn't mean diddly.

The fellow I watched the other evening was one of the new breed of television weathermen. He had all the latest equipment.

He had color radar. He had satellite photos. He gave me the latest information on upper-atmosphere air currents.

He talked about "anomalous propagation," which sounded like something that should be performed only by consenting adults and only behind closed doors, and then he gave a long-range forecast that will last me from now to Groundhog Day.

I don't need that much. I don't want it. I don't understand it. Unless you happen to be a moose, who really cares if a high-pressure system is building over Saskatchewan?

All that Fancy-smancy weather reporting has taken away the mystery of the weather, the anticipation of it. We may as well forget the *Farmer's Almanac* and ignore the old man whose arthritis hasn't missed a rainstorm in fifty years.

Local television news has a basic problem. Because of its competitive nature and because people involved in television apparently do little thinking, it must constantly figure ways to combine show business with some occasional journalism.

That is what brought us giggling weather girls. That is what has now brought us weather reports that are too long and too complicated. That is what will eventually bring us television weather forecasts when somebody will walk out and *sing*.

The Painful Stigma of Roller Skates

This is a good story to read to your children on Christmas. It teaches a number of lessons, including humility, which is an important trait to learn or somebody might bash in your head with a roller skate.

A new movie is out called *Skatetown USA*, and people are flocking to see it because of the recent surge of interest in roller-skating.

I haven't seen the movie, but I have seen the advertisements in the newspaper which show a handsome boy skating with a pretty girl who isn't exactly dressed for cool and damp weather.

All sorts of big-time groups like Earth, Wind and Fire; The Jacksons; and Heatwave, provide the music for the movie; and I suppose what the movie does is portray dancing and skating on wheels as the latest chic activity of the beautiful people.

So maybe it is, but I do want to offer the reminder that roller-skating wasn't the recent brainchild of some Perrier-swilling promotor looking for a way to get the jet set out of their Jacuzzis.

Roller-skating, history tells us, has its roots deep in the nation's poor households, where Christmas was always a low-budget holiday.

When I was growing up, you could always tell the financial status of the community's families by what the kids got for Christmas.

Well-to-do kinds, like Alvin Bates, got bicycles, Erector sets, and air guns for Christmas. Poor kids got roller skates.

Roller-skating, I can imagine, was probably invented by some down-and-out-of-work mechanic who didn't have money for his children's Christmas, so he worked for weeks by candlelight in the dank basement of his three-room house until he had roughed out the first likeness of roller skates for Barney, Shirley, and little Joey.

Now, roller skates cost an arm and a leg, and stars like Cher are performing on them, and little Joey's old man didn't get a dime out of it.

I got roller skates for Christmas for six straight years. So did my boyhood friend and idol, Weyman C. Wannamaker, Jr., a great American.

After returning to school from Christmas holidays, the teacher would always put us through the torturous exercise in which everybody would stand and tell what he or she got for Christmas.

Alvin Bates was always first because he always sat at the front of the room.

"I got a bicycle, an Erector set, and an air gun," he would announce, smirking at the roller-skate segment of the classroom.

"And what did you get, Weyman?" the teacher would ask.

"I'll give you a hint," Weyman would answer. "What has eight wheels, two leather straps, and still costs a lousy three bucks at the hardware store?"

Those were terrible times, but there was one glorious moment I can still recall as if it were yesterday. Soon after Christmas in the seventh grade, Alvin Bates made the terribly stupid mistake of riding past Weyman's house on his new bicycle.

Weyman took it as a personal insult and donned his skates and rolled off in hot pursuit. Color Weyman gone on a pair of roller skates. He caught up in less than three blocks and took off one of his skates and beat large and painful knots on Alvin's head with it.

So let them disco the night away, on roller skates in *Skatetown USA*. Let the bright lights shine, and let the music play.

I will rest in the knowledge it was the poor people who pioneered roller-skating in this country, and it was Weyman C. Wannamaker,

Jr., a great American, who long ago struck the blow for those of us who had to bear the stigma of poverty that roller-skating once carried.

The scene remains so vivid in my mind: Alvin Bates sitting on the curb, holding his aching, bleeding head and crying, and Weyman, filled with sweet revenge, skating away into a hurrying sundown.

Who needs a roller-skating movie when you have already sat in on roller-skating history?

9

STRAY DOGS AND SWEET MEMORIES

The "Marvelous" Le Fevres

After she read this, Eva Mae Le Fevre called me and said if I would drop by sometime she would play me an old gospel song. I've got that down as one of the things I absolutely must do before I die.

I grew up on gospel music, and Sunday mornings have never been the same since there was no more gospel music on the radio to dress for church by.

I'm talking about Hovie Lister's kind of gospel music. And Leroy Abernathy and Shorty Bradford—"The Happy Two"—and a group my daddy loved, The Le Fevres.

You put somebody at a piano, and the sound that emerges is almost rinky-tink. The tall fellow in the back sings a deep, hollow bass, and his short, cherubic friend on the end takes over the high parts.

Gospel music now, I gather, has gone big-time and rhinestone, and send $10.95 for a framed picture of *The Last Supper* that glows in the dark.

I found the obituary in the back pages of the paper last week. I suppose a two-column headline on an obit says the deceased achieved at least some notoriety during his lifetime, but to send Urias Le Fevre away without even a picture seemed an oversight.

He was sixty-nine, and he died last Wednesday of cancer. He spent fifty-four years of his life singing gospel music. And there was even more to him than that.

I talked to one of his neighbors a couple of hours before the funeral Thursday. The neighbor said, "He was a good man, a good father to his children, and a good husband to Eva Mae."

What memories I have. It is Sunday afternoon and the lunch dishes have been cleared away, and supper will be what chicken wasn't eaten and a cold biscuit, if you're lucky. It is the early days of television.

We watched westerns and we watched wrestling matches. And Sunday afternoons, we watched and listened to The Le Fevres.

Eva Mae at the piano. Urias and his brother Alphus in perfect harmony. Only the deaf could resist tapping a toe.

"Marvelous," my father would say, as only he could say it, "absolutely marvelous."

I can even remember the commercials. God bless Martha White Flour for bringing the music of The Le Fevres to my childhood.

Theirs was one of the most successful gospel-singing television shows ever. The show was live for years, but videotape later made it possible for the Le Fevres to syndicate to sixty-five other stations across the nation.

It all began for brothers Urias and Alphus before their teens, when they would sing about the Lord with their sister Maude, back home in Tennessee.

Urias Le Fevre's obituary last week said the group turned down many offers to leave gospel music and go into the more lucrative field of country-western music. The Le Fevres weren't interested; they saw their musical talents as a "Christian calling."

The senior members of the Le Fevre group, Urias, Alphus and Eva Mae, retired a couple of years ago. They had a million miles and a million songs behind them. The younger members of the family are continuing, and one son, Mylon, sings rock 'n' roll.

"I think the family's already left for the funeral," said the neighbor last week as we talked. "I took a half-day off to go myself. Everybody in this neighborhood loved Urias."

But the neighbor had a little time. So he asked, "Want to hear something pretty?"

I didn't have to answer. He already had the record in his hand, and he placed it on the turntable. It was The Le Fevres, and they were singing "He Pilots My Ship."

We listened, and when it was over, I never hesitated with my reaction:

"Marvelous," I brought back from a long time ago, "absolutely marvelous."

Country Mudhole

Journalism students sometimes ask me, "Where do you get your ideas for columns?" They wouldn't believe me if I told them. Inspiration may be found in the strangest of places, even in muddy parking lots.

Statesboro, Ga.

What I happened to be doing in Statesboro has nothing to do with what is to follow. Let's just say Statesboro is one of my favorite stops in the hinterlands, and I have a buddy here who tells good stories and enjoys staying up late telling them.

What this is really all about is mudholes. My buddy and I were going to this place in Statesboro for lunch, and we pulled into the dirt parking lot, and in the middle of the parking lot was a good country mudhole, the likes of which I hadn't seen in years.

We don't have mudholes in the city. We have potholes. There is a difference. Potholes are synthetic. They are caused by cars and trucks driving over cheap asphalt and concrete, and they are a sorry thing that causes much cursing and even damage to the cars and trucks that drive into them.

Mudholes are real. I don't know what really causes mudholes but my guess is they are caused by God's rain hitting God's good earth, and I like that.

Mudholes, like potholes, can be ornery, too. Drive into one with a new wash job on your car, and so much for your new wash job. But anybody stupid enough to drive a just-washed car onto a dirt road where there are likely to be mudholes deserves what he gets.

But mudholes can also offer good times and much recreation. There was a big mudhole in the schoolyard of my youth. When it rained, it was days before the mudhole dried up.

During recess, it was great fun to entice a girl to stand near the mudhole and then throw a large rock into same, thus splashing mud and water all over her dress and shoes and face and hair.

This usually caused the girl to cry, except in the case of Cordie Mae Poovy, the meanest girl in school. Once, in a moment of insanity, I threw a rock into the mudhole and splashed Cordie Mae.

She ran me down on the ballfield and hit me in the mouth and then dragged me back to the mudhole and washed away my sins and the blood that covered my mouth.

Another time, I spotted my dog, Butch, wallowing in the mudhole in my front yard. I jumped in with Butch, clothes and all. My mother beat me for the remainder of the afternoon and through the early portion of the evening.

Butch, the scoundrel who instigated the entire affair, shook himself off and then curled up under my grandfather's truck and went to sleep.

There is one thing you can't do in a mudhole, however, and that is fish. People who fish in mudholes are a little fuzzy, which brings up the name of the legendary "Gums" Garfield, who hadn't had teeth since Roosevelt's second term.

Gums was more than a little fuzzy, and my boyhood friend and idol, Weyman C. Wannamaker, Jr., a great American, enjoyed playing tricks on him.

One day, Weyman said to Gums, "Hey, Gums, you like to fish?"

"I love to fish," replied Gums.

Weyman then explained to Gums about the big mudhole over behind the Baptist church.

"I caught a seven-pound catfish there last week," Weyman said.

Gums immediately went home and got his cane pole and hurried to the big mudhole behind the Baptist church. The preacher, preparing his Sunday sermon, watched Gums for a time from his study and finally could stand it no longer.

He walked out to the mudhole and said to Gums, "Who put you up to this?"

Gums told him.

"Don't you know he was just kidding you?" said the preacher. "There aren't any fish in a mudhole."

"I know that, preacher," replied Gums, as he pulled a clean hook out of the water. "That's why I wasn't using any bait."

I would like to dedicate this column to Cordie Mae, Butch, Weyman, Gums, and the preacher. Also, to my buddy down in Statesboro who bet me a lunch I couldn't write an entire column based on a country mudhole.

"Buddy"

I get sentimental about dogs. I can't help it. If you have ever looked deep into a dog's eyes and felt he was urgently trying to give you a message, then maybe you will understand what I was feeling when I wrote the following.

On a Back Road

My grandfather would have called the dog a "sooner."

"Just as soon stay in the house as out," he would have laughed.

The day was ending, but a long drive home remained. I had stopped for gasoline in one of those all-purpose country service stations, the kind where there is always a little boy with a dirty face and a dog hanging around.

The little boy was buying milk for his mother. The dog was yawning and scratching.

"That your dog?" I asked the old man pumping the gasoline.

"Took up here," he said.

"Fine-looking dog," I went on.

"Smart, too," said the man. "Watch this."

He locked the pump to "on" and walked over to the dog. He held out his hand, and the dog responded by lifting a paw. Smart as a whip, that dog.

"How long you had him?" I said.

"'Bout a week," said the man.

"Any bother?"

"Not a bit. I figure somebody put him our of a car. That little boy that was here buying the milk wants him, but his mama won't let him bring the dog home. Says every dog he brings home gets run over, and it upsets the little boy something awful."

That was an instant memory. I had a losing streak with dogs, too.

There was "Snowball." Every child eventually gets a furry white dog named "Snowball." My daddy bought me mine the day after he got back from Korea. "Snowball" got it from a laundry truck.

"Butch" was later. He chased cars. One day, he caught one.

The vet said "Pokey" had pneumonia. He allowed me to pet my dog one last time, and then he took "Pokey" into a back room, and I never saw my dog again.

I had "Plato." Now there was a dog. I lost him in a divorce settlement, believe it or not. I gave up dogs after that. Missing a dog is a worrisome pain.

"This dog got a name?" I said to the man at the station.

"I call him 'Buddy.'"

The old man scratched the dog, and "Buddy" nuzzled close to the source of affection.

I petted the dog myself. He was obviously of a generous mix, a young dog with patches of white and yellow and black. I tried the paw trick, and "Buddy" responded on cue. Impressive.

I like dogs because they forgive easily, know little or nothing about revenge, and will settle for thirty seconds of care and attention if that is all you have to spare.

I have a house and it is empty, and I have considered adding a dog to the premises. But then I decided that is foolish because I often sleep where I fall, and I do not want a lonely dog on my conscience.

I paid the man for the gasoline and started to get back in my car. The dog was staring at me, or maybe it was just my imagination. Regardless, I stared back.

"You like that dog, don't you?" said the man, smiling.

"That's a fine dog," I said.

"Why don't you take him with you? I got another dog at home."

I gave him five or six excellent reasons why I couldn't and drove away.

It's been a week now. It was dark that night and I wasn't familiar with the road. I doubt I could ever find that country service station again, even if I wanted to.

Which, you understand, I don't.

Saturday Night Fever

News Item: The Ku Klux Klan is on the rise again.

Not much exciting ever happened in my hometown after the trains on the Atlanta and West Point line quit stopping for passengers. This was rural Georgia, early fifties.

But then there was that one week of anticipation, of wonderment, of an amount of sheer terror for boys of eight and nine.

I can still see the posters somebody nailed to fence posts:

"KLAN RALLY."

"SATURDAY NIGHT."

"STAND UP AND BE COUNTED."

"SAVE THE WHITE RACE."

I didn't understand, and neither did any of my friends. I asked my grandfather, the wisest person I knew.

"The Ku Klux Klan," he said, and he explained the best be could, with an unmistakable element of praise in his voice. The Ku Klux Klan, he said, was a sort of private police department.

You take a man who isn't making certain his wife and children have enough to eat, or a man who isn't working when there is work available, or a scoundrel who has left his fields unplowed to escape the sun in a beer joint, then the Klan, my grandfather explained, pays him a visit and suddenly he is more aware of his responsibilities as a father, husband, and citizen.

You don't pass off boyish curiosity that easily.

"What do they do to him?" I wanted to know.

"They flog him," said my grandfather.

"With what?"

I think he mentioned buggy whips and maybe leather straps. He said the visitations normally occurred after dark.

I didn't sleep very well that night. Nor the next, nor the next, because each day more information filtered down about what would happen Saturday night.

Those men, that "Klan," they wear hoods, somebody said. White hoods, with holes for their eyes and their mouths.

They burn crosses.

Sometimes, they burn people. The story was all about, unconcealed from the tenders who hung on every word. A black man—only nobody said "black man"—had been accused of something called "raping" a white woman up the road in the county seat some years before.

The Ku Klux Klan took care of him, the story went. They nailed his scrotum—only nobody said "scrotum"—to a stump and gave him a rusty razor blade and then set the stump on fire.

My grandfather said he doubted any such thing actually happened.

"You stay away from there Saturday night," my grandfather said.

Three of us, on bikes, were the first arrivals. We hid behind a clump of trees.

Spectators began piling in from all over, from as far away as LaGrange and even Columbus. They came in cars and on the backs of flat-bed trucks to an open field that was soon packed with humanity, or something that at least resembled it.

The three of us, we trembled when out of the darkened woods came a marching band of hooded men. Their torches lit the night.

They sang "Onward Christian Soldiers" as they marched.

The men aligned themselves shoulder-to-shoulder toward the crowd. One of the men stepped forward and began to speak about things my grandfather had not mentioned in his explanation. Race-mixing. Mongrelization, whatever that was. Nigger-this. Nigger-that.

An old man sat down front and said a lot of "Amens." Some older boys in the back were drinking something from a fruit jar.

When the speaker finished, the other hooded men set a torch to the ground, and a cross of flame errupted. The rally was closed with a prayer.

My grandfather was waiting for me when I returned home.

"You go to the Klan rally?" he asked.

I admitted my disobedience. It wasn't necessary. I was still shaking.

My grandfather took me into his arms. There was a long quiet. And then he said softly, but firmly, "Don't be afraid. Yellow cowards can't hurt you."

My grandfather, holding a frightened little boy and changing a long-held attitude, needed to hear himself say that, I think now, just as much as I did.

Ode to a Church Fan

After this column appeared in the newspaper, I received nearly a hundred church fans in the mail. This sort of work does have its benefits.

Somebody took a poll the other day concerning how Americans feel about going to church during these trying times, and the published results said the takers and the leavers were split something like 50-50.

I polled myself and decided I still enjoy going to church because it's OK to sing out on the choruses, but there are some things about the modern church that bother me.

In some churches, for instance, sermons are shortened during the football season so nobody will miss a one o'clock kickoff, and let us all stand and sing the first and third verses of "Drop Kick Me, Jesus, Through the Goalposts of Life," which, in case there are any doubters, is a real song.

You can also tithe with a credit card nowadays, and that seems almost too convenient and impersonal, and most churches—even the little white frame country churches where you can still hear an occasional "Amen!" from the back row—have adopted progressive attitudes toward air-conditioning.

So it's more comfortable in church today, but air-conditioning giveth, and air-conditioning taketh away. Gone for good are those paper fans with the wooden handles that were always available in the hymnal racks on the backs of pews.

It never bothered me to be hot in church because I thought being hot in church was a part of God's Great Plan. Sweat it out, brother, because that's just a sample of what awaits the backslider.

Down home on August Sunday morning, the church is packed, and the message from the pulpit is fire and brimstone, and the congregation squirms as one.

You can *feel* the fire. You can *smell* the brimstone, and the closer the preacher gets to the everlasting flames, the faster the fat ladies in their print dresses fan themselves.

But there were other uses for church fans besides fanning away the Devil and the dog-day heat. You could swat noisy children and flies with church fans.

"Goat" Rainwater used to chew on the wooden handles, but "Goat" was always chewing on something like pencils or crayons. My mother said he probably had a vitamin deficiency.

A person could also learn a lot from a church fan. I learned what heaven looks like. The fans in our church were provided by the local funeral parlor, and at election time, a politician or two would bring in a batch.

On one side of a church fan would always be a picture of Jesus sitting with children and a lamb or two and a pony in a soft meadow near a brook.

That was obviously heaven to an eight-year-old, and I would stare at that picture during the sermon and wonder if pony rides were free when you crossed over Jordan. Certainly, I finally decided. That's why they call it "heaven."

On the other side would be the commercial message of the funeral parlor or the politician who had placed the fans.

"Hillside Funeral Home. All Insurance Policies Honored. Twenty-four Hour Ambulance Service. Ask About Our Chapel Rates."

Or, "Elect Buster Knowles State Senator. Veteran. Family man. Deacon. Honest."

Buster Knowles wasted a lot of money providing church fans, because he was never elected. He always included his smiling countenance on his fans, and he looked too much like the crooked Indian agent on "Tales of Wells Fargo."

Fortunately, I have what is probably one of the last church fans. A person who knows of my concern for their demise gave me one, and I am forever in his debt.

One Sunday soon, I may even take my fan to church, and in case the sermon runs a little long, I can stare peacefully at the picture of heaven while the rest of the congregation sweats through a hell of a thought:

God and Jimmy the Greek forbid, but if the preacher doesn't stop in five minutes, there goes the opening segment of "The NFL Today."

The Last of the North Georgia Trout Hounds

Another dog story, mostly true.

Suches, Ga.

Never take a dog trout fishing. I know that; all experienced trout fishpersons like myself know that.

But the dog, who lived up on the hill from where I was hiding from civilization, had followed me around all day and we had become fast friends.

The dog had a number of pleasing characteristics, one of which was he didn't beg or whine when I opened a can of Vienna sausages and a package of soda crackers for lunch.

I despise begging, whining dogs. Plus, I despise sharing my Vienna sausages and soda crackers with any living thing.

Ah! The North Georgia mountains in the springtime. I am in a peaceful valley with a trout stream running through it. In the morning, a mist hangs over the valley, but soon the sun will burn the mist away and the brilliant surroundings will look as if they belong on an artist's canvas.

The afternoons are for rocking on a porch and for dozing off and for wondering why, if such settings are so gorgeous and peaceful, so many of us insist upon living in cities.

Maybe the answer had come from a young member of the family up the hill who owns the dog. She had mentioned that she will be graduating soon from the little high school down the mountain. I asked her what her plans would be afterwards.

"Leaving," she answered. "The only thing to do around here is raise collards."

I said raising collards was an honorable and worthwhile endeavor, but I don't think she heard me. We all go off to cities when we are young, because we don't know any better.

Then, we never quite summon the courage to get back out, because we can't get used to the idea of living more than four blocks from a convenience store.

Back to the dog. As sundown approached, it was time I tried to remove some of the trout from the stream. The dog followed me.

The reason you don't take a dog trout fishing is because dogs bark and scare off all the fish. I didn't read that anywhere. It is just a fact of nature that makes perfect sense to me.

"Go back," I shouted at the dog, but the dog ignored me.

I waded into the stream and made my first cast. The dog waded into the stream, too. One of two things was happening.

Either the dog had become so fond of me, he had to be at my side every moment, or I had stumbled upon one of the rarest of all breeds of dogs, the long-eared, North Georgia trout hound.

I'll keep this short. I waded on up the stream, and the dog waded with me, and, sure enough, the dog had a barking attack and so much for catching any fish.

I gave up after an hour and walked back to my porch and started rocking again, the dog still at my side. Soon, however, I heard the people up the hill call the dog to his dinner.

The dog forgot about our comradeship in the stream and his infatuation with me and left me alone with another can of Vienna sausages and another package of soda crackers, which the dog obviously didn't care for in the first place. Neither did I at the moment. I had planned on trout.

Later, as deep night fell over the valley, I wished for just a moment I was back home in the city. The city does have its advantages, you know. One is that I live only four blocks from a Del Taco.

I hope they fed that damned dog collards.

Gobbledygook

A warm Thanksgiving message about how to get even with a turkey of a neighbor.

I have no idea what finally became of the old coot, but I always think of him around Thanksgiving because he was the first turkey I ever met.

I'm not certain of the exact characteristics of a person who qualifies as a turkey, but I can spot a turkey person when I see or hear one.

Jerry Brown, governor of California, is a turkey, for instance. So are Anita Bryant and Reggie Jackson, the ballplayer, and anybody who would go on television to advertise his used car lot.

The aforementioned old coot was really a turkey, however, because besides being utterly obnoxious and full of any number of unmentionable stuffings, he also raised turkeys.

Turkey turkeys, the kind that have feathers and make dumb, gobbling sounds.

He was our neighbor when I was a kid, if you can call somebody who constantly complains and constantly makes a nuisance of himself a neighbor.

He lived in a large, white house. His backyard was where he kept his turkeys, maybe 300 of them. His pen bordered my grandfather's bean patch.

Let me tell you some things about turkeys:

• Turkeys don't have very much to do, so they gobble a lot.

• One turkey gobbling isn't a problem. Three hundred turkeys gobbling at once, twenty-four hours a day, is enough to wake the dead and drive the living slap crazy.

• Turkeys smell.

• Turkeys are easily spooked.

• A nervous turkey is a skinny turkey. That costs the turkey farmer money and makes him nervous.

• There is nothing more impossible to deal with than a nervous turkey farmer.

One of the local churches saved its money and bought a new bell. Our turkey farmer neighbor complained every time the church rang its new bell.

It spooked his precious turkeys.

My grandfather had a tractor. He used it in his bean patch, which bordered the turkey pen. Whenever my grandfather would plow in his bean patch, out would come the featherbrain, ranting and raving.

The sound of the tractor bothered his stupid turkeys.

I used to play a game in my front yard. I would throw rocks into the air and hit them with a broomstick and make believe I was a member of the 1959 Dodgers lining a shot off the wall at Comisky Park against the White Sox in the World Series.

One afternoon, Duke Snider ripped an Early Wynn hanging curveball over the bean patch and over the fence into the turkey pen.

The rock caught an unsuspecting turkey flush. Now, there was one less turkey to gobble all night, but I had to pay for the damage by handing over my allowance to gobblebrain for six months.

There was, however, one subsequent moment of revenge. In the stillness of the midnight, a child who shall remain nameless crept across my grandfather's bean patch to the turkey pen.

He lit an entire pack of Black Cat firecrackers and threw them in amongst the turkeys.

Gobblegobblegobblegobblegobble!" went the turkeys.

"Arrrrrrrrrrgh!" screamed the angry turkey farmer running out of his house still in his pajamas.

You, of course, will be eating turkey Thursday. I'll just have a ham sandwich and laugh at the satisfying memory of once having watched 299 turkeys and one old buzzard have a group nervous breakdown. Feathers may still be flying.

10

WOMENFOLK

One Rear End to Another

I received a very nice letter from Ann Landers after this article appeared. She thanked me for mentioning her name and then gave me some of her famous advice: "Find yourself another line of work."

I never miss Ann Landers in the newspaper because she always has an answer for any questions you can imagine:

"Dear Ann Landers,

"My husband came home last night with lipstick on his collar. When I asked him about it, he said he didn't know how it got there. I knew he was lying, so I broke his arm.

"Did I react too strongly, or should I have broken his other arm, too?—Big Hilda, Syracuse."

"Dear Big Hilda,

"It depends. If this was the first time your husband came home with lipstick on his collar, I would have to say you may have overreacted. A good punch in the belly would probably have sufficed.

"But if he makes a habit of coming home with such 'evidence' showing, I think you may have let the little worm off lightly."

The other day I was reading Ann Landers' column, and there was a letter from a woman in White Plains who asked:

"What is happening to our culture with so much emphasis on female rear ends? A person can't turn on the TV without seeing a close-up of a woman's derriere."

To which Ann Landers answered, astoundingly: "I don't have the slightest idea."

Imagine Ann Landers being stumped!

Frankly, it wasn't that tough a question. The woman from White Plains told Ann Landers she had seen an ad for jeans on television that had "popped my eyeballs."

She also said she had seen other ads for things like fanny smoothers, fanny shapers, and fanny padders.

"What," the woman went on, "is the explanation for this intense preoccupation with the fanny?"

I'll take it from here, Ann.

This "intense preoccupation" with the fanny is really nothing new. Men have always ogled women's most movable part, and with the new assertive attitude of the modern-day woman, we have learned the male hindpart is quite interesting to the female.

As far as more female rears on television these days, the answer there is simple:

Women buy a lot of things that have to do with their rears—jeans, pantyhose, girdles, diet foods, disco records—and men don't care what is being sold as long as they get a good look at a nice pair of hips occasionally.

There is one commercial that immediately comes to mind. Two women are discussing a particular undergarment that leaves no tell-tale rings or bulges when they walk around in their tight-fitting slacks.

But you never see the two women. All you see is their rear ends.

FIRST REAR END: You don't look like you are wearing anything underneath your tight-fitting slacks.

SECOND REAR END: Of course I am, silly. I'm wearing new Underwonders. No tell-tale rings, no bulges, and the freedom they give me is just fantastic!

A lot of people, like the woman in White Plains, might think a commercial with two walking rear ends is dumb and tasteless, but I'll take it any day over the one where you see the inside of a pipe being unclogged by a glob of Drano.

There is nothing dirty about the human tushy, and unless it reaches double-wide, mobile home proportions, it can be a thing of beauty.

I would advise the woman from White Plains to go water her petunias and stop sweating the small stuff. And I find it rather refreshing, incidentally, that the world's biggest know-it-all, Ann Landers, sometimes falls flat on her can just like the rest of us.

When You Gotta Go

It is my understanding that the female employees at Cagle Poultry Company and their management finally came to an agreement on who could go to the restroom when and for how long. Behold, another victory for human understanding.

I am having a difficult time deciding which side to take in the great debate at a Macon poultry processing plant over employees' restroom privileges.

Nearly two hundred workers have walked off their jobs at the Cagle Poultry Company after the plant manager, a man, sent around a memorandum advising the workers, mostly women-persons, that terrible things could happen to them if they didn't cool it on trips to the company restrooms.

Length of visits also get a mention. One company official was quoted as saying time wasted by employees in the restroom had cost his firm "thousands of dollars."

I don't doubt that. Over the years, I have noticed women tend to spend a great portion of their lives inside restrooms.

You take ball games and concerts. Rarely are there lines to the men's rooms at ball games and concerts. But there are always lines to the women's.

I have no idea what a woman does once inside a restroom at a ball game or concert, but it takes forever if you are waiting for one to come out.

Previously, I have been squarely behind the idea of installing a thirty-second clock inside women's restrooms.

On the other hand, there are some areas where I believe the less rules and regulations, the better for all concerned. Restrooms are one of those areas.

Through one of my reliable sources in Macon, I have obtained a copy of the Cagle Poultry Company memorandum involving "abuse of emergency restroom privileges." Those privileges, notes the memorandum, are spelled out precisely in Plant Rule No. 39.

The memorandum was signed by Malcolm Clark, plant manager, who issued the following new guidelines:

"Any employee will be allowed to visit the bathroom eight times in any four-week period, with a five-trip limit in any two-week period of the four weeks.

"Maximum time away from job is five minutes."

Mr. Clark also stated what would happen to those radicals who didn't follow his new guidelines:

"First offense: Verbal warning.

"Second offense: Written warning.

"Third offense: Three days off without pay.

"Fourth offense: Discharge."

That's not all. The crafty plant manager has also devised a way to insure that workers do not abuse their five-minute restroom time limit.

Each employee is to be issued a "bathroom card"—or "B-card"—to be kept in a rack next to a time clock outside the restrooms. It is to be the responsibility of all employees to clock in upon entering the restroom and to clock out once their business has been conducted.

"Special guards" are to make sure nobody tries anything tricky.

"First offense: Disciplinary layoff.

"Second offense: Discharge."

There is, of course, the sticky situation of employees who have to visit the restrooms in order to take medicine. Mr. Clark thought of that.

The memorandum states that if an employee needs additional visits to take medicine, the employee must have a note from a doctor. If after three weeks the problem is not corrected, the employee gets a leave of absence to correct it.

Company officials weren't talking to reporters Friday. Workers said the rules were "unjust and demeaning." Both sides were meeting—along with Labor Department representatives—to work out a possible solution.

Don't compromise, girls. I think I have decided whom to back here. Work me like a dog. Cut my pay. Steal my pension. But tell me I can't go to the restroom when I'm damn good and ready, and you can take Plant Rule No. 39 and flush it.

Will You Still Respect Me in the Morning?

Quite frankly, I never saw anything wrong with a woman calling me for a date. In fact, I encouraged it. I wonder why nobody ever called?

One of the papers last week ran a series of articles for its women readers entitled "How to Meet Men . . . Now That You Are Liberated."

One part of the series caught my eye because it was about how a liberated, single woman should go about asking a man for a date and what she should suggest they do if he accepts.

"Why should a woman sit passively by the telephone waiting for a man to call her for a date?" the author—apparently a liberated, single woman—asked.

"No reason," she answered herself, "when a woman can make the first move."

I agree. And as a single male, I would more than welcome women calling me to ask for dates. I have spent a great portion of my life calling to ask them.

I want revenge.

I want *them* to hear what mocking, hysterical laughter sounds like on the other end of the telephone.

I want *them* to feel the pangs of regret and embarrassment when a voice says, "You must be outta your mind, Horseface."

I want *them* to experience the intense rejection when the object of their affection suggests further efforts would be fruitless, as in "Bug me one more time, creep, and I'm calling the cops."

It's no picnic asking people for dates, you know, and I simply do not understand why so many of the women I have honored with an offer of my company have thought it necessary to respond abruptly and often downright crudely.

But forget the revenge. I hold no grudges. I will even make it as easy for you as I possibly can.

Don't sit around pondering over what to suggest for our rendez-vous if I see fit to accept your invitation. Over the years, I have suggested a number of fun and clever things I like to do on dates.

As you will see, the dimwitted women who have turned down these opportunities don't know a good time when they are handed one on a silver platter.

When calling, order by number, please:

1. COOKING MY SUPPER: My favorite meal is country fried steak smothered in sawmill gravy, creamed potatoes, butterbeans, squash, spring onions, thinly sliced tomatoes, and unsweetened ice tea.

After supper, do not worry about thinking of something else for us to do. After a meal like that, I would prefer to lie down on the couch and take a little siesta.

2. RUB MY BACK.

3. WATCHING BALL GAMES ON TV: One of my favorite things to do on a date. Make sure the beer is cold and plenty of snacks are within reaching distance of my seat in front of the television.

If you would prefer to do something else while I watch the ball game, that is fine. Just be sure you're back in time to start the fire in the grill.

4. DOING MY LAUNDRY: When you have a break between cycles, maybe I could tell you some of my favorite jokes.

5. HANGING OUT WITH SOME OF MY FRIENDS: We'd treat you just like one of the guys, unless we decided to go to a beer joint, of course. You could wait in the car and read one of those women's magazines that tell you how to avoid getting stretch marks.

6. FISHING: I like to fish, but I do not like to bait my hook, because sometimes when you stick a hook into a Louisiana Pink, they squirt at you. If you will bait my hook for me, I'll let you borrow my new scaler when you clean the fish.

7. WASHING MY TRUCK: Real fun on an afternoon date. Afterwards, we'll go for a spin. I would let you ride up front with me, but that's where my dog sits.

8. LISTENING TO MY ALBUMS: Soft lights and the Statler Brothers. This is what I do when I feel really romantic. Another glass of Ripple, my pet?

9. GOING BOWLING: Lots of laughs and it won't cost you much, except for the beer I drink and shoe rentals.

10. FOOLING AROUND: But promise you'll still respect me in the morning.

Mayor Hot Lips

This was one of my favorite political stories of the year. Incidentally, it had a happy ending. Teddy Kennedy rode Jane Byrne's endorsement to a bellyflop in the Illinois Democratic primary.

Chicago Mayor Jane Byrne's leap from the Carter camp to the Ted Kennedy fold obviously has major political implications for the 1980 presidential election. But it also says something else scary.

It says that men, even the president of the United States, are still stupid when it comes to reading the intentions of women.

To get the full impact of the situation, let us review exactly what happened in the Byrne-to-Carter-and-then-to-Kennedy escapade:

A few weeks ago, President Carter got all dressed up in his tuxedo and flew to Chicago to appear at a fund-raising dinner for Mayor Byrne.

Mayor Byrne got all dressed up too. She wore her white party dress. And a good time was had by all.

Mayor Byrne said she thought the president was a swell guy and knocked everybody on his tomato aspic by saying—so the Carter people thought—she would support her dinner guest for the 1980 Democratic nomination.

President Carter then strode to the podium and talked about what a terrific job Mayor Byrne is doing in Chicago and promised her some big federal grants for her city.

The back-scratching out of the way, Mayor Byrne then kissed the president. I saw her do it on television. She put one smack on the old boy, and he grinned from the Loop to downtown Gary, Indiana.

"Do you think she really meant it when she said she would support you?" an aide asked the president on the flight back to Washington.

"How can you ask such a question?" the president shot back. "She kissed me, didn't she?"

It was only a matter of days before Mayor Byrne had announced she had changed her mind and would now lend her support and that of the Chicago Democratic "machine" to Ted Kennedy.

President Carter should have known better, of course, but then he is just a man, and men are always naive when it comes to being kissed by women.

Men have always thought if a woman kisses you, it means something special. It means she is your girl, she will go with you to the prom, she will give you something nice for your birthday, she will hold your hand in the moonlight.

She won't go around kissing everybody else.

Baloney. I still remember my first kiss. It was from Kathy Sue Loudermilk, the school sex symbol. I felt the earth move.

What I really felt was a half-dozen other guys lining up to be next.

What women have always known about men is that if you kiss one of the big oafs, he'll be eating out of the palm of your hand.

I had hoped that when a woman reached the high position of mayor of a major city, she would no longer resort to such tactics, but Mayor Byrne's plot is evidence I was only dreaming.

The president came courting, and Mayor Byrne played him for the fool. She cooed and smiled and lured him into her web and then "sealed" their new partnership with a kiss.

My Chicago sources tell me Mayor Byrne has used this technique all along. Since she has been mayor, they say, she has kissed practically everybody in town, including a number of city officials who thought getting kissed by the mayor was a sign of job security, only to find their desks cleaned out and the doors to their offices locked while the mayor's lip prints were still fresh on their cheeks.

Whether Ted Kennedy can keep Her Two-Facedness on his side remains to be seen, but at least the Kennedy people are trying to learn from the Carter mistake and the mistake men have been making since the Garden of Eden.

A memorandum has been circulated from Kennedy campaign headquarters to all male Kennedy workers and to the senator himself, detailing rules to follow in case of any contact with Mayor Byrne of Chicago.

"If she puckers," goes Rule No. 1, "run for your life."

Plowing Up the Cornrows

I wonder if women really appreciate it when men take the time to give them guidance and counseling like this:

Normally, I try to refrain from any comment concerning the latest in women's fashions and style. There are a couple of reasons for that.

One, my taste in that area tends to be a bit tacky. For example, I miss the hot-pants-and-white-boots look, and there is nothing like a dame in short shorts and high heels.

Two, it doesn't do any good to tell women what they should wear and how they should look. Women simply won't listen to such constructive criticism.

If women would listen, we would never have had to endure the sack dress and that awful period when all coeds were wearing baggy blue jeans, sweatshirts, and combat boots in an apparent effort to look like female versions of "Skag" on the way to the blast furnace.

Despite all this, however, I no longer can remain a silent observer, because now women are doing something really stupid. I don't care how many letters and calls I get from fire-breathing feminists, I'm going to say this anyway:

The Bo Derek braided look, the "cornrow" hairstyle that apparently is about the sweep the nation, is absolutely hideous.

Allow me to bring those who have been sleeping for a couple of months, or who don't read *People* magazine or watch the Phil Donahue TV show, up to date.

This movie called *10* came out, see. It starred a young woman named Bo Derek, who since has become the nation's latest lust-object, replacing Farrah and the blonde cutie on "WKRP" and other assorted, curvaceous airheads.

The movie's plot would bore you, so all that is really necessary to know is that this "Bo" (silly name for a girl) wore her hair in "tightly woven plaits, laced with beads," as *People* magazine described it.

I can describe it better. As appealing as the child most certainly is from the forehead down, her hair looked like somebody had made a terrible mistake.

Frankly, her hair looked like something the Chinese might use to count on, or the result of shampooing with Drano.

But this ridiculous Medusa-like hairstyle called the "cornrow"—a fairly appropriate name, I might add—is spreading like a bad case of dandruff, and it must be stopped. Otherwise, we might soon be up to our eyeballs in once-attractive women who have all become rope-heads.

There are plenty of reasons, my sisters, not to give in to what is nothing more than a Hollywood-bred fad. Please pay attention while I list them:

1. If you want to make yourself appear to have just hit town from another planet, there is a method much less drastic than having your hair cornrowed. Have one of your eyes moved to the middle of your head, for instance.

2. A cornrow at most Hollywood beauty salons can cost as much as $400, says *People*, and can take up to ten hours to complete. For four hundred smackers, you can have your entire chassis rebuilt with money left over for four new pairs of pantyhose.

3. Cicely Tyson, the brilliant actress, also is a gorgeous woman. There was a picture of Cicely Tyson in *People* magazine with her hair in cornrows. She looked a lot like Stevie Wonder.

4. Cordie Mae Poovy, a girl in my school, was the first female in this country to wear her hair in cornrows. That's because her father ran a dairy farm and one afternoon she got her head caught in one of the milking machines. We used to spend recess throwing rocks at Cordie Mae Poovy.

5. Experts are saying if you wear your hair in a cornrow for too long, all your hair might fall out.

6. I hope it does.

My Angel

I gave Billy Bob Bailey the honor of announcing my third marriage, which occurred on February 10, 1980. At this writing, some six months later, we are still blissfully happy. And they said it wouldn't last . . .

Fort Deposit, Ala.

Billy Bob Bailey is my name and plumbing is my game. People around here like to say, "If it'll stop up, ol' Billy Bob can unclog it."

They got that right. You take Mrs. Arlene Watts' kitchen sink. Mrs. Watts, a lovely child who was once named Miss Fort Deposit Seed and Feed Show Princess, has had all sorts of problems with her kitchen sink lately.

As a matter of fact, that sucker has backed up every afternoon for two weeks, and Billy Bob has been out to her house every day for hours at the time, and I've just about wore my new auger slap out.

I think I finally got the job completed, though, and I'd bet my dog Rooster against a one-eyed mule that sink don't back up again for at least six months, which is just about the time Arlene's—I mean, Mrs. Watts'—husband, Harvey, will have to go out of town again.

But my problem ain't what you're interested in readin' about today, so sit back and get ready for some of Billy Bob's best writin'.

As many of you know, plumbing ain't my only talent. I also write a column for the local weekly called, "The Straight Flush with Billy Bob," and people down here think I hung the journalism moon.

I get to write occasionally in your big Atlanta paper, too, because that scoundrel Lewis Grizzard is always needin' me to bail him out, like the time he said he had come down with some mysterious illness.

He comes down with a lot of mysterious illnesses, just about every time he goes out and tries to drink all the see-through whiskey north of Bainbridge. If it flows downhill, that fool will put ice in it and try to drink it.

But this is a special occasion, indeed. Y'all have heard the rumors.

The boy did it, folks. Got married. It happened right here in Fort Deposit, Aladamnbama, last Sunday afternoon.

Grizzard couldn't get a license in Georgia because up there you have to list all your previous marriages. Georgia doesn't give you enough lines for Grizzard to put all his down.

In Alabama, you just have to list your latest foul-up and the reason for it. By "reason," Grizzard put down, "She kept burnin' the cornbread."

It was a nice ceremony. The bride wore red. I was the best man, of course, and Rooster helped get everybody seated and then bit the bride's daddy when he made a complete fool of himself as soon as the preacher got to that part about, "If anybody here has any objections to this marriage . . ."

After the wedding, there was a reception over at the diner, and everybody in Fort Deposit must have come, because it took six pairs of jumper cables to get that crowd cranked and out of there when it was over.

Rooster said he thought the best thing they served was the individually wrapped Slim-Jims and the fried chicken necks, but don't pay much attention to him because that dog will eat anything he can outrun.

There was also a beautiful ice-carving of a possum, and the cold duck they brought over from the Moose Club was dee-vine.

Of course, everybody wants to know why Grizzard decided to do it again. That boy gets married like most folks eat popcorn.

Well, I can tell you why he did it. I knew the answer when I saw him watchin' his new bride pour quarters in the jukebox with one hand and hold a longneck Blue in the other.

"Listen to what she plays," he said, all moon-eyed.

The girl may not have any taste in men, but she knows her music. She played a little Conway, followed that with Willie, and then she played that new song that goes, "We used to kiss on the mouth, but it's all over now."

"Can she cook, too?" I asked the groom.

"Can George Corley Wallace sing 'Dixie'?" Grizzard asked me back.

That's all I needed to know. Number Three likes country music and her beer in a bottle, she won't burn the cornbread, and I didn't get a close look, but it appeared to me she's still got all her teeth, too.

I thought ol' Lewis put it as good as it could be put when he looked up at me, still sober at the time, and said, "I didn't have no choice. An angel don't come by every day."

You Can Call Me "Papa," or You Can Call Me . . .

Father's Day doesn't have anything to do with "Womenfolk," which is the name of this chapter. On second thought, if it weren't for womenfolk, Father's Day would be just another Sunday.

Sunday was my first Father's Day. What I mean is, Sunday was my first time to be a father on Father's Day.

That's not exactly right, either. What I am is a stepfather, but my stepchildren are young—seven and four—so they didn't know any better than to give me a gift anyway.

I was hoping for a case of imported beer. I got socks. I always get socks when I wish for beer.

Let me tell you about my stepchildren.

The seven-year-old is a girl. The four-year-old isn't. Their average age is 5.5, which means there is a great deal of yelling and screaming and whining and crying at my house. My wife, their mother, is constantly yelling and screaming and whining and crying.

I think that comes with being the mother of two children at the age where they are trying to give everybody around them a nervous breakdown.

I came home from work and found my wife in tears. I asked her what was wrong. She said the four-year-old had run away.

"Don't cry," I said. "He'll come back."

"He already did," she replied. "Why do you think I'm crying?"

Actually, my stepchildren don't bother me that much. Whenever they get out of control, I go down to the bus station and buy a ticket for someplace like Butte, Montana. I never get on the bus, but it is comforting to know I could in case something drastic happened, like the four-year-old finding out where I hid his Big Wheel.

Those of you who do not live around children may not know what a Big Wheel is. It is a tricycle-like vehicle made of plastic. When it is pedaled across pavement by a four-year-old, it makes a sound unbearable to the adult ear.

Gestapo agents used small children riding Big Wheels to force information from captives during World War II.

I've been a stepfather for four months. The first big decision a family has to make when a stepfather moves in is what the children should call him.

We discussed "Papa," but "Papa" sound about sixty and German. I am neither.

"Big Daddy" was one of my suggestions, but my wife pointed out I have nothing in common with Burl Ives in *Cat on a Hot Tin Roof*, including his money, so we threw out that one.

Finally, we decided the children should call me by my real name, "Lewis." My wife, who doesn't have to be that respectful, gets to call me by my nickname, which is "Hey, You."

The first order of business a stepfather must handle when he takes responsibility for stepchildren is to bring a new sense of discipline into their lives.

I am a stern disciplinarian. Last week, the seven-year-old wanted to run away and get married. I said, sternly, "You'll have to ask your mother first."

I must admit children have been an adjustment for me after my years of bachelorhood, and I would not be totally truthful if I said there weren't times I ask myself how the devil I wound up a daddy when my fastball is basically intact.

But being a stepfather isn't something a man should take lightly. If you will pardon my sentimentality for a moment, I know a man who became one twenty-five years ago, and he still offers advice and guidance to a stepson about to ride off the backside of his thirties.

For the sake of the two stepchildren who live under my roof, my Father's Day prayer for 1980 is that I can do half for them what my stepfather did for me.

Don't Sit Under the Grits Tree With Anyone Else But Me

CONTENTS

1

SOCIAL STUDIES

If you hang out around salad bars, work in a bank, have a cute name like "Traci," speak a foreign language, are a professional athlete who says, "Hi, Mom" when you're on television, are overweight, slurp your soup, jog, are a lardbutt, wear padded bras, or don't like old-fashioned soda fountains, maybe you'd better pass up Chapter One and go directly to Chapter Two. . . .

Take This Salad Bar and Shove It

It finally happened to me the other night at dinner in a restaurant. First, the waiter brought water and bread, and then the menu.

After taking my order, he said, "You may help yourself to our salad bar."

It had been some time coming, but the band of restraint inside me finally snapped.

"I DON'T WANT TO HELP MYSELF TO YOUR SALAD BAR!" I screamed.

"SALAD BARS DRIVE ME INSANE!" I continued, my eyes rolling back in my head.

"I think he's speaking in tongues," a woman said to her husband in the booth next to mine.

"Shut up, Gladys," said the man. "He's just high on a jalapeño pepper."

"YOU CAN TAKE YOUR STUPID SALAD BAR AND SHOVE IT!" I went on, now completely out of control.

The waiter, in complete shock, fetched the restaurant manager, who calmed me with buttered saltines.

I have been foursquare against the idea of salad bars since they first reared their ugly lettuced heads in American restaurants.

It is a matter of principle with me.

Whenever I go out to a restaurant, and pay good money, I expect the following:

• Good food.

311

• No loud music or pinball machines in the area where you actually eat.

• To be waited on hand and foot.

If I want to go to the trouble of preparing my own salad, I will do it in the privacy of my own home, where I can eat it in my underdrawers if I so desire.

"But," salad-bar types are always arguing with me, "with a salad bar, you can put exactly what you want, and how much you want of it, on your salad."

I can get the same thing and never move one inch from my seat.

"Waiter, what do you have available for salads in this establishment?"

"Sir, we have lettuce, tomatoes, cucumbers, mushrooms, radishes, peppers, onions, bacon bits, and Italian, Thousand Island, French, and Groovy Garlic dressings."

"I'll have a heaping serving of everything but the radishes (radishes taste like a ping-pong ball would probably taste if it were solid), heavy on the Groovy Garlic dressing."

I sit there while my waiter, who is a trained professional in this sort of thing, prepares my salad.

Frankly, it is difficult to find my sort of restaurant these days, one that doesn't dispense its salads from a salad bar. Even the fast-food chains have come over:

Welcome to El Flasho's Taco Take-Out: Mi Salad Bar Es Su Salad Bar."

Soon, I expect all sorts of other establishments, even those that aren't normally associated with food, to get involved.

"Bubba's Transmission Shop: If We Can't Fix It, It Ain't Broke, Visit Our Salad Bar."

Or, "Henning, Henning, Henning, Watts and Schmedlap, Attorneys at Law. Featuring the Best Salad Bar in Town."

I simply can't understand the appeal of making your own salad in a restaurant. If you think that's fun, try something really dynamite like grinding up your own hamburger.

Which probably is the next fad in American restaurants. You stop off on the way to the restaurant and pick up a few pounds of hamburger, potatoes, and salad mixings.

At the restaurant they show you into the kitchen, where you cook your own dinner, and then you serve your own table. Afterwards, you get to clean your table, and then wash your dishes and mop. Hot water is extra.

And will the last customer to leave please remember to turn off the lights?

All Quiet in the Bank

I often have wondered why more people don't suffer nervous breakdowns when they go into banks. Each time I go into a bank, I emerge with sweaty palms and a pounding heartbeat.

That is because each time I go into a bank, I become so frustrated that I want to rant and rave and scream, but it always is so *quiet* in a bank, which is something else that frustrates me.

Why should people be quiet in a bank? I can understand being quiet in a library or in a funeral home, or even in a doctor's office because there are sick people around, but what's the big deal about keeping your voice down in a stupid bank?

What could they do to you if you suddenly started making a lot of noise while standing in line waiting for a teller?

Is an officer of the bank going to come out from behind one of those wooden doors with the brass nameplates and say, "I'm sorry, sir, but you will have to deposit your money in another financial institution if you can't learn to be quiet while you are in the bank"?

Of course not. Banks just have conned us into thinking they are some kind of big deal where you have to whisper and wear deodorant like when you're in a fancy-smancy restaurant.

Standing in line in a bank is just like standing in line at the grocery store waiting to buy tomatoes. You can chat and sing and even make sucking noises through your teeth and they're still going to sell you those tomatoes because they want their greedy hands on your money.

Next time you're in a bank, break into "The Star Spangled Banner" and I promise nobody will do a thing, except that maybe a few people in your line will think you're nuts and leave the bank, and then you will be able to get to the teller more quickly.

That's something else that drives me crazy about banks. When they build banks, they always build a lot of teller windows. I bank at a small bank. There are maybe ten teller windows at my bank.

Never in the history of my bank have there been more than five tellers behind windows at one time, and three of them always have "Next Window Please" signs keeping customers away while the line stretches out the front door.

If there are ten teller windows, why can't there be ten tellers? Where ARE the other tellers? Probably back in the vault being beaten for making an effort to hurry through transactions with less than fifty people waiting in line.

But let me tell you what REALLY cracks me up about banks. Their pens. The ones that are chained to the penholders that are nailed to the desks where you are supposed to fill out your deposit slips.

Every time I go into my bank, it's the same with those pens. I go to the first desk and one of the penholders is empty because somebody has ripped off the pen.

So I pick up a second pen, but it doesn't work. I shake, rub it across the paper a couple of times, and shake it again. Still, it doesn't work.

I go to the second desk. Same problem. Either the pens have been lifted or they don't work.

Why, I have complained, can't a bank maintain a couple of pens that work? And how can I trust a bank to keep my money safe when it can't even keep an eye on a couple of crummy pens?

But nothing ever changes. The next time I go into my bank, the pen situation will be the same, there still will be two tellers for ten windows, the line will be long and you would think somebodyy just had died the way everybody is being so careful to whisper.

If I had the guts, I would start making sucking noises through my teeth and fill out my deposit slip with a pink crayon.

"T" Is for "Traci"

Lisa, who is in the second grade, was sending out Christmas cards to her girlfriends at school the other evening.

"How do you spell 'Shannon'?" she asked me.

I told her.

"And how do you spell 'Tracy'?" she went on.

I told her that, too. Only it turned out I was wrong. Nobody spells "Tracy" like that anymore. Now, they spell "Tracy" like this: T-r-a-c-i.

Names are like anything else. They come and they go. What has happened since I was a kid is we've had a complete turnover in the sort of names people give to their children.

What the present generations of parents is doing is naming their children "cute" names, like "Shannon" and "Traci" and "Debi" and "Marti" and "Pipsie" and "Amy."

For boys, names like "Sean" are big these days, along with "Chad," "Trey," "Geoff," and "Biff," which is what people used to name their dogs.

Don't get me wrong. I think people can name their kids anything they want. The man for whom the Lear Jet is named, for instance, put "Shanda" on his daughter.

But there are some great names that appear to have been all but forgotten.

When was the last time you heard of a kid named Clarence, for instance? Good name, "Clarence."

Or how about a "Thelma"? There was even a song about a Thelma:

> *"T" for Texas,*
> *"T" for Tennessee,*
> *"T" for Thelma,*
> *Woman made a fool out of me.*

Imagine bringing out the same emotion with "'T' for 'Traci.'"

I went to school with a lot of Arnolds. In fact, one of the craziest people I have even known was named Arnold. Arnold Davenport.

It was in the second grade, I think, when Arnold Davenport found a worm on the playground and ate it. You have to be crazy to eat a worm.

And how many children do you know named Marvin these days? Be careful of anybody named Marvin, too. I went to school with Marvin Millingham, who distinguished himself by allowing a cherry bomb to explode in his hand to show his girlfriend, Imogene Norsworthy, how much courage he had.

Marvin's mother wanted him to be a concert pianist, but so much for that. Imogene Norsworthy, meanwhile, wasn't impressed and started going with Arnold Davenport.

Being from the South, I was used to double names. The possibilities were endless:

BOYS: Billy Bob, Billy Joe, Billy Frank, Bob Billy, Joe Billy, Frank Billy, Jim Bob, Joe Bob, Joe Frank, Willie Joe, Joe Willie, Bobby Earl, Henry Lee, Lee Roy, and one of my all-time favorites, Jack Joe Jenkins, who later married Imogene Norsworthy and moved to Johnson City.

GIRLS: Betty Joe, Bobbie Jo, Jo Jo, Jessie Jo, Jessie Jewell, Jo Beth, Sophie Jo, Sophie Mae, Cordie Mae, Hattie Mae, Linda Lou, Lisa Lou, Betty Lou, Betty Lou Ann Sue, and Kathy Sue Loudermilk, who made Imogene Norsworthy look like a sack of sweet potatoes.

As for me, I was named for my father. His name was Lewis, too. Once, I asked my mother what they would have named me if I had been a girl.

"Same thing," said my mother. "Your father would have insisted."

Thank the Lord it never came to that. Imagine a girl going through life with a name like "Lewis." Some things are worse than eating a worm.

Language Snobs

Most Americans have no interest in learning another language. Learning how to speak English good is hard enough.

There was this one kid from my hometown who went off to the big university and took a lot of French courses. When he got home, he went all over town bragging he had become bilingual.

His entire family was shamed, and the Methodist minister prayed for his retrieval from the deviates who had led him into such a depraved state.

In other countries it is nothing for mere schoolchildren to speak several languages. In high school I took two years of Spanish, but they made me do it.

I hated Spanish. Two years of Spanish, and here is my entire Spanish vocabulary:

> *Si.*
>
> *El beisbol es un juego de Mexico y*
> *Norte America, tambien.*
>
> *Ricardo Montalban.*
>
> *Del Taco.*
>
> *Pepe Frias.*

Pepe Frias, incidentally, plays *beisbol* for the Los Angeles Dodgers. He plays like he just had a bad batch of tacos.

What prompted me to think about all this was a report from the U.S. Embassy in Afghanistan. In case you missed it, a Russian soldier fighting in that country recently sought refuge in the U.S. Embassy.

But there was a big problem. None of the Americans at the U.S. Embassy could interrogate the soldier because none of the Americans spoke any Russian, and the Russian didn't speak any English.

Think about that. About a zillion Russian soldiers came marching across the border in Afghanistan months and months ago, and we still don't even have anybody there who would know what the devil they were talking about if he overheard Russian generals discussing whose border they were going to cross next.

I think the big problem is Americans are snooty when it comes to other languages. Why should WE learn their language? Let THEM learn ours.

That attitude is one of the reasons that when you go to France these days, and a waiter finds out you are an American, he deliberately spills hot coffee in your lap, and if there's not already a fly in your soup, he'll find one.

The point is, the State Department is stupid for not having somebody who speaks Russian in our embassy in Afghanistan, and I just remembered another story that happened in my hometown. It involves a French exchange student and Claude (Goat) Rainwater, who worked at the local service station.

Goat Rainwater had never been outside the county. But he did watch a little television, and he made the tenth grade before he quit school.

Once the church sponsored a French student to come to live in various homes for the summer. The idea was that maybe some of her culture—and language—would rub off on the rest of us.

The first day she was in town, we took her—Michelle—to meet Goat Rainwater.

"Goat, this is Michelle," one of the group said. "She's from France."

"Wellll," replied Goat, realizing this wasn't your everyday, garden variety drop-in at the service station, "*Como esta usted, Senyoreetar?*"

Nobody bothered to correct him, and instead of Michelle teaching us any French, we taught her to cuss like an American sailor who has just been rolled in a bar on the dark side of Tijuana.

Hi, Mom

I have watched a lot of football games on television this year. In some ways, football is a lot better on television than it is in person.

The rest rooms are not as far away when you watch the game on television, for instance.

What else is great about watching the game on the tube is you get to see the players close up. Sometimes they will even show taped interviews of the players while the action is slow on the field.

"While the action is slow on the field, let's show you an interview with Dallas linebacker Eldo (Mad Dog) Rado taped before the game."

"Eldo, what are Dallas's chances of getting into the Super Bowl this season?"

"Well, you know, if we, you know, can, you know, win, you know, a, you know, couple of, you know, more, you know, games this, you know, season, then, you know, we, you know, got a, you know, pretty good, you know, uh, chance, you know."

It doesn't say anywhere in the standard NFL contract that a player must be able to play pass defense and handle the English language at the same time.

What has become a silly practice on televised games, however, is focusing a camera on players while they are on the sidelines, drinking Gatorade, spitting, or eating some of the astroturf.

It is human nature to attempt to perform, or say something clever, when you go one-on-one with a television camera.

But all football players say the same thing in that situation.

They say, "Hi, Mom."

If I have seen one football player say, "Hi, Mom," to a television camera this season, I have seen a thousand.

What is this, "Hi, Mom?" Football players make tons of money. Why don't they pop for a long distance call occasionally and say, "Hi, Mom," then, instead of using up precious time on network television that costs the average sponsor millions?

I would like for a football player to think of something original occasionally when he is before the camera.

"Hi, Dad" would do for starters.

Or, "I would like to take this opportunity to thank both my parents for making me eat the right foods and get my rest so that I would grow strong and tall and be able to come out here on Sunday afternoons and tear my opponents limb from limb."

And why stick to relatives?

"Hi, Bettyann, I know I said I would call, but, golly, the big game was coming up and we had practice all week, and I got this bad case of jock itch, and then I got drunk and lost my playbook, and that girl who answered the phone at my apartment when you called the other night was my cousin from Shreveport who's a nun."

Or why not try to say something intelligent or meaningful to the audience?

"Remember, my fellow Americans, that the game of life is a lot like football. You have to tackle your problems, block your fears, and score your points when you get the opportunities; otherwise, some bad dude like Mean Joe Coca-Cola is gonna come along and stomp your head right into the ground."

The only player who never says, "Hi, Mom" when he is on camera, as a matter of fact, is Dallas' Eldo (Mad Dog) Rado. That's because he doesn't have a mother. They grew him in a forest in northern California, you know.

Abundant Americans

We have studies for practically everything today—studies to see why frogs leap and why rabbits hop and why birds don't fly upside down.

One of my favorite studies lately was the one about fat people. A group in Maryland studied fat people and concluded they are being discriminated against almost as much as blacks and "other minorities."

I didn't know that. See why we have to grant all those tax funds to have studies?

David Tucker, the consultant who directed the study for the Maryland Human Relations Commission, said fat people are victims of discrimination in nearly every aspect of life.

He said fat people have trouble getting jobs because employers don't want them in contact with the public.

He said employers tend to characterize fat people as "lazy, lacking in self-discipline, not well-motivated, sloppy, unclean, and, in one case, smelly."

He said owners of theaters and sports arenas don't make their seats wide enough for fat people, and he probably should also have mentioned airplane seats, because I know a fat person who has to buy two seats every time he flies. If the arm rests won't go down, he straddles them.

We do discriminate against fat people, don't we?

We poke fun at them. There was a guy I knew in college. He was fat as a pig. That's why we called him "Hog-Body"—Hog-Body Spradlin.

I never did know Hog-Body's real name until years later when I ran into him at a cocktail party and he was wearing a name tag. His real name was Norbert, which explains why he never complained when we called him Hog-Body.

We especially poke fun and discriminate against fat women. You never see fat women doing pantyhose commercials or selling shampoo on television.

The first question out of any man's mouth as soon as a blind date has been arranged for him is, "She isn't a fat girl, is she?"

That comes immediately after he has been told she makes her own clothes and "all the girls like her."

I think it was Alex Karras, former football player, broadcaster, and some-time actor, who said the worst thing I have ever heard said to a fat girl.

It supposedly happened at a dance when Alex Karras was a student at Iowa. He was in the clutches of a rather large young woman, but, being the nice fellow that he is, he wanted to pay her a compliment.

He came up with the classic, "You don't sweat much for a fat girl."

Alex Karras is no nice fellow. He is a cad.

We also bicker at fat people about going on diets.

My friend Ludlow Porch, an Atlanta radio announcer, isn't exactly slender. ("The local Little League team," he is fond of saying, "gets in shape by running a few laps around me.")

He hates to go to the doctor because he doesn't want to be told to go on a diet again.

"I went to see the doctor the other day," he was telling me. "He said, 'Ludlow, you're overweight.'"

"I said, 'I know that, doctor, and you're short. I can lose weight, but what are you going to do about your situation?'"

My idea is that we lay off fat people. No more discrimination, no more cute remarks. We could even cut the word "fat" out of our vocabularies.

Instead of saying "fat people," let's say "abundant Americans." "Roly-poly" and "plump" and "rotund" and "obese" and "porky" are words no member of polite society should dare say from now on.

In fact, the only time "fat" should really be accepted is when it refers to a body of our government handing out a "fat grant" so a group of "fatheads" can fool around for six months getting "fat" doing an idiotic study.

No Place for Soup-Slurpers

The question most often asked in this country today must be, "Smoking or non-smoking?" You hear it every time you step onto an airplane or a train, and some restaurants are beginning to separate customers who smoke from those who don't.

That's nothing. When you call for a taxi in New York, you can even request a non-smoking driver.

So determined are we to keep the two groups apart, I wouldn't be surprised if we eventually have smoking and non-smoking states.

The smokers, for instance, could all go live in industrial states where the air already is so foul they couldn't do any further damage to it.

Non-smokers could have what is left, like Montana, where the only pollution problem is an occasional moose with poor personal hygiene.

I happen to be a smoker, and I also happen to be an advocate of segregating smokers and non-smokers. One, I don't want to make anybody around me uncomfortable when I smoke, and two, who wants to be with an uppity group with clean lungs that probably also is into jogging and health foods and never has a light when you need one?

I also would like to take this whole idea a step further. If we are going to separate smokers from non-smokers in public places, why not make the same separation when it comes to other annoying habits?

Like throat-clearing in theaters and non-throat-clearing in theaters?

"Non-throat-clearing," I could answer, and be removed forevermore from the jerk who apparently inhaled a pigeon and the feathers tickle his tonsils every time there is soft dialogue that needs to be followed closely.

I could go on. I think I will:

• Loud-talking in restaurants and non-loud-talking in restaurants.

Put me in the section where people came to eat, not to deliver the Gettysburg Address and other orations with mouths full of zucchini.

• Soup-slurping and non-soup slurping.

Some people don't know how to eat soup. They fill their spoons too full and then, because the soup is hot, suck it into their mouths a small amount at a time.

That makes a slurping sound that is both annoying and crude. I would rather sit next to somebody who smells like a moose than somebody who slurps his soup.

• Nose-blowing and non-nose blowing.

It should be against the law to blow your nose in public. It's not, so let's separate those who do from those who don't, especially when food is being served, soft music is being played, or there is to be a great deal of praying.

• Cosmetic-applying and non-cosmetic-applying.

I detest seeing a woman applying her paint and/or powder in the company of others. Seat those who would commit such a *faux pas* far from ordinary people who get sick at the smell of nail polish and at the sight of pooched lips awaiting a new coating of gloss, especially if it is that ghoulish lavender color disco queens and other vampires wear.

• Gum-chewing and non-gum-chewing.

Gum-chewers make loud, smacking noises, and they have a habit of throwing their gum on the floor when they are finished with it. Then I always come along and get it stuck on the bottom of my sneakers. That makes me want to kill gum-chewers.

For their own safety, put them off by themselves where, if they all want to sound like Secretariat enjoying an order of oats, nobody will hear them.

• Affection-displaying and non-affection-displaying.

You would be surprised how many couples nowadays wait until they are in a restaurant or a theater or on an airplane to play kissy-mouth and engage in all the squeezing and giggling that goes with it.

You don't think that can be disturbing? Look around you. Times, they are a-changin'—and the distraction is even greater when the two with the smoochies both have mustaches.

Running With Rosie

I admit I never had much interest in running until recently when I found out you can cheat at it. Now that I know you can cheat, I accept running as being a real sport.

Heretofore I thought it was just something bored housewives and guys who were in the drama club in high school did occasionally because they had never known the joy of sweating.

You can put in the fix in practically all our favorite athletic competitions. Baseball had its Black Sox scandal, basketball its point-shavings of the fifties, and somebody is always stealing a playbook in football, or doping a horse, or shooting an East German swimmer full of strange hormones.

But running? I never thought anybody cheated at running. I remember when some of my friends first started running.

"Who plays tennis or softball?" said one, an out-of-work actor. "Running is *pure*, man."

But then we come to the case of female runner Rosie Ruiz, the first woman to come across the finish line at the Boston Marathon, the Super Bowl of running.

Other runners, including the woman who finished second to her and spectators, claimed Rosie had not run the entire 26.2-mile course, but had slipped into the pack two miles from the finish line for a record time and a victory that is reportedly worth a lot of bucks in endorsements. Pure, man.

The stink caused a number of subsequent investigations and news conferences and a great deal of confusion. The problem, of course, is that the sport of running never has had to deal with a cheating scandal before and wasn't equipped to handle it.

What running needs to circumvent any such embarrassments in the future is a set of guidelines to follow in checking out finishing runners to make certain they completed the entire course.

The National Union for Running Development has offered a standby list of methods to be considered.

Following are some of the NURD suggestions:

• FOOT TEST: After twenty-six miles, a runner's feet should emit a certain odor. Each finishing runner will be asked to allow a foot judge to smell his or her feet. If the judge is rendered unconscious, there is a good chance the runner completed the entire course.

• JOGBRA TEST: No qualified female runner would attempt twenty-six miles without an official "jogbra." All the top women runners wear them. Any female finisher without such equipment should be detained for more questioning. Any male runner wearing a "jogbra" should be detained, period.

• SHOE TEST: Runners finishing in sandals, disco boots, moccasins, anything a cowboy might wear while walking the pasture, or barefooted should be considered suspicious. Any runner finishing in flip-flops should be placed in the same holding cage with the guys wearing "jogbras."

• BREATH TEST: Finishers who reek of Gatorade or orange juice probably are legitimate. Finishers who reek of gin or vodka probably are just drunks who wandered out of the nearby bar to see what all the commotion was about.

• BURMA SHAVE TEST: "Burma Shave" signs will be posted every five miles along the course, and each finisher must be able to recite what appeared on each sign in order. For instance:

> Here Sits Rosie,
> Brokenhearted.
> She Finished Fine,
> But She Never Started.
> Burma Shave.

Lardbutts Need Love, Too

I went out to the baseball game the other night to watch the Braves lose, and I noticed local fans have formed the habit of booing Bob Horner.

For those of you who do not follow the sport, Bob Horner is this blond kid from out West someplace who is supposed to be some kind of whiz-bang ballplayer.

He's being paid three times what the president makes, but so far he hasn't produced returns proportionate to his pay.

For example, there was his performance the night I caught his act. Four times he came to the plate with runners in scoring position in a tight game. Four times he looked like your Aunt Mildred trying to hit the ball.

There was also his defensive play. Your Aunt Mildred may not have Bob Horner's arm, but I'll bet she can cover more ground at third base.

I've heard all sorts of reasons for why Horner's play has been lacking. There was all that commotion over his contract, then Ted Turner wanted to demote him to Richmond at the first of the season, and he has had many injuries.

I always figured his biggest problem was he's a lardbutt. Lardbutts, because of the way they are built (bottom-heavy), have a difficult time in sports. Plus, despite the fact some of my best friends are lardbutts, they tend to be a little on the lazy side.

Roy Amos was a lardbutt, for instance. In the fifth grade, Roy Amos could hit the ball a long ways during recess games, but he would make somebody else run the bases for him. Also, Roy didn't like to bend over.

So that was my theory concerning Bob Horner: He's a lazy lardbutt who doesn't like to exert a lot of effort or bend over, just like Roy Amos.

But I was wrong, and when I am wrong I want to be the first to admit it. It was Horner's teammate, pitcher Al Hrabosky, who finally discovered the exact nature of Horner's problem.

Hrabosky has this radio show. When it was announced Horner would have to sit out a few days' games recently because of a "stomach disorder," Hrabosky said on his radio show it was not a stomach disorder at all, it was the dreaded "Heinekenitis."

I did some further checking and also learned that Horner picked up the "bug" one evening after a game in St. Louis.

How ashamed we all should be for booing him. A man in his condition cannot be expected to perform up to par.

And I should know. I, too, have had "Heinekenitis" and many other forms of it, such as "PBR Syndrome" and "Strohzema," both of which are just as painful, but don't cost as much to contract.

The symptoms normally begin when you awaken in the morning. They are headache, nausea, dizziness, nervousness, and you want to drink a lot of water, but you don't want to move around a lot or hear any loud noises.

Imagine a person being asked to catch a ground ball or run around a bunch of bases or listen to a screaming crowd in that condition.

When I have "Heinekenitis," it is a chore just to brush my teeth, but I do it anyway because another symptom is your mouth feels like the Chinese army spent the night there.

I think we all owe Bob Horner an apology. He is a sick man, doing the very best that he can, fighting a disease that has brought misery and suffering to millions.

Let us also remember the immortal words of Roy Amos, who said, "Lardbutts need love, too."

This is that apology, Bob. Hang in there, kid, and get well soon.

Forgiving the Bra-Padders

It would be easy to allow the case of Deborah Ann Fountain—the "little something extra girl"—to deflate and pass quietly into the void known as old news.

It never has been the nature of this column to turn its back when it senses that only the tip of a mammoth iceberg has been uncovered, however.

To refresh everyone's memory, Deborah Ann Fountain, Miss New York, went to Biloxi, Mississippi, to compete in the Miss U.S.A. beauty contest.

We all know how beauty contests work. A group of lovely young women strut around in nearly nothing for a couple of days and then a winner is picked, based on her talent and poise.

Miss Fountain decided she could improve her talent and poise by making it appear she had large breasts. So she stuck inch-thick padding into her swimsuit.

Competition can be very keen at a beauty contest. Miss Fountain's attempted trickery was discovered when a contest official, tipped by another contestant, went backstage and ripped down Miss Fountain's swimsuit and uncovered much more than just Miss Fountain.

How many other contest officials volunteered to go backstage and rip down Miss Fountain's swimsuit is not known.

Miss Fountain did what any red-blooded American beauty queen would do after such an experience. She filed suit. In her suit, she contended that four other contestants had silicone implants to boost their bust lines and that twenty other contestants had padded their bras too.

What concerns me is not Deborah Ann Fountain—she has padded her bra and now she must wear it—but just how common is this practice?

If twenty other contestants in the Miss U.S.A. pageant did, in fact, pad their bras, and four more had silicone implants, that means that half the field was cloaked in the dark veil of deceit.

What does this do for the credibility of other women who also are tying to cash in on their, well, talent and poise?

Dolly Parton, for instance. Say it ain't so, Dolly. Jane Russell, still doing bra commercials, and she remembers when Ronald Reagan was breaking in. Is that all you, Jane? And, heaven forbid, but was Janet Cooke wearing falsies when she wrote "Jimmy's World"?

There was a girl in my high school who learned a near-tragic lesson from attempting to be more than she was. During a vacation trip to the beach, she met a charming young man who asked her if she would like to take a swim in the surf.

She'd love to, she said, and met him on the beach in a daring swimsuit. In order to impress the young man even more, she had padded the top of her suit to capacity.

As the two strolled into the surf, they suddenly stepped into much deeper water. The young man went all the way under and came to the surface gasping, only to find his companion not even neck-deep in the water.

Before she could offer an explanation, the padding in her swimsuit sprang loose, and she sank quickly. Only the expert swimming abilities of her young man saved her from drowning.

I would suggest we now grant a National Day of Amnesty for all American women who have the courage to come forward and admit that they have in the past, or are presently, falsifying their pretenses.

This is a forgiving time in which we live. We will forgive Deborah Ann Fountain, of course, and we will forgive any other women who are willing to get it off their chests, so to speak.

We even forgave the girl in my high school, ol' what's-her-name with the floating swimsuit.

One Limeade for the Road

The Last Soda Fountain. Put it up there with *The Last Picture Show*, a marvelous motion picture, and with "The Last Cowboy Song," currently a raging country hit where Willie Nelson joins in on the last chorus.

But The Last Soda Fountain is neither a movie nor a song. It is reality.

The place was Springlake Pharmacy, and it was located near my home in Atlanta. There are memories.

Springlake Pharmacy is where I met Barney, my all-time favorite wino. Barney would sit outside Springlake on a slab of concrete and pour out his bottled dreams from a brown paper sack.

There was the day I saw two punks, they were maybe ten and eleven, throwing rocks at Barney. Barney wasn't bothering anybody. Barney was just drifting away for a time, and he was too weak and too drunk to dodge the rocks.

I chased the kids away. Barney thanked me by asking for a dollar. Barney is dead now.

Springlake is where I bought toothpaste and shampoo and cough syrup and newspapers and once, when I forgot a rather special Valentine, one of those gaudy red boxes of chocolates she pretended to appreciate.

Springlake was where a person could belly-up to the counter of an honest-to-god, just-like-back-home-in-a-small-town soda fountain and ask and receive delights the likes of which are rare and precious indeed in the urban eighties.

Milkshakes. Not milkshakes out of some machine you have to eat with a spoon. That's not a milkshake. At Springlake, you got a milkshake constructed by a human hand scooping real ice cream into a cup with real milk, and you could *drink* the darn thing, as the Lord intended.

Limeade. Real limeade, made out of real lime juice, handsqueezed from real limes. Thousands of limes were rendered juiceless over the years in Springlake. As far as I know, there is no other place in the continental United States that serves as good a limeade as did the soda fountain at Springlake.

I could go on. Cherry Cokes. Coca-Cola syrup, carbonated water and a shot of cherry juice. Good hot dogs. Ham sandwiches with thinly sliced tomatoes.

And nobody behind the counter wore stupid uniforms, and they didn't sell cookies in a funky little box, and the chicken noodle soup was called "chicken noodle soup." At some fastfood establishments today, chicken noodle soup would be called "Soup McNoodle."

My old pal, Estin, was numero uno behind the Springlake soda fountain counter. He spoke only when a grunt wouldn't do just as well.

And then there was the lady who worked with him. I never got her name. Somebody said she was Estin's niece. One day I ordered a ham sandwich and some potato chips from her. She delivered the ham sandwich. She forgot the potato chips, which were located on a rack behind the counter.

"You forgot my potato chips," I said.

"You got two legs," she replied. "Get your own potato chips."

It was that sort of friendly service that kept me coming back to Springlake, hallowed be its name.

Springlake, thirty-odd years at the same location, closed recently to the sound of a bulldozer's snort. A new shopping center went up next door, and the Springlake building was sold, and the Springlake owner decided to move his pharmacy and to pass the soda fountain along to the ages.

I walked inside for one last look.

"We're all just about in tears," said a lady helping dismantle the shelves. "It's a sad day."

The Last Soda Fountain. Let us mourn its leave, for nothing similar remains to take its place.

"Soup McNoodle." How utterly disgusting.

2

CORDIE MAE
AND THE GANG

It has been my pleasure to have known a lot of great, and near-great people in my time: Cordie Mae Poovey, Hog Phillpot, Kathy Sue Loudermilk, Mavis Boatright, all the Rainwaters—especially "Spot" and "Goat"—the late Curtis "Fruit Jar" Hainey, and my boyhood friend and idol, Weyman C. Wannamaker, Jr., a great American, who first showed me my way around a 1957 Chervolet. . . .

Hog Takes a Bride

What fun it has been keeping up with the big news in Britain: Prince Charles, who is thirty-two, is taking a bride, and she is cute, bubbly, nineteen-year-old Lady Diana Spencer, who giggles a lot.

The couple will marry in July, and some celebration it should be. I was trying to remember other big-deal marriages in the past, and I thought of Julie Nixon and David Eisenhower and Ari Onassis and Jackie Kennedy and Grace Kelly and Prince Rainier of Monaco, of course.

And then I remembered the one we had back home, when Harold "Hog" Phillpot married Cordie Mae Poovey, and everybody in town came. Pound for pound, it was the biggest wedding in the history of the county.

Hog tipped the Toledo at nearly 300. Nobody ever knew exactly how much Cordie Mae weighed, but her daddy used to say, "If I could get $1.25 a pound for that child, I could pay off my truck."

Now that I think about it, Hog and Cordie Mae had a great deal in common with Prince Charles and Lady Diana.

Hog proposed in a garden, too, right in the middle of his daddy's collard patch, where Cordie Mae was picking a mess for her supper. Cordie Mae could eat a wheelbarrow load of collards and still want to fight you for yours. When Cordie Mae was hungry, she had the personality of a water buffalo with a gum boil.

Hog also was in his thirties when he married Cordie Mae, who was just nineteen, like Lady Diana. Cordie Mae wasn't one to giggle very much, however. When she laughed she made a sound like a dump truck being cranked on a cold morning.

I don't know the exact plans of Prince Charles and Lady Diana's wedding, but if it is anything like Hog and Cordie Mae's, it will be a dandy. I managed to locate a yellowed clipping from the local newspaper that described the event:

"Mr. and Mrs. Lark Poovey take pride in announcing the marriage of their daughter, Cordie Mae, to Mr. Harold "Hog" Phillpot, son of Mr. and Mrs. Grover Phillpot, at the Mt. Giliad Free Will Baptist Church Saturday, April 11, 1959, at three o'clock in the afternoon.

"The groom is a graduate of the Nuway Recap School and currently is employed by Elroy's Gulf and Tire as Elroy's night manager. The bride, former state high school girls' wrestling champion (heavyweight division), is the popular bouncer at the Gateway Recreation Hall and Beer Joint.

"The wedding service was delivered by the Rev. Vernon 'Jericho' Walls, and the bride was given away by her father, a prominent sheetrocker and dog breeder. Miss Teeter Combs played several selections on the organ, including the traditional 'Wedding March' and her speciality, 'On Wisconsin.'

"The bride's outfit was designed by Arnold's Tent and Awning Co. The happy couple exited the church under crossed lug wrenches, held by employees from Elroy's Gulf and Tire.

"The reception was held in the basement of the church, where the Rev. Walls' wife, Sharinda, served Hawaiian Punch to one and all. Following a wedding trip to the nearest Burger Chef, the couple will reside in the Lonesome Pines Trailer Park, Row Five, Trailer M, a handsome double-wide."

It's hard to believe it's been more than twenty years since Hog and Cordie Mae got married. They're still together, incidentally, but they had to move from Lonesome Pines into a house. Cordie Mae gained so much more weight that she was wider than the trailer.

Mean Mo-Sheen

The Chrysler Corporation has made another big decision. It no longer will produce those big ugly cars nobody will buy—heaps like the Chrysler Newport, the Dodge St. Regis, or the Plymouth Grand Fury, whatever that is.

From now on, Chrysler will produce only intermediate-sized ugly cars nobody will buy. Won't somebody do Chrysler a big favor and pull its plug for good?

I've known for a long time why Chrysler can't sell cars. It has nothing to do with size. It is because Chrysler is trying to sell cars to a generation it never bothered to impress when we were in high school.

Nobody in my school would have been caught dead driving a Chrysler. The principal always drove a Chrysler, or something like it—a DeSoto, for instance, which was worse than one of those fat, black Buicks with the holes in the sides.

The shop teacher, meanwhile, usually was the one with the pale blue Plymouth without chrome or a radio, and the band director drove a brown Dodge.

How can all that possibly affect Chrysler today? Don't you see? It is in high school that a person, especially a boyperson, first gets hooked on cars. It is during that period he forms certain attitudes and makes certain value judgments concerning automobiles that he will carry into manhood.

In the late fifties and early sixties, you couldn't have gotten a date with Cordie Mae Poovey, the ugliest girl in school, driving a Chrysler.

Now we all are grown, but the anti-Chrysler feelings linger, so we're all out buying those little Japanese imports, which we really don't want—but at least there is no chance of being mistaken for a shop teacher in one.

I have a couple of suggestions for Chrysler that could save the farm.

One, forget all the plans for the intermediate-sized cars, or any-sized cars that look like anything you have built in the past two decades. Face it. Those dogs won't hunt.

Two, beg, borrow, or steal the designs to the greatest car ever made. Produce something that at least closely resembles it, and in six months, I promise you will have won over the entire generation of customers you blew twenty years ago.

I am speaking of the 1957 Chevrolet.

There never has been such another car as the '57 Chevy. Its lines were classic, and its back seat was roomy. Its grillwork and fins said, "Here is power, here is speed." And its back seat was roomy.

It was THE car of my youth. A guy driving a 1957 Chevrolet could get a date with ANY girl in school, up to, and including, Kathy Sue Loudermilk, the Collard Festival queen.

I never owned a '57 Chevy, but my boyhood friend and idol, Weyman C. Wannamaker, Jr., a great American, did. A convertible. A red one. Hottamighty, what a car!

He had "Sassy Chassis" written on the hood, and he had flames painted on each door. Weyman called his car his "mean mo-sheen," and occasionally he even would allow me to drive this piece of automotive genius, like when he was busy discussing an upcoming algebra exam in the roomy back seat with Kathy Sue Loudermilk.

I can hear Weyman now, giving me instructions on how to drive his car. "Eyes forward, stupid," he used to say.

So maybe it's a long shot, Chrysler, but nothing else has worked. Give Americans a mo-sheen like the '57 Chevy and maybe they will remember there are some things in a car more important than gas mileage. And maybe they will tell the Japanese to go eat some fish heads.

Besides, their stupid little cars with those cramped back seats have been taking the fun out of American automobiling long enough.

Making Sense of the Census

What I like most about the taking of the census is that it's fair. Once every ten years everybody counts, and everybody counts the same:

One.

Even Bo Derek. Imagine, Bo Derek a "one." Somehow, I can't imagine that.

Something else I like about the census: It's thorough. Most Americans probably mailed in their census reports April 1, but canvassers soon will be going into places like pool halls, dives, and fleabag hotels in big cities to count heads.

That is important because, otherwise, a pool shark or a wino could be missed. The last time there was a census, for instance, my boyhood friend and idol, Weyman C. Wannamaker, Jr., a great American and part-time pool shark and wino, wasn't counted. He was taking a nap (passed out) underneath a load of turnips in the back of his pickup truck when the census-taker came around.

I can't wait for the results of the census to be released. I realize a great deal of the information we gave the government is supposed to be kept confidential, but this census thing is costing the taxpayers a bundle, so why shouldn't we be privy to some of the juicier material?

I just happen to have with me a list of questions I would like answered by the census:

- The 1980 census had the audacity to ask people if they have indoor plumbing. Did any of my neighbors mark "no"? (I have always suspected the Bloomingraths. They spend an awful lot of time going back and forth to Mr. Bloomingrath's "tool shed," and they never have any beer parties.)
- Does anybody really live in North Dakota?
- What is the population of my hometown, Moreland, Georgia? The last time there was a census taken, there were 300-plus but that was before the Rainwater family moved out. (There were so many Rainwaters, they ran out of names for the last four children and had to name then after dogs in the neighborhood. "Spot" Rainwater was one of my closest friends.)
- How many teen-agers are there in America, and when will they all grow up so rock music will finally die out?
- Ten million people live in New York City, where the air is foul, the streets are dirty and the weather is terrible. Hardly anybody lives in Yellville, Arkansas, where the mountain air is refreshing, there are many streams and rivers for fishing and boating and swimming naked, and you don't have to lock your doors at night. Why?
- Who is the oldest person in America, and has he or she ever jogged?
- Under "sex," how many people put down "undecided," and are any of them in my tennis club?
- How many people in America are named "Engelbert Humperdink"?
- Did the name "D.B. Cooper" show up anywhere?
- When is my wife's birthday?
- And, finally, just exactly how many people do live in this country, and with the government doing the counting, how can I be certain that figure is correct?

I can't. If the government knew beans about simple arithmetic, it wouldn't just now be balancing its own checkbook for the first time since it was taking the 1960 census.

Incidentally, they missed Weyman C. Wannamaker, Jr., in 1960, too. He hid in the family "tool shed," which used to be none of the government's damn business.

Pucker Princess of '62

A jeweler friend of mine mentioned recently you can get as much as $150 by digging out your old high school class ring and selling it at what still remains a good price for gold.

I really hate to use this forum for something so personal, but I haven't been able to find my old high school class ring, and I just remembered what happened to it.

What happened to it was Mavis Boatright, a girl in my school, the night at the drive-in movie when I asked her to go steady. Going steady with Mavis Boatright, which really everybody did at one time or the other, meant French kissing her on the mouth if you came across with something of value she could wear to impress her girl-friends.

"How about my letter jacket?" was my first offer, during the intermission between *Gidget Goes Hawaiian* and some Doris Day thing I wanted to French kiss on the mouth through with Mavis Boatright.

"What sport?" she asked.

"Debate," I answered, proudly.

"Pass," said Mavis, who was not exceedingly intellectual, but her parents allowed her to stay out until midnight, thus giving her great bargaining powers.

Plus, the girl could kiss. A Mavis Boatright lip-lock was some-thing to behold.

My next offer was my foam-rubber dice that hung from the rear-view mirror of my car, but Marvin Waterman had made the same offer the night before, and Mavis had told him to go French kiss a bird dog, which is exactly what she told me. Mavis had some kind of quick wit about her.

"How about the ring?" she finally asked.

I was afraid she would ask that. Getting a boy's class ring meant it was something really serious, something that might last as long as a month. I didn't want to spend an eternity with Mavis Boatright. I just wanted to press my lips tenderly against hers and feel the tinge of excitement run down my spine as she bent my head against the movie speaker.

"I can't give you my class ring," I said.

"So we'll sit here and watch Doris Day go on a crying jag for two hours," Mavis responded.

I gave her my class ring, and my lips were numb for a week. It wasn't long after that, however, she ran off with Marvin Waterman and got married, and she never bothered to return my ring.

Now, I want my ring back. I've tried everything to locate her, including calling around in my hometown, but nobody has any idea whatever happened to Mavis and Marvin.

This is simply a shot in the dark, a last-ditch effort. Maybe you will read this, Mavis, and return my ring.

These are difficult times, and, quite frankly, I could use the cash it would bring. I'm planning a small cookout for a few friends, and the 150 big ones would just about cover the buns and pickle relish.

There also is a matter of principle here, Mavis, and you know what I'm talking about. After That Night, you told every girl in school that kissing me was like drinking warm buttermilk.

Do you realize how long it was before I got kissed again after that? Do you realize how many Doris Day movies I had to sit through after that? Do you know I got so sick of Doris Day that every time she started one of her crying jags I wanted Rock Hudson to bash her one?

That's exactly what I would like to do to you, Mavis. Bam! Right in your kisser, legend that it was. Bitter, Mavis, is the man scorned and $150 in the hole for one night of passion with the pucker princess of 1962, wherever you are.

"When It's Refill Time in Heaven"

I stopped for lunch in one of those meat-and-three-vegetables places the other day and, much to my surprise, the waitress brought my iced tea in a quart fruit jar.

You don't see that sort of thing any more, but fruit jars have a significant history, and I even get a little sentimental when I think about them. More about that later.

First, for those who are not familiar with the fruit jar, it is a wide-mouthed, glass container normally associated with the process of canning, as in the canning of vegetables and fruits.

These containers also may be called "Mason" jars for the name of the company that produces state-of-the-art fruit jars. But people who say "Mason jar" instead of "fruit jar" probably are a little snooty and sleep in pajamas.

In the past, in certain parts of rural America, it was quite common for people who couldn't afford regular glassware—and slept in their underwear—to use these fruit jars as part of their table settings.

You take a family in my hometown, the Rainwaters. The Rainwaters were too poor to afford glasses, so Mrs. Rainwater always served beverages in fruit jars.

Claude "Goat" Rainwater was one of my best friends, despite the fact that he rarely bathed. Mrs. Rainwater would serve Goat his food and his fruit jar on the back porch with the dog.

There are certain advantages to drinking from a fruit jar.

The wide mouth allows easy intake of the liquid inside the jar, whether it be iced tea, buttermilk, lemonade, or something more potent.

It is so easy to drink from a fruit jar, as a matter of fact, that it is virtually impossible to keep whatever you are drinking from pouring over your chin, down your neck, and onto the front of your shirt.

There was a man who lived in the woods near my hometown who sold a certain beverage that was so potent you wanted to be careful not to get any on your shirt because it would ruin your shirt. It would eat through sandpaper and cut out engine knock, too.

As I finished my lunch and poured down the last of my iced tea from my fruit jar, my sentimentality got the best of me as I thought of one of my favorite people from my youth.

I am speaking of the late, great Curtis "Fruit Jar" Hainey. Fruit Jar got that name because he was never without one stuck in his coat or in his back pocket.

It usually was filled with the clear liquid—and an occasional bug or leaf the strainer missed—that he purchased from the aforementioned man in the woods.

I can see ol' Fruit Jar now, ambling along.

"Where you headed, Fruit Jar?" we would ask.

"Refill time," he would answer, smiling and holding up his empty jar as he headed for the woods.

Fruit Jar spent so much time drinking there was a notch on his nose from where the top of his jar pressed against it.

"That stuff's gonna kill him someday," the women from the church used to say.

Sure enough, it did. He went one jar over the line one cold night. The blind girl wrote a song for him and sang it at the funeral after the preacher got through. She called it "Lord, Remember Fruit Jar When It's Refill Time in Heaven."

Goat Rainwater even took a bath for the services. A man like Curtis "Fruit Jar" Hainey doesn't die every day.

The Birth of the Jeans Craze

There is an awful lot of conversation these days concerning the case of fifteen year-old actress-model Brooke Shields and her pair of tight-fitting Calvin Klein jeans.

Miss Shields made a commercial in her tight-fitting Calvin Kleins and also made a few, ahem, suggestive remarks.

The public was outraged. The commercials were yanked off television.

This accomplished two things:

• It made Miss Shields, whose talent is not exactly lengendary, into a big star. Her previous accomplishments included playing the role of twelve-year-old hooker and getting stranded on an island with nothing but her ragged loincloth and somebody who was a boy but wasn't her brother. Brooke Shields is fifteen going on thirty-five.

• It sold the diddly out of Calvin Klein jeans.

Frankly, I don't know what the fuss is all about. For years, blossoming young women have been fitting themselves into blue jeans two sizes too small for them. Women just naturally do something to a pair of jeans that a hairy-legged boy can't.

You take Kathy Sue Loudermilk, for instance. It was Kathy Sue Loudermilk who started the blue-jean craze that is now sweeping the world.

She actually wore the first pair of designer jeans ever made to the annual Fourth of July Barbecue and Street Dance in my hometown on July 5, 1954. (July 4 got rained out that year.)

Her jeans were designed by her mother, the former Edna Pearl Simpkins, who fashioned them from a flour sack.

Unfortunately—or fortunately—Edna Pearl didn't quite have enough sack to fit Kathy Sue, and she came up a couple of sizes too small.

When Kathy Sue arrived at the dance, the band stopped playing, people stopped dancing, the Baptist preacher broke into a prodigious sweat, and Goot Niles swallowed a brand-new plug of Brown Mule chewing tobacco.

Of course, there was some outrage expressed concerning Kathy Sue's outfit back then, too. The ladies of the church passed around a petition to ban Kathy Sue's britches from future town gatherings and gave it to the Baptist preacher, who had to drink two quarts of lemonade to cool down every time Kathy Sue's name was mentioned.

"Let's be sensible, ladies," the preacher said. "She's only a child."

"My grandmother's hat," said Goot Niles' wife, Ruby Jean, who also chewed Brown Mule.

Finally the preacher said he would speak to Kathy Sue's mother, Edna Pearl, but by that time she was already working on sack jeans for almost every young woman in town.

Even Cordie Mae Poovey got a pair. Cordie Mae was a big girl who sort of reminded you of a semi hauling hogs. It took five flour sacks and seven yards of elastic for Edna Pearl to make Cordie Mae's jeans.

DON'T SIT UNDER THE GRITS TREE

"The Blob! It lives!" said my boyhood friend and idol, Weyman C. Wannamaker, Jr., a great American, the first time he saw Cordie Mae in her new outfit. She kneed him in the belly and sat on him until it was nearly dark.

When people got too sophisticated to buy their flour in large cloth sacks, Edna Pearl had to get out of the jeans business.

Too bad. Brooke Shields in a pair of Calvin Kleins is kid stuff. Kathy Sue Loudermilk in a pair of Edna Pearls would make a good man leave home, or Cordie Mae Poovey wasn't two sizes bigger than a train wreck.

3

BOY
COLUMNIST

There are many lessons to be learned from the following chapter, such as how to inspect the cap of a wine bottle before your screw it off, where to get a good tattoo, what to do with your polyester leisure suits, how to tell whether or not something that goes bump in the night is about to get you, and where grits come from. This is a very intellectual chapter. . . .

Drinkin' Wine, Spodee-Odee

I have been checking around, and I have unearthed an incredible discovery: Very few newspapers have a wine columnist.

How absurd. Do newspapers not realize more and more Americans are drinking wine these days? Do they not realize there has been a tremendous increase in the number of wine commercials on television? And think how many fat, out-of-work actors that has helped.

Wine. What an intriguing subject. There have been odes written to it, and songs written about it, as the classic Jerry Lee Lewis rendition of:

> *Drinkin' wine, spodee-odee,*
> *Drinkin' wine.*
> *Drinkin' wine, spodee-odee,*
> *Drinkin' wine.*
> *Drinkin' wine, spodee-odee,*
> *Drinkin' wine.*
> *Pass 'at bottle to me.*

Historically, wine-drinking songs rely more on a catchy tune than lyrical quality.

By now you are probably saying to yourself, "Hey, this guy really knows his wine." But, of course.

I go way back with wine, back to when I was thirteen and I went off with my boyhood friend and idol, Weyman C. Wannamaker, Jr., a great American, who had swiped a bottle of something called Eleven Cellars, a rather indelicate port, from the storeroom of the local beer joint.

"Shall you taste, or shall I?" asked Weyman as he unscrewed the cap.

"Be my guest," I said.

"It's a good wine, but not a great wine," said Weyman after the first chug. "The bouquet leaves something to be desired, but its mood is rich."

Indeed. I required medical attention before the day was out. I told my mother I had been eating persimmons.

My knowledge and appreciation of wine was enhanced by a close association with one of the nation's leading wine experts, Ralph (High-Lift) Turnipseed.

When I was a kid, the county in which I lived was dry. That is, you had to buy your booze from a bootlegger in order to keep the church people happy.

One week the local bootlegger went on vacation, and Ralph was left without his normal supply of wine. So he drank Vitalis instead. After that, when he walked, he always picked up one of his legs much higher than the other. Thus, "High-Lift."

High-Lift preferred what he called "walking-around wine," a half-pint of just about anything that would flow downhill. Half-pint bottles would fit in his back pocket, and he therefore would not be bothered by having to carry around a large paper sack.

When he was sixty-five, the doctors told High-Life he wouldn't live another six months if he didn't slow down on his drinking. So he started drinking a lot faster after that and, sure enough, he was nearly eighty when he died. In a motorcycle accident.

Anyway, what this country needs is a good wine columnist and, once again, I must step in to fill the void. Here are a few tips to remember about wine from my very first wine column:

• Always check to see if the seal of the cap is intact before you allow the waiter to unscrew the cap off the bottle. If the seal has been broken, chances are the help has been nipping from the bottle back in the kitchen and may have refilled the portion they drank with water or 7-Up.

• Remember, it's white wine for fish or poultry, red wine for meat. For sardines and soda crackers in the alley, a nice, slightly pink MD 20-20 (any month) is certainly acceptable.

• Never order Wild Russian Vanya unless there is a CPR expert in the restaurant.

• If you're ever in Terre Haute, call EV-7-4433 and ask for Gladys. What's that got to do with wine? Take her a bottle of Gallo Thunderbird and you'll see.

Next time I will discuss what kind of paper cups are best when serving Cold Duck.

The Secrets of My Past

My admiration for Dan Rather, heir to CBS anchorman Walter Cronkite, went up a notch when I read he had admitted in an interview with *The Ladies Home Journal* he has used heroin.

"Not socially," says Rather, but "so I could write a story about it" when he worked in Houston.

Rather also said the experience was "a special kind of hell."

It is only right that a newsman of Rather's stature, who is entrusted with the faith and admiration of millions who watch him dole out the evening news, makes public any previously hidden incidents in his past that would be unveiled later and possibly cause him to lose credibility and respect.

We ask our politicians to open their backgrounds and checkbooks to public scrutiny, so why shouldn't we expect the same from our newspersons?

I'm glad I asked that question, because I am here today to make my life an open book, just like Dan Rather.

As a reader, you have every right to know whether I am a sane, normal person or whether I am some kind of dope-headed sicko who probably has been arrested a couple of times and doesn't like football.

We will do this in the form of an interview. First question, please:

Q. Have you ever "experimented" with drugs?

A. Yes. As part of a general science project in the seventh grade, I fed my neighbor's cat six bottles of aspirin to see what effect the six bottles of aspirin would have on a cat.

Q. And your findings?

A. After eating six bottles of aspirin, a cat will lie very still.

Q. You are evading the real question here. Have you, yourself, ever indulged in an illegal drug, such as marijuana?

A. I cannot tell a lie. Once at a party in Chicago I was with some weird people, and the host, who wore a lot of neck chains and didn't button the front of his shirt, passed around a marijuana cigarette to all his guests.

When it came my turn, the cigarette was very short. I attempted to smoke it, but I sucked the fire into my mouth, instead.

Marijuana causes large blisters on your tongue, so I don't smoke it any more.

Q. Have you ever been arrested?

A. No, but once I received a substantial penalty for early withdrawal from my passbook savings account. The bank teller hit me in the mouth.

Q. Have you ever undergone treatment for a psychiatric disorder?

A. That was in the third grade when the county health teacher was called in to question me concerning why I wouldn't go out of the building during recess to play with the rest of the children.

Q. And what did the health teacher find was your problem?

A. I was scared stiff of Cordie Mae Poovey, the meanest girl in school, who used to pound on my head during recess because she didn't like my looks.

Q. Do you ever drink to excess?

A. Only on weeknights. On weekends, I get blitzed.

Q. Are there any abnormal sexual tendencies in your background?

A. No, but I had a cousin who was a thespian.

Q. Is there anything more you would like to add to this investigation?

A. Just one more thing. When I wrote this column I was high on a plate of Uncle Sam's Red-Hot Texas Chili.

What's Preppy and What Ain't?

If you haven't picked up your copy of The Official Preppy Handbook, you absolutely must do so. Otherwise you might commit some horrid faux pas such as entering the wrong school, thereby being cursed for life as a member of the Great Unwashed.

For those who still are not certain exactly what a preppy is, he or she is a person who was to the manor born, so to speak, who is aware of all the social graces—and disgraces—and who always wears just the right clothing, goes to just the right vacation spots, and, of course, belongs to just the right clubs.

A snob, in other words.

It is important to know who and what is preppy today, since the ruling class has taken over the country again.

The Official Preppy Handbook, currently a runaway best seller, goes for the modest price of $3.95. But even at that, a lot of people probably will never get around to purchasing a copy of *TOPH,* and that concerns me greatly.

Who will lead the masses out of their ignorance? Who will tell the working class to turn up the collars on their pink Izods, to always keep a reserve pair of deck shoes and to name their children Muffy, Corkie, and Topsy (girls) and Chip, Kip, and Trip (boys)?

Many citizens, especially those whose club affiliations are with organizations bearing the names of large, hairy animals found in Canada, don't have the slightest idea that they should always wear gray flannels when having lunch at the Palm Court with Grandmother.

I am here to help these people. "Grizzard's Guide to What's Preppy and What Ain't" is available right here in this very column for free. So save your $3.95 and go buy a couple of six-packs of *brewskis,* an official preppy term for beer. Drinking beer is certainly preppy, as long as you don't do it between bouts at the wrestling matches.

CLOTHING: Throw away anything that resembles polyester, even relatives with stretch marks. A preppy wouldn't wear polyester to a ditch dig. Men, khaki is always safe, and women should stick to shirtdresses, wrap skirts and Calvin Klein jeans.

Women should never wear tank tops, especially if they have tattoos that would be exposed.

SCHOOLING: If you currently are enrolled in the Columbia School of Broadcasting, Harold's College of Transmission Repair, any public school, any barber school, or the University of Arkansas, you probably should commit suicide, or at least stay home nights.

CLUBS: When you hear the term "Junior League," do you think of (a) a spiffy women's service organization or (b) what the Kansas City Royals play in? If you answered "b," the Kiwanis wouldn't have you.

HOBBIES: The favorite hobbies of preppies are things like bird watching and collecting Chinese porcelain and Franklin Mint coins. Sorry, no preppy ever square-danced.

MONEY: You need a lot of this to be a preppy.

Take the following test to see if you qualify:

1. Is L.L. Bean (a) the senior senator from Idaho now that Frank Church is gone, (b) a vegetable, (c) a promising middleweight contender, or (d) a famous place in Maine where preppies like to shop?

2. Is Dom Perignon (a) a baseball player from someplace like Cuba, (b) a disease of the esophagus, (c) the CBS correspondent from Ankara, or (d) a very expensive champagne?

3. Is Perrier (a) Ronald Reagan, Jr.'s, best pal at dancing school, (b) the capital of South Dakota, (c) a nasal decongestant, or (d) bottled water preppies drink when they have a hangover?

If you answered anything but "d" on any question, go wait in the truck, Ripple-breath.

Dr. Feelbad

I was browsing through the papers when I ran across an interesting, but alarming, statistic: twenty percent of the medical costs in the country are being paid out by hypochondriacs—people who are convinced they are sick, but nobody will listen to them, especially doctors.

I have been a practicing hypochondriac for years, and I can't begin to tell you of the suffering. I have had symptoms of every known disease, but never have I been able to find a doctor who agrees with my diagnosis.

Like the time I had toe cancer. Toe cancer is when your little toe becomes swollen and sort of bent out of shape and hurts when you walk.

I went to my doctor, convinced my toe would have to be removed that afternoon, but hoping the leg, at least, could be saved.

My doctor took one look at my toe and said my shoes were too tight. So I changed to a half-size larger shoe, and my toe got better, proving loose shoes to be a definite cure for toe cancer.

This twenty percent thing bothers me because that is a bundle of money for hypochondriacs to be paying out to doctors to be told nothing is wrong with us. Hypochondriacs don't go to doctors to be told nothing is wrong; they go to be assured something most certainly is.

I think I have a solution to the problem. Rather than a doctor, what hypochondriacs need is another hypochondriac—like me, for instance—to tell them they are just as sick as they think they are, which would make them very happy. And think of the money they would save in doctor bills.

Maybe I could write the first newspaper advice column for hypochondriacs. They send in their symptoms, and I use my many years' experience diagnosing my own health problems to diagnose theirs.

Let's give it a practice run. I'll be "Dr. Feelbad, the hypochondriac's best friend," and the column would work something like this:

Dear Dr. Feelbad: After playing tennis, I get a terrible pain in my elbow. My doctor says all I have is common "tennis elbow." But I think it is something much worse. Which of us is correct?
—D.A., Pittsburgh, Pa.

Dear D.A.: You are. What does your doctor know about tennis? You don't have tennis "elbow." You have tennis "arm," and it probably will have to be amputated eventually, and you won't be able to play tennis. You will become a recluse and have to sit around staring out the window all the time. Have a nice day.

Dear Dr. Feelbad: I have a terrible headache. My wife says it is because I got smashed last night, but I know better. I know it probably is a brain tumor and I won't live until morning. How do I break the news to my wife?
—Checking Out, Mobile, Ala.

Dear Checking Out: Your diagnosis is absolutely correct. But wait until you and your wife are in bed and then break the bad news to her gently. But don't keep her up too late. Remember, she has to get up in the morning. You don't.

Dear Dr. Feelbad: I know the seven danger signals of cancer, and I worry about them all the time. But are there any others I could be worrying about, too? I'm getting bored with the first seven.
—Betty, Laredo, Texas

Dear Betty: You bet your boots there are. Here are some of my other favorite danger signals to worry about: Drowsiness toward midnight, increase in bellybutton lint, and sudden loss of memory after a half-dozen tequila shooters.

Dear Dr. Feelbad: Last evening I experienced chest pains and difficulty breathing. Incidentally, my girlfriend, Bearnice, who weighs 300 pounds, was sitting on me at the time. Could I have heart trouble?
—Slim, Terre Haute, Ind.

Dear Slim: Probably not. Bearnice's last boyfriend wrote in about the same thing, but all his problem turned out to be was four broken ribs, bruised kidneys, and a squashed liver. Sorry, better luck next time.

Mr. Cool

A couple of dashing young fellows named Gregory Smith White and Steve Woodward Naifeh have written a book on what men should do to be cool.

The book is titled *Moving Up in Style*, and it teaches men how to dress, what to order in a fancy restaurant, and why scratching your privates in public isn't such a good idea.

The only problem with the book is it is too expensive. It costs $10.95. For $10.95, you could by a case of beer or take a date to the wrestling match.

Who's got $10.95 to blow on some dumb book that gets all involved in what wines are from where and which ones you should drink with what? Just remember not to order a bottle with a screw-off top, and you can't go wrong.

What I am getting around to is this: I know a great deal about being cool myself, having been to three state fairs and to Daytona Beach when I was in high school.

I also know why this distasteful ethnic joke is supposed to be funny:

What are they drinking these days in Poland? Perrier and water.

So there is absolutely no reason to go out and blow $10.95 on Gregory Whozits and Steve Whatshisface's book when, for the price of this newspaper, you can read my occasional "Mr. Cool" column where male readers write in and ask questions concerning style and good taste.

Are you a male? Do you have a question concerning style and good taste? Is so, write "Mr. Cool," in care of me, and if you're lucky, I'll pick your question to answer, and all your friends will get to see your name in print.

Incidentally, a couple of bucks in the envelope and Mr. Cool will personally see to it that you get lucky, which still saves you nearly nine dollars.

Here is the Mr. Cool column for today, jut to give you an idea of how the deal works:

Dear Mr. Cool: I am thirty-two and have been dating my current girlfriend, who is twenty-five, for six months. So far, we have not kissed because I am afraid of where it could lead. Has it been long enough that I should go ahead and give in? Mom says "no."
—Skippy Winthrop III, Spartanburg, S.C.

Dear Skippy: If you're as dippy as you sounded in your letter, I doubt if kissing could lead anywhere but to total revulsion for your girlfriend, who obviously is after you for your bucks.

So tell your Mom to take a hike. Just remember, while you're kissing, it's not cool to peep to see if she has her eyes closed.

Dear Mr. Cool: Me and my woman, Betty Louann Sue, went out drinking the other night. I ordered us two cans of beer, and the waitress brought us two glasses. I know one of the glasses was for Betty Louann Sue to drink her PBR out of, but what was the other one for?—**Ronnie Ray Tucker, Vidalia, Ga.**

Dear Ronnie Ray: The answer to that question would only confuse you. Go put another quarter in the juke box and punch E-4, "We Used to Kiss on the Lips, But It's All Over Now."

Dear Mr. Cool: Is it ever permissible to wear white socks? —**Harley Fingers, Birmingham, Ala.**

Dear Harley: Certainly. While hanging out at the Moose Lodge or attending your bowling team's annual banquet, for instance. Also, white socks may be worn with anything made of polyester, or anybody named Betty Louann Sue.

Dear Mr. Cool: What is the proper wine to serve with Boston Scrod?—**Telly Cervantes, Malibu, Calif.**

Dear Telly: Anybody who would eat something called "scrod" wouldn't know the difference. Start with Ripple and work your way down.

Dear Mr. Cool: I want to get a tattoo. All my friends—Butch, Leroy, and Killer—have them. Butch and Leroy have theirs on their forearms. Killer has his on his chest. Where is the best place to get a tattoo?—**Bevo Scrump, Palatka, Fla.**

Dear Bevo: Pete's Transmission Shop and Tattoo Parlor, West Memphis, Ark.

Wrong Shade of Red

Since I have been writing a column, I have been called a lot of names.

"Redneck" is a favorite among many of my loyal readers.

"You redneck, why don't you ride off into the sunset in your pickup?" they write when they particularly enjoy one of my columns.

"Buzzard" is another favorite, because it sort of sounds like my name. Actually, "buzzard" and "Griz-ZARD," which is the way my father taught me to pronounce my name, don't sound alike at all, but they sort of look alike, which is enough for me to get ten or twenty letters a week that begin:

"Dear Buzzard, I will never read your column again."

What is interesting about that is two weeks later, I receive another batch of hate mail from the same creeps, uh, fans.

Anyway, this is all leading up to something, I think, and that is to inform you that for the first time in my career, I have been called a "communist."

Actually, I have been called even more than that. I have been called a "liberal, socialistic communist," which is really calling somebody something, like when you say a person is a "dumb, hillbilly redneck" or a "lizard, gizzard buzzard."

Robert E. Crout of Greenville, South Carolina, an important textile town located somewhere near Interstate 85, is the one who called me that name.

He wrote a letter to my editor that said, "It is my firm opinion that the majority of readers with common sense are tired of the liberal, socialistic, communist view of Lewis Grizzard."

My editor, who is a close friend of mine, couldn't wait to publish that letter.

What had Mr. Crout so upset, apparently, was the fact that I recently published a copy of the official senility test they are going to give Ronald Reagan, who is nearly as old as baseball, when he starts forgetting things like where he sent Alexander Haig and why.

"It is about time," continued Mr. Crout's letter, "all of us begin to remember a few of the 'Communist Rules for Revolution'. . . .

"Get control of all means of publicity and thereby divide the people into hostile groups by constantly harping on controversial matters of no importance and destroy people's faith in their natural leaders by holding (them) up to contempt, ridicule and obloquy."

My mother read that letter. So did my wife, and my minister, and maybe even both of my ex-mothers-in-law, who probably made copies and passed them around.

I demand equal time:

Mr. Crout, I am a lot of things. A Methodist, for instance. But I am not now, nor have I ever been, a commie. I have never read the

"Communist Rules for Revolution," as you quite obviously have. I don't even know who wrote them.

Furthermore, how could I be a good commie if I don't even know what "obloquy" is? It probably is some swill of a soup they serve to poor suckers who get sent to Siberia.

Mr. Crout, I was a Boy Scout and a Little Leaguer. The only political parties in which I involve myself are election-night bashes with free food and booze. I own two "America: Love It or Leave It" bumper stickers, and I know all the words to Merle Haggard's patriotic ditty, "Walkin' on the Fightin' Side of Me."

I love the memory of John Wayne, the Dodgers, hot dogs with mustard, apple pie a la mode (even when you can't get any ice cream to put on it), my mother, college football, fuzzy puppies, cold beer, and courthouse squares. Walter Cronkite gives me goose pimples.

I don't drink vodka, and I once observed that Russian women give the plain-toed work boots they wear a bad name.

Me, a rotten, pinko commie? That's a hoot. Whoever heard of a commie in a pickup? They ride around in those foreign-made vans with slogans printed all over the side. Everybody knows that.

So go take a brain scan to see if anything shows up, Mr. Kraut, or Mr. Croop, or whatever your name was. Better yet, go stick your head in a bucket of obloquy.

Cooter Brown Award

The time has come to announce the winner of the First Annual Drunk-As-Cooter Brown Award. The award is named for the immortal Cooter Brown, who could get drunker than anybody.

Once Cooter got so drunk he wandered into the middle of a church service and began babbling incoherently.

"Praise the Lord!" somebody screamed out. "That man is speaking in tongues!"

"No, he's not," said somebody else. "It's just Cooter Brown trying to sing, 'There Stands the Glass.'"

"There Stands the Glass," I might explain, is a Webb Pierce classic, a favorite of many a drinking man.

This award, conceived by me, neither encourages nor condones drinking, but I do feel if someone distinguishes himself in that area, he should not go unrecognized.

The winner of the First Annual Drunk-As-Cooter Brown Award goes to a fellow I know, Rigsby, who got so drunk on a recent business trip that he checked into his hotel twice.

"Nobody gets that drunk," I said.

"Yes, they do," said Rigsby. "I got off the airplane, went straight to my hotel and checked in. But I didn't go to my room. I met some business associates in the bar, and we proceeded to drink for several hours.

"We got pretty much oiled and decided to go somewhere for dinner. I drove my rental car. I parked it in front of this brick wall.

"When we came out of the restaurant, after dinner and some more drinks, I cranked the car, the accelerator stuck, and I went smashing into the brick wall."

"Anybody hurt?" I asked.

"No," Rigsby replied, "but the car was totaled."

"What did you do then?"

"Well, my associates suggested I push the car away from the wall, call the police, and tell them that while I was in the restaurant, my car was smashed and whoever did it drove away."

"Did the scheme work?" I inquired.

"I think the police were really going for my story," said Rigsby, "until they found the brick in the grillwork of the car."

"Did they book you?" I went on.

"For being drunk, of course," Rigsby explained, "and also for carrying a concealed weapon."

"A concealed weapon?"

"You're not going to believe this: I had ordered a steak for dinner, but I couldn't eat it all. So I asked for a doggie bag. I also thought of the fact that if I were going to eat the rest of my steak later in my room, I would need a knife.

"When nobody was looking, I slipped my knife into my inside coat pocket. I tried to explain that to the officers, but they didn't believe me, especially since I had been so intent on taking the knife, I had forgotten the doggie bag with the rest of my steak in it."

His associates, Rigsby said, finally were able to obtain his release in the wee hours of the morning. He took a taxi back to his hotel.

"I was still drunk," he said, "so I checked in again. It was the next morning before I discovered I had two keys and two rooms. I should never have drunk those last six tequila shooters."

The selection committee (me) already is looking for candidates for next year's award. If you think you or somebody you know qualifies, enter soon. Remember, the bigger the fool you made of yourself, the better chance you have to win.

"I'll drink to that," said Rigsby, whose latest escapade was getting soused and losing his rental car.

"I parked it somewhere in the Midwest," he explained. "I just can't remember which state."

Cooter Brown, rest his soul, would have been proud.

Journalism Lesson

The $1.6 million libel judgment handed down against the *National Enquirer* in favor of entertainer Carol Burnett may not have sounded like earth-shaking news to most of the nation, but to those of us in the rumor and innuendo business, it was a landmark decision.

Such a thing could lead to the unspeakable: columnists, like yours truly, might have to start dealing in facts.Most of us became columnists because gathering facts is hard work and facts will ruin a good story quicker than anything.

Most readers, I have found, know little about how a newspaper works. In order to show you just how much trouble this Carol Burnett thing could cause, let me give you a little short course in print journalism that you won't get on "Lou Grant."

First, there is the "legitimate" press. Newspapers in big towns like Atlanta, Washington and Boston and New York and Chicago, and newspapers in little towns like Paducah and Moline and Valdosta are "legitimate" newspapers.

That means they actually pay "reporters" to go out and gather "facts." Their columnists are the only ones who can just make stuff up.

(There is an exception to every rule, of course, as in the case this week of the *Washington Post* reporter who won a Pulitzer for a figment of her imagination. Too bad the *Post* editors never noticed her potential as a columnist.)

On the other hand, there is the "illegitimate" press, like the *National Enquirer* and other such newspapers one usually can purchase in supermarkets. Reporters, columnists, the publisher—EVERYBODY—on these newspapers writes gossip, trash, and totally unfounded rumors like Secretary of State Alexander Haig is really a robot and Richard Nixon has the controls.

So they stick it to the *National Enquirer* today. Tomorrow, it could be the "legitimate" press they come after, and who they will come after first are stiffs like me who have to test our imaginations day after day. Anybody can report the "facts."

Prominent local businessman Ernest T. Broomthistle, of Broomthistle and Farkle, was fined $10 in City Traffic Court today for an illegal lane change on Oak Street.

Who wants to read dull garbage like that? Any columnist worth his salt could do a lot more with ol' Broomthistle. Stand back and watch me work:

"So the cops have finally nabbed ol' Ernie 'Big E' Broomthistle, the big-biz bigwig of Broomthistle and Farkle, local manufacturer of women's hosiery, and, according to certain sources, a few other unmentionable garments that are listed only in a 'special' catalog, not readily available to the general public.

"The charge against Broomthistle, who always wears sunglasses and drives a big black car, was 'illegal lane change.' Don't make me laugh. He was stopped on Oak Street, only five blocks from the Three Moons Lounge. What does that tell you?

"A little checking also indicated Broomthistle's partner, Milburn Farkle, lives on Oak Street with his wife, Mona (alias Boom-Boom), former Miss Oklahoma City Rodeo, 1959. Mr. Farkle, it seems was out of town on business the day his partner and alleged best friend, Broomthistle, was caught weaving all over the road just a few blocks up from where his wife was home all alone, probably wearing some of those unmentionable garments from the 'special catalog.'

"The judge who handed down the paltry $10 fine against Broomthistle was Judge Garvin Pendergrass, incidentally. Some interesting connections between Broomthistle and Pendergrass also have been uncovered.

"Pendergrass, for instance, is originally from Virginia. Broomthistle is from Delaware. Both states were included in the thirteen original colonies.

"One other thing. Both men are bilingual."

If they ever do come after me like they went after the *National Enquirer*, I hope the jury will remember just one thing: It ain't easy being a genius.

A Word for Insomniacs

Because of my vast knowledge of many subjects, readers write to me and ask all sorts of questions.

Some of the questions aren't very nice. Like when are you going to leave town? And, how did a creep like you get a job with the newspaper?

However, I do get intelligent, interesting questions, and one that came recently was quite intriguing. The question had to do with insomnia, which millions of Americans, including myself, suffer in varying degrees.

The question was: "Dear Mr. Grizzard, I have insomnia. I lie awake all night long in my bed and hear strange noises which make me very nervous and, of course, unable to sleep. What are these noises and are they really nothing to worry about?"

The letter was signed. "Scared Silly, Tupelo, Mississippi."

I am glad you wrote to me, Scared Silly, and I hope I can help. From childhood, we all are frightened of "things that go bump in the night." Some of us grow out of this fear, others do not.

You obviously haven't grown out of this fear, and neither have I. For years I have suffered from insomnia because I know "something" is out there in the dark. I can hear "it" creaking and crawling and coming to get me.

I especially hear these noises when I have watched the Friday Night Horror Double Feature or when I had lots of garlic for dinner.

I am sorry I can't allay your fears, Scared Silly, but I still may be able to offer some assistance by identifying the noises you may be hearing and explaining what they mean.

Incidentally, do not read this while you are alone or where something can sneak up behind you.

• CREEEEEAK! This is a sound commonly heard in the night by insomniacs and other chickens. It probably is nothing. Then, again, it could be the sound of one of your doors slowly being pushed open by an escapee from a local mental institution who inspired the movie *The Texas Chainsaw Massacre.*

• BLIP! BLIP! BLIP! Probably nothing more than a dripping faucet. But what if it were something else? What if it were the sound of blood slowly dripping onto the floor? Your floor. The floor in the next room. A wounded, mad-dog killer has escaped from the authorities and is looking for another victim. Either that, or Dracula has come to suck the blood from your neck. I'll take my chances with the mad-dog killer.

• BLAM! I hear that sound all the time. It's nothing, I tell myself. A book fell off a table. It's the ice maker in the refrigerator. The wind blew one of the shutters against the side of the house. Burglars are working their way to the bedroom to finish off any possible witnesses. Demons, like the kind that got Linda Blair, are throwing my den furniture around. Killer bees are building their hive in the attic.

• WHOOOOOSH! That's nothing. That just somebody flushing a toilet. But you are alone in the house.

• THUUUUMP! Anybody who has ever been awake at night knows this one. You always hear it as you are just about to doze off. You awaken and you lie there, listening for another sound. You are afraid to move. If you move, "it" will know where you are and "it" will find you. If you should hear a second THUUUUMP, don't even bother to scream.

I hope this helps, Scared Silly, and be sure to write me again if there is anything else I can do. Incidentally, before you go to bed tonight, there is one other thing I should mention.

"It" was last seen near Tupelo, Mississippi. Sweet dreams.

True Grits

I was hoping that four years of Georgian Jimmy Carter in the White House would finally clear up the matter of grits. Grits have been so terribly misunderstood by people who are from parts of the country other than the South.

But, alas, Georgia's Jimmy is only a few weeks from departing Washington in favor of Californian Ronald Reagan, who wouldn't know grits from granola, and I fear grits will never cross the gap that has left so many yet unaware of the history and many uses of one of America's most interesting foods.

As one of the nation's leading experts on grits (my mother served them every morning for breakfast), all I can do is try to light the way for those still blinded by prejudice and fear.

Grits won't bite you. Grits taste good and they're good for you. Just sit back and relax and put yourself in my hands and let's go. "DISCOVERING GRITS: GRIZZARD'S GUIDE TO A SOUTHERN DELICACY FOR FOLKS FROM NEW JERSEY AND PLACES LIKE THAT":

• The origin of grits:

Cherokee Indians, native to the Southern region of the United States, first discovered grits trees growing wild during the thirteenth century. Chief Big Bear's squaw, Jemima Big Bear, is said to have been out of oatmeal one day, so she gathered the tiny grits growing from the grits trees and cooked them in water for Chief Big Bear.

After eating the grits, Chief Big Bear ordered his squaw, Jemima, burned at the stake.

Later, however, Southern planter Jim Dandy found grits taste a lot better if you put salt and pepper and butter on them. Grits really took off in the South after that. Today, grits orchards may be seen from the Carolinas to Florida and west to Louisiana.

At some orchards, tourists may "pick their own grits." If you decide to give it a try, make cetain each grit you pick is ripe and firm. Raw grits tend to stick to the roof of your mouth and have been known to choke even large goats.

• How grits got their name:

From the Cherokee word, *greyette*, which means "corn pebbles." The Cherokee thought grits were tiny versions of corn. They even tried to make bread from grits, which brought about another big run on squaw-burning.

• What does the word "hominy" mean?

It is Southern for "blended voices," as in, "That quartet sure has nice hominy, don't it?"

• How to prepare grits:

First, go out to your grits tree and pick a peck of grits. Wash, then allow to soak in warm buttermilk for an hour. Add two tablespoons Jack Daniel (Black Label) Tennessee sippin' whiskey and one cup branch water.

Stir, bake at 450 for approximately one hour. Cover with sawmill gravy, add butter, then salt and pepper to taste. Cheese (Kraft American) optional.

Must be served hot. Cold grits tend to get gummy. You wouldn't serve cold, gummy grits to communist sympathizers from New York.

• What are some other uses for grits?

Patching blow-outs. Snake bite. Bathroom calking. In some parts of the South it is even believed grits will grow hair. This is doubtful. Grits do make a delightful party punch, however. Just add more Jack Daniel.

• How can I order my grits tree?

By sending $38.95 for each tree desired to "Grits-a-Grow-Grow," in care of me. Add $15 if you want to take advantage of our special offer for our handy "Grit-Picker," which will save time and wear and tear on your hands when you go out to gather your grits off your new grits tree.

• What else may I order from "Grits-a-Grow-Grow"?

A special brochure outlining how you can purchase valuable vacation property at our new Alligator Point resort in Florida and about six zillion copies of Amy Carter's Washington Coloring Book. Order now while they last.

4

ORDINARY
PEOPLE

The best stories are true stories, the real stories about real people. . . .

Team Man

The little boy who lives at my house is about to embark upon his first season of organized baseball. He is barely housebroken, but they have something called Tee-ball for youngsters still only a short pop fly from the cradle.

In Tee-ball, there is no pitcher. The ball sits on a tee, perfectly still, to make it easier for the child to swat it.

A golfer probably invented Tee-ball.

Regardless of how easy they made it for kids in Tee-ball, the little boy who lives at my house is going to have some problems.

First, he doesn't understand the basics of the game of baseball. I thought boy-children were born with the knowledge of how to run the bases, as in you run to first first.

Not so. When he tried out for his team, his coach asked him to run the bases.

He ran to second first, to third second, to home third, and then slid into first last.

Actually, it wasn't a slide, it was more of a *crawl*.

Later, I asked the little boy why he crawled on his stomach into first base.

He said, "That's the way baseball players do it because they don't want anybody to see them sneaking into the base."

Oh.

The biggest problem he is going to have, however, is with his thumb-sucking.

Now, let's go over thumb-sucking for a moment.

357

There is nothing wrong with it. Sucking one's thumb does not make one a bad person.

It is just a habit, a way children relax and relieve tension. Adults have double martinis, kids have thumb-sucking.

If double martinis were suddenly taken away from them, a lot of adults probably would suck their thumbs.

I am certain the little boy eventually will dispense with sucking his thumb, but likely not before his first game of Tee-ball and that's the big trouble here.

I had never thought of this before, but after going out into the yard and tossing a few balls around with the little boy to get him ready for the season, I realized how hard it is to play baseball and suck your thumb at the same time.

Consider: The child is a lefty. He bats, throws, and sucks left.

So, he's playing the outfield and a long fly ball is hit in his direction. The winning run is at third, one out. The runner will try to tag and come home.

The little boy runs for the ball, which is no easy task with a thumb in your mouth. He catches it, but before he can make his throw to the plate, he must remove his thumb from his mouth, hoping the rest of his throwing hand will follow.

The split second he loses with all that wasted motion allows the winning run to score. He is the goat of the game.

I tried to make that point to him.

"You don't want to let the rest of the Cardinals down, do you?" I asked him, appealing to his conscience.

"No," he replied. "I'll try to remember not to suck my thumb when there is anybody on base."

At least the kid's a team man, thumb in or thumb out.

Learning a Lesson

WASHINGTON, D.C.—The kid was twelve, maybe thirteen, and he had sad eyes and a look about him that said he wanted to cry.

But he wouldn't cry, because streetwise kids from the tough neighborhoods are cried out by his age.

He was standing at the entrance to Washington's bustling Union Station, hiding, sort of, behind one of the giant pillars.

All about him were travelers, coming and going, and why he picked me, I don't know. This taxi had dropped me off with my bags. My train would leave in fifteen minutes.

"Can I carry your bags to the train, mister?" the kid asked.

I travel a great deal by train. The way you get your bags down to the train is you find a dying breed called a "redcap," and he puts your bags on the train, and then you pay him maybe two dollars for the service.

Sometimes you can find a redcap. Sometimes you can't. I looked around. I didn't see a redcap. I had more bags than I could handle. Time was running out on me.

I looked at the kid again. Maybe this is some kind of new sting, I thought. The kid takes my bags and when I turn my head for a moment, he is gone, and so are my bags.

But not this kid. Don't ask me how I knew that, I just knew that. Listen, I said to myself, at least he's trying to *work*. He could be out trying to break into a house or into somebody's car.

So just as I was about to turn over my bags to the kid, up walks a redcap.

"Get out of here, kid!" he shouts, and the kid recoils at first, and then makes a stand of it.

"I ain't doin' nothing wrong," the kid says to the redcap, and then they go one-on-one.

"You got no business out here!"

"I'm just tryin' to make a coupla dollars. What's wrong with that, man?"

"Ain't nothin' wrong with that, except it's my two dollars you tryin' to make."

"I got a right to work out here, too."

"You ain't got no kind of rights to work out here. You too young, for one thing."

"I ain't too young."

"The hell you ain't. And you ain't paid no union dues, either, man."

At this point, the kid is stymied. Also, imagine my predicament. Now, my train is leaving in ten minutes, and I'm still standing outside the station.

A station security guard appears out of the air.

"What's the problem?" he asks the redcap.

"Stupid kid's out here hustling my bags, that's the problem," the redcap answers.

Eight minutes to go until train time.

"Don't you know you have to be hired before you can go to work out here?" the security guard asks the kid.

"I just wanted to make a coupla dollars. What's wrong with that, man?" repeats the kid.

"It just don't work that way, son," says the security guard, and by now the redcap has my bags on his cart and he is wheeling them to my train, which I barely will make.

I left the kid with the security guard.

As I handed the two dollars to the redcap for putting my bags onto the train, he said to me, "Don't worry about that kid. He'll learn soon enough. It's every man for himself out here."

Kids. It just takes them a while to catch on, that's all.

Good News

Earl Sheriff, sixty-eight, is custodian at the little high school in the village of Fredericktown, Ohio, which is near Columbus.

You ought to hear them talk about "Mr. Sheriff" around the school.

"He's the sweetest, kindest, most helpful man I've ever known," one of the teachers was saying. "We couldn't get along without him."

Still, nobody knew much about Earl Sheriff's background until one day when some of the students, who were in the midst of a course called U.S. Wars, casually asked the custodian if he knew anything about WW II, the Big One.

Earl Sheriff knew quite a bit. He had lived through it, as a matter of fact, and the students asked him to come and lecture the class.

So here is the school custodian lecturing in the classroom, and Sgt. Earl Sheriff talked about how he had served as a light machine-gun section leader and how he had hit Utah Beach with the 121st Infantry as part of the first replacement unit in after D-Day.

He also mentioned fighting through the hedgerow country of France and into the Hurtgen Forest. And he brought along his Purple Heart—he was wounded three times—and his Silver Star and his Medal of Luxembourg.

"The light machine guns went ahead of the infantry," Earl Sheriff told the students. "We were up there where we could look the Germans in the eyes. It was hell, but we had a job to do, and we did it— and a lot of good boys got killed."

An old soldier remembers, and today's high school students, ages fifteen through seventeen, listen to stories of a fabled time when Americans went to war wearing white hats, and "technical problems" didn't scrub missions. Somebody fixed the machine and the fight went on.

Ancient history, in other words.

When Earl Sheriff finished his lecture, one of the students asked him if he ever saw any of the men he had fought beside.

The custodian said there was an annual reunion of the 121st, but he had never been able to attend.

"Never could get time off from work," he said. Another problem is that his wife is an invalid.

I wondered about those students. Did they really care today how we gave Hitler hell, and what the cost of it was? Have we been on a losing streak so long they could not look at the old man in front of them and sense his pride for having a job to do, and for having done it?

Get the picture here. As the students' teacher put it, "This is still middle America. This is mostly a farm community. These are good kids. They care."

They do. I'll keep this short. What the students did was canvass the school and ask for donations. They raised $250, and they gave it to Earl Sheriff for a round-trip airplane ticket to Macon, Georgia, this week.

There he will attend the reunion of the 121st Infantry Regiment for the first time.

"Seeing all those fellows again," he said, "was always a dream of mine. Now it is coming true."

A group of high school students in 1980 have dug deep into their pockets for an old soldier who fought with our last winner.

You're always clamoring for "good" news out there. This should be a gracious dose.

Forgotten Hero

I heard him tell the story so many times.

He and his men were camped in some godforsaken place in Korea. The Chinese had just entered the war in November. The year was 1950.

"They caught us completely by surprise," he said. "I looked up at this hill and every gook on earth was coming over it."

War was nothing new to him. He had fought his way through France, leading nineteen-year-olds, six years earlier.

"Fighting Germans," he would explain, "was one thing, but fighting these crazy people was something else. German soldiers were intelligent, they thought like Americans. You could figure out their next move.

"These people, the Chinese, were nuts. They didn't value human life. You'd kill one and ten more would come over that hill to take his place." His company was being annihilated. He was sure he would die. He had a wife and a kid back home.

"About thirty of us, the last ones left, dug a pit and held them off for hours," he would go on. "But they finally pitched a mortar right in the middle of the pit. It took off the head of this kid. I'll never forget seeing that. The chaplain got it, too.

"There was so much smoke and noise, I didn't know if anybody else around me was alive. I pulled some bodies over me and prayed they wouldn't notice me."

Maybe it was the prayers. The enemy didn't notice him. He waited under the bodies for hours, afraid to bat an eye, afraid to move for fear of being discovered.

Finally, he stood up. There was total silence around him, a sea of dead. He looked around in the pit. He found a young soldier still breathing. He poured water out of his canteen onto the young soldier's face. He came around.

"I knew he was hurt, but I had to move him," he explained. He carried the soldier as he wandered into the night. When he became so tired he couldn't go another inch, he sat down under a tree and propped the soldier against the tree next to him.

He slept. Sometime in the night, his only companion died.

He continued to wander, now alone, through the next morning. It was a friendly North Korean soldier, who had been forced into duty and was hiding himself, who saw him and befriended him and saved the man's life.

He took the American back to where his family was living in a lean-to at the base of a mountain. He put the American in a hole and covered the hole with boards and straw. Each day for six weeks, he would emerge from his own hiding place to bring the American rice in the hole. The American could hear enemy troop movement around him.

Water seeped into the hole, but the American didn't dare come out for fear of being discovered. His feet froze. When it was finally safe to travel, he said his steps were like "walking on two basketballs."

The friendly soldier eventually led him back to the American lines. The Army notified the man's family that he was no longer missing in action. After a hospital stay in Pearl Harbor, he was allowed to come home.

He had distinguished himself. He had fought two wars for his country. He had a head full of shrapnel, two bullet holes in his hip, and he wouldn't be able to sleep without first emptying a bottle of amber medicine.

His wife and his son and his mother-in-law met him at the train when he arrived home. A local newspaper reporter showed up, too.

But there was no band, no parade, no well wishes, nor a message from his commander-in-chief. He never complained, of course, but later there was little, if any, rehabilitation, either. He never really made it back from that pit in Korea from under the bodies of those dead friends.

His feet bled every day. He died a drunk and a pauper.

We didn't do anything wrong welcoming home the former hostages from Iran. They deserved every yellow ribbon, every hand held out toward them.

But a lot of heroes who preceded them went virtually unnoticed, and for one in particular, I've felt a twinge of bitterness lately. I demand at least that.

Townsend

Jim Townsend died soon after I wrote the following piece. I'm convinced he is presently in heaven, trying to con Hemingway and Voltaire into doing something for the new magazine he's starting.

This will probably read like a book review, but it's not. It's a story about a friend of mine who recently had a book published, a special friend more people genuinely love than just about anybody else I know.

His name is Townsend.

Yeah, he's got a first name, "James," and a middle initial, "L.," but you don't need any of those. He is "Townsend," always "Townsend," forever "Townsend."

His book is *Dear Heart* (Peachtree Publishers), and in his book Townsend takes you from Lanett, Alabama, his hometown, to any number of magic places, with numerous stops in Atlanta, a city he describes as the best city in America for "rearing a family, living in safety, and moving around without unreasonable delay."

One of the reasons so many people love Townsend so much is because he would be optimistic with all four engines out and the tail section on fire, flying through a hurricane.

Townsend, among other things, founded *Atlanta Magazine*. He edited it and nursed it, and he did the same in Cincinnati and in New

Orleans and you name the town, chances are Townsend put his genius to work there at some point.

But Atlanta, how the man loves Atlanta.

In the introduction to *Dear Heart*, fellow author and friend Pat Conroy says of Townsend and what he's meant to this city:

"Atlanta, forgetful city, feisty and brawling and on the go, has not yet honored Jim Townsend, has not paused to thank the man, has not slowed down for one single act of gratitude and appreciation to the man who helped to invent the image of Atlanta.

"But when the history of Atlanta is written, and when they talk about who created the soul of this city, they will have to deal with the brilliant, mercurial, contradictory, and infinitely complex figure of Jim Townsend."

I first met Townsend in a bar. When you met Townsend a few years back, you always met him in a bar.

"Grizzard," he said to me. "I've got a story only you can do." Townsend said that to all the writers.

You didn't always get paid. Lee Walburn, now editor-in-chief of *Atlanta Weekly*, explains on the back of Townsend's new book why that never really bothered you as much as it probably should have:

"Townsend is a lovable old basset hound of an editor whose eloquent cajolery has charmed a million words from hundreds of writers—sometimes for pay, sometimes for promises. The sharing of this collection from his own jewel bag of words pays all debts."

Townsend finally whipped his boozing problem. Now he's got another bear to fight. Cancer.

Still, he's down almost every day on the seventh floor at 72 Marietta Street where *Atlanta Weekly* comes together. He edits. He writes notes. Townsend is the most eloquent note-writer who ever doodled across a scratch pad.

His book sings. There are tent revivals, twenty-fifth anniversary parties at ice cream parlors, and he explains what a "gradualist" is, and you meet H. L. Hunt and Count Alexis de Sakhnoffsky, and there is a piece about Townsend's daddy who was sharecropping cotton in West Georgia when McKinley was shot down in Buffalo.

I just want to say one more thing, and I want to say it directly to Townsend:

I read your book in one easy sitting, and I won't be satisfied until I've read more. You're beautiful, dear heart. Just beautiful.

No Easy Way Out

We aren't, well, close, but we've had a few high times together, enough to keep us reminiscing for a couple of hours at least before we have to start telling the same stories over again.

So I was shocked when I heard the news. This man, a young man, put a .38-caliber pistol to his head. And pulled the trigger.

Say you are just trying to get somebody's attention or sympathy. You take a few pills and wind up getting your stomach pumped out in the hospital.

I'm no shrink, but I know that if you put a pistol to your head and pull the trigger, you are serious about leaving us.

It's like the man's attorney said later: "Imagine his surprise when he woke up and found out he wasn't in the Promised Land after all. He was right back here with the rest of us."

Yeah, he lived. Barely. They were already talking about where to send the remains.

I went to see him in the hospital the other night. I'm not going to mention his name. He's had enough bad publicity in his life already, and there are two children who carry his name.

"You look awful," I said to him.

"Can you believe this?" he laughed. His spirits were surprisingly high. "The last thing in the world I try to do, and I louse it up."

He spared no details.

I already knew about his divorce. Then he ran afoul of the law. Nothing big-time, but enough to bring the heat close enough to feel it.

Then, there was the lady. Stop me if you've heard this one before.

"I thought she was really special," he said.

"They've got that way of fooling us sometimes," I said.

"I just fell apart," he said. "All I could think of was I wanted out. I wanted my ticket punched."

"So what did you do, uh, wrong?" I asked. He held a finger of his right hand to his head and explained to me what the doctors had explained to him.

"They said I held the gun at an angle, so the bullet went through my right eye and out above my left eye. They said most people who shoot themselves in the head hold the gun straight, and it blows their brains out."

Above his left eye was the hole where the bullet left his head. He has lost his right eye. I made some crack about women thinking eye-patches are sexy. He is lucky he isn't blind.

I had to ask. I had to ask what it felt like to nearly die. You've read all those stories of what people saw and felt before they miraculously escaped death's clutches.

"I don't remember anything," he said. "There was a thud in my head after I pulled the trigger, and then, two days later, I woke up and I didn't know if I was in heaven or hell. I just knew I had an awful headache and there were tubes all over me."

There was something else I had to ask. I wanted to know if he was happy he had missed the obit page after all his efforts to make it there.

"I tried to get out, and I didn't make it," he answered.

He is no manner of a poet, and I had never seen sensitivity in him before. But he had something he wanted me to read. On a yellow sheet he had scribbled out the following words:

I am an incurable romantic. I believe in hopes, dreams, and decency. I believe in love, tenderness, kindness, and family. I believe in mankind.

But I must never let my happiness depend entirely on another person's thoughts, whims, or demands. Nor can I forget the value of honesty, the harshness at times of reality, and warmth of life itself, nor the need for love.

Nice thoughts. I got up to leave.

"If you write something in the paper about this," said the man, "will you do me one favor?"

"Sure. What?"

"Tell anybody who's thinking of doing what I did not to do it. It's not the easy way out after all."

Dark Eyes

It's an old story. She was seventeen at the time. She's more than twice that now, but still dark-eyed and beautiful. The first time I saw her, half of my life ago, she nearly took my breath.

It was a small town in the hills, and her mother taught in the little high school. Her father split when she was a baby. Her mother never remarried. There were no more children.

Her mother raised her on grace and good manners.

"Mama," she would say, laughing, "Mama always told me to act like she was looking over my shoulder. I always knew that, somehow, she was."

The child grew to be a beauty, and also a scholar. Besides that, she sang in church and visited the old people.

The boys flocked around her and vied for even her slightest attention. Those were simpler times.

She conquered high school in a matter of days. Cheerleader, clubs, a dozen handsome fellows already left in her wake by her junior year.

She was perfect. Life was perfect. Nothing could go wrong.

Something went wrong. Forget about a drug, booze, or sex angle here, however. This was the early sixties, small town, and Homecoming Night at the high school stadium.

She was one of the finalists, and she would win, of course, because she was the most popular girl in school. The homecoming queen would be chosen by ballot of the student body, the results to be announced at half time.

She was dazzling that night, a girl-child on the fine edge of womanhood.

The results were announced. She won. Her mother beamed; she had done her best under some tough circumstances.

There was another family in the town that was THE family in town. If you worked in town, normally you worked for THE family. They lived in the big house with shade trees framing the drive up to the front door.

And there was a daughter in the family, too, the same age as dark-eyes, and she was a member of the Homecoming Court that night, too.

When the name of the queen was announced, the mother of the loser stormed school officials and demanded that the ballots be recounted. Don't forget, THE family gave money for the new gymnasium and bought uniforms for the band.

The ballots were recounted. At the end of the game, there was a simple announcement. There had been a mistake. There was a new homecoming queen.

They made dark-eyes give back her crown and her roses.

"I thought I would die," she said. "And I think I would have if it hadn't been for Mama. The embarrassment was incredible. Mama said, 'Go back to school, face whatever comes. If you run from this, it could change your entire life.'"

She didn't run. She went back to school. And when it was her time, she caught a bus out of town and never looked back.

We met again by chance the other day. I didn't mention the story, and neither did she. She's been a resounding success. The lady has guts.

I do wish I knew whatever happened to Miss Homecoming, though. I hope she got fat.

5

EATING LIVER AND OTHER SINS

One thing that has always puzzled me: everytime I write a column in which I mention God, at least five people write me a letter and threaten to kill me. . . .

Preacher Jokes

We had the minister over for dinner the other evening, and I think this all is a part of my wife's grand plan to civilize me. Next, she probably will want me to start sleeping in pajamas. Cowboys don't sleep in pajamas, but how could a woman know that?

Anyway, back to the minister coming to dinner. I had all sorts of rules I was to follow:

• You can have a beer or two, she said, but don't get out of your mind and start wanting to sing Maurice Williams and the Zodiacs songs like you do when it's just a regular party with your weirdo friends.

• And above all, don't tell any of your preacher jokes.

My wife was very emphatic about that last rule because she knows I enjoy telling jokes about preachers.

I don't know how I got started collecting jokes about ministers, but I have what must be hundreds in my repertoire, most of which are entirely within the bounds of good taste. You even can tell them at a Rotary Club luncheon.

I have short preacher jokes:

How do you tell the difference between a Northern Baptist preacher and a Southern Baptist preacher?

A Northern Baptist preacher will tell you there ain't no hell. A Southern Baptist preacher will tell you, The hell there ain't!

(For what they pay you to tell jokes at a Rotary Club luncheon, it does just fine.)

I also have long preacher jokes:

Once there was this small town where the Methodist preacher and the Baptist preacher, both of whom were quite young, rode bicycles. One Sunday morning the Methodist preacher was riding his bicycle to church and he spotted the Baptist preacher who was on foot.

"Where is your bicycle, brother?" the Methodist preacher asked.

"My heart is heavy," replied the Baptist preacher, "I think a member of my congregation has stolen it."

The Methodist preacher was appalled. "I think I can help you," he said. "When you're in the pulpit this morning, preach on the Ten Commandments. And when you come to 'Thou Shalt Not Steal,' you bear down on it, and maybe the person who stole your bicycle will get the message and be moved to return it to you."

The Baptist preacher said he would try his colleague's suggestion. Two weeks later they met again. Sure enough, the Baptist preacher had his bicycle back.

"I see my plan worked," the Methodist preacher said.

"Not exactly," said the Baptist preacher. "I did preach on the Ten Commandments, but when I got to 'Thou Shalt Not Commit Adultery,' I remembered where I left my bicycle."

That was the specific joke my wife had in mind when she told me not to tell our minister any of my preacher stories.

It was a marvelous dinner party. Just before we called it a night, the minister turned to me and said, "Hey, did you hear about the preacher who ran off with the church's money and went to Las Vegas?"

I hadn't heard.

"Part of the money he gambled away. Part of it he spent on booze. Part of it he spent on wild women. The rest of it, he just squandered."

Amen, brother.

The Lord's Collection Agent

Rose Emmett, who loved the Lord and didn't mind sharing her meager fixed income with him, received a certified letter a couple of weeks ago in Atlanta from none other than Oral and Evelyn Roberts.

Oral Roberts, of course, is the famous evangelist and faith healer. Evelyn is his wife.

"Dear Sister Emmett," the letter began. "Evelyn and I have knelt and prayed over every word in this letter before dropping it to you."

I probably don't have to tell you what the letter was about, but, for the record, let's go over it again.

Out in Tulsa, Oral Roberts is busy trying to raise money for something called the "City of Faith." What Oral Roberts wants to do is build a sixty-floor hospital complex, which would be the tallest building in Tulsa, as a "testimony to the glory of God."

Oral Roberts' "City of Faith" project has run into problems lately. First, his "partners," donors offering funds for the building, have been a little slow with their contributions. Also, a Tulsa group headed by a local physician has openly opposed Roberts' project as unneeded in the area.

In another fund-raising letter recently, Roberts came up with a real zinger. He says that May 25, he spoke to Jesus and Jesus said he would speak to Oral Roberts' "partners" to assure that the project will be completed.

In his vision, incidentally, Roberts said Jesus appeared as 900 feet tall.

Rose Emmett was one of Oral Roberts' "partners" who had been a little slow in contributing lately. That apparently is what prompted Oral and Evelyn to send her the certified letter.

Mrs. Emmett's daughter sent me the letter. I will quote from parts of it:

"The (City of Faith) construction is standing right outside my window. . . . The enemy is on an all-out attack, and we are facing one of the largest emergencies we have ever faced. Can you imagine what the enemies of this ministry would say if Oral Roberts failed?

"This letter you are now holding can be the greatest letter you have ever held. It can be a door to not only the answer to this emergency we are facing, but also the miracle that you need.

". . . God spoke to my heart to present this emergency to you like this: If you saw a beautiful home or an automobile for sale for $100, you would be foolish not to buy it (even if you had to borrow the $100 and pay it back in small monthly payments.)

"This emergency we are facing is more than just a house, or automobile. It is a crisis for God. If we do not meet it, this ministry will suffer as never before. . . .

"Remember," the letter closed, "if you do not have the $100, we will be praying here in Tulsa that God will lead you, as He did Evelyn and me, to where you can get it."

There was also a P.S., one last plea from Oral Roberts:

"I am going to cancel my plans and wait right here on this (enclosed) envelope from you. . . . Oral Roberts is here praying . . .

waiting . . . watching the mail for the answer from you concerning this emergency for God's work!!!"

You can stop "praying . . . waiting . . . watching" now, Oral. You can also stop counting on Rose Emmett to stroll down to her friendly finance company to pick up the hundred she could have so easily paid back in small monthly payments.

Your letter arrived three months too late. Back in July, Mrs. Rose Emmett, eighty-five, died of a brain tumor in the nursing home where your certified letter was mailed.

"Mrs. Emmett had sent him money before," said her son-in-law. "That's how they knew where to find her. The letter made me boil. Imagine asking an elderly lady like that on a fixed income to go out and borrow the money to give him if she didn't have it."

Just imagine.

The Lord works in mysterious ways, but when it comes to downright chicanery, some of his self-appointed "crusaders"—not mentioning any names—wrote the book.

Interviewing Reverend Falwell

For weeks, this column attempted through legitimate means to reach the Rev. Jerry Falwell, head of the Moral Majority, to discuss his recent "interview" with *Penthouse* magazine.

As most everyone knows, Reverend Falwell claims he was tricked and was not aware that the interview he gave would appear in *Penthouse*, a publication that involves itself with frontal nudity and bad words, and even allows advertisements of liquor.

My attempts to reach Reverend Falwell went for naught, however.

"Does your newspaper print advertisements for moving pictures?" I was asked by one of Reverend Falwell's press aides.

"Of course," I said.

"Even those rated R and X?" the aide asked.

"Those are especially popular with our readers," I answered.

"Then you may NOT interview Reverend Falwell," said the aide, hanging up the phone.

I refuse to be put off that easily. The public has a right to know. Behind these glasses and this frail, unassuming exterior beats the heart of a lion in pursuit of his prey.

I am proud to announce I have just returned from Falwell's Lynchburg, Virginia, headquarters and I got my interview, despite the odds against me.

I disguised myself as a duck.

"Your name?" I was asked at the reception desk.

"A Mr. Chuck Duck to see Reverend Falwell," the receptionist called to Falwell's secretary.

"Go right in, Mr. Duck," said the receptionist.

"What is the purpose of your visit?" the secretary asked.

"I would like to interview Reverend Falwell," I said.

"And whom do you represent?" she continued.

"Duck Daily," I said.

"Does your publication involve itself with any sort of lewdity, such as photographs of naked bodies?"

"An occasional graceful swan in a wading pool," I answered, "but nothing graphic. Mostly, it's just news of interest to ducks."

"Such as?" the secretary persisted.

"Oh, what to do when you get a cold in your quacker, or how to react if your son or daughter starts dating a duckbill platypus."

"I thought you said there was no lewdity in your publication," the secretary said.

"We keep it clean," I said. "We don't even spell out the word 'sex' in our articles. We use the phrase 'you know what.' Last week, for instance, we carried an article titled, 'After Hours Down by the Old Millstream: The You-Know-What Life of a Wild Goose.'"

I could tell I had won the secretary over. She buzzed her boss.

"Reverend Falwell will see you now," she said. I was ushered into the reverend's office. Plush, but not extravagant.

"Chuck Duck of Duck Daily, Reverend Falwell," I said. He was pleasant and open and held steadfastly to his contention that *Penthouse* had hornswoggled him.

"But it won't happen again," he insisted.

As I emerged from his office, a large rabbit sat waiting.

"And whom do you represent, Mr. Rabbit?" asked the secretary.

"*Popular Mechanics*," said the rabbit, winking to me as I waddled out the door.

Out With Sin

Now that the Moral Majority is exercising a great deal of influence upon our government and our society, it should be obvious that sin is out.

During the sixties and seventies, sin definitely was in. Avarice certainly had its moments, but Lust probably was the big sin of that period.

Even women, heretofore believed totally pure, got involved, and women's magazines suddenly were carrying more than recipes for apple strudel.

Lust among women hit an all-time high when a magazine published a centerfold of famous actor Burt Reynolds in the nude.

Maggie Smeltingham, a seventy-seven-year-old spinster from Grove City, Alabama, lusted with such fervor upon seeing Mr. Reynolds' photograph that she swallowed her snuff and had to have her stomach pumped.

"If I met such a man face to face," a local minister said of Mr. Reynolds, "I don't know what word I could use to describe him."

"After I caught my breath," said Maggie Smeltingham, "I would call him, 'Sugar Pie.'"

Now that sin is out, many citizens may have questions concerning exactly what is a sin and what isn't. To help make such distinctions, I contacted my local Moral Majority precinct captain, the Rev. LeRoy "Lucky" Fandango.

The Reverend Fandango is a former professional wrestler who was converted while his head was being rammed into a ring post by his opponent, the Masked Onion No. 2.

"Sin," said Fandango, "is very simple to identify. Just ask these three simple questions:

"1. Is it fun?

"2. Does it feel good?

"3. Is it fattening?

"If you answered 'yes' to any of those questions, you can just bet your boots it's a sin."

"Bet your boots?" I asked.

"Poor choice of words," said Fandango. "Betting, or gambling, offers a certain amount of thrill and excitement, so you can forget it."

I asked Fandango for some more specific examples of sin.

"Gum-chewing, for one," he answered.

"Gum-chewing is a sin?"

"Not in itself," said the Reverend, "but for where it can lead.

"A person starts chewing gum, and the next thing you know, he will go to Lifesavers. After Lifesavers come soft drinks, then booze, and then shooting pool and smoking and cursing and reading filthy magazines."

Moral Majority, of course, has its lists of "no-no" magazines. I asked Fandango to mention a few.

"*Playboy*," he said. I expected that. "And *Hustler* and *Penthouse* and the swimsuit issue of *Sports Illustrated* and *National Geographic*."

National Geographic is a sinful magazine?

"Sections on thatch huts in Ireland are fine," said the Reverend Fandango, "but be sure to stay away from anything having to do with tribal rites or lion hunts."

No drinking, no smoking, no lusting at pictures in magazines. So what does the Moral Majority recommend we do for leisure activities?

"There are lots of possibilities," Fandango explained. "Quiet meditation can be a real hoot once you get into it, and prayer-group softball games are okay, as long as nobody wears short pants. The Rev. Jerry Falwell Coloring Book is available on order, and have you ever just sat and watched milk curdle?"

"Might as well," I answered. "Can't dance."

"Dance?" The Reverend Fandango recoiled in horror. "Don't even say the word!"

Saying Grace

The five-year-old boy who lives in my house is learning to say the blessing.

"LET ME SAY THE BLESSING!" he bellows as we sit down to the table.

"*GOD IS GOOD!*

"*GOD IS NEAT!*

"*LET US ALL THANK HIM!*

"*FOR ALL WE CAN EAT!*

"*YEA, GOD!*"

My stepson is the only person I know who prays in a primal scream. Not only does God get the message, but so does everybody else within six blocks of our kitchen.

The "Yea, God" blessing is his favorite because it is more a cheer than a blessing, and the child is a human megaphone.

But tolerance is very important here because it is a big deal for a child to learn to say the blessing before the family meal. And it's not that easy, either.

First, you have to think of something to say. I remember when my parents first asked me to say the blessing.

MY FATHER: "Say the blessing, son."

MY MOTHER: "And don't mumble."

ME: "ThankyouGodforthemashedpo—"

MY MOTHER: "You're mumbling."

ME: "—tatoesandthegreenbeansandtheporkchopsandthe—"

MY FATHER: "Amen. That was very good, son, but you don't have to thank God for EVERYTHING on the table."

I wasn't going to mention the rutabagas.

After mastering a nice little blessing your mother thinks is "cute," and doesn't hold your old man away from the grub too long, you move into the "clever" blessings stage.

Everybody knew this one:

"Son would you please say grace?" your mother would ask, bowing her head.

"Grace," you would reply, howling at your genius.

"Whaack!" would be the sound of the back of your father's hand across your face.

Then there was the old favorite:

> Good bread,
> Good meat,
> Good Lord,
> Let's eat!

That was good for the backhand across the face AND getting sent to your room without any dinner.

If you really got brave, you could use this one:

> Bless the meat,
> Damn the skins,
> Back your ears,
> And cram it in!

That could get you reform school.

When it came to smart-aleck blessings, my boyhood friend and idol, Weyman C. Wannamaker, Jr., a great American, had no peer.

His all-time classic was the following:

> Thank you, Lord, for this meal,
> We know you are the giver.
> But thank you, Lord, most of all,
> That we ain't havin' liver.

Weyman's father tried to send him to reform school, but the warden was afraid he would be a bad influence on the other "students."

Soon, my stepson will be in the stage of saying "clever" blessings, but I am not going to whack him across the face.

I am going to make him eat liver, smothered in rutabagas.

6

A THIRD LOOK
AT LOVE
AND MARRIAGE

I get letters from people who say, "What have you got against women?" What could I possibly have against women? I've married three of them. . . .

The "Love Boat"

Atlanta is blessed with a number of nearby lakes where people go to fish and swim and sail and ski. It is at a marina on one of these lakes where sits what locals have come to call the "love boat" after all these years.

It is a dreadful little houseboat. Somebody painted it white a long time ago, but now the paint is peeling off.

It has a couple of tiny windows that are always closed. A giant padlock keeps would-be intruders out.

Picture this disaster tied amongst expensive, plush houseboats with three and four bedrooms and air conditioning—floating suites.

"You take somebody for a walk along the marina," one of the lake dwellers was telling me, "and they see beautiful boat after beautiful boat, and then they come to the love boat. They all ask. 'What in the world is this thing?"

For fifteen years, she has appeared at the marina. For fifteen years, every Tuesday and every Thursday, she has arrived in the marina parking lot in an expensive, late-model car.

For fifteen years, every Tuesday and every Thursday, she has gotten out of her car and walked down to the dock, clicking her high heels as she has stridden hurriedly to the love boat.

The locals describe her with awe.

"Beautiful," said one. "An absolutely beautiful woman."

"Stunning," said another.

But she never speaks. For fifteen years, she has never spoken to the others tending to their boats along the dock.

She arrives at the love boat, takes out a key and unlocks the door. She goes inside. In a few minutes, she emerges and sweeps the small deck.

Rumor has it she occasionally will sweep the deck of the boat in the scantiest of pajamas. This is only a rumor.

Soon after she has finished sweeping and has returned inside the love boat, he arrives. He arrives in a sleek cabin cruiser. He is as handsome as she is beautiful.

He docks his boat, ties up and goes to the love boat. He doesn't speak to the others, either.

He has his own key. He unlocks the door and goes inside.

Sometimes, it is an hour before the couple emerges. Sometimes, an hour and a half. But always, they emerge together. She walks with him back up the dock to where his cruiser is tied. They do not speak.

They both step onto the cruiser. He pulls away from the dock and then drops her off at the bank, thus saving her the walk back up the dock.

She goes to her car and drives away. He pulls his cruiser away from the marina and speeds to a nearby bridge that crosses the lake. There, he waits until she drives over the bridge.

As she passes, he stands out on his boat. They wave a final goodbye.

For fifteen years every Tuesday and Thursday, the pattern never changed.

Recently, there has been a change. She is still beautiful, they say. She still drives the nice, expensive car. He still comes dashing up in the cruiser, and they still spend the hour or so in the love boat, and then he waits for one last wave goodby at the bridge.

"It's sorta sad now, though," said a man who docks near the love boat. "After fifteen years, they've cut out Tuesdays."

It Runs in the Family

The big joke around the office lately goes something like this:
"What did you get in the Grizzard pool?"
"The Grizzard what?"
"The Grizzard office pool—how long he'll stay married this time."
That's not very funny, especially when you consider that my secretary, Miss Wanda Fribish, paid a buck to enter and got "eight days."

So I've been married a few times before. Big deal. My Uncle Gaylord, the traveling salesman, recently married his fifth wife, Aunt Mildred, and they are blissfully happy.

Aunt Mildred, incidentally, performs at the Bump 'n' Grind Lounge and Truck Stop near Tulsa, which is where she met Uncle Gaylord one night while she was dancing on his table.

As for me, things are going swimmingly at home. It's been six beautiful weeks, and I had forgotten the difference marriage can make in a person's life.

Hot meals on the table. Back rubs. Clean underwear. And the little woman really seems to enjoy it all.

There will be those detractors, of course, who will continue to insist this heavenly wedlock will never last, no matter what.

But they do not realize how serious I am about making this marriage work. Besides, one more bomb and I'm getting precariously close to double figures.

To prove my rightful intentions, I am about to do something drastic. I am about to reveal publicly the contents of my little black book, the one with all the names of all those delightful lovelies with whom I became acquainted during my single days.

That is a big step for any man, but I am more than willing to take it—and perhaps also provide an opportunity for those lonesome, deprived bachelors in the audience to find the right companion.

Any woman whose name appears on the following list is fair game. My wings, once flapping in the single breeze, have been clipped.

Here goes:

• Marcia Glimstein: waitress. Gets off work at midnight and loves to boogie until dawn. Blonde. Also brunette and redhead, depending on which party ring she's wearing. Shriners welcome.

• Sylvia Mudd: automotive maintenance coordinator. (Works in car wash.) Shining disposition. (Personality of a jar of Turtle Wax.) Bugs on her bumper. (Severe acne problem.) Off Thursdays. (And all rainy days.)

• Shanda Ripplemeyer: stewardess. Sort of. Works air-freight runs in the middle of the night. Wears "Marry Me—Ship Free" T-shirts and sweats a lot. Perfect afternoon date, especially if you need to unload a truck.

• Rhonda de Haven: poet, artist, and checkout girl at Kroger store. Latest works include still life of a cucumber and poem entitled, "Ode to a Frozen Pork Chop." Weird, but cute.

• Mary Jane "Pumpkin" Palmer: cheerleader for professional hockey team. The puck has a higher I.Q., but you ought to see her Zambonis.

- Pauline Gooch: elementary-school teacher. Looking for husband. Wants big family. Could stand to lose a few pounds. Could play linebacker for the Steelers. Fun date if you've never been out with the Goodyear Blimp.
- Natalie Foyt: used car salesperson. Divorcee. Gets dates by running classified ads in personals section. Look under "Clean, 1-owner."
- Tina Marina: crack television news investigative reporter. Won Emmy for in-depth series entitled, "Turning Right on Red: Friend or Foe?" Smart. Witty. Raises chinchillas.
- Alexandria "Bulldog" Mankiewitz: terrorist for local militant women's lib group. Shaves three times a week and then eats the razor blades. Tattoo on left forearm reads, "Born to Raise Hell." Former roller derby star. Idea of a good time is rolling truck drivers.
- Candy Cain: Model, Dancer. Call Sly Fox Escort Agency. Furnishes own film. Uncle Gaylord's fourth wife.

Stand by Your Man

There simply is no way to consider a juicy scandal like the one involving former Rep. John Jenrette of South Carolina and his pretty blonde wife without taking sides.

I'll take his. Rita Jenrette has a big mouth.

Years ago, women who told their husbands' secrets in public would be stripped of their bridge club memberships and, in cruder societies, flogged. Today, they get 10,000 words in *Playboy* magazine and an hour on Donahue.

As if John Jenrette didn't have enough troubles. First, he gets caught in the Abscam web. Then, he loses his bid for re-election and has to resign from the House in disgrace and tears. Then, his loving, trusting wife, who insists she will "stand by his side," turns stool pigeon.

In one magazine article, she calls her husband a "flamboyant womanizer" and spares no details. He's a boozer, she tells the world.

The FBI wants to put the poor guy in shackles, and his wife is calling press conferences to tell about the holes in his underwear.

So John Jenrette decides to split for a few days. Who wouldn't want to get away from darling Rita at this point? And while he's gone, the roof really caves in.

He leaves her a bogus number in Miami, so she calls up reporters and announces she's filing for divorce. Then, she's packing her husband's clothes in their Washington townhouse and she comes across a shoe box filled with large bills that amount to $25,000.

Where do you think the money came from, Mrs. Jenrette?

"Probably my husband's take from Abscam," she answers. Whatever happened to "love, honor, and keep your trap shut while the heat's still on?"

Why didn't she say her husband follows little old ladies to the bank and then robs them of their Social Security payments to get all that money? She couldn't have made it any worse on the poor fellow.

Rita Jenrette has been on my bad side ever since she wagged her tongue at Moose Clubs and said she didn't want to go back to another one because the men all walk around with antlers on their heads.

What does Rita Jenrette know? Think of the good that Moose Clubs do simply by never turning away a thirsty wanderer traveling through an otherwise dry province.

I think Rita Jenrette is trying to attract attention to herself, and I wish she would go away. She is a very dangerous woman, as a matter of fact. What if all wives decided to blow the whistle on their husbands when they caught them in a little hanky-panky?

My wife could tell the world I don't pick up after myself, and that I snore, and that I am afraid to take shots, and that I won't watch horror movies alone, and that sometimes I forget to change socks for days, and that one of my little toes is bigger than the other one.

One of my little toes IS bigger than the other one. That is because one night I was walking through the house barefoot with no lights on and rammed one of my little toes into a sofa leg. And it still is swollen and roughly twice the size of my other little toe and it is shaped sort of like Idaho.

What I was doing walking through the house barefoot with no lights on is, I was headed to the kitchen for a cold pork chop.

There is something comforting about a cold pork chop. Unless, I would imagine, you're married to one like Rita Jenrette.

The Orange Sherbet Room

I promised myself that after I got married, again, I wouldn't write those boring domestic sort of columns nobody really wants to read.

But the other day I came home from work and found my wife with two men who were doing something very strange in the living room of our new house.

They were painting the walls orange sherbet.

"What do you think?" asked my wife, beaming.

"You're doing our living room in early banana split?" I asked.

"You don't love me," said my wife.

I do love my wife, but I never have seen the walls of a living room painted the color of orange sherbet.

You know what orange sherbet looks like. Deer hunters wear vests that color so that other deer hunters can spot them in the underbrush a half-mile away and won't think they are deer and blow holes in them. Nobody will ever shoot a deer hunter in my living room.

Decorating a new house has been a completely unique experience for me. When I was a bachelor, which I have been on a number of occasions, it never took me very long to decorate my living quarters.

I had a black Naugahyde couch I always put in the living room, despite the fact that some liberal got up a drive to do away with Naugahyde couches because of the number of little Naugas they had to hit in the head with lead pipes to make even one Naugahyde ottoman.

I usually mounted a velvet portrait of a bullfighter somewhere, a picture of me shooting a basketball in the tenth grade, a Willie Nelson poster, and the plaque they gave me when I covered the Liberty Bowl football game in 1967 that says I am an honorary citizen of Memphis, even though I never have forgiven that city for not disappearing with the Mississippi riverboats.

Most apartments don't have dens, so I didn't have to worry about decorating my den.

If I had had a den, I probably would have put my collection of twenty-four beer bottles from all over the world there, and I also would have spread some *Playboy* and *Time* magazines around, to say that I not only was with it sexually and socially, but I also knew Hodding Carter was not the name of a new plant food.

My bedroom, you ask? Va-va-voom, my bedroom, they ask! Double mattress with a sag on one side and the Roy Rogers spread my mom bought me when I was ten.

Decorating our new house, I have learned I needed a lot of things I never knew I needed.

Ten zillion houseplants, for instance. *Plants?* In the hallways, my wife has planted a couple of *trees.* They're called *foyerus interruptus* or some such, and the kids want me to build them a house in the top of one.

We have new light fixtures, ceiling fans, French doors that separate this room from that room, more new bookshelves than your local public library, and lots of new trinkets.

I mean, we have *lots* of new trinkets. Little glass doodads that look sort of like the glass blower was on glue or something. In order to get ready for Christmas early, we even have a five-decked, glass-enclosed set of figurines that depict the first fifteen years of the life of Christ.

We have a wood-carved pig, four brass ducks and fifteen paintings of flowers and little girls in bonnets. And nothing made out of Naugahyde.

"What effect," I asked my wife, "are you trying to create with a room the color of orange sherbet?"

"You have no taste whatsoever," she replied. "It's not orange sherbet, it's 'coral,' and I want an outside-indoors effect, Bahamian, sort of Humphrey Bogart in *Casablanca*, Rick's Bar with the ceiling fan and all of that."

I went down to the basement where all my old furniture is stored, dusted off my black Naugahyde couch and took a nap.

Tips for No. 3

When actor Ryan O'Neal gets married to actress Farrah Fawcett, Ryan O'Neal and I will have something in common. We both will be into our third marriage.

Mr. O'Neal and Miss Fawcett plan to tie the knot as soon as possible, the couple announced recently from Venice, which is something Mr. O'Neal and I don't have in common.

I made the announcement of my engagement to No. 3 while standing on the bar in a beer joint located just on the outskirts of Fort Deposit, Alabama.

You would be surprised how many people get married for the third time. A close friend of mine also just got married for the third time.

"Couple more of these," he said to me at the reception after the wedding, "and we'll have enough (ex's) between us for a girls' field hockey team with two cheerleaders."

I didn't think that was very funny, and neither did my friend's new bride, who elbowed him in the belly when he said it.

I wish Mr. O'Neal and Miss Fawcett the very best. They deserve each other, say Hollywood insiders.

I just hope Mr. O'Neal realizes it's different the third time around. The first time you have no earthly idea what you are getting into, and you normally botch it.

The second time, you are a veteran, but still prone to many rookie mistakes. If you go back a third time, you have entered the big leagues, and there can be no more excuses.

Around poker tables, they have a saying: "Put up or shut up, cowboy." The same applies to a man entering his third marriage.

I have nearly eight months of being married for the third time under my belt. It has been a learning experience, from which I now offer the following advice to Mr. O'Neal and to any other man about to go for a three-bagger, an awful choice of words. How to make it work the third time around:

• Go shopping in antique stores with her once in a while, even if it absolutely kills you. It beats shopping for antiques in a bar at midnight, which, you must realize by now, is no fun at all.

• Don't complain if she puts a black sock with a navy blue sock. Life is too short to spend one second worrying about socks.

• Don't come home a-drinkin' with lovin' on your mind. (Loretta Lynn said that before I did, but it's still strong advice.)

• Don't fool around.

• If you are going to fool around anyway, when you get caught (notice I said, "when" instead of "if"), lie like a dog.

• Speaking of lying, tell her she's pretty even when she isn't wearing make-up and her hair is in curlers and she's wearing flip-flops and your old football jersey.

• Don't give her a new blade for her hacksaw on your anniversary.

• Shop for her underwear.

• Pick yours up off the lousy bedroom floor once in a while.

• When you are in a restaurant alone with just her, the champagne, and the candlelight, never say, "You know, this place has really gone downhill since I and (a) my first wife, (b) my second wife, were here."

• Keep a bottle of mouthwash on your bedside table.

• Have some laughing children around.

• Refuse all telephone numbers.

• When there is obviously something wrong with her, and you ask, "What's wrong with you?" and she replies, "Nothing," leave the house immediately. There is something wrong with her.

• Forget candy and flowers. By now you must have figured out what they really like are airplane tickets to places where the sun shines, and Volvos.

• Her back itches, too, dummy. You scratch occasionally.

• Above all, being married the third time means always having to say you're sorry. If you had done that the first two times instead of pouting, there wouldn't have been the need for a third time.

White Bread or Bust

My wife has insisted I give up white bread.

"There is absolutely no food value in white bread," she informed me.

"But it tastes good," I replied.

"Hedonist," said my wife.

I've given up so much already. I'm not supposed to eat a lot of eggs or drink a lot of milk because of cholesterol. Cake and pie and candy do something strange to my blood-sugar level.

Cokes. I used to drink a lot of Cokes, but the doctor said switch to diet drinks. On diet drink cans, there is a warning about saccharin causing cancer in laboratory animals. I assume those animals are rats.

I don't worry about rats getting cancer that much. Rats are little and they just sort of look unhealthy in the first place. When they find out a couple of Diet Pepsis will give an elephant cancer. I'll become much more concerned.

What else? I don't smoke anymore, I gave up vodka tonics out of respect for my head and liver. Now that I'm married again, I'm on the streets a lot less.

White bread was sort of my last holdout. Let me tell you what I like about white bread:

It's soft. I hate hard bread. When I lived in Chicago, all they ever served in restaurants was hard, dark bread.

"What will you have sir?" the waitress would ask.

"Tuna salad, hold the hockey pucks," I would reply.

"Tuna salad, no bread!" the waitress would scream to the cook.

How I longed for some of those marvelous, delicious "brown 'n' serve" rolls, the kind they used to serve in truck stop restaurants of my youth with the $1.25 hamburger steak (which is now the "chopped sirloin" that goes for seven bucks).

White bread makes better sandwiches, too. Take, for example, a banana sandwich, a rare delicacy I used to carry to school for lunch. Cover the inside of two pieces of white bread with mayonnaise, then put the bread around several slices of barely ripe banana, and the result is divine.

Imagine a banana sandwich on dark, hard bread. The mere thought of such a hideous concoction turns my stomach.

"Go ahead and eat white bread and ruin your digestive system and see if I care," my wife says.

"Toast me a loaf of that dark bread and I'll go replace the shingles on the roof," I reply, and the white bread/dark bread debate is off and running again.

She will win in the end, of course. I will give up white bread, just like I did all the other pleasures I miss.

But I have made one promise to myself that I hope I am allowed to keep. It is a dream that is constant:

On my sixty-fifth birthday, I am going to a nice, cool place like the grassy bank of a river. I am going to take with me a carton of Marlboro cigarettes, a quart of vodka, several bottles of tonic, lime, and crushed ice, a loaf of thinly sliced white bread, mayonnaise, a banana, and a nineteen-year-old girl.

I am going to smoke all the Marlboro cigarettes, drink all the vodka tonics I please, and top it all off with a banana sandwich on white.

The nineteen-year-old girl?

After I've finished with all the other stuff and if I'm still alive, I will sing her a love song.

"Love" Versus "Lust"

I always try to listen closely when the pope makes one of his official statements. As I understand it, His Holyship has one of the better pipelines to the Big Rulemaker, and I don't want to miss anything I might be tested on later.

But I, along with millions of others, was caught completely off guard with the recent papal pronouncement that it is a sin to lust after your own wife.

Now there's a real kick in the libido if I ever heard one.

We went all through this lust business four years ago when soon-to-be-elected President Carter admitted he had "lusted in his heart" after women other than the voluptuous Rosalynn.

What is it about the presidential election? Four years later, soon-to-be-unelected President Carter hasn't got time to lust after anybody with Ronald Reagan on his back, but it's the pope, of all people, who brings the subject up again.

I like the pope. He's got a nice smile. He appears to have a sense of humor, and he is a warm, sensitive man of peace.

But he doesn't know beans when it come to love and lust. Otherwise, he couldn't have become pope, if you know what I mean.

But a worldly person like myself, well, I know my share about love, and I have personally lusted on a number of occasions, most recently during the movie *Dressed to Kill*, starring Angie Dickinson.

A man who can watch Angie Dickinson in certain scenes in *Dressed to Kill* and think about needing more salt for his popcorn is badly in need of an oil change.

And as far as lusting after one's wife is concerned, that's been the problem for a long time now. Instead of lusting after their wives, men have been lusting after their secretaries and their neighbors' wives, and the 8.5 at the end of the bar. And if more men would, in fact, lust after what's in their own ballpark, watch the bottom fall out of the divorce rate.

I've read a number of explanations of "what the pope was trying to say." The best one said what the pope meant was a man should "love" his wife and not merely "lust" after her as a "sex object."

Okay, I think most men can certainly live within those boundaries.

But before we put this matter to bed, or rest, maybe we should make some clear distinctions between "love" and "lust."

"Love" is when you bring her home a present and it is not a special occasion.

"Lust" is when you bought it at Frederick's of Hollywood, and Candy Barr wouldn't be caught dead wearing it.

"Love" is when you take a romantic cruise together aboard a sailboat.

"Lust" is when the boat belongs to her husband, who is in Cleveland on business.

"Love" is when you met at a church social.

"Lust" is when she answered your ad in *Hustler*.

"Love" is when she watches "The NFL Today" to learn all of football's positions.

"Lust" is when you have memorized every diagram in *More of the Joy of Sex*.

"Love" is when he invites you to a movie.

"Lust" is when it is playing in his bedroom, the one with the mirrors and burning incense.

Got the picture? What a fun column to write, and I would like to point out just one more thing before I go:

Is it just my imagination that the people who usually are the most vocal about sex also are the people who engage in it the least?

Nineteen Was a Long Time Ago

She was ten the first time I saw her. So was I. She was tall and gangly and put together sort of funny.

"Is that girl going to be in our class?" asked one of my pals as we looked her over the first day of the new school year.

"I hope not," I said. The last thing we needed in the sixth grade, I reasoned, was another girl. What we needed was a good second baseman. Funny how childish priorities go.

But we both grew, she out of her gangliness. Suddenly her proportions were nearly perfect. Me, I was out of my preoccupation with baseball and into a keen interest in the opposite sex.

It was in the ninth grade that the whole blasted thing began. We went on a Sunday school hayride together, and I had never been kissed until I was kissed by her, and so, six years later, I married her.

You don't know a damn thing when you are nineteen. It should be against the law to get married when you are nineteen.

But I was spending every week missing her, and I was absolutely terrible and out of place with anybody else. I knew when I was thirteen that I would marry her, so why wait any longer?

The little church was packed. My best man, as we stood in the anteroom awaiting her arrival down the aisle, said to me:

"Look, stupid. I can have us both 500 miles away from here by morning. Just say the word."

The next morning I was in our honeymoon bed.

We lasted—I forget exactly—four years, maybe. What went wrong? I'll tell you what went wrong. We were kids, children.

I went one way in my head. She went another. It broke our mothers' hearts.

So there I am in this huge department store and people are running all around doing their Christmas shopping, and the last person I figured I would run into, I ran into.

She looked great. Still blonde and thin. Still with the fashion. We talked for fifteen minutes.

She lives in another city. She has a husband and two kids. She was home just for a visit.

"Tell me about your wife," she said.

I raved.

"And how is it with you?" I asked.

"He's great," she replied. "I would have never made it without him.

"You always wanted to be a writer," she went on. "Are you satisfied now?"

"What's satisfied?" I asked back. "The more you get, the more you want. It's human."

We went back and forth like that. In these situations, there is another sense that takes over. You *sense* what to say, and what not to say, and what to ask about, and what not to ask about.

And you *sense*—simultaneously—when it is time to end it. The present reality hovers.

"We were so young, weren't we?" she asked, adjusting her coat to leave.

"We didn't know a damn thing," I answered.

"I'm such a different person now. All that back then is like a dream. God, how did you put up with me? Remember the time I cried when it was my birthday and you went to a ball game? How stupid."

"That wasn't stupid. I shouldn't have gone to the ball game."

"Do you still complain about your socks not being mated exactly right?"

"Yeah. My wife goes nuts when I do that."

"There is one good thing, though," she said.

"What's that?"

"Neither one of us got fat, did we?"

"No, neither one of us got fat."

I took her hand and shook it. She went one way. I went another.

7

CATS AND DOGS

The more I think about it, I really don't dislike cats. It's cat-lovers who are dangerous, and that is explained in detail here. As for dogs, I've never had one to ask, "Where have you been for so long?" "Why didn't you call if you knew you were going to be late?" and "Why do we never talk?" If for no other reason, I appreciate dogs for never having asked me questions I prefer not to answer. . . .

"Butterbean" Goes to Camp

I first thought our dog, who is large and shaggy, was mentally retarded. That is because our dog was doing some strange things. I will list some of the strange things our dog was doing.

• Eating plants. House plants, out-of-the-house plants, also trees and flowers. Imagine this big, shaggy dog walking up to a blooming hybeiwhatzit and eating the sucker, petal by petal. If there were any bugs or bees in the plants or flowers that fell victim to my dog, she would eat them too.

• Wrestling with our youngest child. He is four and about a third the size of our dog. Our dog was making the child's life miserable. Whenever the child made any sort of quick move, the dog would think he wanted to wrestle her, and she would pounce upon the poor little snipper and flip him around like he was no more than a stuffed toy. The child would cry, quite obviously, which would make the dog bark. None of this sort of thing ever happened to me when I was single.

• Running away from home. I spent a great deal of money on a fence for my dog. She would have been out of Alcatraz in eight seconds. My dog would dig her way under the fence and then disappear and I would have to go look for her. Once she escaped and I found her talking to sailors in a bar in Norfolk.

On top of all that, our dog was quite disobedient. "Butterbean" (not her real name) would not come when you called her, nor would she do any tricks, nor would she eat anywhere but seated at the table. (She would wrestle the four-year-old for his chair, then

391

tease and tantalize him with scraps and bites from her plate, poor kid.)

As head of the family, I decided to do something about our dog. I took her to the vet.

"There is nothing wrong with your dog mentally,' said my vet. "She's just a high-strung animal with a dominating personality. You should send her to obedience camp."

Dogs go to camp? Certainly, said my vet, and when they return they don't eat plants, terrorize four-year-olds or hustle drinks off sailors, and actually will eat Alpo off a dish on the back porch.

This I had to see, so I enrolled our dog in an obedience camp. The first week was murder. She short-sheeted two counselors, mugged poodles for their canteen money and called me at two o'clock in the morning, collect, howling to come home.

At the end of the week I had to pay for the damages she had caused (she chewed up all the volleyballs and flushed cherry bombs down the commodes) and then pleaded with the camp director, who once trained killer dogs for combat, to allow her to stay.

"Dogs will be dogs," I laughed.

"Your mutt's a menace to society," he said.

The second week, things began to get a little better. She made a friend—a Doberman. They chased alligators together in a nearby swamp, then shared a large tree for lunch.

Counselors reported her to be less aggressive and even taking part in the crafts classes. She made a leather belt and a wallet with "Dad" etched across the front. I must say I was touched.

The third week, she wasn't the same dog at all. She was elected council representative from her kennel and even had begun helping some of the younger, less experienced campers learn the ropes.

"Dear Mr. Grizzard," the camp director wrote me after the third week. "I am happy to say 'Butterbean' (not her real name) is progressing wonderfully, and she will be able to come home very soon."

Well, that day finally has arrived. This afternoon I will drive out to the obedience camp to pick up our dog. Despite all the problems in the past, we've missed the old girl, and it will be nice to have her home.

The thing with the Doberman never worked out, incidentally. One afternoon he tried to get fresh with our dog and she broke three of his paws, tied a knot in his tail and put him in the camp infirmary for six weeks.

The Comeback Cat

I have a very real problem at my house involving a cat. I don't like cats. I never have liked cats. I never will like cats, and that is the problem.

A cat has moved into my house. I went out of town for a couple of days. When I returned, I opened the front door, and there stood a cat—a brown cat with a speck of white on its tail.

I say "its" tail because I don't know if the cat is a boy or a girl, and I don't know how to tell the difference without resorting to some unthinkable snooping.

First, I asked the cat a question, which was an idiotic thing to do, but have you ever noticed how people are always asking their pets, especially cats, questions?

"Mommie's little darling want some din-din?" Etc.

I asked the cat, "How did you get inside my house?"

The doors had been locked. The windows were secure. Maybe the cat came down the chimney?

"Did you come down the chimney?" I asked the cat.

I did it again. I asked a dumb animal a question. What do you do next, stupid, suggest a couple of games of backgammon?

I shooed the cat out of my house, and so much for my cat problem.

Hardly. The next morning, I awakened to something furry crawling around on my head. The cat was back, and the cat was in my bed. That's impossible. I had put the cat out myself, and I had locked the doors and pulled the damper down in the chimney.

"Who put you up to this?" I asked the cat, obviously no longer in control of my faculties.

I put the cat out again.

But the cat came back. Don't ask me how the cat gets in my house, but it does. I finally reached such a point of frustration that I enlisted the help of one of my neighbors, Mrs. Framingham, a worrisome old biddy who keeps a lot of cats around. I told her how the cat was driving me up a wall.

"You wouldn't hurt the little darling, would you?" Mrs. Framingham asked me.

"I wouldn't consider any permanent injuries," I responded.

"You lay one hand on that cat, and I'll break both your arms," said Mrs. Framingham, who had a typical cat-lover's attitude: Be kind to animals, or I'll break your nose.

"Why not give the poor little creature a chance?" she went on.

"It obviously likes you, and it needs a home. Why not just accept it?"

No way. Cats are sneaky—and try to get a cat to roll over and play dead or chase a stick or do all the neat things a dog will do.

Cats think they are above that. Plus, I don't want a pet that bathes more often than I do.

"Shush," said Mrs. Framingham. "Give the poor dear two weeks. In two weeks you will love it. The two of you will be inseparable. That's the beauty of cats. They grow on you."

I gave the cat two weeks. I still don't want a cat. Besides, while I was typing this, I thought of an obvious solution to the problem.

All I have to do is make the cat feel unwanted. No rough stuff, just a few subtle hints that no purring, meowing little pest is going to get the best of me, no matter what the old bat down the street says.

You don't think I mean it? From now on, daddy's little precious is going to have to sleep in its own room. And our trip to the basketball game next week is definitely off.

Scooter

Kathy Williams is an attorney. She lives in Avondale, a suburb of Atlanta. Until five months ago, she lived alone. Then, Scooter came to live with her.

Scooter was a fuzzy brown puppy. If he had any papers, he didn't have them on him.

"He just walked up out of nowhere," said Kathy Williams. "He was wearing a collar, but he had no license. I fed him. He just stayed. He would hang around in my back yard, except when he walked across the street to play with the children over there. He loved children. And they loved him."

One day she came home from work and Scooter was gone. Dogs often wander away. He would be back.

He never came back.

"What was so funny about this was I had never really cared about dogs before," Kathy Williams explained. "But there was something about this little dog. I called him 'Scooter' because he sort of scooted along on his tummy when he ran. He was just a mixed breed, but after he was gone, I really missed him.

For five weeks, Scooter was missing. Kathy Williams put an ad in the paper, under "Lost Dogs." She watched the papers to see if anybody might have found her dog.

There is a lake in Avondale. Every night she would walk around the lake and call for her dog, hoping he might return.

What else she did was visit DeKalb County Animal Control once a week to see if Scooter had been picked up.

"I was so afraid they would find him and kill him before I could claim him," she said. "I told everybody down there what he looked like, and I had them on alert for my dog."

Last Tuesday, Kathy Williams made her weekly visit to the De-Kalb pound. She found Scooter.

"I've never been so excited in my life," she said. "I couldn't wait to get him out of there."

Here is where the plot thickens.

A woman at the desk told Kathy Williams not to reclaim her dog. When a dog is picked up in DeKalb County, she explained, an officer writes out a citation for whoever reclaims the dog. That person then has to go to court and pay a fine for violating the DeKalb leash law.

"She told me to wait until Thursday, when Scooter had been in the pound for seven days, and then I could just adopt him. That would cost me $41, but he got shots and everything, and I wouldn't have to go to court or pay a fine," Kathy Williams explained.

"I walked back into the cage area, and there was this guy named Jeff, and he told me to do the same thing. I mentioned I really didn't own the dog, that he had just taken up at my house, but he said it didn't matter. If I reclaimed the dog, then I would have to get the ticket."

Kathy Williams took the advice. Before she left, however, she made certain everybody involved knew to make certain nothing happened to Scooter.

"They laughed at me because I went on about it for so long," she said. "But I just couldn't have anything happen to my dog."

Kathy Williams left Scooter at the pound. Thursday morning, she returned to pick him up. On her way, she stopped to buy him a new collar, some flea and tick powder, and a Slim-Jim as a reward.

"When I walked into the place, I could sense something was wrong," she said. "I went back to the cage were Scooter had been, and he wasn't in there." Kathy Williams started asking about her dog. Nobody would give her a straight answer. Finally, somebody gave her a straight answer. There had been a mistake. Scooter had been killed.

"They tried to give me another dog," said Kathy Williams. "I didn't want another dog. I wanted Scooter."

"We made a terrible mistake," said Major Harold Davis, who is in charge of the DeKalb facility. "A note was written and attached to a dog, saying to hold the dog for the lady. But the note was placed on the wrong dog.

"But people ought to think about these things. If your dog got picked up, don't take a chance. Get that rascal out of here. Take the ticket. Pay the fine."

Kathy Williams isn't sleeping so well these nights because she didn't do exactly that. But why was she given advice to the contrary by personnel at the pound?

And how could somebody be careless enough to kill the wrong dog?

"I told that lady," said Major Davis, "when she gets ready for another pet, to call us. We'll help her in any way we can."

A nice gesture. But somehow I get the feeling she won't be calling.

Pet Killer

You have to know basset hounds to love them. I have known and loved two. I lost one in a custody battle. The other, who is three months old, lives in my house now. The dog's name is Barney. Soon he will be the size, and shape, of a canoe.

Somebody else who owns a basset hound was telling me, "They're awful dogs, really. They bark too much, they get their ears in their food and then they get their ears on everything in the house, they won't mind, and they shed all over your furniture.

"But you take one look at those big, sad eyes and you're hooked."

I know the feeling. So do Tom and Diana Thorington of Atlanta. They have a basset hound. His name is Lance. He's two years old and he has national champions on both sides of his family. (If you really love a dog, it doesn't matter if his pedigree is more impressive than your own.)

A couple of weeks ago the Thoringtons took Lance when they went to an afternoon party at a friend's house. The friend has a large lot, so they let Lance out to play with the friend's dog, a mutt. Basset hounds are not snooty.

Sometime later the people at the party heard shots being fired across the way at a neighbor's house. The host of the party and the neighbor were not close friends. Soon you will see why.

The host and Tom Thorington left the party to see what the shooting was about. They saw the neighbor firing away at Lance and the mutt.

When they reached the man, the mutt was already dead. They didn't see Lance.

"Did you shoot my dog?" Tom Thorington screamed at the man.

"Shot two of 'em," the man replied, laughing.

"You are a rotten, no-good son of a bitch," said Tom Thorington, who was being nice.

The man put his rifle, a .22, to Tom Thorington's chest.

"I think I'll shoot you next," he said.

Tom and his friend started to walk away.

"I'll shoot you in the back," said the man.

Tom and his friend kept walking. They got lucky. Crazy with the rifle didn't shoot.

Tom began calling to Lance. A couple of minutes later he heard a muffled sound from the weeds. It was Lance, with four bullets in his throat. And more, all over his body. There were even bullet holes in Lance's long, floppy ears.

"He was shot at least *ten* times," Diana Thorington told me later. "Can you imagine somebody sighting down on a basset hound TEN times?"

I've never heard of a blacker heart.

The Thoringtons rushed Lance to the local vet.

"The vet told us to forget it," said Diana. "He said there was no way Lance would make it. But we begged him to try. We love that dog so much."

Another dog, named Rip, gave some blood, and a miracle happened. Lance lived.

Okay, some nut shoots your dog and then threatens to shoot you. What do you do about it?

"We went to the police," said Diana Thorington, "but they said there was nothing much they could do. The laws about shooting dogs are pretty weak. The police said if we filed charges it would just mean a big hassle, and probably nothing much would come of it. The man was on his own property."

It is not written that life must necessarily be fair. So the Thoringtons' friend's dog is dead, and the Thoringtons' basset hound, with a little help from his friend, barely made it, and el sicko with the gun is still off his leash.

It *is* written, however, that a creep who would kill one family pet and then pull a trigger ten times on what is one of God's most loving creatures will, sooner or later, get his.

Every dog has his day, so to speak. Knowing that, I rest a little easier. Not much, but a little.

8

SPECIAL
OCCASIONS

The holidays. They bring out the best and the worst in people. April 15 is not a holiday, of course, but it should be. It brings out the most in people. . . .

The Morning After

News item: Another New Year's Eve is just around the corner.
"Harvey, wake up, Harvey."
"Whatsmattah?"
"Nothing's the matter, Harvey. I just want you to wake up."
"Whatimeisit?"
"Past 10, Harvey."
"Gladys, why do I have to wake up, Gladys? It's New Year's Day. I wannna sleep until the football games."
"I can't sleep, Harvey. Not after your performance last night."
"What did I do last night?"
"You don't remember?"
"I don't remember, Gladys. I was drunk."
"Drunk? 'Drunk' isn't the word for it, Harvey. You were 'blitzed.' You were 'stoned.' You were sickening."
"What could I have possibly done that was so bad, Gladys?"
"I'll tell you what you did. You made an absolute fool out of yourself at the Blantons' party. I can never show my face in this neighborhood again."
"So I got a little drunk. It was New Year's Eve, Gladys. I always get drunk on New Year's Eve."
"Harvey, you danced with Harriet Blanton's dog all night long."
"So?"
"So you thought you were dancing with Harriet Blanton. You told the dog how much you were enjoying the hors d'oeuvres and you tried to get Harriet to roll over for a sausage ball."

399

"I did that?"

"That's not all, Harvey."

"Omigod. What else?"

"You got into a fight with Ralph Beetleman."

"The skinny guy with the fat wife?"

"Gloria."

"Gloria who?"

"Gloria Beetleman, Ralph Beetleman's wife. She's the reason for the fight. You asked Ralph what he fed his land whale."

"I said that?"

"You said it, Harvey. Then, Ralph Beetleman took a punch at you. He missed, but Gloria kneed you in the belly and you were out for half an hour."

"So I danced with a dog and insulted a beer truck. Big deal, Gladys."

"There's more, Harvey. Your poured a drink on Mildred Pillingham."

"Where?"

"In the living room."

"No, I mean . . ."

"Down the front of her dress, Harvey. Mildred Pillingham is in my car pool."

"I don't want to hear any more, Gladys."

"You're going to hear it, Harvey. I am ruined in this town, and you are going to hear it all. Your burned a hole in the Blantons' new couch with a cigarette. You ate the floral arrangement in the dining room. You put your head in the punch bowl, and when the party was over, we found you in the backyard howling at the moon."

"With Harriet Blanton's dog?"

"With Harriet Blanton. She got just as wasted as you did."

Artie's Tax Service

Some people, believe it or not, actually file their income tax returns weeks and months ahead of the dreaded April 15 deadline. These people are normally well off, and they have their own accountants and use their refund checks to go to resorts in Mexico or the Caribbean.

(You may be asking, "What is a refund check?" Don't bother. It would only confuse you.)

I feel sorry for these people. They don't realize what fun and excitement they are missing by not waiting until the last minute to have their income taxes prepared.

It is the same thrill you get from waiting until the last minute to do your Christmas shopping or to rent a tuxedo for the annual Moose Lodge Dance and Fish Fry.

Procrastinators, like myself, enjoy the adventure and danger of living on the brink of disaster. Only a few days remain before the fifteenth, but I haven't even bothered to look for my W-2 forms yet.

That's because I can do what I always do—wait until a couple of hours before the deadline and pay a visit to Artie (Three Fingers) McGuirk's Friendly Tax Service and Pool and Recreation Hall.

You would love Artie's place. Get your taxes done, shoot a little pool or maybe talk to Artie about important sports questions like point spreads.

This is a special year at Artie's incidentally. Artie is back after a brief absence. Ask where Artie has been, and one of his friendly goons, er, associates, will answer simply, "On a long trip. What's it to ya?"

Of course, there are other places I could go to get my taxes done at the eleventh hour. You hear about them on television about this time every year.

There is Mr. Loophole Tax Service, for instance. What bothers me about Mr. Loophole, however, is all the offices are in trailers sitting in shopping center parking lots. What if I am audited and come back to Mr. Loophole looking for help and there is a shopping center carnival where the trailer used to be parked?

Then, there's H&R Schlock. The man in the three-piece suit, seated in a comfortable chair, comes on the screen and tells you all the reasons you should use his tax service.

"Reason No. 11 for using H&R Schlock Tax Service: If the IRS calls you in for an audit, we'll give you a new tie for your appointment."

Artie and his trained staff of professionals offer even more:

• All preparations and consultations are strictly confidential. As Artie says, "One peep about who fixed this return, and you'll sleep with the fishes."

• All possible deductions are taken. Artie is very careful here. One year he missed some deductions for one of his best clients, Crazy Carlo (The Shark) DeRogatis, and Crazy Carlo deducted two of Artie's fingers as a penalty.

• Each member of Artie's staff has spent years learning about taxes. One spent ten to twenty in Joliet learning you can't hide the fifty Gs you picked up in a land fraud deal.

• If you are indicted and thrown into the slammer, Artie will send you cigarettes and reading material once a month until your release.

• If you do happen to get a refund check, Artie insists you bring it to him to be cashed. You pay only a small service charge of ninety-five percent.

• If you try to cash your refund check elsewhere and take a little trip to Mexico or the Caribbean, Artie will have a member of his staff consult with you further when you return—and your tax problems will be over.

Permanently.

Mayhem and Marshmallow Chickens

Millions of Americans will take part in the annual ritual of the Easter egg hunt today. The adults will hide candy eggs and other sugary surprises, and the children, dressed in their Easter finery, will vie to see who can fill his or her basket first.

Among other bad things that will happen, there will be a lot of arguments.

Larry, eight, and Debbi, five, will happen upon the chocolate bunny prize, hidden in the tall weeds near the swing set, at precisely the same moment.

"It's mine!" Larry will scream.

"I saw it first!" Debbi will counter.

Both children will being to cry and pull at the choclate bunny.

"Now, children," Larry's mom will interrupt. "Let's settle this fairly. Which of you is the oldest?"

"I am, Mom," Larry will say.

"Then you get the chocolate bunny prize," his mother will conclude. Mothers always take care of their own at an Easter egg hunt.

"Waaaaaaaa!" Debbi will scream, running to her mother. "Larry's mother took my chocolate bunny prize and gave it to Larry because he is older than me!"

"Don't worry, darling," Debbi's mom will say. "I'll fix that pushy broad."

A lot of hair-pulling and scratching and screaming later, the two adults will be pulled apart by the cops. Meanwhile, Larry has dropped the chocolate bunny prize onto the ground and the dog is eating it, and Debbi has brained a four-year-old for his marshmallow chicken.

That's another thing about Easter egg hunts. The younger the child, the more hazardous egg hunts can be to both the kid's mental and physical well-being.

Let's say you are two. You barely know how to locate your mouth. And they expect you to be able to run around in an open field and find Easter eggs?

The older kids will find eggs, of course. They'll find 'em by the dozens, but you won't have a blasted thing in your stupid basket, so you will get frustrated and you will start to cry because you feel inadequate. Later, when you flunk out of college and join a religious cult, it will all be because you couldn't find an egg when you were two.

There also is the chance you won't live through the egg hunt in order to grow up to be a total failure. Kids are vicious when it comes to eggs. They will trample other children, hit other children with sticks, kick other children—whatever it takes to wrest an egg from the possession of an opponent in the hunt.

We used to have egg hunts at my school. I hated them because of Frankie Garfield, the school bully. At first, Frankie would go to the trouble of actually making an effort to find his own eggs.

But bending over to pick up eggs was a lot of work for Frankie, so he eventually took to waiting until after school and then searching through every kid's basket and taking his pick of the loot.

Once he caught Alvin Bates hiding a creme-filled duck in his back pocket. Frankie decorated Alvin's face with the creme-filled duck and then hit him in the belly. Alvin always stayed home sick after that on egg hunt day.

The cruelest Easter egg hunt story I know, however, occurred in Philadelphia, where they put on an egg hunt for children in the outfield grass before a Phillies baseball game. The fans booed the kids who couldn't find eggs.

There is something about an Easter egg hunt that brings out the worst in all of us.

A Mother's Side of the Story

Lillian Pye had a son. His name was James Scroggins, and he was an Atlanta policeman, like his daddy before him. He was also a husband and the father of three children.

James Scroggins was thirty when he died last October. Lillian Pye remembers every detail of what happened to her son.

"He had worked his regular day shift at the police department," she began as we talked last week. As we talked, I could hear the hurt in her voice. It still runs deep.

"He went home, and then he got in his car, a Volkswagen, and started for night classes at DeKalb South. He wasn't drinking or anything. He was just going to class.

"There was this other car, and an eighteen-year-old was driving it. A boy. He lost control of his car. He hit a bridge, and then he ran into my son. The boy's car skidded 500 feet.

"It took them two and one half hours to cut my son out of the car. They would never even let me see the car. All he ever said after the wreck was, 'I'm an Atlanta policeman. Take me to Grady.' He knew Grady had the best when it came to emergencies."

When they finally got Lillian Pye's son out of his car, it was too late to do anything more for him.

The other driver wasn't seriously injured. It happens that way sometimes.

"He was drunk," Lillian Pye said. "That boy was drunk." There is bitterness to go with her hurt.

"They told me when they took him out of the car, he was filthy and nasty and he was drunk."

DeKalb County charged the other driver with vehicular homicide. He went to trial. I'll let Lillian Pye tell the rest of it.

"At the trial, you should have seen that boy. His lawyer had told him exactly what to do. He had gotten a shave and a close haircut. He had on a new suit of clothes. He pleaded for mercy from the court.

"And you know what the judge gave him? He gave that boy five years probation and a $1,000 fine. That's it. Five years probation and a $1,000 fine. My son was killed, and that boy got off free. They didn't even take his license away.

"And you know something else? We never heard from him, and we never heard from his family. Not one word. They didn't even want to know if my son's wife and children could keep a roof over their heads, and they had a rough time of it until all the insurance was settled.

"I wrote the judge a letter and I said, 'I know you have a job to do, but you didn't do it very well.' I don't want that boy to get away with this. I don't want him driving around so he can do the same thing again."

I talked to DeKalb traffic investigators about the accident that killed James Scroggins. They agree with Lillian Pye that justice wasn't done.

But there is nothing they can do now. There is nothing anybody can do.

On second thought, yes there is. Lillian Pye admits she's called "everybody in town," television commentators, newspaper people.

All she wanted, I think, was the opportunity to tell her side of the story.

Now, she's had that opportunity, and what we can do for her is listen.

A mother misses her dead son on Mother's Day. What we can do for her is listen and, if just for a moment, share her hurt and her frustration.

It's the least, the very least, we can do.

The Last Hunt

Thanksgiving reminds different people of different things. It always reminds me of the first and last time I went hunting. That is because the first and last time I went hunting was on Thanksgiving Day when I was twelve.

Going hunting after the big Thanksgiving feast was sort of a tradition among the menfolk in my family, and when you were a boy child and reached the age of twelve, you finally were able to go along.

Imagine my glee when my grandfather and uncles and cousins explained what we would be doing on the annual Thanksgiving Day hunt:

First, we would carry these heavy guns and hike over half the county, through briars and under barbed-wire fences and down in gullies, if that was where the dogs took us.

Then, if anybody happened to spot a rabbit, he would promptly blow it to bits.

After the Thanksgiving Day feast the year I was twelve, I hid in the pump house and hoped they would leave on the hunt without me.

"What's the matter, son?" asked my uncle when the dogs flushed me out. "You don't want to go hunting with the rest of the men?" He put a lot of emphasis on the "men."

I'd rather spend the afternoon with my foot caught under Grandma's rocking chair is what I wanted to say, but I didn't say that at all.

"I was just in here checking the pump," is what I did say, and then it was off to the woods on the hunt.

Let me tell you what I think about going hunting:

If you want to take a gun and go out and shoot down defenseless animals in the forest, that's your business.

I just happen to think hunting is unfair. Maybe if they changed the rules of hunting, I would feel better about it.

What I would do is issue guns to all the deer and rabbits and ducks and whatever else people hunt.

If you think hunting is an exciting sport now, wait until your prey can shoot back.

I don't like to hunt, but I do like to fish. "Same thing as hunting," you might be saying.

Not at all. First, there are not guns involved in fishing. Second, the fish has a choice of whether or not to bite the hook.

Hunters will also argue that they go out in the woods and kill for food. I don't believe that, not with a Del Taco on practically every corner in town.

Anyway, back to my first and last hunting trip on Thanksgiving Day when I was twelve:

It was cold and wet, and we must have walked thirty miles.

"Your best bet to kill a rabbit," explained my uncle, "is to find one sitting on its bed. That way, you don't have to shoot a moving target."

I prayed not to find a rabbit sitting on its bed, or on anybody else's bed.

My prayer was answered. As a matter of fact, nobody in the group even fired a shot, and there was a lot of cursing the dratted luck at the end of the day. I think the dogs had a good time, but it doesn't take much to make a dog happy.

When it came time to go hunting the next Thanksgiving, I feigned a strange seizure that affected my ability to keep from screaming at the top of my voice, so nobody wanted to take me on the hunt because I would scare off the rabbits. Every year, I managed a new excuse. When I was eighteen I left home, and the question of going hunting has never come up in my life since.

In summary, what I think about hunting may be likened unto the perspective on the matter of one Ralph "High-Lift" Turnipseed, a man in my hometown who walked funny—he lifted one leg much higher than the other when he walked because of something strong he once drank because the local bootlegger was on vacation.

"Goin' rabbit-huntin' today, High-Lift?" somebody asked him on the street one day.

"Hell, no," High-Lift responded. "I ain't lost no rabbits."

Double-Dose of Hard Times

The response to this plea for help for Betty Hubbard was incredible. She and her son got their kitchen table and much more.

*There is bad in the world and, sometimes, it seems to scream out
to be noticed. But there is much good, too, and Christmas brings
it forth in gushes.*

Betty Hubbard sat on what was a piece of lawn furniture before
somebody bent the frame. Betty's son, Joey, who is fifteen, sat on the
floor. I took one of Betty's two chairs. A second visitor sat in the
other chair.

Betty Hubbard talked about her life. I caught myself looking away
to avoid her eyes when she cried.

"I never thought I would come to anything like this," she said. "We
ain't got a thing."

She is fifty. She looks older. She's been a "widow woman" for ten
years. She has an older son who she says is a "bad influence" on
young Joey.

She moved to Atlanta from neighboring Rockdale County to look
for a fresh start for her and the boy.

She has asthma. She is unemployed. She and Joey live in a hole of
an apartment near Grant Park.

"I apologize for the way this place looks," Betty said. "Me and Joey
got out a bucket of water and scrubbed these floors, but it didn't do
no good."

We are seated in the living room. There is a small table near the
door. On the table are pictures of Betty's sons. Between the two
chairs is a locker. There is a small lamp on the locker. It is the only
light in the house.

There is no table in the kitchen. There are two bedrooms in the
apartment, but only one bed.

"Joey has to sleep with me," said Betty Hubbard. "A lot of folks
might have something to say about that, but if he don't sleep with
me, then he has to sleep on the floor. I ain't lettin' my baby sleep on
no floor. He's all I got."

The sky is gray, the weather is cold. For the first two weeks Betty
and Joey were in the apartment, they did not have the money to have
the gas and power turned on. They huddled under blankets and
burned candles.

Betty gets $400 a month in welfare payments. She hands over $220
for the apartment. She's being robbed. She borrowed from her landlord to put down the deposits for the gas and power.

"We had a home once," Bettty goes on, breaking into tears, "but it
got away from me. It's hard for a widow woman and two boys."

There was a silence in the room.

"I don't lie to my doctor, so I won't lie to you," Betty Hubbard continued. "We've all done some drinking. Me, and both the boys. All it done was cause fighting and misunderstanding. But there were times we didn't have nothing to eat. Where there ain't nothing to eat and somebody comes around with a drink, you just can't help but take it."

Betty Hubbard's apartment is a curse. Crumpled magazines and newspapers on the floor. Towels over the windows. Something caught my eye hanging on the wall, a baby's Christmas stocking marked "Joey," and a Christmas scene torn from a calendar. Christmas finds the darndest places.

Hard times come in different degrees. Betty and her boy Joey have caught a double-dose. They're flat busted and it's Christmas Eve. They don't ask much:

• Some pants for Joey. He has only one pair. He is thirty in the waist and thirty length.

• Some shoes for Betty. Her only pair are worn moccasins.

• A small bed for Joey. And something where the two of them could sit down for a meal.

• Food. They ate sardines and soda crackers for Thanksgiving.

• An old television. "A boy naturally wants a television," said Betty Hubbard. "When I get back on my feet, that's the first thing I'm going to do, get my boy a television."

• Employment. Betty, with her asthma, is limited. She says she is good with children and once worked in a nursery. Joey is strong.

You hear these stories every Christmas. And you can't help everybody. And there are probably people even more deserving than Betty and Joey Hubbard, and, besides, we've got our own families to take care of.

But when the party is over and the wrappings are off the gifts, and Friday brings back reality, Betty and Joey still won't have a kitchen table.

Christmas Moose Smooch

I was driving along and listening to Christmas carols on the radio, and I started thinking back to those wonderful days when I was a kid and we used to draw names for the annual class Christmas party.

What a blast that was. What fun to share Christmas gifts with your classmates.

A bunch of cheap, ungrateful toads, all of them.

In the third grade Alvin Bates got my name. Alvin Bates was the kind of kid who would bring a candy bar for afternoon recess and lick it all over before taking a bite so nobody would ask him to share it.

In the third grade Alvin Bates gave me one of those stupid wooden paddles with the balls and the rubber strings attached. You hit the stupid ball with the stupid paddle and the stupid ball, attached to the rubber string, comes back and you hit it again.

Terrific. Fun for any awkward child under six. For fifty-nine cents, which is exactly what Alvin Bates shelled out for the paddle and the ball, he could have bought me something useful and educational, like a copy of *Stag* magazine they kept on the back shelf at the drugstore.

Stag was nothing compared to the magazines they have today, but in 1954, seeing a picture of a lady in a girdle could make your month.

Later I reaped revenge. I drew Alvin's name in the fourth grade, and I gave him a subscription to *Boy's Life*. Anybody caught reading *Boy's Life* was obviously a complete (a) mama's boy, (b) nurd, (c) sissy, (d) wimp, (e) fruit, (f) several other things I can't mention here.

"Hey, Four-Eyes," we used to taunt Alvin on the playground, "what's the centerfold this month in *Boy's Life*? Picture of a pup tent?"

Alvin spent most of his fourth-grade year crying.

In the fifth grade, Frankie Garfield, the school bully, drew my name.

Having your name drawn by Frankie Garfield was both bad and good. The bad part was Frankie's usual gift wouldn't exactly fit under the class tree.

The good part was Frankie's gift was a promise he wouldn't beat you up for at least a week.

"I let you live, Duck-Face," Frankie would say.

The worst thing that ever happened to me, though, was in the sixth grade when Cordie Mae Poovey, the ugliest and meanest girl in school, drew my name.

Cordie Mae was from a poor family, and she never had much money to spend on a gift. A pair of socks, I figured. Or a box of peanut brittle.

Worse. I opened my gift from Cordie Mae, and all I found was an envelope with a note inside that read, "Merry Christmas. I give you the gift of love. One (1) kiss and one (1) hug. Meet me after school. Cordie Mae."

I'd kiss a pig first. And Cordie Mae was as strong as she smelled. She could break a couple of ribs.

After school I ran as fast as I could, but she finally chased me down, hammerlocked me, and then planted one right on my mouth. Smmmmmmmmack!

"How'd you like that, big boy?" asked Cordie Mae.

"Ever smooched with a moose?" I answered.

"Ever been run over by a herd of reindeer?" replied Cordie Mae, who had no sense of humor whatsoever.

The swelling in my nose went down in a couple of days, but it was a week before my eyes opened again.

9

ELECTION YEAR

I covered the 1980 presidential election from New Hampshire in January to the Republican Convention in Detroit in July to the Democratic Convention in New York in August, and I was standing there with the rain falling on Plains when Jimmy Carter came home on Inauguration Day, beaten and tired. I am convinced anybody crazy enough to go through what a person has to go through to get elected president is very likely about halfway to being completely bananas by the time he spends the first night in the White House. . . .

Too Late for the Duke

The more I think about it, the less I can find wrong with the fact that a movie actor is running for president of the United States.

Look who else has run for that position in the past—surveyors, architects, several generals, a couple of newspaper editors, a bankrupt haberdasher, even a peanut farmer, lest we forget.

But did it have to be THAT movie actor? When this country finally got around to picking somebody off the silver screen to make the mad dash for the White House, did it have to be, as he has been described, "the Errol Flynn of the B-movies"?

Ronald Reagan, for crying out loud? *Love Is On The Air* Ronald Reagan? *That Hagen Girl* (with Shirley Temple) Ronald Reagan? Supporting actor to a chimpanzee in *Bedtime for Bonzo* Ronald Reagan?

Do you realize Ronald Reagan originally was cast for the lead in *Casablanca*? Can you imagine that? Reagan in the role Bogie made a classic?

Let's face it. Ronald Reagan may have been lousy in *Hellcats of the Navy*, but he was terrible in another clunker, as Grover Cleveland Alexander, the baseball player.

Of all the actors we had to choose from to run for president, we took the man who once sold 20-Mule Team Borax on "Death Valley Days"?

411

You're looking for a movie-actor president? Just consider who else was available that we passed up:

• HENRY FONDA: Looks like a president, talks like a president, acts like a president. Did anybody see Henry Fonda in *Fail Safe*? He played the president and wound up ordering the bomb dropped on New York City. I told you he would have made us a good president.

• JIMMY STEWART: Well, ah, it might, ah, take him a long, ah, time, to make, ah, a state of the, ah, union address, but at least, ah, everybody in the, ah, country could do, ah, an impression of the, ah, president, don't you, ah, see?

• WALTER PIDGEON: Tall, distinguished. Plays a lot of senators and other big shots. My mother always thought a lot of Walter Pidgeon.

• CHARLTON HESTON: Normally thought of as an airline pilot or a chariot racer, but be honest with yourself.

You want somebody in the Oval Office who can handle a crisis, right? So would you pick squatty Ronald Reagan with that funky hairdo of his, or tall, handsome Charlton Heston, last seen, incidentally, drowning heroically in a sewer following an earthquake?

• GREGORY PECK: I always have been a big Gregory Peck fan since I saw him in *The Man in the Gray Flannel Suit* and later in *To Kill a Mockingbird*.

Gregory Peck would not waffle on the issues. We elected Eisenhower, didn't we? Then give MacArthur his chance.

• ROBERT STACK: Law and order candidate. Congress starts acting up and Ness and the boys come around to straighten them out.

• CHARLES BRONSON: Want somebody to get tough with the Russians? Here is somebody to get tough with the Russians. "One more word out of you, Leonid, and I'll bust your face in." That kind of get-tough-with-the-Russians.

But what am I saying here? Fonda, Stewart, Heston, etc. Lightweights, all of them, when you consider the man who should be in Ronald Reagan's shoes right now.

Tall in the saddle, he was. A soldier. Tough, but fair. A patriot. What this country needs is a good dose of true grit. He had it.

Ronald Reagan, Ronald Smeagan. This country decides it wants to elevate a movie actor to the threshold of the White House and we pussyfoot around until the Duke is unavailable.

Sort of makes you sick to your stomach, doesn't it, pilgrim?

"What He Meant to Say Was . . ."

To follow the presidential campaigns, one can all but ignore the statements and charges of the candidates and other influential individuals and wait for the clarifications that always follow from aides.

Some notable examples to clip and save:

• Ronald Reagan implies President Carter supports the Ku Klux Klan by making a snide remark about the president opening his campaign in Tuscumbia, Alabama, which, according to Mr. Reagan, is "the birthplace of the Klan."

WHAT AIDES SAID MR. REAGAN REALLY MEANT TO SAY: "Governor Reagan really meant to say he wishes Coach Bear Bryant and the University of Alabama football team another great season.

"He would also like to add he wants to visit Tuscumbia, himself, very soon to see his dearest and oldest friend, Helen Keller, who he remembers so well as such a talented dancer in all those old Hollywood musicals."

• President Carter implies that Mr. Reagan is a racist.

WHAT AIDES SAID MR. CARTER REALLY MEANT TO SAY: "The President really meant to say Mr. Reagan is spending too much time 'racing' round the country making unwarranted attacks on his record. Also he wanted to mention that Mr. Reagan has solicited the campaign help of stock car 'racing' king Richard Petty.

"And just because the President's statements were misinterpreted while he was standing in the late Dr. Martin Luther King, Jr., hometown church, surrounded by every black leader from here to Satchel Paige, it must be considered only a mere coincidence.

• Mr. Reagan says the United States' efforts in the Vietnam War were for a "noble cause."

WHAT AIDES SAID MR. REAGAN REALLY MEANT TO SAY: "'Spanish-American' instead of 'Vietnam.' Just a mere slip of the tongue. It could happen to anybody."

• Mr. Reagan gets his Chinas mixed up.

HOW AIDES EXPLAINED THAT: "The governor didn't have his hand pocket world Atlas with him at the time, and even if he did, 'little' China appears as such a tiny speck, anybody could overlook it, like Rhode Island in our own country.

"Incidentally, the governor will be campaigning in that great state soon, and we hope everybody who can will be out to greet him when his plane lands at the airport in Hartford."

• President Carter charges that Mr. Reagan, if elected, would lead the country into war.

WHAT AIDES SAID MR. CARTER REALLY MEANT TO SAY:
"What he really meant to say was if this nation ever has to go to war,
then Mr. Reagan would be a terrific person to lead us into it. As a
second lieutenant, for instance, up ahead of all the troops, trying to
knock out an enemy machine gun nest."

• *Time Magazine* quotes Miss Lillian Carter as saying, "Sometimes
when I take a look at my children, I wish I had remained a virgin."

WHAT MISS LILLIAN'S FRIENDS IN PLAINS SAID SHE
REALLY MEANT TO SAY: "She really meant to say that sometimes
when she takes a look at her children, she wishes she had remained a
virgin."

• Dr. Bailey Smith, president of the Southern Baptist Convention,
makes the statement that "God almighty does not hear the prayers of
a Jew."

WHAT THE DEACONS SAID DR. SMITH REALLY MEANT TO
SAY: "He really meant to say God doesn't listen to the prayers of
Jews, or of hardly anybody else, on WEDNESDAYS. That's the day
he takes off to listen to blow-hard politicians ask forgiveness for all
the lies they've told the previous week."

Debates and Rat-Killings

The headline in Wednesday's paper said it all about Tuesday
night's debate between Jimmy Carter and Ronald Reagan:

"Carter, Reagan Both Feel Goals Achieved in Debate."

Of course Carter and Reagan both felt their goals were achieved in
the debate. That's the problem with presidential debates. They are
not like wrestling matches where one guy runs another guy's head
into one of the ring posts and you can pick a clear winner.

A presidential debate is more like a rat-killing.

I don't know how many of you have ever been to a big league rat-
killing before, but they work like this:

The rat-killers, armed with .22 rifles, hide behind some bales of
hay in the barn. Some corn has been spread about to entice the rats
to enter the arena. The lights are turned out.

As soon as it sounds like there are a number of rats gnawing on the
corn, the lights are turned on and the rats are momentarily blinded.
The rat-killers then cut down on the rats from behind the hay bales
with their .22s.

This sounds a little one-sided in favor of the rat-killers, and it is,
but the rats do get a nice meal before being blown away, and because
rats are such pests, they don't deserve a fair shake anyway.

And after the rat-killing is over, both sides can always rationalize a victory.

Let's say some of the rats get away:

"A clear victory for our side," says the spokesrat. "Those clowns couldn't hit a bull in the bohunkus with a bass fiddle."

"Another win for us," counters the head rat-killer. "We didn't want to shoot them all so we could have another rat-killing."

Rat-killings and presidential debates. Just alike. Also, throw arguments with your wife into the same category.

I did the only sane thing for the debate Tuesday night. I watched it in a bar. After the debate was over, I polled the joint.

Three drunks were for Carter. Three drunks were for Reagan. The bartender was a Libertarian, and the waitress likes Anderson because he reminds her of her uncle in Tupelo who has the local pocket-fisherman franchise.

I kept my own scorecard. I tried to be as fair as possible. Here is how I rated each man's performance:

• HAIR—Carter's was neatly parted on the side-of-the-week and appeared to have been blow-dried. Reagan, meanwhile, had apparently slicked it down with Royal Crown. Wetheadsville with enough Grecian formula Nine to turn chalk black. HAIR TO CARTER.

• SMILE—Carter, for a smiler, didn't smile much. Perhaps he was having another flare-up of what George Brett had. Reagan smiles like used car dealers smile. SMILE TO REAGAN.

• SUIT—Robert Hall Ronnie looked like he just stepped off the cover of GQ. Unfortunately, a 1953 issue. SUIT TO CARTER.

• FACIAL COLOR—Carter looked like he had just seen Lester Maddox seated on the panel of inquisitors. Reagan had been pancaked a golden brown. FACIAL COLOR TO REAGAN.

• GRASP OF THE FACTS—Neither candidate appeared to know as much as Barbara Walters. GRASP OF FACTS TO BARBARA WALTERS.

What I am going to do is declare the 1980 Great Presidential Debate a deadlock and make only one other observation:

I wouldn't take Barbara Walters to a rat-killing. She'd scare off all the rats.

The Spirit of '76

Four years ago Wednesday morning, I awakened where I had fallen the night before, in an apartment on the thirtieth-some-odd floor of a high-rise apartment building in Chicago. The view was of Lincoln Park and Lake Michigan. The monthly rent was astounding.

I splashed some water on my then-bearded face and opened the front door. At my feet were two of Chicago's daily newspapers.

The message screamed across the front of both:

"IT'S CARTER!"

Thank the Lord I didn't dream it, I remember saying to myself.

Carter. Jimmy Carter. Former governor of that backward outhouse of a state, Georgia. Peanut farmer. Imagine that. Peanut farmer from Georgia running for president of the United States.

They used to ask me about him, Carter, and about Georgia. Chicagoans used to ask. "What's it really like *out there* in the South?"

"Out there" in the South. The West is "out there." The East is "over there." The North is "up here." The South is "down there." We spend millions each year to educate the heathen. And we have such vast ignorance right here in our own country.

A girl in Chicago once asked me. "Do you have any nice restaurants 'out there' in the South?"

"Surely," I answered her. "Mention my name, and maybe you'll get a good seat at the counter."

I took it all. I answered their questions. I assured them cotton wasn't growing in downtown Atlanta.

I explained we do not say, you all," we say, "y'all," and we never use it in the singular.

I explained about grits. Unless you put some butter or cheese in them, they taste awful.

And I hurt a lot. The South was, in fact, rising again. I could read about it every day, I could hear about it on the seven o'clock news.

So why was I, a true son of the red clay whose granddaddy once owned the egg-suckingest dog in Coweta County (dog's name was Edna), stuck in Chicago?

Grizzard Buzzard luck, I supposed. Can't kill nothing. Can't find nothing dead.

I pulled as hard for him as I ever have pulled for anything, anybody. I prayed over it. ". . . And, Lord, if you can't help me, then at least please help Jimmy."

The night he was nominated, I couldn't hold back the tears. I ran up a hundred dollars' worth of phone calls with 404 area codes.

I got Dorsey Hill on the phone. Dorsey grew up in Rome, Georgia. "Sumbitch," he said, "don't it make you proud?"

But that was only half the battle. There was still Ford. This girl with the high-rise apartment gave an election party, and I told her I wouldn't come if any Ford people were going to be there, so we had just a small gathering (Carter lost Illinois in '76, too), but that made the victory just that much sweeter.

Four years ago Wednesday morning, I read both Chicago papers from front to back, but filled with triumph as I was, I was also never so homesick in all my life.

I think you would have had to have been away from the South to see what Jimmy Carter getting elected president in 1976 really meant to the South, and to Southerners.

I caught a cab to my office. Usually, I took a bus. I was celebrating. There was a pink memorandum slip awaiting me in my typewriter. It was from a colleague, local boy, who thought Indianapolis was the Deep South. But the man had some degree of class.

"Congratulations," began the note, "y'all ain't trash no more."

I don't know if Jimmy Carter was a good president or not, and I wish Ronald Reagan all the best.

But four years ago on a cold Chicago morning, Jimmy Carter made me as proud as if I had won the damn election myself. For that, I will always be indebted to him.

Always.

Jimmy Earl Comes Home

PLAINS—Standing here in the pouring rain Tuesday, my feet freezing, I wondered what the Ronald Reagans were doing.

Here in Plains, several thousand of us were waiting for a helicopter to drop out of the gray sky and bring Jimmy Earl home. That's what they call the former president of the United States in his hometown. They call him "Jimmy Earl."

I figured the Reagans were probably finished with their spiffy luncheon that had followed the inauguration. They were to have boneless breast of chicken and California wines.

I suppose they were probably getting ready for Tuesday evening's inaugural ball, or maybe they were having a few pops with somebody like Frank Sinatra or Jimmy Stewart or Liz Taylor. They're all such famous friends, you know.

And while I was thinking about the Reagans, I thought about what Bill Godfrey once said. Bill Godfrey played football for the University of Georgia before Herschel Walker was born. He said, "Ain't folks nice to you when you win?"

To the winner Tuesday went the spoils. Ronald Wilson Reagan became the fortieth president. Jimmy Earl Carter Jr., the thirty-ninth, came home to Plains.

He looked awful. He looked tired and he looked drained. They said he hadn't slept in two days, as he battled to the last minute of his administration to see the hostages freed from Iran.

I think the Iranians waited, on purpose, until Reagan had been sworn in before they released the hostages. I also think the Iranians are lower than camel dung.

The crowd at Jimmy Carter's homecoming day Tuesday was vintage Georgian, vintage Deep Southern. A lady said to her husband, "Hep me, Johnny, I don't think I can get my parasol open." The last person I heard refer to an umbrella as a "parasol" was my grandmother.

A woman from Macon told me, "My boss didn't want me to come over here today, but I came anyway. Jimmy Carter's the only man in the world I'd stand in the rain to see."

A little girl, sniffling, stood on the hood of a truck awaiting the former president's arrival. She held a sign that read, "We love you, Jimmy." The rain had drenched her. ABC nearly ran over CBS to get her on camera.

A sign in front of a store on the outskirts of town read, "New Rooster. Too Many Eggs. Sale. 75 Cents a Dozen. Welcome Back, Jimmy and Rosalynn."

The good ladies of Plains had wanted to turn out the world's largest covered-dish supper, and I think they did it. One table stretched an entire block, and it was filled with Southern delights, including fried chicken, and I saw bowls of collards and cakes and pies that were enough to start a riot.

They almost did. The idea was to form a line across the railroad tracks and to proceed orderly down the table, serving yourself buffet style. But several sweet-tooth vultures would not follow those directins and were pilfering from the table despite the efforts of a lady carrying a butcher knife to keep them away.

Jimmy C. Newman sang Cajun music. Tom T. Hall sang "Old Dogs and Children and Watermelon Wine." Despite the rain, the street dance and the fireworks show were still scheduled for later in the evening. I saw two old boys passing a bottle in a sack back and forth. I didn't see Billy.

When he had finally landed and had made his way to the plastic-covered platform in the middle of town, Jimmy Earl made a nice speech.

He didn't brag on himself too much. He talked about the pride he felt in having been president for four years. He said a wife of one of the hostages had said to him earlier in the day, "Mister President, I hope you can meet my husband someday." And the president replied, "I will be with him in Germany this week, and I will tell him you love him."

He asked us all to support the new president, and he talked about how much the Algerian government had helped getting the hostages released.

That started me thinking again. Here stood Jimmy Earl Carter in the middle of Plains, Sumter County, Georgia, talking about Algeria when most of us in the crowd couldn't find it on a map with directions and a head start. Nobody had come to hear about Algeria.

I got the distinct feeling that the reason that crowd showed up in that awful weather Tuesday was to help soften a hometown boy's abrupt fall from the most powerful office in the world back to private citizen. Let the Reagans dance the night away; Georgians took care of their own Tuesday afternoon.

I mentioned dancing. I will forevermore consider it appropriate that after the new president had been inaugurated, after the hostages had been freed, after dog-tired Jimmy Carter had come back to Plains and had made his speech, the last thing he did before the public eye was stand tall on the platform in front of the cheering crowd and take his wife in his arms and dance with her.

The tune was "Dixie."

Senility Test

Now that Ronald Reagan actually is going to be president, let us remind ourselves of a promise he made during the campaign.

Reagan, who will be seventy by the time he is sworn into office, promised to take a senility test if ever the situation arose where there were murmurings about the "crazy old coot over at the White House."

I think it is important that we hold Mr. Reagan to this promise. Being president is a strain on any man. Look at Jimmy Carter. He was nearly twenty years younger than Mr. Reagan when he took office. But by the time he was blown out, he was so confused, he was discussing nuclear proliferation with his daughter, Amy.

You may be asking yourself what sort of senility test Mr. Reagan would take. I'm glad you asked that. Through various sources in Washington, this column has obtained a secret copy of the Official Presidential Senility Test (Republican Version).

Given after, say, two years in office, could Mr. Reagan then pass the following rigorous examination?

1. Place your hand over your heart. Would you say it is:

(a) purring like a kitten? (10 points). (b) Humming like a Model-T Ford? (8 points). (c) Going "flap-flong-blip-bong"? (2 points). (If you are unable to answer this question because you can't locate your heart, subtract five points and do not attempt to operate an automobile.)

2. How would you describe your ability to hear?

(a) Excellent (10 points). (b) Good (6 points). (c) Fair (2 points).

3. YOU WANT THE QUESTION REPEATED A LITTLE LOUDER?

(Subtract five points and try not to doze off during the remainder of this test.)

4. How would you describe your ability to see?

(a) Excellent (10 points). (b) Good (6 points). (c) Fair (2 points). (d) Last week at a meeting with Leonid Brezhnev you shook hands with your chair and sat down in the premier's lap. (Subtract 5 points and forget about SALT III.)

5. True (subtract 5 points) or False (add 5):

Earl Scheib does your hair.

6. Your lovely wife Nancy comes into the presidential bedroom wearing a slinky nightgown. Your first move is to:

(a) Call the kitchen and order a bottle of champagne (10 points). (b) Look for your old Benny Goodman records (5 points). (c) Phone George Bush to see if he wants to come over and watch one of your old movies on the late show. (Subtract 6 points and say you have a sick headache.)

7. The following question has to do with your memory: Back in 1980 you won a resounding victory over your opponent in the presidential election. Your opponent's name was:

(a) Jimmy Carter. (b) Bonzo.

(If you selected (a), add 5 points to your score. If you selected (b), add 4 points. At least you were close.)

8. Another memory question: You were born in:

(a) 1492. (b) 1776. (c) 1812. (d) 1911.

(If you marked (a), (b), (c), subtract 10 points. If you marked (d), an old fellow like you should probably rest a while before we finish this test.)

9. Your youngest son, Ronnie, Jr.:

(a) Plays football for Notre Dame, like you did. (b) Is a professional wrestler. (c) Drives a truck. (d) Hops around on his toes with pale-looking girls and wears leotards.

(If you marked (a), (b), (c), subtract 5 points for wishful thinking. If you marked (d), subtract 10 points for asking your own son to never visit you in the White House until after dark.)

10. As president, your most outstanding contribution to the country has been:

(a) Getting us into war with Canada. (c) Making Woody Hayes secretary of defense. (d) Pardoning former President Carter.

(No matter what you answered, subtract 10 points and have a glass of warm milk.)

HOW YOU SCORED

70-100: The country survived Millard Fillmore; it probably can survive you.

50-69: Get plenty of rest, avoid press conferences, and drink all your prune juice.

30-49: Move around occasionally with your eyes open. Somebody may get the wrong idea.

Less than 30: We have one chance for survival: If you do decide to push the button, maybe you won't be able to remember where they keep it.

Queen Nancy

A number of women I know never did care for Rosalynn Carter, the outgoing first lady.

"She's cold," one described Mrs. Carter.

"She wore that same horrid green dress for four years," said another.

Needless to say, these ladies are very excited now that former actress Nancy Reagan is taking over at the White House.

"She has dignity and charm," said one.

"She wears nothing but Adolfo originals," added another.

I think Nancy Reagan is a very pretty, well-dressed lady, too. But she's pushy. She reminds me of a woman who used to live in my neighborhood, Mrs. Pratt. Mrs. Pratt was pushy.

She was always offering everybody advice on how to wear their hair, what color drapes to hang in the living room, and where to hang the new picture of the bullfighter.

When you were around Mrs. Pratt, you always got the feeling she was looking down her nose at you. One day Mrs. Pratt told Mildred Elrod she was putting on a little weight. Mildred Elrod was offended and fixed it so Mrs. Pratt couldn't look down her nose at anybody again. It was too crooked after that.

I get the feeling Nancy Reagan is looking down her nose at a lot of us. She was educated at the best schools, of course, and she has spent a lot of her time lunching at expensive Hollywood restaurants, and she is great friends with a lot of rich people like Betty Bloomingdale who go around saying, "dahling."

I first got the idea that maybe Nancy Reagan and some of her aides were snooty when one of her California cronies said, "She will bring more to the White House than Amy."

That is downright catty.

There was another remark about Nancy Reagan's style of entertaining.

"She knows how to entertain, and she'll do it with dignity, the way it should be done. There won't be anymore lemonade, cookies, bare feet, hot dogs, and Willie Nelson."

Willie Nelson, as a matter of fact, has starred in two hit movies, two more than the next president, and he rolled around in the hay with Dyan Cannon, not a monkey.

The clincher came when Nancy Reagan was reported to have said she didn't understand why the Carters didn't go ahead and move out of the White House before the January 20 inauguration so she could begin redecoration.

Jimmy Carter remains president and gets to live in the White House until the inauguration. That's according to some silly document like the Constitution, which is always getting in the way when something important like redecorating comes up.

I don't know a thing about Rosalynn Carter except what I read about her in the newspapers and what I see about her on television, but she seems a nice enough person.

She always came across as sincere. Since I wouldn't know an Adolfo from something off the bargain rack at K Mart, her dressing habits never bothered me.

She doesn't know any movie stars, I don't suppose, and she probably has never lunched on Rodeo Drive in Hollywood, and I doubt she even knows Betty Bloomingdale, much less is friends with her, and Rosalynn talks a little funny, like folks do in South Georgia.

But she appeared to do a good job of being a wife to the president, and a mother to their children, and I would hate to see her kicked out of her house before the lease runs out.

Maybe Nancy Reagan simply needs to be reminded of something before she starts her *reign.*

Just concentrate on being a good first lady, Mrs. Reagan. A queen we don't need.

A Letter to the President

Dear President Reagan,

I purposely waited a couple of weeks before writing you because I wanted some time to think after the attempt that was made on your life. Also, I knew you were up to your ears trying to run our country from a hospital bed.

I am not pretending this will be unique, by any means, but I happen to be one American citizen who is lucky enough to have a public forum, and I see no harm in occasionally using it for expression that is purely personal.

I've got to admit up front I didn't support you in 1980. As a matter of fact, as I stood a few rows behind you as you made your nomination acceptance speech at the Republican Convention in Detroit, I said to a friend standing with me, "He sounds like he's still trying to sell a box of 20-Mule Team Borax."

My friend and I had a good laugh over that. Somehow you seemed unreal to me, too much Hollywood, not enough substance. A man nearly seventy shouldn't look as fit as you do, shouldn't bounce around like you do.

Where was your gray hair? How could you still stand so erect, speak so strongly and keep the demanding schedule those seeking public office must keep?

When you announced you would be glad to take a senility test during your term as president, I said, "Sure he will. If only he can remember where he put it."

I had some problems with your platform, too. I saw you on television night after night, smoothie that you are, telling the American people how you were going to cure inflation, bring down the unemployment rate and give the Russians hell. You sounded great, but I listened to a huckster at a carnival once, too, and it cost me two bucks to learn that what silver tongues preach isn't always golden.

I worried about your feelings toward the poor. I worried about what you would do the first time the Russians tried your hand. Would you react too strongly, foolishly, and get us all blown away?

I've got to admit something else, too, Mr. President. I still haven't been able to warm up toward your wife. When she suggested that the Carters move out of the White House early so she could get to the business of redecorating, I secretly hoped her slip would show on Inauguration Day.

Your son, the one that dances, didn't impress me that much, either, especially when he called President Carter a "snake." I respected and supported President Carter, for a number of reasons:

One, I considered him to be completely honest; two, he talks a lot like I do; three, he is the only president in American history to invite me to drink beer in the back yard of the White House while listening to Willie Nelson sing. A man must have his own priorities, Mr. President.

Anyway, I've said all that to say this: I still don't know if you can pull off any of those miracles you promised, and I probably would vote for Jimmy Carter again, given the chance, but I will tell my grandchildren about the time that creep tried to gun you down in front of the Washington Hilton.

You took a slug in the lung and then walked into the hospital under your own power, cracked jokes with the doctors, went through a two-hour operation, and were signing legislation the next morning. And you're a year older than Arizona.

For right now, at least, I don't care what your politics are, I admire your vigor, your strength, and the way you handled yourself in a crisis of the utmost severity: Your own life was threatened.

Your actions said more than all the words you have uttered as president. The citizens of this country and the rest of the world have no more doubt: At the helm of this ship of state stands the toughest old bird in the valley.

> Your fan,
> Lewis Grizzard

10

NUMBER ONE

I attended the University of Georgia in Athens, Georgia, from 1964 until 1968. When I arrived on campus in the fall of '64, the school's football fortunes were at an all-time low.

But the same year I arrived on campus, so did a thirty-two-year-old rookie coach named Vince Dooley. It took him seventeen years to do it, but on January 1, 1981, in New Orleans, Louisiana, Vince Dooley put a Georgia team on the carpeted floor of the Superdome that was good enough to whip Notre Dame, a team made up mostly of people from north of Greenville, South Carolina, and good enough to win the national collegiate championship.

This made me very happy. In the first piece in this chapter, I will attempt to say why. The pieces that follow will attempt to describe some of the people and places that were a part of what one quite loyal to the Red and Black described as "the second greatest story ever told. . . ."

Georgia on My Mind

I was there that first night when Vincent Joseph Dooley, who was younger then (thirty-two) than I am now (thirty-five), coached his first game from the Georgia sidelines. It was a warm September night, 1964, in Denny Stadium, Tuscaloosa. The opposition was Joe Namath and Bear Bryant's fearsome Alabama.

How I happened to be in Tuscaloosa that night is a fairly long story that can be held in check by explaining I was seventeen at the time, about to enter my freshman year at the University of Georgia. The preceding summer, I had gone to see Ed Thelenius, the Bulldogs' "golden voice," who broadcast the Georgia games on radio.

Ed Thelenius, who died in March of 1981, was nice to me and offered me a job on his football crew. Ten a game and my travel and my room and my food. I would "spot" the opposition, point to the name of who had the ball for the other team. Ed Thelenius had a lot to do with getting my career started. They said he suffered a lot in the end. I hate that.

Early in the game that night in Tuscaloosa, a young defensive lineman from Georgia named George Patton stormed through the Alabama line and made a savage hit on Namath for a loss.

In the Georgia radio booth, I was sitting next to the late Bill Monday, the pioneer sportscaster who did color for Thelenius.

"They're ready!" screamed Monday. "Gawga's ready!"

Gawga wasn't ready. Namath passed them silly. The final score was 31-3. The traffic in Tuscaloosa was so bad it took three hours just to get back to Birmingham. Jim Koger, who did statistics for Thelenius, got out of the car and bought some beer. Jim Koger would teach me about a lot of things that season, including how to enjoy warm beer when there is no cold beer around. Incidentally, Jim Koger later found Jesus. There is hope for all of us.

I started classes at Georgia the next week. A lot of people, including some girls, were very impressed when I told them I worked for Ed Thelenius, who mentioned my name at the end of every broadcast.

The following Saturday, the Georgia team, Thelenius, and I checked into the Holiday Inn in Nashville where Georgia would play Vanderbilt in the evening. Thelenius and I ate a steak. We hung around in the lobby. I remember Dooley and Georgia athletic director Joel Eaves talking together. Both seemed very nervous.

Barry Wilson, a Georgia defensive end, intercepted a Vanderbilt pass that night in Nashville, and it led to the first touchdown ever for a Vince Dooley team. The seven points was enough. Vince Dooley, head coach, and Lewis Grizzard, journalism freshman, had their first victory at Georgia, 7-0, over Vanderbilt. We would go on to be 6-3-1. We would ship Georgia Tech and we would ship Texas Tech in the Sun Bowl. Barry Wilson would later become an assistant coach at Georgia Tech.

I left Georgia in 1968. Each game the Bulldogs played while I was on campus had a special memory. I'll list a few:

—Georgia 7, Georgia Tech 0, in Athens, 1964: Driving to the game from my hometown of Moreland—I had been out of school on Thanksgiving break—a woman plowed into the back of my red 1958 Chevrolet when I stopped for gas near Watkinsville. It was her fault, but my driver's license had expired. The Oconee County policeman said he would have to take me to the courthouse, but I told him I had to be at the game to work for Ed Thelenius. He let me go.

—Georgia 18, Alabama 17, in Athens, 1965: Thelenius pounded his fist on the table in front of him after the flea-flicker game that upset the eventual national champions. It was the only time I ever saw him lose control.

—Kentucky 28, Georgia 10, in Lexington, 1965: The coldest I have ever been in my life. I knocked over coffee onto the spotter boards and all over Thelenius. He never missed a beat.

—Miami 6, Georgia 3, in Miami, 1966: I was married by now and no longer working for the football network. My wife—the first Mrs. Grizzard—and I were parked outside the Dairy Queen in Athens, listening to the game on the radio. My wife wanted to talk about something else.

"Shut up!" I suggested to her.

She dumped a strawberry milkshake on my head. We divorced the year Tech beat Dooley for the first time.

—Georgia 21, Auburn 13, in Auburn, 1966: The first Georgia game I had seen from the stands. I had worked in the press box for all the others. One of my fraternity brothers was sitting next to me in the end zone. He brought along a bottle of Jack Daniels, black. We mixed it with Coke and drank all of it. I found out Georgia had come back in the second half to win, after trailing 13-0, by reading the paper the next day.

In the summer of 1968 I went to work as a sportswriter for the *Atlanta Journal*. Those were great years. I covered a lot of Georgia games. The best one was the '71 game against Georgia Tech in Atlanta when Andy Johnson brought Georgia back in the last minute-and-a-half to win, 28-24.

It looked bleak for Georgia that night. The Bulldogs had arrived at Grant Field with a 9-1 record, heavily favored over the Yellow Jackets. When it appeared there was no hope for Georgia, Tech sports information director Ned West walked over to Dan Magill, his counterpart at Georgia, and said, "Well, Dan, y'all have had a great season. I'm so sorry it had to end this way."

When Jimmy Poulos dived for the winning touchdown for Georgia with fourteen seconds to play, Magill walked over to West and said, "Well, Ned, y'all have had a great season. I'm so sorry it had to end this way."

In the fall of 1975, I did a stupid thing. I took the second Mrs. Grizzard and moved to Chicago to become sports editor of the *Chicago Sun-Times*. The Saturday before I began work, I drove over to South Bend, Indiana, to watch Georgia Tech play Notre Dame. Notre Dame won. I had mixed emotions about the outcome of that game.

It was very difficult for me in Chicago because I didn't care who won the Minnesota-Iowa game, or the annual battle between Northwestern and Illinois. I wouldn't walk across the street to see Michigan play Ohio State, either—two mules fighting over a turnip.

Three weeks after I had moved to Chicago, it was Thanksgiving and Georgia, with another good team, was to play Georgia Tech Thanksgiving night on national television. The second Mrs. Grizzard had gone home to South Carolina to see her parents. I was alone.

Fine, I thought. I will purchase several cold beers, and sit back and watch Georgia play Georgia Tech. The game was to be held on Grant Field in Atlanta.

There was a problem. My neighbor across the hall in the high-rise, Near North apartment building in which I lived, had decided to be my friend. That was fine, except he was from Colombia, and I could barely understand a word he was saying. He thought I was from Zanzibar or someplace with my accent.

He invited me over for Thanksgiving dinner.

"No thanks," I said, "I want to watch Georgia and Georgia Tech on television."

"Who eeze thees Goorgea and Goorgea Tick?" he asked.

I tried to explain. His cat understood more than he did.

"You eeet, jes?" he asked again.

"No," I persisted. "I watch the game."

I cracked a beer and Georgia was scoring like mad. I think the score was 42-0 at the half. I felt wonderful. Maybe I should go have some dinner with my new Colombian friend, I said to myself.

The meal was marvelous. We switched the game on in his apartment. Tech was making a comeback.

I was feeling a bit queezy. Tech cut the final gap to 42-26. I asked if I could lie down.

"Si," said my Colombian friend. "You feel bad, jes?"

"Jes," I said.

"Probably the pot," he said.

"The what?" I asked back.

"The pot. I put eet in the dressing. You like?"

I am 800 miles away from the closest person who loves me, watching Georgia play Georgia Tech with a Colombian who has put marijuana in my Thanksgiving dressing.

I began to make immediate plans to return to Georgia.

I kept up with Georgia football while I was away, thanks to Dorsey Hill, the world's biggest Bulldog fan. Each week I would place a call to his house during the Georgia game. He would make arrangements for someone to be there who would place the receiver next to the radio.

I would sit in Chicago and listen to the Georgia games. I would do this in the privacy of my office at the *Sun-Times*. I would charge the phone call to the company. I kept watching for somebody to come and get me for doing that, but nobody ever did.

I was in Knoxville the night the 1980 season began. I was sitting next to Dorsey Hill, as a matter of fact. Dorsey never gives up. When Tennessee led, 15-0, I said, "Damn, this is a long way to come to see Georgia get beat like this."

"They're going to come back," Dorsey said, I wrote it off as the heat and the many beers working on Dorsey's head. Georgia came back to win 16-15. I would doubt him only one more time.

It was hot in Jacksonville, seven wins later, too. And Georgia had squandered so many chances to put Florida to sleep, I could feel it slipping away.

Florida scored to lead 21-20 with just minutes to play. Georgia's dream of an unbeaten season, a possible national title, were vanishing before my eyes.

"Let's get out of here," I said to the third Mrs. Grizzard.

Dorsey wouldn't budge. "I've come this far with 'em, I ain't leaving," he said.

We were in the parking lot when the third Mrs. Grizzard looked at the people on the top row of the Gator Bowl stadium and said, "Look, the Georgia fans are jumping up and down."

"Probably just a first down," I said.

"But they're still jumping up and down," my wife continued.

I noticed the Gator Bowl was shaking. I finally learned Georgia had scored on a 93-yard play to win, 26-21.

A number of people were very put out with me for leaving the stadium and giving up on Georgia that day.

"You are a disgrace," said Dorsey Hill.

Maybe I can explain. I am a terribly unlucky person. In several million hands of poker, I have never filled an inside straight nor drawn the third king.

With Georgia behind 20-21 to Florida, I reasoned the only chance Georgia had was for me to leave the stadium. With my luck, if I left the stadium, something incredible, something unforgettable, something I could tell my grandchildren about had I remained to watch, would probably happen. I left the stadium, and something did.

Georgia has me to thank for its comeback against Florida.

After Florida, Auburn fell, and then Georgia Tech, and then we all went down to New Orleans to the Sugar Bowl to play Notre Dame.

I don't know what is is about Notre Dame, but I don't like Notre Dame. I pulled hard for Jimmy Carter to win in 1976, because I was living in Chicago, and here was a man who talked like I did running for president. I pulled hard for him again in 1980 because he invited me to the back yard of the White House to drink beer and listen to Willie Nelson sing. But I pulled harder for Georgia to win against Notre Dame in the 1981 Sugar Bowl.

It meant everything to Georgia. The Bulldogs' first national championship was at stake. It meant nothing to Notre Dame save playing the role of the spoiler.

Nobody really enjoyed the 1981 Sugar Bowl game. Georgia people didn't enjoy it because it turned out to be so close, and Georgia had everything to lose. Notre Dame couldn't have enjoyed it because the Irish kept fumbling the ball all over the Superdome carpet and throwing interceptions.

I was frustrated through the entire affair. With six minutes to go in the game, when it was apparent Georgia would never get another first down if we stayed in New Orleans until Easter, I began to use abusive language.

"I can't stand you any longer," said my wife, who promptly left and went back to the hotel.

When it was finally over, tears welled in my eyes. Let me see if I can express what it meant to me and so many others.

Alabama has won national championships. So have Auburn and Tennessee and LSU. And Ohio State or Southern Cal or Texas or Notre Dame is always winning one. But never Georgia.

Georgia. It's where I was born and where my mother and father were born. We've had it rough from the start in Georgia. First we get settled by a bunch of prisoners from England. Then Sherman marches through and burns everything he can see. People call us "redneck." We finally get somebody from Georgia elected president, and nobody likes him.

But on January 1, 1981, the football team representing the University of Georgia, where I went to school, whipped Notre Dame, which gets movies made about its football teams, and won the national championship.

Grown men cried.

A friend of mine was sitting next to his fiancee in the Superdome that day. They were to be married later in the year. The wedding is off now. My friend explained:

"When I finally knew it was over, when I finally realized they couldn't beat us, when after all these years of pulling for Georgia and living with them and dying with them, I realized we had done won the by-god national title, I started crying like a baby. I couldn't stop. I looked over and there was my best friend who was at the game with me. We went to Georgia together in the sixties. We've been all over to see them play. He was crying, too. It was the most emotional moment of my life. I reached over and hugged him and kissed him square in the mouth.

"My fiancee wouldn't speak to me the rest of the day. She was mad because I hadn't kissed her first. We broke up soon after that. I just never could figure out why she thought I would have kissed her first. Hell, she went to Clemson."

Herschel Walker of Clyde's Gulf

This piece was written when Herschel Walker was driving everybody crazy by taking his sweet time about deciding which school would get his enormous talents. He did eventually sign with Georgia, of course, and he led the Bulldogs to their perfect 12-0 season, and the national championship.

Herschel Walker is a wonderful young man, incredibly talented athletically, an excellent student, a polite individual who would turn down $2 million from the Canadian Football League after the 1980 season because he didn't think it was the American sort of thing to do.

Perhaps Herschel Walker isn't from Wrightsville, Georgia, at all. Maybe he's from another planet.

WRIGHTSVILLE—Football star Herschel Walker, one of the nation's most sought-after high school athletes, has ended months of speculation by announcing he is no longer planning to attend college but will remain in his hometown to work for Clyde's Friendly Gulf service station instead.

"I simply couldn't make up my mind where to go," said Walker, "so I decided the heck with all of them."

Walker had received hundreds of offers of athletic scholarships but had reportedly narrowed his choices to three schools before making his shocking announcement.

Those three schools were the University of Georgia, Georgia Tech, and Clemson, none of which were able to win him over completely.

"You ever spent any time at Clemson?" Walker asked reporters at his hastily called press conference around the self-service pumps at Clyde's. "The only excitement there is when one of the fraternities holds a tractor wash or the red light in town goes on the blink."

What about the University of Georgia? Walker was asked.

"Four years of hearing. 'How 'bout them Dawgs!' and they would have had to mail my diploma to the funny farm," he said.

And Georgia Tech?

"Good school," Walker responded, "but I checked out who they have playing in the offensive line. Unfortunately, you can't block anybody with a slide rule. I'm afraid I'd get killed."

Walker had earlier indicated some interest in both UCLA and Southern California, but he explained they were out of the running, too.

"All they had to offer was a place to get a good suntan," Walker explained. "Now, I ask you. . . ."

The youngster's surprise announcement was met with disbelief and amazement from coaches and supporters of the three schools Walker had reportedly been considering for his final choice.

Georgia's Vince Dooley said previous plans to rename Sanford Stadium "Walker Field" would have to be scrapped, but the Bulldog head coach said the jersey Walker would have worn at Georgia will be retired anyway.

"We spent a lot of time and effort and most of our recruiting budget on Herschel," said Dooley. "We've got to have something to show for it."

Georgia Tech's Bill Curry fainted upon hearing the news, and three hairs on his head fell out of place for the first time since he was eleven.

"Why didn't he say he was interested in mechanics?" Curry asked, upon being revived. "Some of our top graduates own their own transmission shops or Brake-O franchises. We could have set him up for life."

Clemson's Danny Ford was also stunned.

"Work in a service station? I thought the kid wanted to be with the FBI. We were flying in Efrem Zimbalist, Jr., for his first game. If he had asked, we would have even let him change the tires on the school president's pickup."

Walker bristled at questions that asked what, if any, illegal recruiting tactics had been used to attract him.

"I didn't ask for, nor did I receive, any under-the-table offers," Walker said. "One school did offer me my own private dorm and a summer job as a bank president, but that is quite legitimate.

"I simply looked at what was available to me, and the decision to stay home and work for Clyde seemed the best. Besides, he's giving me Wednesday afternoons off and an employee discount on tires and tune-ups."

"He starts to work Monday morning," said a beaming Clyde. "I don't expect him to learn everything overnight, but the kid's gonna be a great one."

Big Night in ObKnoxville

Dorsey Hill, the world's biggest Bulldog fan, still hasn't gone back to work.

"I declared Monday 'Herschel Walker Day' in the state of Georgia," said Dorsey, "and, of course, nobody with red and black in his heart would work on 'Herschel Walker Day.'

"Tuesday, I was too hung over from 'Herschel Walker Day' to work. I'm going back Wednesday to open my mail, and then I have to take Thursday and Friday off to get ready for Texas A&M."

I've mentioned Dorsey in this space many times before. He graduated from the University of Georgia in 1966. He drove a 1957 Chevrolet convertible and was one of the first inductees into Bubber's Hall of Fame.

For those who received their higher educations elsewhere, Bubber's is a package store in downtown Athens which is steeped in tradition.

Dorsey would walk into Bubber's on a Thursday night, buy eight bottles of Red Hurricane wine (ninety-seven cents a bottle) and disappear for days.

Enough background. Dorsey's excitement this week is appropriate, of course, after Georgia opened its 1980 season with a 16-15 victory over Tennessee Saturday night in Knoxville.

"It ain't 'Knoxville,'" Dorsey always reminds me. "It's 'ObKnoxville.'"

Dorsey has no love for those of the Volunteer persuasion.

I attended the game myself and can now boast of having been a part of the largest crowd ever to gather for a sporting event this side of Ann Arbor, Michigan.

At last count there were 95,228 of us, bunched together in the sweltering heat. Several hundred were reportedly still sober when the game kicked off.

Quite frankly, I got sick and tired of the Herschel Walker recruiting story. I heard to much about where Herschel Walker, an eighteen-year-old, would attend college I secretly hoped he would stay home in Wrightsville and work for Clyde's Gulf.

But I must admit that after watching his performance in ObKnoxville Saturday night, he is apparently worth all the trouble, and whatever else, that it took for Georgia to ink him to a pact, one of my favorite sports cliches.

Have you ever watched a kids' game of football where one kid was so much better than all the other kids you felt sort of sorry for all the other kids?

Herschel Walker looked like that Saturday night. Clearly, he was the best athlete on the field, and my favorite part of the game was where he ran over the safety from Tennessee and the poor youngster didn't move for several moments.

"He won't be able to run over people in the Southeastern Conference like he did in high school," the smart money was saying only a few weeks back. Give him the ball and he could run over the Russian infantry.

Anyway, it was a marvelous experience, and since I was able to get a seat on a chartered bus, I didn't have to endure any of the traffic problems which are the rule around Neyland Stadium and the infamous local highway system affectionately known as "Malfunction Junction."

I also picked up one other Dorsey Hill gem I must share:

When Dorsey Hill goes to a football game, he makes a full-scale tour of it. Dorsey left Atlanta four days before kickoff and drove around the entire state of Tennessee to, as he put it, "get a feel for the game."

"Did you learn anything from your tour?" I asked Dorsey.

"Sure did," he replied. "I learned the three most overrated things in this world are extramarital sex, home cooking, and Rock City."

God Is a Bulldog

JACKSONVILLE, FLA.—Dorsey Hill, the world's biggest Bulldog fan, left here Sunday afternoon, bound for Auburn, Alabama, where Georgia's undefeated football team next appears.

"I don't think you can get from Jacksonville to Auburn," I had said to him.

"You change buses in Waycross and Columbus," Dorsey answered.

"You aren't going home first?"

"Home?" He screamed back. "I haven't worked since Texas A&M, and I haven't slept since Clemson. You expect me to go back home when we play Auburn in only six more days?"

I lost my head, I suppose.

A lot of people lost their heads here Saturday afternoon. Georgia played Florida. Georgia won the game, 26-21. It's a lot more complicated than that, however.

Georgia came into the game ranked second in the nation. To continue to compete for its first Big Banana ever, the national championship, Georgia had to continue its winning streak.

Florida ("bunch of swamp lizards and beach bums," according to Dorsey Hill) wanted to step on the Georgia dream.

Dorsey arrived here Thursday afternoon with thousands of others who made the early departure south from various points in Georgia. Many of those individuals were drunk as five-eyed owls by the time they reached the Florida line.

As local wit Rex Edmondson says, the Georgia-Florida game is the "annual celebration of the repeal of prohibition."

Dorsey waited until Friday to get into his serious pre-game drinking, however.

"I stopped at the New Perry Hotel Thursday for lunch and filled up on collards," he said. "It's hard to drink on a belly full of collards."

Agreed.

Now that I have had time to digest all that did eventually happen in college football Saturday, I think I can say without fear of charges of blasphemy that the whole thing was a religious experience.

"Deacon Dan" Magill, the "Baptist Bulldog," read a prayer Saturday morning to the Georgia faithful in which he beseeched the Almighty to help the Bulldogs "smite the Florida Philistines."

Then, there was the game itself. Georgia behind 21-20, ninety-three yards away, time running out.

"We need a miracle!" screamed Dorsey Hill, now fortified with more than collards.

Georgia got its miracle. Buck Belue to Lindsay Scott, for ninety-three yards and the winning touchdown with only seconds remaining.

If that wasn't enough, there was the astounding news from Atlanta. Georgia Tech had tied No. 1 Notre Dame. Surely, Georgia will be ranked first in America when the ratings are released.

"A tie was a gift from heaven," said Dorsey. "Notre Dame gets knocked out of number one, but Tech doesn't get a win. God is a Bulldog."

Verily.

I must make one confession here. I did it, and I must suffer the consequences.

I gave up at Jacksonville Saturday afternoon. Florida had the ball. Florida had the lead. There was only three minutes to play. I left the stadium. I was in the street when the miracle came.

"You are a gutless disgrace," Dorsey Hill said to me later.

He detailed my punishment:

"We're going to a tattoo parlor in this very town tonight," he began. "And you're going to have '26' tattooed on one of your cheeks in red. And you're going to have '21' tattooed in black on the other cheek. I don't want you to forget what you did."

I won't, but which cheeks is between me and the tattooist.

Charlie Harris

We're talking about thirty years ago. Sanford Stadium on the University of Georgia campus didn't have those double decks and seated maybe half of what it does today.

The players wore those funny-looking helmets, with no face guards, and they wore those awful high-top shoes Johnny Unitas would never give up.

Herschel Walker hadn't been born. Vince Dooley, the Georgia coach, was just a kid player himself.

Korea was happening.

That wonderful year, 1950. That was the year Charlie Harris arrived in Athens to play football for Georgia. Wally Butts was the head coach. Hard times—compared to the '40s and to the present Georgia season—had set in.

But halfback Charlie Harris would help Butts and the Bulldogs pull themselves together again, so the theory went.

He was fast. He was quick. He was, in the day before the term was used, a "franchise," a 1950s version of Herschel Walker, if you will.

He came in from a place called Goodwater, Alabama. Before he would leave, Dan Magill would nickname him, for his fleet moves, "The Gliding Ghost of Goodwater."

Charlie Harris had an excellent career at Georgia. He never reached the heights of a Trippi, a Sinkwich, a Tarkenton, nor, of course, a Walker, but he had his moments. He even captained the track team.

His four Georgia seasons were to be spread out in seven, however. After the '50 season he went into the Marine Corps and put in three years on the Camp Pendleton team.

"We had a lot of people trying awful hard to make that team," he remembered.

Get cut, get sent to Korea. That's pressure.

Charlie Harris came back to Athens after the Marines, played on the 1954-55-56 teams, had a cup of coffee with the Cleveland Browns, and later gave it a brief shot with the New York Titans, forefathers of the Jets, in the first season of the American Football League.

After that, Charlie Harris became a high school football coach, and that is where I met him. He turned up at Newnan High School at the same time I was John Q. Student. He taught my health class, where you learn not to brush your teeth the way everybody brushes their teeth.

But enough of history. I thought about Charlie Harris all day Saturday. Herschel Walker of Georgia was breaking all-time NCAA freshman rushing records. Mike Kelley of Georgia Tech was drilling passes.

Thousands were cheering. And Charlie Harris lay in his bed fighting a dog called leukemia.

It happened last April. Look at Charlie Harris. He's what they call a physical specimen. Still a long-distance runner at forty-nine.

"I was a runner before it became popular to run," he says. "Twenty miles was nothing for me."

The original marathon man. Never drank. Never smoked. Shamrock High principal. Husband. Father. Church man.

"I hadn't been to a doctor in twenty-three years," Charlie Harris said.

But in April, his endurance went. The ten-mile runs became six-mile runs, and then four-mile runs, and then, "I really didn't know what to do. I played under Wally Butts, and I guess I learned it there. You run everything out. Suddenly, I couldn't run it out anymore."

Leukemia was diagnosed. It got worse, then better. Lately, it has gotten worse again.

Charlie Harris and I talked the other day. I owed him at least a telephone call. Besides trying to save my teeth, he did me another favor seventeen years ago.

We talked about the chemotherapy, and the possibility of a bone marrow transplant, and I said the usual stupid things, like "Get well soon" and "If there's anything I can do . . ."

And Charlie Harris said, "What you learn from all this is nobody is indestructible."

Nobody, the man said. Not even the Gliding Ghost of Goodwater.

The lesson is there for the taking.

Charlie Harris died in the spring of 1981.

Mrs. Walker

WRIGHTSVILLE—The way you get to Herschel Walker's house from "downtown" Wrightsville, county seat of Johnson, is you take a right

on Idylwild Street and then you drive halfway back to Dublin looking for a white house on a hill across the railroad tracks.

You miss the house three or four times. When you finally sight it,
you cross the tracks and drive up a dirt road to the small frame
house where Herschel lived until he departed for Athens and the
University of Georgia and fame and what will likely amount to a
fortune before he quits carrying footballs.

Outside the house, dogs appear from nowhere. Two little dogs,
and one big dog who is a dead ringer for the dog that hung around
Spanky and his gang.

"That's Herschel's dog," says one of Herschel's brothers, who has
emerged from within the house. "That car (a red '55 Chevy) is
Herschel's car, too." That car turns out to be Herschel's "second" car.
His main wheels roll under a Pontiac Trans-Am.

Inside the house is the Herschel Walker Trophy Room. Plaques
cover the walls, trophies stand on every available surface. In the
middle of it all, strangely, hangs a frame that surrounds the faces of
Robert and John Kennedy and Dr. Martin Luther King, Jr.

The house is ten degrees past being warm. It is neat and warm. It
is filled this evening with children and grandchildren, and I notice
that Herschel Walker's family's television is black and white.

In a few years, when Herschel turns professional, he can buy his
family color televisions. Wall-to-wall.

I am here to see Herschel Walker's mother because nobody knows
Herschel Walker any better than she does. It has occurred to me
there could be somebody from another planet reading this who
doesn't know who Herschel Walker is.

Briefly, he's the best college football player alive. He plays for the
University of Georgia. He's just a freshman, and you can watch him
Thursday when he and his team meet Notre Dame in the Sugar Bowl.

Christine Walker, the good wife of Willis Walker, works all day in
a local clothing factory. She is a small, pretty woman with a soft,
reassuring voice. God gives mothers voices like that for a reason.

We talked in her living room. She sat on one end of the couch, me
on the other.

I asked her how much Herschel weighed when he was born. He is
the fifth of seven children.

"Eight pounds and three ounces," she answered. I noticed her face
break into a momentary beam. Mothers do that when they remember
when their children were babies.

I wanted to know what he ate when he was growing up.

"Peas," said Christine Walker.

"Peas?"

"That boy loved peas," she went on.

I asked what kind of peas.

"Red-hull peas," she said. "That's all he wanted to eat until he got a little older. Then he started eating hamburgers. I worry about him getting a balanced diet because all he wants is hamburgers."

Herschel Walker doesn't eat a balanced diet.

And he weighs 230 pounds and he runs like the wind. Put that in your blender and drink it.

I asked Herschel's mother if she ever spanked him.

"When he didn't mind," she answered.

I asked her what advice she gave Herschel when he left for college.

"I told him to make sure he leaves some time for his academics. I always stressed academics to him, and he paid attention to that. He always wanted to learn."

I asked her if she were proud of her son.

"Lord, yes," she answered, and there was that beam on her face again.

One other thing I asked her. I asked her if there was ever a time she was against her baby boy playing football.

"I tried to talk him out of it in the eighth grade," she said.

"Why?" I asked.

"I was afraid he might hurt somebody."

Magill

In the university town of Athens, Georgia, there was a pub called Harry's. Not really a pub. Outside of Atlanta, pubs are beer joints. And they served the beer cold and in cans at Harry's, with pickled eggs and a meaty tasty called a "Slim-Jim."

Later on autumn evenings in a simpler time that was the early sixties, the Slim-Jims were a nickel and there would be an inevitable gathering inside and around one of Harry's wooden booths. The crowd—five, six, sometimes seven or eight—would include an assortment of individuals who had as bonds a daily thirst for the canned brew, at least a fringe involvement with University of Georgia sports, and, perhaps most of all, a love for the spun yarn. Some of the stories told there over the years were true.

The floor was open for the first couple of rounds. The silver-haired English professor would recite his dirty limericks again: "There was a coed from Fitzgerald . . ." began everybody's favorite. A sportswriter from Atlanta had a rumor: Dodd at rival Georgia Tech would soon retire. An ex-Georgia football player who never left town or graduated would insist again that the coaches of the time cussed less on the practice field than they had in his day. "Three years after I played out my eligibility," he would begin again, "I still thought my name was 'Pissant.'"

Soon, however, the chirping of the sparrows would cease. And, as it always seemed the good Lord had intended, the man of every evening hour at Harry's, one Daniel Hamilton Magill, would assume verbal command to speak at great length and with never-ending embellishment of tales that rivaled those of the deaths of kings.

I was a nineteenish sports editor of the local morning journal at the time, no more than tolerated by Harry's regulars. Nearly two decades later there has still been no manner of man to compare with, the Lord-bless-him, Magill.

Magill is a genuine, living legend, although that may not be apparent at first glance. He is balding. He laughs at his own jokes, and he turns red in the face. He is married to a Phi Beta Kappa and could have been one himself. He did as well in school as he did, he says, because he sat next to "A-plus Mason" and "Straight-A Milligan." He has three children. Two are girls, both former beauty queens. His son was a top tennis player at Princeton and is now a heart specialist.

Magill, and it is always simply "Magill," may be further introduced in a number of ways. He was Georgia's director of sports information for thirty years before being named assistant athletic director, as well as director of athletic department public relations. Magill is fifty-eight. He is the University of Georgia tennis coach, and has been since 1955. Magill is also a long-play album on Georgia sporting history, and he has worked seven days a week, week in and week out, at it. All of this may be more commendable than epic, but I have entertained a two-decade-old notion that this man's life was destined for cinematic exposure.

But consider if one were casting a movie of his life and times. One would need, say, a Charlton Heston for Magill's own tennis prowess that continues full-throttle on a senior level. One would need an Ozzie Nelson for Magill's campus stereotype, and a taller George Gobel, in his comedic prime, for the Magill wit. And then go out and find somebody like Will Rogers for tale-bearing qualities.

And remember, too, that here you are dealing with one of the greatest Deep south accents since man drawled the first "y'all." Tex Ritter had a fair-to-middling Southern accent. Charles Laughton, of all people, as Senator Seab Cooley of South Carolina in *Advise and Consent*, was Hollywood's best attempt. But in Magill, you have South-in-the-mouth that is matchless.

Such are the problems that arise when the task is to capture Magill in the limits of the printed word. The beauty of one of his stories, one of his lines, can be mocked by a chosen few. But arriving at a suitable re-creation armed only with a typewriter makes coming close all that is achievable.

Suffice it to say, Magill's "great" is not "grate," but "greyette." His "coach" is more "co-atch."

It is only with the preceding rambling characterization and the subsequent apologetic ground-ruling that Magill may be tackled further. What follows knows no order, either. To pull order to Magill would be nearly disrespectful. Offered next is simply Magillobilia that goes in a thousand different directions, trying to keep up:

Magill grew up in Athens and has been a nonresident only twice: once as a Marine officer in World War II and another time as editor of high school sports at the *Atlanta Journal* in the late forties. His father was editor of the *Athens Banner-Herald*, and, at fourteen, the son became sports editor. He was paid two movie passes a week.

It was during these formative years that Magill took his first step toward a lifetime as a matchless promoter. He had taken a dual interest in snakes and tennis and he saw no reason why the two could not be combined for fun and profit.

Magill had served his snake apprenticeship under Ross Allen, who went on to become snake-handler supreme in Florida. Allen had worked at the Athens YMCA camp and young Magill was one of his students.

Soon afterwards, it fell upon Magill to become caretaker of the University of Georgia tennis courts, honest-to-goodness red clay that they were in those days. Magill chose the courts as the logical site for his first great promotion, a Depression-days snake fight between his own Casper Kingsnake and Rastus Rattler, who had been captured in the north Georgia hills and transported to Athens via bicycle by one of Magill's friends.

A capacity crowd was on hand at a dime a head. "The crowd," Magill can still remember and recount with his special flair, "became so large and noisy it frightened the combatants. Neither Casper nor Rastus would move from their appointed corners. It was touch-and-go for several moments."

The promoter saved the farm, however. Magill's stick-prodding of Rastus brought a strike from the prodee, and Magill's leap in retreat satisfied the customers.

"I don't really know what happened," he was to say years later. "But we finally put my Casper and Rastus in the same cage together

after it became apparent they were not inclined to fight. I returned to
check on them several days later, and only Casper remained in the
cage. There was a rather satisfied look upon his face, and he seemed
to have gained a few pounds.

Magill later promoted successful high school all-star games in
Atlanta while working for the *Atlanta Journal*. He put together a
Jack Kramer–Bobby Riggs tennis match in Atlanta in the forties and
drew more than 3,000, the largest tennis crowd ever in the South at
the time. His Georgia tennis matches have often drawn larger au-
diences than Georgia basketball games in the massive, 10,000-seat
Coliseum. Incidentally, attendance figures at Georgia athletic contests are official: Magill, with a quick glance to the stands, estimates
them.

As sports information director, Magill had the responsibility of
handing out press box tickets, compiling miles of statistics, and
publicizing Georgia athletics. What wasn't a duty, but is now a
tradition, is Magill's conjuring of alliterative nicknames for Georgia
Bulldogs athletes. There have been some classics:

Bobby Walden, who went on to punt for the Pittsburgh Steelers,
was Magill's "Big Toe from Cairo." (Keep in mind that the south
Georgia city of Cairo is pronounced "Kay-ro.")

Kicker Spike Jones was "Sputnik Spike."

Savannah running back Julian Smiley was the "Chatham Chee-
tah."

Halfback Charlie Harris was known as the "Gliding Ghost of
Goodwater, Alabama."

Fullback Ronnie Jenkins, a south Georgian, had a couple of Magill
nicknames. Magill called him "The Wild Bull of the Flatlands" for his
running ability.

"He was a great blocker, too, on the Georgia championship team of
1966," Magill remembered. "He used to literally knock people out
with his blocks. I called him the 'Ebullient Embalmer' because he
always smiled at his opponent before cracking him. He really enjoyed his work."

Quarterback Andy Johnson, now with the New England Patriots,
was Andy "The Unimpeachable" Johnson to Magill. Perhaps Magill's greatest accomplishment, however, was the nickname for
German-born placekicker Peter Rajecki, known as the "Bootin' Teu-
ton."

The 1980 season brought Georgia its brilliant freshman running
back, Herschel Walker, and Magill reportedly went into seclusion in

his back yard vineyard for hours before coming out with "the best I can do right now," that being "Herschel the Unmerciful."

Magill gives credit to one of his understudies in Bulldoggerel, Dewey Benefield of Sea Island, for what he considers an even better nickname for Walker. It was a Benefield poem that followed Walker's debut against Tennessee that referred to the Wrightsville Wonder (my feeble attempt) as "That Goal-Line Stalker, Herschel Walker."

(It's even bettah when you heah Magill pronounce it. "That Goal-Line *Stawlkah*, Herschel *Wawlkah*.")

It was in tennis that Magill's rhyming nirvana may have been reached. It was during the NCAA finals in Athens that the Flouri brothers of Missouri showed up as a doubles act. Long after they had been ousted from the tournament, Magill still delighted in calling them from the press box's public address system: "Will 'Flooorey' and 'Flooorey' from 'Mizoooorey' please report. . . ."

Magill has frequently even been called on by the university to perform duties of great importance. It was Magill who took upon himself the burden of finding a new tennis coach for the university in 1955.

Several turned me down," he recalls. "So finally, I decided I would take the job myself." Later, so the story goes, it was suggested to Magill that Georgia had been lucky he had appointed himself to the tennis position. "Indeed," was his reply.

Indeed, indeed. Magill has built a tennis dynasty at Georgia. His teams have won the Southeastern Conference tennis championship nine of the last eleven years. His 1981 team finished third nationally. Magill was honored in 1980 at the U.S. Open Championships in New York for having recorded his 500th victory as a collegiate tennis coach.

Magill was himself a tennis player and varsity swimmer at Georgia. He has a string of state and Southern singles and doubles tennis titles and still plays every day. It is table tennis at which he may be most adept, however.

He won the state singles championships ten of the twelve times he competed from 1933 to 1958. He also played what legend records as the longest single point in the history of the game, a point he eventually lost. Magill and his opponent were hooked up in a match at the Athens YMCA. In walked an innocent bystander who inquired as to the score: "Three-two, Magill," was the reply. That information in hand, off went the bystander uptown to a movie. He returned to the YMCA some hours later, following a double feature, and was sur-

prised to see the match still in progress. Again he inquired as to the
score. Again came the reply. "Three-two, Magill."

There are those who insist that there should be a special Magill
Practical Joke Hall of Fame. Two of the incidents that belong there
are as follows:

Once Magill was returning with his tennis team from a match in
Tallahassee, Florida. The team, traveling in two cars, stopped for
gas in Thomasville.

"How do we pay for this, Coach Magill?" asked the player who
was driving the car that pulled to the pump first.

"Just tell the man I'll take care of it, and you go on ahead after you
have filled up," Magill, in the rear car, answered.

The player did what Magill told him and drove off. After filling
Magill's car, the attendant asked Magill to pay for the gasoline he
had pumped into the first car.

"Pay for what?" Magill asked. "I've never seen those people in that
car before in my life."

Legend has it that it was in Dublin where the authorities finally
caught up with the victims of Magill's joke. (They were released in
time to win the next match.)

Magill once had a secretary who was the perfect subject for one of
his famous telephone tricks. The secretary had arranged a party—
complete with champagne—for a Georgia basketball coach who had
just completed the school's first winning season since the Roosevelt
administration—Teddy's. In the Georgia governor's house at the
time was Lester Maddox, a teetotaller who wanted everybody else to
be.

Magill answered a rigged call, ostensibly from Atlanta and the
state capitol.

"Well, Governor, I don't think the girls have meant any harm with
having a little champagne at the party even though this is a state-
supported institution," he began. The secretary was aghast. The
argument got hotter. Magill ended it with, "Well, to hell with you,
too, you little ballheaded bigot!" The secretary, swear those who
were there, fainted.

Magill has other accomplishments touching lightly on the near-
athletic.

He has, for a long time, claimed the title of world's fastest two-
finger typist. He was once challenged by a journalism professor,
who typed full fingered. Could Magill's two outdo the professor's
ten? Final score: Magill, fourteen lines; journalism professor, twelve.

Magill also claimed the world's two-fingers-only chinup title as well. He would perform on any available half-in door facing. Tragically, he was challenged one day at lunch after a tuna sandwich.

"My hands were greasy, and I slipped off," Magill contends. A broken collarbone was the result.

Magill refers to himself as a "chain soft drink-drinker." He has his own soft-drink machine, which was presented to him by the Athens Coca-Cola Company and is decked with a plaque that bears his name. His addiction to soft drinks is such that there are those who say that in the days he scored Georgia baseball games, he connected a garden hose from the press box to the men's room directly below for nature's calls at mid-inning.

There is no Georgia fan as dedicated to the cause as Magill. There is no Georgia fan who is any more foursquare against the "enemy," rival Georgia Tech, than Magill.

He contends that Georgia Tech's Grant Field has a slightly higher seating capacity than Georgia's Sanford Stadium because the Grant Field seats are smaller. One must thus be a "squint-ass" to enjoy a Yellow Jacket game. Georgia victories and Tech losses on same Saturdays are praised as "doubleheaded sweeps."

Perhaps no voice in history has ever spoken with more bias or with more pure love than when Dan Magill speaks of his University of Georgia. Breathes there a Bulldog with soul so dead that he doesn't respond emotionally to the standard beginning line of every Magill speech:

"My fellow Georgia Bulldogs, chosen people of the Western world."

Doug Barfield

Auburn University, Vince Dooley's alma mater, attempted to hire him away from Georgia after the 1980 regular season. In all the shouting and anxious moments concerning Dooley's decision—which was eventually to remain at Georgia—the forgotten man was the man Auburn fired in order to make room for Dooley, Doug Barfield. Major college football is a cruel, unforgiving sport that can cast you aside on the whims of fools.

Before the Vince Dooley-Auburn thing is put to rest completely, I wanted to bring up one more name.

Doug Barfield.

I've never met Doug Barfield. Frankly, I wouldn't know him if he walked into my office and asked me to dance. But I have this thing about underdogs, and Doug Barfield qualifies as one. In spades.

He was Auburn's football coach until Monday. He spent a total of nine years at Auburn University, five as an assistant coach and the last four as the head coach.

He never had a chance. Seldom, if you follow a legend, do you have a chance, especially in the fickle arena of sports.

Doug Barfield followed the beloved Shug Jordan as Auburn's football coach and it was just a matter of time before the alumni ax fell upon him.

The same thing happened to Bud Carson, who followed Bobby Dodd at Georgia Tech, and to countless others. The man who follows Vince Dooley at the University of Georgia will probably just be marking time until he is canned.

I don't know if Doug Barfield was a good football coach or not, but the only measure these days seems to be: Did you win all your games? A negative answer to that question can have you in the insurance business overnight.

Pepper Rodgers, who got fired as Georgia Tech's head football coach because the alumni didn't like his hair, said to me once: "Coaching is the craziest business in the world. If you're a brain surgeon and your patient dies, you can walk out to the family, look sincere, and say, 'I'm sorry, but I did all I could do.' And you still get paid.

"In coaching, some nineteen-year-old drops the football and you lose the game, and they'll run you out of town."

They were talking big bucks in the will-Dooley-go-to-Auburn crisis. I read $1.8 million. Imagine that. And here was Dooley struggling with the decision:

Do I stay in my beautiful home in Athens and make all this money here, or do I move into a beautiful home in Auburn and make all that money there?

The human side of this story is, what in the devil was Doug Barfield doing all that time?

Auburn has been his home for nine years. He has two children enrolled at Auburn.

"He was torn asunder by all this," an Auburn man told me Thursday.

I remember back several weeks ago when the rumors started flying that Barfield would be fired. A man named Charles Smith, a member of the Auburn Board of Trustees, made all sorts of noise about finding a coach who would be tougher on the players than Barfield.

Charles Smith runs a laundry in Montgomery. Can you imagine having some guy who runs a laundry deciding how well you were performing in your chosen profession?

More on Doug Barfield from my friend in Auburn:

"He's warm. He has more class than he's ever been given credit for. He's kind. And under all this pressure and criticism, he was a man of steel."

While Auburn officials offered Dooley the farm this week, Doug Barfield quietly resigned. He said, "I don't want to be anyplace I'm not wanted." He also said, "But I don't feel like I have to hide my face."

I wouldn't be a football coach if you gave me the pick of the cheerleaders.

Monday, when all the hoopla about Dooley was at its height, Doug Barfield was in Montgomery. He had been summoned for federal court jury duty.

Each prospective juror was asked to stand before the court and give his name, place of residence, and occupation.

Doug Barfield stood and said:

"Doug Barfield.

"Auburn, Alabama.

"Unemployed."

War Eagle.

This One Is Forever

NEW ORLEANS—I am writing this from the sixteenth floor of the Howard Johnson Motor Hotel in downtown New Orleans. I can see the top of the Louisiana Superdome from this perch. It looks more like one of those ominous nuclear power plants than a sports stadium. The truth is, the place exploded, what is now four hours ago.

I am no stranger to madness. I have attended an Indianapolis 500 automobile race, the annual salute to mental illness. That was nothing compared to this.

This was wild. This was crazy. This was downright scary at times.

A cop on the floor of the Dome said, "Thank God they ain't armed."

A security man screamed to no one in particular, "I've got the damn president of the United States in here and I can't get him out!"

A female member of the Notre Dame band, holding onto her flute as she surveyed the incredible scene before her, said, "If it meant that much, I'm glad Georgia won."

It meant that much. Grown men cried. A man kissed Georgia defensive coach Erskine Russell squarely on the top of his bald head. Erk just smiled.

I saw a man get down on his fours and bark like a wild dog (dawg) and try to bite passersby. A woman I had never seen before lifted her skirt to show me her underpants. "Georgia" was stitched hip to hip.

Let me take you back to when the playing of the 1981 Sugar Bowl Football game between Georgia and Notre Dame first began to show signs of the subsequent emotional explosion that it became.

New Year's Eve on Bourbon Street. It's the Red Sea. If there are Notre Dame people in town, where are they?

The 1 Bourbon Street Inn, in the very heart of the French Quarter, is packed with Georgians. The third floor balcony is Bulldog Central. The bathtubs in the adjoining rooms are filled with ice and champagne.

The people in the street, thousands of them, scream, "HER-SCHEL!"

The people on the balcony respond, "WALKER!"

A chant aimed at what brave or stupid Notre Damers might be in earshot begins:

"YOU GOT THE HUNCHBACK! WE GOT THE TAILBACK!"

"The Pope's a dope" came out a couple of times, too—there's one in every madhouse.

At midnight there was much kissing and hugging and how-'bout-them-dawging and speaking of dogs (dawgs), the Georgia mascot, "Uga," showed up at the party on the third floor Bourbon Street Inn balcony, and I heard one man say to another:

"Hey, how'd your lip get cut?"

To which the second man replied. "I was kissing 'Uga' on the mouth at midnight and he bit me."

When the sun rose on 1981, there were those still partying from the night before. Three hours before kickoff, the city was covered in red. Red hats, red pants, red shirts—red, I was to discover later, underwear as well.

The Game. So close. God bless Mrs. Walker. Thirty seconds are left, Georgia leading, 17-10. Notre Dame can't stop the clock. At :14 showing, the game ends because every Bulldog from Rabun Gap to Tybee Light and Hartwell to Bainbridge has charged onto the floor of the Louisiana Superdome.

They trampled each other. They trampled the players, the coaches, the press, they ripped down a goal post.

The public-address announcer pleaded and pleaded and pleaded: "Please clear the field! PLEASE clear the field!" They turned off the lights, but the Georgia band kept playing, and the people, that delirious mass of people, kept on celebrating.

It got ugly a couple of times. Secret Service men trying to get Jimmy Carter out of the building shoved a few citizens around.

And then there was this group of little girls, the "High Steppers" from Shreveport or someplace, who had competed for the right to perform at the Sugar Bowl. They were cute little girls wearing cowboy hats. They were left out of the pregame show because the teams stayed on the field too long. They were promised they could perform after the game. They lined up, all neat and nice, but there was no way.

One little girl said. "I don't want to go out there. We might get hurt." They finally gave it up and went back to Shreveport. Sad.

But it was also bright and beautiful and boisterous and an All-American sort of thing that other schools have enjoyed, so now it is Georgia's turn to point the finger to the sky. It may be days before the last Bulldog leaves New Orleans. The streets would not be safe Thursday night.

Number One, by God. Number Ever-Lovin'-One. The sign in the Georgia locker room had said it all:

"This one is forever."

11

PEACH OF A STATE

I was born in Fort Benning, Georgia, in the wee, morning hours of October 20, 1946. As an adult, I have left Georgia to live in another place only once. For nearly two years, I was a prisoner of war in Chicago, Illinois, a cold place where it often gets dark at half past four in the afternoon.

Georgia is a diverse state, with spectacular mountains and a sun-splashed seacoast and piney woods and rolling fields and Atlanta, a city in a park. I love the state like I would a good woman. I revel in her beauty and charm, and I forgive her every fault.

I love the way her people act and think and talk. I love her Macons, her Savannahs, and especially her tiny Snellvilles. I love her good ol' girls who will still cook a man a homemade bisuit in the morning, and I love her good ol' boys who weren't bothering anybody, and then Billy Carter's brother went and got himself elected president.

There was that country song, "If I Ever Get Back to Georgia, I'm Gonna Nail My Feet to the Ground." I did. And I have. . . .

Shove It Up My What?

I received an angry note the other day from a Ms. Gloria Schmaltz, who used to live in Atlanta. Now she lives in Portland, Maine.

Believe it or not, I have been to Portland, Maine. It is a seacoast town, a little dingy as I recall, but lobster was cheap.

Ms. Schmaltz's note was brief, but there could be little question as to what had raised her ire.

Me.

It seems some of Ms. Schmaltz's former friends in Atlanta had sent her one of my old columns that concerned what I consider to be a major issue—homemade biscuits.

Ms. Schmaltz read the column and then wrote me the note.

"Reading it," began her message, "helped me remember why, at age thirty, I retired to the North. It is good old boys like you that bring out my hairy-legged worst."

Then, Ms. Schmaltz really got nasty.

451

"You can take your South," she wrote, "and shove your biscuits up your Confederarse."

Pretty talk, Ms. Schmaltz.

I really feel terrible about all this. Here a woman has moved all the way from Atlanta to the dingy little seacoast town of Portland, Maine, just to get away from the strain of Southern male we know as the "good ol' boy."

Shucks, Ms. Schmaltz, was it something we might have said? Was your mother frightened by a pickup truck while she was carrying you?

Perhaps you were offended by our music, Willie and Waylon and Merle and Conway. Sorry, we just like to pat our foot occasionally and hear a song or two about cheatin' and hurtin' and old dogs and children and watermelon wine.

I've got it. You think we drink too much. I guess we do, but a good ol' boy's longneck beer is sort of his security blanket, like if somebody insults the good name of Richard Petty, you are secure in the knowledge you are holding onto something you can break over his head.

We're loud, maybe? I guess we are, but we're colorful. Know how many good ol' boys it takes to screw in a lightbulb, Ms. Schmaltz?

Four. One to screw in the lightbulb, one to write a song about it, and two more to start a fistfight in the parking lot.

And then there's football. You probably don't care a thing about football, do you, Ms. Schmaltz? Good ol' boys do, of course, and that probably bothers you.

But give us that, Ms. Schmaltz. A fellow has to have something to hold his interest when he's not fishing or playing with his dog.

And that column I wrote about biscuits really bothered you, didn't it? You have to understand I wrote it as a public service.

Do you realize the divorce rate in this country? All I did was quote the great philosopher Jerry Clower, who is of the opinion that if more women would cook homemade biscuits for their husbands in the mornings—instead of serving those horrible impostors that come from cans—the divorce rate would go down.

I also wrote that women who wouldn't cook homemade bisuits occasionally probably wouldn't shave their legs, either.

That was just a little joke, Ms. Schmaltz, but I noticed in your note you mentioned something about being "hairy-legged" yourself. That certainly doesn't make you a bad person, but in the words of my boyhood friend and idol, Weyman C. Wannamaker, Jr., a great American, "I wouldn't take a hairy-legged woman to a rat-killin'."

All I am saying, Ms. Schmaltz, is don't judge us too harshly, and please try to understand that good ol' boys need love and understanding, too.

Incidentally, since your heart obviously wasn't in the South you left, I, for one, am glad you got YOUR Confederarse out.

Of Giggling Yankee Girls

I made a 300-mile automobile trip recently, and I noticed the summer's wanderlust has brought out the hitchhikers in great numbers.

I still offer an occasional lift to a hitchhiker, despite the fact that next to "Always wear clean underwear, you might be in a wreck," my mother's favorite piece of advice was, "Never pick up a hitchhiker."

But how can I resist? In my youth I rode my thumb to all sorts of wondrous places, like once all the way from my hometown in Moreland, Georgia, to Daytona Beach, Florida, and back.

I never spent more than two hours at any one stretch without a ride, and a carload of Yankee girls picked me up just outside Palatka and took me the rest of the way into Daytona.

To a Georgia country boy of sixteen, getting to ride in the same car with a group of Yankee girls is a rare and, as I was to discover later, valuable experience.

"Talk for us," they would plead, and I would say things like "yawl" and "dawg" and "grey-its," and they would giggle and talk about how cute I was.

Many years later, standing uncomfortably alone at a bar on the east side of New York City, I recalled that experience, and in a loud voice, began to say "yawl" and "dawg" and "grey-its." Soon I was surrounded by a gaggle of giggling Yankee girls talking about how cute I was.

It doesn't take much to impress Yankee girls, bless their hearts.

The surprising thing about the hitchhikers I saw on my trip was they all looked rather unkempt.

I even saw a young man hitchhiking with no shirt. He obviously was a rookie. There are certain rules every hitchhiker should know, and the first one is: Never try to catch a ride looking like you've just escaped from reform school.

When I was hitchhiking, I always tried to portray the right-young-man-probably-trying-to-get-to-his-grandparents'-house-for-a-visit image.

You don't need a coat and tie for that, but neat clothing and a recent haircut are important, not to mention a look of sincerity about you that will assure the driver trying to decide whether to pick you up that you likely remain after Sunday School for the worship hour and you don't make a habit of cutting throats.

Also, it is important to remember: Once you have gotten a ride, to keep your mouth shut. Let me explain why:

A friend and I were hitchhiking together. My friend was from a very religious family. We caught a ride with a man and his wife.

A few minutes after we had been picked up, the man lit a cigarette. My friend said to him from the back seat, "Please put out that cigarette."

The man said, "Why, kid?"

And my friend said, "Because if the Lord had intended you to smoke, he would have given you a smokestack, that's why."

The man pulled over and put us out of his car. It was the middle of the night somewhere near Eastaboga, Alabama.

"If the Lord had intended you to roll," the man said, "he'd have put wheels on your butts."

We spent the remainder of the night in a cornfield. Big-mouth stayed awake and prayed for a ride that never came. I slept. And dreamt of giggling Yankee girls.

How to Spell "N-e-k-k-i-d"

A picky reader wrote recently to protest the way I often choose to spell the word that means not having any clothes on.

The dictionary way that word should be spelled in "n-a-k-e-d." Sometimes it is okay to spell it that way. Most of the time, however, I prefer to spell that word "n-e-k-k-i-d."

There most certainly is a difference. "Naked" does, in fact, mean having no clothes on. "Nekkid," on the other hand, means not having any clothes on and you're up to something.

For example:

"We all come into this world *naked*."

But, "Let's get *nekkid* and run through the woods."

My point here is that a writer, especially one from Georgia, should not have to be chained to the formal spelling of a word when another spelling and pronunciation conjures a better image of what the writer is trying to portray.

Take the word "police." That does just dandy when you type something like, "Police in Toledo today announced the arrest of. . . ."

But that doesn't work when you want to type, "Why are all the police in Bogalusa so fat?"

In that case, the word must be changed to "poh-lice," as in "Joe Billy hit Marvin on the head with a beer bottle and then Darlene called the *poh-lice*."

I hope this is making sense. Regardless, let's go onward, and, as long as we're in the area of law enforcement, consider the words "motorcycle" and "siren."

I prefer "motor-sickle" and "sireen," as in, "The *poh-lice* were chasing Joe Billy on their *motor-sickles* and their dang-blasted *sireens* were loud enough to wake the dead."

A colleague and I were dicussing this very same matter recently, and he brought up the problem of "threw" and "through."

"If you say, 'He *threw* something *through* something,' it sounds sort of weird," my colleague explained.

And how do you get around such a problem? Simple. By the use of one of my favorite words, "thowed," as in "He *thowed* something *through* something."

I could go on all day:

• "Business": That is fine unless you are describing a Southern male involved in the selling and trading of previously owned automobiles. Then, he is in the used car *bidness*.

• "Ask": There is no such word south of Louisville, Kentucky. The word is *ast*.

• "Sucker": Sometimes that works. Most of the time, *suckah* seems to say it so much better.

Let's end this with a simple exercise: Using the new spellings you have learned for the words mentioned above, make up a cute little story. Okay:

"Joe Billy and Darlene of Bogalusa had a thing going on, but one day Joe Billy caught Darlene and Marvin running *nekkid* through the woods. Joe Billy chased down Marvin and *thowed* him through the bushes and then hit him up side the head with a beer bottle.

"Darlene called the *poh-lice*, and here they come on their *motor-sickles* with their *si-reens* turned up loud enough to wake the dead.

"The *poh-lice* caught Joe Billy and hauled him off to jail. Marvin had fourteen stiches and missed two weeks off from his used car *bidness*.

"Darlene, meanwhile, ran off with Harvey, another poor *suckah* who's *astin'* for trouble."

Snellville: Part I

My father was born in Snellville, Georgia, in a house on a hill that now stands above the Thriftown store off highway 78. When he was a young man, he was in the retail hot dog business here. "I ran a wienie joint," is how he described it.

"One day these two old girls in a '36 Essex coup lost control of their car and ran all up in my little wienie joint," he'd laugh.

Was there any damage?

"Was there any damage? There wasn't an onion left, son. Not an onion."

I went out to my father's grave Saturday afternoon. We brought him home when he died and buried him next to Adolphus and Eugenia, his parents. The cemetery sits in a corner of a pastureland across the road from Zoar Methodist Church, out a ways from town.

I don't really know why people go and stand over graves. It's been seven years. But it was peaceful out there Saturday. Black Angus cattle were grazing to the right, and I hadn't seen that in a while.

Zoar church was established in 1811. It's frame and painted white and probably hasn't changed that much in all this time. They've added on to the back, it looked like, and there may be air conditioning now. That spoiled the memory of a favorite scene—the women fanning themselves on hot Sunday mornings with those fans Zack Cravey used to hand out when he was running for Georgia fire commissioner again.

Snellville is maybe twenty miles from downtown Atlanta. It used to be no more than one of those proverbial bumps in the road to Athens.

You take the Stone Mountain freeway and then two-lane 78 east to get there. Traffic can be tough. Snellville has graduated into a full-fledged bedroom community of Atlanta. Population is 7,000 and growing.

There is a housing development called Lake Lucerne in the area. Lake Lucerne is formerly Possum Pond. Snellville cometh of age. But its pace is more sensible. I was assured the drugstore still serves Coke as God intended: Two squirts of syrup and a dash of carbonated water.

Snellville gave itself a "day" Saturday. There was a parade, of course. Senator Sam Nunn was the grand marshal. It's not an election year, so there were no long speeches.

There was a Jaycee barbecue. Six hundred-fifty chickens went to heaven, and you could have all the iced tea you could drink. The Monroe Girls Drum and Bugle Corps hasn't missed a parade since

Moby Dick was a minnow. They were there. Gordon Tanner and the Junior Skillet Lickers danced, the Matthews Family Gospel Group sang about Jesus, and a Marine band played "God Bless America" while the old men stood at attention.

That evening they had a baseball game. I went with Ludlow Porch of WRNG radio, Snellville's most celebrated citizen. We sat in the Bermuda grass along the rightfield line and fought off the mosquitoes. "Only one thing worse than mosquitoes," Ludlow said, "and that's running barefooted through the pasture and stubbing your toe on a stob."

Snellville's South Gwinnett High played Gainesville. The game was tight. Both managers chewed Red Man and spat a lot. I caught the Gainesville signs. Right hand across the letters and two spits for steal.

The score stood 1-1 in the middle innings when a South Gwinnett batter fouled a couple off behind the screen into a corn patch and then lined a pitch over the centerfield fence into what we used to call a pine thicket; 2-1. In the same inning, another South Gwinnett batter homered to right. The South Gwinnett pitcher, a youth called "Bonut," as in "donut," held off a Gainesville rally in the last inning, and the Snellville team won the game, 3-1.

They build all those big stadiums and pay out all that money. It was here I saw a sixteen-year-old shortstop go deep into the hole, stab the ball, turn completely around and throw the runner out by a half step.

Both teams met in the middle of the field when the game ended and congratulated each other. Admission was free.

Afterwards, there was a street dance up at the Thriftown parking lot.

"I've been everywhere there is to go, and I've done everything there is to do," the old man used to say. "I probably should have never left Snellville."

I used to wonder what he meant by that.

Snellville: Part II

The startling success of "Dallas," CBS' prime-time soap opera, has the other two networks searching feverishly for something to rival the giant hit.

"We don't want a carbon copy of 'Dallas,'" a source at NBC said, "but we do want a program that would offer the same week-to-week suspense."

"Exactly," echoed a high-ranking executive at ABC. "Networks have copied each other for too long. We want our own 'Dallas,' but not really a 'Dallas,' if you know what I mean."

I love that big-time television talk.

I was going to hold back on this for a few more months, but with all the hoopla "Dallas" got over the weekend for finally revealing who plugged J.R., I suppose I should go ahead and release the news:

Yours truly is busy at work on a script for a new television prime-time soap opera that he will sell to the highest bidder, who may then blow "Dallas" halfway to El Paso.

Get the picture. The camera pans the horizon, and then the triumphant name is spread across the screen:

"SNELLVILLE"!

Yes, television fans, "Snellville," the dramatic new series that follows the lives and loves and trials and tribulations of the Gooch family of Snellville, Georgia, bedroom community to the booming metropolis of Atlanta.

You want strong characters, I'll give you strong characters.

Meet Billy Oscar (B.O.) Gooch, the tyrannical eldest son of Grover (Big Tuna) Gooch, who founded the powerful Gooch Fish Market, "Your Channel Catfish and Mullet Headquarters in Snellville and Gwinnett County since 1913."

Then, there is B.O.'s mama, Big Tuna's wife, Pigella (Miss Piggie) Gooch, who can scale and clean a mess of bream in two shakes of a cow's tail.

Which brings up Sophie Jo Gooch, B.O.'s wife, who wasn't bad looking until she got hooked on Twinkies, and now she's the size of the county dump truck.

One day a man was passing through Snellville and saw Sophie Joe standing in front of the fish market.

He walked inside, and B.O. asked if he would like to order a mess of channel cat, fresh from nearby Possum Pond.

"No," said the man, looking out the window at Sophie Jo, "but what'll you take for your whale?"

Also in the script is Wanda Joe, Sophie Jo's dynamite little sister who comes to visit the Gooches for the summer. And then there is B.O.'s younger brother, Norbert (Oyster Face) Gooch, and his wife, Carmelita, whom he met when she came through town doing a motorcycle act for the carnival.

The immediate family also includes Darlene Gooch, precious granddaughter, whose parents deserted her for the nightlife and bright lights of Loganville.

Here's the plot: You put all these people in the same double-wide mobile home at the Bid-A-Wee Trailer Park, and the possibilities are endless.

B.O. is fooling around with Sophie Jo's sister, Wanda Jo. Sophie Jo, meanwhile, is just sitting there feeding her face another batch of Twinkies.

B.O. is also trying to run his brother, Oyster Face, out of the family fish business at the same time Oyster Face's wife, Carmelita, is laid up with three broken ribs and a cracked head from trying to drive her motorcycle up the steep side of Stone Mountain.

B.O. is a no-good creep whose clothes always smell like fish. The only friends he has are local cats who always follow him when he walks down the street.

The plot thickens when, in the last episode of the season, B.O. is beaten senseless with a frozen bass by an unnamed assailant.

Who shot J.R.? Who cares? Who belted B.O. with a frozen bass? "SNELLVILLE"! It even smells like a hit.

The Sweetwater Inn Open

It was something out of a dream urbanites with rural roots probably still have occasionally if they haven't forgotten what home was like.

Saturday afternoon in a small town. It is hotter than the law should allow. Fat folks, old folks, and dogs seek the shade. Nothing is moving with any semblance of speed save the Southern Railway freights that roll through town on their way to the yards in Atlanta.

A number of wise men had gathered at the Sweetwater Inn in Austell—maybe twenty miles from downtown Atlanta out I-20. I can't describe the Sweetwater Inn in any other fashion. It is a beer joint, classic in both appearance and clientele. I mean no disrespect. I hold beer joints dearer than most. I did my undergraduate sin in one.

The juke box is mostly Conway and Loretta and Waylon and Willie. They got a dime for a Tampa Nugget but only eight cents for a King Edward Imperial. A chopped barbecue sandwich is seventy. Sliced is eighty. A longneck Bud is fifty-five. The beer is moving ten-to-one better than anything else on this day.

Inside the conversation ranges from politics to sports to inevitable fishing lies. A man swore he caught 508 catfish out of Sweetwater Creek. Another man cast doubt. It was too hot to take the disagreement any further.

Outside they were pitching horseshoes. A couple of times every year, Don Mitchell—who owns the Sweetwater Inn—gives a tournament. This was doubles only. The Sweetwater Inn Open Horseshoe Tournament. Open because they came not only from Austell, but also from Powder Springs, Mableton, and even Conley. Trophies are the prizes.

From what I could gather, the horseshoe pits in the pine grove out behind the Inn used to be the Forest Hills of horseshoe pitching in Georgia. Once, state tournaments were even held there. But a few years back, pitching on a state level sort of galloped away and now Don Mitchell just gives his own tournaments and the boys get together for the frolic they provide.

A relic of a grander day is still in evidence, however. Underneath the vines and brush that border one side of the pit area, a sign, bearing the names of former state horseshoe champions, has fallen in rust and apparent neglect.

During the tournament Saturday, one of the contestants—several longnecks into the afternoon—relieved himself upon the sign. Other sports send their grand masters to halls of fame and cast statues in their likenesses. Old horseshoe pitchers, it would seem, are not as fortunate.

The game is to fifty. The tournament is double elimination. Ringers count three. Leaners, one. Any deviation from that scoring system is immediately put down. "Barnyard horseshoes," they call it. Some pitchers throw a flop. There are also three-quarter and one-and-a-quarter throws, depending upon the number of revolutions the shoe makes en route to the stob. A competition horseshoe weighs two-and-a-quarter pounds. Don Mitchell gave another tournament a few weeks ago on Austell Day and calculated that three tons of horseshoes went back and forth between the stobs.

The action had been underway a couple of hours by the time I got there. Only three teams were left. Wayne and his partner Mack already had a loss. Gene and Paul had not been beaten and neither had Don and Bud. They were to meet head-on.

There were fifteen in the audience. Fourteen watched from wooden benches. One stationed himself under a pine tree to the rear of the pitchers. It was there he eventually gave in to the beer and the sun, and it was there he missed the Sweetwater Inn Open Horseshoe Tournament as he slept the sleep of the innocent.

Gene wore Bermuda shorts in the showdown match and went to his truck before the first pitch for something to help in the heat. Paul stuck to the beer. By a prior commitment to each other, Bud and Don weren't drinking. Don, said Bud, had been saved recently.

Paul was off from the very start, and Bud and Don jumped to an early lead. Two sets of double ringers off Bud's low, accurate flop throw put his team over the top. Paul and Gene then met Wayne and Mack in the losers' bracket. Wayne is the Frank Tanana of Austell horseshoe pitchers. He and Mack moved into the finals and took Bud and Don twice—50-42 in the final game—for the championship. Wayne threw twenty-eight ringers and three sets of doubles in that final.

I asked him his secret. I think he was serious. "Don't get too drunk," he said. Don't let them put your name on that sign, either, Wayne.

You forget things like this can still happen, that places like this still exist. I had a good time. So did another spectator who had just moved into Austell from Miami. He sat there with a chew in one side of his mouth and a cigar in the other. He drank his beer in long gulps.

At one point he walked over to me and said, "All I need now is a scarlet woman."

"How's that?" I responded.

"I've got everything else," he said. "I'm chewin', I'm smokin', I'm drinkin', and, dammit, I'm cussin'."

We drank a toast to the good times.

Billy

I guess we should have known the Billy Carter story was not going to have a particularly happy ending when we saw him posing for a picture wearing a hat made out of pop-top rings from beer cans.

You may or may not remember that picture, but I do, and I remember thinking at the time I saw it that a man in full control of himself and his destiny likely would not pose for such a picture.

America needed Billy Carter back when he burst through the screen door of the nation's consciousness, grinning that boyish grin of his and pulling on a can of PBR, back in 1975.

We were just getting over stuffy old Nixon and all sorts of other disasters, and here was some redneck galoot who said what he thought, got drunk when he pleased, and would wear no man's necktie, no matter that his high-hatted brother was trying to be the president.

So, the nation took to Billy Carter for a time, like a child takes to a new bauble, and Billy Carter responded to the call by going around doing weird things like posing for the picture with the pop-top hat.

Everybody wanted to drink a beer with Billy Carter in those days. Including me. I found my way to Billy's service station in Plains one afternoon with this good ol' boy from Chicago who was down for a visit, and we must have drunk half a case each, and finally I had enough to ask Billy if he'd pose for a picture with me and my friend.

Billy would have posed for a picture with a snake in those days if somebody would have held its head still. My friend took the picture back to Chicago and showed it around and was a mild celebrity himself for having mixed in such company.

I don't think Billy Carter ever intended to do anything wrong. He simply got caught playing a game in which he didn't understand the rules. Good ol' boys from Plains and other rural outposts know they've done wrong when they spend a night in jail, get fired from their jobs, cuss in front of the preacher's wife, or run their trucks in a ditch.

Making insensitive remarks about this group of people or that group of people or taking silver saddles from this nation or that nation, or relieving yourself under the sky when nature calls, isn't anything to give a second thought about.

But Billy Carter's brother happened to be president, so when the booze got to Billy, and the business deals started to get heavy, and the Libyans started to court him, and instead of being "cute" he was now "tacky," the nation reacted in the typical American way. It dropped Billy Carter like a hot potato.

I was reading the latest about him the other day. The IRS is on his tail for $100,000 in taxes owed.

"They're out to get me," Billy said.

And they'll get him. The IRS always gets its man.

Rosalynn Carter said the other day that Jimmy is doing just fine in his role as ex-president. He'll write a book, of course, and make a lot of speeches, and, in his spare time, there's always his woodworking.

I suppose Miss Lillian will continue to get along, and sister Ruth has her career and sister Gloria still is playing harmonica, I suppose.

Meanwhile, Billy is still trying to make a living and keep the IRS wolves away from his door, and he's not even supposed to have a drink anymore. I wonder if he's still able to muster that boyish grin.

Historians will identify further the legacy of the Carter administration, but already I can name at least one of its unsuspecting victims: brother Billy, who would have been better off if he'd just waited outside in the truck while Jimmy went in to be president.

Moon Over Moreland

MORELAND—This was home for a long time. The lady responsible for me has been sick, but there was still enough left from gardens past to put a gracious plenty on the supper table. We sat up until well past ten. The main topic of conversation was the standard warning from the lady that too many cocktail parties can clear a path to destruction. She's right, you know.

Moreland is in Coweta County, forty miles southwest of Atlanta. The last census said 300 people live here. There are no traffic lights. There are two churches. One is white frame. The other is red brick. They sink you in one. They sprinkle you in the other.

Some of the better memories relate to sport. The Baptist Church sponsored a baseball team. I was a Methodist nine months of the year. Summers, I sang a different ecclesiastical tune for obvious reasons.

We played the games on the field behind the grammar school. It doubled as a rock pile. Anything hit on the ground was an automatic lethal object. Somebody had to stand deep behind the batter's box to save foul balls from being lost in a sea of kudzu and milkweed. An even greater danger was a foul ball landing in a bird dog pen past the weed patch. Bird dogs won't normally bite, but they will chew a baseball beyond recognition and further use in a New York minute.

I won't mention his name because he might still be in reading distance, but the funniest thing that ever happened was an over-weight teammate swinging mightily at a pitch, missing it, and splitting his tight-fitting uniform pants in the rear.

In his haste to make the game on time, he had neglected to wear underdrawers. Moon over Moreland. The game was halted a half-hour while he streaked home to have his mother repair the damage. He never lived it down, of course, but the child also never left home again without one snug pair covering his boobango and a spare in his pocket in the event of another such emergency.

We never heard of tennis or golf. Never *heard tell* of tennis or golf, as went the native tongue. Basketball was an outdoor game. Football was choosing-sides touch in the lot across from the Methodist Church.

The street was one goal line. A sapling was the other. My cousin, a great receiver, went long toward the sapling end of the field. As he turned to take in the pass, he caught the tree flush at full stroke. A brilliant career ended at the same moment. So did prayer meeting, just beginning inside the church, when they heard what my cousin called that sapling after he came to.

I drove around for nostalgia's sake after the lady's breakfast the other day. Even Moreland has changed here and there.

Where we played touch football stands an edifice the county has erected. "That sonufabitchin' saplin'" was gone. I smiled at what might have been my cousin's avowed revenge against it. There are even a couple of tennis courts where I remember a cornfield. Wonders never cease. The old baseball field has lights now and a screen to stop foul balls. I suppose those bird dogs went to their last hunt and chewed the stitches out of their last Reach Official a long time ago, anyway.

I walked out into the dew that covered centerfield. Little Eddie played centerfield. There was the day I was pitching. We led 3-2, or maybe 5-4. It was late in the game, and the other team had runners on. I grooved one and the batter hit a shot to deep center. How can I still recall that sinking feeling? How can I still recall Little Eddie, without a prayer, running a full gait, chasing after what would surely fall to the red clay earth and roll halfway to Luthersville?

A few months after that Little Eddie was dead. The car went out of control, and he was thrown from his seat. He couldn't have been more than fourteen. His folks took it hard. It tore the town apart.

He caught the ball. Little Eddie ran and he dived and, by some grace, he caught the ball.

A Little Piece of Heaven

Except for the time my mother and I were following around the man who gave me this name and the couple of years I was held prisoner of war in Chicago, the splendid state of Georgia has been home.

I love the South. I have few good memories that did not come from within its bounds. I especially love Georgia.

I am a product of its public schools. I attended its state university, just like Herschel Walker, the football player, does now.

I love the incredible diversity of this state, the largest state east of the Mississippi River. (That will win you some bar bets.)

Georgia has miles of beautiful coastline, but the mountains of North Georgia have an even stronger hold upon me. I can lose myself for weeks among them. And Georgia has the massive, piney flat-lands of its broad southern bottom, and it has spectacular, cosmopolitan Atlanta, and it has hundreds of crossroad towns like Hahira and Split Silk and Roosterville and Primrose, where they talk and move slowly, praise the Lord on Sunday mornings, and generally are made of the good, strong stuff that holds a society together.

It hasn't been easy for Georgia. I moved to Chicago in 1975. In 1975, people in Chicago would ask me, "Are there any nice restaurants 'out there' in Georgia?"

I did my best.

"Georgia," I pointed out, "is 'down there.' Omaha is 'out there.' And there are a couple of nice places to eat. Mention my name and maybe you'll get a good stool at the counter."

We've been called "rednecks" and worse. We've been terribly misunderstood. Chicago remains a hotbed of racial contempt, but I was chided during my sentence there for the unfair, stereotype vision of hooded Klansmen walking every street from Rabun Gap to Tybee Light.

H. L. Mencken once described Georgia, and the South, as an "intellectual Gobi." H. L. Mencken made that observation from the lovely city of Baltimore.

But we had our moment in the sun, Georgia and Georgians did. Tucked away in a little corner of the country, the rest of the nation discovered us four years ago, and we enjoyed a brief flirtation with celebrity status.

Suddenly, in Chicago's Division Street bars, my drawl was an object of great interest.

"Say something Southern," they would demand.

"Sumbitch," I would answer. They would howl.

A Chicago friend wanted to try grits. I invited him to my apartment for a Deep South breakfast. Along with the grits, the menu included country ham, red-eye gravy, and biscuits.

As the breakfast was being prepared, the friend walked into my kitchen, took one look at the biscuit dough and said, "So, that's grits?"

How we lost the war remains a mystery to me.

Jimmy Carter brought us out of our relative obscurity. He was our governor, and then he ran for president in 1976 and got himself elected.

I was just sitting here thinking: It all comes to an end Tuesday. Ronald Reagan will become the new president. Jimmy Carter will return home. Georgia will be out. California will be in.

I received a Christmas card with "Jimmy and Rosalynn" stamped on the bottom a few weeks ago. I framed it. A man is lucky to make one presidential Christmas card mailing list in his lifetime. I don't look to do it again.

There probably will be a period of adjustment for us. No more network commentators broadcasting from downtown Plains, no more "Georgia mafia," and Billy Carter gives way to a smart-mouth son who wears very tight pants.

But we will adjust. We always do. And what will be left in the place of all that attention of the four previous years will be what was here all along.

A little piece of heaven, just south of Chattanooga.

Y'all come see us. You heah?

Elvis Is Dead And I Don't Feel So Good Myself

Dedication

To Danny Thompson, Bobby Entrekin, Mike Murphy, Dudley Stamps, Charles Moore, Clyde Elrod, Worm Elrod, and Anthony Yeager — the boys from Moreland, who I hope and pray didn't grow up to be as confused as I am.

And to the memory of Eddie Estes, a great centerfielder.

A Last Toast To The King

WE WERE SITTING on the beach in Hilton Head, South Carolina, me and Price and Franklin. We were mired in those squatty folding chairs, the kind the old people take down to the surf and sit in while the salt water splashes over them. We were drinking cold beer and acting our age.

You can always tell the approximate age of people by watching what they do when they go to the beach. Babies, of course, dabble in the sand and splash around in the shallow water.

When a kid is about ten or twelve, he goes out farther and rides the waves and balks at his mother's motions that it's time to leave.

"Come on, Timmy. It's time to go back to the motel."

"Can't we stay just a little bit longer?"

"No. Your daddy is ready to leave."

"But I want to swim some more."

"I said come here, young man."

"Let me ride just one more wave. Please?"

"Don't make me call your daddy."

"I'll ride just one more and then I'll be ready to go."

"Okay, but just one more."

Parents never win at the beach, at least in these permissive times they don't. A kid can always just-one-more his parents into another thirty minutes of wave riding.

When children become teen-agers, the girls stop going into the water because they're afraid they will get their hair wet. What they do instead is put on tiny little swimsuits and lie on towels getting tanned. Teen-aged boys throw frisbees.

There should be a law against throwing frisbees on beaches. In the first place, throwing a frisbee is a mindless exercise that can't be any fun whatsoever. After you've seen one frisbee float through the air, you've seen them all. They might as well try catching horseflies.

Also, on crowded beaches there isn't room for teen-aged boys to throw frisbees. Frisbees are difficult to control and difficult to catch, so they're always landing on people who are trying to relax in the sun. Sometimes, frisbees even knock over somebody's beer.

A kid knocked over my beer with a frisbee at the beach once. I threatened him with a lawsuit and then put this curse on him: "May your voice never change and your zits win prizes at county fairs." I hate it when somebody knocks over my beer at the beach.

When kids are college age, the girls still lie on towels getting tanned and worrying about getting their hair wet. The boys, meanwhile, have given up throwing frisbees and have joined the girls, lying next to them on their own towels.

They play loud rock music, and when the girls ask them to rub suntan oil on their backs, they enthusiastically oblige ... especially if the girl has unsnapped the back of her tiny top and the boy knows that her breasts are unleashed, for all practical purposes. The beach habits of people this age are basically preliminary sexual exercises, but rarely do they lead to anything more advanced later in the day. As numerous studies have shown, it is quite uncomfortable to attempt to have sex after an afternoon of lying in the sun because of the unpleasant feeling that individuals get when they rub their sunburned skin against that of someone whose epidermis is in the same painful condition.

At about age thirty, most people have the good sense to stop frying their skin in the sun for hours. They know by then that having sex is more fun than having a sunburn; they have heeded all the reports about how lying in the sun causes skin cancer; and they are usually working on their first nervous breakdown by age thirty, and all they want to do at the beach is sit there and relax while drinking cold beer.

The three of us that day at Hilton Head had already tiptoed into our thirties and the beer was going down exceptionally well. I have no idea what women talk about when they're sitting on a beach together without any men around, but when no women are present, men talk about the physical attributes of everything that happens to walk past them — or is lying close to them on a towel — wearing a bikini.

Me and Price and Franklin were doing just that:

"Good God."

"Where?"

"Left."

"Good God."

"How old do you think she is?"

"Eighteen."

"No way. Sixteen."

"Did they look like that when we were sixteen?"

"They couldn't have."

"Why not?"

"If they had, I wouldn't have lived this long. Some daddy would have shot me."

"Yeah, and they got the pill today, too."

"I wonder if the boys their age know how lucky they are."

"They don't have any idea."

"Wonder how old they are when they start these days?"

"Rodney Dangerfield said the kids are doing it so young these days that his daughter bought a box of Cracker Jacks and the prize was a diaphragm."

"Great line."

"Look coming here."

"It's a land whale."

"Damn, she's fat."

"If somebody told her to haul ass, she'd have to make two trips."

"That's awful."

"Hey, we're out of beer."

I remember distinctly that it was Franklin who went back to the condo to get more beer. I also remember distinctly that the month was August and the year was 1977. We had the radio playing. It was a country station.

Franklin was gone thirty minutes. When he came back, he had another twelve-pack. He also had a troubled look on his face.

"What took you so long?" Price asked him. "You didn't call Sweet Thing back home, did you?"

"You're not going to believe what I just heard on television," he answered.

I had just taken the first pull on my fresh beer when I

heard him utter three incredible words.

"Elvis is dead," he said.

Elvis is dead. The words didn't fit somehow. The queen of England is dead. There has been a revolution in South America and the dictator is dead. Some rock singer has been found in his hotel room with a needle in his arm and he is dead. All that made sense, but not *Elvis is dead.*

"They figure he had a heart attack," said the bad news bearer.

A heart attack? Elvis Presley couldn't have a heart attack. He was too young to have a heart attack. He was too young to have anything like that. Elvis Presley was my idol when I was a kid. Elvis changed my life. Elvis turned on my entire generation. I saw *Love Me Tender* three times. He died in *Love Me Tender,* but that was just a movie.

I figured this was some sort of joke. Right, Elvis Presley had a heart attack. And where did they find his body? In Heartbreak Hotel, of course.

The music had stopped on the radio. A man was talking.

"Elvis Presley is dead," said the voice. "He was forty-two."

Forty-two? That had to be wrong, too. How could he be that old? Elvis had to be younger than that. He was one of us, wasn't he? If he was forty-two, maybe he could have had a heart attack. If he was over forty, that meant he probably had wrinkles and maybe his hair had already fallen out and he had been wearing a wig.

But if Elvis Presley was forty-two and old enough to die, what did that say about me and the generation he had captured? He had been what separated us from our parents. He had been our liberator. He played the background music while we grew up.

Elvis is dead. Suddenly, I didn't feel so good myself.

"Damn," said Price, "if Elvis is dead, that means we're getting old, too."

"Damn if it don't," said Franklin.

I asked for another beer.

The announcer on the radio had stopped talking, and the three of us fell silent as an eerie sound came forth. It was Elvis's voice. It was a dead man's voice. Elvis was singing "Don't Be Cruel." It was spooky.

" 'Don't Be Cruel'," said Price. "That was his best ever."

" 'One Night With You' was my favorite," Franklin said. "I remember dancing with Doris Ann Plummer and singing along with Elvis in her ear. 'Oooooooone ni-ite with yuuuuu is all I'm way-ayting fooor.' Doris Ann said I sounded just like Elvis, and soon as I got her in the car after the dance, it was all over."

"Everything he did was great," I said.

Elvis went on singing. I sat, still stupefied from the news, and listened. My friends went on talking.

"My old man hated Elvis."

"So did mine."

"He was always screaming at me, 'Get that garbage off the radio!'"

"Mine was a religious nut. He said the devil had sent Elvis, and anybody who listened to his music was going to hell."

"I wish my old man was alive today to see who the kids are idolizing now."

"Yeah, Elvis wouldn't look so bad compared to some of those weirdos they got today."

"He probably wouldn't even be noticed."

"You really scored with a girl because she thought you sounded like Elvis?"

"Doris Ann Plummer, right in the back seat out behind

the National Guard Armory."

"I always used Johnny Mathis."

"Well, Doris Ann wasn't exactly a great conquest. I found out later she'd do it if you sang like Lassie."

"Everybody had somebody like that in their school."

"Yeah, but just one."

"Imagine if it had been like it is now back then."

"I'd have never graduated from high school."

"I guess we were pretty naive back then compared to the kids now."

"Maybe we're better off."

"Maybe. I wonder if we'd have taken drugs if we'd had 'em back then."

"Hell, I thought drinking a beer was the wildest thing I could do."

"I went to a fraternity party at Auburn when I was a senior in high school. I drank gin and 7-Up and danced with college girls. I didn't think there was anything you could do any better or wilder than that."

"We didn't have it so bad growing up."

"At least we had Elvis."

"He was the greatest ever."

"The King."

"I don't think there will ever be anything like him again."

"Hard to believe he's dead."

"Think he was on drugs?"

"Probably."

"Ready for another beer?"

"Let's drink one to Elvis."

"To Elvis."

"To Elvis."

I joined in. "To Elvis."

The King was still singing on the radio:

"Love me tender,
Love me true,
Make all my dreams fulfilled.
For my darling, I love you.
And I always will."

* * *

I have never forgotten that day at the beach. It was like the day John Kennedy was killed. Like the day Martin Luther King was killed. Like the day Robert Kennedy was killed. Like the day Nixon resigned.

You never forget days like that, and you're never quite the same after them. There have been so many days like that, it seems, for my generation — the Baby Boomers who were minding to our business of growing up when all hell broke loose in the early sixties.

A few weeks after Elvis's death, I heard another piece of startling news. I heard they found Elvis dead in his bathroom. I heard he died straining for a bowel movement.

The King, we had called him, but he had gotten fat and at the age of forty-two he had died straining for a bowel movement. Or so was the rumor. I have spent much of the past seven years hoping against hope that it wasn't true.

When Life Was Black And White

I AM THIRTY-EIGHT years old — it's approximately half-time of the promised three score and ten — and I don't have any idea what is taking place around me anymore.

Lord knows, I have tried to understand. I have dutifully watched "Donahue" in an attempt to broaden myself into a creature adjusted to the eighties, but it has been a fruitless and frustrating endeavor.

How did Phil Donahue do it? He's even older than I am, with the gray hair to show for it, but he seems to understand what people mean when they talk about the new way to live. Me, I feel like an alien in my own country. These new lifestyles seem to be in direct contrast to the way they taught living when I was a child. Back then, *gay* meant, "1. Happy and carefree; merry. 2. Brightly colorful and ornamental. 3. Jaunty; sporty. 4. Full of or given to lighthearted pleasure. 5. Rakish; libertine." (That's straight from my high school dictionary.) Pot was something you cooked in, and back then nobody ate mushrooms. Where did I miss a turn?

The first hint that the world was taking leave of me came after Elvis died. The women who mourned him were *older* and had beehive hairdos and children of their own. Their teeny-bopper, socks-rolled-down days were far behind them. They were my age and they were weeping not only for Elvis, I think now, but for the realization that an era and a time — their time — was passing to another generation. To know that Elvis had gotten old and sick and fat enough to die was to know that their own youth had faded as well.

Elvis, forty-two. Elvis, dead. The voice that sang for the children of the late forties and early fifties stilled, and in its place a cacophony of raucous melodies from scruffy characters playing to the screams of young earthlings of the modern generation, to whom happiness and normalcy was a computerized hamburger at McDonald's and mandatory attendance at earsplitting concerts given by people dressed as dragons or barely dressed at all. Elvis may have shaken his pelvis, but he never by-God showed it to anybody on stage.

Why this gap between me and the younger generation? Why, in my thirties, do I have more in common with people twenty years older than with people five or ten years younger? Where is my tolerance for change and modernization? Why would I enjoy hitting Boy George in the mouth? Where did the years go and where did the insanity of the eighties come from? And why did I ever leave home in the first place?

Home. That's probably it. I don't seem to fit in today because it was so different yesterday.

Home. I think of it and the way it was every time I see or hear something modern that challenges tradition as I came to know it.

Home. I was born in 1946, the son of a soldier who lived through seven years of combat and then drank his way right out of the service, but who still stood and sang the national anthem to the top of his forceful voice at the several hundred ball games we watched together.

Home. It was a broken home. That came when I was six and my mother ran for her parents and took me with her. The four of us lived in my grandparents' home. We warmed ourselves by kerosene, we ate from a bountiful garden, and our pattern of living was based on two books — the Bible and the Sears Roebuck catalog.

Everything came in black and white.

* * *

Moreland, Georgia, had perhaps three hundred inhabitants when I moved there in 1952. The population is about the same today, and Moreland still doesn't have a red light.

Some other things have changed, however. There are two tennis courts in Moreland. Back then, we played baseball and dammed creeks, and that was enough. Cureton and Cole's store, where the old men sat around the stove and spit and imparted wisdom, is boarded shut. I don't know where the old men in Moreland spit and impart wisdom nowadays.

Perhaps spitting and wisdom-imparting around a stove have gone the way of ice cream cups with pictures of movie stars on the bottom side of the lids. I purchased hundreds of ice cream cups at Cureton and Cole's, licking the faces of everybody from Andy Devine to Yvonne DeCarlo. I haven't seen ice cream cups like that in years, but even if they were still around, I wouldn't buy one; I'd be afraid I might lick away the vanilla on the bottom of my lid only to find John

Travolta smiling at me. What a horrid thought.

Those were good and honest people who raised me and taught me. They farmed, they worked in the hosiery mill that sat on the town square, and some went to the county seat six miles away where they welded and trimmed aluminum and sweated hourly-wage sweat — the kind that makes people hard and reserved and resolved there is a better world awaiting in the next life.

We had barbecues and street square dances in Moreland. We had two truckstops that were also beer joints, and the truckers played the pinball machines and the jukeboxes. The local beer drinkers parked their cars out back, presumably out of sight.

The religion in town was either Baptist or Methodist, and it was hardshell and certainly not tolerant of drinking. The church ladies were always gossiping about whose cars had been spotted behind the truckstops.

There was one fellow, however, who didn't care whether they saw his car or not. Pop Towns worked part-time at the post office, but the highlight of his day took place at the railroad yard. The train didn't stop in Moreland, so the outgoing mail had to be attached to a hook next to the tracks to be picked off when the train sped past. It was Pop's job to hang the mail.

Every morning at ten, when the northbound came through, and every evening at six, when the southbound passed, Pop would push his wheelbarrow filled with a sack of mail from the post office down to the tracks. There he would hang the mail, and we'd all stand around and watch as the train roared by. Then Pop would get in his car, drive over to one of the truckstops, park contemptuously out front, and have himself several beers.

One day the ladies of the church came to Pop's house in an effort to save him from the demon malt. I wasn't there when it happened, of course, but the word got around that when Pop answered the door for the ladies, he came with a beer in his hand.

Hilda Landon began reciting various scriptures regarding drunkenness. Pop countered by sicking his dog, Norman, on the ladies, and they scattered in various directions.

Pop, they said, laughed at the sight of his dog chasing off the ladies of the church, and once back inside his house, he had himself another beer, secure in the fact that he and Norman would never be bothered by another tolerance committee.

They found Pop dead one morning after he failed to make his appointment with the mail train, and the ladies of the church all said the Lord was getting even with Pop for all his sinful ways.

I sort of doubted that. Pop always had a good joke to tell and always was kind to his dog, and although I was no expert on the scriptures, I was of the belief that a good heart would get you a just reward in the afterlife as quick as anything else.

We also had a town drunk, Curtis "Fruit Jar" Hainey, but the ladies of the church figured he was too far gone to waste their efforts on. Curtis walked funny, like his knees were made of rubber. Somebody said it was because he once drank some rubbing alcohol when the local bootlegger left town for two weeks and Curtis came up dry and desperate. I figured the Lord could have had a little something to do with this one.

Although Moreland was a small town, not unlike so many others across the country in the early 1950s, we still had plenty of scandal, intrigue, and entertainment.

It was whispered, for example, that Runelle Sheets, a high school girl who suddenly went to live with her cousin in Atlanta, actually was pregnant and had gone off to one of *those* homes.

Nobody ever verified the rumor about Runelle, but they said her daddy refused to speak her name in his house anymore and had threatened to kill a boy who lived over near Raymond. That was enough for a summer's full of satisfying speculation.

For further entertainment, we had a town idiot, Crazy Melvin, who allegedly was shell-shocked in Korea. Well, sort of. The story went that when Crazy Melvin heard the first shot fired, he began to run and when next seen had taken off his uniform, save his helmet and boots, and was perched in his nakedness in a small tree, refusing to climb down until frostbite threatened his privates.

They sent Crazy Melvin home after that, and following some months in the hospital, the Army decided that Melvin wasn't about to stop squatting naked in trees, so they released him in the custody of his parents.

Once back in Moreland, however, Crazy Melvin continued to do odd things, such as take off all his clothes, save his brogans and his straw hat. They finally sent Melvin to Atlanta to see a psychiatrist. When he came back, the psychiatrist had cured him of squatting naked in trees. Unfortunately, Melvin had ridden a trolley while in Atlanta and returned home thinking he was one. Every time you were walking to the store or to church and crossed paths with Crazy Melvin, you had to give him a nickel.

"Please step to the rear of the trolley," he would say, and then he'd make sounds like a trolley bell. The church later got up enough money to buy Melvin one of those coin-holders bus drivers wear, so it was easier for him to make change when you didn't have a nickel.

* * *

Those were the days, when young boys roamed carefree and confidently around the streets of Moreland — Every-town, USA.

We were Baby Boomers all, born of patriots, honed by the traditional work ethic. That meant you worked your tail off and never quit until the job was done, and you saved every penny you could and never spent money on anything' that didn't have at least some practical value. You kept the Word, never questioned authority, loved your country, did your duty, never forgot where you came from, bathed daily when there was plenty of water in the well, helped your neighbors, and were kind to little children, old people, and dogs. You never bought a car that was any color like red or yellow, stayed at home unless it was absolutely necessary to leave (such as going to church Sunday and for Wednesday night prayer meeting), kept your hair short and your face cleanshaven. You were suspicious of rich people, lawyers, yankee tourists, Catholics and Jehovah's Witnesses who tried to sell subscriptions to "The Watchtower" door-to-door, anybody who had a job where he had to wear a tie to work, and Republicans.

We were isolated in rural self-sufficiency for the most part. Television was only a rumor. We kept to ourselves unless we went to the county seat of Newnan to see a movie or to get a haircut or to see the little alligator they kept in a drink box at Mr. Lancaster's service station.

I never did find out how the little alligator got into a drink box at a service station in Newnan, Georgia, but rumor had it that Mr. Lancaster had brought it back from Florida to keep people from breaking into his station after he closed at night. In fact, Mr. Lancaster had a handwritten sign in front of his station that read, "This service station is guarded by my alligator three nights a week. Guess which three nights."

In such a closed, tightly-knit society, it was impossible not to feel a strong sense of belonging. Even for a newcomer.

When I first moved to Moreland at age seven, I was instantly befriended by the local boys. In those idyllic days, we molded friendships that would last for lifetimes.

There was Danny Thompson, who lived just across the cornfield from me, next door to Little Eddie Estes. Down the road from Danny was where Mike Murphy lived. Clyde and Worm Elrod lived near the Methodist Church. Bobby Entrekin and Dudley Stamps resided in Bexton, which was no town at all but simply a scattering of houses along a blacktop road a mile or so out of Moreland. There was Anthony Yeager, who lived over near Mr. Ralph Evans's store, and Charles Moore was just down the road from him.

Clyde Elrod was a couple of years older than his brother Worm, who was my age. Clyde had one ambition in his life, and that was to follow his father's footsteps into the Navy. Clyde often wore his father's old Navy clothes and regaled us with his father's Navy stories. Clyde's father apparently single-handedly won the battle for U.S. naval supremacy in World War II.

Worm got his name at Boy Scout camp one summer. There is only one thing worse than biting into an apple and finding a worm, and that's biting into an apple and finding half a worm, which is what happened to Worm Elrod and is how he got his nickname. Clyde and Worm did not get along that well, due to a heated sibling rivalry. Their father often had to separate them from various entanglements, and Worm invariably got the worst of it. Only when Clyde graduated from high school and left to join the Navy was it certain that Worm would live to see adulthood.

Anthony Yeager joined the gang later. He was the first of us to obtain his driver's license, and his popularity increased immediately. As teen-agers, we roamed in Yeager's Ford and slipped off for beer and to smoke. Once we went all the way to Fayetteville to the Highway 85 Drive-In and saw our first movie in which women appeared naked from the waist up.

Funny, what the memory recalls. The movie was *Bachelor Tom Peeping,* and it was billed as a documentary filmed at a nudist camp. At one point, Bachelor Tom was confronted by a huge-breasted woman who was covered only by a large inner tube that appeared to have come from the innards of a large tractor tire. As she lowered the tube, we watched in utter disbelief.

"Nice tubes you have, my dear," said Bachelor Tom.

Yeager was the first total devotee to country music I ever met, and he is at least partially responsible for my late-blooming interest in that sort of music. Yeager owned an old guitar that he couldn't play, but he tried anyway, and common were the nights we would find a quiet place in the woods, park his car, and serenade the surrounding critters.

Yeager's heroes were Hank Williams and Ernest Tubb. His favorite songs were Hank's "I'm So Lonesome I Could Cry" — later butchered by B.J. Thomas — and Ernest's classic, "I'm Walking the Floor Over You."

Hank was dead and long gone by then, but one day Yeager heard that Ernest Tubb, accompanied by picker-supreme Billy Byrd, was to perform at the high school auditorium in nearby Griffin. Me and Yeager and Dudley Stamps and Danny Thompson went. It was our first concert. Ernest slayed us, especially Yeager.

"I'm walkin' the floor over you.
I can't sleep a wink, that is true.
I'm hopin' and I'm prayin'
That my heart won't break in two.
I'm walkin' the floor over you."

Whenever Ernest Tubb would call in Billy Byrd for a guitar interlude, he would say, "Awwwwwww, Billy Byrd," which Yeager thought was a nice touch. For months, Yeager would say "Awwwwwww, Billy Byrd" for no reason whatsoever. Later he began saying, "Put a feather in your butt and pick it out, Billy Byrd," again for no reason except that it seemed to give him great joy to say it.

Like I said, it's funny what details the memory recalls.

Dudley Stamps. He was the crazy one. He once drove his father's truck into White Oak Creek to see if trucks will float. They won't. There was not a water tower or a forest ranger tower in three counties he hadn't climbed. When he was old enough to get a driver's license, his parents bought him a used 1958 Thunderbird with a factory under the hood.

I was riding one night with Dudley when the State Patrol stopped him. His T-bird had been clocked at 110 MPH, according to the patrolman. Dudley was incensed and launched into an argument with the officer. He insisted he was doing at least 125.

Mike Murphy. He had a brother and sister and his father was called "Mr. Red." Mr. Red Murphy was the postmaster and helped with the Boy Scouts. With the possible exception of the Methodist and Baptist preachers, he was the most respected man in town. Mike had to work more than the rest of us. Mr. Red kept all his children busy tending the family acreage.

"You don't see Red Murphy's children out gallivantin' all over town," the old men around the stove used to say down at Cureton and Cole's. "Red keeps 'em in the fields where there ain't no trouble."

This was the late 1950s, when "gallivanting" meant doing just about anything that had no practical end to it, such as riding bicycles, roller-skating on the square, and hanging out at the store eating Zagnut candy bars and drinking NuGrapes or what was commonly referred to as "Big Orange bellywashers." Gallivanting, like most things modern, seems to have grown somewhat sterile and electronic. Today, I suppose when children gallivant it means they hang around in shopping malls, playing video games and eating frozen yogurt.

The day Mr. Red died was an awful day. It was the practice at the Moreland Methodist Church to return to the sanctuary after Sunday School for a quick hymn or two and for announcements by Sunday School Superintendent Fox Covin. Fox would also call on those having birthdays, and the celebrants would stand as we cheered them in song.

That Sunday morning, Fox Covin announced it was Mr. Red's birthday and asked his daughter to stand for him as we sang. As everyone in church knew, Mr. Red had been hospitalized the day before for what was alleged to be a minor problem.

Soon after we sang to Mr. Red, another member of the family came into the church and whisked the Murphy children away. Something was whispered to Fox Covin, and after the children were safely out of earshot, he told the congregation that Red Murphy was dead.

We cried and then we prayed. Mike was no more than twelve or thirteen at the time. He had to take on a great deal of the responsibility of the farm after that, so his opportunity to gallivant with the rest of us was shortened even further.

"Mike Murphy will grow up to be a fine man," my mother used to say.

Bobby Entrekin. I loved his father. I had secretly wished there was some way my mother could have married Mr. Bob Entrekin, but there was his wife, Miss Willie, with whom to contend, and a quiet, soft, loving woman she was. I decided to remain content with spending my weekends at the Entrekin home.

Mr. Bob worked nights. Miss Willie worked days at one of the grocery stores in the county seat. The Entrekins, I noticed, ate better than the rest of us. While my family's diet consisted mostly of what we grew from our garden or raised in our chicken coops, the Entrekins always had such delights as store-bought sandwich meat and boxed dough-nuts, the sort with the sweet, white powder around them.

The standing contention was that because Miss Willie was employed at the grocery store, she was given discounts on such elaborate foodstuffs others in the community would have found terribly wasteful to purchase.

Whatever, as much as I enjoyed the company of my friend Bobby Entrekin, it may have been the lure of the delights of his family refrigerator and his father that were the most binding seal on our friendship.

Bobby's father was unlike any man I had ever met before. He had a deep, forceful voice. His knowledge of sport was unparalleled in the community. He had once been an out-standing amateur baseball player, and on autumn Satur-days, Bobby and I would join him at radioside to listen to Southeastern Conference college football games — as com-forting and delicious an exercise as I have ever known. My own father, having split for parts unknown, had shared Mr. Bob's affinity for sports and other such manly interests, and Mr. Bob stood in for him nicely.

Mr. Bob also had more dimension to him than any other man I had known. He had educated himself. He had trav-eled a bit. He sent off for classical records, and when I spent the weekends with Bobby, his father would awaken us on Sunday mornings for church with those foreign sounds.

As Beethoven roared through the little Entrekin house out on Bexton Road, he would say to us, "Boys, that is what you call good music." How uncharacteristic of the time and place from which I sprung, but how pleasant the memory.

Bobby was a con man from his earliest days. He slicked classmates out of their lunch desserts, and by schoolday's end, he usually had increased his marble holdings considerably.

Only once did he put an unpleasant shuck on me. Mr. Bob had driven us into Newnan, where the nearest picture show was located. The Alamo Theatre sat on Newnan's court square, across the street from the side entrance to the county courthouse. Admission to the movie was a dime. There were soft drinks for a nickel and small bags of popcorn for the same price.

As we walked toward the Alamo, we came upon a bus parked on the court square.

"Boys," said a man sitting outside the bus, "come on inside and see the world's fattest woman."

"How fat is she?" Bobby asked.

"Find out for yourself for only fifteen cents, kid," said the man.

Bobby started inside while I did some quick arithmetic. I had twenty cents. That was a dime for admission to the picture show and a dime for a soft drink and popcorn. If I paid fifteen cents to see the fat lady, I couldn't get in to see the movie.

I mentioned this bit of financial difficulty to Bobby.

"Don't worry," he said. "I'll loan you enough to get into the show."

We each dropped fifteen cents into the man's cigar box of coins and stepped inside the bus.

The smell got us first. A hog would have buried its snout in the mud to have escaped it. Then we saw the fat lady. She was enormous. She dripped fat. She was laid out on a divan, attempting to fan away the heat and the stench. We both ran out of the bus toward the movie house.

When we arrived at the ticket window, I reminded Bobby

of his offer to stake me to a ticket.

"I was only kidding," he said, as he pranced into the theater. I sat on the curb and cried. Later, when I told his father what Bobby had done, Mr. Bob played a symphony upon his son's rear and allowed me to watch. I took shameful pleasure in the sweet revenge.

Charles Moore. His mother called him "Cholly," and he eventually achieved some renown in high school when The Beatles hit in 1964 because Charles, even with his short hair, was a dead-ringer for a seventeen-year-old Paul McCartney. Charles was never able to make any money off this resemblance — that was before the imitation craze, e.g., the Elvis impersonators after his death and the three or four thousand young black kids currently doing Michael Jackson — but he obviously took a great deal of pleasure from standing in the middle of a group of giggling girls who were saying things like, "Oh, Charles, you look just like Paul."

What I remember Charles for most, however, is the fight we had in the seventh grade over a baseball score. I was a fierce and loyal Dodger fan. Charles held the same allegiance to the Milwaukee Braves.

I arrived at school one morning with a score from the evening before, Dodgers over the Braves. I had heard it on the radio.

"The Dodgers beat the Braves last night," I boasted to Charles.

"No they didn't," he said.

"I heard it on the radio," I continued.

"I don't care what you heard," he said. "The Braves won."

The principal had to pull us apart.

When I went home that afternoon, I called Mr. Bob Entrekin, who subscribed to the afternoon paper with the complete scores, and asked him to verify the fact that the Dodgers had, indeed, defeated the Braves so I could call Charles Moore and instruct him to kiss my tail.

The Braves had won, said Mr. Bob. I feigned a sore throat and didn't go to school the next two days.

Danny Thompson. We were best friends before high school. Danny was the best athlete in our class. At the countywide field day competition, he ran fourth in the potato race. A potato race works — or worked, since I doubt potato racing has lingered with everybody throwing those silly frisbees today — this way:

There were four cans (the kind that large quantities of mustard and canned peaches came in) spaced at intervals of ten yards. The boy running first can dashed the first ten yards, picked the potato out of the can, and raced back and handed it to the boy running second can.

He then dropped the potato into the team can at the starting line and hurried to the second can twenty yards away. The team that got all four potatoes in its can first won the medals.

Danny ran fourth can because he was the fastest boy in our class. We probably would have won the county potato race, had I not stumbled and dropped my potato as I tried to depart from the second can.

Danny was also rather possessive about his belongings. He received a new football for Christmas one year. It was a Sammy Baugh model, and it had white stripes around each end. We were perhaps ten when Danny got the football.

We gathered for a game of touch a few days after Christmas, but Danny didn't bring his new football.

"I'm saving it," he explained.

When I would visit Danny, he would pull his new football out of his closet and allow me to hold it. He would never take it outside, however.

"I'm saving it," he would say again. That was nearly thirty years ago. We never did get to play with Danny's football.

One morning in the fifth grade, I looked over at Danny and his face was in his hands. He was crying. I had never seen Danny cry before. The teacher whispered something to him and then took him out of the room.

Word travels fast in a small town. Danny's mother and his father had separated. He and I were even closer in our friendship after that. We shared a loss of parent uncommon to children then, but we rolled quite well with our punch, I suppose. We spent hours together deep down in the woods behind his house. He talked of his mother. I talked of my father.

Danny wanted us to become blood brothers. He had seen two Indians on television cut their fingers and then allow their blood to mix. I wanted to be Danny's blood brother, but I was afraid to cut my finger. I suggested that we swap comic books instead.

* * *

It was a simple childhood, one that I didn't fully cherish until I had long grown out of it. Only then did I appreciate the fact that I was allowed to grow into manhood having never once spent a day at the country club pool, or playing baseball where they put the ball on a tee like they do for children today, or growing my hair down over my shoulders, or wearing T-shirts advertising punk rock bands, or smoking anything stronger than a rabbit tobacco cigarette wrapped in paper torn from a brown bag and, later, an occasional Marlboro Dudley Stamps would bring on camping trips from his father's store.

It was a most happy childhood, because the only real fear we had was that we might somehow find ourselves at odds with Frankie Garfield. Frankie was the town bully who often made life miserable for all of us, especially any new child who moved into Moreland. There was the new kid with the harelip, for instance.

The afternoon of his first day in school, the new kid rode his bicycle to Cureton and Cole's, where Frankie was involved in beating up a couple of fifth graders for their NuGrapes and Zagnut candy bars.

The new kid parked his bicycle, and as he walked to the entrance of the store, he reached down to pick up a shiny nail off the ground. Frankie spotted him.

"Hey, Harelip," he called, "that's my nail."

Nobody had bothered to inform the new kid about Frankie Garfield. The rest of us knew that if Frankie said the nail was his, the best move was to drop the nail immediately, apologize profusely, and then offer to buy Frankie anything inside the store he desired.

The new kid, however, made a serious, nearly fatal, mistake. He indicated, in no uncertain terms, that Frankie was filled with a rather unpleasant substance common to barnyards. Then he put the nail in his pocket and began to walk inside the store.

He didn't make it past the first step before Frankie began to beat him unmercifully. At first, I think Frankie was simply amusing himself, as a dog amuses himself by catching a turtle in his mouth and slinging it around in the air.

Then the new kid made another mistake. He tried to fight back against Frankie. Now Frankie was mad. When he finally tired of beating his victim, Frankie left him there in a crumpled heap and rode off on the new kid's bicycle.

I suppose Frankie did have some degree of heart about him. He let the new kid keep the nail.

We were involved in some occasional juvenile delinquency, but nothing more flagrant than stealing a few watermelons, or shooting out windows in abandoned houses, or pilfering a few peaches over at Cates's fruit stand.

We went to church, didn't talk back to our elders, studied history in which America never lost a war, and were basically what our parents wanted us to be. Except when it came to Elvis.

* * *

Whatever else we were, we were the first children of television, and it was television that brought us Elvis. He would prove to be the first break between our parents and ourselves. That disagreement seems so mild today after the generational war that broke out in the late sixties, but those were more timid times when naiveté was still in flower.

Elvis was a Pied Piper wearing ducktails. He sang and he moaned and wiggled, and we followed him ... taking our first frightening steps of independence.

Guilt Trip In A Cadillac

RADIO PERHAPS WOULD have made Elvis popular, but television made him The King. We could *see* him, and there never had been anything like him before.

The only music I knew prior to Elvis was the hymns from the Methodist Cokesbury hymnal; "My Bucket's Got a Hole in It" and "Good Night, Irene" from my mother's singing while she ironed; and "Peace in the Valley," which I had learned watching "The Red Foley Show" on Saturday nights after my aunt bought the first television in the family.

But Elvis. Ducktails. His guitar. Uh-uh, Baby, don't you step on my blue suede shoes, and don't be cruel to a heart that's true.

Elvis thrust a rebellious mood upon us. I was ten or eleven when I decided to grow my own ducktails and refused to get my little-boy flattop renewed. As my hair grew out, I pushed back the sides by greasing them down, and then I brought my hair together at the back of my head, giving it the appearance of the north end of a southbound duck. I wouldn't wash my hair, either, for fear it might lose what I considered to be a perfect set.

"If you don't wash your hair, young man," my mother would warn me, "you're going to get head lice."

I didn't believe her. Nothing, not even head lice, could live in that much greasy gook.

I also pushed my pants down low like Elvis wore his.

"Pull your pants up before they fall off," my mother would say.

"This is how Elvis wears his pants," would be my inevitable reply.

"I don't know what you children see in him," she would counter.

I wrote her off as completely without musical taste and suggested that Red Foley was an incompetent old geezer who couldn't carry Elvis's pick.

"I don't know what's wrong with young'uns these days," was my mother's subsequent lament.

My stepfather eventually entered the ducktail disagreement and dragged me to the barber to reinstate my shorn looks. I cried and pouted and refused to come to the dinner table. Why were these people so insistent that I maintain the status quo when there was something new out there to behold?

We fought the Elvis battle in my house daily. Sample warfare:

"How can you stand that singing?"

"Elvis is a great singer."

"Sounds like a lot of hollering and screaming to me."

"It's rock 'n' roll."

"It's garbage."

"It's Elvis."

"It's garbage."

"It is not."

"Don't you talk back to me, young man!"

"I wasn't talking back."

"You're talking back now."

"I am not."

"Turn off that music right now and go to bed. This Elvis is ruining all our children."

I suppose if it hadn't been Elvis who ruined us, it would have been something, or somebody, else. But it *was* Elvis, and it was his music that set us off on a course different from that of our parents.

"That Elvis," the old men around the stove at Cureton and Cole's would say, "ain't nothin' but a white nigger."

"Don't sing nothin' but nigger music."

"That little ol' gal of mine got to watchin' him on the teevee and he started all that movin' around like he does — look like a damn dog tryin' to hump on the back of a bitch in heat — and I made her shet him off. Ought not allow such as that on the teevee."

"Preacher preached on him last week. Said he was trash and his music was trash."

"He's ruinin' the young'uns."

The teachers at Moreland School caught one of the Turnipseed boys, I think it was Bobby Gene, shaking and humping like Elvis to the delight of a group of fifth-grade girls on the playground one morning during recess.

They took him to the principal, who paddled him and sent a note home to his parents, explaining his lewd behavior. Bobby Gene's daddy whipped him again.

"Do your Elvis for us, Bobby Gene," we said when he came back to school.

"Can't," he replied. "I'm too sore."

Bobby Gene Turnipseed may have done the best Elvis impersonation in Moreland, but each of Elvis's male followers had his own version. After my stepfather forced me to have my ducktails sheared back into a flattop, my Elvis lost a little something, but I still prided myself on the ability to lift the right side of my lip, à la Elvis's half-smile, half-snarl that sent the girls into fits of screaming and hand-clutching.

There was a girl in my Sunday School class who was a desirable young thing, and as our Sunday School teacher read our lesson one morning, I decided to do my Elvis half-smile, half-snarl for the latest object of my ardor.

Recall that we were children of church-minded people, and I was quite aware of the wages of sin. I once snitched a grape at Cureton and Cole's, and my cousin saw me and told me I was going to hell for thievery. I was so disturbed that I went back to the store and confessed my crime to Mr. J.W. Thompson, one of the owners. He was so moved by my admission of guilt that he gave me an entire sack of grapes free and assured me I'd have to steal a car or somebody's dog to qualify for eternal damnation. When my cousin asked me to share my grapes with her, I told her to go to.... Well, I ate all the grapes myself and spit the seeds at her.

Stealing grapes was one thing, but thinking unspeakable thoughts about girls while in church and curling my lip at my prepubescent Cleopatra while the lesson was being read probably would bring harsh punishment from above. I couldn't remember which thou-shalt-not such activity fell under — I wasn't certain what *covet* meant, but I figured it had something to do with wanting another boy's bicycle — so I decided to take a chance and do my Elvis lip trick at the girl anyway.

I curled up the right side of my lip perfectly as Cleo looked over at me. I didn't know what to expect. Would she absolutely *melt?* Would she want to meet me after church and go over to what was left of the abandoned cotton gin and give me kisses and squeezes?

She didn't do either. What she did was tell the Sunday School teacher I was making weird faces at her while the lesson was being read. The teacher told my mother about it, and my punishment was to read the entire book of Deuteronomy and present a report on it to the class the next Sunday. I learned a valuable lesson from all that: When you're in church, keep your mind on baseball or what you're going to have for lunch, not on something sweet and soft and perfumed wearing a sundress. Church and Evening in Paris simply don't mix.

Never one to be selfish, I attempted to share my ability to mime Elvis's facial expressions with others, especially with Little Eddie Estes. Little Eddie was a couple of years younger than me and I served as his self-appointed mentor. I taught him how to bunt, where to look in the Sears Roebuck catalog for the most scintillating pictures of women in their underpants, how to tell if a watermelon is ripe (you cut out a plug and if what you see inside is red, it's ripe), and I also attempted to instruct him in mimicking Elvis.

"What you do is this," I said to Little Eddie. "You curl your lip to the right a little bit, like the dog just did something smelly. If you want to add Elvis's movements to this, you bring one leg around like a wasp has crawled inside your pants leg, and then you move the other and groan like when your mother insists you eat boiled cabbage."

Little Eddie made a gallant attempt. He got the lip fine and he groaned perfectly, but he couldn't get the legs to shake in the correct manner.

"I couldn't shake my legs, either, when I first started doing Elvis," I told him. "What you need to do is practice in front of a mirror."

Several days later, Little Eddie's father found his son curling his lip and groaning and shaking his legs in front of a mirror in his bedroom and thought he was having some sort of seizure. His mother gave him a dose of Castor Oil and put him to bed.

* * *

I don't suppose that any generation has really understood the next, and every generation has steadfastly insisted that the younger adapt its particular values and views.

My parents' generation, true to form, sought to bring up its young in its mold, but it also had a firm resolve to do something more for us.

It was much later in my life, perhaps at a time I was feeling terribly sorry for myself and looking for a way out of that constant dilemma, that I decided my parents' generation may have endured more hardship and offered more sacrifices than any other previous generation of Americans.

So they never had to cross the Rockies in covered wagons and worry about being scalped. But my parents, both of whom were born in 1912, would live through and be directly affected by two World Wars, one Great Depression, and whatever you call Korea. And when they had been through all that, they were ushered into the Cold War and had to decide whether or not to build a fallout shelter.

It is no wonder that the men and women who came from those harried times were patriots, were traditionalists, were believers in the idea that he who worked and practiced thrift prospered, and he who allowed the sun to catch him sleeping and was wasteful perished.

These were hard people, who had lived through hard times. But they endured and the country endured, and they came away from their experiences with a deep belief in a system that had been tested but had emerged with glorious victory.

Looking back on my relationship with my own parents and with others from their generation, I think they also felt a sense of duty to their children to make certain that, at whatever cost, their children would be spared the adversity they had seen.

Have we, the Baby Boomers, not heard our parents say a thousand times, "We want you to have it better than we did"?

They wanted to protect us. They wanted to educate us. They wanted us to be doctors and lawyers and stockbrokers, not farmers and mill hands. They hounded us to study and to strive and avoid winding up in a job that paid an hourly wage. They may have mistrusted individuals their own age who had educations and who went to work wearing ties, but that's exactly what they wanted for us. And they made us feel terribly guilty if we did not share their desires.

"Have you done your homework?" my mother would ask.

"I'll do it later."

"You will do it now, young man. I don't want you winding up on the third shift at Flagg-Utica."

Flagg-Utica was a local textile plant.

"I haven't bought anything new to wear in years so I could save for your education," my mother would continue on her guilt trip, "and you don't have the gratitude to do your homework."

Somehow, I never could figure how failing to read three chapters in my geography book about the various sorts of vegetation to be found in a tropical rain forest had anything to do with facing a life as a mill hand. But with enough guilt as a catalyst, you can read anything, even geography books and Deuteronomy.

I suppose our parents also were trying to protect us when they voiced their displeasure with Elvis. They knew he was something different, too, and they were afraid of where he might lead — thinking evil thoughts about girls in Sunday School, for example.

We want you to have it better than we did, they said, and that covered just about everything. They wanted us to have money and comforts; they wanted us to have knowledge and vision; they wanted a better world for us, one free from war and bitter sacrifice.

They are old now, my parents' generation, and I suppose they think they got what they wanted. I did my homework and I got the education my mother saved for, and I live in an air-conditioned house with a microwave oven, an automatic ice-maker, and a Jenn-Air grill on the stove. I also have two color television sets with remote control, a pair of Gucci loafers, and a tennis racquet that cost more than the 1947 Chevrolet my mother once bought. I eat steak whenever I want it, I've been to Europe a couple of times and nobody shot at me, and I have a nice car.

The car. It's a perfect manifestation of having achieved the success my parents wanted for me, but such success can be bittersweet. While we're having it better than our parents did, they now may feel, in some instances, that we've actually gone further than they intended. They may suspect, as the phrase went, that we've forgotten "where we came from."

Allow me to explain.

After I got my first job out of college, I bought myself a Pontiac. Later, I bought another Pontiac, bigger and with more features than the previous one. Then I lost my head and bought one of those British roadsters that was approximately the size of a bumper car at the amusement park but not built nearly as solidly.

After the sports car had driven me sufficiently nuts, I decided to go back to a full-sized sedan, something fitting a person who was having it better than his parents did.

I got myself a Cadillac.

Nobody in my family had ever owned a Cadillac, so I figured if I had one, there could be no question that I had fulfilled my mother's wishes by making something of myself.

I had a former schoolmate who sold Cadillacs, so I went to see him and priced a couple. I couldn't have paid for the back seat, much less an entire Cadillac.

"Have you thought about leasing?" my friend asked me.

As a matter of fact, I hadn't. As a matter of fact, I never had even heard of leasing an automobile.

"It's the latest thing," said my friend, who explained that I wouldn't have to fork over any huge down payment, and for a modest (by Arab oil sheik standards) monthly installment, I could be driving around in a brand-new Cadillac.

I bit.

"You want power steering and power brakes, of course," said my friend.

"Of course."

"And do you want leather upholstery?"

"Of course."

"And how about wire wheelcovers and a sun roof?"

"Of course."

"And eight-track stereo?"

"Of course."

"Let me see if I have this straight," my friend summarized. "You want the kind of Cadillac that if you drove it home to Moreland and parked it in your mother's yard, half the town would want to come by and see it. Right?"

"But, of course," I said.

I drove my new Cadillac with the power steering and the power brakes and the leather upholstery and the wire wheelcovers and the eight-track stereo off the lot and directly home to Moreland.

"It must have been expensive," said my mother.

"Not really," I explained. "I leased it."

"Couldn't you have done just as well with a Chevrolet? I always had good luck with Chevrolets."

"I just thought it was time I got myself a Cadillac," I explained. "I've worked hard."

"I know that, son," said my mother, "but I don't want you just throwing your money away on fancy cars."

Suddenly, I felt guilty for driving up in my mother's yard in a Cadillac. I was feeling guilty because I didn't think a Chevrolet was good enough for me anymore. I could hear the old men sitting around the stove:

"Got yourself a Cadillac, huh? Boy, ain't you big-time?"

"Hey, look who got hisself a Cadillac, ol' college-boy here. Boy, where'd you learn high-falootin' things like drivin' a Cadillac? Didn't learn that from your mama, I know that. She never drove nothing but Chevrolets."

The only person who came by to see my car while I was

visiting my mother was Crazy Melvin.

"What kind of car is it?" he asked me.

"Chevrolet," I said.

"Thought so," said Crazy Melvin as he walked away.

Guilt was a very big part of my generation's adult life. If you didn't do well enough, you were guilty because you'd let your parents down. But if you did too well, and came home driving a Cadillac and wearing sunglasses, you felt guilty because you obviously had forgotten your roots and had turned into a big-city high-roller that you had no business turning into.

The old men at the store: "You drivin' that Cadillac is like puttin' a ten dollar saddle on a thousand dollar horse."

Despite the Cadillac, which now has more than 100,000 miles on it and is five years old (I figure if I drive it long enough, my mother will appreciate the sound common sense I used in not trading for a new car until my old one was completely worn out), despite the education, despite all the gadgetry I own, despite the fact that I didn't wind up on the third shift at Flagg-Utica, I'm not so certain that I *am* having it better than my parents' generation did.

Let me clarify this point: I wouldn't have wanted to go through World Wars and the Great Depression, and I like my creature comforts and the cruise control on my car, but did my parents ever have to eat a plastic breakfast at McDonald's while some guy mopped under their table spreading the aroma of ammonia?

Did they ever have to fight five o'clock traffic on a freeway when they were my age? Did they ever have to worry about getting herpes? Couldn't they eat bacon and all those other foods that are supposed to give me everything from St. Vitus Dance to cancer without worrying?

Did they ever have to put up with calling somebody and getting a recorded message? Did they ever have to make their own salads in restaurants or pump their own gasoline at exorbitant prices in gasoline stations? Didn't they get free glasses when they bought gas, and didn't the attendant always wash their windshield and check their oil without being asked?

Did my parents' generation go to movies and not understand them at all? Did they ever have to deal with women's liberation, gay rights, the Moral Majority, the anti-nuke movement, a dozen kinds of racism, palimony, sex discrimination suits, and Phil Donahue making you wonder if you really have any business on this planet anymore?

Did they have to endure Valley Girls, punk rock, rock videos, the "moonwalk," break dancing, ghetto blasters, and "The Catlins"?

So their kids worshipped Elvis. My generation's children follow Michael Jackson, who wears one glove and his sunglasses at night, and sings songs with names like "Beat It." It also is rumored that he takes female hormones to nullify his voice change. I cannot verify this, but there are rumors he recently was seen hanging his panty hose on a shower rod. My generation's children also follow something called "Culture Club," which features something called Boy George, who dresses like Zasu Pitts.

My parents' generation had Roosevelt for a president. We had Nixon.

They won their war. We lost ours.

They knew exactly what their roles in family and society were. Most of us don't have any idea what ours are anymore.

They had corns on their toes. We have identity crises.

They got married first and then lived together. We do it

just the opposite today.

They fell in love. We fall, or try to, into meaningful relationships.

Did Lou Gehrig use cocaine? Did Jack Benny freebase? Did Barbara Stanwyck get naked on the silver screen? Did they have to put up with Jane Fonda?

I obviously can't speak for all of us, but here is one Baby Boomer who liked it better when it was simpler. My parents sent me out into this world to make for myself a better life than they had and maybe I achieved that in some way. But the everlasting dilemma facing me is that although I live in a new world, I was reared to live in the old one.

I remain the patriot they taught me to be. I like music you can whistle to. If ever I marry again, it will have to be to a woman who will cook. She can be a lawyer or work construction in the daytime, and she can have her own bank account and wear a coat and tie for all I care, but I want a home-cooked meal occasionally where absolutely nothing has passed through a microwave.

I don't understand the gay movement. I don't care if you make love to Nash Ramblers, as long as you're discreet about it.

I don't use drugs, and I don't understand why anybody else does as long as there's cold beer around.

I think computers are dangerous, men who wear earrings are weird, the last thing that was any good on television was "The Andy Griffith Show," and I never thought Phyllis George had any business talking about football with Brent Musberger on television.

In his classic song, "Are the Good Times Really Over for Good?", Merle Haggard says it best:

"Wish Coke was still cola,
A joint, a bad place to be ...
It was back before Nixon lied to us all on TV ...
Before microwave ovens, when a girl could still cook and still
would ...
Is the best of the free life behind us now,
Are the good times really over for good?"

My sentiments exactly. If I could have the good times back, I would bring back 1962. At least, most of it. I was sixteen then. I had my driver's license, a blonde girlfriend, and my mother awakened me in the mornings and fed me at night.

Elvis was still singing, Kennedy was still president, Sandy Koufax was still pitching, John Wayne was still acting, Arnold Palmer was still winning golf tournaments, you could still get hand-cut french fries in restaurants, there was no such thing as acid rain or Three Mile Island, men got their hair cut in barber shops and women got theirs cut at beauty parlors, there was no such person as Calvin Klein, nobody used the word *psychedelic*, nobody had ever heard of Vietnam, and when nobody bombed anybody during the Cuban Missile Crisis, I was convinced that the world was probably safe from nuclear annihilation ... an idea I do not hold to with much force anymore.

1962. It was a beauty.

So what happened to the simple life the boys from Moreland knew? And when did all the change begin?

I think I can answer the second question. It was one morning in November, 1963, and I was changing classes in high school.

Camelot In Bloody Ruin

L "*ET THE WORD go forth from this time and place... that the torch has been passed to a new generation of Americans....*"
John F. Kennedy, January 20, 1961

There was one family of Catholics in Moreland in 1960. They had to drive ten miles to the county seat to go to church. I didn't think there was anything particularly different about them except that on Fridays, when the rest of us were attempting to force down what they said was meatloaf but tasted like Alpo looks, the kids from the Catholic family were eating what appeared to be a tasty serving of fried fish. Had it not been for the fact that it would have put the good Methodists and Baptists in my family into shock and running fits, I might have become a Catholic, too, just to avoid the Friday meatloaf.

The adults in town didn't trust Catholics. One of the old men down at the store said he heard they stole babies. Somebody else said Catholics drank a lot, and half the time they didn't even speak English when they were holding church services.

John Kennedy frightened the local voting bloc, perhaps a hundred-or-so strong. He was Catholic and his daddy was rich, and despite the fact we're talking lifelong Democrats here, they were having a difficult time accepting the idea that a person with religious beliefs so foreign to their own might actually occupy the White House.

The old men around the stove:

"I ain't sure we ought to elect no Cathlic."

"I ain't votin' for him. He'd take all his orders from the Vaddican."

"The what?"

"The Vaddican."

"Where's that?"

"Itly."

"Reckon that's so?"

"'Course it's so. Them Cathlics stick together like buttermilk sticks to your chin."

"You ever know'd any Cathlics?"

"Naw, but I think one come in the truckstop a week or so ago."

"How'd you know it was a Cathlic?"

"He's wearing a white shirt. Who else 'round here wears white shirts?"

If Elvis was the first break between the Baby Boomers and their parents, then John Kennedy — at least in rural Georgia, which was my only horizon at the time — was a second. Kennedy never started the youthful explosion that Elvis had, but there was something about the man that appealed to us. It was later described as "vigah." Although I was too young to vote in the 1960 presidential election, I did my part to elect Kennedy by running down Richard Nixon.

I was born under Truman and then came Ike. The General was okay, but I didn't like the way Nixon, his vice president for eight years, looked even then. He already had those jowls, and when he talked, it seemed like his mouth was full of spit and he needed to swallow.

I also was never able to understand how Nixon fathered any children, because I was convinced he slept in his suit. I suspect Richard Nixon was born wearing a tiny little suit and tie, and his aunts and uncles probably stood around his crib and looked at his beady little eyes and at his jowls — I'm sure he was born with them, too — and said things like, "Well, let's hope and pray he grows out of it."

He didn't, of course. The older he got, the shiftier he looked, and that's why Kennedy beat him in 1960. When they debated, Nixon looked like a 1952 Ford with a busted tailpipe and foam rubber dice hanging off his rear-view mirror; Kennedy was a Rolls Royce in comparison.

All the girls at school liked Kennedy, too. "He's sooo cute," was their usual adept analysis of his platform.

Historians who have looked back on the brief thousand days that John Kennedy was our president have failed to note that Kennedy did, in fact, accomplish an important feat with his looks. Remember his hair? John Kennedy's hair was sort of fluffy. Nixon probably greased his down with whatever it was I used to slick down my ducktails.

In the early 1960s, most men were still using Vitalis and Wildroot Creme Oil on their hair. But I don't think John Kennedy used anything like that on his. In fact, Kennedy may have been the first American male to show off "The Dry Look." It was only a few years after Kennedy became president that we celebrated the death of "The Wethead," and American men poured their hair tonic down the drain and spent millions on blow-dryers and hairspray.

Looks are important to a president, and Kennedy was the most handsome American president since Andrew Jackson — who wasn't any Tom Selleck, but at least he didn't have one of those cherub-looking faces like John Quincy Adams, and he didn't wear a powdered wig.

Look at the appearances of our presidents over the years. The pictures of George Washington that were in our history books made the father of our country look like somebody's sweet little grandmother. Abraham Lincoln was no day at the beach, either, and Rutherford B. Hayes had that long scraggly beard, and William Taft was fat. FDR was fairly handsome, but he used that long cigarette holder that made him appear a bit stuffy, I thought. Truman wore funny hats and bow ties, and Eisenhower was militarily rigid and grandfatherly.

John Kennedy, however, *was* the torchbearer for the new generation. If the times were Camelot, then he was certainly Arthur. He seemed more of an admired, understanding big brother to us than an awesome patriarch ruling from some distant perch.

The youth of the early sixties knew little of the system, other than what we had learned in Civics class, but here was a man with whom we were able to relate — if not to his substance, then most certainly to his style.

The Cuban Missile Crisis brought us even closer to him. He told the Russians where he wanted them to stick their missiles and in the meantime created several marvelously exciting days at my high school. I didn't pay a great deal of attention to the crisis at first. Basketball practice had started, and that had me too occupied to consider the end of the world as we knew it.

I was in Jacobs's Drug Store in Newnan eating a banana split the night the president went on television in October of 1962 and told the nation that we were about this far from having to sink a few Russian ships and maybe start World War III. I hesitated and watched and listened for a few moments, but then I went back to the banana split.

The next day at school, however, our principal, Mr. O.P. Evans, called the student body together and began to prepare us for the nuclear attack he seemed certain would come before the noon lunch bell.

Mr. Evans was a tall, forceful man with a deep, booming voice that was a fearful and commanding thing. He ran the school with a Bible in one hand and a paddle in the other. The school was his passion, and even an imminent nuclear attack would not deter him from making certain that we would be a model of order until the last one of us had been melted into a nuclear ash.

We were told that when (I don't think he ever mentioned an "if" anywhere) the call came to Mr. Evans's office (probably directly from Washington) to inform him that the bombs and missiles were on the way, we would be hastened back to assembly for further instructions. At that point, a decision would be made on whether or not to close school and send us home. In the event we could not safely evacuate, we would remain at school and be given subsequent assignments as to where we would bed down for the night.

That idea caused a great stirring of interest among the boys. Would we get to sleep near the girls? Could we slip around and perhaps catch them in nothing but their underpants? Bring on the bombs and missiles. Mr. Evans quickly dashed our hopes, however, by stating that the boys would be herded to the gymnasium, while the girls would sleep at the other end of the school in the cafeteria and the student activities room, where the Coke and candy machines were also located, damn the luck.

He instructed us to bring canned goods to store in our lockers the following day, presuming there was one, in case the school ran out of food and we had to spend the winter inside the building waiting for the fallout to subside. Students also were to bring blankets and soap, an extra toothbrush, and a change of clothes and underwear. The sacks of clothes and underwear were stored on the stage in the assembly room. Having been shut out of actually getting to see our female classmates down to their skivvies, a group of us went for the next best thing and sneaked into the assembly room during the post-lunch rest period and went through the sacks trying to match girls with panties and bras.

The possibility of an attack did lose some of its glamour, however, when Mr. Evans further announced that as long as a single teacher survived, classes would continue and gum chewing would remain a capital offense.

The attack never came, of course, but we did find out that Gayle Spangler, who always was going off to Atlanta on weekends and was allegedly keeping company with college boys and going to wild fraternity parties, had a pair of panties with the 1962 Georgia Tech football schedule printed on the crotch.

John Kennedy was hailed as a conqueror after backing down the Russians and their missiles, but the triumphant mood of the country was short-lived. One moment Camelot was there, and the next it lay in bloody ruin.

It was the autumn of my senior year. November, 1963. I

was changing morning classes. I had just finished Spanish, which I hated. I particularly hated those silly records they played to us in Spanish class.

"El burro es un animal de Mexico, Espana, y Norte Americana, tambien. Repeata, por favor."

Thirty students with heavy Southern accents would repeat: "El boorow ez uhn anymahl de Mexeecoh, Espainya, why Gnawertee Amuricainya, tambiann."

I was strolling down the hallway toward geometry class. Something was happening. The teachers had come out into the hall and were herding students into classrooms.

"Don't go to your next class. Come into my room. Quickly," said a teacher to me.

The halls were cleared. There was an eerie silence. Is the place on fire? Have the Russians decided to attack after all? Has somebody been caught chewing gum? I noticed the teacher sitting in the desk in front of me. She was holding back tears.

The voice. I had heard that powerful voice so many times, but now it seemed to crack and strain.

"Your attention, please," said Mr. Evans over the intercom. "We have just received word that President John Kennedy has been shot in Dallas. We have no other word at this time. May we all bow our heads in prayer."

I can't remember Mr. Evans's prayer word-for-word. It's been more than twenty years. But I think I can still manage its essence:

"Gawd, Our Father. We beseech Thee. A brilliant young leader has been shot. He is a man we love. He is a man

we trust. He is our president. Our Father, we beseech
Thee now to rest Your gentle hand upon this man and to
spare him, O Gawd. Spare him, so that he can continue to
lead us, to guide us, to keep us safe from our enemies,
to show us how to make our country even greater, to bring
justice to all our people, to make for these students,
who soon will go out into the world alone, a safe and
shining place to live and work and grow fruitful. Spare
John Kennedy, O Gawd. Spare our beloved president.
Amen."

We raised our heads. No one spoke. Some of the girls cried.

"Maybe it's not true," somebody finally said.

"It's true," said someone else, "or Mr. Evans wouldn't have stopped classes for it."

All doubt then faded. It *was* true.

We waited. I don't know how long we waited. Maybe it was seconds. Maybe it was minutes. Finally, the voice came back again.

"Students and faculty of Newnan High School," Mr. Evans began, "President John Fitzgerald Kennedy is dead."

The class idiot was Harley Doakes, whose father hated Kennedy because he had wanted to desegregate the schools. When Mr. Evans announced that the president was dead, Harley Doakes cheered. Somebody in the back of the room threw a book at him and called him a stupid son of a bitch.

* * *

Nothing was the same after that. Ever again. I trace my world going completely bananas back to that single moment when the shots first cracked in Dallas.

What, if anything, has made any sense since? John Kennedy was dead and we were left with Lyndon Johnson, who was low enough to pick up a dog by its ears. He proceeds to get us involved up to *our* ears in Vietnam, and when he finally decides he's had enough, here comes Nixon again. Why wouldn't this man just go away?

I had all sorts of trouble trying to decide who I wanted to be president in 1972. Picking between Richard Nixon and George McGovern was like picking between sores in your mouth or a bad case of hemorrhoids. I wanted Nixon out, but I didn't want McGovern in.

McGovern was the hippie candidate. I had been raised a patriot. I reluctantly voted for Nixon. I admit he did a few things. He opened China, although I'm still not sure what good it did. If you've seen one Chinese urn, you've seen them all; I still don't know how to use chopsticks; and I never did like sweet and sour pork.

It was under Nixon that Vietnam finally came to a merciful end, of course, and there was that marvelous, moving moment when the POW's came home, but it was impossible for me to put heroic garb on Richard Nixon. There always was the nagging feeling each time I saw him or listened to him that he was somehow putting a Bobby Entrekin shuck on me.

Watergate was all I needed. There I had been a decade earlier — a high school senior with a crew cut and even clearer-cut ideals and values. Then the president is shot, and next comes Vietnam, and then somebody shoots Robert Kennedy, and Martin Luther King is gunned down, and another assassin puts George Wallace in a wheelchair for life. And on top of that, we find out the current president is, indeed, a crook (not to mention a liar with a filthy mouth) and he's run out of office practically on a rail.

I no longer had any idea what to believe or whom to trust. I was nearing thirty, and practically every sacred cow I had known had been butchered in one way or another.

Nothing was the same anymore. I had seen students burning campus buildings and students being gunned down on campuses by National Guardsmen.

I had been divorced once by then and was working on a second. Half the country was smoking dope. Gasoline was four times what it had cost before. Men were growing their hair over their ears and wearing double-knit trousers.

And they weren't singing the old songs anymore, either. In fact, it was soon after the death of John Kennedy that the music headed somewhere I didn't want to go.

If Elvis was a break between me and my parents and my roots, then it was The Beatles who forced me back toward them.

5 Where Rock 'n' Roll Went Wrong

A S MOST MUSIC historians know, soon after Elvis became the undisputed King, Colonel Tom Parker hid him out for nearly the next two decades. The only time we were able to see him was at a rare concert or in one of those idiotic movies he began making, such as *Viva Las Vegas,* which featured Elvis singing and mouthing ridiculous dialogue while several dozen scantily-clad starlets cooed and wiggled. Today, Elvis movies normally are shown very late at night after the adults have gone to bed, so they won't be embarrassed in front of their children.

However, the rock 'n' roll storm that Elvis started did not subside after he took leave of the public. As a matter of fact, the music flourished and reached new heights, and when it got its own television show, our parents' battle to save us from what some had considered a heathen sound was over. They had lost.

Dick Clark was apparently a very mature nine-year-old when he first appeared on "American Bandstand," because that has been nearly thirty years ago and he still doesn't look like he has darkened the doors to forty.

Bandstand. I wouldn't miss it for free Scrambler rides and cotton candy at the county fair. The music they were playing was *our* music, and the dances they were dancing were *our* dances. It was live on television, and Philadelphia, from whence Bandstand came, was the new center of our universe. (Previously, it had been Atlanta, where our parents occasionally took us to see the building where they kept all the things you could order from the Sears Roebuck catalog, and to wrestling matches and gospel singings.)

Danny Thompson and I always watched Bandstand together in the afternoons. Danny was not nearly the geographical wizard I was (I had been born seventy-five miles from Moreland in Ft. Benning, Georgia, and had traveled as far away as Arkansas as the quintessential Army brat before my parents had divorced) so anything that had to do with where some place was, Danny asked me.

"Where is Philadelphia, anyway?" he queried one afternoon as we watched the kids on Bandstand do the Hop to Danny and the Juniors's "At the Hop."

"Pennsylvania," I told him.

"How far is that?"

"Thousands of miles."

"Wish I could go."

"To see Bandstand?"

"See it up close."

"Wish we lived in Philadelphia."

"We'd go on Bandstand every day, wouldn't we?"

Besides the music, Danny and I enjoyed watching Bandstand in order to select objects of lust from the group of Philadelphia girls who were regulars. I picked out a blonde with large breasts. Her name was Annette something-or-other. Danny picked out a raven-haired beauty named Shirley, who chewed gum; we could never tell exactly how she voted when she rated a record because in the first place she talked funny, being from Philadelphia, and secondly it's difficult to discern what someone is saying when they're saying it through three sticks of Juicy Fruit gum.

We spent hours discussing whether or not, at their advanced ages of probably sixteen, they were engaging in any sort of sexual activity off camera.

"Wonder if Annette and Shirley do it?"

"I bet Annette does."

"Why?"

"She's got blonde hair. Blondes do it more than other girls."

"How do you know that?"

"My cousin told me. He said you see a girl who's blonde, and she'll do it."

"I'd like to do it with Annette."

"I'd like to do it with Shirley."

"Shirley's got black hair."

"I'd still like to do it with her."

"I'd give a hundred dollars to do it with Annette."

"I'd give two hundred to do it with Shirley."

"You don't have two hundred dollars."

"I could get it."

"How?"

"Sell my bicycle."

"You'd sell your bicycle to do it with Shirley?"

"You wouldn't sell yours to do it with Annette?"

"Maybe I would."

Of course, I would have. The desire to do it strikes young

in boys, and the delicious idea of doing it with a Bandstand regular was my first real sexual fantasy (which must be accepted as proof of our parents' fears that interest in rock 'n' roll did, indeed, prompt the sexual juices to flow).

* * *

The music was good back then. There were The Drifters, and The Penguins, and Paul and Paula, and Barbara Lewis, and Mary Wells, and Clyde McPhatter; and Sam Cook sang about the men workin' on the "chain ga-e-yang." We had Bobby Helms doing "Special Angel," and there was Jerry Butler talking about his days getting shorter and his nights getting longer. There were great songs like "A Little Bit of Soap" and "Duke of Earl" and Ernie Kado singing about his mother-in-law.

We danced and held each other close and took two steps forward and one back to "In the Still of the Night," and later we shagged to beach music — The Tams, The Showmen — and we twisted with Chubby Checker and did the Monkey with Major Lance. We had the soul sounds of James Brown — "Mr. Dynamite, Mr. Please Please Me Himself, the Hardest Workin' Man in Show Business" — and Jackie Wilson sang "Lonely Teardrops," and Marvin Gaye did "Stubborn Kind of Fellow," and Maurice Williams and the Zodiacs did "Stay." And I don't want to leave out Fats (Antoine) Domino and Chuck Berry and Joe Tex and Bobby Blue Bland and Soloman Burke and Jimmy Reed moaning over radio station WLAC, Gallatin, Tennessee, brought to you by John R., the Jivin' Hoss Man, and Ernie's Record Mart and White Rose Petroleum Jelly, with "a thousand-and-one different uses, and you know what that one is for, girl."

There were a thousand singers for a thousand songs. It was truly an enchanted time. But then ever-so-slowly yet ever-so-suddenly, it changed. It seemed that one day Buddy Holly died, and the next day The Beatles were in Shea Stadium.

I'm not certain what it was that caused me to reject The Beatles from the start, but I suspect that even then I saw them as a portent of ill changes that soon would arise — not only in music, but in practically everything else I held dear.

The Beatles got off to a bad start with me because the first thing I heard them sing in 1964 was "I Wanna Hold Your Hand," and it was basically impossible to do any of the dances I knew — the Shag, the Mashed Potato, the Monkey, the Pony, the Gator, the Fish, the Hitchhike, the Twist, or the Virginia Reel— to that first song. About all you could do to "I Wanna Hold Your Hand" was jump and stomp and scream, which, of course, is what every female teeny-bopper at the time was doing whenever The Beatles struck guitar and drum and opened their mouths.

Also, patriot that I was, I stood four-square against the importation of foreign music, just as I have since stood steadfastly against the importation of Japanese cars and Yugoslavian placekickers. The only materials we really need to import from foreign countries, in my way of thinking, are porno movies. It doesn't matter that you can't understand what anybody is saying in those movies anyway, and I like the imagination of, say, the French when it comes to doing interesting things while naked.

But the British? I still have problems with them, especially with the current royal family. I'm sick and tired of Lady Di getting pregnant, I don't care if Prince Andrew is dating Marilyn Chambers, and every time the Queen comes to the U.S., she is always getting offended by something a well-meaning colonist has done to her. I wish she would stay in Buckingham Palace and give the Cisco Kid his hat back.

Even then, I didn't like the way The Beatles looked. I thought their hair was too long, I didn't like those silly-looking suits with the skinny ties they wore, and Ringo reminded me of the ugliest boy in my school, Grady "The Beak" Calhoun, whose nose was so big that when he tried to look sideways he couldn't see out of but one eye. Grady was a terrible hitter on the baseball team because his nose blocked half of his vision.

Soon after The Beatles arrived in the U.S., I started college. At the fraternity house, we were able to hold on to our music for a time. The jukebox was filled with the old songs, and when we hired a band, we had black bands whose music you could dance to and spill beer out of your Humdinger milkshake cup on your date. The Four Tops and The Temptations, The Isley Brothers and Doug Clark and the Hot Nuts, and Percy Sledge (which always sounded to me like something that might clog your drain) were still in demand at college campuses — at least all over the South. A few white bands were still in vogue as well, the most notable of which was The Swinging Medallions. They sang "Double Shot of My Baby's Love," and even now when I hear that song, it makes me want to go stand outside in the hot sun with a milkshake cup full of beer in one hand and a slightly-drenched nineteen-year-old coed in the other.

But the music, our music, didn't last. At least, it didn't remain dominant. Elvis's music was switched to country stations, and every wormy-looking kid with a guitar in England turned up in the United States, and rock 'n' roll meant something entirely different to us all of a sudden.

I didn't like the new sounds or the new people who were making them. I found The Rolling Stones disgusting and The Dave Clark Five about a handful short.

Suddenly came the dissent associated with the Vietnam escalation, and with that came hippies and flower children. And one day I found myself (just as my own parents had done when Elvis peaked) condemning modern music as the hedonistic, un-American, ill-tempered, God-awful, indecent warblings of scrungy, tatooed, long-haired, uncouth, drugged-out, so-called musicians.

I didn't know Jimi Hendrix was alive until he overdosed and died, and I thought Janis Joplin was Missouri's entry in the Miss America pageant.

All the new groups had such odd names. There was Bread, and Cream, for instance. And there was Jefferson Airplane and Iron Butterfly and Grand Funk Railroad and a group named Traffic. I wondered why so many groups were named after various modes of transportation. I theorized that it was because those performers had all been deprived of electric trains as children.

I expected the members of musical groups to wear the same clothing when they performed — like white suits with white tails — and to do little steps together like "The Temptation Walk."

These new groups, however, apparently wore whatever they found in the dirty clothes hamper each morning before a performance. T-shirts and filthy jeans seemed to be the most popular garb. Some, of course, performed without shirts. I found this to be particularly disturbing, since I have no use whatsoever for any music made by a person who looks as if he has just come in the house from mowing the grass on an August afternoon and his wife won't let him sit down on the good furniture because he'll sweat all over it and probably cause mildew.

I didn't like drug songs and anti-war songs, and I didn't like songs that were often downright explicit. Even The Beatles just wanted to hold somebody's hand. The new groups, however, wanted to take off all their clothes, get in the bed, smoke a bunch of dope, and do all sorts of French things that have no business being watched, discussed, or sung about outside a porno flick on the sleazy side of town.

The only piece of raw rock 'n' roll we ever knew about before The Beatles came along was a song by The Kingsmen called "Louie, Louie," and we really weren't certain that what they were saying about "Louie, Louie" wasn't just a rumor.

It was basically impossible to understand the words, except the part which went, "Louie, Lou-eye, Ohhhhh, baby, we gotta go." After that, it sounded like, "Evahni ettin, Ah fackon nin."

The smart money had it, however, that if you slowed the record down from 45 RPM to 33 RPM, you could make out some of the words and that the song was really about doing something quite filthy. Naturally, we all rushed home to slow down the record. I still couldn't make out any of the words. It simply sounded like I was hearing the bass portion of "Evahni ettin, Ah fackon nin."

I made myself a vow never to spend money on any of this new music. But as naive as I was concerning what was taking place in my once placid, sensible world, I was bound to break my vow. I did so by attending an Elton John concert ... completely by mistake.

I was dating a girl who was several years younger than me. I was in my late twenties at the time, but she could still remember where everybody sat in her high school algebra class.

"What do you want to do Friday night?" I vividly recall asking this young woman.

"Elton John is in town," she said.

"He's somebody you went to school with?" I asked, in all honesty.

"You've never heard of Elton John?" she said, an unmistakable tinge of amazement in her voice.

"Well, I've been working pretty hard and...."

"Elton John is a wonderful entertainer. You would love him."

She was a lovely child and had big blue eyes, so I managed to purchase excellent tickets for the Elton John concert — third row from the stage.

I had never been to a concert by anybody even remotely connected with modern rock music. As a matter of fact, the only concert I had been to in years was one that Jerry Lee Lewis gave. "The Killer" came out and did all his hits, and everybody drank beer and had a great time. I didn't see more than a dozen fights break out the entire night.

What I didn't know about attending an Elton John concert was that Elton didn't come on stage until his warm-up group had finished its act. I don't remember the name of the group that opened the show, but I do remember that they were louder than a train wreck.

When I was able to catch a word here and there in one of their songs, it sounded like the singer was screaming (as in pain) in an English accent. One man beat on a drum; another, who wasn't wearing a shirt, played guitar. They were very pale-looking individuals.

"What's the name of this group?" I tried to ask my date

over the commotion. I heard her say, "Stark Naked and the Car Thieves." I thought that was a strange name, even for an English rock group, so between numbers I asked her again. Turned out I had misunderstood her; their real name was "Clark Dead Boy and the Bereaved."

"So what was the name of that song?" I pursued.

"'Kick Me Out of My Rut'," she answered. I was having trouble hearing, however; my eardrums had gone into my abdomen to get away from the noise. I thought she said, "Kick Me Out on My Butt."

After the next number, I asked her to name that tune, too.

"It's called 'I Can Smell Your Love on Your Breath'."

That's what she said, but what I heard was, "Your Breath Smells Like a Dog Died in Your Mouth," which sounded a great deal like "Kick Me Out on My Butt."

Finally, Elton John came out. He wore an Uncle Sam suit and large sunglasses.

"Is this man homosexual?" I asked my date.

"Bisexual," she answered.

That must come in handy when he has to go to the bathroom, I thought to myself. If there's a line in one, he can simply walk across to the other.

I had no idea what Elton John was singing about, but at least he didn't sing it as loudly as did Stark Naked and the Car Thieves.

As the concert wore on, I began to smell a strange aroma.

"I think somebody's jeans are on fire," I said. "Do you smell that?"

"It's marijuana," said my date. "Everybody has a hit when they come to an Elton John concert."

I looked around me. My fellow concert-goers, some of

whom weren't as old as my socks, were staring bleary-eyed at the stage. Down each row, handmade cigarettes were passed back and forth. Even when the cigarettes became very short, the people continued to drag on them.

Suddenly, down my row came one of the funny cigarettes. My date took it in hand, took a deep puff, held in the smoke, then passed it to me.

"No thanks," I said. "I think I'll go to the concession stand and get a beer."

"Go ahead," said my date. "It'll loosen you up."

This was my moment of decision. I had never tried marijuana before. I had never even seen any up close, but now here I sat holding some, listening to a bisexual Englishman wearing an Uncle Sam suit sing songs I didn't understand. I was completely lost in this maze and wanted to bolt from the concert hall and go immediately to where there was a jukebox, buy myself a longneck beer, and play a truck-driving son by Dave Dudley — something I could understand.

I looked at the marijuana cigarette again. Would I have an irresistible urge to rape and pillage if I took a drag?

It was very short. "You need a roach clip," said my date.

"There're bugs in this stuff?" I asked.

"When a joint is short like that, it's called a roach," she explained, pulling a bobby pin from her purse. "Hold it with this."

I took the pin in one hand and clipped it on the cigarette I was holding in the other.

"Take a good deep drag and hold it in," said my date.

"Suck it or send it down," said somebody at the end of my row.

I continued to look at the roach. The smoke got into my

eyes and they began to burn. Suddenly, to my horror, I noticed the fire at the end of the roach was missing. It had become dislodged from the clip and had rolled down between my legs. I quickly reached between my rear and the seat cushion to find it, lest I set the entire arena aflame.

"Hey, man," yelled the insistent one down the row, "where's that joint?"

"It's down here," I said, stooping over like a fool with my hand between my legs, searching for what was left of the marijuana.

"Groovy, man," he said. "I never thought of sticking it there."

Mercifully, Elton John finally completed his concert and I was free to leave.

"Well," said my date when we were in the car, "wasn't he great?"

"Save the fact that I burned a hole in the seat of my pants, burned my eyes from all the smoke, and lost partial hearing in both ears from attempting to listen to a nuclear explosion from the third row back, I suppose it wasn't all that bad."

"Good," she answered. "Let's go hear Reggae next. What do you think of Reggae?"

"I think he's the most overpaid outfielder in baseball," I answered.

That was our last date.

* * *

I honestly didn't think that the music and the people who made it could get worse than it was during the seventies, but again my naiveté was showing. What currently is regarded as "rock" is totally beyond me, especially when I'm switching around on my cable TV and come across one of those music video things.

In the first place, I don't understand what anybody is singing about. I heard a song on a video channel that was, appropriately enough, entitled "Radio."

The lyrics went like this:

"Radio. Radio. Radio.
Radio. Radio. Radio.
Radio. Radio. Radio."

An eleven-year-old child with a stuttering problem, I'm convinced, wrote that song.

Secondly, I do not understand what these people are doing when they're singing their songs on videos. I see people dressed like chickens, people singing while standing on their heads, and people — perhaps I'm using that term too loosely — diving into swimming pools filled with green Jell-O while they're still singing those songs. Every video I've ever seen has reminded me of the nightmares I have after eating too much Mexican food. It's music to throw-up by, I suppose.

I thought the names of the groups and the names of the songs were strange in the seventies, but the eighties have brought total insanity to popular music.

There are groups now like ZZ Top, The Cars, The Dead Kennedys, the B-52's, Run D.M.C., Duke Jupiter, Blond Ambition, Wall of Voodoo, The Cramps, The Razors, The Swimming Pool Q's, Modern Mannequins, Future Reference, The Divorcees, The Pigs, The Fabulous Knobs, Outa Hand, Late Bronze Age, Go Van Go, Riff-Raff, St. Vitus Dance, Kodac Harrison and Contraband, Subterraneans,

Corn, and Wee-Wee Pole.

Wee-Wee Pole? Now, somebody had to think of that name, and my imagination runs in all sorts of directions considering what prompted such a title for an alleged musical group. What comes to my mind first is this scene: There are a few guys snorting airplane glue or something in the back of their van, and one of 'em says, "Hey, why don't we start a band?", sort of a modern-day version of Mickey Rooney's Andy Hardy saying to Judy Garland and the gang, "Hey, why don't we give a show?"

Two other guys think this is a terrific idea, despite the fact that none of them has any musical talent whatsoever, which is no longer important if you want to start a band. The first order of business is to figure out what to call yourselves.

Before they can decide on a name, one of the guys indicates he needs to go to the bathroom, which reminds the others they need to do the same. So the entire group goes outside the van and begins to wee-wee on the first thing they see, which happens to be a telephone pole. The rest is history.

I seem to notice a pattern in names for rock groups today. The names usually either have to do with some sort of animal (The Pigs), something that doesn't make any sense whatsoever (Run D.M.C.) or something totally distasteful or vulgar (The Dead Kennedys and The Cramps).

If this is such a hot item, I would like to get into the business of naming rock groups myself. I likely could make a lot of money doing it, perhaps even start some sort of service. You send me twenty bucks, and I'll come up with a name for your rock group that will embarrass your parents to the point that they'll wish they'd come along when birth control was more widely accepted.

For groups that wanted animal names, I'd have Hog Wild and the Pork Bellies, Rabid Raccoon, Dead Dog and the Bloated Five, and Squid.

For names of rock groups that didn't make any sense whatsoever, the selection would include Oshkosh Ice Cream, Polished Cement, Snarknavel, and MDC Gravel.

In the totally disgusting and vulgar category, you could select from Umbilical Dan and the Chords, Potato Poothead, Battery Acid, Rat Poison, Willie and the Warts, and The Dingleberry Five.

You don't think things could ever get that weird with modern music? Of course, they can. Of course, they will. We've already got Michael Jackson, who sings a lot higher than Mahalia and probably lost his other glove doing something strange with Brooke Shields. (I once opined in another forum that if they ever made a remake of *Gone With the Wind,* Michael Jackson would make a perfect Butterfly McQueen's "Prissy.")

And then there's Boy George and Culture Club, of course. I've seen more culture on buttermilk.

Recently I heard a great curse: "May the next skirt you chase be worn by Boy George." What I want to know is, Does he shave his legs and have a period?

I have a theory about where all these people who make today's rock music came from. Remember when you were in high school and there were always a bunch of kids who were really thin and wormy, back when "punk" meant somebody who had a lot of zits and hung around playing pinball machines and never got asked to parties and never had dates and never played sports?

Well, they all grew up to be rock stars. That's what happened to them. It's the revenge of the nerds.

As much as I despise today's rock music, I must admit that it is even more popular with today's youth than Elvis's music was with my generation. I base this statement on the fact that I could go fifteen minutes to eat or to take a bath or to walk to school or to ride a bus without listening to my music. Kids today can't do that, so they have given the term portable radio an entirely new meaning. I'm talking about, of course, the Sony Walkman and the Ghetto Blaster Age that we are presently living through.

The Sony Walkman, I can take. Some adults even use these machines (which mercifully include earphones so nobody else will be disturbed) to listen to educational tapes and soft music that will put them to sleep in airplanes. I cannot resist the urge, however, when I see somebody tuned out of the regular world and tuned in to a taped version to ask, "What's the score?"

But ghetto blasters — which generally are about the size of a five-hundred-watt radio station — are something else entirely. Young people should be allowed to listen to any sort of music they like, but I shouldn't have to listen to it with them.

When I hear indecipherable music played two decibels above the sound the 4:15 flight to Cleveland makes when it takes off, it makes me nervous, unable to concentrate. And it eventually makes me angry enough to take the ghetto blaster from which the noise is emanating and stomp on it, even if doing so might mean having to defend my life against the owner, who suddenly has been deprived of something to get down on the street and dance on his head to.

Young people play their ghetto blasters on city streets where people with jobs are trying to have nervous breakdowns in peace. They play them on various forms of public transportation. They play them in fast-food restaurants or any time there is somebody else around to offend and render deaf.

There are laws against cursing in public, against spitting in public, against wee-weeing on telephone poles in public, and there should be laws against playing ghetto blasters in public.

* * *

This calamitous change in music, that began in the late sixties and has continued to the point of today's strange lyrics and stranger people, left me with a choice: Either I could totally change my tastes and my way of thinking and follow this metamorphosis, or I could look elsewhere and hope to find musical solace for the soul in another area.

I was lucky, in retrospect, to have had that second choice. The rock 'n' roll I knew was gone; I had absolutely no taste for music sung by fat ladies with high voices in a language I didn't understand; I have never liked any music where any part of it was made by an oboe or flute; I didn't mind a little Big Band now and then, and I could enjoy Sinatra on occasion, but that was my parents' music. Were it not for yet another choice, I might easily have become a musical orphan.

The war in Vietnam and the war against it at home were raging, and Americans had to pick a side. There were doves and flower children on one side and hawks and the guys at the VFW on the other. One kind of music raged against the war, while another kind was saying, "Love it or leave it."

It was Merle Haggard who gave me my new musical

direction. They used to say of Merle Haggard that he did all the things Johnny Cash was supposed to have done, such as serve time in prison.

It really didn't matter. Merle sang it sweet and from the heart, not to mention through the nose. He sang, "When you're runnin' down my country, Hoss, you're walkin' on the fightin' side of me." And he sang, "We don't smoke marijuana in Muscogee," and what I heard, I was drawn to. Now, pop open a longneck and let me tell you the rest of the story ... the best of the story.

They Call It Blue-Eyed Soul

I AM QUITE proud of the fact that I heard of Willie Nelson before most other Americans. This is sort of like being a style-setter and being one of the first people to know when white socks went out.

I'm not certain of the exact date when I first heard Willie sing and attached voice and song to name, but it was sometime during the late sixties after I had made the decision to abandon rock 'n' roll and place my musical interests elsewhere.

What eventually led me to country — before country was cool, if you'll allow me to steal a line from Barbara Mandrell — was, first, an Atlanta radio station changing its format. The station, WPLO-AM, had been a rock 'n' roll station during my youth, but when rock changed, so did WPLO. It went country.

It wasn't just that WPLO began playing country music, it was the way they played it that caught my ear. They avoided the cornball, which had been SOP for all country stations.

Remember the old country disc-jockeys back before country started washing its feet more than once a week?

"Hello there, friends and neighbors, this is your old Cuzzin Cholly, brangin' you some good ol' pickin' and fiddlin'. Yessiree, Bob, we gone have us a good time this here afternoon, and jist remember this here is all brought to you by Lon and Randy's Feed Store on the Pickett Road, yore hog pellet headquarters, and by them good folks over at the Piggly-Wiggly — my ol' Uncle Peahead calls that the Hoggly-Woggly — featuring bargains this week on neck bones, Cardui tablets, and septic tank aroma bars. Now, let's jist sit back and enjoy some good ol' country music. Here's a new'un by Nubbin Straker entitled 'I'm a Floatin' Corncob in the Slopjar of Love.'"

Such was offensive even to a ruralite like myself, who was quite familiar, indeed, with slopjars, the forerunner to the automatic garbage disposal.

I had occasionally drifted across WSM, clear-channel, Nashville, Tennessee, on Saturday nights and listened to the Grand Ole Opry, but even the commercials bothered me there. Somebody was always singing about Black Draught, which I seem to recall was a laxative, and about Goo-Goo Cluster candy bars.

What WPLO did was to put a disc-jockey on the air introducing country music who didn't sound like he just crawled out from under a slopjar, and nobody sang commercials about laxatives and candy, and I could understand the words to the music, and the singers sounded as though they didn't look like something that would crawl under the refrigerator when the lights went on in the kitchen.

Actually, my pilgrimage to country was a pretty short trip.

Despite my early affair with Elvis, nobody could grow up in a small rural town like Moreland, Georgia, in the 1950s and not have at least some appreciation for the way country music sounds when a jukebox is blaring it out from the inside of a truckstop on a hot, thick, summer's night, when the neon is bright and the bugs are bad.

My favorite of the two truckstops in Moreland was Steve's, where the waitress paid off on the pinball machines at the rate of ten cents an extra game; where the cheeseburgers were thick and greasy; where if you were tall enough to reach the counter, you were old enough to drink beer; and where they had an all-country jukebox that played twenty-four hours a day for what must have been fifteen years.

Once I learned in which directions the magnet pulled, I could easily turn fifty cents into a dollar-and-a-half at the pinball machines, and I spent many hours of my youth at that practice alongside the jukebox that was full of coins and country.

There was Hank Williams, still barely cold in his grave, and Faron Young, Little Jimmy Dickens, Eddy Arnold, Hawkshaw Hawkins, Cowboy Copas, Patsy Cline, Loretta Lynn, Hank Locklin, Roy Acuff, Ernest Tubb, Miss Kitty Wells, Gentleman Jim Reeves, the Wilburn Brothers, Lefty Frizell, Lonzo and Oscar, and Webb Pierce singing, among other great hits, "In the Jailhouse Now" and "There Stands the Glass."

In the late sixties, another generation of country stars began to blossom. Johnny Cash put on his black outfit and sang "Ring of Fire," and people talked about the time he had spent in prison, which apparently gave him credentials to wail about life's miseries.

Misery. That's what a lot of early country music was really

all about.

At the same time, former rockers like Conway Twitty and Jerry Lee Lewis were joining the fold, and they brought fans with them. Finally there was music that people like me, who thought Led Zeppelin had something to do with the octane level of gasoline, could listen to without getting a splitting headache.

Back in those days, Willie Nelson was just another short-haired Nashville songwriter. But once I heard him do a song called "Bloody Mary Morning" — she left last night and this is morning, and I might as well start drinking early so I can hurry up and pass out and forget her — I was hooked. He almost *talked* that song in a clear and piercing, if not somewhat nasal, tone. I hummed it for days.

Later, I heard him do "I Gotta Get Drunk and I Sure Do Hate It" and his own "Crazy" and "Ain't It Funny How Time Slips Away," and I became a devotee. I told other people about him, but they sort of looked at me sideways, the way a dog does when he's trying to figure out what on earth you're talking about. Pretty soon I got used to that look.

Despite the growing popularity of country music, there were still those holdouts who felt that all country wore a straw hat with the price tag hanging off (sorry, Miss Minnie). I picked up a date one evening, and when I started my car, the radio began playing George Jones doing the classic "Ol' King Kong Was Just a Little Monkey Compared to My Love for You."

My date immediately reached for the selector buttons on my radio and punched until she found some whiny Simon and Garfunkel song.

"What are you doing?" I asked in genuine horror.

"Somebody put your radio on a country station," said my

date, in the same voice she would have used to tell me a large dog had committed a horrid indiscretion in the front seat while I was out of my car.

This was not the same young woman who later dragged me to the Elton John concert, but they probably were second cousins now that I think back on it.

"*I* put my car radio on a country station," I said proudly.

The girl made a horrible face. Maybe a dog did commit an indiscretion on the front seat while I was out of my car. But no, it was worse. My date was turning up her nose at country music.

"You actually listen to that crap?" she asked.

"Crap?" I said. "You're calling country music crap?"

"That's exactly what it is. Crap."

"And what is that you're listening to?"

"Simon and Garfunkel."

"Hippie music."

"No, it isn't."

"Yes, it is. That kind of music is exactly what's wrong with this country."

"Are you some kind of Bircher or religious nut?" she asked.

"No," I said, "but I like country music and I don't like anybody who doesn't, and I will thank you to keep your communist, unpatriotic, ungracious fingers off my radio."

The girl asked to be put off at the next bus stop, which I was more than happy to do. I left her standing there, and as I drove off, I punched my country station back on and disappeared down the street — alone for the evening, but proud that I would not allow even the stirrings of lustful passion to come between me and George Jones.

This probably is how the Good Ol' Boy fraternity — a

fairly recently identified sociological group — got its start. Smart-aleck women, hippies, and other non-desirables began to make fun of us for enjoying country music, and we sort of banded together in retaliation. The offshoot was that we also went in directions opposite to those who scoffed at us, such as preferring cold beer in longneck bottles to white wine, pickup trucks to Volvos, and, in many instances, our dogs to women who would dare move our radio dials off a country music station.

Before long, country music was appealing to individuals who previously thought they were incapable of enjoying it. This phenomenon was called "crossover," which meant that even yankees had begun listening to country music without remarking about how corny it sounded. The first time I saw this conversion was in Chicago, where I was once held prisoner for three winters.

Powerful Chicago radio station WMAQ had recently changed its format to country and was running away with the ratings. The station even went as far as to sponsor a country concert at the Ivanhoe Theatre on the fashionable, trendy, north side. Billy "Crash" Craddock and Don Williams were the entertainers.

There wasn't an empty seat in the house, which was the first thing that surprised me. I didn't think that more than a handful of Chicagoans had ever heard of either artist. Crash Craddock came out in a red outfit with sparkling rhinestones, and instantly I thought I was back home in the National Guard Armory with Ernest Tubb on stage and every country girl within six counties down in front of the stage taking Ernest's picture while he sang, "It's a long ways from Nashville to Berlin, Honey, so keep them cards and letters comin' in."

Crash did all his big numbers, including the moving ballad "If I Could Write a Song," while midwestern ladies who had the night off from the bowling leagues snapped pictures of him and his funky Santa suit.

It was Don Williams, however, singing soft and low, who stole the show. He came out wearing a floppy hat — the kind Gabby Hayes used to wear — and proceeded to sing non-stop for two hours. When he was done, three thousand frostbitten yankees stood as one and cheered his marvelous, mellow performance.

He had done "Amanda," of course, and "You're My Best Friend" and "She Never Knew Me." And during his encore, I felt I was at some sort of evangelical celebration where the entire audience suddenly had seen the light and had come forward en masse for the altar call.

The entire evening had, in fact, been a wonderful religious experience, and I do not make a spiritual allusion here without basis.

Remember Tom T. Hall's "I Remember the Year Clayton Delaney Died"? Clayton Delaney, so the song went, had been an extraordinary guitar-picker (that's different from "guitarist"), and he also drank a bit and was a rounder. But as he lay dying, the story went on, Clayton Delaney got religion. Tom T. finished the ballad with the suggestion that Clayton's deathbed conversion, and the fact that he could flat pick, probably led him to his just reward. Sang Tom T. in the last verse:

> "I know there's a lot of good preachers,
> Who know a lot more than I do.
> But it could be the Good Lord
> Likes a little pickin', too."

* * *

The pure state of country music — once called "blue-eyed soul" — was bound to go the route of all else once good and simple, of course. I don't know who or what is to blame for the fact that country has forsaken its roots. Today flutists are playing background (and probably oboists, too, although I don't think I would recognize the sound of an oboe if I heard it), country stars are making movies, New York has its own country music night club and radio station, the rhinestones have been replaced by tight jeans and occasionally even tuxedos, nobody remembers Faron Young or Webb Pierce anymore, and half of what you hear that's supposed to be country today isn't country at all, but rather some sort of unholy mix better left for Wee-Wee Pole and the other musical fruits.

We have to start somewhere in tracing what caused country to go cosmopolitan, however, so I think we should start with Dolly Parton's breasts.

It's not Dolly Parton's fault that she has big breasts, and I dare say she still would be a rare talent without her chesty appearance. However, when Dolly Parton became a big country star, people started noticing her breasts more than her singing. Suddenly everybody else wanted to get into the act, and sex subsequently found its way on country stations where once Miss Kitty Wells, in ankle-length skirt and cowgirl boots, had trod.

Pretty soon the Mandrell sisters were wiggling a lot, and the girls on "Hee Haw" were half-naked for each performance, and Conway Twitty was singing, "Pardner, there's a tiger in those tight-fittin' jeans."

Has anyone noticed the sexual overtones that have found their way into modern country music? Conway ought to have his mouth washed out. He sang another song about "Even with your hair up in curlers, I'd still love to lay you down." And there was the one where he sang about the girl "who had never been this far before, bum-bum-bum," and he even had the audacity to remake a Pointer Sisters hit, where he suggests, "You want a lover who will spend some time; not come and go with a heated rush."

Country singers today think nothing of crooning about "the first time we went all the way," and "When we were down to nothing, nothing sure looked good on you," and "If I don't feel like a man, feel again." All of this likely would leave an old pioneer purist like Roy Acuff with his yo-yo in a knot.

I also blame Willie Nelson for a lot of this country-gone-chic. I could overlook the beard and the headband and the ponytails, but then he went one step over the line.

I was at a Willie concert, all ready to cry in my beer and stomp my feet. Then I noticed that the crowd was changing a bit. There was the cowboy-hatted contingent and the GOB's, but there were also people apparently leftover from that Elton John concert, and those weren't Marlboros they were smoking.

Willie put on his usual grand show. He opened, as always, with "Whiskey River," and then he did a medley of his older material. He knocked us over with "The Red-Headed Stranger," which has an ending line that always brings a cheer from the male contingent in the audience: "You can't hang a man for killing a woman who was trying to steal his horse."

It was somewhere in "The Red-Headed Stranger (From

Blue Rock, Montana)," as a matter of fact, that I noticed something strange about Willie Nelson.

He was wearing an earring. Or, at least, he appeared to be wearing an earring. I asked a companion sitting next to me to verify my observation.

"Damn if he ain't," was his reply.

It took me a week or so to figure out how I felt about such a thing. To begin with, I naturally had some doubts about a man wearing an earring, the same sort of doubts I would have had about a man wearing undershorts with pictures of flowers on them. I don't even think Elton John wore an earring, and I'm certain you could have threatened to bash Ernest Tubb's guitar and he still would have refused to wear an earring.

I doubt seriously if there's anything in the Bible that warns against men wearing earrings, but there should be. "Woe be unto ye if ye stick an earring in thy ear and aren't named Rachel or Ruby Ann," is what it should say.

I was pleased at first that country music had become so universally accepted, but did that mean country music eventually was going to lose all its purity? The way Willie Nelson sang, I supposed I could overlook the earring, too, but where would all this eventually lead?

Crossover not only meant their coming to us, I determined, but it also could mean our going over to them. Would we have bisexual country stars and country stars who dressed as bats and stuck out their tongues at the audience? Would country music no longer embrace its classic subjects — cheatin' and fightin' and truckin' and drinkin' and cryin' — but begin to embrace drugs and anarchy? Would the time come when I could no longer differentiate between country music and rock music, because all music would have blended into a form without identity?

These were troubling thoughts. If country music lost its identity, if it were swallowed up into a giant, black hole where electronic gadgets screamed and screeched, where drums pounded out ancient rhythms, who would be left to sing for those of us who fed it during its hungry years?

Willie Nelson wearing an earring. He had told us in "I'd Have to Be Crazy" that he had grown a beard "just to see what the rednecks would do," but did he have to give us this rigid a test?

I never quite forgave Willie Nelson for the earring, but I continued to listen to his music, giving him the benefit of the doubt. I figured he was on the road so much that he didn't get a balanced diet, which caused him to be constipated a lot, which is a direct cause of strange behavior. A person who is constipated all the time suffers great fits of anxiety that go along with it, and maybe Willie had been so anxious that it had affected his ability to think clearly. So one day he said to himself, "I think I'll buy an earring and stick it in my ear, and maybe that'll take my mind off being constipated."

How I wish Willie had consulted me before he did that. A few swigs of Milk of Magnesia probably would have had the same effect and wouldn't have been nearly as unsettling to his fans.

* * *

Here's what I wish would happen to country music: I wish they would give it back to the loyalists and the traditionalists.

I wish somebody would start a new brand of music called "Neo-Country" or "Randy Rural," and anybody who wanted to sing with flutes and oboes and loud guitars, and sing lyrics you would be embarrassed for your mother to hear, could go off and listen to that. The rest of us, including Willie and his pal Waylon, could go on back to Luckenbach, Texas, and get back to the basics of country music.

I want the kind of country music George Jones sings. George sings like a steel guitar sounds. I want to hear more of George singing "If drinkin' don't kill me, then her memory will."

I want Willie to take out the earring and sing more songs like "Faded Love," that he did with Ray Price, and "Railroad Lady," that he did in memory of Lefty Frizell. In recent times, Willie has sung with Spaniard Julio Iglesias, and he's making an album with Frank Sinatra. Where will it end — Willie and Pavarotti singing opera together?

I want more Moe Bandy rodeo songs. I want more pure sounds like Larry Gatlin, more lyrical quality like Tom T. Hall brings to his music. I want Gene Watson and Rex Allen, Jr., and a few Chet Atkins instrumentals and less Eddie Rabbitt. Said my boyhood friend and idol, Weyman C. Wannamaker, Jr., a great American, who is also a country music fan, "If that mess Eddie Rabbitt sings is country, my dog's a P-H-damn-D."

I want Kenny Rogers to take a few months off and never sing another song like "Coward of the County." I want George Strait to make more songs like "Amarillo by Morning," with those mournful fiddles in the background. I never want to hear John Anderson sing "Swingin" again.

I don't want Alabama to do anymore truck-driving songs like "18-Wheeler." Dave Dudley and Red Sovine should do truck-driving songs; Alabama should do "Old Flame" and "She's a Lady, Down on Love."

I want more Joe Stampley and more country songs like "You're a Hard Dog to Keep Under the Porch" and "Don't Come Home a-Drinkin' with Lovin' on Your Mind" and less like "If I Said You Had a Beautiful Body, Would You Hold It Against Me?"

I want country songs with twin-fiddle intros, and I want Charley Pride to do what he does best — sing the old songs Hank used to sing — and I want Hank, Jr., to forget the hard country and try singing the sweet songs that make you want to cry and call your ex-wife and ask for forgiveness, like Don Williams sings.

I want Conway Twitty to clean up his act, but I don't want Merle Haggard to change a thing.

Country music is too much fun to allow it to be spoiled. No other sort of music offers such classic lines:

— "If fingerprints showed up on skin, wonder whose I'd find on you?"

— "My wife just ran off with my best friend, and I miss him."

— "You're the reason our children are ugly."

— "If you're gonna cheat on me, don't cheat in our home town."

— "I've got the all-overs for you all over me."

— "It's not love, but it's not bad."

— And the immortal: "I gave her a ring and she gave me a finger."

I also believe that all country music should fall under one of the following categories:

— CHEATIN' SONGS: She ran off.

— LOVIN' AND FORGIVIN' SONGS: She came back.

— HURTIN' SONGS: The hussy ran off again.

— DRINKIN' SONGS: Nobody here to cook me anything

to eat, so I might as well get drunk.

— TRUCKIN' SONGS: She run off on a train. I think I'll derail that sucker.

— PRISON SONGS: They take derailing trains serious in Mississippi.

— RODEO SONGS: Soon as she got out of the hospital after the train wreck, she took up with a bullrider.

— NEVER-GIVE-UP-HOPE SONGS: I wonder if her sister still lives in Tupelo.

* * *

I've taken a lot of abuse in my lifetime for being a country music fan, but it's all been worth it. Quite frankly, country music has helped me through many tough times. Whatever the problem, there's always meaning in country music, something to lean on.

Want to know what's really important in life? Country music has the answer to that in Tom T. Hall's "Old Dogs, Children, and Watermelon Wine":

"Old dogs care about you,
Even when you make mistakes.
And God bless little children,
While they're still too young to hate.
I tried it all when I was young,
And in my natural prime.
Now, it's old dogs and children,
And watermelon wine."

Freedom. There are times I have paid dearly to get it or to regain it. Perhaps I should have listened to Kris Kristofferson:

> *"Freedom's just another word*
> *For nothin' left to lose...."*

There is something about country music that should appeal to every writer, to everyone who has something in his heart and wants others to feel what he feels.

I've written lots of country songs, myself. Unfortunately, nobody has ever bothered to record one, but that still doesn't stop me from having a few beers occasionally and knocking out a few country lyrics — which is the way most country songs come to be written. People who write rock songs, on the other hand, apparently do so while being stoned (in the Biblical sense).

I've written some very poignant country songs, as a matter of fact. After a six-pack one night, I came up with this one:

> *"Singles bars ain't no place,*
> *Ain't no place for a lady.*
> *It's dark, talk is cheap,*
> *And the men are all shady.*
> *But where does she go,*
> *And is it so wrong,*
> *When a lady's been single too long?"*

Impressed? That's nothing. I also wrote:

> *"You say she gave you her number, friend*
> *Well ain't that just fine.*
> *I know it's Heartbreak six, fourteen-ten,*

'Cause that number used to be mine."

I even wrote a train song once, and it went something like this:

"*Sweet, sweet Jesus,*
I never gave you thanks
That once as a youth,
Through the middle of Georgia,
I rode the Nancy Hanks."

Sometimes when the lyrics won't come, when the beer won't go down easy, I write titles instead. I have some wonderful new titles just waiting for words.

How about, "I'd Marry Your Dog Just to Be a Part of Your Family"?

Or, "Who's Gonna Cut My Toenails After You're Gone?"

I like this one, too: "You Threw Up On the Carpet of My Love;" or, "You'll Never Get Away From Me Darling, Because Even When You're Taking a Shower with Somebody Else, I'll Be the Soap on Your Rag."

The words to that one will probably go something like this:

"*I know I whine a lot*
And occasionally I nag,
But you'll never get away from me, darling,
'Cause even when you're taking a shower
With somebody else,
I'll be the soap on your rag."

I admit it needs a little work, but at least you get the idea.

Perhaps the real point here is that when Elvis and rock 'n' roll came along and caught me as a boy, I followed them off despite my parents' rages against them. But when they led too far, country music called me back, and I forevermore will be grateful. Without it, who knows? I might have wound up one day with hair down to my shoulders, sandals on my feet, a ghetto blaster over my shoulder, and smelling like The Goat Man.

The Goat Man? He may have been the original hippie.

**A Hairy
Ode
To The
Goat Man**

TAKE IT ALL down to the lowest common denominator, shake off all the dust and heave out all the bull, and most of the problems we had with each other in the late sixties and early seventies really were about hair.

Think about it. Let's suppose that student protesters who were burning buildings and marching and demonstrating against the war in Vietnam had shown up at the rallies wearing khaki pants, nice button-down, blue Oxford-cloth shirts, Weejuns, and short hair. I contend we wouldn't have had near the commotion that we did.

Older people would have looked at them and instead of saying, "You godless, bed-wetting, pinko, Commie, nasty, long-haired hippies," they might have said, "Gee, those youngsters certainly are vocal against the war, but isn't it wonderful to see boys and girls that age taking an active interest in government."

I'm not certain why, but most rebellions, however small, usually start with somebody doing something funky with their hair. Remember that at the Boston Tea Party, American revolutionaries grew their hair long, put it up in ponytails, donned feathers, and went out and started a war. Almost two hundred years later, a bunch of actors started a rebellion on Broadway with a musical called *Hair.* Some things never change.

The history of my own hair is one of coming and going.

When I was a baby, so my mother says, I had blond curls. She cut them off and still has them in a box somewhere. She can keep them.

When I was old enough to have my first haircut, my father, the soldier, took me to a barber shop and had them cut all my hair off. I doubt that he asked the barber to sweep my chopped locks off the floor so he could keep them in a small box, because like most military men, my father had no use for hair whatsoever. I never would have attempted to grow Elvis ducktails, had I lived with my father at the time, for fear he would have called me "Louise" instead of the name they gave me.

After I got over the ducktails thing, I went back to a crew cut because that's what all the other boys wore. I allowed the crew cut to grow out before I started college, but I remained a relative skinhead through college and into my early adult years. I didn't want anybody to think I was having anything to do with the hippie and anti-war movements.

Actually, I never saw a live hippie until after I was out of college. Come to think of it, I didn't see any dead ones, either. The University of Georgia was not exactly a hotbed of activism when I was in school there between 1964 and 1968. We were too busy enjoying the school's recent upsurge in football success after a long Dark Age. The only drugs I knew about were those pills you took to stay up all night and study because you'd been drinking beer and partying all weekend, celebrating Georgia's victory over Auburn.

I distinctly remember the first hippie-in-the-flesh I ever saw. The year was 1968. I had just taken a job in Atlanta. One day I was driving along Peachtree Street and entered the 10th Street area, once known for a country music juke joint called Al's Corral. Often had I been to Al's, where the beer was cold and the music made you want to cry.

But by 1968, the 10th Street area had changed. It had become the Deep South's answer to Haight-Asbury.

Hippies were everywhere — tall hippies, short hippies, boy hippies, and girl hippiettes. Gaggles of hippies sat on the sidewalks; one played guitar, while the others sang along or sat quietly listening to the music or picking their feet.

I must admit that I have done, and still do, my own share of foot-picking, but I consider it an exercise that should take place only in private and only occasionally. A person who picks his feet more than twice a month probably has some serious mental disorder, possibly dating back to his youth when he went around barefooted in the front yard and suffered stubbed toes or came down with planter's warts from stepping on places where frogs went to the bathroom. (It is common knowledge that one thing that causes warts is frog pee-pee. You probably could look it up in a medical book somewhere.)

Foot-picking, I also admit, can be an enjoyable experience. When I pick my feet, maybe once every three or four months, I first dig under my toenails and remove any foreign matter such as sock lint. Then I rub my fingers between my toes, which also removes weird stuff that hides in there. Rubbing between your toes makes you tingly all over.

Next, I pick at any callouses on the bottom of my feet. Since I rarely go barefoot anymore, especially outdoors where I might step into some frog pee-pee, I don't have to worry about warts.

I conclude my foot-picking by washing my hands thoroughly.

As I sat at a traffic light on Peachtree Street in the 10th Street area that day back in 1968, I watched one hippie in particular who apparently thought nothing of picking his feet in front of five o'clock traffic on the busiest street in town.

He had taken off his sandals and parked them next to him on the curb. I never could have been a hippie, if for no other reason than because I refuse to wear sandals, the official shoe of hippiedom. Sandals look awful, especially if you wear long, dark socks with them.

As a boy, I had noticed tourists from up north who were driving through Moreland on their way to Florida and had stopped at Bohannon's Service Station for gasoline. Yankee men tourists inevitably wore Bermuda shorts and sandals and long, black socks they pulled up almost to their armpits. Occasionally, however, a yankee tourist would come through and go to the other extreme. He would roll his socks down all the way to his ankles, which made him and his sandals look even sillier. I vowed never to wear sandals, even if it meant walking through a frog latrine barefooted.

I continued to watch the hippie pick at his feet. He dug under a nail with concentration and resolve. Since he wore no socks at all, I knew it wasn't sock lint he was removing. Perhaps it was road tar or some sort of animal leavings. The man looked as if he'd been sleeping with goats.

After completing his nail work, the hippie turned his

attention to between his toes. I don't know what causes strange substances to get between your toes, especially if you're in an urban setting and far from the nearest chicken yard. But I do know from personal experience that if you don't wash your feet often and your feet sweat a lot, you will have a gooey material between your toes. This substance normally is referred to as toe jelly or toe cheese. Since hippies seldom washed their feet, I figured he had a blue-ribbon supply of toe jelly between his toes.

At any rate, the light finally changed, and I drove away convinced that besides the political differences between me and hippies, there was one other major difference: I don't pick my feet in public.

That was just one of the reasons I never considered becoming a hippie, of course. Another was that they reminded me too much of The Goat Man, who is another story.

* * *

Once or twice a year, when I was growing up, The Goat Man would come through Moreland and park his goats and the wagon they pulled in front of the Masonic Hall, where he would camp for a couple of days.

The Goat Man had a long beard and wore tattered clothing and a pair of high-top tennis shoes, which he probably slept in. When, and if, The Goat Man ever got around to picking his feet, he probably found all sorts of things between his toes — even small animals that had gone there to hibernate for the winter.

The Goat Man was a fairly nice person, if you could stand the smell. Herds of goats give out a distinctive aroma, reminiscent of chitterlings while they're being cooked. People who live with herds of goats and sleep in their tennis shoes in the back of wagons take on the smell of their goats, which mixes with their own noxious odor, thereby creating a blend that would shock the olfactory nerves of a buzzard.

The Goat Man always carried around chewing gum for the children who came to see him and his goats, and we normally could hold our breath just long enough to get a couple of sticks of Juicy Fruit from him before we had to run for fresh air.

The Goat Man told great stories, though.

"Been all the way to Alaska and back since I was here last," he would say. "Got so cold, I had to sleep between my goats to keep warm."

Somebody would ask how long it took him to get to Alaska and back.

"These old goats here," he would answer, pointing to his herd, "were just babies when I left. They were great-grand-parents by the time we got back."

The more I think about it, perhaps The Goat Man *was* the original hippie. He spurned the establishment life and indicated that he would rather share his being with goats than with other people.

I'm not certain if The Goat Man is still alive, or if he even lived long enough to see the hippie movement. I sort of hope he did, and I hope he took credit for starting it. A man who has spent his life huddling against the cold between goats needs to know he has left some sort of legacy, no matter how much it might smell.

* * *

There were certain beliefs, whether real or imagined, concerning hippies that were strongly held by those of us outside the movement.

There was the hair thing, of course. It was The Beatles who first hid their ears under their locks, but the hippies took it further and grew their hair over their shoulders and down even to their rears. And they grew long beards. That is, the male hippies grew long beards. Girl hippiettes, most of whom couldn't grow beards, allowed the hair under their arms and on their legs to grow.

In some cultures, men find female underarm hair to be quite desirable. Not so with American men — not even hippies, I would wager. That makes me somewhat suspect of one of those beliefs we had about hippies, that their "Make love, not war" ideas meant they were spending a lot of time having sex with one another.

I really doubt that now. Sleeping with goats is one thing, but making love to a hairy-legged girl with hairy underarms is an even more disgusting notion. I suspect that when we thought hippies were having all that sex, they probably weren't doing anything more intimate than picking one another's feet.

We firmly believed that hippies didn't wash their hair often and probably had cootie bugs roaming around on their scalps.

I'm not exactly certain what a cootie bug is, but there was a boy in my school whose head was allegedly infested with them. He was always scratching at his scalp, and he soon absorbed the nickname (or should I say nickmane?) of "Coot." The teacher finally called the health department and they came and got "Coot" and gave him some sort of treatment. He never scratched his head much after he was de-cootied, which was one of the first miracles of modern medical techniques I ever saw.

It was the fact that hippies wore their hair long and probably had cootie bugs that caused me to begin shampooing every day. Previously, I had not shampooed more than once or twice a week, because when I did my hair would become quite dry and stick up all over my head. A date once remarked that it looked like I was wearing a cocker spaniel on my head. I decided, however, that it would be easier to get another date than to get rid of cootie bugs.

It was the order of that day to make fun of hippies' long hair. The most popular game was to question the gender of a male hippie whose hair flowed down his back like Trigger's tail.

"See that?" somebody would ask, pointing to a nearby hippie.

"I see it, but I don't know what it is," would come the reply.

"Is it male or female?"

"Can't tell."

"It's wearing a man's clothes."

"But it's got hair like a girl."

"Maybe it's one of them she-men. They got those operations now, you know."

"Naw, it's just one of them nasty-headed hippies."

"Yeah, see it doin' that peace sign? All them hippies give that peace sign."

"Yeah, well give the son of a bitch half of it back."

The truth is, those of us in the straight world didn't like hippies and didn't trust them and wanted them to go away so our world could go back to being normal.

We wanted to win the war in Vietnam and bring the boys home victorious and have ticker tape parades for generals and show the evil communistic world that you don't mess with the United States of by-God America. Hippies wanted peace, even a dishonorable one. The cowards.

Hippies smoked dope and took LSD and God knows what else. We wondered why they couldn't be satisfied with beer like the rest of us.

Hippies liked flowers. We liked football.

Hippies listened to musical groups with names like Led Zeppelin and Cream and Jefferson Airplane and Blind Faith and The Grateful Dead and The Moody Blues. We still liked Merle Haggard and "Okie From Muscogee."

> *"Leather boots are still in style if a man needs foot-wear.*
> *Beads and Roman sandals won't be seen.*
> *And football's still the roughest thing on the campus.*
> *And the kids here still respect the college dean."*

Hippies looked filthy. We smelled like Aqua-Velva men.

Hippies didn't work. We busted our tails for promotions.

Hippies wore sandals and patched jeans. We wore wing tips and three-piece suits.

Hippies joined communes. We joined the Rotary Club.

Hippies danced nude in the mud. We worked on our golf games.

There were, of course, many people in my age group who broke away and went off to become hippies. I knew of only one, however. He was Stinky Drake, who was from Moreland and was a couple of years older than me.

As I look back, I can see now that even as a child Stinky showed evidence that one day he might grow up to be a hippie. He never played baseball with the rest of us. He spent his time making belts and Indian moccasins from a kit he had ordered from an ad in the *Grit* newspaper. He did other strange things, too, like the time we went on a Boy Scout trip and we caught a large number of catfish and tied them on a stringer. When nobody was looking, Stinky took the fish off the stringer and set them free.

"What if you were a fish?" Stinky asked his irate campmates. "Would you want to be stuck on a stringer, or to be free to go back to your family in the river?"

We realized there was no point in arguing with anybody who worried about fish being taken from their families, so we tied Stinky to a tree and went back to breaking up fish families for our evening meal. Stinky wouldn't eat that night because he said it would make him feel guilty eating somebody's father or mother.

It wasn't long afterwards that Stinky became the first vegetarian I ever met. At school they served him a special plate; nobody would eat with him and Stinky soon became known as "Bean Breath."

In high school, Stinky joined the Drama Club and wrote a poem for the school paper entitled "An Ode to Vegetables." I remember the closing lines:

> *"Just because I don't eat meat*
> *Doesn't mean that I'm not neat."*

I suppose we were cruel to Stinky, which caused him to rebel against the norm even more. After he graduated from high school, we heard he went off in the mountains somewhere and ate a lot of roots and berries and lived on what he could earn selling the belts and Indian moccasins he still made.

Next, we heard that he had broken his parents' hearts by

growing his hair long and taking up dope-smoking and running off to Canada to avoid the draft. He also was living in sin with a woman who didn't wear shoes or shave under her arms. He had met her at a rock concert.

I don't have any idea what ever happened to Stinky, but I suppose he's still out there in the hills somewhere, dressed like Cochise and munching on sunflower seeds.

* * *

It is odd — and beneficial, too — how time changes ideas and mends feelings. After the war in Vietnam ended, most of the hippies bathed themselves, cut their hair, quit wearing sandals, and quit picking their feet. Today most of them are stockbrokers or fertilizer salesmen.

But they left their mark, and again it was the hair. Do you know who wears their hair long today? Good ol' boys, that's who. You can see it coming out from under their International Harvester and Red Man caps. Know who wears their hair neat and short? Gays and those men you see in clothing ads in the Sunday *New York Times Magazine* (although that may be a redundancy).

As for my own hair, here's the rest of the shaggy story:

After the war, longer hair became the accepted fashion for men, and I followed suit. Sideburns even made a comeback. I had long hair and sideburns, and all of a sudden it wasn't possible to go to a regular barber shop anymore. Men had to go to stylists, and where they once had paid three bucks for a haircut, it was now costing them $12.50 and they had to make an appointment.

The first time I went to a hair stylist — it was around 1974 — I made an appointment with the renowned Mr. Phyllis.

"What on earth have you been shampooing with, my dear boy?" asked Mr. Phyllis.

"Soap," I said.

"Oh, God, no," Mr. Phyllis recoiled in horror. "Soap dries the hair and splits the ends."

I started to say my end had been split my entire life, but I decided it would not be wise to talk about such while I was alone in the room with Mr. Phyllis.

He immediately took charge of my hair. He shampooed it with an odd-smelling substance, put conditioner on it, and then "sculptured" it. Finally he put the blow dryer to me, and when it was over, I paid him the $12.50.

I felt a little cheated. At the barber shop, not only had I been charged a mere three bucks, but the barber usually told me a joke, too.

"Fellow had these two sows he wanted to get mated," went my barber's favorite joke. "He didn't have a boar, but he knew a fellow who did. So he called him up and asked if he could bring his two sows up to his farm and let that ol' boar have a go at 'em.

"The fellow said to bring 'em on up, so he put the two sows in the back of his pickup and drove 'em to his neighbor's farm.

"That ol' boar got real interested in his job and really did some work on the two sows. There was all sorts of gruntin' and oinkin' goin' on, 'cause when you got three thousand pounds of pork in the heat of passion, you got something wild.

"Anyway, when the ol' boar was finished, the man asked his neighbor how he would know if the job had took. His neighbor said to look out at his hogs the next morning, and if they were layin' up in the sunshine, everything was okay.

But if they were still wallowin' in the mud, he'd have to bring 'em back.

"Next morning, he looked out his window and his hogs were wallowin' in the mud, so he put 'em back in his truck and drove 'em back to see the boar again.

"Same thing happened. His neighbor's wife broke out in a sweat watchin' them hogs, and the dogs got to barkin' loud and they had to throw cold water on 'em.

"Next morning', though, it was the same thing. Them two hogs was still wallowin' in the mud. Man took his hogs up there a third time. Next mornin', he couldn't bear to look out at his hog pen, so he said to his wife, 'Honey, look out there and tell me if my hogs are sittin' in the sunshine or wallowin' in the mud.'

"She looked out the window and said, 'Neither one.'

"The man said, 'Well, where are they?'

"The fellow's wife said, 'One of 'em's in the truck ridin' shotgun, and the other one's blowin' the horn.'"

Mr. Phyllis didn't know any jokes, or at least not any like that. He was always too busy talking about his cat or watering the plants in his salon to tell jokes.

After I had gone to the trouble of having my hair styled, I thought it would be wise to take care of what my $12.50 had bought me, so I vowed never to wash my hair with soap again and went out to buy some shampoo.

"Do you have any shampoo for men?" I asked a saleslady in the cosmetics department.

"I think you will like this," she answered, handing me a bottle of shampoo. "It has the faint aroma of apricot."

Apricot?

"If you don't care for apricot," the woman continued, "perhaps you would like something with an herbal essence."

What I really wanted, I said, was something that smelled like soap. I didn't want to go around with my head smelling like a fruit salad.

I also purchased an electric hair dryer, of course. Previously, I had allowed my hair to dry naturally. When I was in a hurry, I would simply shake my head back and forth like a dog does when he's wet. With longer hair, however, I was told that this was impossible, even though I knew I'd seen a collie dry itself off with just two or three good shakes.

After purchasing the hair dryer, I also had to buy hairspray. When I bought it, I said a silent prayer that my father wasn't somewhere looking down upon his only son buying gook that sprayed out of a can to keep my hair in its original, upright and locked position after it had been blown dry and styled each morning.

But it had been so much simpler for my father. He hadn't needed shampoo or hair dryers or hairspray, because nobody else used anything like that when he was a young man about town. Men were men in his day. He would have hit Mr. Phyllis square in the mouth if that dandy had tried to sculpt his hair.

The hair situation is even more confusing today. Mine is shorter than it was when I first allowed it to grow in the seventies, but it still covers my ears. I got rid of the sideburns, but now I've got a beard and a mustache. I'm not certain what my father would think of that.

"Ain't but two kinds of people who wear beards and mustaches," he likely would have said. "That's queers and movie stars, and I ain't seen none of your movies lately."

But if he's concerned about my hirsute appearance, I wonder what he thinks about punk rockers who have their hair styled to look like the back of a horned frog. And I wonder what he thinks of people these days who dye their hair all sorts of colors, including orange and pink. My only hope is that heaven has mellowed him.

But what of me? I'm still here trying to deal with all this craziness. Hair and music have been a problem, but I have managed to cope with them after some degree of agony. But there have been so many other changes and dilemmas in the modern world. For instance, whose idea was it that men all of a sudden were supposed to be sensitive and enjoy fooling around with flowers and were even supposed to cry in front of women if they felt like it?

Each time I thought I knew all the answers to modern-day questions, somebody would up and change the questions.

And just when I thought there was nothing left to go haywire, I lost complete touch with the reality that was once men's clothing.

Excuse me for a moment, while I change into my leisure suit.

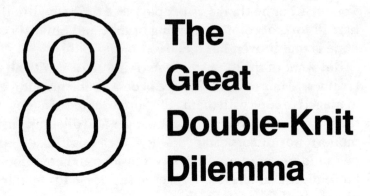

The Great Double-Knit Dilemma

WHEN WE'RE YOUNG, we naturally attempt to dress as our peers do, lest we be ostracized and laughed at. My wardrobe in college, for instance, consisted of the traditional khaki pants and button-down Gant shirts, a couple of V-neck sweaters, a London Fog raincoat, and a pair of Weejuns.

I also had a couple of pairs of socks, but I wore them only to funerals, weddings, or when I had to visit the dean. It was considered quite the fashion not to wear socks with Weejuns. I didn't know this when I arrived on campus at the University of Georgia, but soon after pledging a fraternity, one of my brothers in the bonds, Wally Walrus we called him, took me aside and explained the business about the socks.

The way we dressed on Deep South campuses in the sixties was, of course, quite different from the way students dressed at those schools where there was much dissent about all that was traditional. I'm happy the movement did not hit at Georgia until I was out of school; otherwise, I might have had to find a second-hand store to buy myself some blue jeans with patches and an old Army jacket, like the kids were wearing while they were taking over the administration building at Hofstra or some such place as that.

The way we dressed back then, and the way I continued to dress for several years out of school, is now called the "preppie look." This style of dress is yet the target of much derision from those who still don't understand that it does make a difference what sort of animal emblem appears on one's shirt. Some things, I would say to them, are simply the result of good breeding and cannot be explained to anyone who wears Hush Puppies.

I *would* say that, but I won't, because I admit there was a time when I became totally confused about what to wear, and there was a time when I also allowed myself to stray from tradition as far as my clothing was concerned.

I blame all this on Richard Nixon, too. How could one not go off course a bit with all the disillusionment that came with Watergate? It was about the time they caught Nixon up to his ears in justice obstructing that I went out and did something entirely crazy. I bought a new shirt that didn't have any buttons on the collar.

This particular shirt was a dress shirt, and it was sort of a light brown, as I recall. Men not only had started wearing their hair longer, but they also were wearing colorful dress shirts with no buttons on the collars. Since my peers at that point were mostly a bunch of guys who hung around local taverns and belched a lot, I was without any sort of guidance as to what currently was regarded as proper attire for a young man nearing his thirties.

It was about the same time, unfortunately, that the double-knit polyester craze hit full force. I'm not certain who invented double-knit fabrics, but rumor says it was first manufactured in a clothing plant in Fort Deposit, Alabama. This cannot be verified, however, because some years ago a mysterious fire erupted in the warehouse and 26,000 knit leisure suits were destroyed.

The owner, Delbert Gumbatz, was last seen catching the bus to Montgomery. He was wearing a Big Orange leisure suit — a favorite among Tennessee football fans. The last person to see him was the insurance man who signed the check for the fire, which, incidentally, smoldered for nearly six months.

Most everybody was wearing some sort of polyester or double-knit in those days, especially at bowling alleys and Moose Club dances. Such material was so popular, in fact, that several people were severely injured when they were trampled by a mob of shoppers in Good Sam, Ohio, who had just been informed, "Attention, K-Mart shoppers. On aisle seven tonight we have a special on men's leisure suits — all you can haul out of here for $29.95."

After I bought my brown dress shirt with no buttons on the collar, I lost complete control and bought myself a double-knit shirt. It didn't have any buttons on the collar, either, and it featured pictures of exotic-looking birds. To accent this outfit, I also purchased a pair of double-knit trousers. I looked like Marlin Perkins taking the afternoon off from hunting baboons in the wilds of Africa for Mutual of Omaha.

It could have been worse, of course. I could have bought myself a Nehru jacket and one of those medallions on a chain that people who wore Nehru jackets wore around their necks. What stopped me was an experience I had with a friend on the way to lunch one day. He was resplendent in his white Nehru jacket, a pair of white pants, and white patent-leather shoes. His medallion had a picture of Art Garfunkel on it. I was thinking how sharp he looked when three kids stopped him on the street and wanted to buy Eskimo Pies from him. Then two teen-agers thought he was the leader of some religious cult and offered their week's supply of marijuana and asked him to bless their head-bands.

I chilled on the Nehru suit.

Later, I considered buying myself a leisure suit, maybe a baby blue one to wear with my Marlin Perkins jungle shirt. I went as far as going into a men's store and asking to see their selection.

"I would like to see a leisure suit," I said to the clerk, who was chewing gum and wearing enough polyester to start his own bingo parlor.

"And what color did we have in mind?" he asked me between chomps on his Juicy Fruit.

"Blue," I said.

"Navy, midnight, morning sky, or baby?" he asked.

"Baby," I said.

He brought out something from the newly-created Tennessee Ernie Ford line, perfect for a night of dining and dancing in the Billy Budd Room at the local Holiday Inn.

"It's you," said the clerk.

"No, it's not," I said. "It's a conventioneer from Nebraska sipping a pina colada and trying to get up the courage to ask a fat girl with a beehive hairdo to dance." I left the store and never considered buying a leisure suit again.

Soon, however, I was once again faced with a dilemma

concerning men's fashions: Would I, or would I not, buy myself a neck chain?

Neck chains were big in singles bars in those days. I suppose that was because women were changing, too, and they had shamelessly indicated that the sight of men's chest hairs made them tingle in places they used to deny they even had, until their husbands pressed them on their wedding nights. So men quit wearing undershirts and started leaving their shirts unbuttoned to their navels, and I suppose neck chains and medallions were a way for men not to feel their chests were totally naked.

I happen to be blessed with a great deal of chest hair, and I readily imagined myself at singles bars covered with young women who wanted to run their fingers through it. So I put on my jungle shirt, buttoned only the bottom button, and went out amongst the night.

Not a single young woman expressed a desire to run her fingers through my chest hair, but I did scare off a dog in the parking lot when he saw my shirt.

I decided a neck chain was what I was missing, so I went the next day to a jewelry store.

"Do you have chains for men?" I asked the clerk.

"You kinky devil," he said.

"I beg your pardon," I replied.

"Didn't mean to insult you," the clerk went on. "I like a little S and M myself occasionally."

"S and M?" I said, completely puzzled.

"Don't kid with me," the clerk said. "We don't have any chains here, but I know where you can get a great deal on whips and leather underwear."

I decided that perhaps I wasn't ready for neck chains just yet. Luckily, however, a friend of mine had just returned from California and had the answer — a string of beads. At first, I was a bit wary of them.

"What's that around your neck?" I asked him.

"Beads," he said. "Everybody in California is wearing beads."

"Isn't that a little, well, sissy?" I asked.

"Get off my back with your macho trip," said my friend. "This is 1974."

Macho. What was this *macho*? Some sort of Mexican dish he had eaten in California? My friend explained.

"What *macho* means," he began, "is a man trying to be like John Wayne all the time — aggressive, insensitive, a slave to old traditions and old hang-ups. If a man wants to make a statement about himself, if he wants to wear a string of beads to say he is caring and sensitive and secure within himself, then he can today without fear of being stereotyped. These beads are my way of saying that I am *laid back, man.*"

The entire conversation was far over my head. "Laid back?" I asked.

"Where have you been?" asked my friend. "For years, men have been taught that it's not okay for them to cry, it's not okay for them to enjoy flowers or to dress colorfully or to wear ornamental jewelry. Men who did that were — what was your term? — sissies. Well, we don't have to be like that anymore. Now, we can do our own things. Women really go for guys who can feel, who can share their thoughts, who like poetry and art and antiques and don't mind admitting it. It's even okay for a man to have a cat now."

I was taken aback by all this. True, I had been taught that a man was supposed to be strong and aggressive, and I had always despised cats.

I vowed to change my ways. I borrowed my friend's beads, bought a copy of Kahlil Gibran's *The Prophet,* and took a girl out on a date to the art museum and later to an antique store, where we browsed and looked at brass beds and old pictures of somebody else's grandparents. I thought that was very sensitive of me.

When we reached her house at the end of our date, she said, "I find you so comfortable to be with. You're so sensitive and you don't mind sharing your thoughts. You're so, well, *laid back.*"

I thought I spotted an opening and asked if I could spend the night with her.

"Silly boy," she said. "My cat would be so jealous."

These were trying times for me. With apologies to George Gobel, the world around me seemed to be a tuxedo and I was still a pair of brown shoes.

Leisure suits. Neck chains. Kinky. Macho. Laid back. Men crying and keeping company with cats. Everywhere I looked, there was upheaval and change. And more was on the way.

Women's stated interest in men's chest hairs, which led to the unbuttoned shirts and neck chains and beads, was followed by another shocking admission — they also enjoyed looking at our butts and seeing us in our underpants.

Let's begin with the underpants. The basic rules for men's underpants always had gone something like this:

After a boy-child passes the diaper stage, he moves into what is known as "grippers," or "jockey shorts." These shorts fit very tightly, since small boys have not yet reached the point where tight underwear can cause discomfort and migraine headaches. Before a boy's voice changes, it is perfectly okay for his jockey shorts to have pictures on them, as long as they're pictures of Army tanks or cowboys. Birds and flowers are totally unacceptable.

Once a boy reaches his teens and begins undressing in locker rooms in front of his friends, he still can wear jockey shorts, but forget the pictures of Army tanks and cowboys. Boys at this stage wear plain, white jockey shorts, but they have to be more careful about shorts that fit too snugly because of the aforementioned headaches.

Upon graduation, a young man is fully expected to change into boxer shorts. These shorts are white and they hit just above the knees. A young man should wear this type of undershorts for the remainder of his life, even if he eventually winds up with a truss underneath his clothing, too.

That's the way it used to be, back in a simpler time. Then came Jim Palmer.

Jim Palmer is a famous baseball pitcher who is quite handsome. Some advertising genius got the bright idea to take a picture of Jim Palmer in a pair of bikini-type underwear for men and put it in a lot of magazines. Men, or should I say those men who do not make a habit of looking at pictures of other men in their underpants, ignored these pictures of Jim Palmer, but women didn't.

They began to say to their mates such things as "Why don't you get some sexy underwear like Jim Palmer wears?"

A lot of men went out and did that, but it posed a real problem for others. What good did it do to wear Jim Palmer underwear if you happened to look like Yogi Berra?

I didn't know what to do. I had a couple of dozen pairs of normal, white boxer shorts, and even walking past a display of Jim Palmer bikini-type underpants made me feel quite silly. My wife at the time insisted, however, that I try out a pair, so I dutifully went into the men's underwear section of a large department store.

Why do they allow women to sell men's underwear?

"Can I help you with something?" asked the girl in the underwear department. I wondered if her father knew she had this job.

"Yes," I mumbled, "I would like to buy some underwear."

"And what type would you like, sir?" she went on.

"Well," I said, "I'm not really certain. Do you have any of those like what's-his-name, the baseball player, wears?"

"Oh, you mean the Jim Palmer jockey brief. Yes, we have all colors in four sizes — Small, Medium, Large, and XLC."

"XLC?"

"Extra Large Crotch," said the salesgirl.

I thought of running out the door. I would never see the salesgirl again, and I could tell my wife that when I got to the department store, there were a lot of fruity-looking characters buying Jim Palmer's underwear and I didn't want to be a part of it.

Before I could make my move, however, the salesgirl was standing in front of me with several pairs of Jim Palmer jockey briefs.

"I can see you're a little unsure, sir," she said. "Why don't you step into our dressing room and try on a pair and see how you like them?"

"Incidentally," I said, "what size are these?"

"Well," said the salesgirl, "it's only a guess, but I picked Small."

When nobody was looking, I slipped out of the dressing room and left my Jim Palmer jockey briefs there. I would explain to my wife that they were all out of my size, and she would understand. She would realize that they probably didn't make many XLC's for guys, well, guys like me.

"All out of Small, huh?" replied my wife.

Jim Palmer was recently released by the Baltimore Orioles and his baseball career is likely over, so I hope he'll put his pants back on and leave the rest of us alone for awhile.

The second part of the problem, as you remember, was that women enjoyed looking at men's butts. They even had calendars with pictures of naked men showing off their buns. This feminine interest in men's hindparts led to another problem regarding the wardrobe, but first some background:

Previous to the revelation that women enjoyed the aesthetic qualities of the male hindpart, men spent little time considering the shape of their hips, much less the presentation of same. They selected a pair of trousers on the basis of comfort alone. Consequently, most men walked around in baggy pants, which offered the ultimate in comfort and free movement, but which also totally veiled the male rear and suggested on some occasions that a family of gypsies had moved out of the seat.

Women's liberation came along, however, and the baggy pants industry went bust, but a boom followed in the blue jean game.

Before, only cowboys and young men under the age of seventeen had worn blue jeans. There was an obvious reason for cowboys' wearing this attire. You can get all sorts of substances on a pair of jeans, like what cows leave all over the dusty trail, and still not have to wash them for weeks at a time ... especially if all the other cowboys' jeans are smelly, too.

Most little boys wanted to be just like the cowboys back then, so their mothers dressed them in jeans. I not only wanted to be a cowboy when I was a child, I was convinced I *was* one. As a matter of fact, I was convinced I was Roy Rogers, who was my favorite western star.

Before we moved to tiny Moreland, we lived in a large apartment complex in Virginia while my father soldiered. I got lost one day. I began to cry. (Cowboys never cry unless they're five and hopelessly lost and hungry and want their mothers.) A kind lady attempted to find out where I lived so she could take me home.

"What's your name, little boy?" she asked.

"Roy Rogers," I said.

She called the resident manager's office and asked where the Rogers family lived. There was no family by that name in the apartment complex.

"Are you certain your name is Roy Rogers?" she asked me again.

"Does Trigger have a long tail?" I asked her back.

Finally, the lady began calling all the apartments asking if anybody had a retarded child who thought he was Roy Rogers. Thankfully, my mother claimed me when the lady reached her.

After high school, a male was expected to step out of his blue jeans and into a pair of baggy pants. It was in this style of dress that he then would leave home for the serious effort of educating himself further, learning a trade, or joining the armed forces, which strenuously objected to any form of tight-fitting trousers since they would deter swift movement on the battlefield.

That has all changed, however. Today, men normally have a closetful of blue jeans, because nothing shows off the hips better than a pair of tight-fitting blue jeans, and they're considered appropriate attire for practically every occasion except state funerals.

Most men, raised under the old rules of loose-fitting pants, had to learn a number of new rules about buying jeans:

1. They had to remember to buy their jeans at least two inches smaller in the waist than the jeans and trousers they bought before Women's Liberation. Some jeans advertised a "skosh" more room in the seat, but I don't think they sold very well. That one little "skosh" just might be enough to cause you to go unnoticed by a gaggle of gimlet-eyed legal secretaries hip-watching during a Friday afternoon happy hour.

2. They had to remember that if they decided to bend over for any reason while wearing tight-fitting jeans, they should take a deep breath first to avoid passing out. Rule 2-A is, if you bend over and hear a ripping sound, place both hands over your backside and run backwards towards the nearest restroom. At an outdoor function, cover and run backwards towards the nearest heavy growth of kudzu.

3. It was important to note that tight-fitting jeans could be the devil to remove from your body. Men had to remember always to carry a pocketknife with them when they were wearing their tight jeans, just in case it became necessary to cut them away from their bodies in an extreme emergency ... such as if they were sick and tired of sleeping in them.

4. Men had to accept the fact that while they were wearing tight jeans, they absolutely had to hold their stomachs in at all times, even though doing so would cause their faces to turn red and their eyes to bug out (not to mention the possibility of swollen ankles).

It was in the late seventies that I finally relented and went out and bought my first pair of adult blue jeans. I was surprised at the varieties available. Even the noted snooty designers Bill Blass and Calvin Klein had jeans lines, which suddenly cost what a man used to pay for a Sunday suit.

I bought myself a pair of tight-fitting Kleins and wore them out of the store and headed to the nearest singles bar. I ordered a drink and made certain I kept my backside pointed toward the tables of legal secretaries sipping pina coladas, figuring the sight of my new jeans hugging closely to my hips would knock the umbrellas right out of their glasses.

Unfortunately, no action was forthcoming. A man standing next to me in a pair of tight-fitting Bill Blass jeans finally turned to me and said, "How long you been here?"

"Couple of beers," I answered.

"Me, too," he replied. "I don't think I've gotten one glance."

There was something terribly wrong here. We had both spent half a week's salary on a pair of designer jeans that we had stuffed ourselves into, and all the women who were supposed to go wild at the sight of men's hips hadn't shown the slightest interest.

"I guess it's like my old grandpa used to say," said Bill Blass. "'It don't matter what kind of rifle you have if you ain't got any ammunition to load it with.'"

I finished my beer, went home, and cut myself out of my Calvin Klein jeans. I spent the remainder of the evening attempting to learn to breathe normally again.

* * *

I have never ceased to be amazed by the lengths men will go to satisfy a feminine whim. Take aftershave lotion. God gave men Old Spice aftershave lotion, and that should have been enough. But, no. Women decided that Old Spice, which is what everybody's daddy wore, wasn't nearly the sexy aroma they wanted, and so men had another problem — What sort of aftershave should I use to set my woman's blood to boiling?

There was English Leather. You know what the sexy lady on television says about that — "My men wear English Leather ... or they wear nothing at all."

I can just see it now. I go over to have dinner with her and her parents, and I show up naked as a jaybird.

"Are you crazy?" she screams at me.

"Well," I attempt to explain, "I was all out of English Leather and the stores were closed, so like you say, either I wear English Leather or I wear...."

Somebody later figured out that what a woman really wanted to smell on a man was his natural odor with a little perfume thrown in. The upshoot of that revelation was something called "musk." I could never bring myself to splash anything called "musk" all over my face. It sounded too much like the way it smelled in the kitchen after I hadn't taken the garbage out for a week.

Pete Rose tried to get us back on track and away from all those exotic perfumed potions when he claimed "a man wants to smell like a man" and urged us all to buy Aqua Velva, first cousin to Old Spice. Of course, with Pete Rose's money, he could splash tobacco juice on his face and still make out.

The big question facing men today is, if I use Paco Rabanne cologne, will I score as much as the guys in their advertisements obviously do?

I never have actually smelled Paco Rabanne, but their

ads, which also appear in a number of women's magazines because women are the ones who buy most of the cosmetics for men in the first place, are something else.

Get the picture: This muscular fellow is in bed and covers are all askew. It's obvious that the only thing between him and butt-naked is the sheet he has pulled up just enough to avoid embarrassing his parents, in case they happened to stumble across the ad.

He's on the telephone, talking to the woman who spent the night with him but who had to get up early for an appointment with the board of directors. She is a totally New Woman, who doesn't want children until she has been made a partner in the firm. She also is very open about her sexuality, which means she always carries an extra toothbrush in her handbag just in case.

In a Paco Rabanne ad, you read the dialogue between the man naked in the bed and the woman on the other end of the telephone. It goes something like this:

WOMAN: "You animal."

MAN: "I was just thinking about you."

WOMAN: "You beast."

MAN: "So it was good for you. I was embarrassed to ask."

WOMAN: "My toes are still tingling."

MAN: "Down, girl."

WOMAN: "What are you doing right now?"

MAN: "I'm naked under the sheets."

WOMAN: "You devil."

MAN: "Are you coming back over tonight?"

WOMAN: "Can Burl Ives sell tea?"

MAN: "I'll splash on a lot of Paco Rabanne."

WOMAN: "Forget my career. Forget my partnership in the firm. I'll be right over."

MAN: "Sure you don't mind?"

WOMAN: "My mind might not be sure, you hunk, but the rest of me is."

Paco Rabanne for men. What is remembered is up to you.

How are men supposed to stick to something simple like Old Spice when they can pop for a little Paco Rabanne and maybe stay naked under the sheets for weeks at a time?

Sex. It's everywhere. It's in the music, it determines what clothes we wear, and even what we splash on our faces after we shave.

Do we really have it better than our parents? Sex was simple for them. All they had to do was memorize one position and remember to turn the light off.

But sex has been a whole new ball game for my generation. I'm still not certain if a *ménage à trois* is some sort of French cooking with lots of sauce or something you do naked under the sheets with a girls' volleyball team. And with my luck, about the time I find out, I'll have ulcers and will be too old for it to really matter.

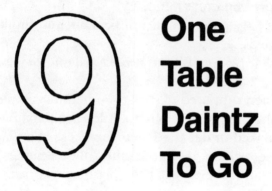

One Table Daintz To Go

SEX TODAY IS just as scrambled as everything else. You can't even talk about it without getting confused. As evidence, I present a glossary of modern sexual terms:

— LOVER: Somebody you aren't married to, but you're sleeping with them anyway.

— COHABITATION: When your lover moves into your apartment and brings all of his or her clothes and starts getting his or her mail at your address. You still aren't married but you're telling your parents that any day now you will be.

— PALIMONY: What you have to pay your ex-lover monthly, even though you never did get around to marrying her.

— GAY: Formerly "queer," "fruit," or "fag." Means you and your lover can go into the same bathroom together when you stop at service stations during long trips.

— AIDS: You and your lover can share the same hospital room together, too.

— PLATO'S RETREAT: Club in New York City where anything goes, including having sex with any number of total strangers.

— HERPES: A little something to remember your last night at Plato's Retreat by.

— RELATIONSHIP: What you tell your friends you're having with your boss because "affair" sounds so tacky.

— G-SPOT: When you touch a woman there, she makes very loud noises. The next morning the kids want to know if there was a panther in your bedroom last night.

— HUNK: What women call exceptionally attractive men.

— RICHARD GERE: Hollywood hunk who has never appeared with his shirt on for more than two minutes at a time in any of his movies.

— BATTERY STOCKS: Really have nothing to do with sex, but have you noticed how much they've gone up since modern women discovered vibrators may be used for more than soothing the tired feet they used to get from standing at the ironing board?

— *PENTHOUSE* MAGAZINE FORUM: Where readers write in to tell of their unusual sexual experiences. Many of these experiences are totally sick and perverted, and the magazine is nothing more than a blight on public decency. Nice people would never be caught reading such trash.

— *PENTHOUSE* MAGAZINE CIRCULATION: It's somewhere in the millions.

— X-RATED: Movie industry rating for film that includes explicit sex scenes.

— R-RATED: Movie industry rating for film that includes explicit sex scenes, but there is some semblance of a plot.

— PG-RATED: Movie industry rating for film where the

sex scenes are not quite as steamy, the plot may actually make sense, and your parents won't be totally embarrassed to watch it.

— *PLAYBOY* CHANNEL: Cable television channel that features X-rated films in your very own home and usually shows the most explicit sex scenes after your parents are asleep. The sound tracks on these films are optional, so there's no need to turn up the volume and risk awakening your parents.

— THE POPE: Powerful religious figure who recently said sex is sinful unless it's being performed for the strict purpose of procreation.

— JERRY FALWELL: Another powerful religious figure who would like to see sex done away with altogether, but he hasn't been able to come up with a viable alternative.

— JOGGING, RACQUETBALL, PLAYING *TRIVIAL PURSUIT,* AND BACKGAMMON: A few activities that have failed miserably as alternatives to sex, but people keep trying them anyway.

— S AND M: Odd sexual activity, involving whips and black leather outfits, which may be traced back to former cowboy star Lash Larue.

— KINKY: Sexual behavior involving the use of duck feathers.

— PERVERTED: You use the whole duck.

See what I mean? That's why so many sex manuals make it to the bestseller list and why the argument for sex education classes in our schools is such a good one. Perhaps if we teach our children all about sex in the schools, then they will be able to explain it to their parents.

We really didn't need sex education classes when I was in

school, because there wasn't that much to learn. You could get about all the sexual knowledge that was known at the time from an older classmate in a very short period of time ... say, just as long as it took for an older classmate to explain that all you'll ever find in a cabbage patch is cabbage and maybe a rat snake or two.

I'm not certain when sex became so confusing, but I think it was when women decided to take part in it. Frankly, I don't blame them for that, because sex — with the afore-mentioned exception of when you're sunburned and also when you're very sleepy or there's a ball game on you want to watch — can be quite a rewarding experience.

But previously, only men had sex. Women were there when all this was taking place, but theirs was basically the role of a waitress who puts the food on the table and says, "I hope you enjoy it," and then goes back to the kitchen to have a smoke.

I suspect that it was a man who got women involved in sex. It probably was the first man who made love to a woman and then wondered if it had been as pleasant for her as it had been for him, so he asked that infamous question: "Was it good for you?"

Men had never wondered that before. You didn't ask your bird dog how he enjoyed the hunting trip or your fishing worm how the water was.

I suppose our previous attitude came from the puritanical belief that sex was basically a rotten thing to do, and if a woman took some pleasure from the experience, she obviously was not the delicate flower she was supposed to be and should be tied to the dunking stool. It took women three hundred years to get over the fear that if they uttered one little sound of pleasure during sex or actually moved, they would be severely punished. I'm not certain, however, if what they feared most was the embarrassment of being dunked in public or the horror of getting their hair wet.

So when the first man asked the question, "Was it good for you?", he created a real dilemma for the woman.

If it *hadn't* been good for her and she admitted it, women's sexual liberation would have been set back another three hundred years, because her sexual partner would have gone out and told all his friends, "Aha! It's just as we expected. They really don't have any fun when they have sex."

But if she *had* enjoyed it and she said so, that same creep would have gone out and told all his friends that she was some sort of brazen hussy who actually enjoyed sex. By the time the gossip got around, the rumor would be that she had said she not only enjoyed sex but often spent ten or fifteen minutes a day thinking about it, and that kind of rumor could get you kicked out of the Junior League.

I admire that first woman who admitted she had, in fact, thoroughly enjoyed the experience of sex. It might have gone something like this:

"Sweetheart?"

"Yes, my dear?"

"May I ask you a question?"

"You want me to run to the store to get you a pack of cigarettes?"

"No, not at all. I just want to ask you a question."

"I really don't mind going to the store. I don't have to start dinner for another half hour."

"That's not it at all, sweetheart. There's just something that has been on my mind."

"You're wondering whether or not I would mind if you went bowling Friday night and then stayed out and had a few beers with the boys and came in all sloppy drunk and passed out in the floor of the living room. Of course, I don't mind, dear. I know you need some time of your own."

"That's not it at all, Sugar Love. See, some of the guys down at the plant and me were talking and this one guy wanted to know, well...."

"If I would bring my delicious brownies to the union hall for next week's meeting?"

"No, he wanted to know, uh, he just wondered if women enjoyed sex, too."

"Marvin!"

"No, Lovey, I mean it's something guys think about a lot. I mean, was what we just did, I mean, you know ... was it good for you?"

"It was great."

"It was?"

"I loved it."

"You're kidding me."

"No, I'm not. It was absolutely wonderful and let's do it again right now."

"I can't right now, Honey. I've got to run down to the plant and tell the other guys."

You can see the trouble this started. Marvin told the other guys, and then they asked their wives, and their wives said they enjoyed sex, too, and soon the word got out all over. Suddenly women all over the world were no longer ashamed to admit their interest in lovemaking, and that's how the sexual revolution began.

The sexual revolution may have liberated women sexually, but it put a great deal of heretofore unfelt pressure on men. Sometime after the first publication of *Playgirl* magazine, where handsome men posed nude for the now-accepted prurient interests of women, women not only were admitting to men that they enjoyed sex, but they were answering the was-it-good-for-you question honestly. Men never have been the same sexually since.

"Sweetheart?"

"Yes, Marvin."

"Was it good for you?"

"Want to know the truth?"

"Of course, my sweet."

"No."

"Do what?"

"It wasn't good for me at all. In a recent article in *Cosmopolitan,* eight out of every ten women polled said their sexual partners did not engage in enough foreplay, were not sensitive enough to the female's needs, and insisted the lights be turned off."

"How would you have voted in that poll, my pet?"

"Turn on the lights, Speedy Gonzales, and I'll show you my ballot."

After this, of course, men had to take special care to please their sexual partners, and this was not an easy thing for them to do because of their backgrounds, and because very few of them read *Cosmo.*

This pressure also resulted in some men suffering from impotence and in the eventual creation of ESPN, the twenty-four-hour all-sports cable television network, which gives men something to do at night after their sexual partners have begun holding up rating cards like judges at diving meets. This, of course, eventually causes them to be too nervous to do anything but watch rodeos and college hockey games on the tube until three in the morning.

The sexual revolution and the revelation that women

actually enjoyed being part of the sexual experience also sent sex into a fad stage, where it remains to this day.

Having simple sex isn't enough anymore. The various sex manuals have revealed there are many kinky positions in which to have sex, such as with your favorite shortstop in the dirt part of the infield so you won't get all scratched up on the artificial turf, and there are all sorts of extracurricular activities that may be interwoven with the sex act.

Today's trendy magazines are filled with examples and instructions regarding such matters. Read the *Penthouse* Forum, for example, and you will wonder if you're the only person left alive on earth who hasn't had sex while riding in a Ferris wheel or standing on your head at a Tupperware party.

It seems that something new and confusing comes out everyday with regard to sex.

And for somebody like me, who was reared in the sexual naiveté of the fifties and who always had a great deal of trouble understanding and getting along with women in the first place, the entire sexual scene has become totally baffling and frustrating.

I'm not certain how I should act around women anymore in order to attract their attention or to arouse any sort of physical interest in me.

I've tried to be sensitive at times by pouring my beer into a glass before I drink it, but all this usually gets me is a long discussion about how her ex-husband used to make love with his socks on.

I've also tried to be like Clint Eastwood and stare at her with my cold yet lusty eyes and not say very much, but all this usually leads to is my being terribly uncomfortable. I mean, sooner or later a man needs to go to the bathroom, but you never saw Clint Eastwood putting the move on a beautiful woman and suddenly announcing that he had to go to the bathroom. He's much too cool for that. Of course, the reason he's always clenching his teeth and has that stern look about him is that he hasn't been to the bathroom in a week, and it's killing him.

I never know what to say to girls in bars anymore, either. Bogart and those guys used to walk over to a woman, light her cigarette, and say, "Sweetheart, where have you been all my life?" and that was it. My generation countered with, "What's your sign?" and "I hate to see anybody drink alone," but then women wised up to those. Now, I think the only men who ever meet women in bars and something actually comes of it are those weirdos who write to *Penthouse* Forum:

"I'm twenty-three and quite a handsome guy, if I do say so myself, and let me tell you what happened to me one recent night when I was on a business trip to Toledo.

"I walked into a bar and there was this gorgeous blonde, wearing a tight-fitting pink sweater and black leather pants and roller skates, standing alone nursing a pina colada.

"I took a spot next to her at the bar and ordered myself a gin and Pepsi. She took off her Sony Walkman and skated closer to me. I could feel her hot breath with the faint scent of coconut against my flushed face.

"We finished our drinks, and without saying a word, this voluptuous creature and I walked (she skated) out of the bar and went back to my hotel room.

"I have never spent such a night of ecstasy. She took off all my clothes and tied me to the bed with a rope she carried in her handbag, and then she skated up and down on me until I was driven out of my mind with passion.

"The next morning, my back looked like they had run the Indy 500 time trials on it, but I will never forget the gorgeous blonde at the bar, and now every time I see Roller Derby on television, I'm aroused. I would be interested to know if any of your other readers have ever had such an experience."

Not me, although a girl did nearly run me down on her Harley one afternoon outside a bowling alley in Houston.

Women are simply too sexually aware today for anybody to sweep them off their feet, especially in a bar where they dress seductively and go to see how many men they can reduce to sniveling idiots. It has been my experience that such women especially enjoy making vulnerable, recently-divorced men feel as though they need to go back immediately and crawl under the rock from which they obviously sprang. This story requires a little background:

I got one of my divorces when I was living in Chicago. I distinctly remember the conversation with my wife when I first learned that she was terribly unhappy being married to me. I called home one evening from work.

"Hi, sweetheart," I began. "What's for dinner?"

"What did you do for dinner before you got married?"

"What kind of question is that?"

"A perfectly good question. What did you do for dinner before you got married?"

"Ate a lot of fish sticks. Why?"

"Here's a hint: Frozen fish sticks are on sale at the Jewell Store. I'd advise you to stop there on your way home."

That was just her funny way of saying she was splitting.

Years later, I figured the whole thing out. Being a house-wife had caused her to lose her identity, and what she needed was to find her own space and establish a relationship with someone who didn't mind preparing fish sticks for *her* once in a while.

At the time, however, I was yet languishing in the idea that it should be enough for a woman that I worked hard and provided for her and didn't talk ugly about her kinfolks. That belief I had picked up from role models during my youth. The old people at home would talk about marriage and the duties of the partners in such conversations as this:

"Heard Clovis Niles is gettin' married."

"Who to?"

"Grover Turnipseed."

"He's a fine boy."

"Don't drink much."

"Works hard, too."

"Don't lay out in beer joints all night."

"Owns his own double-wide trailer."

"He'll make a good provider."

"She's a good cook."

"Sews, too."

"And cans."

In the seventies, of course, women began to want a lot more than a man who owned his own double-wide, but somehow I missed that announcement. So there I was, stuck in Chicago, the snows of winter just around the end-of-October corner, my wife gone, and fish sticks up to my ears.

I had very little luck getting dates in Chicago after my wife left. The biggest problem was that when I went into singles bars on Division Street, I usually was confronted by a lot of people wearing huge furry coats and hats and gloves — they were still trying to thaw out from the cold on the sidewalks outside. (Chicago is the coldest place on earth where polar bears don't roam free.)

The drawback to all that cold-weather gear was that it was often difficult to determine male from female. Everybody looks basically alike when they're dressed like Nanook of the North. That's why Eskimos spend a lot of time cutting holes in the ice and fishing — it's safer than making the wrong move in the igloo and winding up putting the make on the guy with whom you share your kayak.

My next problem, once I had distinguished the men from the women, was my previously admitted inability to think of anything clever to say to a total stranger in a bar. This problem was amplified by the fact that Chicago women — know affectionately as "Michigan Avenue Marauders" — were anything but gentle to poor souls like myself, who were simply looking for someone with whom to huddle against the cold.

Imagine this scene: I'm lonely and far from home. My wife has split and I'm crawling all over thirty, and whatever speed I once had on my singles bar fastball is now only a memory. But a man has to try. A man simply has to try.

She's sitting there on a stool at the bar at Butch McGuire's, and for some girl who's probably from Indiana and works for an advertising firm, she's not bad at all. (She could have been from North Dakota and pumped gas, for all I cared at the time.)

"Gee, it's cold outside," I used as an ice-breaker, if you will.

"What was your first clue, Dick Tracy?"

"That's cute. Could I buy you a drink?"

"Suit yourself."

"What will you have?"

"Cutty rocks."

"Cutty rocks, bartender. I like these Irish bars, don't you?"

"They're okay. Except you have to talk to a lot of weirdos."

"Speaking of Irishmen, hear the one about the two Irish gays?"

"No, but I get the feeling I'm going to."

"Yeah, there was Michael Fitzpatrick and Patrick Fitzmichael. Get it?"

"Thanks for the drink, Tex. I gotta catch the train to Skokie."

There was one night in Butch's when I thought I finally had scored. She was a lovely thing, standing over at the corner of the bar. Just to be sure, I looked down at her feet. She was wearing pink galoshes. Normally, the men in Chicago, even the strange ones, don't wear pink galoshes.

She was staring at me. I was certain of it. I continued to glance over at her. Each time our eyes met, she smiled. This was it! All I had to do was walk over, introduce myself, hit her with a few quick stories, and I would be in.

I didn't want to rush it, however. I ordered myself another drink, casually lit a cigarette, blew out a couple of perfectly-formed smoke rings, and tried to look slightly bored, so that when I said to her, "I really hate these kinds of places; they're nothing but meat markets," she would not doubt my sincerity.

When I thought the time was right, I strolled toward her. Her eyes were still staring directly into mine, her lips curved in a knowing smile.

"I really hate these kinds of places; they're nothing but meat markets," I began.

"I hope you don't mind if I tell you something," the lady said.

"I know you don't usually come on to men like this," I replied, trying to make her feel at ease with her obvious advances. "But don't feel bad about it. It's okay for a woman to do things like that today. We aren't living in the Stone Age anymore, you know."

That would do it, of course. She would recognize me as a very aware person — sensitive, caring, with a beast inside me somewhere, just waiting for the right woman to come along and awaken it.

"I don't want to embarrass you," the woman said, "but your fly is open."

I went back to my apartment, crawled under the bed, assumed the fetal position, and had a nervous breakdown.

* * *

One of the things militant feminists say about men is that we feel threatened by the new feminine aggressiveness and assertiveness. They're right, especially when they say things like that about men who remember women the way they used to be.

We're terribly confused about what women want us to do, when they want us to do it, and for how long. And we aren't certain that one day they aren't going to ditch us altogether, when somebody invents a computer that can do about three or four things at once with the proper mixture of tenderness and boldness, and after women are finished using it, it won't roll over and snore and keep them awake all night.

Do you know what's making a comeback in this country on the sex front? Strip joints, that's what. Strip joints are making a comeback because men can go in there an ogle and whistle and make all those remarks they learned in the

Navy, and the women won't get angry and call their sisters-in-arms and cause the men all sorts of embarrassment and bodily pain.

I wandered into a place one night in Memphis called The Yellow Pussycat. All around me were young women. They were quite naked and they were dancing. I ordered myself a drink and began to watch. Soon, I was approached by one of the young women who had been dancing.

"Wanta table daintz?" she asked. ("Daintz" is the way "dance" comes out when a naked Southern girl with a mouthful of gum says it.)

"What's a table dance?" I asked.

She rolled her eyes as if to ponder what primitive means of transportation recently had dropped me at this address.

"You pay me seven dollars," she said, "and I daintz on your table."

"A sort of private dance, huh?" I probed.

She rolled her eyes again. "Others can watch if they want to," she explained, "but they won't get to see nothin' up close like you will."

Good sport that I am, I paid the seven bucks and experienced my first table dance. The problem was that I am easily embarrassed and often feel quite self-conscious in public, and here I was — a total stranger in a place that obviously wasn't the Christian Science Reading Room, and a young woman I never had seen before in my life was dancing on my table, often moving close enough for me to see the innermost construction of her navel.

I didn't want to stare directly at her and appear like some old lecher, but on the other hand, I had paid the seven bucks and felt obliged to get my money's worth by watching every twitch and strut.

Had we been sipping wine alone together and Table Daintzer had suddenly been so moved by the music and the passion and the subsequent giddiness that she had climbed atop a nearby table to disrobe and move sensuously to the music, I would have thoroughly enjoyed the experience. In this setting, however, I was more than uncomfortable.

After the table dance was mercifully over, she asked me if I wanted another, and I said, "Thank you, but no." Then she said that if I would buy her a bottle of champagne (she split the cost with the house twenty-eighty, she explained, and needed the money in order to pay for her little sister's operation), she would join me at my table and we could talk.

Naturally, I wanted to help all I could with her little sister's operation, so I ordered the champagne and we sat and talked. It was the first time I had had a conversation with a woman in years that we didn't have to discuss her career.

I admit openly and without shame that I am intimidated by today's modern woman. The female role models I had as a child were my mother, who still made homemade biscuits in the morning, and my teachers, who were too busy teaching me how to long divide to tell me that when I grew up, women would be drinking and smoking and sweating in public and telling dirty jokes and would punch you in the mouth if you made a remark they deemed sexist.

Women didn't sweat, or at least I didn't think they did, until the late sixties. I went to school with little girls who wore sundresses and thought it terribly unfeminine to engage in any sort of activity that might indicate they hadn't been born with their sweat glands nailed completely shut, so they could grow up to be cheerleaders and could lift their hands to clap and not be concerned that somebody would see wet spots under their arms. There was even the axiom that "horses sweat, men perspire, and women *glow*."

That didn't change in college, either. The girls there wore cute little outfits and were in school to find husbands. The only ones who were in school to learn anything were the ones who wore thick glasses and played horn. They all eventually grew up to become militant feminists, of course, and they're getting back at us now for all those years the rest of us were busy having parties and picking mates, while they were down at the music room blowing into a stupid trumpet or tuba. The fact that most militant feminists wear thick glasses and have pooched-out lips from too many nights of blowing into horns is proof of my contention.

It was sweat, I think, that finally led to most women's casting aside their previous role as demure little things, to be left in the kitchen while the men withdrew to the study for cigars and brandy to discuss the pros and cons of the designated hitter.

I saw it coming in 1968. The University of Georgia at that time was intent on keeping passion to a minimum on campus. The free-sex movement had started on some Northern campuses, but at Georgia, students had remained in the political and moral status quo. Once you gave a girl your fraternity pin, you might expect a little something more than a kiss goodnight — especially if Georgia had won its football game that week — but nobody ever was late for botany class because they had lost track of the time during a heated moment of noonday passion.

One of the ways the university attempted to keep the status quo was by not allowing coeds to walk around campus in their gym shorts after P.E. classes, thus tempting male students.

For years coeds never muttered a sound about this rule. After P.E., they simply put their raincoats around their gym outfits and went to their next class. They never complained in hot weather, of course, because since *ladies* didn't sweat and smell gamey, walking around in a raincoat didn't bother them, even if they had just completed a rousing game of volleyball and the temperature was over ninety degrees.

In the spring of 1968, however, a young coed named DeLores Perkwater, who wore thick glasses and played horn, passed out in class from heat exposure following her gym session. When they took her raincoat off, they noticed she was perspiring profusely.

Even the more demure coeds from the finest sororities subsequently decided that making them wear raincoats after gym class was cruel and unusual punishment, and the first notice I had of what was to come in the feminist movement occurred soon after. A number of slogan-chanting Georgia coeds, marching in the name of DeLores Perkwater, took over the administration building and refused to leave until the university rescinded the gym shorts rule.

Officials might have won out, but the protest took place late in spring quarter, and after the coeds had been inside the administration building (which was not air-conditioned at the time) for several days without benefit of bathing, the atmosphere became so pungent that the university decided to give in.

"Coeds Free To Sweat!" screamed the headlines in the school newspaper, and soon women all over the country began sweating in public and thinking nothing of it. This eventually led women to begin exercising, building their bodies, and applying for jobs as construction workers and goat ropers and all sorts of other jobs previously performed by men only.

Once women began to do all that, there was no stopping them. And they owe it all to DeLores Perkwater, now commander of the 14th Bomber Wing of the National Organization of Women.

* * *

I'm not certain what my own future will be regarding women. I am currently single, and I don't know what sort of woman I would want to marry if ever I married again.

I still would like to have a wife who cooks a meal occasionally, even if she happens to be the governor. I still like women who don't know everything that I know, so I can tell them something occasionally and they can look at me like I'm quite intelligent. In other words, I want a woman who I stand at least an even chance at beating in a game of *Trivial Pursuit* and who doesn't understand the infield fly rule, so I can take her to baseball games and put my arm around her and say things like, "Well, sweetheart, it's like this...."

I do not want a woman who has hairy legs like mine. I don't want a woman who is in any shape or form involved in the martial arts, and I don't want a woman who comes to bed smelling like a can of Penzoil because her hobby is rebuilding race cars for the Junior Johnson racing team.

I don't want a woman who introduces me to all sorts of strange sexual techniques that she picked up on a recent business trip to the Orient. I don't want a woman who knees me in the belly when I forget to put the top back on the toothpaste, and I don't want a woman who gets into drinking bouts with Marine recruits and maintains a winning percentage.

It's the same old problem for me: I want a woman like women were in 1962, because I remember them as being soft and nice to hold and, like Merle Haggard said, they could still cook back then and still would. I don't mind if girls grow up to be president these days, and I don't think women should be given smaller wages simply because they're women, but what do I do with these old-fashioned feelings that were instilled in me? What can I do about the fact that a woman in a coat and tie carrying a briefcase doesn't do much for me in the area of physical attraction? I didn't come here to take out a loan, madam, I wanted to hug you and kiss you on your mouth.

What I'm doing here is dilly-dallying around. I know exactly what I want in a woman.

I want a woman who was raised in a rural atmosphere and whose mother taught her to bake pies and fry chicken and make gravy and iced tea.

I want her to have no ambition beyond making me very happy and comfortable, including giving me back rubs at night and not complaining when I keep the television on until two in the morning watching a ball game from the West Coast.

I want her to be good to my dog, and I want her to take her own overheads when we play tennis and to lob when I tell her to. I want her to be open and willing sexually, but I don't want her to insist on anything acrobatic that could cause me to have a back injury or get an eye put out.

I want her to like country music and at least understand the basics of college football as it is played in major conferences, and I want her to make devilled eggs to carry to the games for the pre-game brunch, and if it happens to rain, I don't want to hear, "How much longer is this thing going to last?"

I want her to pop me popcorn on cold nights when we're sitting in front of the fire. I want her to make certain there always is cold beer in the ice box and that I never run out of clean underwear. I want her to talk sweetly to me on mornings after I've made a fool out of myself at a party and have a terrible hangover, and I want her to be afraid of spiders and call me to come squish them when she sees one running across the floor in the kitchen.

The sad truth is that I have known and have had such women, but for one reason or other, I have let them get away. I'm not certain there are very many like them left, and it probably would serve me right if I wound up with DeLores Perkwater.

In the midst of this dilemma, I always harken back to the words of my boyhood friend and idol, Weyman C. Wannamaker, Jr., a great American, who once surveyed the changing scene of the roles for women and said, "The whole thing boils down to the fact that the opposite sex ain't nearly as opposite as it used to be."

To further complicate the matter of sex in the 1980s, of course, we are a society attempting to deal with the gay movement. I cannot quote Weyman on his thoughts regarding the gay movement, because he is not at all tolerant in that area. Okay, maybe just one quote:

"All you hear about these days," says Weyman, "is them queers (I'm sorry, but Weyman refuses to say *gay* and it took me months to get him to tone it down to *queer*) and how they have all come out of the closet. I'll tell you one thing — I bet it was a mess in that closet when they were all back up in there together."

Weyman's basic problem with the gay movement, and

mine as well, is that we have had no background whatsoever in dealing with something that seems quite unnatural, occasionally appalling, and, even in my most tolerant moments, something that I one day might be able to accept but never understand.

As far as I know, the first gay person I ever saw was a waiter in a spiffy Atlanta restaurant. I'm not certain why, but it seems there is an overabundant number of effeminate young men working in spiffy restaurants these days. Now, I understand that just because a male is effeminate, it doesn't necessarily mean that he's gay, and just because a man may come on as a rugged, macho-type, it doesn't necessarily mean that he's straight. However (and I promise this is the last time I'm going to quote Weyman on such a sensitive issue), when I see a young man sashay over to me in a spiffy restaurant, and he just sort of floats when he walks and he's what we used to call prissy, I cannot help but harken back to what Weyman says when he sees somebody like that: "Damn, but if I don't believe that ol' boy's about half-queer."

Anyway, some years ago I went into a restaurant, and a young man fitting the above description prissed over to my table and said in a delicate voice, "Hi, I'm Keith, and I'll be your waiter this evening." He sort of put a question mark on the end of "evening," ending his pronouncement with a bit of a wrist movement that you never see from the grill man at an all-night truckstop.

I didn't know exactly what to say, so I said, "Hi there, Keith, I'm Lewis and I'll be your customer."

All that straight, he began by telling me and my party about what *wasn't* on the menu. (I don't know why spiffy restaurants never put their good stuff on the menu, but they don't.)

"Tonight," said Keith, "we have some absolutely *sker-rump-tious* specials."

With that, he delivered an entire litany of dishes I had never heard of. When I said I'd just have the ground sirloin steak, well done, and some fries, he looked at me with a beady-eyed smirk as if to say, "How on earth did someone so uncivilized find my table?"

I think that's what I dislike most about going into an overpriced restaurant and having to deal with gay waiters: If you don't order something that sounds like it ought to have a part in a film with subtitles, gay waiters look at you like you've just broken wind. I try never to break wind in a restaurant, which is why I never order anything that might start my gastronomic network into embarrassing emissions.

There weren't any gay people in Moreland when I was growing up. We thought there was one once, and that led to months of gossip and suspense, but it turned out to be a false alarm.

There was this kid named Donnelle Spinks, who was about my age. His mother named him after his great aunt Donnelle, because he was her eighth and final child and she already had produced seven boys, all ugly and quite useless, and she had prayed for a girl. When Donnelle was born and turned out to be quite male, she figured she would simply make up for the Lord's obvious mistake.

She dressed Donnelle in girl's clothes until he started school and put ribbons in his hair and bought him dolls, and she would have taught him to sew and given him piano lessons had Mr. Spinks not eventually put his foot down. Donnelle, however, had to face terrible abuse from his class-mates because of his name and the way he walked — it was aptly described as walking like he was trying to carry a corncob in his crack.

Donnelle also had a rather effeminate voice with a slight lisp, and when it was discovered during a recess baseball game that his throw back to the cut-off man in the infield was delivered with the wristy technique of a girl, he was further branded as "queer as a rooster that wouldn't set foot in the henhouse."

Donnelle took the blows and the nasty comments until one afternoon in the sixth grade, when Alvin Bates, a smart-aleck teacher's pet, began to chide him on the playground near where the second graders were swinging on the monkey bars.

"Hey, Donelle," said Alvin, "your mother still puttin' dresses on you?"

Donnelle was used to this sort of thing, of course. He continued to do what he always did when somebody started the queer business with him — he ignored Alvin.

But then Alvin got nasty. "Hey, Donnelle," he said, "you going to play dolls after school today?"

Donnelle was still ignoring Alvin, who hadn't had enough.

"Hey, Donnelle, you a boy or a girl?"

"Quit picking on him, Alvin," said Betty Ann Hillback, who had performed a duet with Donnelle in the piano class recital.

"What's he going to do about it, Betty Ann?" asked Alvin. "Why don't you go hide in a closet and improve the scenery around here?"

Suddenly, unexpectedly, Donnelle was walking towards Alvin. "You can't talk to her that way," he said.

"What're you going to do about it, queer boy?" Alvin replied.

Betty Ann, the nervous type, had begun to cry.

"Tell her you're sorry for saying that," Donnelle demanded of Alvin.

"Who's going to make me?"

"Tell her."

"Kiss my...."

It all happened so quickly. Donnelle pounced on Alvin and inflicted facial wounds by the dozens. Donnelle then dragged Alvin over to the monkey bars, doubled him over one, and began giving him a series of quick kicks to his rear. Alvin soon was more than ready to apologize to Betty Ann for his insult.

Later, Alvin told the teacher that Donnelle Spinks had beaten him up, and the teacher called Mr. Spinks in to discuss the violent behavior of his son.

They say that after Mr. Spinks found out Donnelle had severely thrashed another boy on the school playground, he and his son became much closer, and Mr. Spinks bought Mrs. Spinks a little poodle dog, so she would still have something to pet now that Donnelle had become Don and had taken up the habit of walking to church with Betty Ann Hillback and holding her hand. That's when we knew for sure that Donnelle wasn't gay.

Today, I have too much trouble dealing with my own problems in the area of sexual relations to spend a great deal of time being concerned with those of others. That's why if someone chooses to be gay — or can't help it — that's fine with me ... as long as they don't attempt to do whatever gay people do near where I'm eating, watching a movie or a ball game, or attempting to fish, because such antics can be terribly distracting.

I would suggest that if gay people — who seem to have

become more and more vocal and more prone to displays of public affection as their numbers and acceptance into the mainstream have grown — have the sudden urge to love on one another and they can't find a motel room or the backseat of a car parked off in the woods somewhere, they should go back into the closet. It won't be for long, and they can come right back out when they're done.

I also am against gay people as a political force, because it's not wise to mix sex and politics. Had our forefathers known what was going to happen to American sex, they likely would have put something in the Constitution about separation of sex and politics; then sixteen-year-old pages in the House of Representatives could have gone into the cloakroom alone without fear of being accosted by heavy-breathing lawmakers.

On the other side of the coin, had we had a Constitutional dictum against sex and politics, we might also have been spared John and Rita Jenrette, who tried their darnedest to give heterosexuality a bad name ... and with all of us following the sordid saga on television.

10 Eddie Haskell Is Still A Jerk

I MENTIONED EARLIER that Phil Donahue and his television show have been a great source of consternation for me. Five mornings a week, Donahue gets together with a crowd of women who live in Chicago and apparently have nothing better to do, and they discuss strange things.

One morning recently, for example, his guests were two homosexual women and a baby. The two homosexual women, who said they were very much in love, had decided they wanted a baby, so one of them was artificially inseminated with the sperm of the other's brother, and the baby on the program was the result.

One of the homosexual women was black and the other was white, and I think they named the baby something like "Joy" or "Mud." I only remember that the baby didn't have a regular name like we used to give children — a name like Randy or Arlene.

I frankly don't care if a black female homosexual and a white female homosexual decide to love each other, but I do

have some concern for the offspring. Having been conceived in such an unconventional manner and having been
given a name that would embarrass a dog, I wonder if the
child will have the desire or the opportunity to do the things
that are important to most children — such as playing Little
League baseball, eating crayons in school, or laughing at a
clown.

What bothers me about this situation in particular, and
about the Donahue show in general, is where all this might
lead. Television today is probably the greatest single influence on the American public. A recent study showed that
the average TV in this country is on six hours and fifty-five
minutes a day; that's almost forty-nine hours a week. In a
ten-year period, that's almost three years of watching TV!
It's not surprising, therefore, that in many cases society has
become what it watches.

So my question is this: Will all these televised discussions
of aberrant lifestyles eventually make such behavior completely acceptable, and will people start producing babies
with home chemistry sets and giving them names that will
make it difficult for them to survive when they enter the
Marine Corps?

Actually, my problems with television didn't begin with
Donahue. After my Aunt Jessie, who lived next door,
brought home the first television I could watch on a regular
basis, it took me a year to figure out that Howdy Doody was a
puppet. I presumed he had once suffered from some sort of
crippling disease, and that was why he walked funny. He
also had a strange mouth, which I attributed to not brushing regularly. When Howdy talked, the entire bottom portion of his mouth moved like he was trying to eat a large
cantaloupe. Whole.

Finally I noticed the strings attached to him. It was like the day I found out there is no Santa Claus and the day somebody told me they heard Lash Larue was in a porno film. It broke my heart. You know kids, though. I couldn't wait to tell everybody I knew of my discovery.

"Howdy Doody isn't real," I told one of my classmates at school.

"Yes, he is," he replied.

"No, he isn't. He's just a puppet. Somebody pulls his strings and that's what makes him walk and talk."

The kid started crying. I didn't dare tell him that Clarabelle's big red nose was probably fake, too.

Soon I discovered "Superman." I enjoyed watching "The Man of Steel," but I had some problems with him, too. In the first place, I never thought Superman's disguise as Clark Kent was all that clever. Lois Lane had to be a bigger dummy than Howdy Doody not to see right through it.

Whenever Superman decided to become Clark Kent, all he did was put on a coat and tie and a pair of glasses. That's a disguise? Superman and Clark Kent talked exactly the same, were the same height and weight, and if Lois had been any kind of reporter at all, she probably would have noticed that they had the same mole or freckle or other telltale body markings.

In retrospect, Lois Lane had no business working for *The Daily Planet.* She should have been on the obit desk in Topeka.

Something else used to bother me about the "Superman" show. Anytime "The Man of Steel" had a social misfit cornered, the crook would pull out a gun and fire six shots at Superman's chest. Of course, bullets just bounced off, because you couldn't hurt Superman.

Even as a kid, I knew what I would have done after that. I would have gone quietly. But not the crooks on "Superman." After watching their bullets bounce harmlessly away, they would throw their guns at him. Anybody knows you don't further rile a man whom six bullets couldn't stop by throwing your gun at him.

* * *

There were a lot of family shows on television in those early days. There was "The Donna Reed Show," for example. Donna was always so pleasant. I wonder why she never had that-time-of-the-month problems like other women?

"Father Knows Best," another great family show, was one of my favorites. Even so, I used to wonder why Robert Young never took his tie off. When he came home from a long day at the insurance office, he would keep his tie on and replace his jacket with a sweater. He did the same thing later as Marcus Welby, and remember that you never saw him without a tie on when he wound up selling Sanka. He may have been the only man in history to wear a tie more than Richard Nixon.

"Leave It to Beaver" also was a big hit. In fact, it still is. "Leave It to Beaver" reruns are on several cable stations today, and a fellow named Irwyn Applebaum has even written a book entitled, "The World According to Beaver." The book contains examples of the sort of dialogue that was featured on the show. Here's one between Wally and his friend, the ever-obnoxious Eddie Haskell.

EDDIE: "Come on, Sam, time's a-wastin'."

WALLY: "Look, Eddie, I can't go with you guys today. I've got to work out in the yard."

EDDIE: "Work in the yard? Aw, come off it! We got ... Oh, good morning, Mr. and Mrs. Cleaver."

JUNE: "Hello, Eddie."

WARD: "Good morning, Eddie."

EDDIE: "Well, if you've got work to do, Wallace, I don't want to interfere. I was reading an article in the paper just the other day, and it said a certain amount of responsibility around the home is good character training. Well, good-bye, Mr. and Mrs. Cleaver."

WARD: *"Good-bye, Eddie."*

EDDIE (whispering): "Can I talk to you outside, Wally?"

WALLY: "Okay, Eddie, what's up?"

EDDIE: "Come on, Moe, drop the hoe. Lumpy's out in the car and we're ready to roll."

WALLY: "I told you, Eddie. I can't. I got work to do."

EDDIE: "Come on, Isabel, you gonna let your mother and father push you around? Why don't you read them the child labor law?"

WALLY: "Hey, Eddie, isn't it about the time of year you're supposed to shed your skin?"

I take a certain amount of comfort in knowing that Eddie Haskell comes off as just as big a jerk today as he did twenty years ago. There are so few elements of life that have gone unchanged in that period.

"The Adventures of Ozzie and Harriet" was another classic of those timid times. There was Ozzie and Harriet and David and Ricky, and they lived in a big house and everybody was happy and problems were easy to solve. Television of the fifties rarely dealt with anything more intricate than a husband forgetting an anniversary or a wife burning dinner for the husband's boss.

In those days, Ozzie was always around to talk over prob-

lems with David and Ricky. As a matter fact, I still don't
know what Ozzie did for a living; I never recall his going to
work. If they did "The Adventures of Ozzie and Harriet"
today, Ozzie probably would be a dope dealer.

* * *

There are a lot of things I miss about television the way it
used to be. I'll take John Cameron Swayze over Peter Jennings on a big story any day, and has there ever been a better
detective than Sargeant Joe Friday on "Dragnet"?

Joe Friday didn't waste a lot of time keeping Los Angeles
free of crime on his program. All he wanted was the facts.
Today, television cops get involved in a lot of extracurricular
activities, such as fooling around with women.

(Fact: Jack Webb, who played Joe Friday, died not long ago
of a heart attack. Maybe he should have taken a few days off
occasionally and gone to Pismo Beach with a girlfriend.)

"Amos 'n' Andy" was a favorite at my aunt's house. George
"Kingfish" Stevens was always trying to con Andrew H.
Brown, and sooner or late the Kingfish would end up in
court with his lawyer, Algonquin J. Calhoun, representing
him:

"Yo' Honor, it's easy for the prosecutor to talk that way
about my client, George Stevens. It's easy 'cause my client is
a crook, Yo' Honor!"

"Amos 'n' Andy" was classic humor, but unfortunately we
can't watch it on television today. It's allegedly racist.

That's just another example of how confusing the modern world has become. I can't watch "Amos 'n' Andy"
because it's racist, but it's okay to watch "Sanford and Son,"
which is filled with racist situations and remarks.

Remember the time Fred had to go to the dentist? He found out that the dentist was black and insisted on having a white man work on his mouth. And don't forget his classic line, "There ain't nothin' uglier than an old white woman."

There must be some big difference in the two programs, but I swear I can't see it. Maybe it's a matter of perspective.

I remember several years ago when I was working in Chicago, the nation's most segregated city, and caught a cab home one night after work. The cab driver was black, and we began to talk.

"Where you from?" he asked.

"Atlanta."

"Thought so," he said. "I'm from Mississippi."

Here it comes, I figured. A black cabbie is about to give me a lecture on how much better life is away from the racist jackals of the South.

"I'm going back one of these day," he said instead.

I was startled. "You don't like it here?"

"People ain't the same up here," he said. "In Mississippi, they always let you know where you stand. They put up signs down there that say, 'No Niggers Allowed.' Up here, they don't put up no signs. They just let you walk into a place and then tell you you can't stay. I liked it better when I knew ahead of time where I was wanted."

I guess that's how I feel about television these days. I liked it better when I knew what was okay to laugh at and what wasn't.

It is modern television, in fact, that has helped to foster the two most offensive Southern stereotypes — the racist redneck and the belligerent country sheriff. And nothing irritates me more than to see Southerners being portrayed on television by actors or actresses who can't speak the language.

Take *y'all,* for instance. Southerners never say *you all,* and even if we did, we wouldn't use it in the singular sense. The proper word, used when speaking to two or more others, is a contraction, *y'all.*

On television, however, some honey from the Bronx who has landed a part as a Southern belle inevitably says to her lover, "Why don't *you all* come ovuh heah and sit down by lil' ol' me."

I doubt that "Amos 'n' Andy" was near the embarrassment to blacks that yankees trying to portray Southerners is to Southern whites.

* * *

Television actually was responsible for my first encounter with discrimination, because it brought major league baseball into my life.

For the first time, I could *see* Mantle and Musial and Williams and Snider. I became a hardcore Dodger fan — they were still in Brooklyn then — and consequently developed a keen hatred for the Yankees.

I mentioned my love for the Dodgers one day to a cousin, who happened to be a Yankee fan. "The Dodgers!" he said, almost spitting out the words. "They're a nigger team!"

Perhaps I had overheard the older folks talking, or perhaps I had read something in the newspapers about Jackie Robinson, the first black man in major league baseball, but I never considered it when pledging my allegiance to the Dodgers. So when my older cousin made what was obviously a derogatory remark, I was hurt and confused. I pressed my cousin for more information, but all he would say was, "Niggers ain't got no business playing major league ball."

I decided to take the question to my mother. "Do niggers have any business playing major league ball?" I asked her.

"The word," she said in her sternest schoolteacher voice, "is *knee-grow*. I don't ever want to hear you say that other word in this house."

Fine, but that didn't answer the question. Frankly, I was more interested in baseball than in race relations at the time.

"I don't know anything about baseball, son," she said, "but your daddy played with Negroes in the service."

That settled it. If my father had played with Negroes, then there was no problem with Jackie Robinson playing with the Dodgers. Besides, all I wanted Robinson to do was help beat the Yankees, which is exactly what he did in the 1955 World Series.

I was so thankful for the Dodger victory that I said a prayer in church, reasoning that God, in all His infinite wisdom, certainly must be a Dodger fan, too.

* * *

Parents today are concerned that their children see too much sex and violence on television. There wasn't any sex to speak of on TV when I was a child, unless you count watching lady wrestlers tumble around with one another in those tight-fitting outfits they used to wear.

There was violence, but the victims usually deserved the thrashings they got.

Johnny Mack Brown walks into a saloon in the Five O'Clock Movie and says, "Gimme a milk." Heroes in those days didn't drink liquor, you recall.

"Milk?" laughs an ornery galoot standing next to JMB at the bar. "Here, tenderfoot," he continues, pushing a drink toward Johnny Mack, "try a little of this red-eye. It'll put some hair on your chest."

Johnny Mack Brown, after gulping down his milk, of course, would proceed to beat laughing boy to within an inch of his life, and the saloon would be totally destroyed in the meantime. I never thought about it much back then, but now I wonder who paid for the damages after all those saloons were destroyed.

I watched so many westerns as a kid that I'm still an expert on who rode what horse. Try me.

Gene Autry? That's a throwaway. He rode Champion. Hopalong Cassidy? A little tougher, but no problem for an expert. His horse was Topper.

How about the horses of the sidekicks? Tonto rode Scout. Frog Millhouse's horse was named Ringeye. Festus Hagan's mule on "Gunsmoke" was Ruth.

What our parents should have worried about our seeing on television was not sex and violence, but rather a way of life that was totally unrealistic — one that we would never be able to emulate. Just as viewers today are influenced by the whackos on "Donahue," we were given a model of the way a family was supposed to work when we watched early television.

Ward and June never argued on "Leave It to Beaver," and Jim and Margaret knew their roles in "Father Knows Best." Jim sat in the den with his stupid tie and sweater on, while Margaret made dinner. And none of the kids ever got into any kind of trouble that couldn't be handled in a calm family conference.

One of the most unrealistic examples which television

promoted was that of Roy Rogers and Dale Evans (who may have been the first feminist, now that I think about it. She kept her maiden name, and she never rode sidesaddle. Donahue would have loved her).

Roy went off everyday and fought cattle thieves, while Dale stayed home and watched over the ranch. When Roy returned, Dale cooked him something to eat, and then they'd sit around singing "Happy Trails" together. For years, "Happy Trails" was my favorite song:

> *"Happy trails to you,*
> *Until we meet again.*
> *Happy trails to you,*
> *Keep smiling until then.*
> *Happy traaaaails to youuuuuu,*
> *'Til we meeeeeet aaaaagain."*

Of course, it didn't turn out that way at all. "Happy Trails" turned into "Forty Miles of Bad Road."

I came home after a hard day's work one evening and said to my then-wife, "Rustle up some grub, woman, and call me when it's ready. Me and ol' Bullet will be out in the backyard."

"Rustle your own grub, Roy," said my wife. "I'm taking Buttermilk and heading out for a few drinks with the girls."

* * *

I'm not certain when it was that I stopped watching television on a regular basis. I think it was soon after they took "Gunsmoke" and "Have Gun Will Travel" and "Peter Gunn" and "Perry Mason" off the air and replaced them with programs that gave me headaches.

I still search for the old shows — the ones that are being rerun, thank goodness. Give me Andy and Barney and Aunt Bea and Opie over "Hart to Hart" any day. And every time I flip through the channels looking for an old program and run across "Family Feud," I secretly hope that herpes can be contracted by kissing game show contestants.

I never liked "All in the Family." Everybody was always screaming at everybody else, and it made me nervous. Maude was a grumpy old bat, and that program where Tex Ritter's son John lived with those two air-brained women was horrible. Ol' Tex must still be twirling in his grave.

I don't like soap operas, because it's too hard to remember who is pregnant and by whom, and I always had a sneaking suspicion that Laverne and Shirley were gay. But then again, I don't remember ever seeing them on "Donahue."

* * *

The movies. They can get a little crazy, too. I'm all for realism, but the language they use in today's movies is atrocious. Henry Fonda and Katherine Hepburn even used dirty words in *On Golden Pond*. And if they ever made *Gone With the Wind* over again, I can't even imagine how Rhett would tell Scarlett to take a hike this time — "Frankly, my dear, I don't ...."

When it comes to sex, movies are like everything else today — overloaded. I enjoyed sex in movies more when you *thought* they were going to do it, but you were never quite sure.

In those days, when it became apparent that a couple had

more on their minds than playing a few hands of canasta, the leading man and lady would embrace while doing-it music (violins and harps) played in the background. Then before they removed the first stitch of clothes, the camera faded off.

As a matter of fact, whenever you heard doing-it music in a movie, you knew it was safe to leave your seat and go buy a package of Milk Duds, because absolutely nothing was going to happen that you hadn't seen before. Today if you leave your seat for even a couple of minutes, you're liable to miss three gang rapes, two oral sex scenes, and enough skin to re-upholster an entire Greyhound bus.

It doesn't have to be that way, of course. Great movies still can be made without having a nudist colony as the setting. Take *Tender Mercies,* for example; Robert Duvall won an Academy Award for his performance and never took off more than his shirt.

What we need is more movies like *The Natural* and *Patton,* my all-time favorite movie. George C. Scott was even better than his cousin Randolph. I also enjoy action movies where the villains gets theirs in the end — movies like *Walking Tall,* where Joe Don Baker took a stick and destroyed an entire Tennessee roadhouse and everybody inside it.

Unfortunately, I doubt that movies ever will be the same as they used to be. Back then we went for diversion and relaxation and Milk Duds, not for some deep, sensitive message; not to see people butchered with chain saws; not to see things you used to see only in the magazines your older brother brought home from the Navy.

I give credit to the brilliant Chicago columnist Mike Royko for putting today's movies in their proper perspective. Royko sensed that when John Wayne died, the movie industry changed forevermore.

In his tribute to the Duke, Royko cited the way he handled Dirty Ned Pepper in *True Grit,* and he wondered how John Travolta would have dealt with Dirty Ned in the same situation.

"He probably would have asked him to dance," wrote Royko.

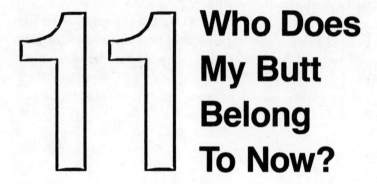

Who Does My Butt Belong To Now?

S IN, LIKE PRACTICALLY every other element of life, isn't as simple as it used to be. And retribution, which always seemed to involve my rear end in one way or another, isn't as firm or as fast as it once was.

Of course, there are many more opportunities to sin today than there were twenty years ago. Combine that with the obvious erosion of discipline and respect for authority, and what you have is a lot of young people running around having loads of fun doing things it never occurred to the youth of twenty years ago to do.

We've already discussed sex. With the pill for safety and the *Penthouse* Forum for directions, who knows what's going on in the back seats of Toyotas these days? Whatever it is, I'm certain that the participants are much more cramped than they would have been had the 1957 Chevy lived on into the eighties.

Peeping Tomism, which was popular with my generation, also has lost its way in the modern world. We used to slip around and snoop in windows to see if we could catch girls in their underclothing. Kids today get their equivalent kicks by using computers to invade the privacy of large corporations. I suppose they see enough skin on television and in the newspaper ads for movies; they don't have to waste their time crouching outside of windows. But if I had to pick, I still would rather watch Kathy Sue Loudermilk do her famous eight-o'clock-every-Wednesday-evening striptease from the tree outside her bedroom than to gaze at the financial records of AT&T in my computer.

The sin of gluttony has even changed since I was growing up. We used to steal watermelons and then gorge ourselves. I was even known to gnaw on the rinds when I was feeling especially gluttonous. Kids today pig-out on Slurpies and Twinkies and Little Debbie Snack Cakes, and they can get pizza delivered to their doorsteps. And not long ago I was at Baskin-Robbins behind a kid who was having trouble deciding which of the thirty-one flavors he wanted, so he finally said, "I'll just have a scoop of each." When I left, he had eaten down through the Almond Toffee and was working on the Fudge Swirl and washing it all down with Tab.

Frankly, I'm glad that I'm not twenty years younger and confronted with all the temptations that the nation's youth face today. I'm glad, for example, that I never had to deal with the issue of drugs.

There certainly were no drugs in my high school, and a real druggie when I was in college was someone who took No-Doz. We knew from seeing Sal Mineo in *The Gene Krupa Story* that a thing called marijuana existed, but we had never seen any. We figured that only kids in New York City smoked it, and that was why they all looked so greasy and undernourished.

The only thing we took to alter our mental state was beer or maybe bourbon mixed with Coke. Even that was only an occasional indulgence, because beginning drinkers (as most of us were) spent a lot of time embracing the stone pony. That means we spent a lot of time throwing up into a commode, and that definitely wasn't cool.

Had drugs been available in my school days, there would have been some to try them, no doubt. Norris Brantley, for instance. He would try anything.

Norris had a big date one evening, but his parents had made him spend the afternoon painting the garage. When Norris finished, he was covered in paint and had only an hour to make himself presentable for his date. He showered and scrubbed, but he couldn't get the paint off his arms and legs.

Norris had heard that gasoline was a marvelous paint remover, so he siphoned several buckets full out of his mother's car and filled the tub. Then he sat soaking in the gasoline, waiting for it to remove the paint.

Meanwhile, Norris's mother was busy hostessing a bridge party.

"Do you smell gas fumes, Marjorie?" one of the ladies said to Mrs. Brantley.

Soon all the ladies smelled the fumes, and Mrs. Brantley began searching through the house to find the source. The closer she got to Norris's bathroom, the stronger the scent became.

She finally looked in the bathroom and found Norris sprawled out in the tub. He had passed out from breathing the gasoline fumes. Moving quickly, Mrs. Brantley pulled Norris out of the tub and, using a fireman's carry, hauled him out of the bathroom, through the den where the bridge ladies were, and out into the yard. After a few minutes, Norris revived.

Mrs. Brantley then went back inside and attempted to revive two of the bridge ladies, who had fainted at the sight of Mrs. Brantley carrying ol' naked Norris through the den.

That was the last time Norris ever tried to take a gasoline bath, but later on he tried something even more daring. He actually ate the "mystery meat" they served us in the high school cafeteria on Wednesdays, which was worse than the Friday meatloaf that had been forced upon us back at Moreland elementary.

Previously, no student had been brave enough to attempt the Wednesday mystery meat. It defied description and categorization. It was a dark, hideous-looking substance which the cooks tried to hide by covering it with gravy. Whenever a student would ask, "What is this?", the cooks would simply look at each other and smile knowingly. They would never answer the question.

Norris, who had eaten an entire package of crayons in third-grade art class on a dare, became so intrigued by the mystery meat that he actually cut a piece with his knife and fork, which required a considerable struggle, and ate it.

"What does it taste like?" somebody asked Norris.

"Sort of like a blue crayon," he answered.

We never did learn the identity of the mystery meat, but Norris later reported that he took a piece home and tried to feed it to his dog. The dog ran and hid under the bed and wouldn't come out until Norris buried the substance in the yard.

Norris would drink anything, too. We were on a camping trip when one of the kids from out in the country produced a pint of his father's white liquor, known to some as "moonshine."

"Let me have a chug of that," Norris said to the kid with the pint.

"You need to strain it first," said the kid. "It's got some leaves and dead bugs in it."

That was no problem for Norris. He took off his T-shirt and strained the pint through it. Then he took a deep pull out of the jar.

When Norris got his breath back, he said, "It ain't much to taste, but next time I got to paint the garage, I sure could use a couple of gallons."

* * *

Most of us were quite satisfied with drinking beer. The only problem was obtaining it. Unless your parents went out of town and left some in the refrigerator, or you had an older brother who would buy it for you, or you had an understanding uncle who would bring you out a case from the Moose Club, you normally had to resort to bribing curb boys.

I drank my first beer when I was six. I found a half-full can on the coffee table one morning after my parents had entertained the evening before. They were still in bed, so I picked up the can and drank what was left in it. Having never tasted cold beer, I wasn't bothered in the least that this was warm. As a matter of fact, I quite enjoyed it, and afterwards I began singing "She'll Be Coming Around the Mountain," my favorite song when I was six. Then I took myself a long nap.

I didn't try another beer until I was fourteen. Nathanial, one of the curb waiters at Steve Smith's truckstop, brought

Danny Thompson and me three tall-boy Carling Black Labels out to the back of the truckstop for the price of the beer plus a dollar for his risk and trouble.

I drank my Carling Black Labels faster than Danny did, so I threw up first. We walked home — both of us quite ill.

It was a warm night. We had no air conditioning at my house, but I was still sober enough to remember how cool the inside of a refrigerator feels on a hot summer night in Georgia. So I sat down next to the refrigerator, opened the door, and stuck my head inside on one of the racks.

Then, just as I had done eight years earlier, I took a little nap. It was in that position, sleeping with my head stuck between lettuce and banana pudding in the refrigerator, that my mother found me a couple of hours later.

"Why are you sleeping in the refrigerator?" she asked.

"I was going to get myself some leftover banana pudding," I answered, "but it was so nice and cool in here that I decided to take a nap."

I always underestimated my mother's ability to tell when I was lying.

"Let me smell your breath," she said. "I think you've been drinking."

I was dead. I let her smell my breath.

"How much did you have?" she asked.

"Two cans of beer that I remember," I answered. "I'm a little hazy on the third one."

"Did it make you sick?"

"As a dog."

"Where did you get it?"

"Curb waiter at Steve's."

My mother put me to bed, and the next morning, as I lay hovering between life and death, she brought me aspirin. I expected her to give me a long lecture about drinking, but instead all she said was, "I hope you've learned a lesson."

And I had. I learned never to drink Carling Black Label beer on a warm evening and never to stick my head in a refrigerator unless I'm wide awake.

* * *

The more I think about it, the more I'm convinced that most of us wouldn't have gotten involved with drugs even if they had been available. Our parents certainly did not condone drinking, but at least there had been beer when they were young, and most of them knew the appeal it held for adolescents.

But not drugs. They would have been outraged, and they would have cracked down hard on us. And I don't think we would have rebelled against them, either, because their disciplinary measures were fast and firm in those days.

These were not people to be trifled with. They had learned from the harsh parenting they had received, and they would stop at nothing to be sure that we understood they were in complete control.

My own dear mother had a strict rule that I was not allowed, under any circumstances, to ride on any mechanized vehicle that had less than four wheels. What she had in mind specifically was Dudley Stamps's motor scooter.

When Dudley was fourteen, his parents bought him a motor scooter. My mode of transportation at the time still required a great deal of pedaling. Dudley would ride into my yard on his scooter and invite me to go for a spin.

"You aren't going to get on any motor scooter," my mother would insist. "You could fall off and break your neck."

I knew I wasn't going to fall off and break my neck, but I couldn't convince my mother of that. When I was younger, she had been the same way about my running with a sharp stick in my hand.

"Put that stick down, young man!" she would scream at me. "You might fall and put out your eye."

For years, I have been following the papers trying to find just one instance of a child running with a sharp stick in his hand and falling and putting out an eye. I have yet to come across one, but I suppose that's the result of the constant vigil of mothers guarding against running and carrying sharp sticks simultaneously.

I rarely disobeyed my mother, but one day Dudley came by on his scooter and my mother wasn't home.

"We'll just be gone a few minutes," Dudley said. "She'll never know you went for a ride."

The thrill of riding on the scooter caused me to lose all track of time. When I returned home three hours later, my mother went into hysterics. She sentenced me to no television for a month, forbade me ever to be in the company of Dudley Stamps again until I had children of my own, and fed me liver twice a week for three months. I considered myself lucky that parents didn't have the right to give the death penalty in cases of such extreme disobedience.

I get the impression that parents of children today, in most instances, do not rule their disobedient young with the strong hand of discipline and authority that once was used.

Some parents think nothing today of allowing their four-teen-year-olds to hang out at rock concerts. Even if it weren't for all the known evils (see earlier reference to Elton John concert), attendance at such events obviously is having a detrimental effect on the hearing of today's youth. Nobody can listen to that much sound without suffering some degree of hearing impairment. Perhaps many of our children already have suffered severe hearing loss, which is why they think the music at rock concerts is appealing.

The schools aren't nearly as strict as they once were, either. If a teacher spanks a child today, she may have a lawsuit on her hands. But that's another reason I don't think many members of my generation would have gotten involved with drugs and dyed their hair orange and exhibited all the rebellious, independent behavior of seventies and eighties youth. If our parents hadn't stopped us from such, the folks at school would have had a field day with our hindparts.

Not long ago I ran into one of my former teachers.

"It was never the same after your class (Class of '64)," he said. "You were the last class that took it as we dished it out. I've missed you."

Certainly the children changed, but I wonder if the teachers didn't, too. I wonder if their growing fears of lawsuits and even their fears of some of the students didn't cause them to lose their grip.

My old high school principal, O.P. Evans, is dead now. Maybe what killed him was living long enough to see discipline erode in the public school system.

Mr. Evans always began each student assembly by reading from his worn Bible, which was held together by a few rubberbands and the grace of the book's main character. I can hear him now, booming out from the Word:

" 'When I was a child, I spoke as a child ... but when I became a man, I put away childish things.' "

That was Mr. Evans's way of saying that any student

caught chewing gum in study hall would be beaten within an inch of his or her life. O.P. had rules and enforced them.

— No gum chewing anytime or anywhere.

— A student caught smoking faced certain suspension. This included smoking on weekends and before and after school. O.P. Evans held that when a student entered his high school, the student belonged to him until graduation.

— No fooling around between male and female students. When walking down the halls with a member of the opposite sex, for instance, a student was to maintain at least twelve inches of space between himself and herself. Those who violated this rule were taken to Mr. Harris's health class, where he lectured about pregnancy, venereal disease, and saving yourself for your life's partner.

— Any student missing time from school must bring a detailed excuse written and signed by his parents. Norris Brantley once was out of school for several days at the same time his parents were conveniently out of town. Norris attempted to write his own excuse. It said, "Please excuse Norris from class. He was real sick Oct. 29, 30, 31, and 32." As punishment, they made him eat two helpings of mystery meat for every day he was out of school.

Mr. Evans's wife, Mrs. Evans to us, was head librarian. She had rules, too:

— No reading a library book before you washed your hands. Any library book turned in with a smudge on any page would bring punishment for the smudger. I always read library books wearing the rubber gloves my mother used for washing dishes.

— No sound whatsoever in the library. This included throat-clearing, sneezing, coughing, and the sound a chair makes when it's pulled out from under a table for the purpose of sitting.

— Boys were required to remove watches and girls were required to remove any rings or bracelets while sitting at a library table, in order that the tables not be scratched.

There were no scratches on the tables in the Newnan High Library, the place was quieter than a cemetery at midnight, and there were no smudges on the books. Students took little advantage of what the library had to offer, however; it's difficult to read *Les Miserables,* for instance, when you feel like somebody is behind you holding a .45 to your head. *Go ahead, punk. Smudge that book and make my day.*

The superintendent of schools was Homer Drake. Mr. Drake wasn't a bad sort, but he had a habit of appearing unannounced in class to check on his teachers. For that reason, the teachers were terribly nervous all the time. They felt the heat of the same .45, I suppose. Consequently, very little of what went on in a Newnan High School class was frivolous. You couldn't even relax and have a few laughs in shop, lest Mr. Drake walk in and catch somebody actually enjoying themselves. The pursuit of knowledge was serious business to Homer Drake.

For added effect, Mr. Drake occasionally dropped into study hall and walked through the rows of desks pulling on boys' ears. Not only is it impossible to work out algebraic equations while the school superintendent is pulling on your ear, but it's also quite painful. One day I noticed that Mr. Drake had very large ears. I reasoned that somebody had pulled on his ears when he was a young man and this was his way of showing us that he was just one of the guys. I would have preferred that he went around goosing us in the belly instead of pulling on our ears.

My high school had traditional instructors, too. There

was Mr. Hearn, the shop teacher, for example.

"Boys," he would begin his classes every year, "the most important thing to remember while working with an electric saw is safety." With that remark, he would hold up his right hand, which was missing its two middle fingers.

We had a wonderful American history teacher named Miss McGruder. She resembled a frog. In fact, her homeroom was called "The Pond." One day she called on Harley Doakes to tell her what he had read the night before in the assignment concerning President James K. Polk.

Harley stammered for an answer.

"You don't know anything about President Polk, Harley?" she pressed.

Harley searched his mind, a brief endeavor, and finally answered, "Was he the one who invented polk and beans?"

Miss McGruder sent a note to Harley's parents, informing them of how he had answered her question.

"I'm proud of you, son," Harley's dad said to him at supper after he read the note. "I certainly didn't know where polk and beans came from."

Miss Garland taught geometry. She was very old and about half-blind. All of her students made high grades in geometry, because if a student could make a few straight lines on the blackboard with a piece of chalk, Miss Garland couldn't see well enough to know whether or not he had solved the problem correctly. She would simply squint at the board for a few seconds and say, "Oh, child, you do such grand work."

Ronnie Jenkins once drew a picture of some unidentifiable four-legged creature on the board. Miss Garland thought he had dissected an angle. She gave Ronnie an A, even though he thought an hypotenuse was a large animal he saw once at the Grant Park Zoo in Atlanta.

The teacher who ran study hall was Mrs. Carpenter, an ex-WAC sergeant. She allowed no foolishness, either. Students were to keep their eyes forward and on their books at all times ... or give her twenty-five quick push-ups.

In the stillness and silence of Mrs. Carpenter's study hall one afternoon, my eyes facing my book, I began to hum. I don't remember why; I just began to hum. The person behind me picked it up and started to hum, too. Soon, seventy-five of us were humming, our eyes still on our books and our mouths closed.

"Who's doing that humming?" shouted Mrs. Carpenter.

We continued to hum.

"Stop that humming right now, or I'll send you all to Mr. Evans's office," she warned.

When we still wouldn't quit humming, she marched all seventy-five of us toward the principal's office.

"I had a good home, but I left, right, left, right....," she called out as we maneuvered down the hallway.

When Mr. Evans could not convince anyone to admit to malicious humming, he decided to punish us by administering an across-the-board, one-letter cut in citizenship grades on our next report cards. He also assigned us to memorize the Beatitudes out of the Book of Matthew. (The meek shall inherit the earth, and woe be unto the fool who hums in study hall.)

Students in future times would burn buildings, smoke dope in the hallways, pull knives on teachers, have frequent sexual encounters with one another, and listen to strange music sung by strange people with pink hair and safety pins stuck through their earlobes. We just hummed.

* * *

Baby Boomers like myself went off to college in droves. Never before had a larger percentage of a generation pursued higher education. More than being what *we* wanted, it was what our parents wanted, what they had saved and scrimped for, what they had dreamed about.

We want you to have it better than we did, they said time and again, and one way we were going to have it better was to be educated. My mother, a teacher, rarely spent money on herself. She watched every penny that came in and went out of the house, and she hoarded many of them for my college.

There were few people in my hometown who had been to college. Among some of the old folks, there was even the classic resentment for and suspicion of someone who had gone, or was going, to college.

I walked into Cureton and Cole's one day, and some of the old men were seated around the stove.

"Heard you goin' off to college," said one.

"University of Georgia," I answered proudly.

"Don't you get too big for your britches and forget where you came from," I was instructed.

"I won't."

"I tell you something, when I come along, there wadn't no way you could go to college. Hell, my daddy jerked my tail out of school when I was twelve years old to help him bring in the crop. I got an education, but it wadn't from no college. I got it from behind a mule."

Somehow, I felt like a traitor. These were my people, my roots.

"I've seen a lot of 'em go off to college and get a lot of book sense, but then they still ain't got no common sense.

Couldn't plow a straight row if their life depended on it."

"Most of 'em go off to college in the first place 'cause they don't want to do a honest day's work."

"Hey, college boy, what you going to study for? You goan be one of them smart-ass lawyers like they got up in the city?"

I said I wasn't certain what I was going to study.

"Why don't you study to be a schoolteacher like you' mama?" somebody asked.

I said school teaching didn't appeal to me. Besides, there wasn't much money in it, I added.

"Money? That's all they think about today is money, especially them damn lawyers."

"Hey, you know the difference between a dead lawyer in the highway and a dead possum in the highway?"

"Naw."

"Dead lawyer ain't got no skid marks in front of him."

I said I'd better be leaving, but before I could go, Harvey (Dynamite) Garfield, Frankie's older brother, walked in.

"Hey, Dynamite," somebody said, "what do you think of college-boy here going off to get an education?"

"Well, it's just like I told that smart sonofabitch foreman of mine at the mill," Dynamite began. "I told him I wanted to get off the third shift and get me one of them day jobs in the office. He said I needed an education for that. I told him I didn't have no edugoddamncation, but I could whip his ass with one hand. He's goan see what he can do about my promotion."

They were still hooting as I walked out the door. I had learned a lot through the years, sitting and listening around the stove. But at that moment, I knew I would never be as welcome again. There was no place for a college boy in the

Order of the Stove. At that moment, I also knew my hometown never would be the same again. I was leaving it, and it would stay the same, but I would broaden.

I wondered if I would miss it. I wondered how often I would come back and, when I did, how I would be accepted — as one to be respected because he had seen the lamp of knowledge, or one to be ostracized because he felt that he wasn't good enough, that he needed to rise above his roots?

I decided two things: (1) No matter how much they had laughed and hooted, no matter what anybody thought, getting an edugoddamncation was important, especially for somebody who couldn't mug his foreman; and (2) I decided I would not go to law school.

* * *

Stories and legends abounded concerning what a young man could expect once he entered the University of Georgia, the nation's oldest state chartered university, which was also known — to those back in the hinterlands high schools — as The Promised Land.

I arrived on the Athens campus in September, 1964, one month before my eighteenth birthday, and was assigned a corner room in Reed Hall. My roommate, who had been selected without consulting me, was a French major who smoked Pall Mall cigarettes. In the evenings, he would sit and smoke and listen to Edith Piaff records in the haze of light coming from a blue bulb in his desk lamp.

We lasted a month together. I finally managed to get transferred to a new room and acquired a new roommate — George Cobb, Jr., from Greenville, South Carolina, whose father built golf courses. George and I got along famously.

After two or three weeks together, we decided to redecorate our room. The university had furnished our tiny cubicle with one bunk bed, two desks, and a couple of hard-back chairs. A monk would have been uncomfortable in that stark environment.

George and I rented a truck and went to a used furniture store in Athens. For fifty dollars, we purchased a used sofa, lounge chair, and ottoman. Fellow freshmen came from dorms all over the campus to view our newly refurbished room.

The University of Georgia had all sorts of rules concerning housing in 1964. Among them were:

— No alcohol inside dormitories.

— No females inside dormitories.

— No used sofas, lounge chairs, nor ottomans inside dormitories.

We had not been apprised of the third rule when we decided to redecorate, so it was somewhat of a surprise when the dean of housing paid George and me a visit one evening.

"What is all this?" the dean, a stern man, asked.

"What is all what, sir?" asked George.

"This ragged furniture," said the dean. "Where did it come from?"

"Farmer's Furniture, sir," George answered. "We think it gives the place a homey look."

"I want it out of here in the morning," the dean continued.

"Sir," said George, a business major, "this furniture represents an investment of fifty dollars on the part of my roommate and I. We also feel it is conducive to improving our study habits, because now that our room is more comfortable, we are more anxious to remain here and do our work. Could you give us some reason why we can't have furniture in our room?"

"I want it out of here by morning, or I'll kick both your butts out of school," the dean said.

Farmer's Furniture gave us only thirty dollars for the used furniture we had bought there five days earlier for fifty. We had, however, learned two new facts:

Fact one: Used furniture depreciates in value at a very fast rate.

Fact two: My butt, which once belonged to my parents and to O.P. Evans, now was under the control of the dean of housing at the University of Georgia.

But despite that unpleasant run-in with university officialdom, George and I were finding out that most of the legends we had heard concerning campus life in Athens were, indeed, true.

The beer flowed freely at Georgia. There was Allen's and Uppy's and Sarge's Place and Harry's and the Black Horse Inn, formerly the legendary Old South, located just across the street from the campus and just above the bus station. The story was still passed around about the student who spent an afternoon at Old South, then walked outside and got into his sports car that was parked in front of the bar.

As he drove to the first stoplight, his brakes failed and he drove squarely into the bus station, his car coming to rest at the ticket counter. Amidst the screams and the shattered glass, he leaned out of his car and said to the man behind the ticket counter, "Roundtrip to Savannah, please."

The best place to buy packaged beer in Athens was at Bubber's Bait Shop, which over the years had become an institution of sorts. Bubber, a gentle man, knew all his

646   *Elvis Is Dead And I Don't Feel So Good Myself*

student customers by name and welcomed them with the same greeting: "Whaddahyouhave?"

"Six-pack of Blue Ribbon, Bubber."

"Bottles or cans?"

"Cans."

"Short or tall?"

"Tall."

"How 'bout a little Red Hurricane Wine to go with that?"

"I don't need any wine, Bubber."

"Ain't but ninety-seven cents a bottle."

"Next time, Bubber."

"That Red Hurricane Wine'll put hair on your chest."

"How much for the beer, Bubber?"

"Two-seventy-five with tax."

"Thanks, Bubber."

"Come again."

Bubber likely became quite wealthy selling beer at the Bait Shop, but he always was the same old Bubber. He was a very trustworthy individual, who also served as an occasional lending agency for financially-down-and-out students. Something else nice about Bubber — whenever a student was kicked out of school and stopped to say good-bye and buy a six-pack for the long ride home, Bubber often would drop a bottle of Red Hurricane wine in their sack for free.

"You going to need that," Bubber would say. "You got a lot of explaining to do."

Allen's was a legendary beer and hamburger joint where, the rumor went, a young man could drink all the draft beer he pleased at twenty-five cents a glass, regardless of whether or not he had sufficient proof that he was twenty-one, the legal drinking age in Georgia at the time.

My roommate George and I tested the rumor one fine autumn evening during our freshman year. Three dollars worth of draft beer each later, we were in a rather festive mood, and George began to do his impression of the sound a mule makes. It was pure genius. First, George would make a whistling sound, and then he would do a rather throaty and low "Haaaaw!" It went something like, "Hrrrrrrrt! Haaaaaw!"

I was terribly impressed.

"You try it," said George.

"Hrrt! Haaaaw!" I brayed.

"More whistle," said George.

"Hrrrrrt! Haaaaaw!" I continued.

"Perfect," said George.

After the manager of Allen's asked us to leave, George decided it would be great sport to go over in front of Farm-House, a fraternity for agricultural students, and make mule sounds.

"Hrrrrrrt! Haaaaaaw!" went George out front of Farm-House.

"Hrrrrrrt! Haaaaaaw!" I followed.

After that, we did chickens and goats and cows and ducks, and George had just broken into his rooster (not as good as his mule but still quite effective) when the smiling campus policeman got out of his car and ordered our drunken butts, as he put it, into the back seat.

He drove us to our dorm room and sent us inside, but not before taking our student I.D.'s and informing us that we would hear from the Dean of Men's office the very next morning, which we most certainly did.

Dean William Tate was a campus institution at Georgia and a gentle person until riled. We had first seen Dean Tate during orientation week, when freshmen men were summoned to his annual briefing about what was considered acceptable and unacceptable behavior of students.

The dean had also told his favorite joke, the one he'd been telling freshmen students for years. It involved Robert Toombs, a Georgia student in the middle nineteenth century who later ran for governor of the state. When the Civil War broke out, Toombs joined the Confederate Army and solicited troops in front of the courthouse in Marietta, Georgia, just outside Atlanta.

"I'll tell you, men, we can whoop them yankees with cornstalks," Toombs had said to his listeners in Marietta.

After the war, Toombs came back to that same courthouse for a campaign speech. In the middle of his many promises to his audience, a man spoke up.

"Mr. Toombs," he said, "I stood right here before the war and heard you ask us to jine up with the Confederate Army. I jined and my brother jined. I got shot in the Battle of Chickamaugua and my brother got shot at Antietam. You told us then we could whoop the yankees with cornstalks. I believed you then, and I paid for it. So why should I believe you now?"

Toombs paused for a few moments and then replied, "Well, we could have whooped the yankees with cornstalks, but the sons of bitches wouldn't fight that way."

We had laughed at his story then, but we didn't crack a smile when we wound up in his office. "What in the hell did you two boys think you were doing last night?" he asked me and George.

"Just kidding around, sir," answered George.

"You boys got a strange sense of humor," said Dean Tate. "I take it you had been drinking to excess."

"We just had a couple of beers, sir," said George.

"Takes more than a couple of beers to make a man stand outside at two o'clock in the morning cock-a-doodle-dooing. You boys were drunk, weren't you?"

We admitted it.

"I ought to kick both your butts out of school," Dean Tate said.

There was a pause as he stared at us over his glasses. I'm certain George was thinking the same thing I was: How do you explain to your parents that you have been kicked out of school for drunken cock-a-doodle-dooing?

Finally, the dean spoke again. "But I'm going to give you boys one more chance. I'm also going to make you a promise: If I see you two roosters in here one more time, you will be only a memory around this institution. Is that clear?"

It was clear.

"We appreciate your faith in us, sir," said George.

We immediately went to Allen's to celebrate our good fortune of being able to remain in school. George lifted his first glass of beer to mine.

"To Dean Tate," he said.

"A fair man," I answered.

"To FarmHouse fraternity," said George.

"Cock-a-doodle-doo," I answered him.

"To our butts," toasted George.

"To our butts," I toasted back.

I suppose what has happened to discipline and authority these days is that most everybody has a lot more control over his or her own butt than they used to. But I'm not so certain that's all for the better.

There have been many times, even recently, when I wished somebody would take charge of mine again, if for no other reason than to render the much-needed service of pointing out to me when I was about to put it on exhibition.

12 Women Don't Wear Jocks

THE CURRENT PERIOD in which we're living is probably the worst time in history to be a man. Just my luck. We had it absolutely made for thousands of years. Cave men did a little hunting now and then, but that was about it, and they ruled their women and their roosts with clubs. If the wife, or whatever cave men called their mates in those days, got a little out of hand, a gentle tap on the head did wonders in readjusting her attitude.

Later, when men became more civilized and learned how much fun it was to fight wars, they all got together on horseback and went and sacked other countries. They raped and pillaged and generally had high times.

Throughout most of history, men stuck together and did manly things and talked about manly things. In an attempt to sustain their elite and separate status over women, they formed male-only clubs, such as the Jaycees. The Supreme Court ruled recently that the Jaycees no longer can exclude women from their membership; that's an indication of how much slippage there has been in the area of male domination.

Some men today feel as though they should apologize for their fathers' attitudes toward women, and many of us have been made to feel woefully inadequate in the face of the rising force of feminism, which seems dedicated to telling men everything that is unacceptable about us.

The litany of our alleged failures is long.

Women are quick to inform us that we are lousy in bed and that we don't know how to satisfy them sexually. There is a feminist joke which says it all. A feminist asks a man, "What does a woman say when she has been totally and completely and incredibly satisfied sexually?"

The man walks into her little trap and answers politely, so he won't spoil her joke, "I don't know."

"I didn't think you would," returns the feminist, and once again the man is made to feel like a fool.

Think of all the other complaints today's women have with men: We work too hard, we're too ambitious, we drink too much, we aren't sensitive enough, and we care more about watching a stupid ball game on television than we do about spending "quality time" (a new eighties term) with them. We sexually harass women in the work environment (formerly known as the "office"), we choose which woman is to be promoted within the firm based on breast size rather than professional ability (That made sense for several hundred years. It's difficult to change overnight), and we refuse to pay women salaries equal to those men get for doing the same job — which isn't fair, of course, but it also isn't fair that men have to shave before they go to work every day, and women don't.

Not only have the Jaycees lost their ability to exclude

women, but it is almost impossible to keep women out of any location formerly reserved for men only. (Location, nothing! Women are even wearing men's underwear these days, and one smart-aleck feminist was quoted as saying, "It's only fair. Men have been trying to get in ours for years," which is a really blatant sexist remark if you think about it. I'm glad I don't have to resort to such a low grade of humor to get my points across.)

I am a former sportswriter. When I was covering sports, all press box tickets included the warning, "No women allowed in press box."

This wasn't because sportswriters didn't want women around when they were busy covering ball games; it was because the people who ran the press boxes knew that sportswriters in general are people who never let work get in the way of a good time. Were women not excluded from the press boxes, there wouldn't be room for everybody to sit down, what with all the writers and the cocktail waitresses they had met the night before.

Excluding women from the press box is against all sorts of laws these days, however, so even if a male writer did bring a cocktail waitress to the game with him, she probably would have to stand, because all the extra seats have been taken up by female sportswriters.

I must make another confession here. I'm certain there are many females eminently qualified to cover and report on sporting events, but I still would rather read a male's report, because I am not convinced, and never will be convinced, that women fully understand the subtleties and nuances of certain athletic events.

Okay, so allow women to cover tennis matches. Tennis is a very simple game. The person who hits the last winning shot wins the match. Professional tennis players like John McEnroe and Chris Evert are always complaining that the press is more interested in their private lives than in their tennis. That's because tennis, although loads of fun to play (I'm an incurable participant in the sport, myself. I have no talent for the game, but playing all afternoon certainly makes the evening beer taste better), is not that interesting to read about. I had much rather know why Chris dumped John than why she won't change her tactics and play serve-and-volley against Martina Navratilova. I already know why she won't come to the net against Martina: She's afraid that big ol' girl will knock her head off with a topspin forehand.

So it's okay with me if women cover tennis, and they can cover golf, too. If tennis is boring to read about, golf is a sleeping pill. Women can also report on other sports that encourage dozing, such as marathon races, bowling, swimming, gymnastics, ice skating, track, field, and soccer. In fact, women can even cover pro basketball and it won't bother me, because pro basketball is simple, too. The team with the biggest black man usually wins ... unless it happens to be the Boston Celtics, who have Larry Bird (the only white man in the last twenty years who doesn't suffer from the dreaded "white man's disease," which causes slowness afoot and the inability to jump very high).

What I strongly object to is women covering football and baseball, because they've never played either sport. Men are born with the innate ability to understand the blitz in football and the hit-and-run in baseball. Women may learn the basics of these sports, but I daresay few really watch anything more than how cute the football players' butts look in those tight pants, or how baseball players spend an inordinate amount of time scratching their privates and adjusting certain necessary athletic equipment that's worn under the uniform.

In fact, that may be the crux of the problem: Women cannot achieve credibility as sports reporters with men because we know they've never worn a jock strap. And if they have, I don't want to read an inside look at the problems of the Atlanta Braves' pitching staff written by some woman who obviously has problems of her own.

If women winning their way into press boxes wasn't enough (and it wasn't), women later insisted that they also be allowed to go into the locker rooms in order to hear the pearls of wisdom that players dispatch to the press following the games. I speak from authority here, because for many years it was my job to go into dressing rooms and to be the recipient of these pearls.

Players say things like: "Well, you know, I, you know, caught the, you know, ball, and then, you know, I ran, you know, just as fast, you know, as I, you know, could, and I, you know, would like to, you know, give, you know, God the credit, you know, for, you know, making me, you know, a, you know, rich superstar."

While the players are, you know, treating the press to these marvelous exhibitions of their ability to express themselves, you know, they normally are quite naked. I'm not certain what it is about ball players, but they like to sit around naked a lot, dangling their participles at whomever happens by to speak with them.

When women first attempted to enter players' locker rooms, authorities tried to block them. But a court order here and a court order there, and suddenly post-game dressing rooms, with the players sitting in front of their lockers and all sorts of women running around with notepads, looked like a Saturday afternoon flea market.

When women no longer could be kept out of dressing rooms, most players were forced to put on bathrobes. I have noticed over the past few years that athletes do not seem nearly as dedicated and don't hustle and give their all as much as they once did. This could be due to the fact that they no longer can look forward to sitting around naked after games.

"I mean, you know, before these, you know, broads started, you know, coming in here, you know, asking a lot of, you know, questions, and looking, you know, at us like we were, you know, just big hunks of, you know, meat, we could, you know, relax after the, you know, game. Man, we could, you know, sit here without no, you know, clothes on, and sort of, you know, mellow out and, you know, think about next year's, you know, contract. You know what I mean?"

I know exactly what they mean. Men enjoy and relish the companionship of other men. They simply need to be off with other men occasionally, with no women around, so they can feel comfortable expressing their thoughts and frustrations and can pass gas without having to apologize for it. (Incidentally, that's how the Jaycees originally grew to be such a large and popular organization. I think women are going to be terribly disappointed when they join the Jaycees and find out that it was nothing more than a bunch of guys getting together once a week to have some lunch and talk about raising money for charities and passing gas in peace.)

Men learn some of the most important lessons in life from hanging around with other men. Let's take baseball, for instance. Baseball is a man's game. Women get more involved with football because it's played only once a week and there's a lot of pageantry involved, but women think baseball is dull.

"Why doesn't somebody *do* something?" they ask when the tension has reached the cutting edge in a baseball game. Meanwhile, the manager in the dugout is flashing signals to the third-base coach, who relays them to the batter; the catcher is trying to keep the runner on second base from stealing his signal to the pitcher; and the pitcher is signaling a ·pick-off attempt to the shortstop. And she asks why doesn't somebody do something.

In addition to that, the hit-and-run is completely lost on most women, and no woman on earth, even an exceptionally smart one, can comprehend the infield fly rule and why baseball simply wouldn't work very well without it.

I played baseball from the time I was five until I was eighteen, and I learned all sorts of manly things that I probably couldn't have learned anywhere else. I learned to cuss, for instance.

There are different curse words for different baseball situations. Let's say you've just led off the game at the plate and the pitcher has struck you out. When you return, bat in hand, to the dugout, the other players always inquire, "What's he got?", meaning, Is the pitcher talented?

Baseball, a *macho* sport, is very competitive by nature. No man who has just struck out to start a game is about to give the pitcher any credit, so he always answers the above question by declaring, "The sonofabitch ain't got a thing."

"Come on!" the other players then beseech the second batter, "base hit him. The sonofabitch ain't got a thing."

There are also appropriate curse words to use when the umpire has called you out and you're convinced you were safe; when you make an error and allow two unearned runs to score; when the manager did not pencil your name into the starting lineup; and when the sonofabitch who didn't have a thing has struck you out for the fourth straight time. I'm making every attempt to keep this a fairly-clean book, however, so please use your imagination to figure out which cuss words fit which of the previously-listed situations.

I also learned a lot of clichés playing baseball — clichés that could be used later in life as well, but clichés that women never understand.

There was "can of corn," for example. When somebody lofts a lazy fly ball to the outfield, the cliché everybody uses is, "can of corn." That means it's a simple out. Later, when another man asks you, "Think you're going to score with Roxanne Smitherington tonight?", you can boast, "Can of corn," meaning, turn out the lights, the party's over.

"Caught looking" is a cliché used when a batter looks at a third strike without swinging. When a man knows his wife is running around on him and doesn't do anything to stop the illicit relationship (such as attempting to beat the other man over the head with a fungo bat) and his wife eventually ditches him for the other man, he is said to have been "caught looking."

"It'll look like a line drive in the box score in the morning," is another great baseball cliché. It also may be adapted to a sexual situation. In baseball, "It'll look like a line drive in the box score in the morning" means you have reached base safely, but you haven't hit the ball very hard. I once hit a ball off the end of my bat. It landed on the rightfield foul line spinning like a top.

The ball spun under the concession stand, and by the time the right fielder retrieved it, I was on third base with a triple. In the box score that ran in the weekly paper, however, there was a "1" by my name under the hit column. For all anybody who wasn't at the game knew, I had knocked the cover off the ball.

Now, for the sex part. Let's say a man is out with his girl and he wants to fondle her breasts. At first, she won't allow it, but then she says she'll let him feel a little, but she won't take off her blouse.

She asks, "Is that enough for you?"

And if he has played baseball at some point in his life, he answers, "Sweetheart, it'll look like a line drive in the box score in the morning." That means, wait 'til you hear how he describes what happened to his pals when he runs into them the next morning.

* * *

Playing baseball also brings men closer together. Men who play baseball together, like men who fight wars together, always have a common bond between them.

When we were ten, Danny Thompson and I went to the county seat of Newnan to try out for Little League baseball. This was official, bonafide Little League, with new balls and bats and uniforms and smooth infields with lights and grown men to coach.

We had played the game before, but only in Danny's yard or over at the school playground, where there was always only one bat and one tattered ball, with electrical tape around it, that would get lost in the high weeds three or four times an hour, forcing the game to halt for a search.

And there were never enough gloves or players to go around. We played four-on-four or, at best, five-on-five. You left the glove you were wearing in the field when it came your time to bat, and since we never had enough players to have a rightfielder, if you hit the ball to rightfield, God forbid, you were out.

I wanted desperately to make the Little League team in Newnan. I was shaking in my Keds the afternoon Danny's father drove us for our first tryout.

The city kids from Newnan looked so much bigger than I felt, and some even wore regulation caps and baseball shoes with rubber cleats. We had heard that Newnan had a lot of rich people, but we didn't know they were *that* rich. Every kid had his own glove.

I got cut the first day, but Danny made the team. It broke my heart. I was ashamed that he had made the team and I hadn't, and I missed him those summer afternoons when he was in Newnan playing official Little League baseball and I was stuck at home swatting rocks with a broomstick out in the gravel driveway.

A summer later, however, I got a break. Of all the wonderful things that ever could have happened, the Baptist church in Moreland decided to sponsor a boys' baseball team, and it would play teams from other Baptist churches around the county.

Of course, I was a Methodist at the time, but I was fully willing to become a Baptist in order to make the team.

Before I could go through with my plan to switch denominations, however, the Baptist deacons voted to allow any boy in town who could run, hit, catch, and pitch to play on the team, thus saving me a dunking in the Baptist pool which always seemed to be covered with green scum, water bugs, and an occasional dragonfly.

We even were provided uniforms and new bats and new balls, and such was the excitement around town that several members of the team even received new gloves from their parents. I did, too, but the story isn't that simple.

My stepfather, H.B., had been a permanent member of our household for approximately a year when the Baptist church started its baseball team. He and I were not getting on together. My real father had been a pushover, but H.B. insisted on regular chores, on regular bedtimes, and on cleaning my plate, even if we were having liver.

In contrast to my father, H.B. knew little of sport. He attempted one afternoon to play catch with me, but I quickly noticed that he threw the ball with far too much wrist. "You never played baseball?" I asked him.

"Never had time," he answered. "There isn't time for anything else but work on a tobacco farm."

I wasn't impressed. With my childlike reasoning, I even lost some respect for the man. I think he sensed that.

I had a baseball glove, but it was old and the rawhide strings that held it together were falling loose all about it. I came home from the first practice with the Moreland team in tears. I had seem all my teammates sporting new gloves. I cried in my mother's arms.

"Maybe you'll get a new glove for your birthday," she suggested.

A lot of help she was. My birthday wasn't until October.

I knew what sort of glove I wanted. I had seen it at the hardware store in Newnan. It was a fielder's glove with a deep pocket, and it was autographed by Pee Wee Reese of the Dodgers. It cost thirteen dollars. I often went to sleep dreaming of that glove.

A couple of days after my tearful scene with my mother, she told me that H.B. wanted to see me in their bedroom. I presumed the worst. He had something for me to do that would involve wheelbarrows and digging around in the dirt.

I walked into the bedroom as he was putting on his tie. "Look in the sack on the bed," he said to me.

I picked up the sack and looked inside. It was a new baseball glove, but it wasn't the glove I had wanted, the glove I had dreamed about. I had never even heard of the bush-leaguer who had lent his name to it.

"That what you wanted?" H.B. said.

"I wanted a Pee Wee Reese glove," I answered.

"Who is Pee Wee Reese?" he asked.

That settled it. The man was totally without portfolio when it came to baseball. I threw the glove down and ran to my room crying.

I'm not certain when I realized that I had done something wrong. Perhaps it was in the night sometime, when I recalled the look on my stepfather's face as he watched me peer into the sack.

He had made the move. He had known that his lack of baseball expertise had disappointed and frustrated me, so he had tried to surprise me with the new glove. He had reached out to me, but I had been ungrateful.

I never got over that awful thing I did to my stepfather — it grieves me even now — but I did attempt to make amends. I told him I was sorry. I even tried the glove. It wasn't that bad a glove. The first game we played, H.B. came. I pitched and we won. After the game, he said, "You have a nice fastball."

It is amazing what bonds baseball can develop between men ... and between boys and men.

* * *

It has been nearly thirty years, but I remember the Moreland Baptist lineup as vividly as ever: Danny Thompson played first; Bobby Entrekin was at second; Wayne Moore, the coach's son, was at shortstop; Danny Boswell played third; Dudley Stamps caught; Charlie Moore was in the outfield with Mike Murphy and Eddie Estes. I pitched.

Pete Moore, "Mr. Pete" to us, was the coach. He was a short, heavy-set man of great baseball wisdom and patience. Perhaps his greatest move was to devise a plan to save our supply of new baseballs.

The problem was this: We played our home games on the Moreland School playground field. There was a wire backstop behind home plate, but it wasn't much of one. Foul balls went over and through the backstop and usually landed inside a birddog pen directly behind the field.

Given the opportunity, birddogs will chew a baseball right down to the cork in a matter of seconds.

After the birddogs had chewed up enough foul balls to threaten possible cancellation of the rest of the season, Mr. Pete decided to station team reserves in the pen to retrieve the baseballs before the dogs could get to them. We called that position, naturally enough, "birddog."

That's how Eddie Estes, who later became one of the all-time great Moreland Baptist outfielders, learned to play the game. Eddie was two years younger than the rest of us. He was also a thin child but quick as a cat. And Eddie was persistent. He came to every practice and to every game, even though he never could break into a lineup made up of older boys. That was before Mr. Pete put Eddie at "birddog."

Every game, when the rest of us would head out onto the field to take our positions, Eddie would go the other way and crawl inside the birddog pen behind the backstop. The training he got fighting birddogs for foul balls eventually made him into a defensive whiz.

He made the starting lineup the next season in center-field. We were playing rival Grantville, as I recall, and I was pitching. The game reached the late innings tied.

Grantville had runners on with its slugger, one of the Massengale boys, at bat. What little curve ball I had, I hung to the Massengale boy.

The ball shot toward centerfield. Eddie turned his back toward the infield and ran. There was no fence, only a gully and a dirt road that was the centerfield boundary. A few steps before he reached the gully and the road, little Eddie jumped into the air and flung his glove skyward. When he came down, he tumbled into the gully out of sight.

He quickly emerged from the muddy pit, scratched and bleeding, but the ball was in his glove. The umpire called Massengale out. We won the game.

Mr. Pete embraced little Eddie when he returned to the bench. Mays robbing Wertz in the '54 Series hadn't been as dramatic.

"Eddie," said Mr. Pete, "that was one of the best catches I have ever seen."

"I was afraid not to catch it, Mr. Pete," Eddie responded.

Mr. Pete asked him why.

"I was afraid that if I didn't, you'd put me back at 'bird-dog.'"

* * *

There are instances now, of course, of girls actually play-ing Little League baseball. If she can go to her right and hit line drives, then I suppose it would be terribly unfair to keep her off the team. But I'm still old-fashioned enough that I'd be shocked if I heard a nine-year-old girl, who had just struck out to start the game, come back to the dugout and tell her teammates, "The sonofabitch ain't got a thing."

What concerns me even more is, I'm not certain how many boys are playing baseball today. It seems to me that too many of them are playing soccer.

I dislike soccer immensely. It's a dull sport and it is not American. They play it mostly in those weird countries where the government changes hands every two or three days, supporting my suspicion that soccer is also a game that encourages political upheaval and anarchy.

All a person needs to play soccer is wind enough to run up and down a field for several hours and agility enough to bounce a ball off his head. Anybody can learn to run up and down a field for several hours, and I've watched seals in the circus bounce balls off their heads. On the other hand, I've never seen a soccer player who could dive underwater and come back with a dead fish in his mouth.

Kids are playing soccer all over America today, but are there any great soccer clichés? Of course not. People are too busy running up and down the field to think of any. As I explained before, in baseball there's all sorts of time to sit around in the dugout and think of clever things to say, like when an opposing player makes a stupid error and you say, "Nice move, Ex-Lax."

In baseball, you not only have to be able to run, but you also have to learn to bat and to catch and to throw and to slide and to spit. All baseball players spit. I doubt they ever spit in soccer, except when they fall down and get a mouthful of grass.

Once I was in London and, because there was nothing better to do, I switched on the BBC and watched the English soccer (they call it football, which is ridiculous) champion-ship game. (After you've walked through Harrod's and been over to Buckingham Palace, London can be even more boring than soccer.)

One side would kick the ball down to the end of the field, and then the other team would kick it back. I've seen more excitement at county fair pick-up-the-duck games. The crowd, a hundred thousand or so, sang during the entire game. They apparently were just as bored as I was.

The players kicked the ball around for a couple of hours, and finally it hit a guy who wasn't looking in the back of the head and went into the goal. After much running and kicking, the guys in green finally had themselves a soccer championship by the score of 1-0.

I'm afraid that when today's young soccer players become adults, they're going to be terribly boring people and per-haps even a little fuzzy from having soccer balls bounce off their heads for so many years.

What *really* worries me, however, is the great number of today's youth who don't play baseball *or* soccer. They're in shopping malls playing those damned video games. They're all going to grow up, I fear, to have big buglike eyes from staring into too many video screens. Just listening to the infernal beeping noises those games make is enough to drive kids goofy. And trying to shoot down all those asteroids in a matter of seconds also will make a child extremely nervous and frustrated, and they may all wind up with the same bad case of the shakes overworked air control-lers get.

We played indoor games when I was a kid, too, but we played educational games like rotation pool and nine-ball, which teach a youngster such important lessons as how to put reverse English on the cue ball while squinting through the smoke coming out of the cigarette he's holding in his mouth at the time.

There weren't any women allowed in pool halls, either, which offered further opportunity for male development. Girls today walk into video game arcades big as you please, and there's even a female version of "Pac-Man" — "Ms. Pac-Man," if you will.

I haven't checked to see, but if there's still a *Boy's Life* magazine, it probably carries advertisements for feminine hygiene spray these days.

* * *

One of the few remaining all-male holdouts is college fraternities. So far, women have been content to remain in their sororities. Belonging to a fraternity offers all sorts of opportunities for companionship with other men without women around. You can drink beer together and play cards together and think up nasty Homecoming floats together, and the older brothers will be available to keep you abreast of the proper way to conduct yourself as a young gentleman on campus.

I pledged Sigma Pi fraternity my freshman year at the University of Georgia. They were a great bunch of guys, the frat house was a beautiful old Southern mansion, and it was the only fraternity that offered me a bid.

Fraternity rush in my day was helpful to a young man, because it gave him the opportunity to test his fragile male ego, and it supported his theory that the more macho he acted, the better chance he had of making other young men like him.

Basically, rush worked like this: You walked into a large house filled with strangers. You had worn your best suit — your only suit, in my case — and you had doused yourself heavily with Old Spice, which your father wore. You went around shaking hands with members of the fraternity you happened to be visiting.

If your father had been a member of the fraternity and also was wealthy, you didn't have a lot to worry about. You probably could have managed a bid wearing pajamas and flip-flops. If you had no such legacy, then it was important that you did everything possible to make a good impression on the brothers.

"The most important thing," I had been told, "is to make certain you squeeze hard when you shake hands."

Nothing, of course, gives a man away like a soft handshake. Girls and wimps and nerds have handshakes that feel like you've just grasped a recently-departed grouper. Real men, the kind of men you would want in your fraternity, squeeze your hand firmly. Strength of grip was second only to size of genitalia in determining manhood. All this likely dates back to the days of the cave men, when they ran around naked and choked each other.

Each time I was extended a hand during rush, I made certain that I offered a firm shake in return. By the time I walked into my third fraternity house, my hand felt like a beer truck had run over it. I continued to squeeze firmly anyway, doing my best to ignore the pain and taking a certain amount of comfort in the fact that it was the handshake, not the aforementioned first measure of manhood, that was being checked.

There was something else I had been warned about when I went through rush. If you are included in a group that is taken on a tour of the plumbing system of the fraternity house, that particular fraternity probably doesn't want you even to be seen on its property, much less want you to be a member.

The first house I visited was SAE. From various sources, I had learned that SAE was a very prestigious fraternity and that girls from the spiffier sororities loved to date SAE's. The SAE house was nice. I especially enjoyed seeing how the water pipes in the basement were insulated so they wouldn't freeze during the wintertime.

Next, I went to Sigma Nu. They didn't show me the pipes, but they did herd me over into a corner with two exchange students and a kid with a case of terminal acne.

I didn't do any better at Phi Delta Theta, either. One of the brothers took me and two other rushees — one of whom wore thick glasses and stuttered and the other who was wearing white socks — back to the kitchen and left us with the cooks, who were peeling potatoes.

I thought I might do much better at Kappa Sig. My first cousin happened to be chapter president. When I finally was able to corner him, however, he not only disavowed our kinship, he also swore — in a very loud voice so his brothers could hear him — that he had never seen nor heard of me before. My keen deductive senses alerted me to the fact that I might as well write off any future as a Kappa Sig.

At the Kappa Alpha house, they sang "Dixie" and told stories about Robert E. Lee. The brothers there treated me like a direct descendant of William T. Sherman. I got the pipe treatment again at Sigma Chi, and at ATO they asked me to wait out on the porch until the bus came back to pick up the rushees.

I was close to giving up on any chance at becoming a

fraternity man when I walked up the stone pathway to the Sigma Pi house, an impressive antebellum structure with large white columns and rocking chairs on the front porch. To my utter surprise, the brothers never mentioned one word about the Sigma Pi plumbing system and they seemed generally interested in me and what I had to say.

They showed me the party room and the jukebox, and they took me downstairs to something called the "Boom-Boom Room," which featured a sawdust floor, booths in which to sit, and all varieties of neon beer signs. This, I determined, was where the brothers of Sigma Pi brought their dates.

"This is probably where you bring your dates," I said knowingly to the brother giving me the tour. I might have been fresh out of high school, but I wasn't a complete dummy.

"Good thinking," said my guide. "Now, let's go over here to the toilet and see if you can figure out what we do there."

I figured I was dead after that. But, to my complete surprise, I was invited back to Sigma Pi the very next night, and when the bids went out, they offered me one. I was elated but also quite concerned. If nobody else wanted me, why would Sigma Pi, and did I really want to be a member of a fraternity that would accept the likes of me? My ego was in shambles, again.

I asked a friend, who had just accepted a bid from Phi Delt, what I should do.

"Take it," he said, "before they change their minds."

I pledged Sigma Pi and was later initiated and eventually became totally content with my membership. At my fraternity, we had a rigid code regarding responsible, manly behavior. I'll just hit a few high spots.

— AT A PARTY: Never throw up on your date. If you feel like you must throw up, go outside and do it in the parking lot. We'll make the pledges clean it up the next morning.

Never attempt to climb onto the bandstand and sing with the band until everybody is bad drunk and won't notice you making a total fool of yourself.

If you think you have the opportunity to engage in amorous activity with your date, do not take her to any of the upstairs bedrooms. We do not want coeds to see the scummy conditions in which we live.

If you have to go to the bathroom, do not go on the shrubbery outside the fraternity house. Shrubbery is too expensive to replace. Go on the tires of somebody you don't like.

— AT FRATERNITY HOUSE DINNERS: If you do not like a certain dish, such as asparagus stalks, do not hurl it at members sitting at another table. Also, do not spit English peas at tablemates and do not drink directly from the syrup container.

— WHEN PARENTS VISIT: Hide all booze, 8mm skinflicks, condoms, love dolls, firearms and explosives, poker chips, dead animals, roach collections for Saturday night roach races, and any stolen goods.

If you have any books, spread them around your room, and if somebody's parents ask your major and you can't remember, say you're undecided between pre-med and animal husbandry.

— PROPER ATTIRE: Never wear socks with your Weejuns.

— IN CLASS: If it is absolutely necessary that you go, sit in the back of the classroom and do not ask any questions, so when you don't come back for another two weeks, perhaps the professor won't notice that you're missing.

If you thought you had a copy of the exam the night before, but then the professor hands you a test that has questions you've never even heard of, pretend to have some sort of fit and maybe they'll take you to the infirmary.

— WHEN ARRESTED: Never indicate you were part of a conspiracy involving other members of the fraternity. We are a loyal brotherhood and will make the pledges fork over enough money for your bail.

My fraternity brothers were a rather diverse lot. I had one brother who rose to the presidency of the Interfraternity Council, a rare and prestigous honor. I had another who pilfered wallets. We called him "Robin Hood."

I had fraternity brothers who majored in pre-Law and pre-Med. I had others who majored in Bubber's Bait Shop and threw up on the sawdust floor in the Boom-Boom Room. I had a fraternity brother known as "Odd-Job" because of his physical likeness to the Oriental goon who was an aide to Dr. No in the James Bond movie of the same name. I was frightened of Odd-Job, especially after I saw what he did to another fraternity brother's stereo.

It was an otherwise quiet evening on the second floor of the house where Odd-Job, for the first time in his collegiate career, actually had decided to study. This was difficult for him, however, because his roommate, who was known as "Seaweed" because his father had been a famous Marine war hero, was playing Sam the Sham and the Pharoahs's "Wooley Bully" over and over again on his stereo. Several times, Odd-Job had informed Seaweed that if he didn't quit playing the record he would tear Seaweed into small pieces and let God sort them out.

Seaweed was a stubborn person, however. Also, a stupid

one. When Odd-Job had finally had enough of Seaweed and "Wooley Bully," he walked over to the stereo, took the record off, and began biting it into tiny pieces, spitting out the pieces directly at the startled Seaweed. Odd-Job then picked up the stereo, ripped the plug out of the wall, and threw it out the second story window, rendering it a crumpled mass of electronic innards. He had Seaweed, himself, halfway out the window when cooler heads informed Odd-Job that if he murdered Seaweed, Dean Tate probably would put us on social probation and we couldn't have a party for the entire fall quarter.

"Then, you live, swine," said Odd-Job to Seaweed. He then went back to memorizing the Emily Dickinson poem he had been assigned in English Lit class.

* * *

Belonging to a college fraternity, as playing baseball had done, provided me with wonderful memories, lifelong friends, and even the opportunity to see racial harmony at its best.

As near as I can remember, a white band never set foot in the Sigma Pi house party room between the years of 1964 and 1968. White bands simply couldn't make a party come alive and turn into a raging inferno of dancing and screaming the way a black band could.

The civil rights movement was at its peak in the early sixties, but when the music was good and the beer was cold, everybody in the party room was in it together.

It was a start to the sort of feelings that eventually led Ray Charles and George Jones to record an album together; that is the very essence of racial harmony, and music was the medium.

Fortunately, this discussion can end on a further positive note. Kids today may be playing a lot of soccer when they should be playing baseball, but I hear that fraternities and the Greek system, much maligned in the seventies, are making a comeback on college campuses. I even hear that the kids are out of Army fatigues and back into Weejuns and khakis, and that many of them are now shunning drugs for beer.

These are good signs, my fellow Americans, good signs, indeed. Not all elements of modern life have gone to hell and rust.

Now, if somebody would just tell me where I could get the sort of French fries that God intended, the kind that are cut fresh in the kitchen and have never been frozen, I might even be able to see a small, twinkling of light at the end of this tunnel. "God Save the French Fry!" Won't somebody hear my plaintive cry in the wilderness of gastronomic silliness?

Romancing The Turnip Green

THE FRENCH FRY is a marvelous creation. I think that perhaps God, Himself, created the French fry, say on about the twelfth or thirteenth day. And it was good. French fries stayed that way for several thousand years, but then modern man started monkeying with them.

I suspect God is quite angry about it, and that may be one reason why the weather has been so loused up lately.

Here is the way the perfect French fries should be prepared:

You take an Irish potato. You wash it and then you peel it. God didn't leave the peelings on His original French fries. That may be in the Bible someplace. Probably Leviticus.

After washing and peeling the Irish potato, you cut it into slices — not too thin and not too thick. The proper size for a slice of potato soon to become a French fry is somewhere between the size of a felt-tip pen and a baby carrot.

After slicing the potato, you drop the slices into a frying pan that has been filled with cooking oil. You fry the slices until they're sort of crispy on the outside but still nice and mushy on the inside. Some people drain the grease off their French fries once they're through cooking them, but in my estimation, the greasier the French fry, the better. And remember, God is on my side in this one.

My mother, a devout Methodist, could prepare wonderful French fries, and so could the cook at Steve Smith's truckstop, who served them with a hamburger steak that cost $1.25. Today that same piece of meat is called "chopped sirloin" and costs $6.95, and the French fries you get with it are awful. They also serve hard, dark rolls with it, rather than soft, white ones, and if you want a salad, you have to get up and go make it yourself at the salad bar. This borders on sacrilege.

I'm not sure who first loused up French fries, but I hope he's able to beg forgiveness on his death bed. One day we had great French fries — fresh and crispy on the outside and gushy in the middle — and then the next day they were all gone, and we were eating those French fries with crinkles that had been frozen.

Why would anybody want to put crinkles in sliced potatoes? Isn't it a lot of trouble? And why freeze something that's available fresh year-round?

French fries today are hard and have no flavor. All those fast-food places advertise that their French fries are wonderful, but the truth is they're terrible, a disgrace. I'll go down the list of fast-food French fries and tell you exactly what's wrong with them:

— McDONALD'S: Come on, the French fries they serve at McDonald's probably aren't even made out of potatoes. McDonald's probably has devised some scheme whereby they recycle those styrofoam containers the hamburgers come in back into French fries. You know how Ronald McDonald got so ugly? Eating all those styrofoam French fries, that's how.

— WENDY'S: Wendy's French fries are not as tasteless as McDonald's, but they aren't anything to write home about, either. The only thing that makes Wendy's fries halfway edible is that compared to Wendy's chili, the French fries won't make you think you're eating something that came from the mop bucket.

— BURGER CHEF AND BURGER KING: Someday, God is going to get Burger Chef and Burger King for what they've done to His French fries. I suspect they're actually crinkle-cut zucchini.

— STEAK 'N' SHAKE: What is Steak 'n' Shake trying to do — save a few bucks by cutting their French fries into tiny, thin slices? They don't think we notice that? Steak 'n' Shake could take one potato and feed half the state of Missouri. Show me a Steak 'n' Shake French fry and I'll show you what is really a potato "stick." Remember potato sticks? They were awful, but Steak 'n' Shake is trying to bring them back. They should be ashamed.

— KRYSTAL: Krystal's home office is in Chattanooga, Tennessee, so they should know better than to serve the frozen French fries they use. I love Krystal cheeseburgers; I can eat a dozen. I hate Krystal French fries. You could put them in Wendy's chili and it wouldn't improve it.

— HARDEE'S: Worst French fries on earth. I take that back.

— ARTHUR TREACHER'S FISH 'N' CHIPS: Worst French fries on earth. So bad they had to change the name to chips. I have heard it said that even the cows wouldn't claim them.

The demise of the French fry probably began when Americans decided they didn't care what they ate as long as it was prepared in a hurry. Americans do not like to wait. They would eat French fried hog snouts if they could get them without waiting.

"Hey, Martha, want some French fried hog snouts? They taste awful, but we won't have to wait for 'em to cook."

Fast food. It has become an American tradition, like getting a divorce. First, fast food did away with good French fries. Then the hamburgers went. Somebody (probably in New Jersey) started mashing out thin, flat hamburger patties, then they froze them and shipped them all over the country to fast-food hamburger places. Because they were so thin, they took only seconds to cook, and impatient Americans flocked in and bought these mass-produced burgers.

McDonald's even went a step further and started putting a "special sauce" on their hamburgers. I don't trust anything that doesn't have a name. "Special sauce" doesn't really say what's in it. It's like the "mystery meat" Norris Brantley once ate in the school cafeteria.

Why doesn't McDonald's say it's their "special pickle relish" or their "onion-based special sauce with mayonnaise"? They either don't know what's in it themselves, or they're afraid to tell us. I've eaten a McDonald's hamburger with "special sauce" only once, and that was by mistake. It tasted to me like something you'd get if you mixed Thousand Island salad dressing and Wild Russian Vanya.

The way God intended, you don't put any sort of sauce on a hamburger, special or otherwise. What you put on hamburgers is mustard and catsup, tomatoes, lettuce, onions, mayonnaise, dill pickles, or any combination thereof.

And I'll tell you what else you *do not* put on hamburgers — mushrooms. They'll put mushrooms on your hamburger if you order one in those cutsie places where there are a lot of house plants and they serve salads that cost up to $6.95.

I went into one of those places recently and ordered a simple cheeseburger. The waitress asked if I wanted it on pita bread. I didn't have any idea what pita bread was, but I knew I didn't want it covering up my cheeseburger. I asked for a regular bun like you're supposed to serve a cheeseburger on, and the waitress went off in a huff. She brought the cheeseburger back on the right bun, but she also covered it with mushrooms.

"My God!" I exclaimed. "Somebody has put toadstools on my cheeseburger."

"Those aren't toadstools," said the waitress. "They're mushrooms. We always put mushrooms on our cheeseburgers."

"Do you know, young lady," I replied, "that these are, in fact, toadstools, and do you know how toadstools got their name?"

She didn't know.

"Frogs go to the bathroom under them when it's raining," I explained to her. "Imagine how awful it would be to have warts on your tongue."

* * *

As long as we're on the subject of fast food, I must make mention of biscuits, too. All the fast-food places sell biscuits these days, and they advertise them as "just like your mother made."

I don't like for anybody to insult my mother that way. She

certainly didn't make biscuits like those they serve in fast-food places. She made biscuits with an old-fashioned sifter and a rolling pin, and she took each individual biscuit and patted it and shaped it with her own hands. What could McDonald's know about biscuits in the first place?

As anyone with any sense knows, the only thing you're supposed to put on biscuits is either gravy or syrup. Ask some sixteen-year-old behind a McDonald's counter to put something on your biscuit, and she likely will throw on a mess of that special sauce.

Frankly, this entire McDonald's thing bothers me. Do they really know how many billions of hamburgers they've sold? Do the managers call into some central office each night to report?

"Central, this is Topeka. We sold 406 today."

"Central, Joplin here. We did 382. We dropped three on the floor, but we washed 'em off good and sold 'em anyway."

What concerns me about McDonald's and the like is that they've brainwashed our children. Kids today have grown up with fast-food food. They don't know what a real hamburger should taste like. They enjoy going to McDonald's because they see it advertised on television, because all their friends go there, because of that silly clown, and because McDonald's serves cute little food for cute little children in those cute little boxes and containers.

The Communists don't need to bomb us to take over. All they have to do is take over the McDonald's franchises one by one, and we'll fall into their hands like a ripe plum.

I have one other complaint about McDonald's — they serve fish sandwiches. What kind of person would eat a fish sandwich? What kind of fish is it? It could be monkfish or carp, for all we know.

I have never eaten a fish sandwich at McDonald's or at any place else. The only person I ever saw eat a fish sandwich was an ol' boy down in south Georgia one night, when they had a fish fry at a beer joint I often frequent during trips into the region.

This ol' boy walked up to where they were frying the fish, picked up a bream, put it between two pieces of white loaf bread, and ate it, bones and all.

"That's one of them Dewberry boys," the man frying the fish said. "They're hog farmers. Hog farmers will eat anything."

* * *

There is all sorts of food that confuses me today. Take one of those fifty-three-item salad bars, for example. There's the lettuce, I know that, and there are those little red tomatoes and the onions and the cucumbers in the back. (Ever notice how they always put the good stuff at a salad bar way in the back where it's hard to reach? They really don't want you to have it, that's why. They're saving it for themselves to eat after we all leave.)

But what is all that other stuff at a salad bar? Is that yellow dish an egg or scrambled squash? What about the brown stuff? Is it the house dressing or Alpo with water added? I have even seen salad bars where there were anchovies. Now, I ask you, who would put an anchovy on a salad? Have you ever looked at those little things closely? They've got hair on them; I swear they do.

The same confusion exists in other areas. I know by now that real men don't eat quiche, but what is quiche in the first place, and why isn't it pronounced "Kwi-chie" like it's spelled?

What are bean sprouts? They look like something that washed up on the beach.

One of the new items that practically every restaurant is serving today is chicken fingers. I didn't know chickens had fingers. I knew they had toes, but I didn't know they had fingers. I guess what they're really selling is chicken toes, but how much meat can there be on one of those scrawny things?

What I secretly have always wanted to be is a restaurant critic. The mistake most restaurant critics make is assuming that we're all gourmets like they are, and that we know what they're talking about when they order *Coquille St. Jacques.* I thought he was a wide receiver at LSU.

I would aim my restaurant criticism toward people like myself, who simply want to know whether or not the food is fit to eat. I would review restaurants like this:

"I walked in and this guy in a tuxedo says to me, 'Walk this way, please,' and I said to him, 'I don't think I can walk that way,' which he didn't think was very funny.

"I had myself a beer before I ordered. It was cold, but before I could tell him to stop, the waiter had poured it into a glass. Beer tastes better out of the bottle, but I suppose they don't want any bottles around in case a fight breaks out.

"I couldn't make out a blasted thing on the menu because it was all written in a foreign language. Since I was on expense account, I told the waiter just to bring me one of all the most expensive things on the menu.

"While I was waiting on my appetizer, I noticed there was butter on the table but there weren't any crackers. I like to eat butter and crackers while I'm drinking my beer. I complained and the waiter brought some crackers, but they were the kind women put out on the coffee table when they have little get-togethers, not the kind you eat with butter or with raw oysters or crumble up in your chicken-noodle soup.

"The waiter brought out the first appetizer. It smelled like the back of the supermarket where they keep the mullet on ice. It didn't taste all that bad, but I kept thinking about those mullet that still have their eyes, and they just sort of lie there in the ice on their sides with one big eye looking up at you. I was afraid there might be a fish eye in that appetizer someplace, so I just sort of picked at it.

"Then, they brought the soup. The man said it was *vichysoisse*. I complained that it was cold. The waiter said it was supposed to be. I asked, 'Well, do you have any still in the bottle?' He looked at me funny and walked off. I crumbled up some of those crackers in my soup, but it didn't help. If I wanted to eat cold soup, I'd go down to the Mission and eat what they dish out to the winos.

"Speaking of wine, I had some. It was white. 'Would you like to smell the cork, sir?' asked the man who brought the wine. I smelled it. 'That's cork, all right,' I said. Then he poured a little in my glass, and I knew what I was supposed to do then. I tasted it.

" 'Assertive, but not offensive,' I said to the wine man. That was something I heard a guy in a movie say once. I didn't have any idea what it meant, but you're supposed to say things like that whenever there's no screw-off top on the wine bottle and you aren't drinking it out of paper cups.

"I had a salad. There wasn't anything really wrong with it, except they served those little red tomatoes on it. You ever try to eat one of those suckers? If you bite down on one, you'd better put the whole thing in your mouth. I tried biting one in half, and the juice shot all over a fat lady at the table next to me. I apologized and offered her what was left of my cold soup, but she declined.

"The main dish came out. It was chicken with some yellow sauce on it. After I scraped the sauce off to one side, it was passable. I didn't want to leave unless my plate was clean, so they wouldn't think I hadn't enjoyed whatever it was they picked out for me, so I took one of those hard rolls they served and tried to sop up the sauce. It's hard to sop sauce with a hard roll, I found out, so I put what was left of the sauce into my cold soup. I didn't taste it, but it looked like egg custard after I did that.

"As far as dessert was concerned, it was cheesecake and it stuck to the roof of my mouth. The whole meal cost $112.17, and I put on a big tip for everybody and said good-bye to the fat lady.

"I wouldn't go back there again if I had to spend my own money."

I could understand a restaurant review like that, but you never see them. What has happened to me in food, as in most everything else, is that I have gone back to basics.

I still eat lunch at my mother's house in Moreland once a week. She always apologizes when I walk in.

"Son, we don't have hardly anything to eat today," she says.

So what am I going to get here? A piece of toast and a radish? Then I go to the table and there's enough food to feed the Chinese infantry: country fried steak smothered in gravy, mashed potatoes with no lumps in them, all sorts of fresh vegetables from the garden, and hot cornbread and maybe even some coconut pie.

People who live in towns where there isn't a McDonald's (Moreland is one of the five remaining towns on the face of the earth where there is no McDonald's. The other four are in Afghanistan) do not realize how good they have it. The dogs that eat the scraps at home eat better than I do in the city.

I don't like fancy food anymore. If the truth be known, I never did, but when I was younger I pretended that I liked it so nobody would think I was a misfit. I don't care what anybody thinks anymore.

I ate at Maxim's in Paris once. It took four guys to hand out the dessert — strawberries and cream. One guy held the bucket of strawberries, another held the dish of cream, and a third dipped the strawberries and the cream onto my plate. The fourth guy played the violin. You could buy a late-model used car, fully equipped, for what that meal cost, and yet it wouldn't touch what I can get at my mother's house for free.

This book was not designed to be a culinary guide, but because I consider myself an expert on eating (I took it up as a very young child), I'm going to offer you the benefit of my years of experience. I would ask you to clip these guidelines and attach them to your refrigerator door, but with the price of books today, maybe you should just turn down the ear of the page so whenever you're hungry or need advice about eating, you can turn to this spot readily.

GRIZZARD'S GUIDE FOR EATERS

1. Never eat barbecue in a place that also sells Dover Sole. Neither dish will be any good.

2. Never eat any place where they mark the restroom

doors in any fashion but "Men" and "Women" or "Ladies" and "Gentlemen." Especially do not eat in a restaurant that specializes in seafood and marks its restroom doors "Buoys" and "Gulls," because they have been too busy thinking up cutsie names for the restroom doors to really pay attention to the food.

3. Never eat in a restaurant where nobody speaks or understands English. You might get boiled horse or roasted dog if you're not careful.

4. As per our recent discussion, avoid any place that offers French fries and then serves you those with crinkles in them. Any place that doesn't have the decency to serve its customers hand-cut French fries doesn't really give a damn if the rest of its food is fresh and tasty, either.

5. Never eat anything that resembles a house plant, like asparagus, broccoli, or Brussels sprouts.

6. Never eat soup with chunks moving around in the bowl when you aren't stirring it.

7. Avoid "broasted" chicken. Chicken is supposed to be fried to a heavy crisp on the outside, and anybody who tries to cook it any other way is again toying with God's Master Plan.

8. Don't go into French restaurants. They charge you extra for drowning the food in all sorts of sauces. If the food was good to begin with, why would they need to put sauce on it?

9. If the waitresses are skinny, go somewhere else. If they won't eat the food, why should you?

10. Never eat in a restaurant where the maitre d' is a cop.

No. 10 deserves some further embellishment. I checked into a hotel late one Sunday evening. The hotel restaurant had been closed for hours, so I asked the lady behind the counter where I might get something to eat.

"How hungry are you?" she asked.

"I could eat the bellman's hat," I answered.

"In that case, you could walk across the street to The Cave."

"Is the food good?" I inquired.

"Let me put it this way," the woman answered. "Stephen King is thinking of basing his next novel on their menu, but you said you were hungry."

The Cave was located in the basement of an apartment building. I opened the door and the first person I saw was a policeman.

"How many?" he asked.

"One," I said.

"Are you a member?" continued the policeman.

"Of what, Officer?" I asked.

"This is a private club," I was told.

I knew all about private clubs. Private clubs are an ingenious way to get around a lot of sticky rules about selling booze after hours. The policeman explained that I could join The Cave for a dollar and have all the rights and privileges of other club members, such as being able to drink until four in the morning.

Such a deal. I paid my dollar and the policeman handed me a membership card. Then he took me to my table in a cozy little corner near the bandstand. As I was being seated, the thought occurred to me, Why is there a policeman here?

"I hope you won't take this the wrong way," I said to the policeman, "but are you expecting trouble here?"

"About twice a week," he answered, "somebody tries to cut the cook."

I considered going back to the hotel and munching on some of the plants in the lobby, but the waitress had already arrived and handed me the menu. It was printed on an air-sickness bag.

There is another rule to follow when you're eating in a place where the food is obviously of questionable quality: Order as simply as possible. As a matter of fact, that's probably a good rule to follow anytime you're eating out. I never order anything I can't pronounce.

"I'll have a steak," I said to the waitress, figuring that it's difficult for anybody to louse up a steak.

I waited for the waitress, who probably hadn't been nearly as ugly ten years and fifty pounds ago, to ask me how I wanted my steak cooked, but she didn't, so I said, "... and I would like it cooked medium well."

"Folks in hell would like some ice water, too, honey," she answered.

"I can't get my steak cooked medium well?"

"Depends on how sober the cook is," she said.

As I waited for my meal and silently prayed for at least some semblance of sobriety in the cook, I surveyed the scene around me. There were all sorts of individuals at the bar, including a very fat woman dressed in an extremely tight pair of red pants that had the words "Roll Tide," the University of Alabama war cry, written down each leg. I made a mental note to speak to the club officers about a stricter dress code for the members.

There also were several couples shuffling around the dance floor as the band blasted away. Bands that play in such places are always loud, because they follow an old musical adage: If you're going to sound terrible, do so as loudly as possible. Bands in such places always play the same songs, too, and they're songs that I hate. These include "Proud Mary," "Jeremiah Was a Bullfrog," "Tie a Yellow Ribbon," and "Feelings."

The band was butchering "Proud Mary" when the waitress returned with my steak. It may have been a good steak at some point in its existence, but when it reached me it resembled a shingle. I reached for my knife. Out of the corner of my eye, I noticed the policeman move his hand toward his gun.

"I'm just going to try to cut my steak," I said. I honestly had no desire to tangle with the cook. Anybody who would do what he had done to my steak obviously was not the sort of person you'd want to face with a knife.

I had a difficult time cutting the steak. In fact, I couldn't. Finally, I asked the waitress for a couple of packages of crackers and attempted to fill up on them.

As I left, the fat girl in the tight pants winked at me.

"Roll Tide," I said, trying to be nice to a fellow member. I said the wrong thing. The band had just cranked up on "Feelings."

"How 'bout a slow dance, Sweetie?" said the fat girl as she moved toward me. I hid behind the policeman, who convinced her not to drag me to the dance floor as she obviously intended to do.

I thanked the policeman, gave him my membership card back, and made myself a promise never again to go out of town when I'm hungry. If the food don't get you, a fat girl might.

* * *

It's odd how time and circumstances change the taste

buds. I travel a great deal these days. Therefore, I eat a lot of airline food and hotel food (which we eventually will get around to passing laws against). But all the while, I find myself craving the food my mother reared me on. I find myself even craving turnip greens, which is a fairly complicated story with a happy ending.

I hated turnip greens when I was a child, but they were a staple for the family. My grandfather grew them in his garden and used to make me help pick them, which was like making the guest of honor at a hanging help build the gallows.

In the first place, turnip greens emit a foul aroma when they're cooking. And they do not look appetizing. As a matter of fact, they look like something that grows on top of a pond. And the very words *turnip* and *greens* are a turn-off to the appetite as well. *Turnip* sounds like something they would find growing on your pancreas.

"Am I going to make it, doctor?"

"Removing a pancreatic turnip is a serious matter, but we'll do everything we can."

Greens. That sounds like something to do with loose bowels.

"Sarah just hasn't been herself lately."

"What's her problem?"

"Got a bad case of the greens. She's been afraid to leave the house for three days."

Now that I'm older and forced to eat modern foods, however, I enjoy the occasional turnip greens that I get. My Aunt Jessie makes them for me when I visit her. Recently, Aunt Jessie had a sort of family reunion at her house, and she cooked a huge pot of turnip greens. As I was saying how tasty they were, Aunt Jessie's daughter, cousin Glenda, spoke up and said turnip greens are sort of how she came to meet her new husband. I enjoy a good love story, so I asked her to explain.

"Well," she said, "I was working at a Hardee's and Owen was working at a gas station next door. One day, I stopped to fill up my tank and he came out to wait on me.

"While the gas was pumping, we started talking and I casually asked him how he was getting along. He said everything was fine, except that somebody had given him a mess of turnip greens and he didn't have a pot to cook them in.

"I said, 'Well, I've got a pot if you've got the greens,' and next thing you know, we got married."

You'll never find that moving a love story in *True Romance*. And isn't there a country music song in all this somewhere? We could call it, "You're the Greens in My Pot of Love."

* * *

Just one more note about food (which should lead me nicely into the next chapter). One of the worst things that has happened to food in the past ten years is the microwave oven. I have one in my kitchen, but it came with the house.

I worry about food that has been prepared in a microwave oven. What is a "microwave" in the first place? Does it have to do with radiation? Whenever I eat something that has been cooked in a microwave, I feel like I should be wearing a lead vest instead of a napkin at the neck.

And why do restaurants that use microwave ovens put a sign on the door that says, "Warning: Microwave Oven in Use"? Somebody told me that if you have a pacemaker in your heart and you stand around a microwave oven, the rays or waves or whatever is inside one of those ovens can throw your pacemaker out of kilter. If a microwave oven can do something like that, what else can it do? My car occasionally won't start in the morning, usually after I've cooked some bacon in my microwave oven. You figure it out.

And you've heard that rumor about the woman who gave her cat a bath and then put him in her microwave to dry him, haven't you? Besides, if God really intended for us to have microwave ovens, why did He give us Ol' Diz charcoal?

Questions like that are always popping up these days. It's the price we pay for living in a world of modern technology. And just to be on the safe side, if I was a cat, I'd stay the hell out of the kitchen. Now, if everyone will kindly climb aboard the turnip truck to the next chapter, we will continue this discussion of modernity.

14 Somebody Pull The Plug On Modernity

I WAS VISITING the folks at home, and my stepfather walked outside to hang the week's wash on the clothesline. I went along for some fresh air.

The winds of early March flapped the sheets and pillowcases and the freshly-washed underwear. Both the sight and the sound were comforting, even reassuring. One of the things that's wrong with our society today, I thought as I watched my stepfather, is that most people are too pretentious to hang their underwear out to dry on a clothesline that any passerby can see.

Today, people prefer to dry their underwear inside their houses in a gadget called a dryer, which spins the clothes in vicious cycles, pumping electrically-heated air to them. As the clothes tumble, odd sounds come from the machine, and when they're finally dry, the machine stops automatically and gives out a signal that it desires to be unloaded.

But why would anybody want to be summoned by a machine?

Clothes dried outside by the sun and the wind and without buzzers (in Smith Barney parlance, the "old-fashioned way") have a certain feel to them. Underwear dried outside, for instance, is less likely to cause itching and, because of the natural freshness, it may not even ride up quite as readily. There's also a wonderful smell to naturally-dried clothes — the smell of the building warmth of early morning.

Maybe one reason people are more grumpy these days is that their underwear smells like coils and filters instead of like fresh sunshine. And it also rides up more aggressively, and we all know that nothing saps a person's friendliness and comfort quicker than underwear creeping into certain crevices.

Just think about a society that didn't mind hanging out its underwear for the world to see: It was a society that accepted the cards it was holding, a society that said, "My privacy is dear, but my refusal to bow to pretense is to be cherished even more." Or, put more simply, it was a society that said, "I'll hang my drawers on the line if I want to, and if mine happen to be more holey than thou's, so be it."

I wouldn't want to leave the impression that I spent an inordinate amount of my childhood staring at other folks' underwear on their clotheslines. I will admit, however, that there was occasional good sport to be had on wash day.

Miss Nellie Bascomb hung her clothes on a line in her easily accessible back yard. She wore those pink bloomers that struck just below the knee and had legs large enough for a fully-grown man to crawl through. When Miss Nellie hung out her entire compliment of bloomers, they looked like flags flapping on a mainsail.

Prissy Betty Ann Hillback, who played piano and sang solos at funerals (and who, you will remember, saved Donnelle Spinks from homosexuality), lived near Miss Nellie. One evening, a commando team of pimply-faced young men, who shall remain nameless, sneaked into Miss Nellie's back yard and took her bloomers off the line.

The raiders then slipped into Betty Ann Hillback's back yard and took her cute little step-ins, with the days of the week embroidered upon them, off the Hillbacks' clothesline and replaced them with Miss Nellie's pinks. The next morning, when Betty Ann's mother sent her out to bring in the clothes, the perpetrators of this foul deed strolled up to Betty Ann and made all sorts of hooting remarks, such as, "Hey, Betty Ann, how about loaning us a pair of your bloomers? We need a tent for a camping trip."

Betty Ann turned pinker than Miss Nellie's underpants and ran into the house. The Hillbacks, incidentally, were the first family in my hometown to buy an electric clothes dryer.

* * *

Please understand that I'm not indiscriminately opposed to modernity. Some modern inventions and conveniences, I fully condone. Here are a few:

— AIR CONDITIONING: There is absolutely no reason to sweat anymore, unless you absolutely want to, which I don't.

— AUTOMATIC TRANSMISSION: I still don't know where reverse is on a straight stick, and remember what an awful time you had with the clutch when you were stuck on a hill in traffic?

— AUTOMATIC ICE-MAKERS: Thank you, whoever invented the automatic ice-maker, for delivering me from those ice trays that froze harder than Chinese arithmetic. The lever always bent when I tried to pry open the ice.

— AUTOMATIC COFFEE-MAKERS: They would be even more automatic if somebody would think of a way to make the thing remember to go out and buy the coffee, too, but you can't have everything.

— HAAGEN-DAZS ICE CREAM: I know this doesn't exactly fit here, but I love Haagen-Dazs ice cream.

— TWENTY-FOUR-HOUR AUTOMATIC BANK TELLERS: Three times a week, I run out of cash at precisely 11:30 p.m.

— BIC PENS: You lose one, so what? For a pittance, you can buy another.

— SCREW-OFF TOPS ON BEER BOTTLES: You never have to worry about keeping a church key handy again.

— OVERSIZED TENNIS RACQUETS: You don't have to bend over as much to hit the ball anymore. Bending over is something I hate about tennis.

— ELECTRIC POPCORN POPPERS: Remember when you had to shake the pot to get the kernels to pop?

— ROACH MOTELS: They don't smell up the house like Black Flag used to and they're quite effective against roaches. I checked my Roach Motel recently and found a dozen dead roaches inside, including three in the lounge and one out by the pool.

— VIDEO CASSETTE RECORDERS: This certainly is a wonderful modern invention. You can tape television programs and watch them later, and you can rent movies and watch them in your very own home. Unfortunately, I have had a video cassette recorder for four years and I still haven't figured out how to work it. I'm waiting for a fully automatic one that you don't have to monkey with and that will mail off for X-rated movies on its own.

— THE THERMOS BOTTLE: A truly amazing invention. In the summertime, I put iced tea in my thermos bottle. Thirty minutes later, I pour out the iced tea and it's still cold. In the wintertime, I put hot coffee in my thermos and thirty minutes later, I pour it out and it's still hot. In the immortal words of my boyhood friend and idol, Weyman C. Wannamaker, Jr., "How do it know?"

— REMOTE CONTROL FOR TELEVISION: This invention has changed my life. Before, when I watched television, I had to sit through all those commercials because I didn't feel like getting up and switching channels. With my remote control, I can change channels any time I want without having to leave my chair.

Do you realize what this means? I haven't had to watch a Drāno commercial — the one that shows the inside of that pipe with all the hair and various other sorts of goo inside it — in years. I also haven't had to watch any commercials advertising feminine hygiene spray or mini-pads. (Has Cathy Rigby reached menopause yet? I certainly hope so.)

And hemorrhoid commercials — I don't have to watch them anymore, either. Do they still run the one where the woman is talking about her hemorrhoids and underneath her face it says, "Roxanne Burgess, Hemorrhoid Sufferer"?

I used to wonder how they found that woman. It's not the sort of thing you hold tryouts for, I don't suppose. How would you keep each contestant's score?

Do you know what *really* would be a marvelous invention? A remote control device for life. Whenever you found yourself in an unpleasant situation, you would pull out your remote control and switch around until you found a situation you liked better.

Let's say you've been out half the night with your rowdy friends. You come home singing drunk, and your wife greets you at the door and begins calling you horrible names. Not to worry. You simply pull out your remote control and ZAP!, you're right back with your rowdy friends drinking beer and telling lies again.

* * *

So, you see, there are a few modern inventions that I enjoy, but there are many more that have weasled their way into our lives and have become great nuisances.

Take airplanes, for example. I realize that they date all the way back to the Wright Brothers, but airplanes didn't come into my life until after I was old enough to understand that anything going that fast and that high is inherently dangerous.

I fell in love with trains as a small boy. Somebody — it may have been what's-his-name, the guy who writes the daffy poems — once said, "After spending a day watching trains, baseball seems a silly game." (I just thought of his name: Rod McKuen, and that's the only thing he ever said worth remembering.)

Trains make sense to me. The engine moves and the cars attached behind it follow.

Trains are also romantic, especially their names. I mentioned earlier that I wrote a song about a train called the "Nancy Hanks." It ran between Atlanta and Savannah on the Central of Georgia line. Once, while riding the "Nancy Hanks" from Atlanta to Savannah, I drank fourteen beers in the club car — which was not that big a deal, but getting up and walking to the restroom twenty-six times on a train that is rocking back and forth may yet be a record for American railroads.

Another time I rode a train called the "San Francisco Zephyr" from Chicago to Frisco. (A "zephyr" is a west wind, incidentally.) Somewhere between Denver and Cheyenne, Wyoming, I met an Italian fellow in the club car. He spoke very little English; I spoke no Italian. I did, however, manage to get his name and to ask, "What do you do for a living in Italy?"

"I am painter," Oscar said.

See how romantic it is traveling by train? Have you ever had a drink with an Italian artist somewhere between Denver and Cheyenne, Wyoming, while traveling in an airplane? Neither have I.

"And what do you paint?" I asked my Italian friend. "Landscapes, still-lifes, pastels?"

"Houses," Oscar answered. "I am house painter."

Okay, so how many Italian house painters have you met on airplanes?

Eventually, my profession led me to travel a great deal. When you write books, you have to go many places in an attempt to sell those books. Also, people will invite you to make speeches in front of large groups (that frankly would rather have skipped the dinner and the speaker and kept the cocktail party going).

It soon became evident to me that either I would have to give up the rails as my primary mode of transportation or get a new profession, such as working in a liquor store.

In a more civilized time, a book publisher would say, "Could you be in Bakersfield, California, by Friday?" They would say that on the previous Saturday.

"Certainly," you would answer. "I can connect with the

'Super Chief' in Chicago and be there in plenty of time."

But book publishers don't say that anymore. Now they say, "Can you be in Bakersfield by five this afternoon?", and they say that at ten in the morning. And you answer, "No problem. I'll shave and shower and catch the noon flight, and with the time change, I'll be able to get a haircut at the the airport in L.A."

Anyway, the guy at the liquor store said he didn't need any help, so I had to take up flying.

The main reason I've never liked flying is that I'm terrified at the very thought of it. My friends have all attempted to make me feel better by pointing out that more people die from slipping in the bathtub than in commercial airplane crashes. If there were any way to travel by bathtub, I tell them, I certainly would do it.

If airplanes are so safe, why do they make you strap yourself in the seat? And why do they always point out, "Your seat cushions may be used for flotation"? If I had wanted to float to Bakersfield, I would have chartered a canoe.

And I still don't understand how those big suckers fly. I have a friend who is brilliant in the area of engineering and such. One day, we were riding near the airport and a large plane took off over our car.

"What makes those big suckers fly?" I asked him.

"Well, you see, there is the air foil and lift and blah, blah, blah, technical, technical...."

"I know all that," I said, "but what I really want to know is, What makes those big suckers fly?"

Faced with the option of either flying or drawing unemployment, I searched for ways to control my terror. For the benefit of others who may feel the same, here is how I cope with my own fear:

— I drink a lot before getting on the plane. I'm not talking about having one drink or two. I'm talking about joining all the airlines' private clubs, where the booze is free, and drinking six or eight double screwdrivers and then calling for one of those buggies they carry handicapped people in to take me to my gate.

— I drink a lot while I'm in the air, and I ask the stewardesses to allow me to mix my own drinks, so they'll be very strong. The only problem with drinking this much is that sometimes when the airplane lands, I get off and cannot remember what city I was traveling to. So I ask and somebody tells me, but then I can't remember what I was supposed to do when I got there, so I go back to Delta's Crown Room or Eastern's Ionosphere Lounge and have another drink.

— When I have a choice, I prefer to fly with the airline that has had the latest crash. I figure my odds are better on an airline that isn't due.

— I never fly on the national airlines of Communist countries, or countries where they think cows are sacred and allow them to wander around in the streets.

— I never fly on commuter airlines. If the pilots are so good, why are they stuck flying for Air Chance ("We'll take a chance, if you will")? Besides, you know what they serve you to eat on airlines like that? The stewardess passes around an apple and a pocket knife.

— No matter what, I never go to the toilet in an airplane to do anything I can't do standing up. This eventually may lead to a very embarrassing situation for me, but I don't want them to pick through the charred remains of a crash and find me with my pants down sitting on a toilet.

— I call the pilot the night before takeoff to make certain that he isn't drinking and that he is in bed early.

— I am able to relax a bit after the seat belt sign goes off and the pilot comes on the intercom. If they've turned off the warning light and the pilot doesn't have anything to do but talk on the intercom, I figure all is well in the cockpit. On some flights, the pilot never comes on the intercom. I order another drink when that happens.

— I pray a lot. There are no atheists in a foxhole, and I doubt there are any in a 727 that is passing through heavy turbulence after takeoff from Philadelphia at night. I try never to have any dirty thoughts on an airplane, so God will like me and listen to my prayers.

Even if airplanes weren't frightening, they still would be a large pain. The food, of course, is awful; all airports are crowded; and there's usually a baby crying on every airplane (must be some sort of FAA regulation).

Planes are also frequently late, they can't take off or land in heavy fog, and sometimes too many planes are waiting to land or take off. Waiting to take off isn't that unsettling, but circling around waiting to land, knowing that a frustrated and overworked air controller is the only thing between you and a mid-air collision, is not a happy thought.

Keeping up with airline fares these days is also a big headache. I always feel guilty when I fly because I might not have gotten the best fare. You have to be careful trying to get too good a deal, however. I saw advertised recently a flight between Atlanta and New York for $26. I called the airline to inquire. The hitch was that you had to ride in a crate in the cargo hold.

Think how much better the world would be today if the

airplane had never been invented. There wouldn't be any threat of nuclear war. How are the Russians going to drop a bomb on us without an airplane? They sure couldn't throw it out the back of a panel truck.

And if flying had never been invented, we wouldn't have spent all that money on the Space Program, in which we sent a bunch of people to the moon to find out that it looks a lot like Nevada.

If we didn't have airplanes and still took trains, we would know a lot more about our country. You would be surprised how much of the country you can see from a train window. Did you know, for instance, that there are more piles of junk in Newark, New Jersey, than anywhere else in America?

If there were no airplanes, we wouldn't have to put up with Frank Borman, and no matter what a terrorist threatened to do, there is no way he could hijack a train to Cuba. And did you ever lose your bags on a train trip? Of course not. I took a flight between Atlanta and Charlotte once, but the airline sent my bags to Caracas.

Planes cause people to be in a rush. They cause them to go a lot of places they probably wouldn't go to if they thought about it long enough — places like Nassau and New York City and Cannes, France, where I flew to once. After about an hour, watching barebreasted women gets boring; then you have to go back to the hotel, where every Algerian and his brother-in-law is in the lobby having a loud argument.

And finally, if we hadn't been smart enough to invent airplanes, we likely wouldn't have been smart enough to invent computers, either; and I definitely could do without computers. In fact, I may be one of the last holdouts against computers, and I can prove it by explaining that I am typing these very words on a 1959 manual Royal typewriter for which I paid ninety bucks and wouldn't sell for five times that, because I don't know if I would be able to find another one.

People in the swing of modern ways often say to me, "Why don't you get yourself one of those word processors? It would make writing a lot easier for you."

No, it wouldn't. First, I would have to sit for hours at a time staring at a television screen with words on it. It would be like watching one of those cable television stations where they play music in the background and words appear on the screen, giving you the news and baseball linescores.

If I watch one of those stations for longer than ten minutes, I get sick to my stomach. It's the same feeling I get when I try to read in a car.

Also, I don't know where the words go in one of those word processors. You type a lot of words onto the screen, which will hold just so many, and then they disappear. What if they accidentally went into somebody else's word processor? Not that anybody else would want my words, but some things I write never appear in print and would tend to embarrass me if somebody else were to look at them.

All of journalism has gone to computers these days. In fact, nobody types on paper anymore. When I was an editor, we had paper all over the place, especially on the floor. It gave the office a homey look. Now, there is no paper and there is carpet on the floor. I walk into a newspaper office today and I feel like opening a checking account.

When I write, I like to hear some noise. I enjoy hearing the tap-tap-tap of the keys on my Royal manual. When I hear that sound, especially if I hear it without interruption, I know I'm getting something accomplished. As with any machine, however, minor problems occasionally occur with my typewriter. For instance, I once wrote an entire book without the letter "e" available to me, because the "e" character had broken on its key.

When I handed in my manuscript, the editor said, "What are all these blank spaces on your manuscript?"

"Wherever you see a blank space," I said, "that's where an 'e' goes."

There's also the small matter of maintaining a fresh ribbon in a manual typewriter, and sometimes the keys get stuck together and you get ink all over your hands trying to pry them apart. I'm constantly getting the "g," "j," and "f" keys stuck together, because I have bricks for hands. But at least my manual typewriter can't be knocked out by lightning and won't go on the fritz if I happen to spill coffee on it.

Frankly, I don't dislike computers as much as I dislike people who spend a lot of time operating them. They speak to one another in a language I don't understand, and I'm convinced they think they're a lot smarter than people who don't know anything about computers. I have a feeling that these are the same people who carried around slide rules when I was in high school and college and thought spending an afternoon discussing logarithms was keen fun.

Computers also have become an excuse. For example, "Pardon me, but is flight 108 to Cleveland on time?"

"Sorry, sir, but our computer is down."

I think what they really mean is that they have lost flight 108 to Cleveland but won't admit it. That's something else I never had to deal with when I rode trains.

"Is ol' 98 running on time?"

"She was about two minutes late into Steamboat Junction, but she's highballin' now."

Once, a large company owed me some money. It never

came. I called and inquired about my check.

"Our computers have been down," I was told.

"Isn't there a company officer somewhere who can simply write a check and then you could mail it to me?"

"All our checks and mailing are done by computer."

I know what they were doing. They were using my money to pay for the repairs on their stupid computers.

I'm afraid we are ruining an entire generation of Americans by getting our children involved in computers at a very young age. In some elementary schools today, kids bring their own computers to class. All I needed in elementary school was a box of crayons and milk money.

You give a kid a computer and strange things can happen. One of the little boogers eventually will figure out how to launch a Pershing missile, and try explaining to what's left of the Kremlin that little Johnny Manderson of Fort Worth, Texas, was just kidding around on his computer. I say put a twenty-one-year-old age limit on computers and send the kids outside to play ball or go drag racing. Should a kid really know his user I.D. before he knows how many fingers to hold up for his age?

My first experience with computers came when I entered college. They handed me computer cards as I enrolled in different classes. Each computer card had written on it, "Do not fold, bend, staple, or mutilate." I wondered what would happen if I should fold, bend, staple, or mutilate one of the cards.

My curiosity finally got to me, so I bent and folded and stapled and mutilated and even poured catsup on my computer card. There were no serious injuries or substantial penalties forthcoming, but it took me two quarters to get my standing as a home economics major changed.

All sorts of things puzzle me about computers:

— Computer shopping: Do we really want to shop by computer? The instant you see a TV commercial, you press a button on your computer and a conveyor belt delivers Ginsu knives to your kitchen and deducts $14.95 from your account. Could you really tell if a pair of loafers would fit by looking at them on a video monitor?

— Easy-to-use computers: That's easy for somebody else to say. I can barely operate a bottle of aspirin.

— Talking computers: Now there are even cars that talk to you. "You need gas, you need gas," says your car. Talking cars give me gas.

— Understanding computers: Where do all those cables on computers go to? Is there a little Oriental guy in a room somewhere with an abacus going a mile a minute? What's the difference between "software" and "hardware"? Is one part wool and itches a lot? Is a "semiconductor" a person who works for the railroad part-time?

— Computer dating: What if the computer doesn't mind girls who don't shave their legs and gets me a date with one? I'm the one who has to kiss her goodnight, not the computer.

— Personal computers: I don't want to get personal with a computer. I wasn't compatible with three wives. How am I supposed to be compatible with IBM?

You know something else about computers? There's nothing funny about them. In doing research for this chapter, I looked in several computer magazines. There was not a single joke section or cartoon in any of them.

The big question we must all ask is, Where is this computer business going to end? How much of our lives are they going to take over? The first computer filled a warehouse.

Now, a computer the size of your fingernail can do the same amount of computing. Will they eventually be like contact lenses, only worse? You see somebody down on their hands and knees and you say, "Lose something?"

"Yeah," comes the answer. "I dropped my computer. I know it's here in the grass somewhere."

Computers can even talk to each other now, so what's to keep them from plotting against us? And here is something else to worry about: What if all the computers on earth went down at one time? Life as we know it would come to a standstill all over the planet. The only people who would know how to carry on would be natives who live in the African bush who never have heard of computers, and me, who has steadfastly refused to learn to operate one.

Frankly, I'm sort of looking forward to that day. I could dress up in a loin cloth with my friends from the bush, and we could dance up and down and I could laugh and say, "I told you so," and poke all those uppity computer-types in their butts with my spear.

I want to get even with computers and the people who build them and the people who run them. That desire peaked recently at the airport in Jacksonville, Florida.

I was awaiting a flight. I went into the airport lounge to have my normal six or eight pre-flight double screwdrivers. There was nothing that looked unusual about the bar — just a couple of barmaids serving a weary traveler here and there.

"Can I help you?" one of the barmaids asked me.

"Double screwdriver, please," I said, "and a little heavier on the screw than the driver, if you will. The weather's bad out and I have to fly."

The barmaid didn't understand my little joke.

"What I'm trying to say," I explained, "is could you give me a little extra vodka and a little less orange juice in my drink. I'm nervous when I fly, and the more I drink, the more comfortable is my flight."

"All I can give you," replied the barmaid, "is what the computer shoots out."

"I beg your pardon?" I asked, somewhat in shock.

"The cash register has got this computer in it, and it's hooked up to the little hoses that we pour the liquor out of. All I do is mash the button, and the computer squirts out a shot, and it all gets rung up on the cash register."

"Let me see if I have this straight," I said. "You have no power whatsoever over how the drinks are poured? A computer measures the amount of booze I get in my drink, and there's no way you can change that?"

"Right," said the barmaid.

"In that case," I said, "bring me the coldest beer you have."

"Ain't got no cold beer," said the barmaid. "The cooler's busted."

The flight was delayed two hours because of the bad weather. I caught a cab to the nearest convenience store, bought two quart bottles of beer, and drank them out of a paper sack, eating peanuts and Slim Jims and watching the rain fall. Computerized drinking is the final straw, I thought to myself, and I prayed silently for the day that somebody, or something, would pull the plug on all this madness.

* * *

My incompatibility with modernity does not cease with

airplanes and computers. Here are some other modern conveniences that aren't.

— Telephones: Do you really think we've made a lot of progress in telephones? We haven't. Telephones, when I was a kid, were very simple to operate. You didn't even have to dial the blasted things. You just picked up the receiver, and when somebody else came on the line, you said, "Hilda, get me the courthouse."

Gossip was a lot easier to keep up with then, too, if you were on a party line. And telephone operators would make long distance calls for you, and if the line was busy, they would say, "Would you like for me to keep trying and call you back?" That was service.

I'm very confused about telephones today. I am not certain who's in charge of the telephones anymore, and there are all sorts of things you have to decide when you have a telephone installed.

Telephones used to be black. That was it. They were sort of short and squatty and black. Today, you can have a telephone in the shape of a pretzel if you so desire. A pink pretzel. "Watson, come here, you *savage.*"

Telephone numbers used to be fun, too. You dialed PLaza 7-3622, or WEird 9-6238 (if you were calling somebody in California). There weren't any area codes, either, and there were no such things as credit card numbers.

I have a friend who has one those new Sprint calling services. First, he has to dial a local number to get himself a dial tone (or should that be *punch* tone?) in order to make a long distance call. Then he has to punch in something called an "access code." Then he has to dial the number he's trying to reach.

"First," he was explaining to me, "I punch in the local

number, 355-0044, which is seven digits. Then I punch in my access code, which is 525-833-611, nine more digits. Then I punch in the number I'm calling, say, 1-817-423-5578. That's another eleven digits, and that's a total of twenty-seven digits. And just about the time I'm punching the last of them, my finger always slips and I have to start over."

I hate recording devices that answer telephones, too, because they entice people to create cute recorded messages.

"Hi, this is Bob. Well, actually it's not. This is Bob's machine. Bob got it from his mom for his last birthday. Mom said she was going to get Bob a puppy, but she was afraid it would just mess all over the carpet and Mom is very clean-conscious, so she got him this machine. Bob is out right now, but he will be back later, so at the sound of the tone, please leave your name and number and any message, and when Bob comes home he will call you back ... Beeeeeeeeeep!"

I can't help it. Whenever I call a number and get one of those recordings, I always leave a message designed to frighten whoever owns the contraption:

"Bob, this is Davenport at the IRS, and we urgently need to see you. Do not make any plans that can't be broken for the next seven years."

Whoever invented call-waiting for telephones should be taken out and shot. Nothing infuriates me more than to be talking to somebody on the telephone when that little click goes off, and they say, "Would you mind holding for just a second?"

Damn right, I mind holding. You called me; I didn't call you.

People who have these devices on their telephones have

large egos. So what if somebody calls and gets a busy signal because the person is on the phone talking to me? Who could be calling that is *that* important? I suspect that they really don't work. People simply have clicking noises put in their phones so that when I'm talking to them, I'll think they're very important and popular because a lot of other people are trying to reach them.

— Showers with complicated knobs: These are found mostly in hotels. Remember how simple showers used to be to operate? There was a knob with an "H" on it and one with a "C" on it. You turned the "H" knob for hot water and the "C" knob for cold water, and you could get your shower just right.

I go into hotels now where it would take a degree from MIT to figure out which way to turn the handle to get hot and cold water. I'm surprised that scalding hasn't reached epidemic proportions in this country.

— Self-service gas stations: You go to one pump if you have a credit card, another if you have the correct cash, or another if it's Tuesday and you're wearing green slacks. I have closed deals on houses in less time than it takes to figure out how to pump ten gallons of gasoline into my automobile.

— Beepers: You can run these days, but you can't hide.

— Eyeglasses that are supposed to turn dark when you walk outside and then clear up when you go back inside: They never clear up enough when you go back inside. I had some glasses like that. Every time I walked inside a building, somebody tried to buy pencils from me.

— Talking soft drink machines: I like to put my coins in the machine and get a soft drink. If I wanted conversation, I'd talk to my car.

— The designated hitter in baseball: This has nothing to do with gadgetry, but it's another ridiculous modern idea. It keeps too many old, slow, fat people in the game.

— Electric shoe shiners: They don't work. When I have my shoes shined, I want to hear a rag pop.

— Beer with lower alcohol content: This allows too many sissies into good beer joints and taverns.

— Automatic pinsetters in bowling alleys: They put a lot of good pin boys out of work, and how do those things operate in the first place?

— Commodes in public places that flush automatically: I think it is my right as an American to be able to flush any commode I might be using when I'm good and ready.

* * *

There rests in most of us, I suppose, a longing for the simpler past. I'm convinced that simplicity breeds contentment, but how can one be content when constantly befuddled by a thousand different electronic gizmos that we really don't need, and by a constant stream of new ideas that don't give a national damn for tradition?

As I grow older, I become more and more comfortable ignoring these changes and trends. I don't have to do things any more just because everybody else is doing them. Who knows? Maybe by the time I'm forty, I will be able to tell somebody who wants me to be in Bakersfield by five o'clock to go stick their head in their Jacuzzi; I'm taking the train.

The thought is a delicious one.

15 You Can't Trust A Psychiatrist With Cats

I HAVE A theory about time: The longer you live, the faster it passes. When I was fifteen and wanted my driver's license more than anything in the world, it took me exactly seventeen years to reach age sixteen. After I finally became sixteen, I wanted to be twenty-one so I could go into a bar and order a beer without fearing the Gestapo would show up at my table and take me off somewhere and beat me with rubber hoses. They could have rerun the Thousand Years War during the period it took me to go from sixteen to twenty-one.

Then things began to speed up. It took about six months for me to become twenty-five; twenty-six through twenty-nine went in about a week; and the next afternoon, I turned thirty.

Turning thirty does have some benefits. For one, it means you can smoke cigars. I have never smoked cigars, but I don't think it's appropriate for anyone to smoke them until after they've turned thirty; there's nothing more obnoxious than some juvenile puffing on a big cigar and pontificating about world affairs — which inhaling cigar smoke apparently makes people do. After thirty, however, a person is finally old enough to light up a Cuesta Rey, lean back in his chair, and say the president is an idiot. Even if he is completely misinformed, people will listen to what he has to say and nod in agreement.

Another good thing about turning thirty is that you're finally old enough to realize the truth about life: It isn't fair. All young people think that Moses brought down an extra tablet from the mountain, and written on it by the hand of God was, "Life is Fair."

When my cousin got more banana pudding than I did after supper because she had eaten all her turnip greens and I had just picked at mine, I would complain to my mother, "That isn't fair."

When I was twenty-five and had cornered a beautiful young woman at a singles bar and was regaling her with my interesting tidbits of knowledge, but she wound up leaving with some guy who had large muscles and a Porsche, I turned to the bartender and said, "That isn't fair."

By the time I turned thirty, however, I had learned that what actually was written on that other tablet was, "If life had been meant to be fair, there never would have been such a thing as a proctoscopic examination."

There are some negative aspects to being thirty, of course. For example, young girls start calling you "Mister" and asking you if there was such a thing as television when you were growing up. Your parents and friends stop forgiving you for doing stupid things because you were too young and didn't know any better.

When you're thirty, you finally realize there is no chance

you're still going to be discovered by a major league scout while playing recreation league, slow-pitch softball and wind up in the big leagues and on the cover of *Sports Illustrated.*

When you're thirty, in case it hasn't happened already, you know the time is coming when you will be unable to perform sexually one evening, because your older friends have already started talking about it. The simple knowledge that it *could* happen to you will eat away at your mind, and soon that evening will come and it will go something like this:

"What's the matter?"

"I don't know."

"Is it me?"

"Of course, it's not you."

"It must be me."

"I don't know what's the matter."

"Has it happened before?"

"Of course, it hasn't happened before."

By this time, a cold sweat has covered your body and what you really want to do is hide under the bed in the dark until she leaves, and then have a nervous breakdown in private.

"Why don't we wait until morning," you say.

"I have to be up early for work."

"You don't hate me, do you?"

"Of course, I don't hate you."

"It's just that I've got a lot on my mind."

"I understand. I really do."

She doesn't really understand, of course, and she really hates you and thinks you're a wimp, and what if she goes around telling everybody? This is the stuff suicides are made of.

I had flirted a bit with adulthood before I hit my thirties. I got married for the first time when I was only nineteen. An insurance man followed me around for a month and made me feel guilty until I finally took out a policy that would make certain my bride would be kept financially secure should I die.

Should I die? The thought that I might actually die one day had never occurred to me until I took out that insurance policy. Realizing mortality is a giant step toward adulthood.

I got my first divorce when I was twenty-three. Something like that will wear off a little of your tread, too. I got married again when I was twenty-six and got divorced again when I was twenty-nine. Then something quite adult happened to me: I stopped for a few moments and had a long talk with myself to determine what it was about me that had led to two marriages and two divorces before I turned thirty.

Self-analysis is a very adult maneuver, although in my case, self-analysis did me little good. I couldn't come to any conclusions because I always was arguing with myself.

"Maybe it's because my parents divorced when I was six, and I really haven't had a role model to teach me how to fashion a happy marriage," said my ego.

"Quit making excuses. The truth is, you're a selfish, insensitive person, and nobody can live with you more than three years," said my alter ego.

"But I really tried to make a go of it."

"Tried nothing. You never tried until it was too late and you were afraid of being alone."

"I wasn't afraid of being alone."

"Yes, you were. You realized all of a sudden that if you were alone, there wouldn't be anybody around to keep your underwear clean."

"I can take care of my own underwear, thank you."

"How? You've never washed a pair of dirty underwear in your life. Your mother washed it for you and your wives washed it for you. When you weren't married and your underwear got dirty, you simply went out and bought new."

"So look what I did for the underwear industry. I'm basically a good person."

That sort of thing went on for months without resolution, so I did something that all modern adults eventually do. I went to see a psychiatrist.

I didn't tell anybody about this plan, however, because I was reared to believe than anybody who went to see a psychiatrist was admitting that he or she was some sort of screwball, soon to be admitted to a home where they would be kept very still and quiet. Milledgeville, a pleasant little village in central Georgia, was where the state sent its loonies when I was a kid. Anybody who went to Milledgeville for observation or admittance automatically was deemed completely out of focus.

The old men at the store:

"Heard about Tyrone Gault?"

"What happened to him?"

"They done took him to Milledgeville."

"When did he go crazy?"

"Said it come on him real sudden. He come in the house from the barn one day and told his wife one of his cows had just told him to go to town and buy a new tractor, and he thought it was the Almighty that was talking to him. He was back in a hour on a new John Deere."

"I heard about a fellow could make animals talk."

"You ain't never heard of no such thing. You ain't crazy like Tyrone Gault, are you?"

"Naw, it's a true story. There was this Injun and he was sittin' out by his tepee and this fellow walked up and said, 'Can your horse talk?'

"The Injun said of course his horse couldn't talk, so the fellow turned to the horse and said, 'Horse, is this Injun good to you? Does he ever put you up wet? Does he feed you plenty of oats?'

"Well, the horse spoke right up and said, 'Yeah, I can't complain one bit. He's pretty good to me.'

"The Injun couldn't believe his ears. Then, the fellow asked the Injun, 'Can your dog talk?' The Injun said of course his dog couldn't talk.

"So the fellow turns to the dog and says, 'Dog, does your master treat you all right? Does he give you plenty to eat and does he scratch your ears?'

"The dog said, 'He treats me just fine. Ain't a thing in the world wrong with the life I got.'

"The ol' Injun was amazed. The fellow asked him then, said, 'Can your sheep talk?', and the Injun said, 'Yes, sheep talk, but lie like hell.'"

"Get away from here with your foolishness."

"It's a shame 'bout Tyrone Gault, though."

"I feel sorry for his wife and children. Don't reckon he'll ever get out of Milledgeville. They say once you're down there, you don't ever get back right."

"I heard tell the same thing. I wonder what his wife would take for that new tractor?"

Even from a background of complete misunderstanding about mental health, I figured I had no choice but to seek psychiatric help. I decided, however, to pay cash for my treatments and not give my real name, in case the psychiatrist wanted to have me committed.

I was living in Chicago at the time, which added to the possibility that I might be crazy. I looked in the yellow pages, found a psychiatrist's office near my apartment, phoned him, and made an appointment.

I should have expected something was wrong the moment I stepped into the psychiatrist's office, which wasn't an office at all but the man's apartment. There were two cats sitting on the couch. A cat never has done anything all that terrible to me personally, but I don't like cats because they're sneaky and snooty, especially if you're a man. Women and cats seem to be able to get along together, to understand each other. Most men don't understand either one.

I sat down on the man's couch between the cats and immediately got cat hairs all over my slacks and the back of my shirt.

"Irene, you and Sparkle leave the room, please," the psychiatrist said to his cats. Not only did the man keep cats in his apartment, where they could get cat hair all over everything, but he had named them "Irene" and "Sparkle."

The psychiatrist looked a bit feline-like himself; he was thin and had beady eyes. We began by talking about my childhood. I told him about my parents' divorce and the fact that I was having problems staying married.

"Did your mother give you a lot of attention as a child?" he asked.

Yes, I answered.

"How about affection?"

I said yes to that, too. Once my mother came to school to pick me up in the third grade and she kissed me, and my friends saw her do it and made fun of me the next day at school. I didn't tell the psychiatrist that, however. He looked as if he had been a big sissy when he was a kid, so I didn't want to offend him by telling him how much I tried to avoid being connected to that description in any manner.

"Did your mother read you stories when you were a child?" he asked.

Sure, I said. "The Little Engine That Could," "Billy Goat Gruff," and "Little Black Sambo," because it wasn't considered racist and you could even name a restaurant chain after it in those days.

"Did she put her arm around you when she read you those stories?" he continued.

I honestly didn't remember.

"Don't you think that would have been a warm, pleasant memory if she had?" asked the psychiatrist.

He was getting fairly personal. I asked him his point.

"Perhaps," he began, "you have been looking for someone to share an intimate relationship with, and because your mother never put her arm around you when she read you stories, you never felt an intimate relationship with her. So now you aren't able to construct one with anyone else."

How could I overcome this obstacle, I asked the doctor?

"Perhaps we could start now," he said. "How would you like for me to read you a story?"

Whoa, Jack, I thought to myself.

The psychiatrist reached into his bookshelf and pulled out a book. "May I come sit on the couch with you and read you a story?" he inquired.

Okay, so I was a little nervous about the way my first psychiatric session was coming along, but I figured I might as well get my money's worth. The doctor sat down on the couch with me and got cat hair all over his slacks and the back of his shirt, too.

Then he began reading me a story. It was a story about a couple of rabbits — I remember that. It might even have been quite a good story, but I was having a difficult time concentrating. Sitting on a couch covered with cat hairs, listening to another grown man read me a story about rabbits was a unique and somewhat unsettling experience.

About halfway through the book, the psychiatrist asked, "Do you want me to put my arm around you while I read you the story?"

He had dialed the wrong number this time.

"I think that's about all the therapy I can take today," I said as politely as possible as I stood up from the couch.

"But we still have fifteen minutes left," he said.

"If it's all the same to you," I replied, "I think I'll be leaving."

"But you haven't heard the rest of the story," he insisted.

"Heard all I want to hear."

"When will we see each other again?" he asked.

I was halfway to the door by then. I threw a couple of twenties and a ten on a table and tried to figure out what was happening. The man wanted to put his arm around me and read me a story. I wondered if somebody had tried to do that sort of thing to Tyrone Gault in Milledgeville. He might have talked to cows, but I was willing to bet that Tyrone was sane enough to avoid this sort of thing.

"Probably never," I answered belatedly.

As I opened the door to leave, Irene and Sparkle appeared in the hallway. I made barking sounds and growled at them, and they ran away. If I didn't get anything else for my fifty bucks, at least I got that.

I never went back to another psychiatrist. What would the next guy want to do? Put a pair of diapers on me and make me suck on a pacifier?

* * *

I suppose I was thirty-one, nearly thirty-two, when I left my apprenticeship and became a full-fledged adult. That's how old I was the day Elvis died. After Elvis — whose music had launched my generation into another direction from our parents' — got fat and died, I realized that adulthood was squarely on me, whether I liked it or not. I was growing old and the world was driving me toward the grave. I was convinced it would be a short trip.

Although my childhood was filled with nothing more than the usual maladies — chicken pox, mumps, measles, etc. — I became a hypochondriac at a very young age. For example, since I was eleven years old and found a wart on the side of my wrist, I've been certain that I have cancer. It was a big, ugly wart, and when I heard that a change in a wart or a mole was one of the danger signals of cancer, I never took my eyes off it.

When I was fourteen, the wart suddenly went away, but then I worried about a mole on my back. I made the mistake of mentioning my fears to my mother. She suggested that when my uncle, a doctor, came to visit, we should have him burn it off.

Burn off my mole? You mean, set fire to it? This is modern medicine? I had seen witch doctors perform the same procedure on television. Cancer or no cancer, I wasn't about to go through anything like that. When my uncle came to visit, I hid in the pump house. Later, somebody told me that the way to get rid of warts and moles was to rub them with a dishrag and then bury the rag.

I followed those directions to the letter. The mole still hasn't disappeared, but you have to give these things time.

Most hypochondriacs enjoy going to the doctor. It gives credibility to their belief that they're seriously ill. But I'm a weird sort of hypochondriac. Although at various points in my life I have had (or thought I had) tuberculosis, leukemia, malaria, and several strokes, I always have avoided going to a doctor. I simply have chosen to sit in a dark room somewhere brooding over the possibility that I might be seriously ill.

Doctors and doctors' offices spook me. I hate sitting in a waiting room — not only frightened out of my wits that I'll soon find out I have only weeks to live, but also nervous about catching whatever the other people in the waiting room have.

That's another of the health problems I've had. Whenever anybody else has a disease, I automatically presume that, with my luck, I soon will have it, too.

A guy at work came down with kidney stones.

"He was fine one minute," somebody said, "and then he was in terrible pain."

I began to feel gnawing pains in my back and stomach and stayed out of work three days drinking beer (for medicinal purposes only) to flush out my kidney stone. I'm not certain if I got rid of the stone, but for three days, I felt absolutely no pain, save a severe headache that disappeared somewhere in the middle of my second beer of the day.

I knew another man who was having trouble with his prostrate gland. He said it hurt when he went to relieve himself, and that the biggest problem was he couldn't always finish, which resulted in a terribly embarrassing circumstance each time he wore khaki pants. "All men begin to have problems with their prostate after they get older," said my acquaintance.

All men? Older? When I was thirty-two, I had managed to avoid doctors for years. But maybe the odds finally had caught up with me. Maybe I had it, too. I decided it was time to get a professional opinion, so I looked up another doctor in the yellow pages and made myself an appointment.

I was quite proud. I had made my own doctor's appointment without anybody forcing me to do it, and I would walk in there and face whatever medicine the doctor dished out. I thought of cancelling the appointment no more than two or three hundred times, the last of which was when the nurse stuck her head into the waiting room and said, "We're ready for you now."

I could bolt away from here, I thought to myself. It's not against the law to run out of a doctor's office and refuse to take an examination. This was something I had to pay for.

The nurse sensed my hesitancy. "Be a big boy and come on in," she said.

Women do that sort of thing to you. They question your manhood in tight situations. If I had walked out of the doctor's office, it would have been a sign of weakness, so in I went.

Did you ever notice that the doctor is never ready to examine you when the nurse says he's ready to examine you? After you get out of the waiting room, there's another wait in a tiny cubicle they call the "holding room."

It's always very quiet in there, and everything is made out of cold metal, and the chair you have to sit and wait in is very uncomfortable, and I always have the feeling that I'm being watched.

"Watch him through the two-way mirror, nurse," I imagine the doctor saying, "and see if he does anything weird."

That idea, of course, makes you even more nervous, and if you have to scratch your privates, say, you're afraid the nurse might be watching you. So you just sit there in that quiet room, in that uncomfortable chair, nervous and frightened with itchy privates.

The doctor finally came in. He checked everything, including my prostate gland.

"Bend over," said the doctor.

I bent over.

Oh, God.

"Do you feel pain or pressure?" the doctor asked me.

"Both!" I screamed.

"Is it more pain or more pressure?" the doctor asked again.

"Pain! It's pain!" I shrieked.

"Are you certain?" asked the doctor.

I was certain by now. It most certainly was pain, the worst I had ever felt.

"You can straighten up now," said the doctor.

"That's easy for you to say, doctor," I replied. "You haven't just had an intimate experience with the Jolly Green Giant's first finger."

After finally conquering my fear and going to the doctor, I decided I ought to try to do something about my problem with dentists, too. I gathered all the courage I could muster and went to have my teeth checked and cleaned.

"When was the last time you went to a dentist?" he asked me.

"I was fifteen. Why do you ask?"

"No reason," replied the dentist. "It's just that I'm going to have to use an acetylene torch to get down to where I can clean these things."

The dentist asked if I wanted gas.

"I woke up with it," I answered. "I always get gas when I'm nervous."

"I mean nitrous," the dentist explained. "It'll help relax you."

I didn't know what nitrous was, but if it would ease my terror, I would take it.

"How much do you want?" was the dentist's next question.

I said two shoulder tanks should do nicely.

When I came out of my trance, the dentist said he was through cleaning and checking my teeth and that I needed seven fillings, two caps, four extractions, and a root canal.

"Soon as my prostate clears up," I said, "I'll be back."

* * *

I remember that as a child I would read things that said, "By the year 1980....", and the "1980" would look so strange to me.

"How old will we be when it's 1980?" my friend Danny Thompson, not exactly a mathematical whiz, would ask when we were boys together.

"Thirty-four," I would answer him.

"Think we'll ever really be that old?" he would ask.

"Not before 1980," I would say.

I had a feeling even back then — and the feeling grew with each passing year — that the 1980s might be somewhat traumatic for me. The sixties were turbulent, the seventies disillusioning, and what on earth would the eighties bring?

I got married again in 1980 ... for the third time.

In 1981, I went to Europe for the first time. The trip cost

me a lot of money, and I saw a lot of cathedrals and concierges with their hands held out.

I also turned thirty-five in 1981. I awakened in a motel room in Birmingham, Alabama, on my thirty-fifth birthday. I was alone. I called practically everybody I knew and mentioned I was alone in Birmingham — that's why they hadn't been able to reach me to wish me a happy thirty-fifth birthday.

"Please don't go overboard on my gift," I cautioned them all. They didn't.

Turning thirty-five also had its ill effects on me. It depressed me a bit to know that I was only five years away from forty, but I was uplifted by the thought that I was now the age my father had been when I was born, and I could easily recall his vitality during my days on his knee. I figured I still had a ways to go before it was time to put on a baseball cap and go to the park and feed pigeons and wet my pants (an indiscretion society allows to old men with worn out prostates).

In 1982, when I was thirty-six, I made another of my infrequent trips to the doctor, and this time he did find something wrong with me. My hypochondria had been vindicated; I'd been telling people for years that I wasn't well. I soon had heart surgery to repair a damaged valve.

I was convinced I was going to die, but I didn't. So what if I don't like Boy George, hair dryers, and airplanes? I'm impressed with medical science, and if there was any sort of computer involved in helping me live through my operation and making me fit again, then I vote that's one we spare when we get around to destroying the others.

I got another divorce in 1983, and that sort of brings my confused life up to date. I'm single again. I live alone in a large house with my dog. My mother is still concerned that I can't stay married and haven't produced any grand-children.

Aging in any type of world has its negative effects — the hair grays, the eyes and legs go bad, the back hurts, the hangovers linger, and the mind starts to drift. But aging in this modern world is even worse, I think, because the older people get, the more they tend to worry, and we have every-thing from the killer bees heading north from Mexico to getting wiped out by nuclear war to worry about.

Next to worry, guilt is the most obnoxious part of aging.

I have a friend named Billy. He is forty-two and feels guilty and gets depressed a lot, like I do. Sometimes, we visit each other and feel guilty and depressed together. This usually is after we've gone out the night before and done something to feel guilty and be depressed about that was a lot of fun while we were doing it.

Billy and I are both divorced; we feel guilty and get depressed about that sometimes. We feel guilty because quite often being single is a wonderful state in which to live, but it was instilled in us in a simpler time that we weren't supposed to wind up in our middle ages still acting like we were nineteen. We get depressed because we tried to do what our parents taught us to do but failed, and damned if we know what to do about it now.

We feel guilty because we really don't have all that much ambition anymore. We both have concluded that the best way to live is not to have a lot of things you worry about losing, but our parents wanted us to have it better than they did, and if we just hauled off and went and lived on a boat somewhere, we would be letting them down. We get depressed because we don't know how to deal with those feelings, either.

Depression, says Billy, often takes the form of a tall man with a hat pulled down over his eyes and wearing a raincoat. Billy calls him "Mr. D."

He starts on you in your thirties, according to Billy. "He's the voice you hear in the morning after you've been out having a great time the night before. You never hear that voice when you're younger. Your conscience is basically still clear then.

"But after you get a little older, he starts on you. You remember that Christmas song you used to sing when you were a kid — 'He's making a list and checking it twice, gonna find out who's naughty and nice'? Well, it isn't Santa Claus making the list anymore. It's Mr. D."

I've had my own bouts with "Mr. D." He gets me when I awaken in hotel rooms far away from home in the morning. He's always peering around the corner at me when I'm doing something my mother and the old men at the store wouldn't approve of. He's there when I get involved in the Sunday Morning Academy Award Theater movie and don't make church. He's there after I drink too much, and he's there when I eat animal fat, reminding me that it causes cancer.

He's there whenever there is a dilemma in my life, whenever I don't know whether to go or stay, whether to join or not to get involved, whether to use my heart or my head.

Dilemmas. Has any other generation ever had to face as many as mine has? Sometimes, in recent years, I have felt that modern life is like a giant ice cream parlor with innumerable flavors. Do I stick with vanilla or go for something more exotic? And if I eat tutti-frutti, will it make me gay?

My mother could have read me rabbit stories and hugged

me until I turned blue in the face, but I don't think it would have helped.

16 Maybe Someday, Rainbow Stew

FOR MOST OF my adult life, the only thing that has been perfectly clear to me has been the booze I've used to steady my nerves. You name it and it has confused me, because usually I was right in the middle of the issue, leaning towards both sides.

We could start with Vietnam. I was born a patriot of patriots, and I don't give a rat's tail for the Commies, but I also didn't want to be sent off to get shot in some rice paddy, and I didn't want anybody else to, either.

And drugs. There I was, standing off on the fringes, clinging to the cold beer in my hand while others sat in a circle and passed around a marijuana cigarette and appeared to be having a wonderful time. All I could do was seek refuge with my own kind in some beer joint, playing country music and the Bowl-A-Matic machine.

We've been all over the music. I took off after Elvis, but had I known where he and his music eventually would lead — there's a rock singer today who bites the heads off bats as part of his performance — I likely would have stayed with Red Foley.

And free sex. It has its good points, but what if I get herpes?

Constant dilemma, the legacy for my generation — the In-Betweeners — is a wearisome thing, and I don't mind admitting that I'm weary of it.

God knows, I have tried my best to fit into modern life. I bought a new house a year or so ago, and it has a Jacuzzi in the bathroom. One simply has not arrived today unless one has a Jacuzzi (which sounds like the Italian word for getting bubbles up your butt).

I've been in my Jacuzzi twice. Once, I had hurt my back playing tennis, and the doctor had said that if I had a Jacuzzi, it would be a good idea to get in it and soak my back in the hot, bubbling water.

The problem came when I tried to get out of the Jacuzzi. My back hurt so much I couldn't lift myself out. I was rescued several hours later by sheetrock workers who had come to repair a hole in the wall of my bathroom — which was the result of the first time I got into my Jacuzzi and felt those bubbles in my rear. I thought there was something strange in the tub that wanted to make friends, and in my haste to get out, I fell and knocked a hole in the wall.

So if I really am that tired of the dilemmas of modern life, what can I do about it?

First, I have to come to grips with the fact that I soon will be forty, and it's time I stopped trying to understand all that is strange and new to me. By the time a person is forty, it's much too late to comprehend anything young people are doing or thinking, and we look silly when we try.

The best thing to do is what our parents did — write off

the younger generation as totally gone to hell. If you need evidence, cite the children out in Texas who put dead bats in their mouths in an effort to emulate that nut rock singer I mentioned earlier. These children had to take rabies shots for biting bats, and our parents thought we were strange because we listened to Elvis. (I hope most parents of In-Betweeners now realize that Elvis wasn't that bad after all, compared to what is happening today. If they have, then rest well, Elvis, wherever you are; all is forgiven.)

But if kids today want to eat bats, there's nothing I can do about it, so I might as well relax and worry about something I can control. Nothing that I have control over comes to mind right off, but at least that's something else I can worry about.

After I have accepted the fact that I'm out of step with modernity, I must then look for a niche in which to crawl and rest contentedly with the idea of retirement; I'm too far gone to run in the fast lane.

I don't know if I'll ever take what seems to be a drastic step for someone who has been an urban creature for more than half his life, but I do occasionally dream of going home. Back to my roots. Back to Moreland.

Somebody once said to me, "We spend the first half of our lives trying to get away from home. We spend the second half trying to get back."

Growing up in Moreland is the primary reason I am what I am — a premature curmudgeon, longing for the simple life — and I wonder if moving back would fulfill that longing.

The boys from Moreland. Some of us got away, others didn't. Dudley Stamps is still living there. He built himself a house on the land where he was reared, and he works on cars. He steadfastly refused to budge from where he was when the changes came.

He built a stereo system in his new house that piped music into all the rooms, and he issued a dictum to his wife that never, under any circumstances, would there be anything but country music on his stereo system. He caught her disobeying his order one day — she was playing a rock 'n' roll station on the radio — and that may have been one of the things that led to their divorce. At least the man had his priorities in order.

Danny Thompson and Anthony Yeager stayed around home, too, and Clyde Elrod came back. He did just what he said he was going to do; he spent twenty years in the Navy, retired, and now drives the butane truck in Moreland. I was home for a visit not long ago, and he came by to fill my parents' tank. He told me that he used to go out on a ship for days and sit there and look out on the Indian Ocean, and all he could think about was getting back to Moreland one day.

"We didn't know how good we had it growing up," he said.

I enthusiastically concurred.

The other boys from Moreland, like me, still haven't given in to the urge to return. Bobby Entrekin has a wife and a daughter and he travels, too, so I rarely see him. I've lost track of Charlie Moore. Mike Murphy has three kids and his own business, and Worm Elrod is a hairdresser.

I suppose I also should mention Little Eddie Estes. Soon after he made that marvelous catch in centerfield to save the game against Grantville, he died in an automobile accident. He was only fourteen. His mother and daddy buried him in the Moreland Methodist cemetery, about three long fly balls from the exact spot where he made the catch.

* * *

While the rest of the world went bananas, Moreland changed very little at heart. Today, Cureton and Cole's store is boarded shut, and they're trying to refurbish the old hosiery mill and turn it into some kind of museum that reflects life in the village a hundred years ago. Moreland still respects its past, and I like that.

Steve Smith's truckstop is gone, but the interstate took most of the truck traffic anyway, and that makes Moreland even quieter. There is still no traffic light and no police department, and they still have dinner-on-the-grounds at the Methodist and Baptist churches. And you still have to drive to Luthersville in the next county to buy a bottle of whiskey. It would do me good to live someplace where the nearest bottle of whiskey is a county away.

They're still neighborly in Moreland. My Aunt Una and her husband, John, live just up the dirt road from my parents. John came down sick and they didn't know what they were going to do about plowing their garden.

"One day," my Aunt Una was telling me, "we heard this commotion out in the garden, and we looked out and there was one of our neighbors — a pilot who bought a farm down here — on his tractor plowing our garden for us. I don't know what we would have done without him."

They still plant gardens in Moreland, too, and if I lived there, there would be no reason to set foot in a McDonald's again. My Aunt Jessie, who lives on the other side of my parents' house, continues to work her own garden despite her age.

I had lunch with her recently. She served fried chicken, baked chicken, baked ham, cornbread dressing, butterbeans, field peas, green beans, fried okra, sliced home-grown tomatoes, creamed corn, mashed potatoes with gravy, several varieties of cake and three pecan pies she had baked herself, and a large container of iced tea. We sat under a big tree outside and feasted upon her offerings, and there was peace in the moment.

But even if I never take the final plunge and move back home, I know that Moreland is there, mostly yet unspoiled, and that settles me when I'm caught in a traffic jam or waiting for a light to change in the city, as I stand next to a kid with a ghetto blaster on his shoulder, beating out sounds to have a nervous breakdown by. In Moreland, the music you hear is that of one of the church choirs, drifting out the open windows on a soft, still Sunday morning.

And although I remain fearful that the world eventually will go crazy enough to spin off its axis and fly into space somewhere, there are, in fact, occasional glimpses of hope that manifest themselves.

We have a popular, conservative president who once played cowboy roles in the movies. Sigma Pi, my old frater-nity at Georgia, was kicked off campus in the seventies, primarily because of drug use in the chapter. It currently is making a comeback. There was even a recent letter to the editor of the Atlanta papers written by a disgruntled Uni-versity of Georgia student. His complaint was that the uni-versity faculty was too liberal for the mostly conservative student body.

I read somewhere that sales on white socks are up twenty percent. Pick-up truck sales have been on the rise for years, and more and more bars are selling beer in longneck bot-tles. There's a joint I go to in Atlanta where they have an all-country jukebox, including a complete study in George

Jones, and, right there on Peachtree Street in trendy Buck-head, the place is packed every night.

Tobacco chewing and snuff-dipping are in style again, and ridership on America's passenger trains is at an all-time high. There was a recent month in which there were four separate passenger train accidents, including one in New York where two trains collided head-on. One person was killed and a hundred were injured, and people who prefer planes made a big deal of it. But if I'm going to be in an accident while traveling, I still would prefer it to be on a train. Let two jets run together and see how many walk away.

Traditional clothing is in again. In fact, you're called a "preppie" if you wear button-down collars today. But I still contend there would be less crime and craziness in this country if everybody dressed nicely. You never hear of anybody robbing a liquor store dressed in a Polo shirt and a pair of khakis and Weejuns with no socks. Check police records if you don't believe me.

Some changes, like air conditioning, have been good for us all. Even people who live in the most rural areas of the country have air conditioning now. I have an acquaintance in a small town who sells air conditioning. He told me about getting a telephone call at his office from a lady who lived so far back in the country that the sun went down between her house and the road.

"She wanted to know what kind of air conditioners I had and what they cost. I was telling her about one air conditioner with this many BTU's and another air conditioner with that many BTU's. When I finished, she said, 'All I want is an air conditioner that will cool a b-u-t-t as big as a t-u-b.'"

Still, if we don't someday cut back on radical change and unchecked progress, we may all get our b-u-t-t's blown away or replaced by robots. Or else we might end up taking off all our clothes and squatting naked in trees, like Crazy Melvin, from worrying about it.

Maybe it will be us, the In-Betweeners, who finally make some sense out of the world again. We're still young enough to have the energy to do it, and, as we get older, perhaps we will have the wisdom, too. We've seen the old way of life that we were reared in, and we've seen the new one that has given us ulcers; maybe we can pick the best of each and produce a world where everybody has a fair chance and an air conditioner. But salad bars will be unlawful.

And if we're able to do that — if we're able to lead the way out of the wilderness of frightening modernity and back into the land of simplicity and contentment that we knew as children — then having lived with the dilemmas will have been worth it. Somebody has to do something before the Democrats nominate Phil Donahue for president and he up and picks Billie Jean King as his running mate.

But until that day comes, play me the old songs, bring around my old friends, keep the beer cold, and constantly remind me to cling to the immortal words of the man who sings now in the void left by Elvis, Merle Haggard:

> *"One of these days,*
> *When the air clears up*
> *And the sun comes shinin' through,*
> *We'll all be drinkin' that free Bubble-Up*
> *And eatin' that Rainbow Stew."*

SHOOT LOW, BOYS— THEY'RE RIDIN' SHETLAND PONIES

LEWIS GRIZZARD
In Search Of True Grit

To Chuck Perry, the editor's editor.

— 1 —

Walk a Mile
In the Duke's Boots

HERO. IT WAS a word I heard often in my youth. Even
before I knew what it meant, what it stood for, I liked
the way it sounded. HEro, as in strong and masculine. You
almost grit your teeth as it rushes from the back of the
mouth.

I think the first time I heard it used was in reference to my
father. He was recently back from Korea, where he had been
wounded and captured before escaping and being sent
home. All the men who fought that war were heroes, but
my father's Purple Heart certified his status.

I remember sitting in his lap with my arm around his
neck and feeling the back of his head. "What are these
lumps, Daddy?" I asked.

"Shrapnel," he said.

"What's that?"

He tried to explain. It all sounded so exciting, so heroic,

to a five-year-old boy. He never complained about the pain, but my mother said he used to get awful headaches. Maybe the booze helped to ease that pain. And when it beat him down and left him in ruin, they called him "hero" again as a sort of explanation. It was years before I knew what they meant.

The next hero I encountered was Roy Rogers. At age six I saw my first Roy Rogers movie, and afterwards I rode with him and Trigger and Bullet and Dale and Buttermilk on a thousand vicarious adventures through the woods near my house and once even into my mother's flower garden.

"Get out of that flower garden!" my mother screamed.

"Quiet, Mom," I whispered back. "They're about to rob the stage."

My grandfather (who was quite heroic to me, too, since all the neighborhood dogs followed him around) was also a big Roy Rogers fan. Once when we were watching Roy on TV, a collection of range riffraff kidnapped Dale and took her to the line shack. I never knew exactly what a line shack was, but there was always one in every western, and nothing good ever happened there.

As the villains tied up Dale, my grandfather yelled to the television screen, "Don't worry, Dale! Roy'll get those sons of bitches!" Which he most certainly did.

Years later I had the opportunity to interview Dale Evans, and I asked her whatever became of Trigger and Bullet. "Roy had them stuffed and put into his museum when they died," she said.

For Dale's sake, I hope Roy goes before she does.

Norris Cole was another of my early heroes. He was a year older than me and one of the greatest climbers of all time. After observing that squirrels had unusually long claws which enabled them to climb trees with ease, Norris grew his fingernails and toenails extremely long. He soon became known as Norris "Claws" Cole.

"Claws is a real good climber," his little brother Fred used to say, "but he's awful to sleep with." About twice a month Fred would have to go to the doctor for stitches after Claws had rolled over during the night and snared him. Fred eventually took to sleeping with the dogs.

Claws didn't care how tall a thing was or how much danger was involved; if it was there, he climbed it. Trees were his specialty, but he also climbed the town water tank, Confederate war memorials, forest ranger towers, the Methodist church steeple and every telephone pole in town.

All of his climbing wasn't recreational, however; he also did public service climbing. Mrs. Loot Starkins's husband, Jake, used to get very drunk, and when Mrs. Loot started screaming at him, Jake would climb to the top of the tree in their front yard to get away from her. One day Mrs. Loot screamed so much that Jake, perched safely in his tree, swore he was never coming down again. Somebody called for Claws, and he climbed up and talked Jake down out of the tree.

"How'd you do it?" one of the neighbor ladies asked.

"Told him if he didn't come down, I was going to teach Mrs. Loot how to come up," said Claws.

I heard several years ago that Claws died in a climbing accident, although more than likely it was the falling that got him.

"Reckon Claws went to heaven?" one of the locals asked when he heard about the accident.

"If they tried to keep him out," said an old man, "he'd just climb right back in."

Then, of course, there was my boyhood friend and idol, Weyman C. Wannamaker, Jr., a great American in the truest sense of the phrase. It was Weyman, for example, who taught me to shoot pool and to use the big end of the cue to hit folks over the head with in case of a disagreement.

"You had one foot off the floor when you made that shot," an unwise opponent said to Weyman one afternoon in the pool hall. Words were exchanged, and then the other fellow called Weyman a "do-do pot who doesn't love the Lord."

Weyman turned his cuestick around and raised a large lump on the head of the source of the insult. Then he pulled the victim's mouth open and inserted the five-ball. Afterwards, Weyman could have climbed onto the table and kicked balls into the pockets, and no one would have spoken on behalf of the rules of billiards. A man has to do what he has to do.

There was almost no end to Weyman's talents and his heroism. His most heroic act, however, was single-handedly removing the snake from Kathy Sue Loudermilk's dress. Of course, it was Weyman who put it there in the first place. A man has to do what he has to do.

It was just a little garden snake, but after Kathy Sue flailed around for awhile, screaming and shrieking, Weyman began to feel guilty. So he pushed everyone aside and took it upon himself to remove the snake. As the serpent worked its way south toward Kathy Sue's lovely hiney, Weyman shouted, "Don't worry, Kathy Sue. I'll stop it before it tries to make a U-turn!"

Weyman grabbed for the squirming snake, but all he came up with was a handful of Kathy Sue's shapely buttocks. The terrified snake crawled past her step-ins and headed for the apparent security of her ample bosom.

Weyman, ever vigilant in his attempt to save the lovely Kathy Sue, reached down the front of her dress in search of the snake. Five minutes later, he snatched the devil from a pit the likes of which it would never find again.

"Are you OK?" Weyman asked Kathy Sue.

"Fine," she answered, smiling at Weyman.

"Are you gonna tell your father what I did?"

"I sure am," said Kathy Sue. "I'm going to tell him you dropped a snake down my dress twice. You do have time, don't you?"

My father, of course, was a super patriot throughout his life, and one of his great pleasures was singing "The Star-Spangled Banner." He was one of the few people who could sing it without bruising the ears of those around him, and he missed no opportunity to bellow it out loud and clear.

Once at a baseball game we attended together, he sang so loudly that everyone around turned and stared. When we sat down, I said, "Daddy, it embarrasses me when you sing the national anthem that loud."

"Son," he replied, "it embarrasses me when you don't."

Years later someone came up with a term that described the sort of heroism I had come to revere. They called it True Grit, and they made a movie by the same name starring John Wayne, "The Duke," who dramatized it as well as anybody could. It was a great movie, a classic, an "outside movie."

Maybe that needs some explanation. You see, there are inside movies and outside movies. An inside movie is where most of the scenes take place inside a house, and there are a lot of women in the cast and a lot of lovey-dovey talk.

Or, worst of all, an inside movie could be an English movie. Every English movie I ever saw had all the "action" take place in a library with a group of people, dressed for dinner, jabbering nonsensically about whether Mrs. Witherington-Kent had done in Mr. Witherington-Kent with poisoned kidney pie.

Outside movies, on the other hand, always involve guns and horses or tanks and planes, and there are a minimum of women. If the hero wants a kiss, he can kiss his horse or tank.

The problem with women in outside movies is that they're always turning their ankles. Hero is trying to get out of a tight spot, and he's dragging Sweet Thing behind him, and suddenly she turns her ankle. So now he's got to pick her up and carry her.

I was watching an outside movie once with Weyman C. Wannamaker, Jr. Alan Ladd was the star, and his horse was dead, he was out of water and he was trying to get through the desert with this dancehall dolly who was tagging along behind him. Sure enough, she turned her ankle.

"What am I going to do with you now?" asked Alan Ladd.

"Leave her for the buzzards!" Weyman screamed from the audience.

Alan Ladd, gentleman that he was, picked up the girl and carried her all the way back to town. Weyman never went to see another Alan Ladd movie. *True Grit*, on the other hand, he saw forty-seven times. Now, that was the quintessential outside movie.

John Wayne played Marshall Rooster Cogburn, a one-eyed, whiskey-swilling, foul-mouthed old coot who goes riding off into Indian territory with Mattie Ross (Kim Darby) and a Texas Ranger named Le Boeuf (Glen Campbell) to find the galoot (Jeff Corey) who shot Mattie's dad and who is also a member of a gang led by the notorious Lucky Ned Pepper (Robert Duvall).

Young Mattie, an expert on human character, picks Rooster Cogburn to lead this mission because she believes he has "true grit." Or, as he is described by another member of the cast, "He's the big fella with the eye patch, and fear don't ever enter his mind."

What eventually happens is that Rooster Cogburn tracks down the varmint who killed Mattie's pa, and then he faces the entire Lucky Ned Pepper gang in a four-against-one shootout.

What a scene! What grit!

Rooster Cogburn advises Ned Pepper that he's taking him in, and Ned Pepper says that's big talk for a one-eyed fat man. So Rooster puts the reins to his horse between his teeth, cocks his rifle with his right hand and draws his pistol with his left and says, "Fill your hands, you son of a bitch!" Then Rooster charges straight ahead even though he's bad outnumbered.

Horse galloping. Hat swept back by the wind. His guns blazing, their guns blazing. Three members of the gang go down and Ned Pepper is filled with holes, but he still has the strength to fire a shot at Rooster, killing his horse.

The horse falls on one of Rooster's legs and traps him. Here comes Lucky Ned aiming to finish him off, but before he can pull the trigger, Glen Campbell picks him off and The Duke escapes another tight spot.

True Grit. John Wayne had it, all right. But so do a lot of other people of far less fame. Folks who have overcome overwhelming odds, have fought and won and fought and lost, have spit in the devil's eye, have soared with eagles despite being surrounded by turkeys, have kissed innu-

merable frogs in search of a prince, have been bloodied and
bullied and tricked and tangled and peed on and pissed off.
They're out there everywhere, these unsung heroes. None
has ever wiped out an entire gang of outlaws like Rooster
Cogburn did, but in their own ways they have robed themselves in The Duke's heroic garb for a moment or two.

There was the morning I drove into Tellico Plains, Tennessee, and walked into a beer joint. I asked the barmaid
where I could get breakfast. She said for two dollars she
would go to the grocery store and buy the fixings and cook
me up something in the back.

It would have been a bargain at any price. Fried eggs.
Bacon. Potatoes. I paid her the two dollars for breakfast and
then handed her a two dollar tip. She smiled a toothless
smile and said, "God bless you, young'un. I been savin' six
months and I was just two dollars short."

"Of what?" I asked.

"Of enough to buy me some store-bought teeth," she
said. "I ain't chewed nothin' in fifteen years."

I have walked the streets of Yellville, Arkansas, nodding
at strangers; I have bought fresh corn from a farmwife in
Lodi, Wisconsin; and I have drunk beer with a one-armed
man in a beer joint in a town I can't remember somewhere
in Oklahoma. I had one too many and asked him where he
lost his arm. He said he couldn't remember for sure, but he
was certain it would turn up any day now.

I even proposed marriage once on the road. I ate the best
fried chicken on earth in the Foley Cafe and Bakery in Foley,
Alabama, and I sent the waitress back to tell the woman
who cooked that chicken that I would marry her on the
spot.

"Doris is already married," said the waitress, "but I ain't."
I wiped the grease off my hands and left Foley, Alabama,

behind me as quickly as possible.

These are the people I have come to honor. Not those who bask in the spotlight, but the strong, the swift, the courageous who huddle among the masses. True grit comes in many different shapes and sizes, and it often turns up where you least expect to find it.

— 2 —

Profiles in True Grit

A Free Spirit On the Road

I MET AL BERGMAN completely by chance. I was driving through one of Atlanta's spiffiest neighborhoods when I noticed a police car pulled off to the side of the street, blue lights flashing. The policeman was talking to a bearded man of advancing years who appeared to have made a camp in a wooded area just off the street. I figured the policeman was running him in for vagrancy.

"I stopped to investigate a wreck and saw him," the policeman said. "I told him some of the ladies in this neighborhood might complain about him, and that he'd be better off on down the street near the park."

I walked over and introduced myself. His beard was long and full and white. He was sitting next to what appeared to be an old-fashioned wagon. His dog, a German shepherd named Jamie who was tied to a nearby tree, was finishing her supper.

Al Bergman told me he was sixty-nine and that he had
retired from the real estate business in Nashville. What he
was doing was walking around the United States, pulling
the wagon that held his supplies.

"Been thinking about doing something like this for a long
time," he said.

Got any family?

"Wife, three kids and nine grandchildren."

And what does the wife think of this odyssey?

"Let's just say it wasn't a joint decision," he answered.

Al Bergman volunteered more information about himself. Said he didn't smoke and that he had jogged for years,
which was how he was able to pull his wagon. "I make
fifteen miles a day on flat land and about ten when it's hilly."
He said he had parachuted into Greece with the OSS during
World War II, and that he had been a roadbuilder in South
America and later in Vietnam.

I asked if he was afraid camping all alone.

"Jamie's a trained attack dog," he said. "And they taught
us how to handle situations in the OSS. I still know how to
put a piece of wire around a man's neck.

"Tell you the truth, though, I haven't had one minute's
trouble. There are an awful many good people left in this
country. They've offered me money and food for me and
Jamie, and some of 'em want me to spend the night in their
houses. But I don't want to take a thing. I want to do this all
by myself."

Al said he was going south out of Atlanta and when he
reached the Florida Keys, he would head back up the west
coast of Florida, continue along the Gulf and on to California.

"Got to see this country one more time before I'm gone,"
he said. "And I want to see it the right way — from the

ground at one mile an hour."

I asked Al if he were going to heed the policeman's advice and move on down the road to the park.

"No," he said. "I could make it, but I think Jamie's too tired to walk another step."

WEARING HER STORY ON HER BACK

It wasn't the sort of place I would want my mother to catch me in, but there were a few more stories to tell and we didn't want to give up the night quite yet. That's how we ended up in the strip joint.

It didn't take long to figure out the hustle. After each girl danced, she would pick out a table and join those assembled, asking to be bought a drink, which probably was nothing more than Kool-Aid but cost a cool four bucks.

"Hi, I'm Mikki," she said. "Buy me a drink?" She was blonde and young and, judging from her performance on stage, quite athletic. As she sat at our table, I noticed the tattoo on her back.

"It's a horse with wings," she said. "Me and my first husband had 'em done at the same time. He had an American flag done on his back. He was real sexy when he took his shirt off."

For four bucks I figured I might as well get the entire story, so I asked what had happened to her first husband.

"He got blowed up in a factory," she said. "Him and a lot of others. We didn't have no insurance on him, so he left me broke."

"And that's when you started stri — , I mean, dancing?"

"I got married again after that. To a soldier. But he run off."

"So then you started dancing."

"I saw an ad in the paper. I auditioned and got the job. It beats waitin' tables."

"You don't mind dancing in front of all these people without your clothes on?"

"Don't bother me. The more that watches, the more tips I get. I made $200 last weekend."

It was an orderly process: While the girls danced, the men slipped bills under garters worn at the thigh. After their routines, the dancers rewarded the tippers with a kiss.

Mikki said she wasn't going to stay in town much longer, that she was heading to Las Vegas to be a chorus girl. "I hear they make two thousand a week out there," she said.

"And you won't have to kiss anybody for tips," I added.

"Kissin' don't bother me," she said. "Kiss enough frogs and you might find a prince."

She put down her glass, winked and went back to dance and kiss again. I wondered if she would ever make it to Vegas. I wondered if she would ever find a prince. I doubted it, but tattooed strippers have a right to dream, too.

SAYING AN AGE-OLD GOODBYE

There were maybe half a hundred of us in the airport concourse waiting for the call to board. Some read. Some stared. Some stumbled through awkward goodbyes.

Jets have taken away some of the romance of saying goodbye. When you said goodbye at a train station, there were tears and long last kisses. Saying goodbye at an airport, I thought, is like leaving to go to a convenience store for a box of cereal.

Then I saw the kid and his mother. She had to be his mother. The kid was a Marine but obviously hadn't been one for long. His uniform was ill-fitting and seemed to itch. He had some hair but not much.

The kid was leaving on the plane. His mother had come to say goodbye. I let my imagination run at its own pace.

He looked nineteen, tops. She was in her late thirties or early forties, still a pretty woman. She never took her eyes off him, trying, I suspect, to memorize every detail of him so that when she missed him, which would be every day, she could recall his face and maybe ease the pain a little.

He seemed terribly uncomfortable. I guessed him to have boot camp behind him. He had been home on leave. Now he was being sent to his first assignment — adult sort of stuff. The last thing he needed was a doting mother who wouldn't take her eyes off him at the airport.

He smoked a cigarette as they talked. Or, as his mother talked. He only nodded, or grunted, or gave an occasional yes or no and then took another pull off his cigarette. He was new at cigarettes, too. He tried to flick the ashes off with a finger but flicked the fire instead. The hot ashes landed on the jacket of his uniform.

His mother quickly brushed off the fire before there was any damage to the government-issued fabric. That embarrassed the kid, too. A Marine doesn't flick the fire from his cigarette onto the jacket of his uniform, and even if he does, his mother doesn't brush it away.

I wondered about the kid's father, the mother's husband. Why hadn't he come? He was probably dead. No. He had probably split, and that's why the mother hovered about her son so and wished that he didn't have to leave her and dreaded the loneliness that surely would follow.

Their time ran out.

"When do you think you'll be back?" the mother asked.

"Christmas, I guess," the kid answered.

"It's a long time to Christmas," she said.

"Yeah," grunted the kid.

"You'll write me?"

"I'll write you."

"Be careful."

"OK."

"I love you," she said.

The kid mumbled back all that would come out. His mother kissed him. He let her, and then he disappeared down the walkway to the plane.

She wiped something from the corner of her eye and went home to wait for Christmas.

A MEMORY GOOD FOR A LIFETIME

We had only one real Christmas together, my mother, my father and I. Only one Christmas when we were actually in our own house with a tree, with coffee and cake left out for Santa, with an excited five-year-old awakening to a pair of plastic cowboy pistols, a straw cowboy hat and an autographed picture of Hopalong Cassidy.

My first Christmas I was only a couple of months old; that doesn't count. Then we were traveling around for a couple of years. The Army does that to you. Then there was Korea. And then we had that one Christmas together before whatever demons my father brought back from Korea sent him to roaming for good.

That one and only Christmas together, my father had duty until noon on Christmas eve. I waited for him at the screen door, sitting and staring until that blue Hudson, "The Blue Goose" as my father called it, pulled into the driveway. I ran out and jumped into his arms.

"Ready for Santa?" he asked.

"I've been ready since August," I shouted.

But before we could settle in for our Christmas, my father had to take care of a problem. He had found this family — the old man out of work, in need of a shave and a haircut, and his wife crying because her babies were hungry. My father, whatever else he was, was a giving man. He couldn't stand to have when others didn't.

"They're flat on their butts and it's Christmas," I remember his saying to my mother. "Nobody deserves that."

So he somehow found a barber willing to leave home on Christmas eve, and he took the old man in for a shave and a haircut. Then he bought the family groceries. Sacks and sacks of groceries. He bought toys for the kids, of which there was a house full. The poor are often fruitful.

We didn't leave them until dusk. The old man and the woman thanked us, and the kids watched us with wondering eyes. As we drove away in "The Blue Goose," my father broke down and cried. My mother cried, too. I cried because they were crying.

We all slept together that night and cried ourselves to sleep. Next morning, I had my pistols and my hat and my picture of Hopalong Cassidy.

Maybe the three of us had only one real Christmas together — my father had left by the time the next one rolled around — but it was a Christmas a man can carry around for a lifetime. Each year at Christmas, with my father long since in his grave, I thank God that one is mine to remember.

GETTING WHAT HE DESERVED

There were seven or eight of us in line, waiting to pay the cashier for our lunches. We were all in a hurry because that's the way of the American business-day lunch. At the front of the line was a woman with a small boy of about eight. He was a cute little fellow wearing jeans, sneakers and a pullover sweater. A shock of dark hair fell over his eyes.

As the woman fumbled in her purse, looking for money to pay her check, the kid noticed a display of candy bars beside the cash register and immediately wanted one.

"You can't have any candy," said his mother. "You had pie with your lunch."

"But I want some candy," said the kid. His tone was surprisingly insistent. Almost belligerent.

The mother continued her search for money in her purse, and the kid continued to whine about the candy. Then he began to stomp his foot.

The rest of us in line were beginning to get restless. We bunched a little closer together and several folks began mumbling under their breath.

"Ought to snatch him bald," said one man quietly.

The kid by now was reaching for the candy display in open opposition to his mother. She grabbed his arm and pulled it away, but not before he clutched a Snickers bar in his hand.

"Put that back!" said his mother.

"No!" shouted the child, his lips pooched out in a classic pout. It was an arrogant "No!" A why-don't-you-try-and-make-me "No!"

The line bunched even more closely together, and the man who had suggested snatching the kid bald appeared ready to do so himself. So much for the kid's shock of dark hair, I thought.

But the mother moved suddenly and with purpose. She paid the cashier, took back her change and dropped it into her purse. Then with one quick motion, she grabbed hold of the child's pullover sweater and lifted him off the floor. The moment his sneakers came back to earth, she turned his back toward her and began flailing his backside. She flailed and flailed. A look of disbelief came across the kid's face. His eyes filled with tears. He tried to break away, but that incensed his mother more, and she flailed him again.

When she had finished administering the punishment, she turned the child around and pointed a finger squarely in his sobbing face. With a voice strong and certain, she said, "The next time I tell you to do something, young man, will you do it?"

The child looked at the floor. Meekly and sincerely, he replied, "Yes, ma'am."

The mother turned to go. The child returned the Snickers bar without further hesitation and marched dutifully out behind her.

The rest of us in line broke into spontaneous applause.

A NOBLEMAN IN RAGS

Alvin was a thirty-year-old black man. He was one of the street people in our nation's capital, Washington, D.C. He had no job. No money. He slept and ate in shelters for the poor. He told horror stories about some of the folks in those shelters.

I met Alvin on a cold, fall day as we both stood in Lafayette Park across from the White House. Within sight of that great edifice and all it represents, I was a soft touch when he asked me for a handout. As I gave him a dollar, I asked how he got in the shape he was in.

"I'm from Dayton, Ohio," he answered freely. "I moved to Maryland with this woman who was in the Navy. One night I came home drunk and she started hittin' on me.

Look here at this knot on my arm. That's where she got me with a stick.

"I was drunk and I got mad and whipped her ass. The police came and got me, and I was in jail for two months. When I got out, my woman had moved off with another man. I still miss that woman. Especially at night," he said.

"I came here to look for a job, but there ain't no jobs. I had nearly 'bout a thousand dollars when I got here, but that ran out pretty fast and I started sleeping in them shelters. I called my mama in Dayton and told her a lie, and she sent me fifty dollars. She thinks I'm doin' good here, and I don't want to break her heart and tell her I been in jail."

Alvin apparently had been drinking again. When he talked about his mother, tears welled in his eyes.

"I'm gonna stay here until I get me a construction job or something like that. I ain't never gonna let my mama see me like this."

There was no way to listen to his story in the shadow of the White House and fail to see the shocking contrast between the two Americas — the one within and the one without. Across the street, Ron and Nancy and the king of Saudi Arabia, drinking champagne and eating caviar. In Lafayette Park, Alvin in his rags, begging for a handout.

I asked him if he was angry with Ronald Reagan, who is supposed to be heartless when it comes to the poor.

"He ain't the one that got drunk and beat up his woman and got throwed in jail. That was me," Alvin said. "I got myself into this mess, and I got to get myself out of it now."

I think I said something stupid like, "Well, hang in there," but forgive me. It's not every day that I'm confronted with nobility in rags.

***

Al Bergman, the sixty-nine-year-old free spirit on the road

with his dog Jamie, looking for peace and the soul of America. Mikki the stripper, a third his age but already in search of the same dream. One mother sending her Marine son off to the real world, far from her protective bosom; another trying to teach her young son discipline. And Alvin, down on his luck but not on himself or his country.

In their own ways, each of these people is an embodiment of true grit. You can hear it in their voices, see it in their eyes, feel it in their stories. It's there just as surely as it was when Marshall Rooster Cogburn took those reins between his teeth and rode out to face Lucky Ned Pepper and his gang. And yet as real as it is, it seems indefinable.

What is true grit? Where does it come from? How did it get there? These are the questions books are made of.

— 3 —

Never Go Camping With A Man Who Drinks Whiskey Sours

ONE OF THE THINGS John Wayne had going for him in *True Grit* (and in real life, for that matter) was that he looked the part. Tall, strong, ruggedly handsome and tough to the bone. The way he walked, the way he talked, the clothes he wore — all these things added to his aura.

The same was true of another of my childhood heroes, Superman. When he was dressed as Clark Kent, mild-mannered reporter for a large metropolitan newspaper — black-rimmed glasses, white shirt, striped tie, blue suit and wing-tipped shoes — nobody paid him any attention. Certainly not Lois Lane. But the minute he switched into that tight-fitting Superman costume and started leaping tall buildings in a single bound, Lois was on him like bark on a tree.

So maybe "the look" is part of the recipe for true grit. I'm not arguing that clothes make the man, but I've dated enough women hiding vast quantities of themselves under muumuus to know that diversionary tactics can work.

It's easy enough to chronicle the traditional manly characteristics which The Duke embodied. For one, he always seemed to have a couple of days worth of stubble on his chin and a little hair hanging over his collar.

I have more than a couple of days worth of stubble; I've got a beard. I decided to grow it several years ago after someone called me "fishface." I think the implication was that I have a weak chin. I found that a beard made me look more mature and even gave me an air of pseudo-sophistication. I liked it.

So I took the look one step further and started smoking cigars. They, too, I reasoned, made me look mature and urbane. One day while smoking my cigar, I accidentally knocked the fire off the end. I didn't immediately see where it fell, but I soon discovered that a burning beard gives off a terrible odor.

I gave up cigars after that frightening experience and started carrying a copy of the *Wall Street Journal* under my arm. It gave me the same aura of authority and, whereas a cigar lasts no more than an hour or so, I could carry the same *Wall Street Journal* around for a week or more before it started turning yellow and I had to buy another.

Anyway, I have the beard, and I also have the hair over the collar. In fact, I've been wearing my hair long for years. It's like a muumuu for my ears.

I never noticed that I had big ears until I was in the fourth grade and Alvin Bates pointed them out to me. "Your ears poke way out," he said. I looked in a mirror and discovered that for once in his life he wasn't lying. I also had a lot of freckles on my nose, and when I smiled I bore an amazing resemblance to Howdy Doody, the late puppet. I hoped that no one else noticed the similarity.

"How's Clarabell?" asked Alvin Bates in a loud voice the next morning when I walked into class. That was only the beginning of the abuse I took from my classmates.

"Mind putting your head down on your desk?" the girl who sat behind me asked one day during an arithmetic lesson.

I didn't have any better sense at the time than to ask her why.

"Because, Howdy," she said to the delight of the jackals sitting around her, "I can't see the blackboard for your ears."

I tried everything to make my ears grow closer to my head. At night I slept with a rubber band around my head to hold my ears in. Can you imagine how much it hurt when the rubber band broke in the middle of the night? I even tried gluing my ears to my head. Inevitably one of them would come unglued, leaving me looking like I was giving signals to a train.

My only salvation came years later when long hair, fashionably trimmed over the ears, came into style. But even that caused me some trauma.

You will remember that my father was a military man and consequently was not fond of long hair. Many times his cohorts told me the story of how he dealt with a young recruit sporting more than regulation locks:

"We had some new recruits come in to Fort Benning," the story began, "and they sent the Captain, your old man, out to look them over and get them checked out for their first day on post. He came to this little ol' skinny boy with hair down over his eyes and way down on the bottom of his neck. That wouldn't be anything today, but back then he looked real strange.

"Your daddy looked him up and down real slow and then

made a horrible face and said, 'Son, as soon as I dismiss you, I want you to go over to the hospital and check yourself in. Have the doctors give you a thorough going over.'

"The kid said to your daddy, 'Do you think there's something wrong with me, sir?'

"Your daddy said, 'Yes, indeed, soldier. I think beyond a shadow of a doubt that if the doctors look close enough, somewhere on you they will find a vagina.'"

Even after all these years, I can handle the guilt better than my uncovered ears.

***

Another thing common to men like Rooster Cogburn is that they're bad to drink or chew or do both. You can tell a lot about people by noticing what they drink. For instance, I was in a restaurant recently when a man walked in and asked the hostess, "How long before I can have a table?"

"About fifteen minutes," the hostess said.

"Good," the man answered. "That'll give me time for a whiskey sour at the bar."

I can't explain why, but a whiskey sour is a drink for a man whose mother made him practice piano a lot when he was a kid. A man who drinks whiskey sours also probably throws a baseball like a girl — limp wristed. A man who drinks whiskey sours and then eats that silly little cherry they put in the bottom probably has a cat or a poodle for a pet. In other words, I wouldn't go on a camping trip with a man who drinks whiskey sours.

Scotch drinkers are aggressive. They order like they're Charles Bronson trying to have a quick shot before returning to the subway to kill a few punks and thugs.

"What'll you have, sir?" asks the bartender.

"Cutty. Water. Rocks. Twist," growls the Scotch drinker. I think maybe Scotch drinkers wear their underwear too tight.

You have to watch people who drink vodka or gin. "Anybody who drinks see-through whiskey," an old philosopher once said, "will get crazy." Indeed. Vodka and gin drinkers are the type who leave the house to get a loaf of bread, drop by the bar for just one, and return home six weeks later. With the bread.

I wouldn't go on a camping trip with anyone who drinks vodka or gin, either. They're the types who would invite snakes, raccoons and bears over for cocktails and then wind up getting into an argument about tree frogs.

Bourbon drinkers never grow up. Eight out of ten started drinking bourbon with Coke in school and still have a pair of saddle oxfords in the closet. Bourbon drinkers don't think they've had a good time unless they get sick and pass out under a coffee table.

Then there are the white wine drinkers. Never get involved in any way with them. They either want to get married, sell you a piece of real estate or redecorate your house.

As for myself, I'm a beer drinker. We're usually honest, straightforward people. We also are usually kind and quite sentimental and will get cryin'-about-our-daddies drunk with one another. That's just before we destroy the establishment in which we're drinking because somebody made an offhand remark about Richard Petty or the memory of Patsy Cline.

Never go camping with a beer drinker, either. We're really no fun unless there's a jukebox around, and we belch a lot, which might frighten the snakes, raccoons, bears and tree frogs.

I occasionally get an urge to chew tobacco, and snuff-dipping is a part of my heritage, but I have a distinct problem with both. I'm talking about the mess they make.

There used to be two popular commercials promoting snuff, one featuring former professional football player Walt ("Just a pench between yo' cheek and gum") Garrison and another starring famous fiddle player and singer Charlie Daniels. The commercials always showed these fellows smiling as they snuffed up, but they never showed them spitting. If you dip, you spit. If you dip and don't spit, you have swallowed your snuff and soon will die a slow, agonizing death unless somebody has a stomach pump handy.

My grandmother was a snuff user. She used to send me to the store to buy her "medicine," as she called it. Then she would sit for hours with her Bible in her lap and a dip behind her lip. I knew it wasn't medicine. If it had been, no one would have kept it in their mouth that long.

One afternoon while returning from the store with my grandmother's "medicine," I decided to sample it. The convulsions began immediately. I managed to spit some of it out, but most of it went in my nose and eyes. The remaining portion I swallowed. If there had been a doctor nearby, I would have been pronounced dead on arrival at home. Month-old lettuce looked better than I did.

If there were truth in advertising, manufacturers of snuff would be required to print a warning on the side of the cans: "Dip or chew if you want, but know that you're going to have to spit every eight seconds or so and probably will get it all over your shoes."

Not only do those snuff commercials fail to show people spitting, they also never show them with spittle curling out of the corners of their mouths. "Dip or chew if you want," another warning should say, "but be prepared to look like you've been eating mud."

I have a friend who has been chewing tobacco for years. Like all other chewers, he spits a lot and juice runs out the sides of his mouth. His wife tried to get him to stop because she was offended by the little spit cups she found all over the house. There's nothing more unappealing than a cup of day-old tobacco spit.

Finally she said to him, "That's it. I've had it. Either the chewing tobacco goes or I go."

"Honey," my friend replied, "I don't have but one vice. I don't stay out drunk, I don't chase women and I'm kind to children, old people and dogs. But my daddy chewed and his daddy before him, and chewing is in my blood. Asking me to give it up is like asking a dog to stop licking his privates. I couldn't stop even if I wanted to."

His wife studied on his statement for a few moments and said, "OK, if it means that much to you, I suppose I can live with it."

Soon afterwards they were celebrating their wedding anniversary. My friend's wife gave him a leather pouch for storing his chewing tobacco and he gave her the promise that he'd go outside whenever he needed to spit.

That compromise took guts on both their parts — so much, in fact, that I was inspired to write a poem about it. It went like this:

True love.
True grit.
You need 'em both
When you've got to spit.
Ptui.

***

Another ingredient of true grit, judging from most of The Duke's movies, could be body odor. Think about it: Except for when he wrestled some galoot into the river and knocked him senseless, did you ever see that pilgrim bathe? No, sir. The Duke liked to smell like a man . . .or at least like a man who had been riding the range for a month without a bath.

Back before air conditioning became one of the elements essential to life, it was perfectly all right to sweat a little and to emit an aromatic scent. Everybody did. Your mother sweated over a hot stove. Your father sweated at work and then came home and sat around in his underwear and sweated some more. At the end of a long day, nobody asked, "Where did you park your goats?" Nobody said, "Isn't it about time you looked for a reliable underarm deodorant?"

Today, sweat stains under the arms are considered only slightly less offensive than Joan Rivers. They can lead to the loss of a big account: "Sorry, Wilson, but we're going to have to find ourselves a new boy. Those perspiration stains on your shirt are a disgrace to the firm." Or to the loss of a lover: "I'll always love you, Marvin, but you've got the Okefenokee Swamp under your arms." Or even to the breakup of a family: "I'm filing for divorce, Donna. Those underarm stains on your tennis blouse are ruining the children's chances at a full and happy life."

Mandatory air conditioning not only did away with underarm sweat stains, it also led to the demise of a great tradition: the paddle fan. In the little Methodist church in my hometown, there were always Cokesbury hymnals and paddle fans along the back of each pew. The fans generally were provided by either a funeral home or an ambitious politician, with their message on one side — "Arnold's Funeral Home/Free Parking" or "Vote for Grover (Shorty) Turnipseed, County Commissioner" — and a four-color biblical scene on the other side (usually the Last Supper).

It wasn't necessary to listen to the minister's words to know whether or not he was reaching back for one of those you-had-better-change-your-evil-ways sermons. All you had to do was watch the congregation. The faster they fanned themselves, the closer to home the preacher was hitting.

The mere mention of the evils of alcohol was certain to speed the fanning strokes, and when the minister began to describe the warm climate that one who imbibed could expect at his final address, a draft no manner of air conditioner could match would roar through the sanctuary off those paper fans.

If I were a minister today, I would use a two-prong attack to challenge my backsliding flock. First, I would turn off the air conditioning some hot Sunday morning, and then I would explain the major difference between the two possible destinations that awaited them: hell for companionship, perhaps; heaven for its climate. Then I would quietly take my seat and let them sweat out their decisions without benefit of paddle fans. Now, that's the sort of situation that develops true grit.

Our preoccupation with smelling any way except natural doesn't end with air conditioning and deodorant, of course. "Is your mouthwash doing the job?" asked a commercial on television the other night. I don't know the answer to that. I brush my teeth every day whether they need it or not, and I even gargle on occasion. But how do I know if my mouth has that awful medicine smell they were talking about on TV?

I can hear my friends now: "He's a decent guy, but somebody really ought to tell him he has medicine mouth."

The same is true of shampoo. According to current commercials, if the shampoo you're using doesn't clean your hair, remove all dandruff, and leave your hair bright and shiny and full of body and smelling like a flower shop, people might not allow you in the same room with their children. You could infect the little boogers.

The new shampoos, of course, are highly scented, and one even leaves your hair smelling like apricots. Here's a hint: If you happen to be a man, never walk into a truck stop with your hair smelling like apricots. Someone likely will make fruit salad out of your head.

Come to think of it, that's probably the kind of shampoo that Lucky Ned Pepper was using, and that's why the marshall was so riled. That and the fact that just before their big shootout, Ned yelled across to Rooster Cogburn, "Hey, big guy, what's your sign?"

***

Another quality I associate with The Duke is that he was always friendly with his critters. His horse loved him. His cattle loved him. And in several movies he had a dog by his side. A man needs a good dog — one who'll fetch a stick and lick his hand. Don't forget what Bullet did for Roy Rogers and what Rin Tin Tin did for Sergeant Preston.

I'm not talking about those highfaluting purebreds who have been pampered by their owners and registered with the American Kennel Club. I don't like pampered children, and I don't like pampered dogs. I want a dog with character and personality, one who had to turn over a trash can once in a while just to keep food in his stomach. And I like a dog who knows enough about where puppies come from that he can choose his own mate and take care of business without waiting for some high-hatted human to "arrange" a canine tête-à-tête for him.

Allow me to explain the types of dogs that I like and probably the kind The Duke liked, too:

• YARD DOGS — A yard dog, usually found in the rural South, is a likable sort who hangs around the back door waiting for table scraps and who crawls under trucks to get in the shade on hot days. Yard dogs are recognizable by the oil and grease on their backs and by the humble way they walk sideways toward the individual calling them.

- HOG DOGS — These are fat little dogs who come from a union of Lord-knows-what and will eat anything that is put before them. They will lick the pan clean and beg for more. In rare cases, these dogs have been know to suck eggs. On the positive side of the ledger, such dogs make the expense of a garbage disposal unnecessary.

- LAP DOGS — These are very loving dogs who crave attention and leap onto your lap and lick your face and shed all over the sofa. They especially enjoy lying on their backs and kicking their legs back and forth while you scratch their bellies. I had a great lap dog once. My wife used to scratch the dog's belly for hours. When I asked her to do the same for me, she called her mother and told her I was perverted.

- A.J. FOYT DOGS — These dogs enjoy standing on the side of the road and racing with cars when they drive by. Every neighborhood has at least one. The problem with such dogs is that they tend to become frustrated after never being able to outrun passing cars, so they resort to gnawing the tires on your car when it's parked in the driveway. They also tend to have short life spans, because sooner or later they catch one of those cars.

- SHOE DOGS — These are dogs with a shoe fetish. Leave a pair of shoes out one night and by morning they'll have them chewed back to the raw material stage. Never take a shoe dog into a Gucci store; you could be bankrupt within minutes. Regional variations of this dog will chew eyeglasses, leather-bound books, remote control devices and Tupperware.

***

Finally, one of The Duke's most obvious characteristics, and an essential element, it seems to me, of true grit, was his self-sufficiency. He didn't need nobody for nothing.

I've always tried to emulate John Wayne in that regard. I've tried to learn to feed myself, clothe myself and fix leaky pipes. After all, you never know when your wife may leave and take your dog with her.

The first thing a breathing, self-sufficient male has to learn to do is feed himself. I'm not talking about eating out or ordering pizza. There was a time when I ordered out for pizza so many times that the delivery boy started getting phone calls and his mail at my house. But that's cheating; self-sufficiency means doing it yourself.

So, armed with determination and an unused kitchen in a new house, I set out to cook for myself. The first thing I did was buy one of those amazing food processors. "This food processor is the state of the art," said the saleslady. "You can make your own mayonnaise with it."

Why would anybody want to make their own mayonnaise, I wondered, when the Hellman's people are perfectly willing to do it for them? Self-sufficiency, I answered.

The next morning I decided to make myself a hearty omelette. I had never made one before, but I knew I needed at least eggs, onions, tomatoes, ham and cheese. First I decided to chop the onion in my new food processor. In less than ten seconds, I had a food processor full of onion juice. I have no idea what happened to the onion itself.

I immediately deleted onions from the recipe and proceeded. Next I put a piece of uncooked ham in my microwave oven and set the dial for five minutes. When I returned with the morning paper under my arm, the ham looked like Sherman had passed through Atlanta again. I mean, to a crisp.

Not to worry. Ham is high in cholesterol and unnecessary for a good omelette anyway. Remembering my experience with the onion and the food processor, I decided to slice the tomato by hand. Meanwhile, I put the cheese in the microwave to soften it.

When I had stopped the bleeding on my first two fingers, I checked the cheese in the microwave. That afternoon, it took the Roto-Rooter man only forty minutes to get the cheese unstuck from the sides of the oven.

I judiciously decided to forget about the omelette and simply have scrambled eggs with fresh orange juice. If the food processor would turn a fresh onion into onion juice, I reasoned it would do the same thing to an orange. I was correct. In seconds I had fresh orange juice. It tasted terrible, however. I later figured that maybe I should have peeled the orange.

I still had the eggs. The part that didn't stick to the bottom of the pan tasted like Silly Putty, so I threw the entire mess into my new garbage disposal which promptly clogged.

I waited until the pizza place opened and ordered a medium with everything except anchovies. It came with anchovies anyway, so I scraped them off the top of my pizza and electrocuted them in my microwave oven. I felt momentarily vindicated — after all, the microwave did what I intended it to do — but I felt far from self-sufficient.

That evening while watching television, I saw a commercial for a book that promised to save me hundreds of dollars a year in home repair and improvement bills. If I ordered one of these books, the announcer said, I would be able to fix my plumbing and even build myself a new patio.

No I wouldn't. I don't care how many of those books I read, I can't build or repair anything. A hammer is high technology to me.

When I was a kid, my mother bought me an erector set. I

read the instructions and tried to build a crane. "Oh, look," my mother exclaimed when I finished. "You've built a 1948 DeSoto with both doors missing."

I was so inept they wouldn't allow me to play with the garden hose. "Get away from that hose," my mother would say. "You know you don't know nothing about machinery."

I carried this lack of knowledge into high school, where I enrolled in shop class in an effort to improve myself. As my term project, I decided to build a chair.

"What is it?" asked the shop teacher at the end of the quarter.

"It's a chair," I said.

"Looks more like a wooden model of a 1948 DeSoto with both doors missing to me," he said.

As an adult, I've always had the same problem, particularly with automobiles. "What seems to be the problem with your car?" the auto mechanic asks me.

"It's broken," I answer.

He opens the hood and looks inside at all that infernal wiring and all those other doflatchies and what's-its that make a car run. "Here's your problem," he says. "Your lolabridgelator isn't gee-hawing with your double-low, E-flat commodgelator."

What does that mean? And how did he learn that?

Around the house I'm equally confused. When I moved into a new house and tried to take a shower, there was no hot water. I called the plumber. "Here's your problem," he said. "The letters on your shower knobs are wrong. The 'H' is on the cold knob and the 'C' is on the hot knob."

It cost me nearly $200 to have the plumber move the knobs on my pipes so I would have hot water when I turned the "H" knob.

I did think I could at least build a stand for my mailbox at the new house. I went out and bought lumber and nails and bolts. I now have the only mailbox stand in town that looks like a 1948 DeSoto with the doors missing.

Finally I did find one thing mechanical that I could fix when it broke. I can stop a commode from making that annoying sound it makes sometimes after you flush it. What you do is lift the lid off the top of the commode and fiddle with the rubber dohickey until the sound stops.

Try finding that kind of information in a stupid book.

My last attempt at self-sufficiency almost proved fatal. I had a bad case of the flu, but I resolved to lick it myself without running to the doctor to have him laugh at me. Real men stick it out.

I felt worse than a five-eyed goat in a sandstorm. I was so sick my toenails turned black. I couldn't breathe, I couldn't eat and my tongue itched. I turned to would-be friends for help and advice.

"Here's what you do," one said confidently. "You pour a glass full of bourbon and then you take a tablespoon of sugar. You eat the sugar and chase it with the glass of bourbon and then go to bed. You'll feel great the next morning."

He was partially right. I felt great while I was in the coma caused by the sugar and bourbon. When I came out of it, however, I felt just as bad as I did before.

Somebody else told me to eat lots of mustard. "It's an old custom in my family. A cup of mustard a day will cure anything."

Anything, that is, except the flu. Eating a cup of mustard without hot dogs will make your ears water.

The next advice I got was to eat honey and chase it with a heavy dose of castor oil. "Honey and castor oil will purify you and cleanse all the poison from your body," I was told.

Maybe so, but eating honey and chasing it with a heavy-duty dose of castor oil also will keep you from sitting in one place for more than five minutes for days. Captured enemy spies were threatened with the same treatment during World War II by Allied interrogators. It always worked.

Still another friend suggested that an afternoon in a sauna would be just the thing to put me back in the pink. "You get into a sauna for about an hour," said the friend, "and then you come out and drink a strong vodka tonic. Go back into the sauna for another hour and then come out and drink two vodka tonics. You return to the sauna for a third hour, then come out and finish off the bottle of vodka."

"Sounds great," I said. "A sauna should really help me."

"You kiddin'? Saunas are awful for a man in your condition, but after a bottle of vodka, who cares?"

Chicken soup was the final suggestion. "Do I put vodka or castor oil in it?" I asked sheepishly.

"No, silly. Chicken soup by itself has tremendous curative powers."

I ate so much chicken soup that I had the urge to go peck corn, but I was still too sick to get off my tail feathers and go outside.

Eventually I cured myself by doing what any real man would do in a similar situation: I pulled the covers up over my head, whined and felt sorry for myself. In a couple of days, I was fine. A victory for self-sufficiency.

***

So is it the stubbly beard, the long hair, drinking and chewing, sweating and stinking, loving dogs and being self-sufficient that gives a person true grit?

There must be more to it than that. Otherwise, how would you explain the likes of Eugene Ellis?

— 4 —

A Heaping
Helping of Grit

Setting A Shining Example

IT USED TO BE that there were a lot of people around —
on street corners, in barber shops, in train stations and
airports — who would shine your shoes for a price. But
shining shoes got to be a social stigma, a sign of subser-
vience in some people's minds, and so shoe shining has
gone the way of service at gas stations: It's there, but you
have to look for it.

When I met Eugene Ellis shining shoes in Macon, Georgia, I asked him if it bothered his self-image that he was still
shining shoes for a living. He answered my question by
looking at me like I was crazy.

Eugene Ellis is sixty-two years old. He's black. He's short,
which he says is helpful when you shine shoes because you
don't have to bend over as far. Eugene Ellis is an orphan, a
husband and a father of five. He shines shoes all day in a
barbershop, and then he shines for a good part of the

evening in a local jazz bar.

He started shining shoes on the streets of Macon when he was five. Years later at the Atlanta airport, he shined the shoes of a young senator who hoped someday to be president of the United States. John Kennedy told Eugene that when he was elected president, he would give him a job shining shoes at the White House.

"Said he'd come back and get me," recalled Eugene, "but I didn't think he would."

Eugene Ellis shined shoes at the White House for three presidents — Kennedy, Lyndon Johnson and Richard Nixon — before he decided it was time to go back home. He brought memories with him:

On Kennedy — "A good Catholic man. Real quiet. I was in the eighth car back when they shot him."

On Johnson — "If he was still president, I'd still be shining his shoes. He always took me to the ranch with him."

On Nixon — "He was a little different from the others."

Eugene shined the shoes of Hubert Humphrey, Gerald Ford, Muhammad Ali, Don McNeal and Elvis Presley. He said Elvis paid the best of the bunch.

The worst shoe to shine? "Patent leather. Can't see what you've done."

Favorite shoe to shine? "Anything in bad shape. I like to see my work when I'm finished with it."

It would be easy to try to attach some social significance to this story and say that what this country needs today is more people shining shoes like Eugene Ellis does, and wouldn't that solve some of the unemployment problem? But "let 'em shine shoes" isn't exactly my style, so I'll just let it pass with this:

Eugene Ellis, who has put three daughters through college, gets salary plus tips at a regular job. And when he

pulled out his wallet to show me a card some prince gave
him at the White House, it was filled with what he called his
"lucky twenties." His work is inside and requires no heavy
lifting, it beats scraping dead bugs off windshields, and he
says that when he's got a good pair of shoes to shine and his
rag is popping just right, "it's like I'm making music."

Yeah, I think that's enough said.

WISDOM IN RETROSPECT

The courtesy van showed up to take me to the airport at
Salt Lake City. The driver was a woman, probably in her late
thirties. They had been hard years. You can see it in a
person's face sometimes.

She asked where I was headed, and I told her Atlanta.

"That's where you live?" she asked.

"Don't I sound like it?" I answered.

She just laughed. "Yeah, you do. I was married to an ol'
Georgia boy once."

"Where from?"

"Albany."

There was a story there. "How in the world did someone
from way out here in Utah get hooked up with someone
from Albany, Georgia?"

"Met him on the bus," she said. "I was just nineteen. Was
going to Boise, Idaho, to visit my grandparents. He was in
the service on his way to Anchorage, Alaska. He sat down
next to me when we left Salt Lake. He was a real quiet boy
and shy. Didn't say a word the first hour, but then he
started talking a little. I could tell he was homesick.

"He showed me some pictures he had in his wallet. When
we got to Boise, he helped me get my bags off the bus and
asked if he could write me some time. I said he could. Then

one day he wrote and asked if I would marry him. I accepted. I was nineteen and had the moon and the stars in my eyes. We got married and drove all the way to Albany for our honeymoon," she continued.

"We had seven years together and two kids."

"You got divorced?" I pried.

"He was Baptist. I was Mormon. That was one of several things that were wrong. After I split with him I stayed single for seven more years. Then I got to figuring my kids needed a daddy, so I went out and found them one."

"How did that work out?"

"Bad. You can't make a daddy out of just anybody, I found out."

We were getting close to the airport. "You married now?" I asked, hoping for an end to the story.

"I'm living with a fellow now," said my driver. "I guess we moved in together about two years ago. My mother is shocked because we don't go ahead and get married. She says what we're doing is sinful. It might be but we're happy. I guess I'm as happy now as I've ever been. I don't want to take a chance of messing up again. Getting married don't solve any problems, it starts 'em."

As I stepped out of the van, I asked her name.

"It's Dixie."

I didn't have time to find out why. I simply said, "Stay happy, Dixie."

She smiled, nodded and drove away. Somebody in Utah has himself a good woman, I thought to myself. I just hope he knows it.

EXERCISING DISCRETION IN TENNESSEE

My friend Stephens and I were returning from a camping

trip somewhere in the hills of Tennessee when we developed an urgent thirst. He pulled into the first place with beer signs he spotted — a cement-block building with a lot of pickup trucks parked outside.

"Let's go in here," Stephens said.

The first thing I noticed inside was a pool table. Pool can be a dangerous game when played in a church basement. When played in a place like this, customers should be issued hockey helmets.

The crowd gave us the ol' they-ain't-from-around-here look as we moved quietly toward a table. I noticed a sign over the bar which said, "It is a felony to carry a weapon where alcoholic beverages are served." You didn't put a sign like that on your wall, I reasoned, unless there had been a previous incident, or incidents, to warrant it.

I usually can pick out a troublemaker, and there's one in every bar in America. In this instance, he was standing at the counter. He had long sideburns and his cigarettes rolled up in the sleeve of his shirt, a sure sign of a belligerent personality.

The tough guy picked up his beer and walked toward us. I drew a bead on the front door.

"Either of you shoot pool?" he asked.

"No," said Stephens.

"No, sir," I said.

The tough guy just grunted. "Guess I'll have to shoot by myself," he said.

Pool can be a very macho game. A man attacks a pool table, especially on the break when he makes every effort to shatter the balls.

The tough guy knew every eye was on him. He chalked his stick confidently, aimed the blue tip toward the rack of balls, closed one eye and came forward through the cue ball with an enormous grunt. But there was no ear-splitting sound of balls colliding. The tough guy had whiffed the cue ball.

The room fell silent. Nobody dared move a muscle. The tough guy, fighting to keep his cool, lined up the cue ball again as quickly as possible and this time scattered the balls around the table.

Stephens and I finished our beer, paid our tab and drove away.

"How far we been?" I asked him a little later.

"About ten miles," he said.

"Think we're safe?" I asked.

"Nothing out here but the bears and possums," he answered.

Then, and only then, did we allow ourselves the marvelous relief of howling laughter.

THE GIFT OF LOVING A CHILD

"I just want one thing," Sherry said to me. "I want people to learn of the tragedies we have been through so maybe they will understand how important it is to love their children with all their hearts and souls. To love a child is one of God's greatest gifts."

Sherry and D.A. were just kids themselves when they married nearly twenty-one years ago. Their first child was Lex, a boy. Then came another son, Allan.

"After Allan," Sherry explained, "we felt, in this day and time, that two children were enough. I was having some health problems, too, so I agreed to have my tubes tied."

They settled in the small town of Calhoun, Georgia, an hour or so north of Atlanta. Sherry taught elementary school, and D.A. became high school head football coach.

When he was four years old, Allan was diagnosed as having

leukemia. After several years of treatment, doctors determined that there might be hope for him if he underwent a bone marrow transplant. The family went to Seattle, Washington, for the operation. Lex was the donor for his little brother. The transplant was considered a success, and the family returned home in good spirits and resumed their lives.

"We sort of grew up with the kids ourselves, especially with Lex," said Sherry. "We always did everything together."

Several years later, Lex won a football scholarship to East Central Junior College in Mississippi. The whole family was jubilant. And when his team won a big game on the last day of September, 1983, he called his mother at three in the morning to tell her about it.

"He was so excited, and we shared that excitement," Sherry recalled. "He said he thought his team would be nationally ranked. He was on his way home for a visit before the next game."

Lex never made it home. Just a few miles outside of Calhoun, he fell asleep at the wheel and hit a truck head-on. He was killed instantly.

"On the way to the cemetery for Lex's funeral," Sherry continued, "my husband asked little Allan to look for a sign in nature that would show us that Lex was still with us. After the service at the graveside, a beautiful monarch butterfly flew between us. We believe it was a sign, and I can't think of anything more fitting than a butterfly. It is constantly on the go, just as Lex was, and it is not aggressive, and neither was our son."

When the family later redecorated their house, the wallpaper they selected was filled with butterflies.

Within a year after Lex's death, doctors discovered that Allan's leukemia has spread to his brain and spinal column.

His medication had to be discontinued to prevent further damage. The second son was dying.

"He knew he was dying, but he wasn't afraid. He knew his 'Bubba' would be waiting for him."

But Allan wasn't the only courageous member of his family. His mother and father were determined to carry on.

"We talked about the future. I even thought of seeing if I could have an operation that would allow me to have children again. But I'm too old for that," Sherry explained. "We also checked into the possibility of adopting, but there's a waiting list of several years. We have so much love to give, and we want to channel it somewhere. We know there are so many children who need it."

I asked Sherry how she and her husband had coped through their ordeal.

"We live with one thought," she said. "That God has something else planned for us. He must. He simply must."

AN OLD FOGEY WITH CLEAR VISION

My Aunt Jessie has lived in rural Georgia since 1931. She is widowed now and spends most of her time watching her "stories," which is what she calls the television soap operas. I'm not certain how old she is, and I never intend to ask, but it's a fact that she's a great-grandmother.

One of the grandchildren offered recently to take her to Atlanta to see Kenny Rogers in concert. Aunt Jessie, a lifelong devotee to country music, accepted.

Those of us who live in large urban areas learn to accept the dramatic changes which occur around us almost daily, but Aunt Jessie was shocked when she ventured from her rural security for a modern concert. It was refreshing to hear her view of it all:

"I never seen so many people in one place in my life. And when the concert finally got started, you couldn't hear a thing. Every time Kenny would start to sing, everybody would scream and holler.

"The rest of the time I couldn't see because somebody was always crawling over me to get something to eat. Looks like they would've had supper before they came to the concert, or at least brought themselves a sandwich so they wouldn't have had to leave their seats."

Aunt Jessie was amazed at the actions of some of the women at the concert. "I saw these two young girls, in britches so tight I don't know how they breathed, running all over the place, touchin' the ground just in the high places. I don't know where their mamas were. But if they had been mine, I'd have wore 'em both out for dressin' and actin' like that.

"Then there was a woman so drunk she couldn't stand up, holding a big ol' cup of beer in each hand. She could have at least stayed home if she was going to act like that.

"At the intermission I was standing in line to go to the restroom and this woman got tired of waiting, so she just pranced right into the men's room, big as you please. I thought, 'Lord, what's this world comin' to?'"

I tried to explain to Aunt Jessie that women have changed a lot since her time, and nowadays they smoke and drink in public and occasionally use profanity and generally have come a long way, baby.

"I guess I ought to be thankful for one thing," said Aunt Jessie.

"What's that?"

"That I'm still an old fogey, country woman," she said.

I'm thankful for that, too, Aunt Jessie. There aren't many of you left.

WAVING HER FLAG OF FREEDOM

We were waiting for a couple of planes. She had two, maybe three drinks. We shared a story and an opinion or two, and then she asked, "How old are you, anyway?"

"Thirty-nine," I answered.

"Same age as my husband, the sorry bastard," she said.

Ever perceptive, I asked, "You're mad at your husband?"

"Actually," she said, "he's now my ex-husband. Ran off with a girl half his age."

I made no comment. I'm old enough to know better.

"You know what's wrong with men your age?" she continued.

"Yeah," I said, "but what do you think is wrong with men my age?"

"You're all afraid of getting old, so you start chasing around after young girls." She ordered another drink. Scotch.

"How long have you been divorced?" I asked.

"Six months."

"Kids?"

"One. He's twelve. Do you know how old I am?"

When a woman asks a question like that, I always subtract five years from my best guess. "Late twenties," I answered.

"Thirty-five, and you know what's wrong with women my age?"

I had several ideas, to be sure, but the best answer at the time seemed to be shaking my head no.

"We were brought up so differently from young girls today," she began. "You take me. My mother has dominated my life. All the time I was growing up, she used to harp on me to always be a 'good girl.' And I was. I didn't dare do anything my mother wouldn't approve of. I never had a drink until I was married. I've had sex with only one man, my husband. I've been a 'good girl' all my life, and all I've got to show for it is a broken marriage and a lot of guilt."

"Yeah," I said awkwardly, "our parents sometimes leave us with a load to carry into adulthood."

"Know what I did today, though?" the woman asked. "I got dressed up in this outfit and went by my mother's house. She said, 'Oh, you look so lovely, darling. Are you going to a party?' I said, 'No, mother, I'm not going to a party. I'm going to leave here, get on an airplane and meet a man. Then I'm going to commit adultery for the first time in my life.' I thought she was going to faint. She was absolutely bewildered."

"Did she try to talk you out of it?" I wanted to know.

"I wouldn't let her. Every time she tried to preach to me, I just told her it wouldn't do any good. It's my life and I've missed so much. I've got to start being my own person, and now is as good a time as any."

She ordered one last drink. "What's so funny," she said, "is that all my mother could say to me when I left was, 'Don't do anything that will cause you to hate yourself.' If I don't do this, then I'm going to hate myself."

They called the woman's plane. She downed her drink, smiled and boarded. I hope she had a great weekend.

***

So maybe true grit has less to do with things physical and more to do with things mental. It seems to come from many sources: from religion, and sports, and living with women and dealing with living. In the words of Erskine Caldwell, "Call it experience." I've had my share.

— 5 —

Sinning and Grinning
And Knowing The
Difference

I GREW UP HEARING that good things come to those who love the Lord; the Moreland, Georgia, Methodist Church was deeply and comfortably seated in the traditional interpretation of The Word. But religion, like so many other things, isn't as simple as it used to be. Nowadays the good guys sometimes wear black and white striped hats instead of just one or the other.

Almost every day in the mail I receive a letter from some television evangelist asking me for a donation to help buy a new truck for his television equipment or to pay off the debt for the new gymnasium at New Testament University. The implication is that if I don't send them the cash, I'm on the express train for hell.

Will I end up down there with Hitler and Attila the Hun and Bonnie and Clyde just because I didn't send them five bucks for a new wrestling mat? Then again, is hell actually *down* there?

"Can you dig your way to hell?" I asked the preacher when I was a kid.

"Guess you can," he said, "but I can tell you how to get there a lot quicker."

Frankly, thinking about hell scares the you-know-where out of me. I'd much rather think about heaven. Just the other day my mail included a pamphlet entitled, "Heaven: Are You Eligible?" I took the test and scored "too close to call."

With that kind of rating, I pay close attention to all those groups who predict the coming of Judgment Day. If some guy says he has it on good authority that the end of the world is due on October 11, then I'm particularly careful that day not to do anything awful, like telling big lies, attending an adult movie or coveting my neighbor's new Porsche.

Otherwise, can you imagine your chances of getting aboard the glory train when the first question they ask you at judgment is, "For starters, what did you do today?"

"W-w-w-well, f-f-first I lied to my boss about having to go to the doctor and I went instead to see *Flesh Dance* at the Porn Palace. Then I went home and kicked the tires on my '73 Ford wagon because that's what I'm stuck with when Thorndike across the street has a new Porsche."

Take a seat, boy. The southbound leaves in just a few minutes.

I know in my heart that most of these forecasts are poppycock, but my old-fashioned upbringing always keeps me just a little uneasy. Remember, everybody thought Columbus was nuts when he bought a round-trip ticket. You just never know.

That's why I started early in life being careful not to get caught in mid-sin at the precise moment of His return. I

remember my first beer. I tried to chug it down but suc-
ceeded only in gagging myself.

"What's your hurry?" asked my companion in evil.

"Beer is better when you drink it fast," I answered
between coughs.

Truth is, I just wanted to finish that beer quickly so I could
throw the can away and get rid of the evidence in case the
Second Coming were to occur in the next five to ten minutes.

I guess it is possible to overreact to these predictions.
Anytime I hear another Judgment Day date, I'm reminded
of the story my grandfather used to tell about an Elmer
Gantry-type preacher who came through town with his
tent.

"The end is close at hand, my children," the preacher
screamed one night. About that time, a small boy who had
just been given a toy trumpet for his birthday walked past
the tent and gave his new horn a mighty toot.

The congregation panicked and bolted out of the tent.
The evangelist grabbed the cash box and cut down the
street at full gallop. The little boy, wondering where everybody was headed, followed the preacher.

The preacher ran faster and faster, afraid to look back, but
the little boy matched him step for step, still tooting on his
new horn. Finally the preacher stopped, whipped out a
switchblade and said, "Watch it, Gabe, or I'll cut you!"

My grandfather wouldn't have cared much for today's
bigtime television preachers. In his oft-stated opinion,
preachers were supposed to marry folks, preach funerals,
mow the grass around the church and administer to the
needs of the flock (that meant consoling the poor soul who
lost his job, whose wife ran off, and whose trailer burned all
in the same week). Our preacher even used to knock down

the dirt dobbers' nests in the windows of the sanctuary so the inhabitants wouldn't bother the worshippers while he was trying to run the devil out of town on Sunday mornings.

Do you suppose that Oral Roberts or Jerry Falwell ever knocked down any dirt dobbers' nests?

My grandfather also didn't like it when younger preachers used note cards to deliver their sermons. "They ought to get it straight from the Lord," he said many a time. "Politicians use notes."

The preacher at Moreland Methodist when I was growing up suited my grandfather just fine. He drove an old car. He had only one suit. He did the yard work around the church, didn't use note cards and always attempted to answer the questions of a twelve-year-old boy when things didn't add up. Once he even preached a funeral for a dog because that little boy, who loved the dog very much, asked him to.

What would Pat Robertson say over a dog?

What bothers me today is that for every glamour boy of the pulpit, there are thousands out there who tackle the devil daily, one-on-one, with little or no audience, against long odds, and occasionally on an empty stomach.

God bless them. And God, please don't let my grandfather — I know he's around there somewhere — find out that we've got preachers down here today who use cue cards and hang out with politicians.

***

I had a dream about all this the other night. Maybe it was my grandfather passing along a little inside information. This is how it went:

God called in the angel who is in charge of keeping an eye on what's going on in the United States. "What's all this fussing about religion and politics? I thought I had Ben

Franklin and his friends work out the separation of church and state a couple of weeks ago," God said.

"Actually," said the angel, "it's been a couple of weeks heaven time, but to folks on earth it's been more than two hundred years. But every so often, they decide to argue it again."

"Who started it this time?"

"I suppose it was Jerry Falwell and the Moral Majority," answered the angel.

"Jerry who and the Moral what?"

"Jerry Falwell and the Moral Majority. Falwell is a television evangelist and he heads a fundamentalist organization called the Moral Majority. They support President Reagan because they think you are a Republican."

"Whatever gave them an idea like that?" asked God.

"They think you sent President Reagan, a Republican, to save the morals of the country because he believes in a lot of the same things as they do."

"For instance?"

"Well, President Reagan believes in prayer in public schools, and so does the Moral Majority."

"So what's the big deal? I get thousands of prayers a day from students in public schools. Here, look at this one that came in yesterday. Pretty creative for a tenth grader:"

> O Lord, hear my anxious plea.
> Algebra is killing me.
> I know not of 'x' or 'y,'
> And probably won't until the day I die.
> Please, Lord, help me at this hour
> As I take my case to the highest power.
> I care not for fame nor loot,
> Just help me find one square root.

Latin and Grammar are also trouble.
Guide me through this daily double.
And, Lord, please let me see
One passing mark in Chemistry.

Lord, why am I such a dope in school?
My teachers think I'm such a fool.
One said, 'Son, you're a horrid flop.
You bent the saw and failed at shop.'
My days in class are filled with remorse.
I can't even pass the easiest course.
I hunkered down and bowed my neck,
But I burnt the cake and flagged Home Ec.

In English Lit, I studied hard
And read all the words of the Bard.
But my mind is like a hateful Judas.
It couldn't recall, 'Et tu, Brutus?'

Lord, will there ever be
A tougher subject than History?
Into the past I steadfastly delve,
From Plymouth Rock to 1812.
I learn of all those patriotic folk,
From John Q. Adams to James K. Polk.
But test time comes and I fall on my tail.
Was it Patrick Henry or Nathan Hale?

Lord, must I offer an apology
For three times failing Biology?
Why is it I'm in such a fog
Concerning the innards of a frog?
I push and strive and strain and grope

To come to terms with the microscope.
Lord, please forgive my derision,
But who gives a hoot for cellular division?

Lord, I wish that I could vanish
When the teacher calls on me in Spanish.
And I promise, it's a cinch,
I'll never learn a word of French.

Down in gym I take P.E.
Calisthenics will be the death of me.
I have all the grace of a mop.
I made an 'F' in side straddle hop.

Lord, is there anything I can't flub?
Will I ever be in Beta Club?
I have never found the key to knowledge,
And my folks want me to go to college.
Oh, such a thing I constantly dread.
I'd as soon join the Marines instead.
Lord, please give me a sign
That you've been listening all this time.
If you will help, I'll give my all,
And won't even chew gum in study hall.
Please lead me out of this constant coma,
And give me a chance at my diploma.
Let others fight about church and state.
I pray only to graduate. Amen.

"Now, that's a prayer worthy of my time," said God. "But apparently that's not good enough for this Falwell fellow. Tell me more about him."

"Well, he has his own television show."

"When does he visit the sick?"

"He doesn't have time for that. If he's not preaching on the air, he's busy fund raising for his ministry or else he's on one of those news shows like, 'This Week With David Brinkley,' telling people where you stand on this and that."

"Just what I needed," said God, "another spokesman." God thought for a moment and then said to the angel, "I want you to do something for me. I want you to deliver a few messages. First, tell both sides that I don't want to be any part of their political squabble. Their forefathers had the good sense to leave me out of politics, and I don't see why they can't.

"Also, tell Reagan to forget about school prayer for awhile and instead find a way to talk to the Russians before they find a way to destroy what I've created. Then tell that Falwell fellow to stop using my name to boost his television ratings and stop trying to run the country from his pulpit. Can you handle all that?" God asked the angel.

"Yes, ma'am," the angel replied.

***

Apparently that message I dreamed hasn't been delivered quite yet, because the Moral Majority is still busy trying to convince us that they have all the answers. Me, I'm more confused than ever. It's gotten to the point that I'm not sure I know sin when I see it. Or hear it. According to the Moral Majority, music is one of the major mediums of the devil today, and nowhere is the temperature hotter than in country music.

I'll be the first to admit that some questionable lyrics have sneaked into country music in recent years, but are the dials "down there" really tuned to WSM? In an attempt to get this disturbing issue cleared up, I contacted Mrs. Debbie Sue Ann Betty Jo Jenkins of Blue Ball, Arkansas. She's the

Moral Majority's expert on the state of country music.

"May I call you Debbie Sue Ann Betty Jo?" I asked when I reached her on the phone.

"Call me anything but 'Barracuda,'" she replied. "That's what Conway Twitty called me when I tried to stop his show in Little Rock."

"You tried to stop the Conway Twitty show?"

"He was singing that trashy song about meeting a woman in a bar who was wearing tight britches," Mrs. Jenkins explained.

I know the song in question, entitled "Tight-fittin' Jeans," and I suppose it is a little suggestive. I asked Mrs. Jenkins which part of the song offended her most.

"The part where the woman tells Conway Twitty, 'Pardner, there's a tiger in these tight-fittin' jeans.'"

I quickly realized that Debbie Sue Ann Betty Jo, Mrs. Jenkins, was a bit of a tiger herself. Anybody who would try to stop Conway Twitty as he groaned to his legion of fans is not the sort of person to be taken lightly.

"What other songs offend the Moral Majority?" I asked.

"Anything by Barbara Mandrell," she said.

Barbara Mandrell a musical filth peddler? I couldn't believe it.

"Imagine such perversion as inviting a man to eat crackers in bed with you in a song," explained Mrs. Jenkins, referring of course to Ms. Mandrell's hit song, "You Can Eat Crackers in My Bed Anytime." She continued, "Decent people would never do such a thing. Beds are for sleeping and nothing else."

"What does Mr. Jenkins think about that?" I asked.

"He doesn't even like crackers," she said.

Mrs. Jenkins went on to list several other songs which the Moral Majority disapproves of:

- "My Favorite Memory" by Merle Haggard. One line recalls "sleeping all night long on the floor." "Probably ate a bunch of crackers before they dozed off," said Mrs. Jenkins.

- "Best Bedroom in Town" by Tammy Wynette. "Doesn't anybody ever get out of bed in Nashville?" asked Mrs. Jenkins.

- "If I Said You Had a Beautiful Body Would You Hold It Against Me?" by the Bellamy Brothers. "Utter trash," said Mrs. Jenkins. "I'll bet their mother, Mrs. Bellamy, hides herself in shame every time she hears that song. If Mr. Jenkins had ever said anything like that to me, I would have bashed in his little worm head."

- "My Baby Thinks He's a Train" by Rosanne Cash. "More perversion," explained Mrs. Jenkins. "Mr. Jenkins decided he was a Greyhound bus once and that he was leaving."

"What did you do?" I asked her.

"Bashed in his little worm head, of course."

Finally I asked Mrs. Jenkins to name the one song which she feels is most harmful.

"It's by Glen Campbell," she said.

"Glen Campbell?"

"Yes, I know it's hard to believe, but he sings a song called, 'I Love My Truck.' Can you imagine a nice boy from Arkansas getting involved in something like that?"

No, ma'am, I sure can't.

***

Gospel music, thank the Lord and Mrs. Jenkins, is still safe from such perversion, and I listen to it with gusto and a clean conscience. I get my interest in gospel music honestly. My late father could hunker down on a piano and make it sing a joyful noise as long as there was somebody around to listen.

My Uncle Dorsey on my mother's side rarely missed an all-night gospel sing at the old Atlanta Municipal Auditorium. He favored the bass singer, the tall fellow in the back who always let go on the "Wellawella's," as in, "Wellawella, evuhbody's gon' have a livin' in glowry...."

I grew up in my maternal grandmother's house, and each Sunday morning I awakened to her radio blaring out the "Gospel Jubilee." My grandmother preferred the inevitable short, baby-faced tenor in the quartet who could pop up there higher than a kite with a nearly operatic, "He's my Jeeeeesus!"

Recently I attended the National Gospel Quartet Convention in Nashville, Tennessee, and it was a glooorious event. The auditorium was encircled by those rolling motels that once were Greyhound buses, carrying groups from date to date. On the sides were the names of the groups — the Singing Echoes, the Kingsmen, this family and that.

The auditorium was maybe half full when I entered, but before the night was over it was bulging. In the hallways were booths where gospel fans could buy tapes and albums and autographed photos of their favorite performers. As each quartet left the stage, a spokesperson was given the opportunity to plug the group's wares:

"We're right over yonder at booth fifteen," a man shouted into the microphone, "and we got a three-album-for-fifteen-dollar sale on. Y'all drop by to see us."

There was passion in the music. It jumped and even rocked a bit, and it set toes to tapping and occasionally brought the audience to its feet, heads held toward the heavens, hands clapping.

"We ain't the stars of the show," a fellow said. "Jesus is the star. Let's all stand and give Him a hand!"

Another group walked on, and the lead singer said, "I

seen on the marquee out front that the Talking Heads are coming to this auditorium. There's gonna be dope-smokin', pill-poppin' and rock music. But you ain't gonna get none of that here tonight. All you gonna get high on is Jeeeesus!"

The crowd loved it.

The last group appeared on the stage and sang its hit song, "Call Me What You Want To, But When He Calls Me, Call Me Gone." The crowd roared following a rousing rendition.

"Sort of gives you glowry bumps listenin' to 'em, don't it?" said the woman sitting next to me.

It does at that. It sure does.

— 6 —

Are You Non-Essential, Undesirable, Unmentionable Or Just Undone?

SOMETIMES YOU DON'T have to go out of your way to find opportunities to develop true grit. They'll come to you. Just surviving the lunacy and frustrations of the modern world is evidence of some degree of character. Isn't that why our society always makes such a big deal out of golden wedding anniversaries?

In my particular situation, I travel a lot. Thirty years ago that would have meant many pleasurable train rides with good food, good drink and plenty of time to read or relax. Today, however, it means airports and airplanes and endless delays and migraine headaches. It starts before you even leave home.

"Good morning. Wingandaprayer Airlines. May I help you?"

"Yes," I said to the voice on the phone. "I'd like to make two round-trip reservations for the Sunday evening flight to

Pittsburgh, please."

"Will this be first class, tourist or Wingandaprayer's new cargo class?" she asked.

"Cargo class?"

"Certainly, sir. In an effort to attract your business in these competitive times, Wingandaprayer Airlines is offering an innovative and inexpensive way for you to travel by air. Cargo class simply means you ride in the cargo hold with the baggage at a huge savings in cost. This is available, however, only to those passengers who will fit into their own hanging bags."

"I'll just take tourist," I said.

"Oxygen or non-oxygen?"

"I don't understand."

"Another Wingandaprayer option in our effort to offer passengers a variety of ways to save money and still not have to take the bus," she explained. "If you prefer to bring your own oxygen tank, then your seat will not be equipped with an automatic oxygen mask release in case of sudden cabin depressurization. If Wingandaprayer doesn't have to provide you with oxygen, it can save money and pass those savings along to its customers in the form of reduced fares."

"But I don't have my own oxygen tank."

"In that case, sir, how long can you hold your breath?"

"I'll just take two seats with oxygen."

"Will you be traveling with your wife or another adult?"

"No, I'll be traveling with my nephew Robert, who's six."

"Does he chew Rootie-Tootie Bubble Gum?"

"Is that the kind that turns his teeth blue?" I asked.

"Exactly, sir, and Wingandaprayer now offers free tickets to children if they show eight Rootie-Tootie Bubble Gum wrappers when they go to the agent for their boarding passes. 'Get 'em while they're young and they're yours forever,' is what we always say at Wingandaprayer," she explained.

"So what is the adult fare?"

"Depends, sir. Will you be cashing in coupons on this trip?"

"Coupons?"

"Check your local newspaper for Wingandaprayer cost-cutting coupons. Bring the coupons with you to the ticket agent and trade them in for savings on your fare."

"OK. Now, will dinner be served on the evening flight to Pittsburgh?"

"Not in tourist, sir. Wingandaprayer lost millions last year, and in an effort to keep our own costs down, we've cut out all meal service except in first class, where passengers are allowed to bob for apples."

"I'll pack a sandwich for me and Robert. Now, will you please see if there is space available on the evening flight to Pittsburgh?"

"I have you confirmed on our 7:20 flight to Pittsburgh, sir. May I have your home address?"

"Why do you need my home address?" I asked.

"So Wingandaprayer can mail you your green stamps and toaster."

When we finally arrived at the airport and boarded the plane, we were immediately greeted by two delays. The first, said the captain, was due to "a minor mechanical problem. We should have it cleared up soon." If an airplane is going to develop a mechanical problem, whether major or minor, the best time to do so is when it's still on the ground. Nonetheless, it can be extremely unsettling to the passengers.

For example, what does the captain consider "minor"? It could be anything from a wing being loose to the navigator's pen being out of ink. Secondly, how can the captain or the passengers know for sure that the problem has been fixed? It's not exactly like dealing with someone's pickup truck, where the mechanic opens the hood, pulls at a few wires and hoses, and then says, "Try it now." If the truck doesn't start, the mechanic pulls at some different wires and hoses. With an airplane, you don't get a second chance.

I expressed my concern to a passing stewardess.

"Don't worry," she said, "our mechanic knows this plane from front to back."

If he knows so much, I thought to myself, why isn't he in the cockpit flying this sucker instead of underneath it pulling at wires and hoses? I looked out the window and saw a fellow who looked like a mechanic scratching his head with a big wrench. On his breast pocket I could read the name, Bobby Earl. Would you trust your life to a man named Bobby Earl?

Another concern was that we were flying on Sunday. Have you ever tried to find a mechanic to work on your car on Sunday? The only ones I've ever found had just been fired from Brake-O. Bobby Earl worked on the plane for about an hour. Then I heard him yell to the pilot, "Try it now!" Sure enough, it started. I didn't know whether to be happy or sad.

As we backed away from the terminal (Why do they have to call it that?), the chief stewardess announced another delay.

"Due to heavy traffic here at the airport, we are presently 108th in line for takeoff, which means we're going to spend approximately the four hours and ten minutes either taxiing slowly or sitting in line with a bunch of other planes waiting to take off," she explained.

"Wingandaprayer Airlines would like to apologize for

this inconvenience. We realize that some of you have con-
nections or important meetings in Pittsburgh and that this
sort of delay could cause you to lose your company's biggest
account, among other disastrous occurrences. But please
do not whine, because we can't help it if thirty-five other
airlines decided to schedule takeoffs at the same time we
did.

"We will do everything in our power to make up for this
excruciating experience. For those of you who might want
to read while we are taxiing out, ask your flight attendant to
bring you something from Wingandaprayer's in-flight
library. Available today are *War and Peace*, *The Rise and Fall of
the Third Reich*, and *The Complete Works of Victor Hugo*.

"Later in our taxi out, we will be offering at no charge our
'Movie While You Wait.' Our feature in first class will be the
original, uncut version of *Gone With the Wind*, while our
coach passengers will enjoy viewing *Rocky I, II* and *III*.

"If we still haven't taken off by that time, Wingandaprayer has other means of killing time for our passengers.
There will be a bridge tournament in rows twenty-five
through thirty. For those who prefer bingo, cards may be
purchased at a nominal charge. First officer Willard Smith,
who is just as bored as the rest of you, will be calling the
games in rows seven through twenty-four.

"In first class there will be Trivial Pursuit games and mud
wrestling for any passengers who are interested, as well as
a musical performance by two of our flight attendants,
Ramona Dentz and Glenda Jane Chastain, singing songs
they actually wrote, such as, 'I've Got the Air Sickness Bag
Blues.' Other pre-takeoff performances include a lecture by
Captain Allis Chalmers, who will explain how to hot-wire a
747, and a demonstration on in-flight macramé by navigator
Marco Polonski.

"Also, because of our long delay, our smoking passengers may wish to step outside to smoke. If so, please remember to walk along with the aircraft in case it moves so you don't get too far behind. Thank you for ridin — , I mean flying, Wingandaprayer Airlines, and have a pleasant flight."

***

If dealing with airlines doesn't test your mettle and cultivate a little true grit, then try buying or selling a house. Real estate agents are God's curse on mankind when locusts are out of season.

When you're trying to buy a house, there are basically three parties involved: (1) a large lending agency which employs no people, only computers, (2) a real estate agent, who is one of seventeen zillion housewives who got bored with Tuesday morning doubles and went out and got licensed to sell houses, and (3) a working stiff with a wife and two kids.

Here's how the game is played:

The stiff and his wife and two kids have outgrown their modest, 2BR, 1BA, brk. rch. w/o fpl. They are looking for something a little nicer and with more space. They contact a real estate agent, an attractive person named Delores who smokes a lot and drives a late-model Mercedes.

Delores takes the stiff and his wife and his two kids to look at houses that are for sale. The stiff is shown a house with three bedrooms, two baths and a fireplace in the den, which is exactly what he had in mind. Last year it cost $17,000. But that was last year.

"This honey of a place is one-five," says Delores. "One-five" is real estate saleslady talk for one hundred and five big ones. I'm talking thousands.

The poor stiff, meanwhile, is holding about half of the downpayment and facing an interest rate that would make

Shylock cringe.

"But, Darling," says his wife, "it's just perfect, and Marvin and Arnold (the two kids) can each have their own bedroom."

"Yeah, Dad," echo Marvin and Arnold.

This is where the real estate game gets interesting. There's no way the stiff can do what his father probably did — plunk down ten percent and make reasonable payments the rest of his life — so he has to engage in what is termed "creative financing." That's real estate saleslady talk for, "No way you can afford this house, turkey, but I haven't had a good commission in a month, so here's the way we're going to rig it."

There are all sorts of ways to finance a house creatively. Here are a few:

• LOAN ASSUMPTION — That's where you assume your brother-in-law, the doctor, will lend you the money for a downpayment, but he laughs in your face and asks if Marvin and Arnold can come over to help him clean his pool.

• WRAPAROUND MORTGAGE — That's where a bunch of fast-talking guys with cigars wrap you around their little fingers and you're in so deep you have to take a night job and Marvin and Arnold forget you exist.

• GRADUATED PAYMENTS — The first year you pay ten dollars a month. The next year you pay ten thousand dollars a month. The following year you live in a tent.

• STARVATION MORTGAGE PLAN — You can make your house payments, but you can't afford food for the first two years of the loan. Marvin and Arnold go to live with your brother-in-law.

• BLACKMAIL — You find out the owner of the house you are trying to buy had a sex-change operation in 1963.

"He" gives you the house for free and buys Marvin and Arnold a dog.

● ROB-A-LIQUOR-STORE PLAN — Just what the name implies. You rob liquor stores until you can afford the house. The real estate firm locates the stores and furnishes a stocking to go over your head. Marvin and Arnold watch the doors. Delores drives the getaway car.

Selling a house can be equally frustrating. First the house sits for six months without a single person coming to look at it, but Delores is still nauseatingly optimistic.

This house will sell. I guarantee it," she says, jingling the change in her pocket and rocking back and forth on her heels.

"Yeah, but during my lifetime?" asks the stiff.

"Trust me," says Delores, popping her gum. Didn't I buy a Pinto from her several years ago? Or was she the travel agent who sold me the Braniff charter to West Beirut?

Finally one afternoon the phone rings and Delores says, "Will it be OK to show the house later today?" What that really means is, "I'll be there in four minutes. These turkeys (prospective buyers) could be hot."

Delores's timing is magnificent. The United States Army Mule Team and its drivers were over for lunch and have just left, and she wants to show the house in four minutes.

"It'll just take me a week to hose the place down," you argue.

"Trust me," says Delores. The Pinto was lemon yellow and the engine sounded like it had emphysema.

The stiff immediately starts throwing things under chairs, under the sofa, into cabinets, and his wife puts something on the stove to boil. That's another tip from Delores: boil cinnamon to give the house a "homey" smell.

"What's that god-awful smell?" asks the man as soon as

he walks through the front door.

"Smells like cinnamon to me," says his wife.

"I can't stand the smell of cinnamon. Let's go back and take another look at that house that smelled like garlic. You know, I just love garlic."

Another trick Delores suggests is to have a fire burning in the fireplace. Gives the house a "cozy" feeling, she says.

Only problem is that stiff forgets to open the flue.

"Stay close to the floor and there's plenty of air," says Delores to the prospective buyers. "Now, in there is the master bedroom...."

"Let's get out of here," the man says to his wife. "I'll call the fire department at the first pay phone we see."

I once had a house that sat for nine months without selling. Without so much as thinking about selling. So I did what any self-respecting syndicated columnist would do: I wrote a column about an eccentric old bird who lived there before me and buried $200,000 in cash somewhere on the property just before he died. With my bad back, I couldn't even lift a shovel, I wrote, but . . .

In the words of Delores, "Trust me."

***

Unfortunately, those sorts of shenanigans are not limited to the real estate industry. Deception and misrepresentation are more prevalent today than Boy George. Our very language is twisted and distorted daily so that it's hard to know exactly what phrases mean anymore. Take politics, for example.

When a politician says, "We're still checking the results of our latest poll," what he really means is, "I paid a fortuneteller fifty bucks to predict my chances, and she said that if I got two thousand votes she'd eat her crystal ball."

Here are some of their other favorites:

- "A heavy turnout will help us." If all my cousins bother to vote, I might hit double figures.

- "I think bad weather on election day would definitely benefit my opponent." My support is so weak that I'll lose half my votes if there's more than a ten percent chance of rain.

- "We haven't had any attention from the media." I bought drinks for two television reporters and a newspaper columnist, and all I got in return was stuck with a fifty-dollar tab.

- "I don't know how my opponent could stoop so low as to bring up something like that." You rig just one little million-dollar construction bid and everybody wants to make a federal case out of it.

- "We've run a clean, honest campaign." I spent $25,000 on private detective fees and couldn't come up with a damn thing on my opponent.

- "No matter what the outcome of the election, we've made a lot of new friends all over the country." Especially the blonde at the bar at the Hyatt in San Francisco.

- "I have nothing to be ashamed of." I gave the blonde a ficticious name.

- "You can't run a campaign as inexpensively as you once could." Votes aren't nearly as cheap as they used to be.

- "I'm just a simple country boy." The closest I ever got to a cow was ordering Steak Diane at the country club.

- "It's too early to make any sort of definitive statement on how the election is going." My campaign manager hasn't returned with the booze yet.

- "I want to thank my wife for all her support during the campaign." She believed the story about the lipstick on my shirt after the campaign trip to San Francisco.

- "I would like to congratulate my opponent on his vic-

ARE YOU UNDESIRABLE OR JUST UNDONE? 817

tory." All I want is five minutes alone with that sorry SOB.

● "Now that the campaign is over, I'm looking forward to getting my life back to normal." I'm not going to sober up for a week.

● "The people have spoken." If I'd known I had that many enemies, I'd have carried a gun.

Politicians and their aides also are forever coming up with catch words or phrases which I find terribly confusing. For example, not long ago President Reagan sent home a lot of "non-essential" government employees because he was fighting with Congress about getting a budget approved.

After his announcement, I couldn't help wondering, What do all those non-essential government employees do? I suppose they handle all the non-essential work the government has to do. But if thousands of government employees are non-essential, what about me? How do I know if I'm essential to the country or not?

To help myself and other Americans answer this crucial question, I devised a test to find out if you're non-essential or not. Just answer the following questions.

1. Is it absolutely necessary that you stay awake and in an upright position while performing your duties?

2. If you walked into the boss's office and demanded a raise, would he (a) give you the raise? (b) throw you out of his office? (c) mistake you for Killingsworth from accounting who died last year?

3. If you took a leave of absence and hiked the Appalachian Trail for six months and came back to work with a full beard, would anybody notice that you had been away, or, if you're female, remark how it's not everyday that you see a woman with a full beard?

4. Are you with the Ford Motor Company and presently designing a diesel Edsel?

5. If you called in sick, would the boss hire a temporary to fill in, or would he say, "Killingsworth from accounting can handle things until you get back"?

6. If you said, "But, sir, Killingsworth from accounting died last year," would the boss respond, "Too bad, he was a good man," or, "I know. That's why he'd be perfect for your job"?

7. Are you Woody Allen's weight coach?

8. If one day you didn't come to work but sent your dog instead, what most likely would happen? (a) Nobody would notice the difference; (b) The SPCA would cite you for unnecessarily boring a defenseless animal; (c) Your dog would be promoted because he was overqualified for your job.

Finally, if you had the time to take this test while at work, it's a good bet you're non-essential.

Another category of people frequently referred to by the Reagan Administration is "undesirables." You might recall several years ago when a former Secretary of the Interior suggested that The Beach Boys might attract "undesirables" to a Washington concert. The Beach Boys, incidentally, are still going strong; the former Secretary now is a fur trapper on the upper east side of Manhattan.

About that same time officials at the University of Texas opposed a Willie Nelson concert on campus because he might attract "undesirables." Since I am one of Willie's biggest fans and attend his concerts at every opportunity, does that make me an undesirable?

Once again, I devised a test to help me and other confused Americans to discover if we are, in fact, undesirable.

Just answer truthfully the following questions.

1. When you hear Willie Nelson sing "Up Against the Wall, You Redneck Mother," does it make you want to (a) beat up a hippie; (b) drink beer from a quart jar; (c) take off your shirt; (d) call your mom?

2. Does The Beach Boys's "Little Surfer Girl" make you want to (a) take narcotics; (b) quit your job and go live at the beach; (c) insult a policeman; (d) ice down some Pepsi and build a sand castle?

3. If you were to attend a Beach Boys concert, which of the following would you likely wear? (a) half a bikini; (b) T-shirt with an obscene message; (c) it doesn't matter because you're going to take it off as soon as you get good and drunk anyway; (d) Gray Flannel cologne.

4. The last time you saw a Willie Nelson concert, which of the following best describes your behavior? (a) loud and obnoxious; (b) nasty and mean; (c) it took a dozen cops to get you into the paddy wagon; (d) you read the latest issue of the *New Yorker* between numbers.

5. Which of the following do you think would come in most handy at your next Beach Boys concert? (a) a hand grenade; (b) your coke dealer; (c) assorted birth control devices; (d) an uncrowded restroom.

6. Which of the the following would you be most likely to do after attending a Willie Nelson concert? (a) get tattooed; (b) burn a city; (c) rape and pillage; (d) watch "Nightline."

That's it; you can relax now. If you answered (d) to all of the questions, you most certainly are not an undesirable. If you did not answer any questions with (d), you're invited to a party at my house next Saturday night. Dress is not required.

***

It seems to me that a lot of old-fashioned jobs have been declared non-essential or else those who worked them have been deemed undesirable. For example, what has happened to movie ushers?

It used to be that you bought your ticket and some popcorn and a nice young man in a uniform would lead you with his flashlight to an available seat. You think that wasn't an essential job? You walk into a dark movie theater these days and there's no telling what can happen. You might sit next to a weirdo who makes sucking noises with his teeth. Or worse, you could sit on top of somebody. I walked into a dark theater the other day and was about to comment on how soft and comfortable the seats were when I realized I was sitting on a fat woman's lap.

"Get off me, you weirdo!" she screamed. I scrambled away and landed in another seat on top of a small child, who pinched me. I finally found an empty seat and made sucking noises with my teeth so that I'd be left alone.

And whatever happened to the old-timey car washes? Who declared them non-essential? Years ago people at a carwash would attack your auto with brushes and rags, and then they'd sweep and vacuum the inside of the car. Not even the Methodist Youth Fellowship car washes do that anymore. It's important to have the inside of your car cleaned occasionally. I did so recently and found two dollars in change, a missing tennis shoe and an old friend I thought had moved to Wyoming.

In today's automatic car washes, I feel like I'm trapped inside a giant washing machine like a pair of soiled pajamas about to be rinsed to death. If the inside gets cleaned, it's only because my windows leak and the jet sprays soak the interior.

And where, pray tell, are the old door-to-door salesmen?

Nobody comes to my house selling magazines or encyclopedias or vacuum cleaners anymore.

"Hi," the young man would say. "My name is Harvey and I'm working my way through college and I'm trying to win this contest...."

I don't remember ever buying anything from those salesmen, but at least it kept them off the streets and gave the dogs a little sport that was safer than chasing cars. What could be more essential?

In place of those important old jobs, we now have people doing the most absurd jobs imaginable. Just who are those people in the bathrooms everywhere I go? Do their wives know what they're doing?

I've been able to go to the bathroom without assistance since I was five or six, but lately every time I turn around I'm confronted by a smiling, grown man bearing towels. For the use of one, I'm expected to drop something spendable into his tip dish. I admit that I'm not very mechanically inclined, but I can usually figure out a towel dispenser or even one of those electric blowers without help.

There are, of course, ways to avoid restroom attendants. You can leave quickly without washing your hands, or you can simply hand the towel back to the attendant, smile and say thank you. If he still wants a tip, tell him to plant his corn early next year.

Not washing your hands can be unsanitary, however, or even unsociable. I was standing at a urinal beside two fellows at a Georgia-Auburn football game once. The Georgia fan, dressed in red and black from head to toe, finished his business, zipped his pants and headed for the door.

"Hey, Bulldog," shouted the Auburn fan, "don't they teach you guys at Georgia to wash after using the bathroom?"

"No," said the Bulldog fan, "they teach us not to piss on our hands."

I'm a dyed-in-the-wool Bulldog, and that's why I don't need anybody in the bathroom handing me a towel.

***

Being non-essential, undesirable or even outmoded is minor compared to the shame that can result from being associated with unmentionables. I'm not referring to disreputable characters, but rather to women's lingerie. Buying it, even for your wife, can be more embarrassing than urinals that splash.

In the first place, you never know who might see you.

"Guess who I saw in Willoughby's buying lingerie," says one busybody to another.

"Who?"

"Harvey Nelson, that's who."

"Never would have figured him for the kinky type."

"I feel sorry for his poor wife and children."

You can't walk into a lingerie department with a big grin on your face and say, "I'm not buying these for myself," because everyone will assume that you certainly are; neither can you walk in announcing, "These are for my wife, you know," because everyone will assume that they certainly are not. In such situations, I recommend a disguise, such as wearing dark glasses and speaking with a foreign accent.

"May I help you, sir?" the saleslady will ask.

"*Si,*" you answer. "I would like to look at your nightgown collection, *por favor.*"

The saleslady will have no idea she is selling good ol' Harvey Nelson something that the Catwoman on Bourbon Street wouldn't wear.

"I'll tell you something, Mildred," she'll say to her friend at lunch. "Those French are everything they say they are."

There are a couple more "don'ts" which I would recommend to any man who finds himself in this situation:

- Don't ask the saleslady to try on lingerie "since you're about the same size as my wife."
- Don't inquire about the possibility of purchasing the especially attractive mannequin in the black nightie. This could lead to an embarrassing arrest.
- Don't buy your wife or mistress colored underpants with the days of the week or the Clemson football schedule printed on them. For some reason, most women don't like them.

***

One of the greatest personal adversities I must endure, one that develops patience and grit in me, is the frequent abuse of my last name. A man's name is his birthright, and to have it besmudged is a terrible thing.

Only recently someone sent me an advertisement from the local newspaper in which a grocery store was offering "Fresh Chicken Grizzards" at seventy-nine cents a pound. The loving folks who sent me the ad included a notation: "Know the difference between a gizzard and a grizzard? One's just part of a chicken. The other is the whole thing."

To think that riffraff like that are allowed to use the public mails.

What obviously happened in the ad was that someone made a small error. By inserting an *r* in gizzards (which aren't worth seventy-nine cents a pound, no matter how you spell 'em), they libeled my proud name. It's not the first time, I must admit. People of little breeding often pronounce my name without the *r*. In restaurants they're always blurting out, "Gizzard, party of four. The Gizzard party, please." I save a lot of money on tips when that happens.

Other people simply mispronounce the name by making it rhyme with lizard. It does not. Notice the two z's, which means that Grizzard should be pronounced GrizZARD, which is French in origin and means "wild stallion."

There have been some very famous GrizZARDS down through the years who have made the name synonymous with noble deeds and glory. There was Pierre GrizZARD, a famous French sheetrocker who is given credit for many of the aesthetic qualities of the Palace of Versailles.

Then there was Jean Paul GrizZARD, the French trapper who single-handedly introduced several different strains of venereal disease to the North American Indians in the middle of the eighteenth century.

And, of course, there was my great, great, great grandfather, Brigadier General Beauregard GrizZARD of the Confederate Army, who successfully defended Miami Beach against the yankees during the Civil War, something no one else has been able to do since.

Yes, mine is a proud name, steeped in history and tradition. To have it abused in some grocery ad is a personal affront to me and my kin. And for anyone who is thinking about writing me a letter referring to that insidious joke about Mr. BuzZARD who's in the yard, and Mr. TurTELL who's at the well, and Mr. RabBIT, etc., don't bother. Mr. GrizZARD has already heard it a million times.

***

Of all the trials and tribulations I face, one of the most difficult certainly is Sunday nights. I hate Sunday nights. I think this hatred goes back to my childhood.

Sunday mornings when I was growing up were wonderful. We got up early with the radio blaring gospel music through the house, ate a wonderful breakfast of homemade biscuits and ham or bacon and then got ready for Sunday school.

I had only one white shirt and wore it every Sunday. My mother would wash it, hang it on the line to dry in the Southern sunshine and then iron it by hand. There is a special place in heaven for women who spent days of their lives ironing.

Sunday school itself was a social event. They put us kids in the basement and for an hour we sang songs like, "Do, Lord, oh do, Lord, oh do remember me, praise Jesus!" The sermon hour wasn't as easy. I watched the hands on my mother's watch crawl as I drew hills and birds on the title pages of the hymnals. I hope the Great Scorer doesn't hold that against me; I was only nine.

Then came that wonderful Sunday lunch, featuring fried chicken and rice and gravy and plump prizes from the garden. And, of course, more homemade biscuits. My mother always let me fork the first piece of white meat. I hope someday I love a child enough to let them do the same.

On Sunday afternoons my friends and I dammed creeks and watched trains or rode bikes or hit rocks with broom handles. Then as the sun got low in the sky, we'd gather on the front porch and start talking about supper. But it was never an organized meal — just leftover chicken and biscuits whenever you wanted it.

I think that's where my problem with Sunday evenings began. I was a grown man before I stopped pouting that my mother made me get my own supper on Sunday evenings. Inevitably there was no white meat left, only dark. And the only thing on television was Ed Sullivan with seals and jugglers. It was a depressing way to end what had been a wonderful day.

Sunday nights still feel the same way. They depress me. I take a lot of Sunday night meals alone these days, and many times I would be thankful for a cold piece of dark meat. There's still nothing much on TV, just an occasional "60 Minutes" piece on germ warfare that depresses me even more.

There's a distinct quiet on Sunday nights. A lonely quiet. I get sentimental. I call a few old friends, we talk, hang up and the quiet is even quieter. I try to work a lick but my mind won't have it. It's too late to call anyone else. I eat some tuna fish straight from the can.

I also pray on Sunday nights, whether I feel the need to or not. Give Monday a little shove, Lord. Do.

***

Finally, for those citizens of the world who endure it daily, who confront idiocy and walk away from it a better man or woman for having done so, I offer some questions and answers that don't necessarily match but are worthy of your consideration nonetheless.

THE QUESTIONS:

• Why is it that no matter which lane you're in on the expressway, the other one is always moving faster?

• Who ate the first oyster?

• Who said convenience stores are convenient? As compared to what?

• Why do service stations lock the bathroom door but leave the cash register unlocked?

• Is it really necessary for bowling balls to be that heavy?

• Do animals go to heaven when they die?

• Did Michael Jackson or Boy George every play any sports?

• What are chicken fingers that so many restaurants are

serving these days? I didn't know they had fingers.

- Why is it I have sixty channels on my television and still can't find anything worth watching?
- What makes popcorn pop?
- What happened to the power in modern automobiles? They're wonderful for funeral processions but no match for a strong headwind.
- Why aren't there any black hockey players?
- What are those little green things in fruitcake?

THE ANSWERS:

- Most of the things your mother told you are true. Disregard the part about eating liver to live longer; it's not worth it.
- Life isn't fair. That's what makes it so interesting.
- Money doesn't grow on trees, and if it did somebody else would own the orchard.
- If you have to shoot it, don't drink it.
- The greatest benefit of going to college is learning to get up in the morning without somebody making you.
- Going to church on Sunday morning will make you feel better no matter what you did on Saturday night.
- The best things in life aren't free. Just ask any poor person.
- Never buy anything from a man who jingles his change.
- If you can't flow, flee.

— 7 —

One Man's Hominy Is Another Man's Grit

Another War, Another Legacy

HE CAME WALKING ACROSS the lobby of the hotel. He was scraggly and his jeans were in need of a washing. He carried a paper sack.

He hit on the cashier first. She shooed him away with a flick of her wrist. A woman sat reading in a chair. He approached her. She looked up from her magazine only for a second and then went back to reading, ignoring his pitch. Then he saw me. If you panhandle long enough, I suppose it becomes easy to spot a soft touch.

"Sir," he began, "I wonder if I could speak with you for a moment?"

Most beggars are very polite. They can't afford not to be. He started to reach inside his sack.

"What are you selling?" I asked.

"I'm not selling anything. I'm just asking for a donation for this."

He handed me a lapel pin, a tiny American flag. The pin was attached to a card which read, "Show your colors and help a disabled veteran."

"You're a disabled veteran?" I asked the man.

"Got my card to prove it."

He pulled a tattered wallet out of his back pocket and drew out a small card. On the card, he or someone else had scrawled, "Charles Ienberg, Disabled Vet."

"World War II?" I continued.

"I ain't that old," he said. "Korea."

His breath smelled like stale beer. I thought of another man I knew who also fought in Korea and drank after he came back.

"Were you wounded?" I went on.

"See this fingernail?" he said, pointing the index finger on his right hand toward me. "They pulled the fingernail off and burned my hands with cigarettes."

"Who is 'they?'"

"North Koreans," he answered. "I jumped into South Korea and they got me and these three other fellows just like that. When we finally got out, they sent me to Seattle and I was in the hospital for a long time. I never have been the same since. They told me to quit drinking, but that ain't no easy thing to do."

"You're still drinking?"

"I'll be honest with you, sir," he said, "I need me a drink pretty bad right now. I ain't gonna lie to you. I'm hungry, but I need a drink a lot worse than I need something to eat."

I appreciated his honesty. "This is all you do, ask for donations for these pins?" I asked.

"Used to do some house painting, but I can't get no work no more. Guess I'm too old."

"How old are you?"

"Fifty-two."

He looked twenty years older than that. I pulled a five out of my pocket and handed it to him. He handed me a lapel pin. Then he thanked me for my donation, tucked his sack back under his arm and shuffled away to buy his pint.

I mentioned another lonely old soldier. I used to give him whiskey money, too. I buried him next to his mother.

Damn wars. Damn them all.

LIVING UP TO HIS CREED

When Chuck joined the Boy Scouts at age fourteen, the kids at school gave him a lot of grief about it. It wasn't exactly a groovy thing to do, joining the Scouts, especially at that mature age. "It was pretty rough on him," Chuck's scoutmaster told me.

I've forgotten all of the Boy Scout creed, but I remember that "kind" was in there somewhere. Chuck's scoutmaster recalled the time his troop was on a camping trip and Chuck found a dead mother squirrel with a lot of hungry babies in the nest. He took the babies home and fed them with an eyedropper until they were strong enough to tackle the forest on their own. That sort of thing gets out at school and a fellow might never live it down.

Chuck joined a scouting group called the Leadership Corps, where older kids teach intermediate Scouts special skills. Chuck's special skills were canoeing and swimming. So not long ago Second-Class Scout Chuck of the Leadership Corps took off on a trip to a nearby lake with some younger kids.

The group was joined by a couple of non-scouts, one a fifteen-year-old who turned out to be a lousy swimmer.

While everyone else was having fun, this kid was drowning in fourteen feet of water in the middle of the lake. The only person close to him was Chuck, who was forty yards away.

The scoutmaster told me the rest of the story:

"I was on the shore, and I saw the kid go under for the first time. Then I saw Chuck turn back toward the middle of the lake to go after him. I knew for sure I was about to see a double tragedy. I didn't see how Chuck could swim all the way out there and then save both of them.

"I jumped in my canoe, but I knew there was no way I'd get there in time. I just hoped we could pull them off the bottom of the lake and resuscitate them in time to save their lives.

"When Chuck got there, he was immediately pulled under by the struggling kid. A drowning swimmer has tremendous strength. Then I saw them come up again and Chuck had gotten away, but he wouldn't give up. He circled around the kid, talking to him, trying to calm him down. Then he went after him a second time. This time he managed to grab an arm and dragged the kid to shore. I don't know how, but he saved him."

Chuck was hesitant to talk about it, but I persisted until he told me what happened. "When we went under, I hit him in the stomach and he let go of me. I just couldn't let him drown."

"Chuck never had a lifesaving course," said the scoutmaster. "What he knew, he learned from reading the manual. He's dedicated to Scouting. He never thought of the danger. He never thought of his own safety."

I remember from the creed that Boy Scouts are also brave. Somebody ought to tell the kids at Chuck's school that you can't get much groovier than that.

DEARLY DEPARTED IS GLADLY DEPARTED

This is a true story. Believe me.

There was an automobile accident and a woman in her late thirties was killed. A local funeral home agreed to handle her service.

As friends and relatives were settling into their seats in the funeral home's chapel, a bearded man walked in and took a seat in the front row near the casket. He was dressed like Abe Lincoln, wearing a black suit and a tall black hat. The man, as it turned out, was the common-law husband of the deceased.

The service began and the minister decided to bring a full-length, no-holds-barred, fire-and-brimstone message to the mourners. As he bellowed forth, a man and a woman arrived in the chapel quarreling loudly. It was obvious to the funeral home personnel that they had been drinking.

"All I could do," said one employee, "was hope the preacher would quit soon and we could get out of the chapel before there was a ruckus."

Turns out the woman involved in the quarrel was the former common-law wife of Abe Lincoln, who was still sitting down front, and the man with whom she was at odds was her current husband.

The plot thickens.

The preacher had no intention of ending his service quickly. As he continued his message, the mourners became restless and several of them ventured into the hallway outside the chapel to stretch their legs or have a smoke. Meanwhile, the rowdy couple continued bickering in the back.

The preacher finally brought the service to an end and everyone adjourned to the cemetery for burial. As the preacher began his closing prayer at graveside, the funeral director thought to himself, "This thing is finally over. We're going to get out of here without an incident."

He was wrong. Suddenly, Abe Lincoln and his former wife's current husband squared off. They took off their coats and shouted at each other as calmer heads held them apart. Then Abe's former wife decided to get into the act and began to give him a piece of her mind. Before anybody could put out that brush fire, Abe decided he had had enough verbal abuse for one day and hauled off and decked his ex-wife.

"Cold-cocked her," was the description given by one witness.

Finally order was restored, the service was completed, everybody went home, the tent came down, the chairs were folded, the flowers were loaded on the truck and the deceased was buried.

A week later, however, a shooting was reported in town. When police arrived, Abe was firing shotgun blasts into a van occupied by his ex-wife's new husband. The fact that the van was borrowed didn't matter to Abe. He shot it anyway. Police finally subdued him and hauled him away.

All that's left to ponder is whether or not the dear departed will ever be able to rest in peace after all that's taken place since she left us.

DANCING THE NIGHT AWAY

You find these joints when life is a road trip. There in the Holiday Inn in Texarkana, or two blocks down to Shoney's and then hang a right in Rock Hill or Tupelo.

There's a bar and a bandstand, and they pour in off the main road when the darkness catches them tired and lonely. A man peddles industrial lubricants all day and his needs at night are simple: a drink, a dance and then you take your chance.

"Grover and the Groovers" are on the bandstand playing "Proud Mary," the anthem of the just-off-the-interstate roadhouse.

"Beer in a bottle," I shout to the waitress. Grover and the boys are waking the dead for miles around.

"All we got is draft," the waitress shouts back. She's early to middle forties. She outgrew her outfit when Ford was president. Somebody left her and there's the kids to feed and the "Z" she can't afford needs new tires. The story is always the same.

I can't believe they don't have beer in bottles.

"Don't want nobody to get knocked in the head," she explains.

I accept the draft. Grover asks for requests.

"Feelings!" yells a woman from across the room. Grover nods approval. I think, Oh no, not again.

The men are mostly married. Maybe a few clean one-owners, but mostly married. Their wives trust them. The women just came here to dance. They tell themselves that over and over.

Lots of beehives. The aroma of Spray 'n' Set is rampant.

I watch the phenomenon as Grover and the boys launch into "Feelings." The men, who have gathered securely at the bar as a covey, are flushed out toward the tables where the women are sitting, usually two by two.

The procedure is tough on women. Say nobody asks you to dance. Or say a man walks over and asks your friend ("If there was more light in here, he'd have asked me"). Or, worse, the one who asks is wearing a jacket with "Rockwell Power Tools" emblazoned across the back.

It's even tougher for men. I watch one of them — his shirt is a collector's item — give it a try. He takes a pull off his draft, hitches his pants and walks the long mile to where she is sitting. As he stands in front of her, his weight shifts from one foot to the other. She smiles, but her head and the beehive shake, "No."

Years ago I was sitting in such a bar with a friend. He tried. She said no, too.

"Toughest thing in the world is walking over and asking a woman to dance," I philosophized to him later.

"No, it isn't," he said. "It's walking back."

GUTS AT AN EARLY AGE

Larry has a little boy named Joe, who is six years old. When Larry talks about his son, the look in his eyes changes and the love shows through.

Little Joe is a man's kid. He's tough. Women often tell men that the problem with us is that we try to run through too many walls instead of just walking around, but Little Joe would run through a wall if his dad asked him to. There are just some things women don't understand.

Although he's only six, Little Joe joined a Midget League football team with some of the neighborhood kids. Larry told me what happened:

"Joe's the kind of kid most coaches hate to see coming," he said. "He doesn't have any talent yet, he's flat footed and slow as mud, and he weighs only about forty-five pounds. Other kids his age weigh fifty-five to sixty-five pounds. But he's tough."

The first week of practice, Joe had an accident on his bike and had six stitches taken in his leg. "But he never complained," said Larry. "He did all the running and drills. He never missed a practice. He enjoyed the drills that the other kids hated. But the thing he enjoyed most, and the thing he did best, was hitting."

"Hitting" is football talk for tackling, except it's more than that. It's tackling with unusual aggression.

"The coaches decided to put Joe in at middle linebacker. In the first game, although the other team ran us ragged, little Joe made ten individual tackles and assisted with five others. I told him how proud I was of him."

But after the team got trounced again and again, the coaches finally decided that part of the problem was little Joe — he was just too small — so they benched him.

"I was at practice when he came off the field. He tried to tell me what had happened through his sobs. I don't think the coaches knew how hard he had worked. They never knew about his injury, either. It broke the kid's heart, and mine, too, to see him play above his ability and stand and fight when other kids might have given up," said Larry.

"I would tell him that his heart will carry him farther than his legs, that you can't measure desire, that the fastest horse doesn't always win the race, that if he fights hard enough and long enough his reward will come . . . but in the form of a broken heart?"

I am not a father and by no means an expert, but what I would do is forget the poetic approach. I'd turn in his pads and helmet, tell him I love him and send him out in the back yard to play in the dirt, which is what a six-year-old, bless his little heart, should be doing with his spare time in the first place.

A GAMBLER ON A ROLL

I wandered into a local bar and sat next to a man who was

nursing a drink. There were two quarters sitting by his glass.

"Want to match for a drink?" he asked.

A perfect stranger wants to play a small game of chance. I was hesitant.

"I just want to see if I'm still hot. You see, I'm on an incredible roll. I've just gotten off a plane from the Bahamas where I was up over $20,000 playing blackjack. I want to see if my luck is still holding," he explained.

I told him I'd be glad to buy him a drink if he'd just tell me how to win twenty grand at blackjack. The only time I get lucky playing that game is when I get sleepy and have to go to bed.

"I just sat down at the table at six last Friday afternoon," he began. "I started off with $200. When I woke up Saturday morning, I was up $20,000. The only thing I did was not take a hit if the dealer had six or less showing. It was ten percent knowledge and ninety percent luck.

"On Saturday morning, I realized if I continued playing, I might lose all I had won, so I decided to buy something while I still had some money. I got a security guard from the hotel to go with me, and I went to downtown Nassau and bought a Presidential Rolex watch. Cost me six thousand," he continued.

"I started playing again at six Saturday night. In the first twenty minutes, I was up another $11,000. But by ten I had cooled off and was down to only $12,000, so I decided to take the money and run. The hotel paid for my room, gave me free meals with Dom Perignon and drove me to the airport in their limo."

Counting the $12,000 in cash and the six in a Rolex, he walked away an $18,000 winner.

"It was the most incredible thing that's ever happened to

me. Now, let's match for a drink."

What the heck. We both flipped.

"Same," he said. And they were.

"Once more?" he asked.

I agreed and we flipped again. He won again.

"One more time?"

"I'm already down two drinks," I said, "but let's just go to see how long this streak can last."

We flipped. He called same. I had heads. He had tails.

"Maybe the streak is finally over," I said.

"Maybe," he answered, and I thought I detected a sigh of relief.

REACHING OUT A HELPING HAND

I received a letter in the mail recently which deserves to be shared.

"I don't have much education," began the writer, "but I've got something inside me I want to get out. I thought maybe you could help me."

Not much background is necessary. The man works in a K-Mart. His wife is a nurse. He moved out of the city a few years ago so he could put some cows in a pasture and raise his kids, four of them, on a farm.

"Here I sit, pulling on a longneck beer. I'm not trying to get drunk, just trying to understand. Ten days ago my wife, myself and our four-year-old daughter visited Atlanta to see a doctor that had been recommended to us. The problem was that my little girl has crossing of her eyes. Our oldest daughter had the same problem when she was five or six, so we figured this one had the same thing.

"The first doctor referred us to another and then he sent us to another and after four doctors, my little girl was finally admitted to the hospital. Just to make sure, they said. Just a few tests. The next day we waited. We waited all day. The tests would come the next day, they said. Finally she was taken down for a brain scan. The machine was down so we waited some more.

"About six on the second day, one of the doctors came and told us that she had a tumor at the base of her brain stem. Because of its location, it is inoperable. The tumor affects her motor functions. Before she was a vivacious little blonde, looking forward to life. Now she drools and stumbles and slurs her speech. She's undergoing radiation therapy, but her prognosis is not good. My only hope is to make these last few months as enjoyable for her as possible.

"But this is not really what I wanted to say to you. I wanted to get across how I feel about those who have helped this family since this tragedy struck. We moved here from the city, and I didn't know the local people had accepted us. But I have never seen such an outpouring of love.

"I didn't know things like this went on anymore. I didn't know there were so many people who still care and love their neighbors. They have brought food. They have helped my wife. They have even contributed money.

"I wish I had the talent of a writer to really get across what is in my heart. I am so moved by how much love and kindness others have shown me, my wife and my little girl that I just want to share it with somebody else. I'm not asking for handouts, but if you see fit to use any of this letter, just tell your readers to look around them. They probably have friends they never knew they had before, friends just waiting for the chance to help them.

"And one other thing. Tell them to love their kids. One day they might not have them anymore. Thanks."

No. Thank you.

— 8 —

What's the Penalty For An Illegal Upchuck?

SPORTS HAS ALWAYS BEEN a great proving ground of character. Kids grow up hearing clichés about the values of sports:

- When the going gets tough, the tough get going.
- Quitters are always losers and losers are always quitters.
- It's not whether you win or lose but how you play the game.
- Show me a good loser and I'll show you a frequent loser.
- It ain't over till it's over.

One of the first sports a kid is exposed to is fishing, since dad is always dragging a son or daughter along to carry the tackle box. As a result of my childhood memories of fishing from the banks of various lakes and rivers, I have always maintained my affection for wetting a line.

Not long ago I was standing along the bank of a creek that runs through one of the golf courses of the magnificent Greenbriar Hotel in White Sulphur Springs, West Virginia. I was there because a man at the pro shop assured me I could catch a huge rainbow trout from that bank. I have never caught a rainbow trout — huge or otherwise. I have watched those television fishing shows where somebody is always landing a big trout, and I've read the magazine articles about techniques, but the closest I've ever been to landing one is in the fish department of the Kroger.

The man at the golf shop rented me a spinning rod and some sort of lure that looked like a roach dressed up for a night out at the disco. "This drives 'em crazy," said the man, who also explained that I could keep any four fish I caught and that the cooks up at the hotel would fillet them for me and serve them for my lunch.

Imagine the thrill: out in the wilds of West Virginia, casting for rainbow trout, and later I would dine on my own tasty catch. Eat your heart out, Gaddabout Gaddis.

The water was so clear that I could actually see the fish swimming around in the creek. They were beautiful and just the right size for eating. I made my first cast and got ready for the tug. Nothing. I cast again. Still nothing. As I was reeling in for my third cast, a trout almost had a head-on collision with my lure but managed to swerve out of the way at the last minute.

About that time, a small boy appeared and began fishing next to me.

"Toss it right in there, Scottie," said the kid's father.

Scottie was dressed in official trout fisherman's garb: floppy hat with flies stuck in it, fishing jacket with lots of pockets and a creel over his shoulder. A creel is what trout fishermen put their fish in. The guy at the pro shop had given me a plastic laundry bag for my catch. I didn't care for Scottie the minute I saw him.

Scottie cast where his dad had advised and almost immediately yelled, "Look, Dad! I've got one." The little brat reeled in a gorgeous rainbow. I reeled in and moved down the bank a little farther.

"Dad," I heard the kid say, "I've got another one!"

"Good going, Scottie," his dad answered.

Get out of my life, Scottie, I thought to myself.

I never did catch a rainbow trout that day. In fact, I didn't catch any fish that day. Not only that, I hung my line in an overhanging tree and lost that funny looking roach lure.

"Look, Dad," said Scottie. "That man has caught a tree." Dad and Scottie had a big laugh. I reeled in my line and started to head back for the pro shop with homicide on my mind.

"Would you like to have these fish Scottie caught?" the dad asked as I was leaving. "We still haven't eaten the ones we caught yesterday."

"No thanks. I hate fish," I said.

Of course, by the time I arrived back at the office, my catch was considerable and never had I enjoyed a finer meal than those rainbows I had pulled from the creek. That's another thing kids learn early about fishing — lying is part of the sport. Consider these standard examples:

QUESTION: So, how were they bitin'?
ANSWER: Had to stand behind a tree to bait our hooks.
TRUTH: The mosquitoes didn't even bother us.

QUESTION: Did you have a guide?
ANSWER: One of the best.
TRUTH: Luckily, the day we got hopelessly lost my five-

year-old kid remembered the way back to the dock. I found the bar on my own.

QUESTION: Anybody get sunburned?
ANSWER: Are you kidding me?
TRUTH: I was out of intensive care in no time.

QUESTION: How many did you catch?
ANSWER: Filled up two ice chests.
TRUTH: With beer. The fish fit in my shirt pocket.

QUESTION: What were you fishing for?
ANSWER: Trophy bass.
TRUTH: I'd have been happy with a small frog.

QUESTION: See any snakes?
ANSWER: Big moccasin fell off a tree limb into my boat, but I killed it with the paddle.
TRUTH: A Louisiana pink worm crawled out of the bait box. I made the kid put it back.

QUESTION: So what did you catch?
ANSWER: Largemouths, mostly.
TRUTH: One carp and a turtle.

QUESTION: What did you catch them on?
ANSWER: Top-water plugs.
TRUTH: The carp had a heart attack and floated to the top of the water. My kid caught the turtle and took it home for a pet.

QUESTION: Can't wait to get out there and get at 'em again, huh?
ANSWER: Next chance I get.
TRUTH: I traded my tackle box for two six-packs.

***

When I got older and more sophisticated, my friends urged me to join them in a sport more appropriate for that time in our lives — golf. I later figured out that the people who encouraged me to play golf disliked me very much. It has to be the most frustrating game ever invented.

Because of my history of heart problems, I try not to play more than once a year. In that length of time I usually forget how awful it was the last time and am willing to take another swing.

Golf, I'm convinced, was conceived by real estate developers so they would have an excuse for ruining perfectly good forests and pastures. After the golf courses are completed, these scoundrels further ravage the countryside by building condominiums along the fairways. Rich Republican retirees move into the condos and become even stuffier than they were before.

In fact, stuffiness is probably the no. 1 characteristic of golf. Have you ever listened to the announcers broadcasting the Masters golf tournament? They sound like they're doing the play-by-play for a state funeral. Golf would be more fun if somebody would belch occasionally.

My most recent annual swing at golf came in Myrtle Beach, South Carolina. A companion and I paid a week's salary for green fees, rental clubs, an electric cart and a half-dozen orange golf balls (I could have sworn they were white the last time I played, but maybe that was tennis).

On the first tee my playing partner and I made a small wager, another integral part of the game, and then proceeded to tee off. Unfortunately, my first drive sliced into the backyard of somebody's condominium where a Tupperware party was in progress. I got a free container suitable for serving congealed salads and a free drop off the coffee table.

My second shot, a three wood, caught a tree limb and bounced back toward the Tupperware party, coming to rest on a plate of cheese and crackers the ladies were munching with their white wine. This time I bought six cups and a casserole container to pay for the damages and pitched back into the fairway. I took a twelve on the first hole. My companion went one-up with an eleven.

We both went into the water on the second hole — the water in a swimming pool located behind somebody else's condominium where a woman sat reading a copy of *Cosmopolitan*. My companion removed his tennis shorts and waded into the pool to retrieve our errant shots. The woman went inside and fetched her husband, a very large man, who threatened to call the authorities if we weren't off his property in thirty seconds.

In our haste to leave, we drove the cart over one of the pool chairs, which wouldn't have been all that bad had it not been the one the woman was sitting in at the time. Luckily, the poor woman was unhurt, but her *Cosmo* got caught under one of the cart wheels and we scattered a series on unsightly liver spots for several hundred yards.

I finally shot a sixty-six on the front nine. My companion had a sixty-two and took me for a dollar. We intended to play the back nine, too, but my friend had decided to take his shirt off and catch a few rays. As we made the turn, the head pro requested that we leave the course immediately. We might have resisted, but he made the request while drawing back a four-iron.

Undaunted, we drove to the strip on Myrtle Beach and got in a quick eighteen holes at Jungle Jim's Carpet Golf, where they don't care if you take off your shirt just as long as you don't steal the scoring pencils.

Relieved to get away from the stuffiness of the regular

links, I got my dollar back on the last hole by sinking a long putt that rolled into the monkey's mouth, out through his tail, then under the giraffe's legs, dropping squarely into the cup.

Actually, golf would be a lot more fun if the rules were a little more flexible. For example, I have come up with my own rules guaranteed to add enjoyment to your round:

• THE MILLIGAN RULE — Most golfers know what a mulligan is. That's when you get to hit a second shot off the first tee because your first shot went into the next county. The "milligan" takes that a step further. If you don't like your first shot off any tee, hit another one. If that shot is lousy, too, then hit a "McMilligan," which is a third shot. If that shot is also poor, drive the cart out into the middle of the fairway about 250 yards and drop your ball there. That's called a "Grover McMilligan," named for a famous card cheat who died in a lynching accident.

• MOVING THE BALL IN THE ROUGH — Under my rules, you may not only move your ball in the rough, you also may ignore rough altogether and put your ball back in the fairway ten yards closer to the hole for each form of reptilia spotted while you were in the weeds looking for your ball. A snake and two turtles can make a long hole play much shorter.

• LOST BALL RULE — Let's say you hit your ball into the water and it can't be retrieved. What you do is subtract two strokes from your eventual score on the hole. You deserve it. You just paid three bucks for a brand-new golf ball, and now it sleeps with the fishes.

• SAND RULE — Whose idea was it to put sand on a golf course in the first place? When your ball goes into the sand, remove it as quickly as possible to a nice flat place on the green. That's called a "sandie" in golfing lingo.

• TREE RULE — If you were aiming at a tree and hit it, then you must play the ball as it lies. However, if you were aiming down the middle of the fairway and hit a tree, don't let it ruin your round. Move the ball fifty yards closer to the green for each variety of pine tree you can name.

• TWO-PUTT RULE — If you still aren't in the hole after two putts, pick up your ball and place it in the cup. If your opponent complains, put his head in the hole.

• BEER RULE — At the end of your round, count up the total number of beers you drank during your round and subtract that number from your score. If you had been sober, that's probably what you would have shot in the first place.

***

Golf is not the only game that could benefit from a few adjustments in the rules. Professional tennis, basketball and baseball also could be made more exciting.

In tennis, for example, one of the biggest problems today is players berating the officials. Every time they disagree with a call, they question some linesperson's parentage.

I propose arming each linesperson and the umpire with a big stick, just the kind you would take along on a walk in the woods in case you had to beat a snake. Let's say John McEnroe, one of the most frequent offenders, is playing. He serves, rushes to the net, hits a backhand volley which his opponent returns down the line. The linesperson signals that the ball is in.

"What?" screams McEnroe, turning red in the face. He stomps the ground, breaks his racquet and pulls his hair. Then he calls the linesperson a dirty, rotten so-and-so with everybody in attendance listening. At that point, the linesperson gets out of his or her chair, walks over to McEnroe and bashes him over the head with the stick. A couple of times having a tune played on his noggin will improve his behavior immensely and thereby make the game more enjoyable for the rest of us.

My friend and step-brother Ludlow Porch, a great philosopher, came up with a similar plan to bring baseball more in line with popular tastes.

"Americans love rough contact sports," Ludlow explained, "like football and boxing and hockey and pool."

Pool is a rough contact sport?

"Not the game itself," he said, "but the knife fight that breaks out every night in any decent pool hall certainly is."

So Ludlow has a plan to put more rough stuff into baseball.

"You add two new players. One plays behind the shortstop. That's your left-mugger. Another plays behind second base, and he's your right-mugger. Now, say the batter hits the ball to the third baseman. He throws it to the right-mugger. The runner is not allowed to stop on a base, so he is chased by the right-mugger, who, in order to get the runner out, must knock him to the ground and hit him square in the mouth with the ball and hold him down long enough for the umpire to count to three."

But isn't that terribly unfair to the baserunner, not to mention dangerous?

"There is one other thing," Ludlow said. "The guy who hits the ball gets to carry something with him for protection when he meets a mugger on the basepaths."

And what is that?

"His bat."

The biggest problem with basketball is that all the players have outgrown the game. Guards used to be quick little fellows who could dribble through a church picnic without getting potato salad on the ball. They shot two-handed set shots from the cheap seats and married squatty home-ec majors, and they produced more guards and squatty home-ec majors.

Today guards are so tall they don't even need a ladder to get arrested for peeping into the third floor of the girls' dorm to see if the home-ec majors really have thighs as big as their own.

The big man in basketball used to be any awkward boy over six feet tall who didn't mind being called "Stretch." Today, the big men are what former coach Al McGuire calls "aircraft carriers." You could land on them. They marry girls nobody used to want to dance with and together they produce more "aircraft carriers."

What I propose is legislation to prohibit anyone over six-five from marrying anyone over five-six. That way we won't have to ruin the game for future generations by raising the basket (or, if you're a Democrat, by lowering the floor).

A second way to improve basketball is to do away with the clock. Without a doubt, the "stall," designed to run time off the clock, is the worst thing ever introduced to basketball. It's about as exciting as watching cabbage boil. The rule should be that the first team to score one hundred points wins the game. Clean and simple. And the wives of the losing team have to provide punch and cookies following the game.

***

After my bad experiences with golf, I gave up participatory sports and became a professional spectator. I started with one of the loveliest spectacles of all — the Kentucky Derby.

I reached Louisville, Kentucky, site of "The Derby," after

sixteen hours on an Amtrak train. I could have made it faster in a wheelbarrow but probably wouldn't have had nearly as much fun. The club cars are pretty small in most wheelbarrows. Upon my arrival, my hosts informed me that we did not actually have seats at Churchill Downs. Instead, we were going to leave at six A.M. to attempt to fight off fifty thousand others for a spot in the infield to watch a five o'clock race.

"Will we be able to see any of the Derby from that vantage point?" I asked.

"If you actually wanted to see the race," my host said, "what are you doing in Louisville? You could have stayed home and watched it on television."

So I trekked out to the track at sunrise the next morning and pretended to have a good time until the preliminary races started sometime after lunch. That's when I broke away from my group to try out the new system I had devised for betting and winning on the horses.

My plan was to bet on horses with names that began with an *l* or an *m* or a *g*, which are my initials. That meant that I bet on Lollipop, Milky Way and Gone for Good.

Lollipop couldn't have won on six legs. Milky Way melted in the stretch and Gone for Good is exactly what happened to the two bucks I bet on him.

In the next race I bet on a horse named Liar's Poker. If anybody sees Liar's Poker, tell him to find another line of work. Later I heard two guys talking about a horse that was supposed to be a good mudder. Mudder starts with an *m*, so I bet two dollars on him. Unfortunately, it was a clear day at Churchill Downs and the stupid horse came in last — in the next race.

In desperation I went down next to the track and leaned on the rail, hoping to pick up some tips that way. One of the guys who rides the horses that accompany the thoroughbreds to the gate rode past.

"Hey, fellow, got any good tips today?" I asked him.

"Yeah," he said, "we just painted that rail."

Now I hate horses, too.

***

I finally decided that the best sport for me was good ol' American football. Nothing frilly, no condominiums along the sidelines, just cold beer and fried chicken on a tailgate before the game.

I started with college football and was having a great time until I became disillusioned. I discovered quite by accident that some college football teams were actually cheating. Obviously they never heard another of those childhood clichés: Cheaters never win.

What happened was that this kid in my hometown was being recruited by the University of Florida, a school which has been caught more than once with its hand in the proverbial cookie jar. He received a letter from the head coach and brought it over to Bogator Green's mechanic and body shop for us to see. Here's what the letter said:

"Dear Prospective Florida Football Recruit:

"Soon you will be deciding where you will be playing college football for the next four years. As head coach at the University of Florida, I thought you might like to know what to expect when you visit with our recruiters and when you visit here on the Florida campus.

"Our recruiters are very nice people and they are very generous. Let's say, for instance, that you really like the new Corvette that one of our recruiters drives when he visits your home. You might try asking if he would mind if you took the car for a spin. The recruiter might surprise you by saying, 'I really don't need a car like this, so why don't you borrow it?'

"This, of course, would not mean the coach was actually giving you the car, which is against NCAA regulations; it would mean he was lending it to you. Simply remember to leave the keys in the car following your final year of eligibility.

"Since NCAA regulations allow only one official visit to each campus, we want your stay on the Florida campus to be a memorable one. Make certain you do not miss the Florida School of Forestry's famous 'money tree.' On the tree you will find bills of various denominations that always seem to blossom during recruiting season. The bigger bills, incidentally, are toward the top for all you blue-chippers who excel in the vertical leap.

"You may also be asking yourself, If I sign with Florida, how many tickets will I get? We will provide enough tickets so your parents and relatives will be able to see you play. Let's say you received twenty tickets per game. You give your parents one each and your sister and her boyfriend one each. That leaves sixteen tickets. What should you do with them? Why not sell your remaining tickets to a wealthy alumnus? It is against NCAA rules to sell the tickets for more than the price marked on the ticket, but if a wealthy alumnus happens to drop a couple of hundreds out of his pocket during the transaction and you happen to find them after he walks away, is that your fault?

"Some of you might also want to earn money in the off-season. At Florida we offer a complete job placement plan for our student athletes. For example, you might be in charge of making certain the house plants in the head coach's office always have plenty of water. This will teach you how to handle responsibility, as well as earn off-season bucks. This job, incidentally, is currently paying $400 per week.

"You may also want to meet some of the top Florida alumni and boosters. We could arrange for you to meet George Steinbrenner, the wealthy owner of the New York Yankees, at his Bay Harbor Inn in Tampa. If there should be a mix-up at the reservations desk and you are not charged for your three-bedroom suite, leave quietly by the side door so as not to embarrass anyone..

"You may want to know, too, If I sign with Florida, will I be playing for winning teams? We are installing a new system at Florida that should guarantee us many wins. I can't go into details, but it was designed by a loyal Florida alumnus currently working with the CIA.

"Finally, you may be wondering if you are academically qualified for a football scholarship to Florida. Here's a test: How many teams are in the Big Ten? If your answer was ten, no sweat. If it wasn't, we'll think of something.

"See you soon, and go Gators!"

***

I also have a problem with professional football — I can't

understand the terminology that the announcers use. After many Sunday afternoons in front of the tube with diction-ary and notepad at hand, I have come up with a guide to modern football lingo which I hope will help others:

• HANG TIME — What time they will be hanging this or that coach for failing to win his division. Sometimes head coaches are hung in effigy. This year they probably will be hung in Denver and New Orleans as well.

• NICKEL BACK — Fifth-round draft choice out of Arkansas State whose agent got him a $150,000-per-year, no-cut contract and he isn't worth a nickel.

• "HI, MOM!" — The most intelligent statement an NFL wide receiver can think of on the spur of the moment when the television camera catches him picking his nose after a long touchdown reception.

• ERIC HIPPLE — What gets in a player's bellybutton after he crawls around on artificial turf for a couple of hours.

• AHMAD RASHAD — Disease a player can get between his toes if he doesn't change his socks often enough.

• TWO-MINUTE WARNING — When a player is caught in a compromising position with a teammate's wife in the teammate's house and the teammate pulls into the drive-way unexpectedly. The player has approximately two min-utes to get dressed and sneak out the back door before his teammate catches him and breaks his face.

• ILLEGAL CHUCK — Illegally impeding the progress of a receiver named Chuck who is more than five yards down the field.

• ILLEGAL UPCHUCK — Throwing up on the playing surface. Five yard penalty if the surface is grass, fifteen if it is artificial turf.

• ATTACKING UNDER THE COVERAGE — How to

make friends with a Dallas Cowboys cheerleader.

● BUMP AND RUN — What to do in case you smash into a Rolls in the parking lot before the game in your 1973 Plymouth Fury.

● 3-4 — How many beers a Pittsburgh Steelers fan has before breakfast on the day of a big game.

● HOWARD COSELL — The end of the horse you never saw when "Mr. Ed" was still on television.

For anyone who doesn't know, the preceding terms apply to American football, not rugby which the English call football and not to that half-breed which the Canadians mistakenly call football.

Several years ago when the National Football League went on strike, American television stations broadcast several Canadian football games to try to satisfy the public's appetite, but I don't think it worked. I was standing in Sonny Bryan's barbecue joint in Dallas, a hotbed of football if ever there was one, when two ol' boys came in talking about a Canadian football game they had seen on TV.

"Frank," the first one said to his buddy, "I believe that was the worst thing I ever saw. I'd just as soon watch a soccer game from Afghanistan."

"Earl," said the other, "I don't think they play soccer in Afghanistan."

"Well, I'd just as soon watch it anyway. When I turned on my set the score in that football game was 14-1. I'm talking about *one*, Frank. How in the hell can you score just one point in a football game?"

"I think it has something to do with not being able to run a punt out of the end zone," said Frank.

"That's another thing," said Earl. "Them end zones are big enough to graze a hundred head of cattle in. And the dad-blame field is 110 yards long. Didn't they read the rule book when they started playing football in Canada?"

"Well, at least it was football," said Frank.

"Wasn't no such a thing," answered Earl. "Listen to me. I been to ever' Cowboys game since we got us a team. I seen Meredith. I seen Staubach. I seen 'em all. And I ain't interested in watching no bunch of castoffs who couldn't play for TCU run around on no oversized football field in some foreign country where all they got is snow and gooses."

"You mean snow and geese," said Frank.

"Them too," said Earl. "And I'll tell you something else. They got strange names for their teams up there. They got a team called the Argonauts. What do you reckon an Argonaut is?"

"I think it's some kind of moose," said Frank. "They got lots of mooses in Canada."

"Mooses?" asked Earl.

"Mooses," answered Frank.

"Let me ask you something, Frank," said Earl. "If gooses is geese, then how come mooses ain't meese?"

"Dang if I know," said Frank. "I don't speak a word of Canadian."

My sentiments, exactly.

— 9 —

Fill 'er Up?
Regular or Harold?

IT'S TOUGH BEING a male chauvinist these days. Talk about something that will build character and develop grit. I can't even joke about it for fear that some woman will do severe harm to my person (body would be a sexist term in that context). The only reason more men aren't being beaten up by women these days is that no matter how far they've come in other areas, most women still can't run very fast and they'll take a double-pump fake every time.

The fact of the matter is that I don't have many chauvinistic attitudes myself, but since some of my friends do, I decided to help them by starting a Male Chauvinist Hotline. Through my newspaper column, I answered questions regarding men's and women's rights. Following are a few of the more helpful selections:

QUESTION: What makes you think you're such an expert on women?

ANSWER: I have been married three times, and I was deeply involved with several other women who auditioned for the part.

QUESTION: Isn't it true that women are more easily frightened than men?
ANSWER: Just because they always go to the restroom in pairs? Of course not.

QUESTION: I work in a steel mill. My foreman says he is going to have to hire some broads. Do I have to put up with that?
ANSWER: Yes, but look on the bright side. Maybe one of your female co-workers will let you have one of her stuffed celery stalks for lunch one day.

QUESTION: My girlfriend is always telling me what great athletes women make. I don't believe that because I still haven't seen a woman who can slam dunk a basketball. How can I overcome such a sexist feeling?
ANSWER: Next time you want your dinner cooked, call Julius Erving.

QUESTION: My wife says I never do anything to make her feel younger. Her birthday is next week. What should I give her?
ANSWER: A six-pack of Oil of Olay.

QUESTION: How many women does it take to replace a lightbulb?
ANSWER: Three. That's one to call her mother for advice on the subject, one to mix the strawberry daiquiris, and one to light the candles when mother doesn't answer.

Despite my vast knowledge of feminine ways, I confess

I've had my share of problems with them, too. I was once married to a young woman who became angry at me for missing a dinner party she was giving for her parents. I missed the dinner because I was playing tennis and the match went three sets and then we had to drink a beer.

The next morning I awoke to find my wife had taken one of the Ginsu knives I had bought for her birthday and cut the strings out of my tennis rackets. I learned my lesson well: I never bought her any more sharp instruments for her birthday.

But that incident was nothing compared to what happened to some of my friends. One fellow's girlfriend discovered he was fooling around with somebody else, so she slipped into his apartment while he was working, took a jar of honey from the refrigerator and poured it all over the kitchen floor. Then she opened the kitchen door and invited in every ant within three counties.

My friend Rigsby probably got it worse than anybody. When his first wife caught him messing around, she went into his closet and cut the ends off all of his ties and one leg off of each pair of pants.

"My second wife topped that," explained Rigsby. "She took all my suits and loaded them into the trash compactor. Take my word for it, a trash compactor adds new meaning to the word wrinkle. Then my third wife scored the coup de grâce. I had a convertible that I kept parked in the garage. She got so mad at me one day that she called a concrete company and had them fill my convertible with cement."

"Well," I said, "it looks like you're doing all right. You must have gotten a sympathetic jury for your divorce case."

"Sympathetic?" said Rigsby. "They came back in after a couple of hours of deliberations and asked the judge for more instruction."

"What could they want after two hours?"

"They wanted to know if they could give the death penalty in an alimony case."

I get pretty much the same treatment from my secretary, the lovely Miss Wanda Fribish. Behind every successful man, one can usually find a pleasant, agreeable, supportive secretary. Behind a failure like myself, however, you take what you can get, which is how I came to hire Miss Fribish.

To keep her from pouring glue over the keys of my typewriter or pulling some such feminist prank, I usually buy her off each Christmas by taking her to lunch at the place of her choice. Last year she chose El Flasho's Burrito Barn, famous for its all-you-can-drink frozen margarita special.

We settled in at a table in El Flasho's and ordered our first round of margaritas. After the third round, Miss Fribish started fidgeting and I could tell she had something on her mind. On the fourth margarita, it spewed forth.

"Come here, Four Eyes," she said, wiping the salt off her mustache and grasping me in a hammerlock, a technique she learned in the Militant Feminist Karate, Kung Fu and Secretarial School, of which she is a proud graduate. "There's a few things I want to get straight with you, you little pencil-necked geek."

"Please continue," I gasped, offering myself, as usual, as the open-minded, willing-to-listen employer.

"I'm sick of working for you," she went on. "The pay's lousy, the hours are miserable, and I have to talk to your creepy friends on the phone. Besides that, I'm tired of your constant sexual harassment."

I normally wouldn't argue with a person holding me in a hammerlock, but I asked Miss Fribish what she was referring to.

"You know what I'm talking about, you lecherous leech," she patiently explained. "Every time I walk into your office, I can feel your eyes undressing me."

I assured Miss Fribish that when I stared at her, it had nothing to do with any sexual intentions or desires. I tried to explain that she often startles me with her attire, like the time she came to work wearing a pair of steel-toed combat boots and a camouflage outfit.

"You know perfectly well why I wore that," she said. "Some of the sisters and I were launching a commando raid on an all-male Rotary Club luncheon, and I didn't want to have to go home and change."

After Miss Fribish reminded me, I remembered the incident well. When the cops arrived, they found her with a Rotarian under each arm, ramming their heads together in time to "Camptown Races," which the organization's piano player was performing to open the meeting.

"One more 'doo-da,'" said the investigating officer, "and the two victims might have suffered permanent brain damage."

Recalling the plight of those two Rotarians, I decided it was an opportune time to give Miss Fribish the small raise I had been considering, and I promised never to look at her with anything but business on my mind.

Of course, Miss Fribish's commando unit finally got what they wanted a couple of years ago when the Supreme Court ruled that the Jaycees and other such groups could not exclude women from their memberships.

Shortly afterwards, I received a call from my old friend Gilbert, who had a novel idea. "Listen to this," he said excitedly. "I'm going to start a club that will be for men only."

"Listen, Gilbert," I said, "you obviously haven't been keeping up with the news. You can't exclude women from clubs anymore."

"No," he argued, "you don't understand. I'm not going to exclude them. I'm just going to start a club that they won't want to belong to. We'll do only the things they don't like. We won't say we're for men only, but as soon as any woman joins she'll be so disgusted that she'll quit. It's a great plan!"

I asked what sort of disgusting and appalling things the members of Gilbert's club would do.

"Just the usual stuff we used to do in the old days," he said. "First of all, we're not going to serve white wine in the bar. That'll cut out two-thirds of the women who might want to be members. Then we're going to drink a lot of beer and belch and fart whenever we feel like it, and we're going to smoke big cigars and blow smoke all over the room. Women hate cigar smoke. And finally, we'll tell all the sexist jokes we used to, like the one about why God created women in the first place."

I asked Gilbert what he intended to name his new club, but he didn't get to tell me.

"I don't have time to talk anymore right now. My wife is having the girls over for a Tupperware party, and if I don't have this house cleaned up by six, she'll kill me."

Admission to previously all-men's organizations was just one of many equal opportunity advancements women have made in recent years. In fact, I can't think of any place between here and outer space where they're not.

Just the other day I stopped into a service station and a woman attendant came out. She seemed quite capable of handling her job and opened with the standard dialogue, except for a small change.

"Fill him up?" she asked.

"Please," I said.

"Regular or Harold?"

"Harold? What happened to Ethyl?"

"She's running for Congress."

I was watching television and a female evangelist came on asking for donations. "This broadcast is run on faith alone," she said. "Send us what you can, we'll take a check or money order, and the Lord will bless you. She told me so Herself."

Next day I walked into a hardware store and there was a woman behind the counter.

"I'd like a garden hose," I said.

"What shade?" she asked.

"I'm not certain," I replied, somewhat taken aback.

"So what color is your lawn?" she continued.

"Green."

"Then I'd suggest something in a soft pastel," she said, "either a melon or perhaps this delightful pink."

I also asked if she knew where I could pick up a used winch.

"Try the bus station about midnight," she replied.

***

One of the few remaining places where men can still be left alone with other men is the old-fashioned barber shop. These are the places that kept their names — the Sportsman Barber Shop, or Haynie's Barber Shop — when others became "styling salons." A man can be as sexist as he wants in such a setting.

"Heard about the two young bulls that met at the fence?" asked my barber, who always has an off-color joke. "One bull says it's great where he is. Plenty of grass to graze on, lots of shade trees around and plenty of heifers to keep him company. He says it's just like heaven on his side of the fence, and he asks the other young bull what it's like on his side.

"The other bull says it's awful. There's not much grass, no trees to stand under when it gets hot and there aren't any heifers at all. He says the only company he's got is an old washed-up steer and all he wants to do is talk about his operation."

My barber also trims my mustache, which qualifies me for another story.

"I got a friend," he says, "who grew himself one of these long, handlebar mustaches. Fellow asked him, 'Don't that mustache bother the women when they kiss you?' My friend said, 'Not a bit. They don't mind going through a little briar patch to get to a picnic.'"

The barber finished my trim and slapped the back of my neck with some cologne. "You need a little of this boy-dog smell," he said.

Yeah, I reckon I do. Don't we all?

***

With the possible exception of the old-fashioned barber shop, women are gaining equality with men in all areas. But lest there be any confusion, I should point out that women themselves are not equal in all respects. As one who has traveled and researched across this great country of ours, I must confess that there are considerable inequities between Northern women and Southern women.

First, there is the matter of yankee women not shaving their legs. This, according to the famous Southern author Homer Southwell, is a custom that began in Buffalo, New York, during the Great Snow Storm of '26. Women found that by not shaving their legs they were afforded natural protection against the snow and cold, and so the entire female population of Buffalo went hairy-legged that winter.

This led, incidentally, to a dramatic fall in the birth rate in Buffalo and also led to the popular folk song, "Buffalo Girls, Won't You Come Out Tonight (And Graze by the Light of the Moon)?"

Most Southern women, of course, wouldn't be caught dead without shaved legs — even big, fat, ugly Southern women who bark at the moon and run rabbits.

Southern women also make better cooks than Northern women. There are even women left in the South who will arise early in the morning and cook their men hot biscuits. Not "whomp biscuits," where you whomp the can on the side of the table, but real biscuits as the Lord intended man to have.

Northern women make good cooks if you like to eat things that still have their heads and eyes, cooked in a big pot with carrots and asparagus and other houseplants.

Southern women aren't as mean as Northern women. Both bear watching closely, mind you, but a Southern woman usually will forgive you two or three times more than a Northern woman before she pulls a knife on you.

Most importantly, Southern women know how to scrunch better. Scrunch is nothing dirty. It's where on a cold night you scrunch up together in order to get cozy and warm. Southern women can flat scrunch. I tried once to scrunch with a yankee girl, but she hadn't shaved her legs and it was like trying to cuddle with a hundred-pound Brillo pad.

So I admit it — even though I'm pretty much an expert on women and certainly open-minded to a new order, I've had my share of trouble with them. But who hasn't? John Wayne had about as many run-ins with them in real life as he did on the silver screen. Heck, even the president of the United States has trouble with women.

I read just the other day where Ronald Reagan and a group of his advisers had a midnight session trying to come up with a plan to bridge the president's gender gap.

"Criminy," said the President, "no matter what I do or say, I can't seem to make America's women happy."

The room was quiet as the President paced. Suddenly he stopped and said, "I think I've got it! Why don't we send every woman in America a big bouquet of flowers with a nice little card attached?"

"Not a bad idea, Mr. President," said one of the advisers. "What would the card say?"

"Something very sweet and tender," said the President. "Women are pushovers for flowers and sweet, tender cards. It could say, 'Roses are red, daisies are yellow, your loving President is a really sweet fellow.'"

"I don't think it would fly," said another adviser. "Women would think you were just trying to buy them off with flowers."

"How about candy then?" asked the President. "Once Mrs. Reagan got very mad at me for talking to a visiting emissary's wife too long at a party, so the next day I bought her a big box of candy and she forgave me."

"Same problem," said the disagreeing aide. "The days when you could woo an American woman with candy and flowers are over."

"Fur stoles are even out of the question?" asked the President.

"You'd lose the conservationist vote if you did that," said another presidential confidant.

The President thought some more. "I think I have it this time," he said. "Whenever candy or flowers or a new fur doesn't work with Mrs. Reagan, I always take her out to a nice restaurant. What if I took all the American women out for dinner? We could go to a real nice place and have champagne, and they could order anything on the menu they wanted. Maybe afterwards, we could go some place romantic for a glass of cognac."

"Now you're really getting some place," another aide spoke up. "You could make it a very intimate evening. Just you and a few million American women."

"It would be very charming," said the President. "I would look into their eyes and tell them how beautiful they all were this evening, and we could have strolling violins to play 'Moonlight Becomes You' to increase the romantic effect."

The adviser who earlier had been against flowers and candy lit a cigarette, blew a puff of smoke and asked, "How long would it take to put something like this together? We're running out of time, you know."

"I don't think it would take too long," said the President. "Of course, we would have to wait long enough for all the women in America to have their hair done and maybe buy a new dress for the occasion."

"I know the maitre d' at Tiberio's," said another aide. "I could find out when he could take a party of several million."

The plan was put into place. The President would phone each woman to be invited and ask her to a quiet dinner with him, "so we can get to know each other a little better." The President would wear his best tux and dash on a little Paco Rabanne cologne, and before the evening was over, the women of America would be eating out of his hand.

Just then Mrs. Reagan came down from the presidential bedroom in her nightgown. "Isn't it time you came to bed?" she asked the President. "My feet are cold."

"Not now, honey," he said. "We're holding man talks."

***

It's been said before, but I agree that bucket seats may have done more to separate men and women than the Baptist church. Back when cars and trucks were equipped with bench seats, women cuddled up next to their men so that sometimes you couldn't tell who was driving.

My boyhood friend and idol, Weyman C. Wannamaker, Jr., a great American, once nearly totaled his 1957 red Chevrolet while out on a date with Kathy Sue Loudermilk. They were driving along a back road looking for a place to stop and discuss one of Weyman's favorite philosophical questions — Is wrestling fake? — when Kathy Sue inched her way over to him. She kept inching, as a matter of fact, until she was slap dab in his lap behind the wheel. Then she proceeded to kiss him squarely on the mouth in a most passionate fashion, which was the only way she knew how.

By the time Weyman managed to bring the '57 Chevy to a halt, he had run over two road signs, three possums and Curtis "Fruit Jar" Hainey, the town drunk. The road signs were demolished, two of the three possums passed away and "Fruit Jar" swore off drinking for an hour.

The man who invented bucket seats obviously never dated Kathy Sue.

There's an old story which says it best:

A man and his wife are riding along and his wife spots a younger couple huddled close together in another car.

"We used to do that twenty-five years ago, honey," she says to her husband. "Why did we stop?"

"Don't ask me," he replies. "I haven't moved."

That's sort of how I feel about the women's movement in general — I haven't moved.

— 10 —

Profiles In
Gray Grit

AS AN ONLY CHILD in a traditional Southern family, I grew up around adults. Not just my parents, but grandparents and uncles and aunts as well. It was an extended family long before anyone decided to call it that.

While they sat on the front porch rocking and shelling peas and telling tales, I picked beggar lice off my pants legs and listened closely. That was probably the best education I ever received, and as I look back on it now from the perspective of near-middle age, I realize there was more wisdom on that porch than I ever imagined.

Listen to a few of these stories of senior citizens and you'll see what I mean.

A PRIVATE WAR ON HUNGER

My grandmother, Willie Word, declared her own war on

hunger years before it became the international issue that it is today. "Every stray dog and cat in the county seems to wind up here," she used to say. It was easy to figure out why. Every stray dog and cat in the county had gotten the word that when all else failed, you always could get a handout at Willie Word's house.

My grandmother also made certain that birds around her yard never went hungry, and when my grandfather complained that the worms had gotten to his tomatoes, she would say, "Even worms have to have something to eat, you know."

She fed her family well, too, of course. My favorite from her table was pork chops. Biting through the flaky crust and succulent meat remains my taste buds' unanimous choice as childhood's best culinary memory. I was an admitted glutton when it came to Mama Willie's pork chops. She always cooked two each for every member of the family, but I always managed to get three.

"Want my last pork chop?" she inevitably asked me, and I inevitably accepted.

One afternoon as I was walking home from a friend's house, I spotted an old man, a tramp, I supposed, lying on the front steps of the Baptist church across the street from where we lived. When I got inside, I told Mama Willie about him.

"He's probably hungry," said my grandmother, who promptly went across the street and fetched him.

He was hungry. You could see it in his eyes as he watched Mama Willie prepare dinner, to which she had invited him. A pork chop dinner. I counted heads and pork chops as we prepared to deliver the blessing. There were five people and only eight pork chops. I was immediately concerned about my usual three.

Mama Willie passed out the pork chops. She placed two on my plate, two on my mother's plate and two on my grandfather's plate. Somebody, I reasoned, is going to miss out on a marvelous pork chop dinner if this trend continues. Then my grandmother gave the ragged old man the other two chops, denying herself any meat that night.

Where, I wondered, is my usual third chop coming from? I ate my first one in a hurry. As I started on my second, I noticed my grandmother staring at me. I looked down at the second pork chop. I looked back at Mama Willie. She motioned her head toward the tramp, who had gone through his two chops in record time and was now attacking the bones. I knew what she wanted me to do.

I had to spit out the words. "Would you like my last pork chop?"

"I'd be much obliged," he said.

I looked back at my grandmother. She was smiling at me.

I haven't sent any money to help the starving people in Ethiopia yet, but I think I will. The memory of that smile demands it.

STILL A FLAME IN THE FIREPLACE

The Atlanta Braves were playing the Toronto Blue Jays in a spring training game in West Palm Beach, Florida. Three or four thousand of us sat blissfully in the sun and watched.

There was more to watch than just the game, however. For instance, there was the girl, a young blonde thing. She wore high heels and tight white pants that came to a few inches below her knees. Had we been hit by high water, she would have been prepared. Call her "The Walker."

She sat for an inning before she started strutting about the stands. To quote William Price Fox, when she moved, the motion in her high-water britches looked like two bob-cats fighting in a croker sack.

When I wasn't watching The Walker, I was watching the old men. What better way to while away a retirement after-noon than to sit and warm yourself over a leisurely baseball game that really doesn't count anyway? If and when I become an old man, I want to come to these games and sit with others my age. I'll probably say a lot of outrageous things. Old men can get away with such as that.

The kids today idolize the current players and go for their autographs like a hound on a good scent. Their heroes still wear the uniform. We middle-agers are losing our heroes in a hurry. Pete Rose and Phil Niekro are still around, but how can I get excited about Dennis Lamp when Sandy Koufax is still fresh on my mind? The old men have their memories, too, and you can hear them in the stands still praising Williams, DiMaggio, Gehrig and even Ruth.

"Now, those were ballplayers," the old men say. "You never saw those guys sitting out a game with a hangnail or a little cold."

There were probably eight of them, the old men, sitting together near me. They sat through the last innings like crows perched on a powerline, silent and staring. When the game was over, they moved slowly out to the aisle. Two needed assistance in walking. They were held on each side by the steadier hands of their companions.

When they reached the walkway out of the stadium, they said their goodbyes. A friend next to me observed, "They seem very sincere about saying goodbye. I guess when you get to be that age, you never know how many empty seats will be on your row tomorrow."

At precisely that moment, The Walker came by. The old men looked at the curves she was throwing, and one smiled at his friend and gave him a knowing wink.

Yeah, they're all getting on, I thought to myself. But bless their hearts, with apologies to Charlie Dressen, they ain't dead yet.

NEW TRICKS FOR AN OLD DOG

My friend Milton is sixty-six. He looks sixty-six. He's been around, Milton has. He was a newspaper copy boy once. He was in the Army. He has seen the world. He has seen this country, all of it, twice — both times from the window of a Greyhound bus.

His first trip was in 1966. It cost him $99 for an unlimited travel ticket, and he used it. New York. Chicago. Seattle. Los Angeles. Back home to Atlanta.

"I mooched off relatives whenever possible," Milton told me. "Other times I'd see a town I liked, get off the bus and stay a couple of days. If it turned out I didn't like the town, I'd grab the next bus out."

Several years ago, Milton took the grand tour again. This time it cost him $159. "I did thirty states and probably one hundred cities," he said. "You get used to the bus. Last time I checked, I still had my spine."

On Milton's first trip, one of his stops was Iowa City, where he walked the campus of the University of Iowa. "I was just walking around looking, waiting for another bus. But something about that campus struck me. It was winter. I looked up at all those towers of learning. I studied all the statuary, and I got an inspiration. I even said a prayer about it. I was determined to get back into college, even at my age."

Almost two decades later, he did it. The Georgia legislature passed a bill granting free tuition to anyone over sixty-two who wanted to attend college.

"It was a dream come true," said Milton. "I really just wanted to see if I could do the work. I didn't know if my brain cells had deteriorated to the point where I couldn't retain anything. I haven't done a lot to prolong them, you know. I've done some riotous living, and I've knocked around half the world on planes and buses and trains, and I've been hit in the head a lot with baseballs. But I'm amazed at what I'm learning. I never knew I was so stupid before."

Milton, of course, isn't stupid at all. He's wise even beyond his years. Old dog Milton is learning new tricks. Don't get old, he advises, just get busy.

"I feel like Alice in Wonderland. I'm in my third childhood. Now, all I want to do is live long enough to graduate."

Any man who can survive two bus trips around this country is a good bet to live through four years of college. Give 'em hell, Milton.

A SOLDIER FOR LIFE

Major Harvey Banks of the Salvation Army retired from active duty way back in the late 1930's. His health was failing, and he was well into his sixties anyway. He tried taking it easy for awhile. Maybe for the first couple of days. But Major Harvey Banks wasn't one to sit still if somebody could use his help.

He visited jails and prisons and sang songs and played music for the inmates. He tried to convince them that his God was theirs, too. He got involved with caring for unwed mothers, and he worked tirelessly in welfare and disaster relief.

"The only difference between Major Banks when he was

retired and Major Banks when he was active," a friend of his told me, "was that after he retired, they put an *R* at the end of his name."

You see these people who work for the Salvation Army and you wonder about them. What prompts a person to spend his or her life wearing that silly uniform, standing on a street corner tooting a horn or ringing a bell? It's certainly not the money. The base pay for a married Salvation Army officer is approximately $150 a week. If you've got forty-five years in and you're married, you pull in a cool $175 or so a week. Single officers get about sixty percent of those figures.

"We do get our housing," said one member of the Army.

After his retirement, such as it was, Major Banks received a small pension, and his working daughter helped him make ends meet. An old friend said of him, "He lived on faith. The extra energy God gave him, he used in the interest of other people."

Major Banks was born in 1873 in Ontario, Canada. The Salvation Army had been started in London in 1865. It came to this country when Major Banks was six years old. Thirteen years later he joined.

In August of 1982 in an Atlanta, Georgia, nursing home, more than forty years after he had retired from "active duty" due to health reasons, Major Harvey C. Banks died. He was 109.

"He was just as lively as ever, still had a great sense of humor, still had a twinkle in his eyes, still loved to sing and listen to music," said another friend at the Salvation Army headquarters.

There was no long period of suffering for Major Banks. His illness and his subsequent death came quickly. He was the oldest living Salvation Army officer in the world, a man who first gave one life to the assistance of the lost and failing, and then turned around and gave another.

The good die young, they say. Not always, thank God. Not always.

CAMPAIGNING FOR THE LORD

The first time I met Ottis "Smokey" Bailey, he was standing on a corner of Peachtree Street in downtown Atlanta handing out Bibles. Smokey holds that everybody ought to own at least one.

"I don't care what kind of misery you got," Smokey says, "the Book can set you free."

Smokey was doubling as a janitor in an apartment house at the time. He had one room in the basement, and that's where he kept his stacks of Bibles he gave away to anybody who would take one from him. "People are always giving me Bibles to give away," he said, "but I don't never take one from nobody unless they got an extra. If you ever get without a Bible, you're lookin' at the devil right in his eyeballs."

Smokey and I eventually sort of teamed up in his handing-out-Bibles venture. He was the brains and the legs of the operation. I took over the financial and public relations parts. First I wrote a newspaper column about him, asking for spare Bibles. They came in by the truckloads. "I made sure that everybody who sent one in had an extra," I assured Smokey. He seemed relieved.

Later, the management company at the apartment house decided that Smokey was handing out Bibles when he should have been replacing screens, so they put him and his Bibles out on the street. That's when I got involved in the financial end of our business: I gave Smokey twenty dollars.

He's still handing out Bibles, and he'll preach anytime anybody will listen. And I still pass him a twenty occasionally.

"You know, things been tough on me since my mama died back in '78." Smokey doesn't need to remind me, but he always does just the same.

After a considerable absence, Smokey reappeared in my office just the other day. Outside the streets were flooded with an April Atlanta monsoon.

"You lookin' well," Smokey said.

"You, too," I answered. "How's it going with the Bibles?"

"Couldn't be better," he said, "but I'm having a little trouble at the hotel where I'm living."

"Rent trouble?"

"Yeah. I could use about thirty," he said. Inflation, I reasoned. I asked Smokey if he could come back later since I was out of cash.

"Could you just give me a check now, brother? It's doing some powerful raining out there."

Try that line the next time you visit your banker for a loan.

I wrote the check. Smokey blessed me a couple of times and headed for the door. I looked out my office window a few minutes later and saw him walking down the sidewalk, bound for the nearest bank, I suppose. At that very moment, the sun peeked out from behind the clouds for the first time in days.

SERVICE THE WAY IT OUGHT TO BE

David Poole and his brother Robert opened their little garage back in the sixties. They were tired of getting somebody else's grease under their fingernails, so they decided to give it a shot on their own. Working a mechanic's flat rate for a greedy dealer can be a going-nowhere treadmill.

For a time it was a good life and a good living for the Poole brothers. They are good, honest mechanics, and they aren't interested in ripping off their customers.

"They've been servicing my cars about as long as I've been driving," a customer told me. "If everybody operated the same way they do, this would be a better world to live in."

A couple of honest, hard-working mechanics satisfying their customers. What a nice little scenario in today's grab-what-you-can scheme of things. Only this story doesn't have a happy ending. A couple of years ago, the break-ins started.

"Had five or six in one year," David Poole said. "We figured we knew who was doing most of it, but we couldn't prove nothing. Police said we'd have to catch him with the goods. It was this little boy, about sixteen. He cleaned us out one time. I mean, he took everything we had, including an old wood step stool and even the nozzles off the air hoses."

The burglaries continued, so the Poole brothers started taking their tools home with them. "Then somebody came in one night and stole all our antifreeze," David said. "Finally we just decided we'd had enough."

After more than twenty years in business, the Poole brothers gave up, victims of urban crime, victims of a judicial system that couldn't stop a two-bit kid burglar from robbing a couple of hardworking, grown men.

"I'm sixty-one," said David Poole. "They've taken things we can't afford to replace now, and I don't feel like starting over anyway. So we just closed for good."

To show the Pooles how much they were appreciated, many of their customers got together and gave them a surprise party at the garage just before it closed. "That was really something," said David Poole, choking on the emotion.

"You know what worries me most about closing?" he asked. "It's the older ladies who have been coming in here ever since we started in business. They don't know a thing about what's wrong with their cars, or what needs to be done. I don't know where they'll go now. I just hope nobody takes advantage of them."

Me, too, David. But I wouldn't bet the nozzle off an air hose that somebody won't.

A WEAK BODY BUT A STRONG WILL

The old man was born in 1888. That's five wars ago, from the Spanish-American to Vietnam. Think of the changes in his lifetime, from horse and buggy to men walking on the moon.

He farmed nearly all his life. Even as he reached the age where he couldn't farm on a large scale anymore, he still maintained his garden.

One of his grandchildren was saying, "I can remember twenty years ago when my mother used to say, 'We've got to go visit Grandpa and Grandma. They won't be around much longer.' That was two decades ago, and they were both in their seventies then."

The grandchildren and great-grandchildren loved the old man. He handed out quarters every time they drove to the country to visit with him, and he obviously took pride in seeing his children's children frolic on the good earth.

He had white hair and wore thin, wire-rimmed glasses until he was well into his nineties. Then he had the cataracts removed and didn't need his glasses anymore. When he took the test to get his driver's license renewed a couple of years ago, his eyesight was nearly perfect.

He had been married to the same woman for more than seventy years. She doted on him. She took care of him. The kids used to wonder what would become of Grandpa if anything ever happened to Grandma.

It came on her slowly. Senility creeps in at first, but then it gains momentum and devours its victim. She started to forget little things. Then she couldn't remember what day it was, who had come to visit last week, where she had put things in the kitchen. When she reached the state where Grandpa could no longer care for her, the kids tried hiring a housekeeper, but Grandma couldn't understand why there was a strange woman in her house and once chased away the housekeeper with a broom.

Without his wife to tend his needs as she had done for most of his life, the old man's health began to deteriorate, too. Just like that. The kids decided their only recourse was to put the couple in a nursing home. In some instances, nursing homes serve a good purpose, I suppose. Neglected and lonely old people are able to get the care they need and are able to have companions.

But sometimes when old people are uprooted, it doesn't work so well. Their roots run too deeply into their home places to pull them away. I remember when my own grandfather died. My grandmother, although she was in ill health herself, couldn't be budged out of the tiny house she had shared with the man she loved.

The old man didn't take to the nursing home. His wife reached the point where she didn't know who he was anymore. The children of four generations visited when they could, but they always found the old man lonely and depressed.

"Every time one of us would go to visit him," one of the grandchildren recalled, "he would beg us to bring him a gun. He'd say, 'Let me get this thing over with now.'"

The old man stopped eating. He brooded and cried. He begged to die. Without his wife and away from his home and garden and his dog, he saw no reason to live. They found him in bed one morning not long ago. He had died in his sleep. He was ninety-five.

"He just willed himself to death," said the grandchild. "I guess it was a blessing that he was able to do that."

Medical science has developed all sorts of means to keep people alive, but maybe sometimes it is better to die than to live on beyond your time. The old man was able to make that choice on his own. Maybe that is a blessing, rest his weary soul.

HONEST, MOM, IT'S NO TROUBLE

It's the same story every year at Christmas.

"Son," says my mother, "you don't have to get me anything for Christmas this year."

And I say, "I know that, Mother, but I want to get you something for Christmas."

"Well, I just don't want to be any trouble."

"It won't be any trouble, Mother. That's part of the enjoyment of Christmas, buying gifts."

"There's just no reason to waste your money on me, son."

"Buying you a Christmas present isn't exactly wasting my money," I argue.

"But there's really nothing I need."

"There must be something you need or want."

"You gave me pajamas last year. I have plenty of pajamas."

"So how about house shoes, the fluffy kind?"

"I have a closet full of house shoes already," she says.

"How about a nice nightgown?"

"I'll never use all the nightgowns I have now. Why don't you just take the money you would have spent on me and buy yourself something nice? Do you have a warm coat?"

"Yes, Mother. Three of 'em."

"How about sweaters?"

"I could start my own line of sweaters, I have so many."

"How about a hat?"

"I don't wear hats."

"Well, how do you keep your head warm?"

"My head doesn't get cold."

"You need a hat in the winter. You might catch a cold if you don't wear a hat."

"This is ridiculous. We're supposed to be talking about what I'm going to get you for Christmas."

"What could you get me? I never go anywhere anymore."

"How about a jacuzzi?"

"A what?"

"You'd love it. A jacuzzi is a tub that you fill with hot water, and there are all these jets shooting out water. You sit in there and it's very relaxing. It would be great for your arthritis."

"I never heard of such a thing," she parries.

"What we could do is knock out a wall and extend the bathroom and put the jacuzzi there."

"I don't want a bunch of carpenters sawing and hammering and tracking mud into the house. Don't get me a bacuzzi."

"Jacuzzi."

"However you say it, I don't want it."

"I know there must be something you'd like to have for

Christmas," I persist.

"OK. What I really would like is a pantsuit to wear when I go to the doctor."

"Great. Why didn't you say that in the first place?"

"I didn't want to be a bother."

"It's no bother. What size?"

"Sixteen. Don't let 'em sell you a fourteen, because that's too small."

"What color?"

"Any color, except red."

"Why not red?"

"I'm too old to wear red."

"OK, one non-red pantsuit. Anything else?"

"That's plenty, son. I don't want to be a bother to you."

The pantsuit I bought my mother is blue. It was no bother whatsoever.

— 11 —

Ugly Goes Clear
To the Bone

AMERICA AND MOST of the civilized world has a fascination with health and beauty. When was the last time you saw a billboard or a television commercial featuring a fat, ugly person? For those of us not blessed with an attractive countenance, these can be very trying times.

I've had this problem for years. In fact, when I was born they called in a vet. My mother was caught two days later in the nursery trying to switch my ID bracelet with that of another child. As I was growing up, she tried the old trick of tying a pork chop around my neck so the dogs would play with me. The dogs preferred to dig for turnips in the garden instead.

When my sight started failing in grammar school and I had to get glasses, that didn't help my looks much either. My classmates always called me "D.U." That stood for "double ugly."

"Beauty is only skin deep," I would argue.

"Yeah," they would reply, "but ugly goes clear to the bone."

In the seventh grade we had a Halloween masquerade party at school. The scariest costumes were awarded prizes. The kid who placed first went as me.

Finally in high school my looks became an asset. I was asked to join the Future Farmers of America because they needed a scarecrow for the Spring Corn Festival.

In college everybody went to the beach during spring break, but I was afraid to be seen with my shirt off. So I joined a health spa and asked the instructor what I could do to build up my muscles.

"You want my honest opinion?" he asked.

"Give it to me straight," I said.

"You're wasting your time. It would take you six months just to get into shape to take your 'before' picture."

Not long ago I was showing a friend some of my childhood pictures. "You looked like that?" the friend said.

"That's the way I looked."

"Well, let me ask you something. Did any of your mother's children live?"

***

When the graze craze hit in the late 1960's, the favorite war cry of the health food set was, "You are what you eat." If that were so, I would have been a stick of bologna by the time I was ten. Ugly bologna.

"What's for lunch today?" I would ask my mother.

"Bologna sandwiches," she inevitably would reply.

After six years of the same dialogue, I finally stopped asking. And if I complained, my mother made it into an international incident.

"This stuff makes me want to throw up," I would argue.

"How can you say that with all the starving children in China?" she would counter.

"Name one and we'll send him some of this bologna."

"There's nothing wrong with bologna," she would say. "It's nutritious, it's a bargain and it sticks to your ribs."

What good are fat ribs unless you're a side of barbecue? I always wished it would stick to the roof of my mouth so I wouldn't have to swallow any more of it.

One day while eating yet another bologna sandwich, it occurred to me to ask, "Just what is bologna?"

A hush fell across the room. You would have thought I had asked for an explanation of sexual reproduction. "Well, son," stammered my mother, looking for a way out, "you're not old enough to be asking about such things. Just hush up and eat your bologna."

I don't know if my mother really ever knew what was in bologna, because I still don't know myself. I'm almost afraid to find out for fear that it's something awful. All I know for sure is that I ate a horsecart full of it in my youth. (Why did I say horsecart?)

As I look back on it now, I realize that I learned a great deal from eating all that bologna. I'm sure it has made me a better person. While other kids brought ham sandwiches to school, I ate bologna and learned humility and courage. Believe me, it takes courage to eat that stuff day after day.

But eating bologna, as distasteful as it was, didn't compare to the trauma of being forced to try liver. I knew what it was, and I didn't want any part of it.

"Just try it with a little onion and pepper," said my mother. "You'll find that it's pretty good."

I would have put Forty Mule Team Borax on it if she had let me — anything to kill the taste.

Years later I devised a plan to eradicate crime in America,

and liver formed the guts of the plan. (Why did I say guts?) My unique plan called for crime to be punishable not only by a prison term, but also by being made to eat a food befitting the crime.

For example, a person convicted of first-degree murder would be sentenced to life in prison with nothing to eat except liver three times a day. Manslaughter would get you twenty years of liver, only with onions. Armed robbery would be five to ten of macaroni and cheese, the kind they used to serve in the school cafeteria. Talk about sticking to the roof of your mouth . . . Kidnappers could look forward to ten years of Brussels sprouts, embezzlers to ten years of pork and beans straight from the can and a conviction for fraud would net a sentence of ten years of nothing but Jello — with bits of bologna inside.

Is your kid a wimp or a troublemaker? Does he hang out with punk rockers and whine about everything? Fill him up to his pierced ears with bologna and liver and you'll see an immediate improvement in his character.

It's time to get back to basics, America. Stand up and be counted.

***

Growing up eating bologna and liver may have helped my character, but it didn't do a thing to improve my looks. I still scared cats. But leaving home and not eating bologna and liver didn't seem to help either.

"Gee, I didn't know you'd been in a wreck," people used to say. I hadn't.

Part of the reason for my ongoing uglies may have been my bad eating, drinking and smoking habits. Apparently I was not alone, however, since most people who live by themselves tend to have bad eating habits, I've read. There-fore, in my endless effort to help my fellow Americans, several years ago I developed "The Grizzard Diet for Single Non-Cookers Who Are in a Hurry."

The staples of this revolutionary diet are Maalox (the family-sized bottle), cold tuna salad sandwiches from vending machines, pizza to go and large quantities of alcohol. Of course, you are offered a number of choices to avoid monotony. For example, here's a typical day on "The Grizzard Diet for SN-CWAIAH":

BREAKFAST — Order out for pizza, preferably pepperoni and scrambled eggs. If you can't find anything open at that time of day, eat the cole slaw left over from the night before's Kentucky Fried Chicken dinner.

LUNCH — Rolaids and a large Pepsi.

AFTERNOON SNACK — Maalox and a pint of chocolate milk.

DINNER — Go to a bar and drink yourself silly. Then ask the bartender for a bowl full of olives and maraschino cherries.

LATE-NIGHT SNACK — Call a married friend and ask if they had anything left over from dinner.

The advantage of this diet is that all of the meals are interchangeable. The disadvantage is that after about three months, you look like a prisoner of war; this diet will either kill you or make you tough (see earlier reference to, "When the going gets tough, the tough get going"). After six months friends assume you have anorexia nervosa and feel sorry for you. A single female friend of mine who adhered to this diet for several months was very nearly killed in an accident at a fast-food restaurant. A nearsighted cleaning woman mistook her for a mop and had done half the kitchen floor with the girl's head before she realized the mop was making gurgling sounds when it was raised out of the bucket.

I also lost too much weight on the "Single Non-Cookers Who Are in a Hurry" diet and had to visit weight-gaining expert Cordie Mae Poovey, an old acquaintance from my school days, to get help. When Cordie Mae was eleven, she was already a herd. She once hijacked the local ice cream wagon and ate nine sundaes and seventeen Eskimo Pies before releasing the driver, who was unharmed except for the black eye Cordie Mae gave him when he initially refused to tell her where he kept the chocolate syrup and whipped cream.

Cordie Mae, currently employed in the Broken Bottle Lounge as a bouncer and stand-in when the mechanical bull goes on the blink, was more than happy to share with me her can't-miss, five-day, weight-gain plan. "Indulge and bulge," she told me.

MONDAY

BREAKFAST — Pancakes with heavy syrup, a dozen eggs, a loaf of toast and a large watermelon, if in season. If not, substitute a pizza with extra cheese.

LUNCH — A pone of cornbread crumbled into a gallon of buttermilk with a six-pack of tall Pabst as a chaser.

DINNER — A barbecued goat and six Twinkies.

TUESDAY

BREAKFAST — Same as Monday, only add bananas. Enough to feed a family of gorillas for a week.

LUNCH — A school of catfish. Fried. With hush puppies, French fries and enough volume and variety of Girl Scout cookies to buy the local troop an Oldsmobile.

DINNER — A dozen biscuits, smothered in gravy, mashed potatoes with four sticks of butter, a coconut cake and two quarts of Buffalo Rock ginger ale to wash it all down.

WEDNESDAY

BREAKFAST — Grits, served in a large trough, hot with butter and cheese. If you're really hungry, mix in a mess of collards.

LUNCH — Three bowls of chili, a box of Oreos and a long nap.

DINNER — An entire pig, cooked any way you like it. Do not try to put the entire pig in your mouth at once.

THURSDAY

BREAKFAST — A chocolate milkshake, four Hershey bars, three fudgesicles and a half-dozen Reese's Peanut Butter Cups, including the wrappers.

LUNCH — Pig out at McDonald's. If the clown shows up, eat his shoes.

DINNER — Eat a large T-bone steak with all the trimmings. Then drag the bone out in the yard and howl at the moon. Be careful of ticks.

FRIDAY

BREAKFAST — An omelette the size of a Chevy pickup and a large pickle.

LUNCH — A dozen cans of Vienna sausages, a large package of soda crackers and a raw Vidalia onion twice as big as the pickle you had for breakfast.

DINNER — Go to an all-night diner and eat until the sun comes up, or until they run out of food, whichever occurs first. If you get hungry on the way home, stop and buy four dozen Moon Pies and a large jar of mayonnaise.

***

Between the "Single Non-Cookers" diet and Cordie Mae's advice, my body was more confused than I was. Neither of us would have recognized a healthy lifestyle if it had been naked at the beach. In order to save my sanity, I returned to my typewriter and devised "Grizzard's Rationalization Chart of Overeaters, Smokers and Boozers," to be used whenever you slip off the wagon but don't feel like unloading the guilt.

Here's how it works. Food, for instance, will not cause you to gain weight if:

- You eat it standing up.
- You eat it off someone else's plate.
- Your mom cooked it.
- You offer it to the dog first.
- You eat it in the dark.
- You do not chew it.
- You are eating because you're depressed about all the starving people in the world.
- It is smaller than a regulation NBA basketball.
- It's your birthday.
- It's Chester A. Arthur's birthday.

For smokers, there are some equally effective rationalizations. For example, another cigarette won't hurt you if:

- You don't smoke it all the way down to the filter.
- It's not your regular brand.
- You bummed it.

- You throw away the rest of the pack.
- You make a contribution to the American Cancer Society.

Been hitting the bottle a little too hard? One more drink won't hurt you if:
- It's a special occasion, like Happy Hour.
- Something from your past has been eating at you lately, like the death of your dog Skippy when you were four.
- You drink to a worthy cause, like finding a cure for Leon Spinks.
- You use lots of ice.
- The bottle was a gift.
- It was almost empty anyway.
- You make it last longer than the National Hockey League season, which is the only thing that lasts longer than pregnancy.
- You drink it out of a coffee cup.

***

Starting from where I did — that is, uglier than a '47 Packard on blocks — I don't suppose my bad eating, smoking and drinking habits really did all that much harm. They were just a logical extension of me, sort of like clothes.

My clothes. Now, there's another problem. I never could figure out what was in and what was out. When the hippies were wearing sandals, jeans and T-shirts in the late sixties, I was still in my penny loafers, slacks and oxford cloth shirts. By the time my outfit came back into style in the early eighties, I was wearing popsicle-colored leisure suits. In fact, the only people still wearing leisure suits then were me and Slim Whitman.

What did everybody else do with theirs? I admit I haven't been to any bowling league awards banquets or wrestling matches or Moose Club dances lately, but it seems that even that crowd has dumped the leisure suit.

So where are they? They didn't just sprout little polyester legs and walk away. In an attempt to answer this permanent press-ing question, I tried to contact designer Leon "The Needle" Tackeeinksi of Fort Deposit, Alabama, who first introduced the leisure suit to America. Unfortunately, Mr. Tackeeinski could not be located.

"One day," said a man who answered the phone at the Fort Deposit bus station, "he got on the three o'clock north-bound and we haven't heard from him since."

When I asked if Mr. Tackeeinski had closed his leisure suit factory before leaving town, the man told me about a mysterious fire the night before his departure which destroyed the entire factory.

"It was a horrible thing," he said. "Half the town was overcome by polyester fumes and couldn't resist the sudden urge to go to Sears-Roebuck and order white shoes and belts."

Perhaps that's the clue I've been looking for to explain what happened to all the leisure suits in this country. Maybe American men, in a burst of fashion consciousness, all went out in their back yards and burned their leisure suits.

"That is highly possible," said a local scientist I contacted about my theory. "As you no doubt have noticed, we have been having strange weather the past few years. One explanation could be that the fumes from all those leisure suits burning rose into the earth's atmosphere, creating what could be called the 'Polyester Zone.' This layer of gases could have a strange effect on our weather. During the hurricane season last year, for instance, I recall that we had one named Delbert that swept in off the Gulf coast and headed straight to the nearest K-Mart."

There is one other possibility about what happened to all the leisure suits. Maybe the Japanese recycled them and are using them to make seat covers for Isuzus. I'm considering using my leisure suits for the same purpose; I'm just not sure how my car will look with orange sherbert-colored seats.

***

The beautiful people of the world, those whose pictures appear on billboards and in television commercials, seldom have to worry about their clothes. If their faces are pretty enough, nobody looks any lower. Or if they have great bodies, nobody cares what they're wearing or even *if* they're wearing. And if they show up dressed in something terribly out of date, people just presume they're being trend-setters.

So why is it that when I show up wearing a blazer with five-inch lapels and Guccis without socks, everybody presumes I'm tacky instead of trendy? Why? Because my face gives it away. No one who looks like Alfred E. Newman can be a trend-setter.

Kathy Sue Loudermilk never had that problem. She was the first real beauty queen I ever knew. She won the coveted Miss Collard Festival Queen title seven years in a row, breaking the record of Cordie Mae Poovey who had won four consecutive titles by threatening the judges.

Kathy Sue turned her victory into a bigtime modeling career and later appeared on a billboard advertisement for Cleghorn Dairies buttermilk. "Cleghorn's Buttermilk — Buy It By the Jugs" is what the copy under Kathy Sue's picture said.

She was justifiably proud of her looks. A reporter for the local newspaper once asked Kathy Sue, "Do you consider yourself a sex symbol?"

She answered him by asking, "Does a duck have lips?"

But many of today's beauty queens can't decide if they're proud of their bodies or embarrassed by them. Half of the contest winners, who've paraded around in bathing suits that wouldn't create suntan lines, say, "I can't stand a man who wants me only for my body. I have a brain, too, and I can use it. I know the capitals of six states and I went to a museum once."

A former Miss Universe from Venezuela said her looks were secondary to her mind. "I want to be an architect and design beautiful buildings," she said. "But buildings with a purpose — for the poor." I'm sure the poor people in Venezuela appreciated that. Give them a few beautiful buildings and maybe they'll quit complaining about being cold and hungry.

Then there are the other beauty queens who are so proud of their endowments that they sometimes forget to keep their clothes on. I recently wrote a treatise on the subject, which I will read at the upcoming Coweta County Moose Club Convention, entitled, "I've Seen England, I've Seen France, I've Seen Miss America Without Her Underpants (With Apologies and Thanks to Vanessa Williams)." I wonder where this new trend will lead?

***

ATLANTIC CITY, NEW JERSEY — DECEMBER, 1999: Twenty-one-year-old Roxanne "Boom Boom" LaTouche, Miss California, was crowned Miss America for 1999 here Saturday evening, becoming the first stripper ever to win the prestigious title.

Miss LaTouche brought both the audience and the judges to their feet with a nude break dance in the talent competition. As pageant emcee Bob Guccione sang the traditional

Miss America theme song, "There She Is, Money in the Bank," Miss LaTouche bumped and grinded down the runway wearing her new crown and, again, to the delight of the all-male audience and male judges, nothing else.

"It just goes to show you," said the beaming Miss LaTouche, "that any girl in this country can become Miss America if she has the correct ideals and values and a new breast implant."

For the last three years, Miss LaTouche has been the star performer at the Yellow Pussy Cat Lounge in Encino, California, where she became famous for her widely heralded ability to strip completely nude while juggling three large cats. Asked if she would return to her position at the lounge, Miss LaTouche announced that she would be attempting instead a career in the movies.

Her agent, Marvin "The Shark" Perronowski, who is also part owner of the Yellow Pussy Cat, said his client is expected to sign a contract with Sin Flick Productions in Hollywood and will star in the full-length porno film titled, "Deep Throat Meets Bert Parks."

Miss LaTouche attended Candy Barr Memorial High School in Encino, where she was captain of the cheerleading squad and became the first cheerleader in the history of the school to have her sweater retired upon graduation.

First runner-up in the pageant was Miss Indiana, who was given temporary parole from the Indiana State Women's Prison in order to compete in the event. She was doing five to ten for armed robbery. Upon learning that she had not won the crown, Miss Indiana pulled a knife on two of the judges but was quickly whisked away by her parole officer.

Second runner-up was Miss Nevada, a stunning Las Vegas showgirl who was named Miss Congeniality by a unanimous vote after a closed-door session with the judges, two of whom — both elderly — were treated and released at a local hospital following the performance.

Third runner-up was Miss New York, daughter of former Miss America Vanessa Williams. Immediately following the contest, Miss New York announced her engagement to Miss Alaska. Former Miss America Williams, incidentally, attended the pageant and told reporters that she plans to enter politics and hopes to be the vice presidential candidate on the Ducks Unlimited ticket in the 2000 presidential election.

Miss LaTouche, meanwhile, begins a national tour next week in which she will make appearances on various talk shows, including the popular NBC "Tonight Show" with host Harry Reems.

"This is one of the best Miss America pageants ever," said Guccione, "and all of our contestants are to be congratulated." Speaking for all contestants, Guccione also said he has more than three thousand nude color photographs of the fifty young women and will run them in the upcoming January edition of his *Penthouse* magazine, which has sponsored the Miss America pageant since 1985.

— 12 —

You've Got to Bend Over To Pick Grit

FOLLOWING JIMMY AND Billy Carter's rise to national prominence in the late 1970's, the term redneck became very popular with the American public. It was a term of derision in the mouths of some uneducated people, but to those of us born and bred in the South, it was most often used to refer to just good ol' down-to-earth folks. Those of true grit.

Let's say it is your lot in life to have to pick butterbeans. Picking butterbeans is a thankless job that requires long hours of bending over and getting hot and dirty, but somebody has to do it. After a couple of weeks under such conditions, the back of your neck will be redder than the home crowd at a Georgia football game.

Rednecks, or butterbean pickers and others who work the land, have always had trouble with those who see themselves as being more sophisticated just because they happen to live where the bus stops, even if nobody is getting on or off. These people are referred to by rednecks as city slickers. In the mouth of a redneck, city slicker can be a term of derision.

"Hey, redneck," city slickers used to say to a farm boy who ventured into town, "what brings you to civilization?"

"Paw's truck," the redneck inevitably would answer, and the city slickers would have a good bellylaugh. That is, until the redneck plowed on their heads with his fists, which is how rednecks got the reputation of being overly hostile.

Ed Koch, the mayor of New York, is one of those city slickers who doesn't care much for rednecks and the rural way of life. In fact, he once was quoted in a *Playboy* interview as saying that country living was a "joke." My friend Billy Bob Bailey, who was one of the original rednecks and a great American, took offense at Koch's remarks and wrote to tell him so. Billy Bob has given me permission to share his letter, which is now enshrined in cellophane wrapping on the bulletin board at Bogator Green's mechanic and body shop:

Mayor Ed Koch
New York City

Dear Mr. Mayor,

My name is Billy Bob Bailey and I live in Fort Deposit, Alabama, which is so far back in the country that the sun goes down somewhere between here and Montgomery, the state capital.

I was over to the store the other evening and they had the television on and I heard what you said about living out in the country. You said driving around in a pickup truck and driving twenty miles to buy a Sears-Roebuck suit was a waste of time. You said living in the country was a "joke." What kind of fumes have you been inhaling, your honor?

I drive a pickup truck, and one advantage to living out here in the country is the only time I ever get stuck in traffic is when there's a funeral and the hearse breaks down. Those of us in line have to wait until Junior (he's the funeral director's son) goes back to the plant and gets the jumper cables. You got that wrong about Sears-Roebuck suits, too. I don't wear no suits, period. No need to. They don't care what you wear to the Moose Club, long as you ain't barefooted.

They started requiring shoes because of Hoot Dingler, who used to come in regularly to drink beer and shoot pool and was always barefooted. Hoot didn't even own any shoes. Didn't believe in 'em. "Might slow me down if I needed to get somewhere in a hurry," Hoot explained. Problem was that Hoot's a pig farmer and he's always walking around where the pigs live. We might be country, but we don't like to drink beer, shoot pool and smell hog at the same time, so they changed the rule about coming in barefooted. Hoot started drinking with the Elks after that.

They showed a picture of you on television, Mr. Mayor, and you look right slack-eyed and loop-legged to me. Been a little bilious and goofy-headed lately? Sometime when folks don't feel good, they say things they don't mean. I hope you didn't mean what you said about living in the country being a joke, 'cause my dog Rooster heard about it, too (he reads the Montgomery newspaper), and Rooster don't like nobody from New York City throwing off on the way we live. "I wouldn't shoot a rat trying to crawl out of New York City," is what Rooster always says.

If I were you, Mr. Mayor, I wouldn't come around Fort Deposit or Rooster for awhile, because I'm afraid that dog would take a plug out of your leg and I couldn't stop him with a stick.

Rooster and me ain't never been to New York City, but it ain't exactly Hog Heaven either, is what we hear. Vonda Kay Potts from right here in Fort Deposit was state dairy queen one year and won a trip to New York City. She said she liked it fine except that when you went outside, the streets and air were so dirty that the whole place smelled like Hoot Dingler's feet.

We hear that you want to further your political career after you're through being mayor. Maybe be governor or president or something. But I wouldn't count on a lot of support from the rural parts of the nation, Mr. Mayor. It's like Rooster always says: Country people all have one thing in common. They know a rat trying to crawl out of New York City when they see one.

Thanks, all,
Billy Bob Bailey

***

Billy Bob's right when he says that life in the country can be awfully good. I was reminded of that fact recently when I ran into an old friend I hadn't seen since college. He now owns a small drugstore in a small South Georgia town. He has the same wife he started out with and two babies and a dog, a cat and a number of hogs.

"My hog farm is my hobby," he says. "When I'm out there with them, I can really relax."

Maybe Mayor Koch and everyone else who struggles to survive in our cities should take note. Give everybody a small hog farm and maybe there would be less crime and fewer heart attacks.

My old friend also is a member of the city council in his town. "I get $75 a month, and it's rare I get cussed out more than twice a week." He is involved in local charities and organizes an annual tennis tournament which raises money for the county retardation center. My friend donates the hogs for the barbecue which is held in conjunction with the tournament, and the ladies in town bake pies and cookies and make potato salad and cole slaw, and somebody slices a mile of tomatoes. The only thing wrong with any of this lifestyle, my friend says, is the gnats. "We call 'em the South Georgia Air Force."

Comparing my life in the city with his in the country makes me stop and think. He lives the solid rural life and helps sick folks and tries to make his community a better place to live. And in between all that, he raises hogs and children and breaks his butt trying to help those who have trouble helping themselves. Me, I rattle around with a couple million hurrying souls and we fight traffic and each other. Sometimes all I get from the effort is the blues.

They might not believe it on the flat, piney plains of South Georgia, but there are worse things in life than gnats.

***

Of course, life in rural America can be filled with excitement, too. There are more characters in most small towns than gnats in South Georgia. Just the other day a friend was telling me a story about a fellow named Paul in his hometown.

"Paul was having some trouble with the IRS, something about an unauthorized deduction. So when these two IRS men wanted to meet with him, he told them to come down to where he lives — in a trailer way back in the woods with the snakes and armadillos and albino possums — to have lunch.

"Paul, you know, eats about a quart of mayonnaise every day, so he reached into his mayonnaise jar, pulled out a handful, and started spreading it on bread. That's all he wanted on his sandwich, but he put a slice or two of meat on those other fellows'. He sat down at the table, pulled out his gun from one pocket and his brass knuckles from another and laid them on the table. Then he asked the two IRS men to join him in prayer.

"'Lord,' he started, 'please keep these two fellows safe while they're here with me, because you know how much I want to shoot 'em. But, Lord, don't let me do that, much as I want to....' When Paul looked up from praying, the two IRS men were gone. He ain't heard a word from them since."

***

Rural Americans, especially those in the South, have long been misunderstood by other segments of the population. Some folks think just because a fellow has a gun rack in the back window of his pickup that he's on his way to shoot a bunch of liberals. They think grits grow on trees and poke salad is a weed. And possibly their biggest misconception of all is that the pink plastic flamingos positioned in many front yards are "tacky."

Nothing could be further from the truth. Tasteful, well-bred individuals normally paint the trunks of the trees in their yards white; line their driveways with old tires, also painted white; plant flowers between the tires; and place at least three pink flamingos strategically about the lawn.

Common riffraff, meanwhile, decorate their yards by taking the tires off a '52 Studebaker and putting the automobile on cement blocks beside the house.

I remember the day my family moved into a new home. How I swelled with pride when my parents allowed me to stick the legs of our new plastic pink flamingos in our front yard.

"Does this mean we are a tasteful, well-bred family and no longer common riffraff?" I asked.

"It does, indeed, son," answered my mother.

How could anyone, even an unenlightened yankee person, refer to plastic pink flamingos as "tacky"? They lend a tropical flair to any yard. They are graceful in their posture, and their pink color blends most pleasingly with the green hue of the grass, just as a red shirt accentuates a black polyester suit.

My boyhood friend and idol, Weyman C. Wannamaker, Jr., a great American, had a dozen plastic pink flamingos in his yard. Weyman's mother was president of the local garden club, and her yard was the annual winner of the "House Beautiful" award in our community.

Mrs. Wannamaker, being a woman of exceeding taste and breeding, complemented her flamingos with a ceramic hen being followed by her baby chicks, and various other lawn statuary including ducks and deer and one marvelous piece in the form of a fat Sumo wrestler, which she got for free when she purchased four chenille bedspreads.

Mrs. Wannamaker's yard was also quite impressive at Christmas. Her annual decoration included Santa's sleigh being pulled by — you guessed it — eight pink flamingos.

When asked about his mother's Christmas decorations, Weyman said, "My mother is a very sick person."

I would like to add in closing that I have just purchased a new home and have ordered two pair of pink flamingos from the Sears catalog. I haven't decided for sure, but I think I'm going to put them next to the little birdhouse that says, "See Rock City" on the roof.

My neighbors will be pink with envy.

***

So country ain't so bad after all. And if you don't believe it, try calling Ed Koch the next time you have a craving for a big pot of butterbeans.

— 13 —

The Bigger They Are, The More They Weigh

NOT EVERYBODY GETS out of life what they put into it. Some folks work hard all their days and never free themselves from the bog of poverty. Others just bounce through life like a pinball, taking the easiest path but lighting up things and racking up points all the way. Yet from one end of the tax scale to the other, from Who's Who to the welfare rolls, real character looks the same.

A GENTLE BEAR OF A MAN

I spent an afternoon drinking with Paul "Bear" Bryant once. I had been to Athens, Georgia, with him for an autographing session for the book he wrote with John Underwood of *Sports Illustrated*. When we returned to the Atlanta airport, there were still a couple of hours before his flight to Tuscaloosa, Alabama.

"Let's get a drink," he said.

The weather was awful. Rain. High winds. Lightning and thunder. Bad flying weather. Good drinking weather. He took me into the Eastern Ionosphere Lounge, where he ordered double Black Jack and Coke. Two at a time.

I probably got the best interview of my life that afternoon, but I don't remember much of it. However, I do remember walking him back to the departure gate two hours later. At the gate, the Bear ran into a doctor from Tuscaloosa who was booked on the same flight. The doctor was also an amateur pilot.

"Coach," said the doctor, "I don't like this weather."

"You a drinking man, son?" Bryant asked him.

"Yes, sir," said the doctor.

"Well, good. Let's get us a couple of motel rooms and have a drink and fly home tomorrow."

There were fifty or sixty would-be passengers awaiting the same flight to Tuscaloosa. When they saw Bear Bryant turning in his ticket, all but a handful did the same thing.

"If Bear Bryant is afraid to fly in this weather," one man said, "I sure as hell ain't about to."

That was the last time I was with the Bear. On January 26, 1983, he died of a heart attack. As soon as I heard the news, I knew I had to get in touch with a friend of mine.

She had met Bear Bryant through her profession, public relations, several years earlier, but their relationship had grown far beyond that. I'm not talking hanky-panky here; grandfather and granddaughter comes closest to describing it.

They were an unlikely pair. He, the gruff, growling old coot of a football coach. She, a bright, young, attractive woman with both a husband and a career and a degree from the University of Texas, of all places.

He would call her even in the middle of football season and they would talk, and he would do her any favor. Once a friend of hers, a newspaper columnist, was having heart surgery. She called the Bear and had him send the fellow a scowling picture with the autograph, "I hope you get well soon. Bear Bryant." The picture still hangs in my home.

I called her the minute I heard that he had died. I didn't want her to get it on the radio. She cried.

"I loved him," she said, "and he loved my baby."

My friend had had a baby a few years earlier. Had it been a boy, she would have named him for the Bear, David Bryant. But it was a girl, and so she named her Marissa.

"I had no problems with naming my son David Bryant, but I wasn't about to name a little girl Beara," said my friend.

Of course, a busy, big-time college football coach like Bear Bryant didn't give it a second thought that somebody else's little girl wasn't named for him. He still sent her gifts. Gifts like a child's Alabama cheerleader uniform, and then an adult-size uniform for use later. He sent her footballs, dolls and probably a dozen or so letters that her mama read to her.

It's funny, though. When he sent his packages and letters, he always addressed them not to Marissa but "To Paula."

LAUGHTER IN THE SKY

Great big ol' Jerry Clower was signing an autograph when I spotted him in a busy airport. Great entertainers need neither stage nor special occasion as opportunity to perform. An airport or an airplane, for instance, is just as good as any.

For the uninformed, Jerry Clower of Yazoo, Mississippi, used to go around telling funny stories and selling fertilizer. Then somebody from Nashville discovered him and signed him to a recording contract. Now all Jerry does is go around telling funny stories, although some insist that he's still spreading verbal fertilizer.

On the plane, Jerry took a seat in front of me, turned around and began to spout forth his philosophy on any number of subjects in a voice loud enough to be heard throughout the plane. With Jerry Clower around, E.F. Hutton would never get a word in edgewise.

I asked him about a mutual friend, a writer.

"We agree on lots of things," he said of the fellow, "but we're a lot different, too. Like, I've been married to the same woman (Homerline) for thirty-seven years. He's been livin' with one about two years and says he don't know if they're going to get married or not because he ain't through trying her out yet."

I mentioned something about college football and his eyes lit up. Jerry used to play a little offensive line at Mississippi State.

"What I like most about college football," he said, "are the rivalries. I was down at the University of Texas the other day. They don't like Texas A&M one bit, you know. Fellow down at Texas told me the Texas A&M men are so lazy that they marry pregnant women."

The passengers, all of them, were his by now, so he kept rolling.

"These network news fellows always amaze me. Big reservoir down in Mississippi has been flooding for years, but up until last year it was just the poor blacks and poor whites who were being flooded out. Then some of them $200,000 houses started gettin' a little mud inside 'em, and it all of a sudden is a big story.

"This network news fellow went down there to one of them big houses and asked this proper woman what she thought caused the flood. She said it was the bass fishermen. She said they hadn't lowered the reservoir enough just so them bass fishermen could still catch fish. Then he interviewed this real intelligent man. He blamed the whole thing on the Corps of Engineers, said they hadn't planned the watershed right.

"Course, them network fellows try not to interview no good ol' boys when they come to Mississippi, 'cause they think they don't know nothing. But one of 'em slipped up and interviewed this ol' boy he figured was highfaluting 'cause he happened to be wearing a coat and tie. He asked him what he thought caused the flood. 'Sixteen inches of rain caused it, and if we get that much rain next year, we'll have another flood.' "

Jerry also told his boots story. He was on a Hollywood talk show one time and a lady producer noticed his boots.

"She jumped up out of her chair like a wasp had done stung her," he said, "and she commenced to hollering about my boots. She said, 'What kind of boots are those, Mr. Clower?' And I said, 'These here are lizard boots.'

"She said, 'I can't believe you would wear such boots. To think that somebody killed an innocent little animal just so you could wear those boots.' I said, 'No, ma'am. This particular lizard was run over by a Greyhound bus. I even stood out there in the road and helped fight the buzzards off him.' "

There was a pause and then Jerry Clower added, "You know, I sometimes get the feeling some people are educated far beyond their intelligence."

And anyone who has spent much time with Jerry Clower

has been blessed far beyond his due.

HE'S THE ONE IN OVERALLS

They buried Junior Samples in his favorite pair of overalls on a cold Georgia day, dark and damp, in November 1983. Junior's bronze, flower-laden casket was closed during the services, but a man standing outside the church confirmed that Junior's family wasn't about to send him across the river wearing anything else.

"All Junior ever wore was overalls, anyway," said the man.

"One thing's for sure," said another, "he's a lot more comfortable than he would have been in a pair of britches."

Junior Samples, Forsyth County's claim to fame, died of a heart attack at age fifty-six. Slow talking, slow moving Junior turned a fish story somebody recorded back in the sixties into a career as a bungling bumpkin on television's "Hee Haw."

Junior's funeral was inside the little white-frame Roanoke Baptist Church out on the Buford Dam Road. An Atlanta television cameraman remarked what a pretty picture the little church made, perched atop a hill, its steeple and cross reaching toward the gray sky.

"These folks up here had a lot of respect for Junior," said a local reporter. "What they liked about him, he didn't change after he got on TV. He still got out amongst folks. He was one of them right until the end."

It was generally agreed that Junior's was one of the biggest funerals in the county's history. Early arrivals got seats inside the church, but by the time the Jenkins Family, local gospel singers, opened the services with "One Day at a Time, Sweet Jesus" and "Just a Rose," there were more gathered on the porch of the church and in the muddy driveway than were inside.

A man from the funeral home told me about Junior's flowers.

"We loaded up a truck plumb full," he said, "and we still got just as many back at the funeral home."

I asked if he had known Junior personally.

"Knowed him all my life," he answered proudly. "People thought he was trying to be funny on television, but he was just being Junior."

Another group of Junior's friends gathered under a barren tree outside the church. The blue hearse pulled up first. Junior's tearful family followed. Next came a Tennessee sheriff's car with some of "Hee Haw'"s other stars.

"There's LuLu," said one of the men. "She looks as fat in person as she does on television, don't she?" She did.

Nobody knew her real name, but the toothless woman who's always beating her husband over the head on the program came, too.

"I thought they made her up to look that ugly," said another onlooker. "Lord, she's just natural ugly."

A tall, blonde woman they identified as Misty Roe, one of the "Hee Haw" girls, got the most attention. She wore high heels and a black miniskirt, and her hair had been teased into a frazzled, frenzied mane.

"Looks like she'd knowed not to have dressed thataway," somebody said.

The boys outside said Junior hadn't been drinking as much the last few months since he had been so sick. The preacher told mourners inside the church that Junior hadn't been doing as much fishing lately, either.

"He knew the final hour was upon him," the preacher said. "And he spent his last days praying. I can tell you

Junior Samples was saved. His name was recorded on the Lamb's Roll of Life."

The Jenkins Family ended the service with "Shall We Gather at the River," and everybody went home, content that Junior was with the angels.

In case you don't watch much television, Lord, he's the one in overalls.

A STORY OF COURAGE AND DIGNITY

She said she remembered the first time she ever saw him. "I was in a seventh-grade music class in my hometown of Provo, Utah," she began. "The teacher introduced us to a new boy who had just moved into town from New York. He was wearing knickers. He had on a pullover sweater and a little cap. He wore them every day. I found out later he was so poor that's all his mother could afford."

They became friends. They moved on to high school together, and they attended dances together.

"He told me there were two reasons he took me to dances," she recalled. "He said he liked me, of course, but I also had paid for my activities card, so he didn't have to pay a nickel to get me in."

Una Clark is a bright, pert lady with an easy smile. She lives in Seattle, Washington. Does her name sound familiar? That's right, Mrs. Barney Clark, widow of the first human recipient of an artificial heart. Dr. Barney Clark, the little boy in knickers, grew up to be a dentist. He developed heart problems, and when there was no alternative, he agreed to try the artificial heart. It kept him alive 112 days.

"We did hope there would be personal gain if we agreed to the artificial heart," said Mrs. Clark, "but Barney also felt this was something he could do for his fellow man. Somebody had to be first."

I wanted to know more about Una and Barney Clark's life together. After Dr. Clark died, his doctor said one of the reasons he was able to live as long as he did was because of the strong support he had from his family, because he had a wife who loved him dearly. I wanted to know how such a relationship came about.

"Barney never had much confidence," Mrs. Clark said. "He never told me how he felt about me. His father had died when he was very young, and he had been so insecure, so poor. I think that's what caused his lack of confidence. Maybe if he had said he cared about me, something would have happened when we were younger, but I never had any idea he wanted anything serious between us. I married his best friend."

That was just before the outbreak of World War II. Una Clark's husband was a flier. He died in action.

"Barney called me when he heard what had happened," she said. "It wasn't long after that when we found out we loved each other."

Dr. Barney Clark was a bombardier during the war. It was his service record, said his wife, that gave him the confidence he had never had before. He went to dental school after the war and established a successful practice.

"Everything he did, he went after it hard," said Una Clark. "If there was anything about him I could criticize, it would be that he was selfish with his time. He was a workaholic. If I could have changed him, I would have made him spend more time with me."

The man showed awesome courage in agreeing to become the first artificial heart recipient. His last days were spent in the discomfort of tubes and tests. But as his wife said, somebody had to be first. As one who has benefited directly from heart research, Una and Barney Clark are heroes to me.

One more thing I had to ask. "Do you miss him?"

"Yes," she answered softly. "I miss him very much."

We all do.

FORGIVE HIM AND TOAST HIS MEMORY

Marvin Griffin was governor of the State of Georgia from 1955-59. When he died in 1982, most of his eulogies included an apology for the fact that he once stood tall for segregation.

Running for political office has a lot in common with show business. You give the people what they want. When Marvin Griffin ran for governor, what the people of Georgia wanted — at least those who could vote — was a segregationist. If you felt differently in those days, about the only thing you could run for was the state line.

I'm not launching a defense of Marvin Griffin's politics; I'm just pointing out that he wasn't singing a solo.

As a person, I liked him very much. I first met him a dozen years ago in a bar. I introduced myself and told him my grandfather had been one of his most ardent admirers.

"What is yo' granddaddy's name, son?" he asked me.

I told him.

"Yes, indeed," said the former governor. "A fine man. I know him well. And how is his health?"

"Been dead ten years," I answered.

"Sorry to hear that, son," said Uncle Marvin. "Let's toast his memory."

Some are born to politick, and I've never drunk with a better practitioner of the art. He had a million great lines, and he growled them in a classic Southernese. He was a big man, robust and full of life. When he talked, he played with each word, milking it for all it was worth.

He was asked once, after his term as governor was over, if he had any advice for young politicians. "Tell 'em to remember just two things," he said. "Keep yo' mouth shut and yo' bowels open."

The last time I saw him was at a banquet before a big Georgia football game. He was the opening speaker and forgot at least the first part of his advice to young politicians. The thousands assembled nearly missed the kickoff of the football game, but I loved every minute of it. There'll be other games, but only one Marvin Griffin.

"Man came up to me one time when I was campaigning in Fayette County," he reminisced, "and said, 'Governor, let's me and you go have a little drink.' I said, 'My friend, soon as I see to it that everybody in Fayette County knows my name, I'll go drink a mule's earful with you.' "

Forgive him his opportunistic bellowings for segregation. Forgive him the improprieties of his administration. He added color to our lives and made us some memories, he did. A mule's earful.

— 14 —

Please Adjust
Your Set

EVERY TIME I HEAR about the modern communications explosion, I keep hoping that somebody has finally blown up most of the television and radio stations and about half of the newspapers in this country.

We are, in fact, besieged with words, spoken and written. There probably are more satellite dishes in rural America today than there are tractors. In the words of a sixties rock hit, "Signs, signs, everywhere signs, funking up the scenery, breaking my mind. Do this. Don't do that. Can't you read the signs?"

Being able to decipher all these communications, to cull the good from the bad, the useful from the useless, the helpful from the harmful, is one of the traits of those who possess true grit. The rest of us merely dog paddle through this alphabet soup. Me, I've progressed to the back stroke.

Just driving to work and reading the signs along the way

can overload your circuits. "Watch for Falling Rocks," says a frequent one. But how, I ask myself, can I watch for falling rocks and at the same time keep from running my car off the accompanying cliff?

"Low Flying Aircraft" is another of my favorite highway signs. Why are they telling me that? It's not flying that low, is it? And what am I supposed to do if I see a low-flying aircraft? Blow my horn and wave? My policy regarding low-flying aircraft is I won't bother them if they won't bother me.

There are signs on many entrances to interstate highways which read, "Take Gap, Give Gap." In public? Sounds like something that ought to wait until you get to a motel room.

I was in a radio station in Austin, Texas, recently. In the vending and coffee area was a sign that read, "Your mother doesn't work here, so clean up after yourself."

Here are some other favorites I've encountered along the way:

- In a Hilton Head, South Carolina, health food store: "Anyone having the audacity to smoke in here will be flogged unmercifully with an organic banana."

- Above a pool table in a roadhouse in Oklahoma: "No gambling. Anybody caught gambling will be prosuted." It's bad enough when they prosute in a doctor's office, much less in a pool hall.

- Handwritten on the front window of a South Alabama service station: "This here is a service station. It ain't no bank. Don't come in here and ask me to cash no checks. And that includes kinfolks."

- In front of a large Baptist church in Atlanta: "Caution: Blind People Crossing."

- In front of a used car lot in Spartanburg, South Carolina, which had closed for the night: "This lot is guarded by armed security three nights a week. Guess which three."

Of course, the most common signs of all are not printed but scrawled — graffiti. And New York, where everyone is handed a paint brush as they cross the East River, is the graffiti capital of the world. Writing on the sides of subway cars is as much a tradition in New York as a $14.95 breakfast in a hotel restaurant.

What I've never understood is how somebody can run alongside a speeding subway train with a can of spray paint and still be able to write "BJ Is One Bad Hombre" legibly. The trains don't stop long enough in the stations to get a shot at them standing still, so I assume BJ is also one fast hombre.

If it weren't for the damage done to public and private property, I would be in favor of graffiti. Not everyone in America can write a column for a newspaper or be a television or radio commentator. There are even a couple of people left in the country who have never spoken to a Rotary Club. For those Americans, graffiti can be an invaluable source of expression. Let me give you an example:

There is a freeway overpass near Atlanta's Hartsfield Airport, by some counts the world's busiest. A message has been painted on it. In black paint and in a scraggly handwriting, it says, "Betty. You Are Missed."

Betty. You are missed. I can't stop my imagination when it comes to that message. The guy is almost dying. He's tried everything. He's called all her friends. Her mother. She didn't even leave a note. Just up and went east. He came home from work — he drives a cab nights — and she was gone. Took her clothes, the albums, the pictures of the bullfighter, and left him with an empty bed and that awful pain that crawls down in your belly and does a dance that won't let you eat, sleep or put two sane thoughts back to back.

Regrets. First he goes through all his regrets. He never took her out. Maybe twice a month they would go get a pizza. Even then she would want anchovies, and he hated anchovies, so they wouldn't order them, and she would get that disappointed look on her face and pooch out her lips. God, she was cute when she pooched out her lips that way. If he could just find her, he'd buy her a truckload of anchovies.

He forgot her last birthday. He should have been more tender. He should have kissed her on her nose occasionally and said mushy things to her. He'd wanted to, but it's tough for some men to do things like that, and he thought she knew that he felt it but just didn't know how to get it out.

He goes for a few beers one night. Alone. Somebody punches B-6 on the jukebox. Willie Nelson. "You Were Always on My Mind." He drinks half a case, remembers the can of spray paint in his cab, drives to the overpass and, with a shaking hand, does the last desperate thing he knows to do. "Betty. You Are Missed."

Maybe one day, I always think, she will see the message and recognize his handwriting and come back home and be up to her ears in anchovies and kisses on the nose. Or maybe she won't. But I have to believe that man felt a little better that night after he sprayed his message on the freeway overpass. As long as the message is there, as long as some yo-yo from the highway department doesn't come along and remove it, he has hope, some slight shade of hope.

I haven't yet succumbed to writing my messages on freeway overpasses, but I've cried out in a similar way. I have a lingering case of Black Cord Fever. This ailment is easily diagnosed. All you have to do is check your monthly long-distance telephone bill. Is the total $11.16? Then relax, you don't have it. Is it $133.28? Does it include calls to places like Anchorage and Hershey? If so, you've got it bad.

Black Cord Fever is a condition that causes people to get an irresistable urge to make long distance calls in the middle of the night. Let's say it's two o'clock in the morning, you've had a couple of toots and start missing your old girl friend Gloria, who stole the mattress from your apartment and moved to Toledo.

"That you Gloria?" you ask when the ringing finally stops.

"Izme," she answers.

"Are you asleep?" you ask. Another symptom of BCF is that you ask stupid questions. Of course, she's asleep. Everyone in Toledo is asleep at two in the morning.

Turns out Gloria is now living with Freddy, who has the phone by this time, and he threatens to reach out and touch your head with a large stick if he ever gets the chance.

Realizing the love of your life and that creep Freddy are probably sleeping on the very mattress she stole from your apartment, you become very sad and call your ex-wife in Omaha. The only thing she didn't take when she left was the mattress that Gloria got. A man suffering from BCF can run up a huge long-distance bill in one night of tracking down ex-girlfriends, ex-wives and ex-mattresses.

I'm convinced that the telephone companies are directly responsible for BCF in this country. Those conductors of words are the ones who're always trying to embarrass us into calling somebody. That's really your mother they picture in their commercials, looking sad that she hasn't heard from her darling in months. "He's forgotten all about me.

He doesn't love me anymore. I know because he never calls," is what your mother says in those commercials.

So you give in and call. Turns out your mother is at the wrestling match and you get Uncle Willie, who just had his gallbladder removed. And it costs you twenty-six bucks to hear him describe his operation. In detail. You'd just as soon talk to that creep Freddy.

Next time Black Cord Fever strikes, I may just reach for a can of spray paint. Another couple of words won't matter at this point.

Another way phones contribute to media pollution is telephone solicitation. I answer and a woman's voice asks, "Are you the man of the house?" I know I don't sound like Broderick Crawford, but I sure don't sound like Aunt Sally come to visit from Shreveport, either.

Usually they're selling portraits. If you can answer a question — "Who was the only American president to resign from office? His initials are R.N." — you win a free family portrait worth $17.95. The idea, of course, is to sucker you into taking the entire family down to the studio for one free portrait, but by the time they've finished taking individual shots of all the young'uns, they're into you for big bucks.

The other day, however, I got a different scam. A woman who sounded about fifteen years old asked, "As you prepared to invest $29.95 for a selection of coupons worth thousands of dollars if you went out and bought each item for yourself?"

Before I could answer, she was off and running.

"I'm certain you are, so allow me to describe what you will be receiving by purchasing these valuable coupons from Earl's Midnight Merchandising Company. First, you

will get a free lube job, wheel balancing, front end align-
ment, wash and wax, two tanks of gas, an oil change including a new filter, one set of spark plugs and three quarts of
transmission fluid.

"You also will receive a free membership to the Reverend
Leon Goforth's Spiritual Health Spa, including one free
consultation with Reverend Goforth hisself, who will tell
you how you can find salvation through deep knee-bends.
This offer also includes free Putt-Putt golf, four trips down
Willie's Wild 'n' Wet Water Slide, a case of ping-pong balls
and a year's free bowling at Lucky's Pin-o-Matic Lanes,
including shoe rental.

"Don't think this is all you will receive from this once-in-
a-lifetime opportunity, however, 'cause there's much, much
more. You will also get one honey-baked ham, a case of Diet
Pepsi Free, three packages of luncheon meat, a free subscription to People Magazine and nine baby chicks, guaranteed live on arrival. Then you'll get a night's free stay at
Purdy's Bide-a-Wee Motel in the fabulous Rock City resort
area, a pet goat, a nine-by-twelve color photograph, suitable for framing, of the Wilburn brothers and volumes A
through M of the Encyclopedia Britannica."

The girl had not breathed in five minutes, but I was afraid
to stop her.

"And that's not all. You will be receiving a man's and a
woman's Timex watch, a Tennessee Ernie Ford album collection of inspirational hymns, two bamboo steamers, a
pocket fisherman, a tea strainer and three live Maine lob-
sters.

"For one payment and one payment only of $29.95, you
will be entitled to all that and more, including a free estimate from the Mug-a-Bug man, a Hertz once-a-month flea
and tick collar for your dog or cat, a year's supply of Prepa-

ration H, a package of Velveeta cheese, a road map of Idaho, the complete works of Zane Grey, a dozen personalized No. 2 lead pencils, seven pairs of ladies' underpants with each day of the week printed on the backs and a Shetland pony named Arnold.

"Now, will someone from your family be at home for the next hour so that one of our sales representatives can drop by and allow you to take advantage of this fabulous offer?"

I asked her if she would mind reading the list to me one more time, that I thought I had missed a couple of important things. When she got to the part about transmission fluid, I softly depressed the button and hung up.

***

Television obviously is the biggest culprit when it comes to communications pollution, and nowhere is the pollution more evident than in TV weather reports. You can actually see it. Those high-priced meteorologists (a week before, they were slapping hoods in used car commercials) don't call it pollution, of course; they refer to it as "ground clutter."

"Looking on the hundred mile scan of our Super-Duper Weather Scooper, you'll see that it's completely clear. All those patches of color that look like torrential rain are really just ground clutter that the radar is picking up."

I'm still not sure what "ground clutter" is. Will it stick to the soles of my shoes? Will it cause ring worm? If there's nothing on the radar, why do they spend so much time showing it anyway?

Ludlow Porch, who included a weather report in his popular radio talk show, had a better way of dealing with the weather. He'd send his dog outside. "If Rover came back wet, I knew right away that it was raining. If he came back with ice on him, I knew it was cold. That's really all anybody needs to know about the weather. The rest is just pollution."

The best weatherperson I ever knew was my grandmother, Mama Willie. She watched the weather like a hawk.

"Looks like it's about to come up a cloud," she would say. "Come up a cloud" is Deep South for, "It's about to rain."

Mama Willie always knew when it was about to rain because the corns on her little toe would ache. When the corns on her big toe ached, it meant fair to partly cloudy. Mama Willie also had a unique way of forecasting cold.

"Going to turn cold soon," she would say.

"How can you tell?" I would ask.

"Saw a hog frowning today," she would answer. "He knows what's coming."

I've never seen a hog frown or smile, but by the time they get to the stage I like them — sausage, bacon and barbecue — facial expressions are pretty much a thing of the past. Then again, maybe they smile only in the summer; if that's so, I also never would have seen one, because nobody in his right mind goes near a hog dwelling when it's hot.

Late one spring we had a frost which Mama Willie failed to predict. "It's them satellites," she said. "Fouls up the weather. Shame none of them astronauts don't have any chickens to worry about. Maybe then they'd think about staying on the ground."

Then again, maybe chickens are responsible for ground clutter.

***

Television soap operas are another form of television pollution. Does that stuff really go on in the suburbs? And if so, what kinds of vitamins are those guys taking?

I haven't spent much time watching them, but it seems to me that all the soaps I've seen follow the same formula. So I figured if other folks are getting rich from packaging the same sleaze over and over, I might as well give it a try myself. Thus, Grizzard Entertainment proudly presents "General Popsicle" — love, lust and other steamy stuff you used to have to go to the movies to see, set in a Baskin-Robbins ice cream parlor in a shopping center on the outskirts of Bismarck, North Dakota.

The cast:

• NORENE — Sexy eighteen-year-old vaporhead who works the counter during the early shift. Still has trouble telling the difference between chocolate and vanilla. "I know one is dark and one isn't," she says, which at least indicates a step in the right direction. Wears tight-fitting uniforms and brings in customers from miles around who have no interest in ice cream but enjoy watching Norene shake her pistachio.

• DORENE — Sexy eighteen-year-old vaporhead who works the counter during the late shift. Gets confused when a customer asks for more than one scoop of any flavor. The mop has a higher IQ. Also wears tight-fitting uniforms and is so well endowed that she once reached deep into a bucket of almond toffee and was stuck there for nearly an hour until the Roto-Rooter man could be summoned to free her. There was no charge for his services.

• ARNOLD — Assistant manager who flunked out of the Bismarck School of Bartending. Twenty-ish, handsome, smiles out of the corner of his mouth and steals out of the cash register to support his Clearasil addiction.

• MR. PALMER — The manager. Forty-ish, balding, former wrestler and veterinarian. Friendly and fatherlike to his employees, especially Norene and Dorene. Likes Arnold, too, but is suspicious of him. "I wouldn't trust him as far as I could throw the mop," says Mr. Palmer.

• THE MOP — Has more acting ability than anyone else in the cast.

The show opens as Norene and Dorene vie for Arnold's attention. They get into a huge, hair-pulling, name-calling fight behind the counter over near the chocolate mint, and Mr. Palmer has to break it up. During the confusion of the fight, the refrigeration system is accidentally shut off and six thousand gallons of ice cream melt and begin to run all over the floor and out into the parking lot of the shopping center.

As the melting ice cream shorts out the center's lighting system, Arnold goes from store to store cleaning out the cash registers and then splits for Fargo in Mr. Palmer's black 1958 Buick.

Norene and Dorene, their uniforms torn in revealing fashion during the fight, both tell Mr. Palmer they are pregnant and that Arnold is the father of their babies. Mr. Palmer marries both Norene and Dorene because that's the only honorable thing to do, and the Roto-Rooter man reappears to demand payment for freeing Dorene from the almond toffee.

Millions of dollars in lawsuits result from the ice cream meltdown, and Mr. Palmer is now completely broke. He decides to commit suicide by sticking his head in a bucket of chocolate syrup. Before he can do so, however, Arnold, who has used the money he stole from the shopping center to stage a successful campaign and become governor of North Dakota, returns to the scene and pays off all of Mr. Palmer's debts.

Norene and Dorene find out they weren't really pregnant after all, and they run away with the Roto-Rooter man. The mop falls off the wall in disgust.

Next on "General Popsicle": Mr. Palmer hires a new counter girl. Or is she? Guest appearance by Renee Richards.

***

Actually the soap operas are no more offensive than the television commercials which run with them. Take those feminine hygiene products, for example. One manufacturer touts the fact that its products are disposable. Now, I ask you: Who would want to keep such a thing?

Deodorant commercials are the same way. "Oh, Marge," says one Junior Leaguer to another, "how do you manage to stay so dry?" I'll tell you how Marge manages to stay so dry. She lies around in bed all day eating bon-bons and not hitting a lick at a snake, that's how.

I saw a commercial the other day for medicine to remove canker sores. What on earth are canker sores and where do they come from? Do you get them on your canker, and if so, where is mine?

Recently attorneys have gotten into the act. They show pictures of rear-end collisions where everybody ends up with whiplash. Then they follow with a cute little jingle, like,

Wilson, Jones, Morris and Pate, The ones to call when you lit-ah-gate.

May they get sores on their cankers, and may their wives dispose of their feminine hygiene products by storing them in their husbands' golf bags.

And then there's the commercial for burial plots which begins, "We started not to make this commercial...." So why did you, casket face? It was that commercial which convinced me to give my body to science when I die. I want them to figure out how a man in my condition could live so long.

***

But to paraphrase an old adage, there's some good in the

worst of everything, even television. Amid all that harmless (or is it mindless?) clutter, there occasionally is a program that can make you think. And squirm.

The best squirmmaker of them all, I suspect, is "60 Minutes." Sunday after Sunday, Mike Wallace always gets his man.

"And so, Mr. Ferndorf, you say you know nothing whatsoever about the falsified expense reports," Mike Wallace says, and his victim, that lying cheat Ferndorf, thinks he's about to get off the hook.

"I know nothing about it, Mike," says Ferndorf, who is sadly mistaken.

"Then what about these?" asks Wallace, suddenly producing from some unknown place the falsified expense reports. And guess whose signature is all over them.

Ferndorf, dead duck, begins to squirm.

"We're waiting, Mr. Ferndorf," says Wallace, twisting the knife.

"Well...I, huh," explains Ferndorf, who by now is perspiring and turning blue while all of America watches.

"Look at this, Martha," says the average "60 Minutes" viewer in Des Moines. "Ol' Mike just got another one!"

As a squirmmaker, Perry Mason was small time compared to Mike Wallace.

I have this recurring dream, part of the Mike Wallace Syndrome, where "60 Minutes" gets in touch with me and says they would like to get some footage for a possible future profile. This is my big break, I think, and soon all the cameras are there and I'm sitting across from Mike Wallace and we're having a lovely chat.

"Well," I say, "after knocking out my column each day, I enjoy a few sets of tennis or maybe I relax at home with a good book and . . ."

Then Mike Wallace interrupts me and says, "That's enough beating around the bush, Mr. Grizzard. Why don't you come clean?"

Startled, I begin to stutter. "Wwwwwwhat on earth are you talking about, Mmmmmmike?"

"This," says Wallace, holding a copy of an essay I did in high school on the Clayton-Bulwer Treaty, an essay which won first place in the county literary meet. "Did you actually write this essay without notes, as the rules of the literary meet specified, or did you, in fact, smuggle in your history book and write your essay by copying word for word from the book?"

I'm squirming from side to side in my chair.

"Look at this, Martha," says the guy in Des Moines.

I did, in fact, smuggle in my history book. How else could anybody write five pages on the Clayton-Bulwer Treaty? But how did Mike Wallace? . . .

"You're probably wondering how we found out about this fraud," says Wallace. "We were first contacted by Arthur Norbest, who finished second in that contest and who just happens to be Harry Reasoner's nephew."

I usually awaken before breaking down in front of the cameras, disgracing not only myself but all my family. Not to mention everybody who signed the Clayton-Bulwer Treaty.

Wouldn't it be ironic, I often catch myself thinking, if one day somebody got something on Mike Wallace, like maybe he wet his bed at camp, and then made him squirm before the entire country? That's a better dream than the one I've been having.

***

I have spent more than half my life working for newspapers. Like many other things in this world, our relationship has been one of love and hate. I love newspapers, but I hate it when they misplay their hands.

I have my own ideas about what should and shouldn't be in a newspaper and about how a newspaper should look. I've never found anyone who was particularly interested in my ideas, but I have them nonetheless. You never know when some wealthy eccentric might leave me a major metropolitan daily.

First of all, if I owned a newspaper, I wouldn't run any color. There is something to be said for good ol' black and white. "It's right here in black and white, Gladys," a man says to his wife when he wants to assure her that something is true beyond a doubt. He would never say, "It's right here in orange and green, Gladys."

I would never run stories in my newspaper about how many fatalities the highway patrol is predicting during the holiday weekend. Too gruesome. If you're going to run that kind of story, why not run one where local cardiologists predict how many people are going to croak from heart attack over the same period?

I wouldn't run scoring summaries from hockey games in my newspaper. They don't make any sense.

I wouldn't allow lengthy interviews with twenty-year-old defensive linemen who, given the choice, probably would rather eat a newspaper than attempt to read one.

I would run follow-ups to society marriage announcements in my newspaper: "Mr. and Mrs. Arnold Crampton announce the divorce of their daughter, Heide Mildred Crampton Millingham III, son of Dr. and Mrs. William Harvey Millingham, Jr. Grounds for the divorce were that Mr. Millingham III whomped his former wife on the head with his polo mallet whenever she complained about his riding his pony in the house."

I would tell my movie critics to cool it on all that imagery and symbolism be-bop and just tell the readers whether or not the movie is worth seeing and how the popcorn is where it's playing and what time the darn things starts.

I would allow precious few interviews with artists. They're more boring than twenty-year-old defensive linemen.

I wouldn't give Ted Kennedy any more publicity. Let him take out an ad.

I'd run fewer stories about abortion, dieting, sex after seventy and before seventeen, how to dress if you're a career woman and have decided being married and having kids is not for you, sperm banks and what to do about liver spots. We have Phil Donahue to cover those things.

I would run more stories about little boys who lost their dogs and then found them, and I'd run eighty percent of all political stories next to the comics page.

Finally, I would watch my columnists very closely. They can be real troublemakers.

— 15 —

Are We Missing
A Few Cards?

I **HAVE ALWAYS SUSPECTED** that some of my friends are not sane. Of course, I would never come right out and say that to them, but in the polite South we have several euphemisms for getting the point across. For instance, we might say of such a person that he's not playing with a full deck. Or, she doesn't have both oars in the water. Or, his lights are on, but there's nobody home. Or, his elevator doesn't stop at all floors. Such phrases seem to be more civil than saying, "He's crazier than a billy goat at mating time."

Although I seldom invite such people to my house for fear they might not leave, I keep them on my Christmas card list to demonstrate to the world how open-minded I am. Besides, in the eternal quest for the origins of true grit and two socks that match, you never know when there might be a gem hiding inside a rock. So, with hammer in hand, allow me to present a few of my rock-headed friends.

***

Not long ago, I decided it was time to invest some of my very small fortune in the stock market (it's the only form of legalized gambling in Georgia). I called my broker friend, Willard "The Bull" Saperstein of Saperstein, Silverman and Simpson, Inc., the brokerage house with the famous slogan, "Yes, yes, yes, buy from SSS."

"Cat food," Willard said the minute he answered the phone.

"Cat food?" I asked.

"Cat food is hot," he said. "More and more people are owning cats these days, and a cat has got to eat."

So I invested heavily in companies that manufacture cat food. A week later, a rumor circulated that Morris the cat had a severe case of indigestion. Nine Lives cat food plummeted two and a half down to just six and a half lives, and the bottom fell out of Puss 'n' Boots as well.

"Just an unlucky break," said Willard, who then suggested that he buy IBM stock for me. IBM has always been a sound company, so I gave him the go-ahead. Sure enough, a week later IBM announced a major breakthrough that sent the stock soaring.

I called Willard and told him to sell, expecting to make a handsome profit on my investment.

"You don't have that IBM," said Willard.

"What other IBM is there?" I asked.

"I bought you International Banjo Makers. It's down eight points and falling fast."

I should have learned my lesson but didn't. Willard soon called with another hot tip.

"American Chinchilla," he said.

"Chinchillas?"

"You should buy every share of American Chinchilla you can get your hands on," said Willard. "It's going to be a cold winter, and there's going to be a heavy demand for chinchilla coats."

It wasn't long before that investment went sour, too, when American Chinchilla discovered that seventy-five percent of the male chinchillas it had bought for its large breeding farm in Oklahoma were gay.

"Don't buy me any more risky stocks," I told Willard.

"Well, why didn't you say so?" He immediately placed an order in my name for one hundred shares of Asbestos Toys. I lost another bundle.

"Get away from me," I said to Willard the next time he called.

"You've just had a few bad breaks," he said. "Give me one more chance and I'll make it all up to you."

Fool that I am, I trusted him once more. Willard came back to me with a new portfolio of can't-miss stocks. He had International Cranberry; a blight killed most of the crop.

He had a new company that had perfected a way to breed worms for fish bait in half the time and at half the cost; one night the worms all crawled out of their boxes and disappeared into the ground.

He had stock in a company that manufactures salt. Salt took a bad health rap. When it rains, it pours.

He had me invest in a company that had developed a chemical that would cure runny nose, itchy throat, stuffy head and that ache-all-over feeling. Unfortunately, it also would inflame your hemorrhoids.

He had Royal Lippizan Stallions, Inc. Several mares came down with herpes and the stallions all had nervous breakdowns.

He had Chrysler. I panicked after all my other stocks fell through the floor and sold two days before it started to soar.

Willard, meanwhile, got out of the stockbroker business.

He's now my bookie.

***

Contrary to what some people have said about me, I don't hate all liberals. I have a very good friend named Blanton who is one of the country's leading liberals.

Blanton is, of course, anti-nuke, except for the one bomb he would like to drop on Ronald Reagan's Civil Rights Commission. He supported George McGovern in '72 but has dropped George like a bad habit in '85. The ticket he would like to see the Democrats offer would feature Jesse Jackson and Jane Fonda. Blanton is against prayer in school, tax write-offs for the rich, capital punishment, boxing, designer clothes and Senator Jesse Helms. He is for passage of the Equal Rights Amendment, the legalization of marijuana, the impeachment of Nancy Reagan, a national holiday honoring John Lennon and giving the Russians the benefit of the doubt.

"You don't agree with President Reagan that Russia is the 'Evil Empire'?" I asked him.

"Conservative claptrap," he answered.

"But what about the Russian invasion and occupation of Afghanistan?"

"Nothing worse than what we did to the American Indians," he said.

I had forgotten about Blanton's interest in the plight of the American Indians. For starters, he wants to give back the land we got in the Gadsden Purchase and make Marlon Brando the new Secretary of the Interior.

What stirs Blanton's liberal blood more than anything, however, is environmental issues. He fought tirelessly to save the snail darter. He has protested vigorously against the slaughter of baby seals. He tried to get chicken put on the endangered species list when a Mrs. Winner's went up next door to a Popeye's in his neighborhood.

Last time I saw Blanton, he was loudly spewing forth his usual tirade against The Right when I asked him what was new.

"Pelicans," he answered.

"Pelicans?"

"Somebody has got to do something for the pelicans in this country."

I had no idea pelicans were in any sort of trouble, but Blanton set me straight.

"Do you know what causes pelicans to die?"

"I don't even know what causes them to get sick," I said. Blanton did not laugh.

"It's the most horrible thing I've ever heard," he explained. What happens is that pelicans have to keep their eyes open when they're diving for fish, and after diving into salt water day after day with their eyes open, they become blind and can't see the fish. Consequently, they eventually die of starvation.

I asked him what we were supposed to do.

"I'm going to Washington to demand that the government provide a pair of goggles for every pelican in America," he said.

Can Blanton save the pelicans? The hell he can. But at least he has a cause, and I know enough about his kind to know this: A liberal without a cause is like, well, a pelican without goggles. What good is a big mouth if you can't find anything to aim it at?

***

Scientists have been trying for years to talk to porpoises, supposedly the most intelligent members of the underwater crowd. Me, I've never understood why there's so much interest. If you could talk to a porpoise, what would you ask him? How's the water?

I once tried to talk to a girl in a singles bar who bore an amazing resemblance to a porpoise. She had a large nose and wore lots of blue eyeshadow.

"What's your sign, sweetheart?" I asked. That one was hot for awhile.

"Pisces," she said.

"I thought so."

"Why is that?"

"Easy," I said. "You look a lot like something that lives underwater." When the swelling went down in about a week, I could see as well as ever.

I really don't find it so incredible that animals might be able to communicate with people. That's because I grew up with the legendary Claude "Goat" Rainwater, who not only smelled like an animal but could also talk to them. Dogs were his specialty. He would talk to any dog in town, except poodles.

"Don't talk to no poodles," said Claude.

"Why not?" I asked.

"Had one once," he explained. "Dog wouldn't talk but one time a year. First year, he said the food I was giving him was bad. After another year, he said he didn't like sleeping outside with the beagles. Third year, he said he wanted to leave and find a new place to live."

"What did you tell him?" I inquired.

"I told him, 'Go ahead. All you've done since you've been here is gripe.'"

Goat also once had a bird dog he bought from a fellow in Texas.

"Dog's a big football fan," said Goat. "Every time he sees a game on television, he raises his paw and says, 'Hook 'em, Horns!'"

"Hook 'em, Horns," incidentally, is the battle cry for University of Texas football fans, a rather rowdy bunch.

I tried to get Goat to make his bird dog do that trick for me, but Goat said it wouldn't be right since it wasn't football season. He said I'd have to wait until the fall. When fall came, however, the dog was gone. Word was he'd been dognapped by a bunch of Oklahoma fans.

I probably didn't miss much anyway. If a drunk Texan can fall off a bar stool in Austin and bellow "Hook 'em, Horns!" twice before he hits the floor, I don't know what's so special about a perfectly sober bird dog being able to do the same thing.

Goat also talked to cows, horses, pigs, chickens and mules. And he also smelled like cows, horses, pigs, chickens and mules.

"Hate trying to talk to a mule," he once said.

"Too stubborn?" I asked.

"Like trying to talk a tomcat into staying home on a Saturday night."

I remember asking Goat what was the most unusual animal he had ever talked to.

"Girl skunk," he said.

"What did she say to you?"

"'What's your sign, big boy?' "

***

My friend Fred was complaining about his children.

"All they do is beg for things and then bellyache if they don't get them," he said.

"What are they begging for?" I asked.

"My son wants a sports car and my daughter wants a trip to Europe."

"How old are your children, anyway?"

"The boys is six," he said, "and the girl is nine."

I used to employ the same strategy with my parents. I'd ask for things like an air rifle, or a Flexy racer or a motor scooter — things I knew they'd never give me. But the idea was to inflate the request so that what I ended up getting was still pretty good.

Actually, I didn't figure out that strategy alone. An older playmate explained it to me one day. I was six at the time and wanted a dog, but my parents weren't ready to take care of one, so they refused. I ran off crying and bumped into the older kid.

"What's wrong?" he asked.

"My parents won't let me have a dog," I sobbed.

"Did you ask them for a dog?" he asked.

"Of course I asked them for a dog."

"Dummy," said my wiley playmate. "That was your mistake. You should have asked them for a little brother. Then they would have given you a dog."

I tried to explain the old ruse to Fred, but he wasn't listening. He seemed preoccupied and generally irritated.

"Come on," I said, "what's really bothering you?"

"Well, it's my fortieth birthday today," he confessed.

"Hey, congratulations! Are you going out tonight to celebrate?" I asked.

"Why should I celebrate?"

"Because it's a milestone in your life, that's why."

"Not to me," said my friend. "It's just another year I didn't get a pony."

***

Rigsby is one of those people who will try anything once. And if he likes it, he'll try it several more times.

He was having dinner at a Mexican restaurant recently when someone suggested a round of straight tequila shooters.

"I'll try anything once," said Rigsby.

He tried one straight tequila shooter, liked it, and proceeded to drink a dozen more. Before finally passing out in his cheese enchilada, he did a Mexican hat dance on the table, sang three verses of "La Cucaracha" and tried to ride a fat lady with shaggy hair because he was convinced she was a burro.

Rigsby has tried sky diving, mountain climbing, square dancing, snake charming, body painting, goat roping and escargot, so I shouldn't have been surprised when he told me he also had tried cocaine. "You know me," he said. "I'll try anything once."

I've never tried cocaine myself, but I'm fascinated by the number of people who apparently think it's worth going to jail for. I asked Rigsby how he came to try it.

"I was at a party," he said, "and somebody introduced me to this fellow from Southern California. He had buttoned up just enough of his shirt so you couldn't see his navel, and he had enough chains around his neck to open a hardware store. We started talking and all of a sudden he looked around the room to see if anybody was watching us. Then he leaned over and asked me if I wanted some coke.

"I told him I'd just stick to the beer, but that there was plenty of Coke and Tab and even some 7-Up in the refrigerator. He thought I was pulling his leg, so he insisted that I come out to his car for a toot. I wasn't sure what a 'toot' was, but you know me — I'll try anything once," continued Rigsby.

"We got to his car and he pulled out one of those bags you wrap sandwiches in. I asked, 'What's in your bag?' He said, 'It's cocaine, man. You want some?' And I said, 'Sure, I'll try anything once.'

"He poured some of it out on this little piece of glass and

then handed me a straw and told me to sniff it up my nose. About two sniffs and I had this powerful urge to sneeze. My sinuses are always giving me trouble, you know. I let out this big one and that cocaine went all over this fellow's car and in his hair. He started cussing me hard and told me I had just blown away $300 worth of cocaine. I said, 'Well, that's show business, Hoss,' and went on back to the party for another beer."

I asked Rigsby if he thought he would ever try cocaine again.

"Once was enough," he said. "But if that fellow paid $300 a sniff for that stuff, I sure would like to meet the man who sold it to him, because, brother, there goes a salesman."

***

My friend Worthington was scared to death when he got the call last week that the boss wanted to see him immediately. He was still shaking when he told me about it.

"Worthington," the boss said, "how are things out in Shipping and Receiving?"

"Fine sir," he said. "We could use an extra forklift, but . . ."

"I'll check into it next week, Worthington. Frankly, I didn't call you in to discuss forklifts. I understand you are the chairman for this year's company Christmas party."

"I am, sir. I'm replacing Van der Meer from Personnel."

"What happened to Van der Meer?"

"He got run over by a forklift."

"What's the damage?"

"Darn thing will probably be out of service for another month, sir. That's why I was saying that we need another forklift."

"I'm not talking about the forklift, Worthington. I'm talking about Van der Meer."

"Oh. He'll be back in a couple of weeks but not in time to

coordinate the Christmas party."

"Well, I know this thing has been practically dumped in your lap, Worthington, but what are your plans?"

"Well, sir, I thought we'd get drunk and chase the secretaries around."

"I'd expect that from somebody in Personnel, Worthington, but you're from Shipping and Receiving. Can't we do something a little more original?"

"Like what, sir?"

"Like drawing names and exchanging gifts."

"Don't you remember, sir? We tried that three years ago, but Whipple from Accounting drew Beulah Riddick from Quality Control and gave her a pair of underpants from Frederick's of Hollywood."

"So?"

"So, Beulah Riddick's husband who worked in Building Maintenance was at the party, and when he saw what Whipple had given his wife, he tried to pull off one of Whipple's ears with a pair of pliers."

"Whatever came of all that?"

"Nothing, really. Beulah and her husband got back together, and if you speak up, Whipple can hear you just fine."

"OK, so forget the gifts. What about we have some coffee and cake and sing Christmas carols?"

"We tried that two years ago, sir, but a couple of the stock boys slipped in some beer and cheap wine, and everybody started throwing cake and a fight broke out and the cops came and the whole thing made the newspapers the next day."

"I seem to remember the headline, now that you mention it, Worthington: 'Workers Deck Each Other in Halls of Local Factory.' "

"You fired Himmerman in Public Relations over that one, sir."

"Himmerman schimmerman. There must be something decent we can do for the annual company Christmas party. What about a dance? We can rent a hall and get a band and have a Christmas dance."

"Tried that last year, sir."

"And?"

"I'm surprised you don't remember, sir. Beulah Riddick got stewed and did a strip number, and when she got down to her unmentionables, her husband started looking for the creep who had given them to her."

"And who was the guilty party? My memory is so bad these days, Worthington. I'm getting on up there, you know."

"Well, sir, Beulah spilled the whole story. You gave them to her."

"Did her husband come at me with those pliers?"

"No, sir. You promoted him to manager of the Houston plant before he had a chance to go out to his truck for his toolbox."

"Worthington?"

"Sir?"

"Let's go with the getting drunk and chasing secretaries. And if I happen to catch one, please remind me what I'm supposed to do next."

***

The majority of my life has been spent either learning to be or being a newspaperman. In the course of that pursuit, I have encountered a plethora of unbelievable and unbelievably talented people.

One such person was John E. Drewry, dean of the Henry Grady School of Journalism at the University of Georgia

when I arrived there in the mid-1960's. Founder of broadcasting's revered Peabody Awards, Dean Drewry was a
master of the language with a wit that one sees today only
in such distinguished gentlemen as Sir John Gielgud and
John (Smith-Barney) Houseman.

The Dean wore round glasses that gave him the appearance of an owl, and he wore three-piece suits with a long
watch fob hanging from the vest. His accent was aristocrat-
ically Southern, making it a joy to hear him pronounce
polysyllabic words such as, "im-proh-pri-uh-tee."

As he lectured one day to our class of approximately three
hundred students, he walked back and forth across the
room that had an exit door to either side of the podium.
Each time he reached one of the doors, he would peer out.
This routine went on for about forty-five minutes before he
offered an explanation.

"Class, I know there are those among you who are wondering why I have made regular visits to each of these doors
today, peeking out each time in search of, you are no doubt
saying, God knows what. My purpose for this effort is quite
simple, my young friends.

"I, as I am sure you have, have become quite interested in
our country's missions into outer space. I have said to
myself, 'Is it not pompous on the part of all earthlings to
consider that we are the only intelligent beings in this
universe?' The answer can be only one: of course, it is, and
there must be other civilizations out there who, as we are
they, are trying to contact us at this very moment.

"Let us consider what might happen if these beings from
another planet landed on earth for the first time here on the
campus of the University of Georgia. It is certainly not
unthinkable that these beings would want first to see the
environs of our nation's oldest state chartered institution of

higher learning.

"It is further apparent to me," he continued, "that once they removed themselves from whatever contraption it might have been that brought them here, they would first want to visit the School of Journalism where we specialize in the art of communication.

"That being the case, I have been walking to each door today assuming that this might be the day for our first encounter with the extra-terrestrials. Were they to arrive here in our building, I would not want them to have to wander the halls with no one to greet them. As dean, I think that certainly would be my duty."

A couple of years later, when I had taken my college journalism education and put it into practice at the Athens Daily News, I encountered an equally fascinating and talented character in my editor, Glenn Vaughn.

One afternoon when I reported for work, Glenn asked me to step into his office. "What," he asked, "would be the biggest story we could have in this newspaper?"

I thought for a moment before answering. "Coed dorms at the university."

"Bigger than that," said Glenn.

"A four-lane highway to Atlanta."

"Even bigger," he prompted.

"Georgia signs a quarterback who can pass."

"Close," said Glenn, "but that's still not it. The biggest story we could have would be the Second Coming."

I did not argue with him.

"So just in case it breaks while we're here, I've gone ahead and designed page one."

He had the page neatly drawn in green ink on a layout pad. There would be a large file photograph of Jesus on the front, although Glenn was hopeful that the wire services would provide a photo of the actual moment of touchdown. He also had written the headline as well. In bold, 124-point type, it would say, "HE'S BACK!" Underneath that headline would be a smaller one reading, "Details on Page 2."

To this day, I don't know whether Glenn was joking or not.

Billy Bob Robinson was another character spawned by newspapers. He was a member of the Atlanta Journal sports staff when I went to work there in 1968. Robinson's beat was auto racing and outdoors, and he was one of the finest writers in the business . . . even when he didn't make it to an event. "Never let the facts stand in the way of a good story," was one of Robinson's favorite lines.

Once he wrote a piece about fishing for bass with his good pal, ol' so-and-so down in South Georgia. "Fish are bitin' so good down here," he quoted his friend as saying, "we have to hide the bait to keep 'em from jumpin' in the boat."

Several days after that article appeared, I fielded a phone call in the department.

"Let me speak to that Robinson fella," said the voice on the other end.

"I'm sorry," I said, "but he's out of the office right now."

"Well," said the caller, "just give him a message. Tell 'im that there fella he was supposed to have been fishin' with down here in South Georgia the other day's been dead for six months."

Another Robinson quirk was that he never showed up for work on time. He carried a flat tire around in his trunk to use as an excuse anytime he couldn't think of something more exotic.

Finally the boss told him that if he was late one more time, he would be fired. Sure enough, the next morning Robinson appeared two hours late.

"OK, you know what I told you," said the boss. "You're fired and I don't want to argue about it. But just for the record and for one last time, why were you late?"

"Well," began Billy Bob, "you know that Maria and I have been married for almost nine years and that we have eight children."

The boss nodded in agreement, waiting for the rest of the story.

"Well, this morning was the first time since we've been married that Maria has had a period, and she was too sick to take the kids to school, so I had to do it."

Instead of firing Robinson, the boss took a week off to regain his composure.

***

I had this roommate named Charlie once. We lived in what was basically a dive, but it was our first home away from home, our first taste of independence, so it was special.

We did what all anxious young men do when they first leave the nest — we played our music loud, stayed up late and sought the company of women. I got lucky and met a dazzling young thing. The fact that she had another year of high school left and I was headed off to college seemed to impress her considerably.

I cleaned all the trash out of my car, bought a bottle of English Leather cologne, and even bought a new pair of yellow Gold Cup socks to go with the yellow shirt I planned to wear on our big date. Gold Cup socks were a fashion must in those days. They came in a variety of colors and cost $1.50 a pair, an obscene price even now.

As the time drew near for my date, I showered, shaved

and splashed English Leather all over my body. Then I started putting on the clothes I had meticulously laid out on my bed. But my new yellow Gold Cup socks were missing.

"Have you seen my new yellow Gold Cups?" I yelled to Charlie, who was watching "Bonanza" in the living room.

"Haven't seen 'em," he answered, never taking his eyes off the screen as Hoss Cartwright thrashed a man to within an inch of his life.

I never found those new socks, and my date turned out to be a total bust. I don't know if one was the result of the other, but I spent a good deal of the evening pulling up a stretched-out pair of white socks.

More than twenty years later, I was speaking at a public gathering when a woman came up and asked me if I remembered Charlie, my old roommate.

Of course, I told her.

"Well," she said, "he's a friend of mine, and when I told him I was going to see you here tonight, he asked me to bring you something."

She reached into her pocketbook and pulled out a pair of yellow Gold Cup socks.

"Charlie said he stole a pair of these from you once, and it's been worrying him ever since. He said to give you these and ask you to please forgive him."

I don't wear yellow socks anymore, but there's a pair in my sock drawer anyway.

— 16 —

Grit Is In the Eye Of the Beholder

A Little Old-Fashioned Justice

IT WAS ALAN'S BIRTHDAY. He met his girlfriend for lunch and they had a few drinks, and then a few more, and then she gave him his presents, one of which was a bouquet of flowers. They had one more for the road before she went back to work and Alan headed home.

On the way, a policeman pulled him over. "Have you been drinking?" he asked.

Alan admitted to having a couple at lunch with his girlfriend. "It's my birthday," he added.

The policeman apologized for ruining Alan's birthday, but he told him he obviously was too drunk to drive, so he loaded Alan into the back of the patrol car.

"I don't know why I did it," Alan explained later, "but I decided to take my flowers with me."

At the police station, they booked Alan for drunken driving and put him in a cell with several others. Again, he took his flowers.

"As they were opening the cell door for me," Alan said, "I realized I shouldn't have brought the flowers with me. One fellow yelled right away, 'Hey, Flower Boy, did you bring those for me?'

"There was a group of black guys sitting in one corner of the cell. When I looked at them and smiled, they smiled back, so I went and sat down with them and tried to make friends," said Alan.

"I told them it was my birthday and that my girlfriend had given me the flowers. They sang, 'Happy birthday, dear Flower boy.' I've never been so embarrassed and so scared in my life. I tried again to make friends.

"I asked one guy what he was in for. He said he was hungry and didn't have any money, so he went into a convenience store and put a can of Spam in his pocket and walked out. He said he didn't even get a chance to eat it before the police stopped him and brought him in with the Spam still in his pocket."

Alan spent the night in jail. At his hearing the next morning — both he and his flowers were somewhat wilted from the experience — the judge was hard on him despite his first-offender status. He received a hefty fine and was placed on probation.

"I learned my lesson," he said. "The quickest way to get people to stop drinking and driving is to make them spend a night in a jail cell holding on to a bouquet of flowers. It's a frightening experience."

Alan was released along with the man who had stolen the can of Spam. "I thought it was a nice gesture," he said. "They gave him the can back."

A citizen learns his lesson about drinking and driving and the Spam bandit, hungry enough to steal for his supper, is allowed to eat the evidence. Just a little old-fashioned justice goin' round.

LOYALTY EVEN UNDER DURESS

Tom first met blue-eyed Mary nearly forty years ago when they both were students at Auburn University. They eventually married and had three daughters and a son.

The family settled in a small Alabama town where Tom began a successful business. Mary took care of the kids and dreamed of finishing her degree, which had been cut short by the kids. Maybe when they were grown . . .

Three of their children ended up with degrees from Auburn, and the family became loyal supporters of the school and especially of the football program. Mary was the biggest War Eagle fan in the entire family. She often clipped headlines about her beloved team and taped them to the refrigerator door.

When the kids had finished their educations, Mary decided it was time to fulfill her dream of returning to school. "School's so hard when you get as old as I am," she told friends, but she wanted that degree. Her grades were high and her family and friends were proud of her.

It all came on suddenly. One day Mary was bounding with energy and enthusiasm; the next day she was in the hospital after suffering a heart attack. A week later, she died at age fifty-seven.

As a friend of the family, I attended the funeral. The preacher talked about how much Mary loved that family but about how she also was her own person: "Completing her education was so important to her," he said. He also talked about her love for Auburn University: "She was fanatical," the preacher said lovingly, and the family even broke into smiles as they remembered the woman's loyalty.

As they rolled Mary's casket from the church, the family followed it down the aisle. Tom held to one of his weeping daughters, trying to comfort her. As he passed, I couldn't help noticing the tie he had chosen to wear to his wife's funeral. On the front, in blue script, were the words, "War Eagle."

"At first," one of the children told me later, "we couldn't believe Daddy was wearing that tie to Mama's funeral. But then, it just sort of made sense somehow."

Yes, it did. It certainly did.

ONE VOTE FOR A POKE

Jason, who is eleven, was walking home from school with a friend. They were doing what all kids that age do — walking through vacant lots, throwing rocks and dirt bombs, "anything to get dirty," his mother said.

Behind a convenience store, Jason accidentally stepped on a board with a rusty nail protruding through it. The nail penetrated his shoe and lodged in his foot. In such excruciating pain, Jason could not get the nail out of his foot, so his friend had to pull it loose.

Bleeding badly and still in pain, Jason limped into the store, showed the clerk his wound and asked for a Band-Aid or some sort of bandage.

"Yeah, I got plenty of Band-Aids," said the clerk. "But have you got a dollar?"

Jason said he didn't have any money, and neither did his friend.

"Sorry," said the clerk. "No money, no Band-Aids."

There was no money for the telephone either, so Jason, still bleeding but aided by his friend, limped the half-mile home.

His mother rushed him to the doctor's office, where he received a tetanus shot. He spent the rest of the weekend hot-soaking his foot. Jason will be fine, but his mother may never be the same again.

"I know now how wars start," she said, "how people get murdered, how hate grows from a tiny little thing into a monster. Ever since this happened, I have wanted to walk into that store and poke that man's eyeballs out. I have wanted to stay home from work and march in front of that store with signs saying, 'Do not buy anything from this store; you might bleed to death.'

"So far I haven't poked anyone's eyeballs out, and to my husband's relief I haven't picketed the store, either. I haven't even called the company to complain; they'd probably just tell me the man was doing his job. I did pray for the man, but I worry about this rage I can't shake.

"You've seen those containers near cash registers that say, 'Take a penny, leave a penny.' Well, I've given enough pennies in this same neighborhood store to buy a large box of Band-Aids. And I would have gladly paid for anything Jason used. I would have appreciated it if the clerk had even allowed him in the bathroom to pack his shoe with toilet paper. And I certainly would have appreciated it if he had called me so I could have picked up my injured child.

"I'm just a mother whose child has been done wrong, and I just don't know about people sometimes....I just don't understand, and I don't know that I ever will."

Me either. And, Lord, forgive me for wishing she had gone for the guy's eyeballs just once.

A DEAL IS A DEAL, SOMETIMES

A man was walking along the river that flows behind a

expensive neighborhood when three guys told him he was trespassing. He argued briefly, but when one of them pulled a gun, he left and went for the police.

He returned later with a police cruiser following him. Behind the police car just happened to be eighteen-year-old Nuno de Almeida, a native of Portugal who had recently come to live with his American-born stepfather.

The man in the lead car stopped when he reached the scene of his trouble and spotted two of the guys who had pulled the gun on him. The police car then stopped, and so did Nuno de Almeida. Suddenly, the police cruiser backed up and crashed into the front of Nuno's car. The cop jumped out of his car, rushed to Nuno's window and accused him of following too closely.

The cop called his sergeant, who arrived on the scene a few minutes later. They conferred and then told Nuno that if he would forget the whole thing, there would be no ticket for following too closely and no chance of losing his license.

Nuno wouldn't make the deal. His car was damaged, and there was still his stepfather to answer to. The two fellows who had pulled the gun had witnessed the whole event. The cop walked over to them, mentioned they could be in big trouble, and asked if they had seen the accident.

"The inference was there," said one of the fellows named Kenny, "that if we backed him, he wouldn't do anything about the gun."

So Kenny and his buddy said they hadn't seen anything. No charges were filed against them for the incident with the gun. The fellow in the lead car also said, truthfully, that he hadn't seen anything.

Nuno de Almeida was given a court date. His stepfather, despite the advice of three lawyers to forget the matter and take the fine, urged his son to fight. "Nuno doesn't lie," he said.

Nuno pleaded not guilty. The policeman gave his side of the story, then Nuno told his version.

"Are you saying the officer is lying?" asked the judge.

"He hit my car when he backed up," said Nuno.

The courtroom laughed. Kenny was then called to the witness stand to testify against Nuno. A deal is a deal. Nuno looked to be in big trouble. It was his word against the cop's and the cop had a witness.

But Kenny and his friend had talked things over. "We just couldn't live with our consciences if we didn't tell the truth," he said. "Why should this kid look like a liar when he wasn't?"

Kenny told the judge the truth about what had happened, that Nuno was not lying. The courtroom broke into applause. The judge dismissed the charges. The officer was left to his superiors.

Only in America.

A LESSON IN SAVING

Brad, age eight, and his sister Linda, age eleven, recently received gifts of fifty dollars each from their grandparents. Brad wanted to spend his money on candy; fifty smackers will buy a lot of Reese's Cups. Linda wanted to spend hers on rock tapes; fifty dollars worth should keep her gyrating till she's sixteen.

Brad and Linda's mother, however, didn't want her children blowing their first serious amounts of money on frivolity. "I wanted them to use their money to learn a lesson," Karen said. "I convinced them that the way to accomplish the American dream was to put their money in a savings account. I explained that the bank would pay them for using their money."

The kids agreed, and so the next morning they all headed down to the bank to open an account. At the bank, however, the kids were told they couldn't have their very own savings accounts because the minimum amount needed was one hundred dollars. Bank policy, it was explained to Karen.

She tried to talk them into pooling their money and opening a single account, but sibling rivalry won out and the kids wouldn't go for that.

A few days later, the grandparents heard of the ordeal, were impressed and decided to give each child another fifty dollars so they could have their own savings accounts. Back to the bank.

This time they were told that Brad and Linda couldn't open their own accounts because they didn't have social security numbers. "The government is afraid somebody will make some interest and they won't get any of it," explained a bank official. Frustrated for a second time, the kids burst into tears.

"I didn't know what to tell them after that," said Karen. I thought teaching the children to save now would make them more likely to do the same when they were older."

To try to make amends to the kids, Karen took them on a shopping spree for candy and rock tapes. It was the only thing left to do. Besides, the children will learn another valuable lesson about money: Easy come, easy go.

— 17 —

From Sea To
Shining Sea

A S I'VE TRIED TO demonstrate, true grit is not indige-
nous to any group or any place. Some of the best
examples of the developing and the finished product I've
seen, for instance, appeared in Italy.

I was there for three weeks of R&R (Note to IRS agents:
That stands for Research and Reflection. I worked night and
day, as this chapter proves, and that's why I was forced to
list the trip as a deduction). Like most tourists, the first
challenge I had to face was the language. To better prepare
myself, I bought one of those Berlitz guides of "two thousand helpful phrases."

They were right. The guide would have been very helpful...if I had been having a convulsion. The way to say, "I
am having a convulsion," in Italian is, roughly, "Io ho le
convulsioni." But who's got time to look it up if they're
having a convulsion face down in the pasta? If they really

wanted to be helpful in those books, they would tell you how to say, "Last night I went out and got drunker than a four-eyed Italian dog, and I desperately need something for this hangover." I couldn't find that phrase anywhere. And I needed it. Bad.

The book did provide me with a useful phrase for the train. The way to say, "I think you are in my seat," is, "Penso che questo sia il mio posto." What it didn't do, however, was tell me what to say when the fellow in my seat was the toughest hombre in Genoa, and he replied with an Italian phrase which I interpreted to mean, "One more word out of you, salami-face, and I'll slice you up like so much prosciutto."

What I finally did was what most Americans do when they can't speak the language. I started using American-Italian, which means putting a vowel on the end of each English word and waving your arms a lot. For instance, if you want to say, "You are standing on my foot," in Italian, you say, "Youo areo standingo ona mya foota." If you look down and point at your foot, it will helpo.

Italians, to their credit, will attempt to speak English with you, thus making it easier for visitors in their country. There is a problem here, too, however: Italians, especially taxi drivers and waiters, know only certain English phrases, and they use them for a multitude of responses.

"If you don't slow down," you might say to the taxi driver, "you are going to kill us all!"

To which he will reply, "Dank you berry much."

Or, to your waiter you say, "This soup is rancid."

"Meddy Chreestmas," he replies.

All the communications problems I had in Italy reminded me of a similar qroblem Bogator Green, the world famous mechanic from my hometown, once had. An Italian couple was driving through in a rental car when it developed engine trouble. A local deputy sheriff came to their rescue and had the car towed to Bogator's "garage," a large shade tree behind his trailer.

The couple spoke no English, and Bogator was only slightly better versed in Italian. After checking their car, Bogator said, "Your manifold's busted."

The man shook his head in bewilderment.

"He's Italian, Bogator," said the deputy sheriff. "He doesn't understand you."

"Oh," said Bogator. He then cupped his hands around his mouth and screamed in the man's ear, "YOUR MAN-IFOLD'S BUSTED!"

***

Once you've mastered the language, another way Americans build character in Italy is by walking the streets.

"You go out for a walk?" asked the bellman at my hotel in Rome.

"Yes," I replied.

"Be careful," he suggested. "The drivers are very aggressive here." And the Pope is Catholic, he might have added.

In a matter of minutes, I had figured it out — it was a game of demolitionio derbyo. The buses try to run over the cars. The cars try to run over what seems to be everybody and his Italian brother on a motor scooter. And all three try to run down the helpless pedestrians, who are nothing more than human bowling pins. The taxi driver who drove me from the train station to my hotel narrowly missed picking up a 7-10 split on the Via Condetti, and he left an easy spare on the Via Veneto when a shopper dived away from his speeding taxi just in time.

"An Italian taxi driver," said another man at the hotel,

"would try to run over his grandmother if she got in his way." I guess that explains the shortage of Italian grandmothers I noted in Rome. I finally figured out that red lights are merely for decoration in Italy, brakes routinely last 100,000 miles since they're seldom used and the quickest way to become rich is to open a body and paint shop.

"Why do people drive this way in Rome?" I asked the bellman.

"Because," he laughed, "ninety-five percent of the Italian people think they are Beppe Gabbiani."

"Beppe Gabbiani?" I asked.

"Richard Petty, to you."

That cleared it up nicely.

***

In Florence, my traditional American values were challenged on every corner. You see, there are a million statues in Florence, and every one of them is naked.

There's "David" by Michelangelo, a masterpiece completed in 1504 when the artist was only twenty-five years old. David makes Bo Derek look overdressed.

There's "The Rape of the Sabine Women" by Giambologna. Children under seventeen must be accompanied by a parent or legal guardian to get a gander at this one.

"Hercules and Diomedes" by Vincenzo de Rossi apparently is a tribute to the sport of wrestling. If you liked watching Argentina Rocca throw Lou Thesz out of the ring, you'll adore "Hercules and Diomedes."

"Perseus" by Cellini is another example of a woman losing her head over a man, and "Bacchus's Fountain" is a sculpture of a fat man riding a turtle. Must be some sort of tribute to Italian turtle racing.

We are not accustomed to such rampant nudity in the United States, and any time it appears, there is always some group stepping forward to protect us. I remember when Marvin Knowles, a fellow from my hometown, made it big in professional wrestling. Using the name "The Masked Pork Chop," Marvin wrestled in National Guard armories and high school gymnasiums as far away as Tupelo, Mississippi.

Because of the acclaim he brought to our town, the local ladies club arranged for "Marvin Knowles Day," which would feature the unveiling of a statue of Marvin in his ring crouch, to be placed on the elementary school ballfield where Marvin got his start wrestling Cordie Mae Poovey, the ugliest and meanest girl in town. The day before the unveiling, however, some of the ladies dropped by to inspect the statue and were shocked to find Marvin wearing nothing but his wrestling tights. They had the sculptor back the next morning before dawn, carving Marvin a pair of loose-fitting underdrawers that reached all the way down to his wrestling boots.

I think maybe they were right. Try as I may, I just can't picture Stonewall Jackson on his horse in the town square wearing nothing but his sword. It ain't fittin'.

***

By the time I reached Venice, I was delighted to hear Americans talking at a table beside me during dinner. It was an elderly couple grappling with noodles and salmon and drinking white wine from a pitcher. I asked where they were from.

"Massachusetts," said the lady, obviously someone's grandmother.

"Originally from Arizona, though," her husband added. He had the look of an ex-soldier.

Apparently they also were glad to hear a voice from home, and we swapped stories over dinner that night. They were both widowed, the lady said, but had been friends back in Arizona before their mates had died. Living alone had not appealed to either of them, so they had married recently. Their eyes met and stayed together as she talked about their marriage.

"So this is a honeymoon?" I asked.

"Just a nice, long trip," the man said. I think I noticed a blush as he spoke. He had started slowly in the conversation, but now the wine was beginning to take effect. They were to be in Europe for three months, he said. First they had visited Germany, then it was on to Austria. The old man told me about the archbishop who once ruled over Salzburg.

"He built a large house," he explained. "And why would an archbishop need such a large house? For the woman he kept there who gave him fifteen illegitimate sons!"

The old man roared with laughter. There's at least a spark left there, I thought.

"Newspaperman," I answered when they asked. The old man brightened again. What a coincidence, he said; his brother-in-law used to be a newspaperman, too.

"He was the music critic for the Washington Post, the one Harry Truman threatened to kick where you don't want to be kicked when he questioned Margaret Truman's musical talents. Years later, my brother-in-law was visiting Independence, Missouri, and was going through the Truman library. Somebody recognized him and asked if he would like to say hello to the former President. Well, of course he would, and do you know what Truman said to him?"

No, I couldn't imagine.

"He said my brother-in-law was right all along. He said his daughter Margaret really didn't have much talent as a musician." The man roared again with laughter.

It was getting late. The man started into the story about the archbishop again.

"You've already told that one, dear," his wife said.

I offered my goodbyes and said maybe we would see each other again sometime. Of course, we wouldn't, but Americans always tell each other that sort of thing. As I left, I heard the man ask his wife, "One more half-liter of wine before bed?"

"OK, let's have one more half-liter," she answered, smiling at him.

Oh, to be young — relatively or otherwise — and in love as night falls on Venice. Or even on Cleveland.

***

I can't think of anything, short of gun-totin' federal marshalls, that would make me move out of the United States. But if for any reason I ever had to pick another country to live in, I think it would be Switzerland.

In the first place, it's a naturally beautiful country with mountain peaks and crystal clear lakes. It's also very clean, the banks are discreet, it's a nice place to shop for cheese and watches and the taxi service is wonderful.

Most of the cabs in Switzerland are late model Mercedeses or BMWs. I've ridden in taxis in the U.S. that were so old the driver had to pull off the road to reshoe his mule. Also, when a taxi picks you up in Switzerland, the driver gets out and opens the door for you. In the U.S., most taxi drivers are surlier than Mr. T with a bad case of hemorrhoids and wouldn't open the door for their grandmother if she were carrying a steamer trunk.

Here are some other nice things about Switzerland:

• When you cross the street, motorists stop and allow you to pass. In most American cities, it's open season on pedestrians.

• When you swim in a Swiss pool, you must wear a bathing cap. I asked the pool attendant why. "You shouldn't have to swim with other people's hair floating in the water," she said. Darn straight.

• There are very few billboards along the Swiss road-ways. You can actually see the countryside.

• While I was in Switzerland, I didn't see a single snake or mosquito.

• The air in Switzerland doesn't burn your nose, and when the temperature reaches eighty, they think they're having a heat wave.

• I don't think they have much of a crime problem in Switzerland, either. I base this assumption on an experience I had in Lugano. I noticed a man down on his hands and knees drawing a beautiful picture of the Virgin Mary on the sidewalk with colored chalk. Around the man were several shoe boxes in which those who appreciated his artwork had dropped coins. The following evening I happened to pass by the same spot. The artist was gone, but the shoe boxes were still there along with the day's collection. "You mean to say," I asked a native, "that he can leave his coins out there all night and nobody will steal them?" The man looked shocked. "Steal from a poor artist?" he asked. "Who would steal from the poor?"

That's another thing I like about Switzerland: It still has a ways to go to catch up with the rest of civilization.

***

Of course, if Italy or even Switzerland isn't your cup of wine, there are many other options for interesting vacations closer to home which can also teach you about the world and the wonderful characters who populate it. Here are just a few American vacation packages I could recommend:

• GALA ARKANSAS — Four days and five nights in the

"Land of the Razorback." Learn to stand on a table in a restaurant and scream, "Sooooooooie Piiiig!" like the happy University of Arkansas football fans do when they go out of town. Learn to jump-start a pickup truck like the University of Arkansas football fans do when they try to get back home. Visit the lovely Ozarks and stay in a real mountain shack near Dogpatch, USA. See firsthand what outdoor plumbing is all about! The kids will love it! (Soap, towels, heat, lights, snakebite kits and ammunition NOT included.)

• THE OTHER FLORIDA — Tired of crowded beaches and fancy hotels? Then this might be just right for you. A trip off Florida's beaten paths to lovely, exciting Bugspray Swamp Resort, located in the mysterious Everglades. Explore the hidden world of reptiles and insects with guide, cook and medicine man. Take a hike in Quicksand Alley. (Who got left behind?) See mosquitoes the size of eagles and gnats as big as bats. Four days, five nights and six chances out of ten that at least one member of your family gets eaten by an alligator.

• OLD SOUTH TOUR — Get a real feel for the Old South with a tour of Fort Deposit, Alabama, and meet Fort Deposit's leading citizen, Billy Bob Bailey, and his dog, Rooster. See the local diner where Governor George Wallace once had lunch during a campaign trip. See the local hospital where the governor recuperated. Visitors from New Jersey and other places Up North will want to ask Billy Bob about his special deals on souvenirs, like water actually carried by soldiers during the Civil War, dirt from historic Civil War battlefields and trained boll weevils. And, if you're lucky, Rooster might even do some tricks for his northern friends, like removing their distributor caps. Don't worry. Billy Bob's Service Station, located next to the souvenir shop, is open twenty-four hours a day.

• NUDE BEACH — Just think of it! Nude swimming, nude tennis, nude golf and nude volleyball. And we know just the rock you can hide behind to see it all. Film extra.

• DINOSAUR WORLD — Located off Highway 78 near beautiful downtown Snellville, Georgia. Huge replicas of dinosaurs and other prehistoric animals. Great fun for the kids and educational, too. Would you like to own Dinosaur World yourself? Ask for Harvey and make him an offer. Any offer.

• DUDE RANCH — Here's a dude ranch with a new twist. Instead of riding a bunch of smelly horses, ride dinosaurs and other prehistoric animals. Located off Highway 78 near beautiful downtown Snellville, Georgia. Tell Harvey, the dude who got stuck with this joint, to "saddle 'em up!"

***

If your tastes run more to the great outdoors, I could recommend a rafting trip down the raging Colorado River. But before you sign up for such an arduous undertaking, you may want to ask a few questions — to which I already have the answers.

1. How do I get to the Colorado River? Fly from Las Vegas out into the middle of the Arizona desert in a small airplane (envision a '53 Ford with wings) and land in a wide place between two cacti. Then ride a mule down the treacherous ledges of the canyon to the river and pray the mule doesn't make one false step, because mules, unfortunately, don't have wings.

2. How can the Arizona desert best be described? Ten zillion acres of dust.

3. Is there ever a change of scenery? Occasionally you see a cow pie.

4. Once on the river, are the rapids exciting? Lie down on a water bed and get a small child to jump up and down on it. Same thing, except you don't get as wet.

5. How hot is it on the river? During the day, about 120 degrees, but at night it cools down nicely to maybe 102.

6. Where do you camp? On sandy river banks.

7. What is it like camping when the wind starts blowing at night? Think of a blast furnace.

8. What do you eat on the trip? Mostly sand.

9. How did the brochure describe camping at night along the river? "...Drift slowly off to sleep under the starry western skies as you are caressed by a cool breeze, the restful sound of rushing water and the pleasant blend of guitars and mellow voices."

10. Has the person who wrote the brochure ever actually taken the trip? No.

11. Was there anybody interesting along with you? Yes. A newlywed couple on their honeymoon.

12. What do you call people who take a rafting trip down the raging Colorado for their honeymoon? Weird.

13. Did you encounter any scorpions? Yes, but the red ants were worse. Scorpions sting only in self-defense; red ants bite because they enjoy it.

14. What about rattlesnakes? Don't worry. We never found more than one at a time in a sleeping bag.

15. What are the restroom facilities like in camp? A little green tent.

16. What is the most important thing to know about camping on the Colorado River? Never spread your bedroll near the little green tent.

17. Will you ever take such a trip again? Sure, as soon as mules sprout wings and fly.

***

I used to recommend Hilton Head, South Carolina, as a wonderful getaway spot, but not long ago a friend sent me a clipping from the island's newspaper which warned of trouble. For the sake of an informed public, following is a reprint of that article:

Members of an elite corps of South Carolina state militia stormed the beach here Saturday and reclaimed the plush resort from thousands of Northern vacationers who took over the island several years ago after surrendering Miami Beach.

"Hilton Head is a part of the sovereign state of South Carolina," declared Governor Willis Peabody, "and nobody else has any right to any part of the soil our forefathers grabbed off the Indians. Any attempt to retake the island will result in the gravest of consequences."

The governor would not elaborate on what he meant by "gravest of consequences," but the South Carolina militiamen have put the island under what some of the Northern vacationers are referring to as "the next thing to martial law." One new order disallows the sale of piña colada mix to anyone who cannot prove he or she was born south of Richmond, Virginia.

Hilton Head Island, with miles of beach, numerous golf courses and tennis courts and Ralph Lauren's coastal headquarters, is just off the South Carolina mainland near the Georgia port city of Savannah.

The pre-brunch raid which reclaimed the island was believed to have been launched from Williams' Seafood Restaurant in Savannah in bass boats rented from the Thunderbolt Marina, Bait and Tackle. "We even brought our own beer," said Captain Charlie "Swamp Fox" Ravenel, head of the Carolina militia.

It is believed that the militia also included volunteers from the neighboring state of Georgia, which has had a recent problem with a growing number of Northerners moving into its Golden Isles resorts of Jekyll Island, St. Simons Island and Sea Island. This belief was stimulated by reports that some of the militiamen, upon storming across the beach and reaching the lobby of the Hilton Head Holiday Inn, cried out, "How 'bout them Dawgs!" — a familiar Georgia exclamation for any occasion, including selected funerals.

The Northern-bred occupants of the island, including visitors from the Canadian province of Ontario who were on the island looking for reptile farms and glass-bottom boats, were caught completely off guard by the attack. There apparently was only one casualty, however; a lady from Akron, Ohio, on the beach to catch some early rays, was stepped on by an attacking militiaman and suffered a pair of broken sunglasses.

"You can spot yankee men on the beach from a mile out in the ocean," Captain Ravenel said. "They all wear Bermuda shorts, sandals and black socks pulled up to their armpits. But yankee women, they put on those white bathing suits and they haven't been in the sun in so long, then blend right into the sand. My man said he thought that lady was some kind of jellyfish that had washed up on the beach. If he'd have looked a little closer, he'd have seen her mustache and probably would have missed her."

Reaction came swiftly from the North. One possible retaliatory move, said Governor Fitzhugh Stratsworth III of Ohio, was to move the Ohio National Guard south to Hilton Head to meet the Carolina militia head-on. "If we don't have to stop every time somebody has to go to the bathroom, we could be in the Hilton Head area in three to four days," Governor Stratsworth said.

Meanwhile, Secretary of State George Schultz has already landed in Hilton Head and announced that he is prepared to "stay as long as necessary" to help mediate the dispute. Told at a ninth-hole briefing that rumors were flying that the Carolina militiamen were feeding some of the yankee inhabitants to the many alligators that live on the island, Schultz quipped, "I thought they only ate grits."

***

Not long ago I was strolling down New York's Fifth Avenue with a native. He pointed out things I'd never thought to observe before.

"Watch the Japanese tourists," he said. "They'll take pictures of anything, even the sky."

That made sense to me. I explained to the New Yorker that in most other parts of the world the sky is blue, and that the visitors from the East probably were intrigued by the fact that the sky in New York has a brownish or yellowish tint to it.

Then my guide told me how to distinguish a native New Yorker from a tourist. "Watch their eyes," he said. "New Yorkers never look up. They either look down or straight ahead. Only visitors to the city look up."

In addition to being bored with tall buildings, I suspected that most natives had suffered some misfortunes with pigeons and therefore did not look up.

My friend further explained that if I watched closely, I would observe that three out of every five New Yorkers would be wearing headsets. "It's our way of dealing with noise pollution," he said.

But if their ears are plugged with loud music, how are they going to hear the two-second blast of the horn which taxi drivers politely give before driving over pedestrians?

Further down Fifth Avenue, my guide showed me yet another point of interest. Along the sidewalk, a crowd gathered to watch large amounts of money changing hands in a little card game being played on top of cardboard boxes. It was like the old shell game: three cards face down, two black and one red. The dealer switches the cards around; the object is to find the red one. I saw people betting as much as a hundred dollars.

"Don't get involved," said my friend. "The people you see winning are shills for the dealer. The tourists see them win and so they give it a try, but they almost always lose."

"Isn't that illegal?" I asked.

"Of course, it is," said the native, "but they have look-outs for the police. If a cop heads their way, they simply grab their box and go to another street."

"You said tourists almost always lose. Does that mean some occasionally win?"

"Yes and no," he answered. "If they do happen to win, one of the shills follows them down the street, mugs them and gets the money back."

About that time we passed a group of Japanese tourists. I nodded and said hello to them. They all took my picture as if I were unusual.

***

They told me about Old Faithful, the world-famous geyser that's the main attraction at Yellowstone National Park in Wyoming, when I was a kid in school. I wasn't much impressed. So every hour on the hour this hole in the ground spews out a lot of steam and hot water. That's a big deal?

Rock City and Disneyland certainly were on my list of things to see when I could afford it, but Old Faithful wasn't in the running. My traveling companion through the wilds of Wyoming, however, had a different idea.

"People come from all over the world to see it," he explained. "We're crazy to come this far and not get a look at it."

I checked the map. We were 120 miles roundtrip from Yellowstone. "You want to drive that far just to see hot water and steam?" I asked. "Why don't you just turn on the shower and close the bathroom door tonight?"

He responded by questioning my patriotism, so the next thing I knew we were on our way to Yellowstone, where bears eat people, to see Old Faithful. We arrived just after eight o'clock.

My friend explained that since a major earthquake in the area in 1983, Old Faithful — which previously had been spewing forth on the hour for more than a hundred years — was running as much as eighty-two minutes between eruptions.

"You mean we've come this far and the thing might not even go off?" I complained.

"It'll go off," he said. "That's why they call it Old Faithful."

There must have been three thousand people sitting on

benches patiently waiting for the show. Me, I went for an ice cream cone.

"You might miss it," warned my friend.

"So I'll see the highlight film," I quipped.

When I came back with my cone, Old Faithful was smoking a little steam but nothing more. The crowd still waited quietly. Then, at about half past eight, it happened. There was steam, and more steam, and then there was a roar and I think the ground trembled. Old Faithful belched forth with a boiling, steamy column of water that reached over a hundred feet into the sky.

The crowd gasped in awe. The explosion seemed to go higher and higher, and when it ended a few minutes later, the crowd fell silent for a moment before bursting into spontaneous applause.

Later, as we were driving in the darkness of the park, my friend asked me how I felt when I saw Old Faithful come through for her audience.

"Proud to be an American," I answered.

I can't explain why. You just had to be there.

***

From New York to Dallas, from Florence to Yosemite, there are men, women and children walking around with hearts full of true grit. It may be hidden beneath the surface of poverty or tattoos or behind the face of wrinkles, but it's there just the same, pure and clear.

So what if they might be riding Shetland ponies instead of gallant steeds? They all could have ridden alongside Marshall Rooster Cogburn, hallowed be his name and theirs.